Raves for *The Dragon Quartet*:

THE
DRAGON QUARTET

THE
DRAGON QUARTET

THE BOOK OF EARTH

THE BOOK OF WATER

MARJORIE B. KELLOGG

DAW BOOKS, INC.
DONALD A. WOLLHEIM, FOUNDER
375 Hudson Street, New York, NY 10014

ELIZABETH R. WOLLHEIM
SHEILA E. GILBERT
PUBLISHERS
http://www.dawbooks.com

First Paperback Printing, December 2005
1 2 3 4 5 6 7 8 9

DAW TRADEMARK REGISTERED
U.S. PAT. OFF. AND FOREIGN COUNTRIES
—MARCA REGISTRADA
HECHO EN U.S.A.

PRINTED IN THE U.S.A.

INTRODUCTION

In memory of Denise Frances Farquharson Bryan.

When I was twelve or thirteen, my best friend's British mother introduced me to a new kind of literature. Casually, on some rainy day when we were racketing about the house, bored and irritable, and driving her crazy.

"You girls might enjoy this."

No pressure. No fanfare. She just handed over well-thumbed copies of *Childhood's End* and the C.S. Lewis *Perelandra* trilogy. It may even have been Denise who first suggested this curiosity from England called *The Lord of the Rings*, long before it was available in every library and bookstore, and now on every supermarket shelf.

And so, I was hooked, and have remained so ever since. Perhaps the ground was prepared by my paternal grandfather, who had read Lewis Carroll aloud to me yearly since I was old enough to walk. But it wasn't until I'd exhausted the Bryan book collection and went looking for more than I understood that the world had a pocketful of nasty words for this sort of writing.

Escapist. Just-for-kids. Genre-lit. Not relevant to the "real" world.

As if the imagination has played no role in history and the evolution of mankind . . .

Yet what have the ancient civilization left behind, besides a lot of ruins and broken pottery? Their myths, their dreams, their stories of gods and heroes. And weren't these stories created to encode values and behavior, knowledge and insight about the "real" world, in order to pass it down through the generations in a form accessible to all?

Is the tale of Medea less valid as a lesson in the ravages of oppression and jealousy just because she flies off at the end in a chariot drawn by dragons?

Well, to some, perhaps.

But when we open up the borders of a narrative to admit the mythical, the fantastical, the speculative, we enlarge that narrative. We expand its potential for relevance to the widest—and the most diverse—population. We create, in effect, a more public space.

But why, specifically, *The Dragon Quartet*?

Borders have always interested me. Transitions. The tidal zone. The edge of the forest. The exhaled breath between waking and sleep. And especially, that slippery place between the real and the unreal, where mystery presides. Before *The Dragon Quartet*, I had written only science fiction. When my friend and publisher Sheila Gilbert suggested that I come up with a fantasy project, I realized that what I really wanted to explore was not "pure" fantasy or science fiction, but a more ambiguous territory that might include them both.

Readers often ask where the ideas come from. I believe they are sparked by what nags at the writer the most. So, it was inevitable that I would be drawn again to the concerns that underlie all my written work so far: a hope for social justice, and for greater human responsibility to our habitat, the Earth. And for this, a series would be ideal: a chance to observe both the causes and the result, over time. I could begin my tale in the past, where our destructive habits of being were laid down long before we were aware of the harm they would cause, and develop it through the present and on into the future, where the consequences of our behavior lie grimly in wait for us.

Thus, the quartet could start as a traditional fantasy, generally associated with an idealized low-tech or magical past, then morph gradually into science fiction, generally associated with a high-tech future. Many will argue that the presence of dragons keeps the series from ever crossing over fully into the realm of SF, but the dragons themselves evolve and by the end have stepped into the role filled in SF by an alien species.

The symmetry of all this appealed to me, and kept me going throughout the long process of writing—longer to many readers, I know, than seemed reasonable. Always, even when I was wound in a tangle of plot and details, this symmetry—the Larger Design—provided a dose of clarity. I hope that these new omnibus editions will, by rejoining the sundered parts of a single narrative, offer the reader some of that greater clarity.

Marjorie B. Kellogg
Franklin, New York 2005

THE BOOK OF EARTH

TO SEATHRÚN ÓCORRÁIN

poet, sibling, old soul—but not necessarily in that order:

In addition, a very special helping of gratitude and appreciation to my editor, **Sheila Gilbert**, for her great faith, bright ideas, and patience well beyond the call of duty.

Burnt offerings also on the altars of other friendly deities of perseverance and good advice: Lynne Kemen and Bill Rossow, Barbara Newman and Stephen Morris, Antonia Bryan, Vickie Davis. Thanks to you all.

"Mythology is psychology misread as biography."
—Joseph Campbell

The Creation

IN THE BEGINNING:

In the Beginning, four mighty dragons raised of elemental energies were put to work creating the World. They were called Earth, Water, Fire and Air. No one of them had power greater than another, and no one of them was mighty alone.

When the work was completed and the World set in motion, the four went to ground, expecting to sleep out this World's particular history and not rise again until World's End.

The first to awaken was Earth.

PART ONE

EARTH

The Summoning of the Hero

CHAPTER ONE

Balanced on the sill, she watched the distant jagged crest of rock where the road climbed up out of the forest. Finally the riders appeared. Banners at first, ghostly white and limp in the dank mountain air. Horses next, also white, cloud horses etched pale against the distant gray of the upper peaks, puffing vapor that rose like departing spirits past the night-black firs.

Erde shivered. She dreaded this priest's coming, this stranger with his entourage and his dire prophecies, even though it meant ceremonies and feasting and the chance for news from outside her father's isolated mountain domain. The news would be bad, she knew it would. It was always bad these days. But fresh faces would be a welcome relief. At the ripe old age of nearly fourteen, Erde already believed it was true that a young person could die of boredom.

A cry caught at her ear, thrown up from the cobbled yard below. The apple-cheeked crone who watched the chickens with her one good eye and pressed card readings on anyone who'd listen, stared up from her perch on the stone wellhead. The gray light turned her rheumy gaze to silver. Erde hated the chicken-crone. The old woman always seemed to be expecting something of her and would never say what. Erde looked away and pulled the casement tight.

"My lady?"

Forehead tight to the rippled glass, Erde let the cold seep into her furrowed brow, and contemplated the novelty of an unfamiliar face—how gratefully you noticed the peculiar arch of an eyebrow, the odd shape of a lip, how the color

of an eye surprised you because maybe no one you'd
known yet had eyes exactly that color. She had seen her
own eyes in a shard of polished steel that her grandmother
kept in a robing trunk. They were very dark, almost black.
Her mother's, she was always told, though Erde could not
remember. She cracked open the window for another stare
across the battlements.

"My lady?"

Far off along the stony path, the cloud horses resolved
into living horses, material banners and corporeal men in
white robes, a greater number of them than had been expected. Erde could see no pack animals. This priest was
very sure of his welcome, to arrive without provisions in
such a time of hardship.

"My lady!"

Erde started. "Pardon?"

"Come down from that drafty old window!" Her
chamber-woman poured water from a kettle into a stoneware bowl. The steam rose into the chill room like the
mist come in off the mountain. "You'll lose your balance
and fall!"

"No, I won't." Erde searched the distant blur of bodies,
hoping to make out a face, any face, in that line of faceless riders.

The kettle clanged to the floor. "Then you'll catch your
death, you with only a shift on! I met three ravens in the
stable yard this morning and I've been fearing the worst
ever since! Such tales you hear! My grand-auntie Hildy
vows she's never known a time so full of ill omens!"

Erde had seen those ravens, all puffed up in the cold and
looking grim. She had wondered about them. "Oh, Fricca!
I'm in my shift because I'm supposed to be getting
dressed!"

"Well, indeed you are, miss, so come down this minute
and wash yourself clean!"

"Why should I? Nobody else will. It's too cold to be
clean!"

"It's not for you to be caring what everyone else might
do."

Her chamber-woman was what Erde had heard referred
to as "comely": golden-haired, fair-skinned, and plump, all
the things that Erde wasn't. Sometimes she suspected that

"comely" really meant kind and silly, for Fricca was both. Like now—venturing no farther than the limit of heat from the fireplace, the chamber-woman pressed her palms to her cheeks until her mouth was a soft red rose of anxiety. "Just think of it, my lady! The baron your father's first Occasion as Tor Alte's lord! Oooh, he'll be so displeased if you're not ready and at his side when the holy brother arrives!"

" 'Sooo displeased . . .' " Erde mocked. "My father's displeased whenever he sees me."

"Not so! Your father loves you. Surely, he's very busy just now, becoming baron, but you're all he has in the world and it wouldn't hurt you to humor him a bit."

"Why do you pretend it matters what I do?" Erde pivoted on the high stone sill and jumped down, her bare feet slapping against the planking. She knew a proper lady would step first to the window seat, toes pointed, then float daintily to the floor. But even if she could manage such a performance, Erde would never allow Fricca the satisfaction of witnessing it. "As if my father's humor was ever as mild as displeasure."

Fricca made clucking noises as she sponged Erde's face and arms. "Oh, yes indeed, and aren't you just your father's own child!"

"No!" The thought horrified her. "I am my mother's!"

"That's as may be, God rest her soul, sweet sweet lady."

Erde's chin lifted. "And my grandmother's granddaughter."

"And rest hers also." Fricca touched the corner of her apron to her eye. "So recently departed."

"It feels like forever!" Erde moaned.

But it had only been three days. Three impossibly long days. Erde fought another turn of the nausea that had plagued her all morning. How sad and empty those three days had been, without her best friend, her boon companion. Perhaps she so dreaded the priest because he came to lay her dear grandmama in the holy ground, putting thereby to rest her own mad hope that the old woman might yet rise off the cold stone bier in the chapel where only a single tallow candle kept her company. If she could have faced her father, she would have complained. How dare he claim he couldn't afford the beeswax to light his own mother's road to eternity?

"Now don't you be going all stiff on me! It's only water!" Fricca tossed the wash-felt into the basin with dispatch. Her solemnity, like a fair-weather cloud, quickly passed. "There! It's time to make ourselves beautiful!"

Erde hunched her shoulders. Why did the whole world not mourn this death as she did? "I'm not beautiful."

"Nonsense. Look at the magnificent long hair on you!" Fricca caught up the heavy shining darkness that flowed down Erde's back and let it slide through her hands like water. "Who about here has glory hair like this?"

Erde shook her head irritably. People always talked about your hair when they couldn't think of anything more important to say about you. "I don't care if I'm beautiful."

"Of course you do! Every girl wants to be beautiful! You're just gloomy with the baroness' passing, but life goes on, you know." Fricca bustled to the bed, where a white velvet ceremonial gown lay in state under the canopy, on a length of sun-bleached muslin.

Like Grandmama in the chapel, Erde mused, cold white on white. The gown had been her mother's, packed away for twelve years. Suddenly her father had insisted it was a waste to let it molder in the chest. The seamstress had hardly needed to alter it at all.

"Draw tight the bed curtains," she intoned grimly. "Let the dead rest in peace!"

Fricca waved her hands as if shooing hens. "Such things you say!"

"Grandmama would never make me wear that."

"Rest a piece, yourself, and come off with that dull rag, now." Fricca held up a new silk shift trimmed with delicate gold. She dangled it this way and that, letting it catch the firelight. "Oooh, what a wonder! Fit for a young virgin bride, which, God willing, soon you'll be! Come, lucky girl, slip it on."

The slick cool silk was like eelskin in water, like icy hands touching her all over. Erde plucked at it fitfully. "It hardly covers me at all! And it clings so!"

"Doesn't it though!" Fricca eyed it with sly envy. "And will come off as smartly as it went on."

Erde reddened. "I'll wear my old one."

"Oh, don't be prudish! If you think a bed's just for sleeping, it's time you learned better! Lots of girls your age are married by now." Fricca tugged the shift down and smoothed it across Erde's thin back. "Look at the great height of you, and you not even bleeding yet! Sometimes I think you're keeping it back on purpose!"

Erde wished Fricca did not feel that, due to the sudden demise of her lady's only female relative, it had fallen to her to supply a proper education of the bedchamber. But this suggestion was certainly more interesting than most of Fricca's notions. "Could I do such a thing?"

Fricca's mouth formed a small plump "o" of distress. "Of course not! That's black witches' business and none of yours! We may be all sorry sinners, but I am a good Christian woman and there'll be no talk of witchery in this house!"

"It'll be awfully quiet down in the kitchens, then."

"Oh, aren't we the big ears! Well, people will talk when there's news to be shared, but that's just talk and harmless, too."

"But you said I . . ."

"I only meant that when I brought my auntie's special lady's tonic, you poured it out!"

Erde's blush deepened. "I don't want to get married yet!"

"Tch! With such a temper, who'd have you anyway? Come on, now." Fricca shook her apron at her. "You must wear your father's gifts. Just think of the cost!"

Erde hardly could without shame, for despite the "official" word about court, she knew the countryside was in dire circumstances. Her father insisted that the people needed to see their lords well fed and in proper array to prove that all was still well with the world. But all was not well with the world, and Erde knew she could feed an entire village for the price of that silk shift. She imagined bartering all the hated garments in her robing chest for dried meat and potatoes to fill the farmers' empty larders. But who could be found these days with surplus enough to barter? "I wish he'd give me a pair of leather riding breeches instead!"

"And I suppose you'd wear such a thing, right out in public?"

"Everyone knows the only sensible way to sit a horse is astride."

Fricca's eyes rolled skyward. "Holy angels, don't hear a word she says!"

Erde hid a vengeful smile. She'd hit upon something truly shocking at last. She liked Fricca well enough and the woman did show a talent almost equal to her grandmother's for deflecting the baron's sudden bouts of wrath. But she couldn't help tweaking Fricca for her cotton-wool thinking. In addition to missing the comfort of the baroness' company, Erde missed the reassuring clarity of her mind. She felt cast adrift, and angry that lesser mortals lived on while her grandmother had left her, so terribly alone. She tried actually picturing herself in men's breeches. Perhaps her father would have loved her better if she'd been born a boy.

A sharp rap on the door sent Fricca scurrying to snatch up the shining gown from the bed as if rescuing a sleeping child. "Oh, dear, that'll be Rainer—poor lad, how my lord does order him about these days! There, see? He's come to fetch you and you not half ready!"

But Erde knew Rainer's knock and she knew her father's. She could only wish it was Rainer. "It's my father."

"Never it is!" Fricca frantically readied laces and sleeves. "My lady will be out in a minute!"

The heavy door swung on silent hinges and thudded against the stone. "And where is the Beauteous Flower of Castle von Alte?"

Fricca spread the gown and her substantial self screenlike in front of Erde. "Please, my lord! My lady has not finished dressing!"

"What! Not yet? His horses are already at the Dragon Gate! Shall we let a mere priest catch us napping?"

Erde watched her father carefully as he strode past her to the window. Unable to suffer both her own grief and his constant dissatisfaction, she had mostly avoided him since the baroness' death. But she knew well enough that he did not think of this priest, whom rumor preceded like distant thunder, as a mere anything. Yet here he was doing his hearty act, so perhaps he was both sober and in a reasonable mood.

Seeing her father, Erde was always astonished. How could she be related to this giant? He was tall and deeply barrel-chested, with a waist that tucked in beneath his ribs as neat as a woman's, barely widening at the hips. Almost top-heavy, she decided. He had a big head and affected a clean-shaven style peculiar for a man well into middle age but, since his accession, spreading rapidly to the rest of the court. The castle barbers were uncharacteristically busy. The baron's strong, naked chin and his penchant for dark shades of rich velvet offered—when properly brushed and aired—a flattering contrast to his thick, prematurely silver hair. Today he was freshly barbered and wore burgundy finely stitched with that same silver. It occurred to Erde that her father was a little vain.

He flung the casement wide. "Wind's come up again."

In the tall stone hearth, flames dipped and roared as the high-vaulted room inhaled the draft. The tapestries billowed on the damp-streaked walls. The baron sucked air noisily and licked his lips as if tasting something unpleasant. "Might get snow tonight. Perhaps this priest's prophecies are true."

Snow, Erde marveled. People of the upland domains were by long tradition held to be particularly skeptical, but snow in August? In *early* August. No wonder the countryside was so rife with black rumors.

"Please, my lord! My lady will catch her death!"

"Please, my lord," the baron mimicked, and Erde felt a pang of guilt, for it was her father's own habit of mockery that she had inherited. When he turned from the window, she noted how bright and hard his blue eyes were, above his practiced amiable smile. Like a frozen bit of sky. Sometimes the brightness meant he'd been drinking but not enough to really show. Right now, she wasn't sure what it meant. He folded his big velvet-shrouded arms. "Now let's see."

Fricca plumped the white gown awkwardly, still holding it to Erde's chest.

"Not the dress, woman, the girl!"

"Oh!" Fricca bobbed her head and Erde saw her grin foolishly as she gathered the gown to her own chest and stepped aside.

"Well," murmured the baron, "How does our little flower grow? Are our dainty rosebuds swelling yet?"

Fricca giggled. "Oh, just a little, my lord!"

Erde studied the floor, her big toe tracing the cracks

between the worn planks. Her father often looked her over
as if she was one of his prize warhorses, but since her
grandmother's death, something new lurked in his appraising stare. She saw her narrow shape reflected in his eyes:
dark hair long to her waist, long face, long slim body more
proper for a boy than a young girl. The firelight flickered
behind her, as if she was aflame. *I look like a witch at the
stake,* Erde thought. She wondered what her father saw.

"Well," he said again, and walked around to observe her
sidelong. Then he did something he had never done before.
He moved close and rested a finger on her shoulder, then
drew it lingeringly down her naked arm. Erde caught her
breath. She must not flinch from his touch, and anger him.
He had never struck her, though he had often threatened,
but before, there had always been the baroness to answer
to. "Skin like butter and olives," he mused. "Like your
mother's."

Abruptly he dropped his hand and his glance, and turned
away with a sharp gesture to Fricca. "Too thin, though,
don't you think? What are you feeding her?"

Fricca held up the gown for Erde to step into. "She's a
fine eater, my lord, I promise you." She dared to smile at
him over one shoulder as she fastened laces. "Surely it's
our long walks out on the mountain in this devil's weather
that's wearing her out."

Wearing *you* out, more likely, thought Erde irritably.

The baron let the ends of his mouth curl a little. "How
is it these walks don't leave you scrawny, woman?"

Fricca rounded her shoulders until her cleavage deepened, and giggled. Erde suddenly felt invisible and ignored.
"Ha! You'd never catch Fricca out there in the forest getting her shoes dirty!"

Her chamber-woman shot her a warning glance, but too
late. The baron frowned. "Forest? You walk in the forest?"

Fricca shrugged helplessly. "My lord! As if I could keep
up with her, racing all through the trees like a boy-child!"

"*Alone* in the forest? This is no boy-child! Where does
she go?" He spun on Erde. "Where do you go?"

She almost could not answer. "Nowhere special. I
just . . ."

His eyes went dark as winter oceans. "Who do you meet
out there? Some boy from the villages?"

"Boy?" The notion astonished her. "Of course not! Everyone knows about my walks!" Her careless spite had stumbled her into trouble. She could never tell her father the real reason she ventured alone into the forest, where the great trees swayed far above her head, and the amber-coated deer ate from her hand. So many of the herd were falling to the Baron's Hunt as it ranged ever deeper into the forest in search of meat for her father's table. Erde studied the huntsmen's routes and led the deer away from them. Of course Fricca could not come. Fricca would betray her, and the deer. "I need the exercise. The guardsmen watch me from the gate tower!"

Miraculously, this seemed to soothe him. He blinked and gruffly waved a dismissive hand. "Brigands and bears! It's too dangerous! I can't allow it." Fricca knelt with her back to him to arrange the lustrous folds of the gown, and the baron took in the round shape of her and her trim waist. A small distracted smile touched his lips. "Well, that's it, then. No more hiking about."

"But, Papa . . . !"

"Would you have the whole court whispering that my daughter is not a lady? Walk the battlements, if you must exercise. Stroll the yards."

"But that's so boring!"

The baron set his jaw. "Your grandmother indulged you." His velvet robe sighed about him as he made for the door. "Fricca! I'll see you outside for a moment!"

The look he threw from the open doorway left Erde fearful and confused. Why should a few mountain walks make him glare so fiercely? *It can only be,* she decided, *that my father hates me.*

CHAPTER TWO

Erde forced herself erect in the huge high-backed chair. It was carved and dark, with its own little vaulted roof to shadow her head. It had been, for the short while she lived, her mother's ceremonial seat. Erde felt strange sitting in it, dressed in her mother's own gown. The chair had sat empty in the great-hall for most of her life.

But this was her first High Ritual at her father's side. She supposed she was now, in title at least, the female head of household, though she wasn't quite sure what that meant. Her grandmama's final illness had swooped in so suddenly, like a hunting hawk. The old woman hadn't had time to instruct her in practical matters.

To her right and a step higher, Erde's father sat rigid in his own larger chair, with its taller, more elaborate canopy. He stared off into the clerestory of the great-hall, his impatience beginning to show. Erde thought it served him right. While her grandmother held the baronial throne, she stood by the entrance herself to greet most humble or most high. A woman ruling a baronage, she told Erde, must take pains to prove she is no mere figurehead. She must meet head-on the day-to-day challenges to her authority. Meanwhile, handy by the door, the Baroness would usher her visitors right on in, and there was none of this endless preening out in the hallway or jockeying for the best moment to make an Entrance.

But the new baron preferred to rule from a distance. His tastes ran to pomp and formality, to the ritual show of power. By your public image are you judged, he insisted, by both your enemies and your friends.

Erde did not care about power, though her grandmother

had labored long and hard to pique her interest, brazenly including her in discussions of policy from a very early age. The court thought it eccentric at the very least; at worst, unwise. "Putting ideas in the child's head," some muttered, as if the hiatus in patriarchy represented by their current liege was too anomalous to be considered a serious precedent. Erde listened because it annoyed the mutterers, and because her beloved grandmother wished it, but she often complained to the baroness that power seemed to be about limiting life rather than encouraging it.

"I only hope you learn to appreciate power before you have need of it," the baroness would reply.

"But I have no need of power," Erde would insist. "Papa will marry me off to some other baron's son, and he will protect me."

"Do you think life is so predictable? What if Josef dies before you marry, like my father did? You are a von Alte and his only heir. Have some thought to your responsibility."

Erde could hear the melodious raspy voice inside her ear as if the baroness stood right beside her, instead of lying so still in the chapel. She gripped the velvet folds of her mother's gown and willed the dead to get up and walk. Down along the wall to her right, a small door carved with linen-fold paneling led from the hall to the chapel. Staring at it, Erde could almost see it move.

"Erde? Hsst! Daughter!" Baron Josef leaned over the high arm of his throne, reaching past carved reliefs of heroic von Alte ancestors to jog her shoulder roughly. "Remember: he will be humble before you, but you must treat him as you would the highest lord."

"Yes, Papa."

"He is the Church's representative among us."

"Yes, Papa." Her grandmother's honest piety had been broad enough to include the notion that the Church was a power to be feared on Earth as well as loved in Heaven, but Erde had thought her father feared nothing. As of today, she was not so sure.

She pushed herself upright again and tried to sit like a lady. Like her mother would have, despite chronic boredom and the dank chill of the hall. The fine silk velvet of her gown was slippery on the polished wooden seat, and Fricca had pinned the pearled headpiece too tightly in her elaborately braided hair. Erde wanted to rip it all out and run off to the comfort of the stable. *Oh, Mother,* she mourned, *I fear I am unruly.*

Gazing about the hall always inspired her, so she tried that out for a while. The great-hall of Tor Alte was a grand and elegant edifice. Like the long, rhyming verses of the von Altes' history-saga, it spoke of a grand and glorious past that Erde wished she had been a part of, for it had surely had battles and dragons in it and must have been more interesting than her life was now. The hall was high and gracefully narrow, and filled with gray light from the clerestory windows. Beneath the tall side galleries, two vast roaring fireplaces surmounted with the von Alte crest faced each other across the width, insufficient to warm so large a hall but cheering in their aspect. The walls were of light-colored stones from the south, of matching size and smoothly dressed. The stout beams and rafters were cut in the shape of branches and polychromed in green and gold. The twenty wooden columns that supported the galleries were trefoil in cross-section and as big around as Erde could reach, like great trees stretching upward to a leafy vault.

Best of all were the column capitals: twenty carved and painted dragons, fierce and magical, each one a masterful expression of the artist's imagination. Now here was power that Erde was interested in. As soon as she could talk, her grandmother had taught her the dragons' names and their long lore-histories and all their aspects. Erde made up stories about them as if they were her dolls. Recalling those idyllic fantasy worlds soothed her now and drew her deeper into the memory. For instance, Glasswind, the third from the right. You wouldn't know it to look at her, but Glasswind had translucent wings that tinkled when she flew, like the glass-maker's chimes, and she was the great Mage-Queen's favorite. In the history-sagas, Erde's ancestors had slain dragons, winning the right to include the figure of a dragon in the family crest. But in Erde's games, the dragons were her staunchest allies. She had flown Glasswind in the service of the Mage-Queen many times.

Erde recalled now that she'd dreamed of dragons the night before, for the first time in ever so long. She tried, but could summon up no detail, only a formless memory of hulking dragon-presence. Another ill omen, like the three ravens? There was talk of dragons in the countryside, fired by the rumors of witchcraft and sorcery, but nobody claimed to have actually seen one. Real dragons. Despite her childhood preoccupation, the possibility alarmed her. She suspected a real dragon would not be as reasonable as Glasswind.

"Don't slump, girl," Baron Josef hissed.

"No, Papa."

Erde pulled herself up once again and tried to mimic her father's haughty, unfocused stare, straight out into space above the heads of the waiting court. But inevitably her eye was drawn downward. Anything was more interesting to look at than the vacant air, even the floor, the vast floor of the great-hall, paved with reddish slates and worn smoothly lustrous by two hundred years of the booted feet of soldiers and courtiers.

Currently, the entire household of von Alte was arrayed across that floor, in two lines with an aisle between, all decked out in the warmest and best clothes they had, from chambermaid to visiting vassal, now beginning to wilt and shift from the fatigue of standing about in the cold, waiting for something to happen. Even the smartly plumed and black-armored honor guard had relaxed from attention. When the baron had first arrived in the hall, with his dark-haired daughter resplendent in her mother's white dress, the priest's horses had just clattered into the castle yard and the opposing lines of courtiers ran straight and clean from the great wooden doors of the grand entry to the foot of the dais at the far end of the hall. One long hour later, the visiting entourage milled about in the courtyard. The court herald came and went from anxious conferences with a huddle of the baron's advisers, and still the priest did not make his entrance. Erde was losing patience with decorum. She wished her father would charge down off his throne and drag the man bodily into the hall.

"Papa," she whispered. "What *is* he doing?"

The baron rearranged his wine-colored robes over his knees. "Playing with me, girl. What else?"

"Oh."

His frank reply was a measure of his irritation. The next

obvious question was why, but Erde sensed that the answer
had something to do with an unequal balance of power,
and might make him angry. She returned to the safety of
studying the waiting crowd. Even the chicken-crone was
there, staring at her still.

Then she spotted Alla, the only face she really wanted
to see, her old nursemaid and her father's before her. Alla
was watching, too, just so that she could wink and make a
face when their eyes met, to test Erde's powers of concentration, for sitting in her mother's chair she must never
giggle or grin. Alla was the castle midwife and Erde's only
remaining confidante since the death of her grandmother.
With a straight back and a forthright manner, Alla was
sneaking into her eighth decade with every intent of living
through it. Even so, Erde was glad someone'd had the respect to find her a stool. *Alla will know,* she told herself,
what it means to dream about dragons.

At last, there was a stir near the grand entry. The courtiers neatened their lines abruptly. The elderly court herald
dipped back into the hall with a relieved nod, straightened
his green and black tabard, and gestured to the guardsmen.
It took two strong men to swing each tall wooden door
wide on growling iron hinges. Erde heard the herald cough
and clear his rheumy throat, and worried for him. Fricca
had told her he was in bad health. She'd also said that the
baron thought it was time to replace him with a younger
man more in keeping with the style of the new court.

The herald faced the outer hall. "Gentlemen of the
Cloth! To the court of Josef Heinz-Friedrich, fifteenth
Baron von Alte, be welcome!" He turned toward the dais,
graceful despite the years crooking his spine. "My lord
baron! May I present the envoy from the Church of Rome,
Brother Guillemo Gotti!"

Trumpets shrilled from the galleries. Necks craned. At
last, a release from boredom and the creeping chill!
Through the august columned doorway marched a pair of
white-clad, hooded men. Four even paces back, another
pair. Another followed, then another. Ten, twenty, thirty
tall sturdy men with dark beards deepening the concealing
shadows beneath their cowls. The hall filled with their bulk
and the wet-wool stench of their robes. Their every step
was matched. Their uncanny alikeness made Erde dizzy,

suffocated, as if there was no room within their sameness for so much as a breath. On the baron's right, the young guard captain Rainer came to full alert, shrugged his black ceremonial armor into a less uncomfortable position on his shoulders and signaled his men to move in close and be ready. Erde decided not to try to catch his eye. Not now, while he was working so hard to appear mature and in command.

When the first pair of robed men reached the foot of the dais, the entire entourage halted as one, as if at an unheard command, then knelt. Silence fell. The court's attention turned toward the door, awaiting Brother Guillemo's grand entrance. After a long moment, the old herald peered sidelong into the courtyard, then caught the baron's attention with a head shake and a subtle shrug.

The baron pursed his lips darkly. He studied the men kneeling before him. "Welcome to Tor Alte, gallant servants of the Church," he said finally. "Bring you word of your master, Brother Guillemo?"

"I do," a deep voice intoned from among the paired ranks.

"Step forward then, good brother, and be delivered of it."

"That I cannot, my lord. For I am he, and no man's master."

The baron flushed and the court murmured, for as yet no individual rose to officially identify himself. The baron rearranged his robes some more and settled himself more comfortably. "Your pardon then, sir. But may I know your face, to better welcome you in person?"

Court talk, thought Erde. She often wondered if her father practiced it in his rooms in secret. Nobody talked like that when they were sitting around at ease with each other.

With a rustle of sandals on stone, the entourage rose, and one of the second pair in line moved forward to stand before the dais, arms spread wide as if in supplication. "You honor me, my lord baron, with your understanding that we mean no discourtesy. I should explain that our vow of humility asks of us a ritual anonymity."

Erde suppressed an instinctive frown. She hated to admit to her father's brand of paranoia, but surely Tor Alte's chaplain would have informed the baron ahead of time of such an unusual Church protocol. Besides, how could this priest speak of anonymity, when the name of Brother Guillemo Gotti was already famous in a world where news traveled fitfully if at all? She peered at him more closely. Is that what a famous man looks like, so indistinguishable from his fellows? She stole a quick glance to her right, but her father gave no indication that he noticed anything amiss.

"The House of von Alte cherishes all dedicated servants of God. Welcome again, noble Brother. If your ritual is now satisfied, may I present to you my beloved daughter Erde?"

If the baron had hoped that chivalry would overwin humility, his gambit failed. The robed man bowed deeply but did not remove his hood. "My lady."

This is not Guillemo Gotti, Erde decided suddenly. *How peculiar. Why doesn't the priest speak for himself?* She was sure her grandmother would have rooted out the real man right away, or coaxed him into revealing himself, but Baron Josef chose to play along, launching immediately into a detailed recitation of arrangements for the funeral and the subsequent festivities. He may not have known how many servants worked for him but he knew all the proper protocols.

Meanwhile, Erde surveyed the other twenty-nine white robes and made her own choice. Four pairs from the back, within a few quick strides of the open door, one man seemed slightly shorter, slightly broader than the others. She had first picked him out by the quick gleam that his eyes made, catching the silvery light from the clerestory as they flicked about the hall. Mapping out the exits, or counting the guardsmen? Taking the measure of their young captain so prominently displayed by the baron's side? The other brothers kept their eyes fixed forward. Erde pondered this mystery. Brother Guillemo might willingly ask shelter and board of Josef von Alte, but perhaps he did not trust him. Was it because he came from so far away in Rome, and therefore did not trust any stranger?

She studied her candidate further, taking care not to be noticed. He was older, too, than the others, with pockmarked skin only partly hidden by his thick black beard and anonymous cowl. She could make out a narrow ferrety nose and full red lips. The priests Erde had known from the churches in the villages were mostly pale, dry creatures with bovine dispositions. The castle chaplain was reserved and precise. But this man's face was worldly and manipulative. He reminded her of some of her father's vassal lords, the sort who'd drink with him late into the night and the next day, scheme against him behind his back. She knew they did so. Her chamber-woman had told her all about it. Sometimes Fricca's gossipy nature had its uses.

"And so, my lord baron," the false-Guillemo was saying, "with your noble permission, we poor mendicants will retire to rest after our long journey and pray, in order to properly prepare for this solemn occasion and to be received into such high-born company."

The baron nodded. "My permission, good Brother, and gladly."

The priest bowed and melted back into the ranks of his fellows. When the entourage had proceeded grandly and irritatingly slowly into the courtyard, Baron Josef rose, signaling his guard captain to follow, and strode from the hall. The court relaxed into a hubbub of debate and discussion. Suddenly invisible, Erde slipped from her ceremonial chair and darted through the crowd.

"Alla! Alla!" She caught up with the nurse-midwife as the old woman struggled up the circular stair toward her chamber off the gallery. "Alla! Such a thing I have to tell you!"

"Hello, moonface. Don't be tearing that fine dress, now." Beneath her midwife's white head cloth, Alla's hair was thinning, but her eyes were bright and her round fine-seamed face demanded the same frank honesty that it offered. "Really knows how to lard it on, that one, doesn't he?"

"Listen to me, Alla, listen!" Erde squeezed past on the narrow stair and faced her, mounting the steps backward with the velvet gown hiked up past her shins. "You know what? It's not really him! I mean, that's not him, the one who spoke!"

"Slow down, lightning, so a poor ancient can understand."

Erde gained the top step and took a breath. Seeing Alla always reduced her self-image to that of an eight-year-old, until she caught herself and remembered she was nearly fourteen. "The monk who spoke to Papa is not really Brother Guillemo!"

"And no monk, either, I suppose," the old woman muttered. She scaled the final stairs with a soft groan for each rise, frail but erect, then limped determinedly along the gallery.

Erde dogged her heels. "But I'm sure, Alla, I'm really sure! Why would he do that? Maybe he's not even there! Oh, maybe something has happened to him, and they don't want anyone to know!"

"Hush, bluejay, before your tongue and your wild imagination race you neck and neck to nowhere!" Alla gripped Erde's arm and drew her off the tapestry-hung open gallery into the side hall that led to her room. "Now listen: do you want the whole mountain to hear how its liege lord allowed himself to be drawn into Fra Guill's silly game?"

"But couldn't they see?"

"Perhaps they were not looking. This man bears the imprimatur of Rome itself."

"But, Papa . . ."

"Perhaps he was looking *too* hard."

This last remark Erde did not understand, but Alla's brisk manner made one thing very clear: that this priest came disguised might prove he feared or mistrusted her father, but it also meant that the baron had cause to fear or mistrust the priest.

"And surely he does fear him," said Alla later, when they were safely behind closed doors. "This is no parish priest come begging for Christmas alms. We've not seen his like for a while hereabout." She set herself to brewing rose-mint tea at the tiny hearth that was barely enough to heat her draft-ridden room. Erde thought her father should provide his old wet nurse with better rooms, but Alla claimed she never felt the cold because she came from a much colder place far to the east, called the Russias. "Though he'd never show his fear, not my Iron Joe. He'll be pacing his study now, snapping the ears off our poor Rainer lad for not divining Fra Guill's trick ahead of time. You know how your father hates surprises."

"Why do you call him Fra Guill?" Erde hoped her father wouldn't yell at Rainer too much. She thought it odd to raise a fine young man like Rainer to a position of responsibility, then bully him all the time. The baroness would not have allowed it.

"That's Fra for *fratello,*" Alla explained. "It's Italian for 'brother.' But don't you be picking that one up, pipsqueak. It's what they call him in the villages, those that don't favor his doomsday preaching. Mark my words, this one's too dangerous for the likes of us to show him anything but the most obvious respect."

"Is that why Papa was polite, even when the priest was rude?"

"All part of the game, chipmunk. Josef's been looking to turn this visitation to his advantage since he first heard of it. Now he'll be plotting to return the challenge, or figuring out some way to make Fra Guill beholden to him. I only hope he truly comprehends what kind of swamp he's playing in."

Erde sipped at her tea pensively, inhaling scents of spring leaves and wood smoke. She loved Alla's room, with its spare furnishings and the wooden drying racks tied with flowers and herbs. She felt safe there, and welcome. She hitched her stool closer to the little fire. "Alla, is it true Fra . . . er, Brother Guillemo prophesies the coming of dragons?"

"Oh, well, yes, dragons," Alla agreed darkly. "Among other things. It's the other things we should be worrying about. The suspicion he encourages, the fires of doubt he fans in the hearts of the villages."

"I dreamed about dragons."

Alla nodded approvingly. "A good dream, I hope."

"I can't remember. Isn't it a bad omen to dream about dragons?"

"Nonsense, moss-nose! A von Alte has every right to dream about dragons."

"Does it mean they will come?"

"Here?" Alla cackled uproariously. "Just think of it! What self-respecting dragon would hang around here, with no livestock in the fields but some starved milch cow to steal for his dinner?"

Erde grinned at her old nurse over the glazed rim of her tea bowl. "Well, couldn't he just eat people?"

"Of course not!" Alla set her own bowl down. "Where'd you get that idea, calfbrain? Dragons don't eat people."

Erde nodded. Just what the Mage-Queen would have said. "Brother Guillemo says they do, least that's what Fricca told me."

Alla's smirk dismissed both Fricca and Brother Guillemo. "This priest talks about a lot of things he knows nothing about. But don't you go telling *anyone* I said so. Now be off, starling, and ready yourself for the baronessa's final ritual."

Erde's grin fell away like a leaf in the wind. For a moment, safe in Alla's little room, she had almost forgotten that her grandmama was dead.

Cold rain fell as the funeral procession wound down among the jutting rock ledges toward the alpine meadow where ten generations of von Altes slept the long sleep beneath rough-hewn granite slabs.

The rain became sleet as the wind picked up. In the lead, the baron quickened his pace, though the broken scree was icy and treacherous underfoot and his gait was not particularly steady. The court lagged behind, but the thirty robed brothers tightened their cowls about their dark faces and urged the pallbearers onward, though their white-shrouded burden swayed precipitously atop its heavy wooden bier.

Erde left off her searching for the real Guillemo among the hoods and robes and concentrated on keeping her balance. The guard captain Rainer paced beside her, his hand ready at her elbow.

Rainer was from Duchen, a town far to the south. He'd come to Tor Alte as a motherless boy of seven, traveling with his father who was a courtier on the king's business. Erde's only memory of the man was a toddler's misty vision of a tall figure dressed in red, for the same illness that claimed her mother took Rainer's father soon after he arrived. Because the orphaned boy was mannerly and intelligent, the baroness took him into her service, but soon became fond of him, and raised him more like a younger son than a servant. Erde had grown up with Rainer, fighting and playing and sharing secrets as if he were the older brother she very much lacked.

He had grown tall like his father, slim but strong and adept with his sword, and was now working too hard at the business of being an adult to have much time for a younger sister. Though he made sure to pause when they met, to tease her a little and exchange a few words of gossip, Erde missed their giggling and chasing, and lately she sensed a new formality in him, an unacknowledged distance that puzzled and dismayed her. She suspected it was because she was just a girl and Rainer was newly made guard captain, upon her father's succession. Just turned nineteen was a young age to have risen so high, so perhaps he had become overly full of himself.

But not today. Glancing sidelong at his pale, solemn face, Erde was sure that the baroness' death had grieved Rainer as much as it had her. She brushed sleet from her eyes. "If only it would go ahead and snow. Grandmama always loved a fresh fall of snow."

Rainer nodded wordlessly. He slipped off his heavy woolen cloak and draped it about her shoulders without asking, like the solicitous brother he'd once been. Erde's own cloak was warm enough but she knew Rainer worried about people taking ill in the cold, never thinking to worry the same about himself. He was too thin, she decided, too taut across the cheekbones, as if the anxiety she often read in his eyes were absorbing his flesh from the inside. How is my father treating you, she wanted to ask, but now was not the time for conversation, nor this place, so grim and chill, the proper place.

The grass was brown in the meadow, as shriveled as if summer had never happened. The granite marker waited to one side, the size and shape of a stable door, and as gray as the leaden sky. The grave was shallow, a mere depression in the mountain rock scraped bare with pick and hand. But the baroness had been tall and thin, as Erde would be also.

"There will be room enough," she murmured sadly.

Beside her, Rainer shifted, cleared his throat, and said nothing. She wished they could hold hands like they used to in church, keeping each other awake on cold mornings during the sermon. She wanted to weep and lean into him, as she would do with her great horse Micha, exchanging her grief for his warmth and solidity. But she knew if she slipped her hand into his, Rainer would stiffen and ease his hand away. Besides, her father would be angry if he spied her disgracing him with childish tears and displays of emotion. Erde sighed deeply and kept her eyes dry.

The white-robes ranged themselves before the grave like a military escort, at rigid attention in two rows of fifteen, waiting for the stragglers to arrive. To Erde it felt as if she was their prisoner, instead of them being guests of the castle. When the court had finally assembled, one white-robe stepped forward as Brother Guillemo would be expected to do. He signaled the pallbearers to set down the bier. Four of the baroness' most favored retainers, the old herald among them, took up the damp embroidered edges of the linen to lift the slight still weight and lower it into the shallow pit. The fifteenth Baron von Alte stood at the head of the grave and gazed down at his mother's shrouded remains, frowning.

The white-robe who had come forward began the ritual of burial. He kept his head down and his voice low and reverent until the section of the rite where the priest addresses the congregation. Then he let both rise, and augmented his performance with gestures. His cowl slid back a bit as he warmed to a lecture on the wages of sin, warning of a nearby day of reckoning. Erde waited for him to mention dragons but he only decried the wickedness of the worldly in a more general sort of way, exhorting all present to stand beside him in the coming battle against the evils abroad in the land, to take responsibility and clean out the "sinkholes of depravity" in their own back gardens.

Erde was disappointed. She thought his harangue a standard one and over-rehearsed. Tor Alte's own chaplain was also dull but at least he'd known the baroness, and would have done better by being able to say something personal. What did catch her interest was noting that the haranguer was not the same man who'd passed as Brother Guillemo a few hours earlier. Covertly, she located her own candidate in the back rank, but this time she forgot herself and stared too long. His eyes, darting about, met hers and held piercingly until she could gather her wits enough to glance away.

Her heart thudded. She felt short of breath. Throughout the rest of the long, sleet-sodden ceremony, Erde pressed as close to Rainer as he would allow, and did not look up again.

CHAPTER THREE

At the funeral feast that evening, a third false-Guillemo took the place of honor at the baron's right.

Candles flared at the high table and the hearths burned bright. Precious oil smoked in every lamp on the three great wagon-wheel chandeliers. Three days had passed since word had come of Brother Guillemo's offer to reroute his pilgrimage in order to bury the baroness in the full authority of the Church of Rome. The baron's chamberlain had been frantically gathering food and arranging the precise protocols of seating and serving. Household and guests crowded the long horseshoe of stout wooden trestles, grateful for the ceremonial excuse to eat all they could get their hands on.

Tray after tray of roasted meats and sauced vegetables paraded past the high table for inspection. Meanwhile, the new false-Guillemo engaged Baron Josef in a peculiarly one-way conversation. Seated to her father's left, Erde listened while pretending not to. This man's voice was deep like the other two Guillemos', but more nasal. Her girl-child's enforced experience as a listener told her he spoke German like a native. It was his foreigner's accent that was learned. She stored this detail away to pass on to Alla later.

Erde had no trouble searching out her real-Guillemo, but now she was painfully cautious in her surveillance. She did note that he placed himself well inside the ranks of his brothers, along the right side of the horseshoe, and that while the robed and hooded man to her father's right spoke of the cold summer and bad harvest and made an elaborate show of taking a spartan meal of bread, cheese, and spring water, the platter in front of her chosen Guillemo bore only a nibbled crust and some apple parings. But Erde spied him helping himself covertly from his neighbors' bowls and flagons—and only from those portions they had already tasted. Now and then, she caught him staring in her direction.

She herself could barely eat. She considered the group gluttony of feasting to be the least appealing aspect of ceremonial occasions, and resented the probability that this noisy throng of red-faced, greasy-fingered eaters had struggled through the wet, unseasonable cold not to bid the baroness a loving farewell but to stuff themselves with a good meal.

Tonight, particularly, she felt heavy and stupid from the unaccustomed heat in the hall. The din of forced joviality beat harshly at her ears. She drank some wine to wet her nervous throat, and wished the priest would stop looking at her. She knew that, as a baron's daughter, she would always be stared at and would always have people seeking to use her somehow, but she particularly hated feeling drawn into this man's game. It was like being sucked into a current too strong to swim against.

For relief, she watched Rainer as he wandered the circuit of the tables, restless, a mug of ale in hand for camouflage. She found herself thinking how fine he looked, as if she had never really noticed before, how tall and bronze-blond he was in his black captain's tunic. Fricca had once called Rainer "delicate," and it was true that he was not brawny like most of the baron's Guard, the beefy bearded men whom the chamber-women cooed over. His shoulders were not overbroad and he often had to be reminded to stand up straight. But Erde had watched him spar with his men in the stable yard. He was easily their equal in strength and agility, and his greater height gave him an added advantage. What Fricca thought overanxious and fragile, Erde saw as sensitive and elegant. Certainly he was the only member of the baron's Guard who'd learned how to read. The baroness had seen to that. After all, Rainer's father had served His Majesty the King.

How steadfast he seemed to her now as she watched him pace along the tapestried wall, how concerned and reliable. She considered taking him into her confidence and pointing out the real-Guillemo to him, but what if he didn't believe her? Or worse still, what if Alla was right, that both Rainer and her father had noted the deception long ago, and only she, a foolish little girl, thought it was such a big secret? She wouldn't want to seem foolish to Rainer.

"Your table is a marvel, my lord, in times of such hardship." The false-Guillemo drained his cup and refilled it from a clay pitcher of springwater.

"Hospitality is one of our Lord's commandments, is it not?" returned the baron dryly, gesturing for his own cup to be filled with hearth-warmed wine.

Erde fanned herself covertly. Was her father calling the hooded band's bluff with this merciless indoor heat? She found his forbearance with his lecturing guest to be quite remarkable, even as the man detailed far beyond courtesy the plight of the lands he had traveled most recently, how the fertile river plains were plagued with drought and the uplands so unseasonably cold and wet that the frost-killed crops rotted in the fields before ripening.

"Peasant and lord, they're declaring it a punishment from God, my lord baron, and being God-fearing folk, they wonder what it is they've done to deserve such misfortune. One or two bad seasons they're used to, as good men of the land, but my lord, this year makes it six in a row!"

The baron set down his knife, with which he had just speared a prime chunk of venison and paired it with a small potato. His eyes sparkled with drink, but his voice was neutral. "I have petitioned to the king for relief for the villages."

"The king?" The false-Guillemo let just enough space fall between his words to invite comment. "You will surely pardon a visitor's ignorance, lord baron, but from what we have heard in our travels, you will be lucky indeed if help comes from that quarter."

Erde was shocked. The king had surely had his troubles of late, but in her grandmother's court, such disrespect would not have been allowed, even from a foreigner who could be supposed not to know any better. But Baron Josef merely reclaimed his knife and ate, his glance steady on his guest.

"I mean, of course, from which of your king's empty storehouses is such relief to come?"

The baron chewed thoughtfully. "Ah, yes, from where is relief to come? Nearer at hand, perhaps."

"Perhaps, my lord." Again, the pause. The false-Guillemo's hands were folded tightly on the table in front of him. "But we must not hope for help from an earthly king when the Church is our only salvation. Six bad years. Six, you know, my lord, is the Devil's number."

The baron speared another morsel, nodding.

The false priest leaned closer, the folds of his cowl falling about his face so that his deep voice resonated out of pure darkness. "It is not Heaven who punishes us, my lord, nor chance who visits with these plagues. God has sent his Word to our brethren, and we have received it. The true cause is Nature, the Devil's fancy woman, and her host of beasts and sorcerers, turning our own lands against us. A conspiracy of mages, lord baron, of mages, witches, and women, that God calls us to rise up against and vanquish in His Name! What do you say to that?"

A conspiracy of mages, indeed. Erde found herself wishing she could call up the Mage-Queen herself to spirit this horrible man away, all the way back to Rome with every one of his so-called brothers. She noted her father's faintly arched brow and watched his interest, captured initially by the priest's political innuendo, fade before this onslaught of religious rhetoric.

"Good brother, I await further enlightenment."

The not-priest heard the invitation but not its skepticism. "There are dark forces abroad, my lord! Dark forces that thrive on our weaknesses. We've been too careless of Nature, sir. We've relaxed our guard, let her evade our discipline, let her emissaries invade our lives, our very homes. Our women talk of cycles of the moon instead of gifts from God. Our children run loose in the land like young animals, empowering the very forces that seek domination over us! Nature readies herself, my lord. She calls her creatures to her, and soon . . ."

Through the drone of the false-priest's tirade, Erde became aware of a door opening, a scuffle, of shouts rising above the chatter of the diners, a man crying out Brother Guillemo's name as he was subdued by three guardsmen who'd been handy to the entrance. The candle flames danced on the high table and she heard the soft rasp of Rainer's sword easing from its sheath.

The false-Guillemo broke off his speech and sprang from

his seat, arms spread wide. He stood for a moment, poised, letting his cup spill and roll to the floor, its clatter punctuating the sudden silence his gesture created. "Soldiers, I beg you! Let this good man be! He does no harm to call my name!"

The other white-robes rose as one to second his protest.

The three guardsmen looked to their captain. In the breathless hush, the pinioned man worked an arm free and reached toward the false-priest with a desperate cry. "Brother, they have come! Protect us, poor sinners all! Have mercy on us!"

Ladies giggled and whispered as the false-Guillemo pushed back his chair and shouldered his way through the throng of his hooded brothers toward the door. "Who comes, friend? What has you so frightened?"

"The dragons! The dragons come!"

In Erde's breast, hope stirred along with apprehension. Dragons? The white-robes murmured and stirred, flowing like a frothy torrent in the false-priest's wake.

"My lord?" asked Rainer quietly from beside the baron's chair.

"Religion's his bailiwick." The baron sipped his wine. "Let him handle it, if he's so eager."

Rainer raised his sword, letting the blade flare in the lamplight, then sheathed it. The guardsmen let the man go.

"You know this man?" the baron asked Rainer. A hovering servant filled his cup again.

"No, my lord. But I'll ask around later."

The newcomer was middle-aged and pasty, as if his job kept him well out of the sun. He fell to his knees on the slate floor, weeping at the false-priest's feet as the other white-robes converged around them, hiding both from sight. The courtiers waited, tittering among themselves, eager for the excitement.

"What now?" the baron murmured, easing forward in his chair.

"Another switch?" Rainer suggested, and Erde breathed a sigh of relief that she hadn't blurted out her Great Discovery to him. Had the entire court been aware of it? She reminded herself to listen to Alla more. Clearly, not saying anything was just part of the game.

"He'll have to get down to business sooner or later,"

said the baron. "Now that he knows I'm not going to poison him."

"But can you trust him to tell you what his business is, my lord?"

The baron offered his guardsman an icy profile. "I can trust myself to figure it out, Captain."

Rainer's head dipped. "Of course, my lord."

"Brothers!" A new voice rose from out of the throng around the door. "Give the man room to speak!" The white-robes drew aside. Erde's real-Guillemo now knelt beside the weeping man, his hood thrown back, revealing a bald head and large, commanding eyes. He pressed the man's hand piously to his chest. A guffaw from one of the guardsmen's tables against the far wall was quickly hushed.

"Yesss!" hissed the baron thickly. "Now we'll see what he's about."

"It's really him now!" Erde whispered before she could stop herself.

Rainer grinned and nodded, but Baron Josef turned and stared her into silence. The wine sparkle in his eyes was blurred and watery.

"Holy father, help us!" the weeping man pleaded.

"We are all brothers here, my friend," Guillemo reproved gently. He rose, pulling the man up with him. His hands were small, Erde noticed. Darkly furred and delicate. "Have you your voice back now? Can you tell us what you saw?"

"Ohhh!" Ragged sleeves fell back from the palest flesh as the man waved his arms and tried to cover his head. "A great rush of wings past the wheat field, Brother, and a shadow like blackest night falling over the barnyard! And an awful stench, like a hot wind from the very bowels of hell itself. It's the evil come hunting us, surely, just like you prophesied! See, here, its terrible mark!"

"Where? What?"

The man offered his forearm. "Its awful spittle fell in flaming gouts and burned me."

Guillemo grasped the arm with both hands to display to the crowd like a relic. A few red welts marred the hairless skin. "Lo!" the priest exclaimed. "The mark of Satan!"

In the clamor of derision and dismay that followed, the baron tapped his front teeth with the point of his knife and gestured to his captain to move closer again. "Do you believe in dragons, Rainer?"

"Actual dragons, my lord, or convenient ones in our neighborhood?"

The baron chuckled. "Just so! The man is clever, though."

"Sly. Send him packing."

"Not until I've plumbed his uses."

"I'd say it's you he seeks to use, sir."

"Don't cross me, boy!" the baron snapped. "You think I don't see what he is?"

Rainer straightened abruptly. "Your pardon, my lord!"

Erde dared a glance. Rainer's mouth was tight with shame, and she understood his confusion so well. It was like that with her father. Often he tricked you with invitations to intimacy, when really all he wanted to do was to hear himself talk. Sometimes it seemed the baron preferred his subordinates to be crafty rather than intelligent.

Guillemo sat the raving man down on one of the benches emptied by his entourage. His small hands soothed the man's thin shoulders. "Now, my friend, I have no doubt you believe what you saw, but perhaps you were only napping and woke from a bad dream, burning yourself on the hearth grate . . ."

"Oh, no, Brother, I swear . . ."

"Tch, man! Never swear unless you've a Bible to hand!" The priest cocked his head and offered his audience a worldly glance. "Perhaps, brother, you felt a particularly dark cloud passing over?" His gesture was derisive, and the court laughed with him.

"No, I . . ."

"Do you think we are so important, so special here in Tor Alte that the Devil would choose to single us out?"

The man became confused. "But how," he wailed, "are we to know?"

Brother Guillemo smiled at him then, a smile like embers bursting into flame on a darkened hearth. He smoothed back the man's disordered hair as if he were a child and kissed his pale brow. "Oh, my good brother, hear the Truth. No one is too small to avoid the Devil's attention and . . . you will know because I will tell you."

Guillemo was bulky but agile. Levering off the man's

shoulder, he sprang onto the bench and spread his arms.
His abrupt move, so like an attack, drew gasps around the
horseshoe. Swords clanked among the baron's Guard and
nearby, a woman shrieked.

"Listen, oh my people! For what if this man speaks
true?" His voice was as deep as his fellows' but more resonant. Erde felt it vibrate within her chest. Beside her, the
baron sat forward with renewed interest. Guillemo slewed
his riveting glance around the hall and pointed at the most
crowded table. "Do you know him?"

"Aye!" shouted someone, but Erde thought it came from
among the white-robes.

"Is he a good man?" Guillemo demanded.

"Aye!" several more voices answered.

"A humble man?"

"Aye!"

The priest reached behind him to grab the man's burned
arm and exhibit it once again. "Then are we not fortunate
for this good and humble man who brings us the first true
sign? He did not cower in terror of the Darkness but came
straightway to report its approach!" He looked down, over
the thick brush of his beard, pacing the length of the bench
and scowling. "Be wary, oh my people! Be alert to every
sign, to every chance of a sign, to every possibility that the
Moment is come!" He let his voice drop, as if speaking in
private meditation. The only other sound in the hall was
the crack of the hearth fires and the chicken-crone snoring
in a corner. "For this evil is everywhere, and the innocent
are the most easily corrupted." He looked up, singled out
a pretty woman nearby. "A young soldier's wife had a
sickly child. Instead of bringing him into God's church for
a holy blessing, she buys a talisman from an old hag who
lives at the end of the village." He stamped his foot, pointing suddenly at the entrance. "And thus, the Devil has a
foot in her door!"

Several people glanced nervously behind them.

Guillemo paced along the bench again, turned, and paced
back. "Remember, oh my people! The Devil's only foot-
hold in this world is in our hearts! If we would deny him
there, he would never triumph! But we do not deny him!
Every day without thinking we let him in! A child talks

back to his father! A woman argues with her husband! A young girl buys a love charm and, oh my people, see how we suffer for it! See how the lands dry up and the babies starve! See, see . . ."

Guillemo reached both arms above his head as if grasping for the sky, then clapped his palms to bulging eyes and fell gasping to his knees on the tabletop. "See! Oh, I see, my good people! I see the winged servants of Satan abroad in the land, searing the fields with their foul breath, blackening the waters with their reptile slime, setting them to boil with the acid of their tongues! I see demons marching against us, led by the secret army of witches and warlocks who hide now among us waiting for the Devil's call! Oh! I see the air aflame with dragons! I see the witch-child and the Devil's Paladin . . . oh . . . !" His face scarlet and swollen, the priest doubled over on the wide boards of the trestle, moaning, scattering cups and platters. Several of the white-robes rushed to aid him, raising him bodily, settling him back on the bench, brushing at his robe and plying him with water and wine. Erde sat frozen in her chair. She hoped she had only imagined that, the moment before he'd collapsed, this final, real, and terrifying Fra Guill had caught her eye.

When it was plain that the priest's vision had passed, the court relaxed, having finally been granted the spectacle they had sat down to receive in his company. On his bench in the midst of his solicitous brothers, Guillemo contrived to look ordinary once more, nodding and smiling, wiping his brow on his sleeve, blotting the saliva from his beard.

The baron watched him fixedly. He drained his wine cup and signaled for more. "See how well he plays them."

Erde wondered if his envy was as clear to everyone around him as it was to her. She wished Alla was there, but the castle midwife was not invited to formal events, and nobody else was listening. The real Guillemo had enraptured them all.

When the priest recovered himself, he asked for the man who had brought the dragon sign and led him to a seat himself, boldly setting him down to a meal at the baron's table. Then he made his way to the place his former self had vacated, bowing deeply before easing into the broad velvet-cushioned chair. "Your pardon, my lord baron, for this untimely disturbance . . . I fear God does not warn ahead when he sends his Holy Word to me."

Baron Josef studied him for a moment with pursed lips. Unlike his substitutes, the real Guillemo returned the stare unflinchingly. Finally, the baron nodded, as if some negotiation had passed between them. He signaled for wine to be poured for them both, and the priest did not refuse.

"God's Word must not be denied," agreed the baron. "Tell me, does God fear we harbor witches at Tor Alte, Brother Guillemo? Should I be checking my stables for dragon scat?"

Erde could not decipher the priest's cocked eyebrow. Was it the expected disapproval or was it amusement?

"The Devil's minions are everywhere, my lord."

"Indeed they are." The baron eased himself back into the velvet cushion of his chair. "I don't recall hearing before of a Devil's Paladin, Brother. Who might he be, fallen angel or human man?"

"He is in the vision, my lord. I myself do not yet comprehend it."

The baron swirled the wine in his cup. "Sometimes I think my mother was a witch."

"God forbid, Baron, for today she lies in holy ground!"

The baron's laugh was careless. "Well, I mean, how else could a woman hold a throne so long? But you were speaking of the children." He waved an unsteady hand. "Before all this. Pray do continue."

"Was I?" Guillemo smiled guilelessly. He tasted his wine, then drank deeply. "With all the excitement, I've quite forgot."

"The *naughty* children," the baron prodded. "Running loose in the woods."

Guillemo chuckled. "The woods, my lord?"

"Yes, yes, like little animals. Erde, my sweet, are you listening?"

"Of course, Papa." Erde sipped at her wine. Hoodless, Brother Guillemo was ugly, with his ferrety nose and his pockmarked skin. But his transforming innocent smile could make you question whether you'd misjudged him. Then he leveled a predatory eye on her and Erde was sure she had not. A true priest in God's grace should not stare so.

"Not your children, of course, my lord," said Guillemo.

"I've only the one, Brother, was widowed early. A motherless child, you know, can run a bit wild. Yes, I think even my daughter could benefit from some proper schooling."

Erde sipped again, to appear occupied. She wished they wouldn't talk about her as if she weren't sitting right next to them.

Guillemo contrived to look both sympathetic and disapproving. "Surely, my lord, a girl her age already has what schooling befits a woman."

"Ah, yes, but her grandmother had her own ideas. So, needless to say, there's work left to do. Fortunately, she's hardly grown. But growing fast, very fast." He threw Erde the odd look he had earlier, from her chamber door, only this time he smiled, as if at a secret between them.

"She's very dark," the priest remarked. "Unusual."

"Her mother's blood."

"Lovely . . ." the priest murmured.

No, a priest should not stare so. Erde looked down, breathless and sick under their shared regard, wanting to rush from the hall and not stop until she was away from the heat and the smoke and breathing free in the sharp mountain air. The need seized her until she was dizzy with it. She grasped for her wineglass and missed.

The baron saw her color go, and raised his arm with a quick snap of his fingers. "Captain!"

Rainer was ready behind the baron's chair. "My lord?"

"I think the child has had enough feasting for one evening. Please see her to her room."

"Of course, my lord."

Erde summoned enough presence of mind to say her proper good nights at the high table, but she was glad of Rainer's steady arm as she tottered from the hall. In the outer corridor, her vision swam, her knees buckled. Rainer caught her about the waist and picked her up without thinking.

"Shall you carry me, then?" she asked foolishly.

The guardsmen stared straight ahead. "It appears I shall, my lady, you not being much able to walk and all."

"Am I not too heavy?"

Rainer laughed softly. "No. Not too heavy."

"I could walk, you know." But it felt better to rest her head against his chest as he paced down the long side hall, to be with someone who was not always judging her and finding her lacking. The dizziness subsided, though the nausea remained. She wanted only to go to bed.

"I hope you're not picking up the drinking habit, my lady." He paused and readjusted her weight to carry her up the broad central staircase.

Erde snorted rudely. "It's my father who's drinking too much!"

"Ah, but my lord baron can drink most of us under the table."

She marveled that men seemed to find this so admirable a quality in each other. "I think the priest could drink more."

"Yes, you would think that, if you're not watching him carefully. But his cup hardly empties."

Erde frowned. Perhaps she'd been feeling too poorly to be truly alert. "Well, I only had one cup of wine."

"Even one can be too much for some, you know."

"It made me sleepy."

"Are you feeling better?"

"My stomach aches so oddly."

"I'll fetch Fricca for you when we get there."

Erde nestled into the dark fabric of his tunic as if it were her pillow. The rhythm of the stairs was soothing. She could hear his heart beating. "Try my father's rooms."

Rainer nearly missed a step. "What?"

"Oh, you know what I mean. That's where she is most times now. She's more his chamber-woman than she is mine."

"Erde! . . . my lady, I mean . . . ?" He shook his head helplessly.

"I'm not blind, you know."

"Of course not."

"I'm almost fourteen, for heaven's sake!"

"So you are, my lady, so you are."

She heard herself giggle and knew the wine truly had gone to her senses. Her only hope was to lie back and enjoy the ride. "Oh, Rainer, you're so proper!"

"I am not," he replied indignantly.

"You are! You used to call me princess."

He paused again for breath on the top step, gazing down the dim curving corridor that led to the tower stair. "I used to call you a lot of things that aren't right for us anymore."

"Who says?"

"Well, uh . . . you know."

"I want to know who says such things! I hate it when you call me 'my lady.' "

"But that's what you are."

She knew that now was the time to ask him, now that the wine had loosed her tongue. "Rainer, are we not friends anymore?"

He headed down the corridor. "Friends? Sure we are."

This was somehow not a satisfying answer, but his long-legged stride quieted her, made her thoughts drift. Her head ached as she thought about Fricca and her father and what they did together in his rooms. Was it the same as love? She knew she could question Fricca, who would eagerly supply every detail. But Erde couldn't bear the thought of knowing such things about her own father.

However, her curiosity, being suppressed, was the more intense.

"Rainer, have you ever kissed anyone?"

"Hey! Are you *trying* to get me in trouble?"

Well, finally. She had shocked the formality out of him. "We used to talk about that sort of thing all the time."

A pretty serving girl came out of a room ahead of them with an armful of linens. Seeing Rainer, she propped her load against the wall and smiled. He nodded stiffly and strode past. "Okay, sure, yes, I have."

"Who? Friends?"

"That is none of your business."

"Well, would you only kiss someone who's beautiful?"

He glanced down at her quizzically, made a turn, took a breath, and started up the next flight of stairs. "That depends. Why?"

"Would you kiss me even though I'm not beautiful?"

The guardsman caught himself just before he sent them tumbling on the stone. "Shhh! What are you saying! Damn, Erde, you are drunk, after all!"

Erde looked up at him earnestly. "No. It's my new idea. If there's something I'm shy about, I learn it from a friend."

"If there's anything you're shy about, I sure don't know what it is."

"But doesn't it make sense?"

"It'd make more sense to be thinking about what your father would say."

Erde frowned. "My father hates me."

"Of course he doesn't."

"He hates me because I'm alive and my mother isn't."

"He loved her," said Rainer simply.

"I miss her as much as he does!"

"Perhaps. But in a different way."

She relaxed against him. "Please, Rainer . . . would you?"

"What? What?"

"Kiss me."

"Don't be silly."

"Please! Just once, so I know what it's like. I'll never make you do it ever again, I promise."

Rainer made his voice deep and serious. "This is unseemly, my lady."

Erde laughed and wriggled in his arms. She closed her eyes and puckered up her mouth until it was a tiny hill above her chin. "Please, please, pleeeese . . . ?"

Rainer sighed. He slowed at a landing, glanced around, then dipped his head and brushed her lips lightly, the barest feather touch with a dry tense mouth. "There." He raised his head and continued upward resolutely.

Erde opened her eyes to the firm smooth line of his jaw and the bronze glint of his hair as it curled around his earlobe. The sculpture of his lower lip was so finely wrought, so like a statue, that she felt the urge to slide her fingertip, just the very tip, slowly along beneath its shadow. A surge of her father's quicksilver envy seized her, sharp as a knife in her befuddled heart. She couldn't quite keep back the tears. "It's because I'm not beautiful, isn't it?"

"What is?"

"You won't really kiss me because I'm not beautiful, like you are."

"Like . . . ?" Rainer stopped and gazed down at her. "What's going on here?"

Erde was suddenly nervous. She had pushed and pushed at something she didn't quite understand until an unseen

boundary had been crossed. "Oh, Rainer, I didn't mean
to . . ."

"Yes, you did."

"Well, I mean . . ." She twisted her face into his chest.
"I'm so confused."

"Erde . . ."

She glanced up, and he tightened his arms around her,
gathering her unsuspecting mouth into his, quickly, hun-
grily, running his tongue along the inside of her lip before
letting go abruptly with a soft groan and a shake of his
head, like a man coming up through water. "Who says
you're not beautiful? Don't let anyone tell you you're not
beautiful!"

Erde stared at him in wonder. "Oh."

He gulped a breath, let it out, then laughed harshly.
"Holy God, I've surely lost my mind." He resettled her
more formally, as if he could hold her at a distance from
him, hurrying along in silence until they had reached the
door to her room. "I'm going to put you down now. Can
you stand? Can you manage until I find Fricca?"

She nodded, tongue-tied, wanting him to go, wanting to
cling to him. He let her slide gently to the floor, supporting
her still with one arm. As he reached for the door latch,
Erde heard him gasp softly. There was bright blood on
his hand.

Erde was mystified. "What happened? Are you all
right?"

Rainer stared at his hand a moment more, then at her,
craning his neck to look her over. "Oh, Princess," he whispered. "It's yours."

"What? Mine?" Then Erde understood. "Oh no!"

"Fricca!" Rainer shouted, no longer equal to the situation. He shoved open the door. "Fricca! Damn! Where are
you, woman?"

Thoroughly awake at last and mortified beyond imagining, Erde slipped out of his encircling arm and pushed him
away from the door. "No! I'm, uh, all right! I'm . . . oh,
God, just leave me alone!"

She darted behind the door and shut it in his face.

CHAPTER FOUR

Erde recalled her chamber-woman finding her in the middle of the floor, but not much else until she was bathed and in bed by firelight with Fricca patting her hand and telling her not to worry, that was how it was being a woman. For all her voluble advice-giving, Fricca had neglected to warn her that when this much awaited time arrived, she would feel so completely awful.

"Oh, that'll pass." Fricca was plainly delighted by the turn of events, though she did cast the occasional troubled glance at the ruined white gown now discarded in the corner. She pressed her giggles back into her mouth. "Poor Rainer! Oh, such a face on him! You'd think these young soldiers would be used to the sight of a bit of blood!"

Erde relaxed into the feather bed and let her breathing slow. Perhaps if she feigned sleep, Fricca would go away and leave her alone with the thousand new thoughts raging in her head. She didn't think of Rainer. She couldn't without squirming. He would never speak to her again, and surely she would never dare speak to him. Yet his face filled her vision when she closed her eyes. She had not expected his lips to be so soft.

In the breaks in Fricca's monologue, Erde could hear the sleet ticking at the window glass. In the forest, the deer would be seeking out their winter shelter, the young ones too slight yet to withstand the early weather. Shouts from the feasting echoed up the stairwell. Brassy music and the distant clash of steel.

"Listen to them still going on!" exclaimed Fricca. "You'd think it was a battle won, not a poor good woman laid in the holy ground."

Erde pictured her father, well into his cups with the slimy priest. She wondered if Rainer had returned downstairs as well, to drink too much and joke with the rest of the Guard and make fun of the baron's daughter, the silly skinny child who couldn't hold her wine. She knew Rainer was always a moderate drinker, but she wouldn't blame him for wanting to lose himself in drink tonight. She turned over with a groan and curled tighter around the source of her unfamiliar ache. "Is Alla asleep already?"

"Nay, the captain went to fetch her. She'll be making up something special for you, that's all that keeps her." Fricca rose to stir the fire and pile on several unnecessary logs, then came to close the bed curtains. "Go to sleep if you can. I'll sit till she comes."

The warm bed soothed, and the flame-flicker on the sheer linen drapes was mesmerizing. Erde dozed but it could only have been a while, for the firelight was still bright on the curtains when sudden noises woke her, loud voices in the outer hall, her door opening.

"Where is my daughter? Is she well?"

Her father, and fully drunk by the sound of him. Erde did not move.

Fricca sputtered out of her nap by the hearth. "Oh, fast asleep, my lord." She gave a small womanly laugh. "After her ordeal."

"What? What ordeal?"

"Ummm . . ." Fricca faltered. Erde guessed there was someone else in the room.

"Out with it, woman," her father ordered.

"Shhh, shhh, my lord!" There was whispering, and Fricca's maddening giggle.

"What? When?"

"Just now! I found the poor child fainted dead away in the middle of the floor." Fricca sobered. "But I fear your fine gift is ruined, my lord. And my dear lady's gown as well."

"Pfft," said the baron. "Just a dress. Her mother would be delighted. Let's see this trophy!"

"Surely not, my lord, with . . ."

"Bring it!"

Fricca reluctantly retrieved the stained garment. The baron snatched it from her and shook it out. He was silent

for a long time. Erde heard him walking about in the staccato way of a drunk determined to appear sober.

"Well, Brother," he declared finally. "What do you think
of that? My daughter is a woman at last."

"Cause for joy indeed, my lord."

The priest. In her own bedchamber. Erde thought of the
deer again and tried to be as still as they were when hiding
from the hunters.

"My only daughter," mused the baron thickly. Then he
roused himself. "We must announce it. We must have a
celebration!"

But Erde detected no celebration in his voice. She heard
the scrape of the priest's sandal, his light-footed careful
step, as he moved toward the heat of the fireplace. "Certainly you should, my lord, once the usual rituals have been
observed." He lowered his voice, which made him sound
threatening. "I assume, my good woman, that you've taken
appropriate steps, in order to be able assure his lordship
that he's hearing the truth of the matter?"

"Steps?" Fricca replied blankly.

"I mean, woman, have you properly examined the girl?"

"Oh, oh, she's fine, your reverence, I mean, she will be,
just tuckered out, you know."

"Don't play with me, woman!" the priest growled.

Fricca made inarticulate noises, then fell silent.

The baron snorted. "She hasn't a clue what you mean,
Brother. We are a bit less formal here in the benighted
provinces. But rest your mind." The gown rustled as he
tossed it to the floor. "Truth is in the evidence."

"But evidence can mislead, my lord."

The baron hardly seemed to hear him. "A celebration,
then! Fricca! Let's have some wine here!"

"There's a tray already laid in your chamber, my
lord . . ."

"But none here. I see none here! Now, woman! Here
and now!"

Fricca rustled away. The baron lowered himself with an
explosive sigh into the chair by the hearth. The leather
creaked and for a while, Erde heard only the snap of the
fire and her father's wine-heavy breathing. Then the
priest stirred.

"May I speak, my lord?"

"Aye, speak, Brother. You've shown no reluctance so far. In fact, I've been impressed, yes, even moved by your knowledge and concern for the minor political details of a fiefdom that could hardly be of importance to a great man from Rome." He shifted and the leather groaned again. "What's on your mind?"

"Concern for your own interests, my lord, now that I have come to know you personally. And for God's holy commandments."

The baron chuckled. "Are they all under attack?"

"You may mock, my lord, but the Devil lurks behind every door."

"Enough simpering behind priest's rhetoric, Guillemo! We've done with that, you and I, have we not? Leave it to your army of subordinates. If something's bothering you, spit it out!"

"With your permission then, my lord . . . in cases like this, the ritual examination is no mere formality. It . . ."

"Cases like this?"

The priest was silent a moment, offering a reluctance to continue so obviously a ploy that Erde could barely keep silent. She wanted to shout at her father that if he weren't so drunk, he'd see how this man was manipulating him. At length, Guillemo cleared his throat politely. "My lord baron, I sense something irregular here. Could the servant be protecting the girl?"

"Protecting?"

"Well, for instance, you said she never informed you of the girl's unseemly gamboling in the woods."

"Protecting her for what?"

"For your daughter's reputation," the priest prodded silkily, "and for yours. The woman clearly, well . . . favors you, my lord. It's only natural that she'd . . ."

Erde thought she would stop breathing altogether. She could almost hear suspicion clicking into place in her father's wine-sodden brain, like the gears of a clock readying itself to strike.

"For what *reason*, I mean!"

Guillemo's sandals slapped softly against the stone, back and forth in front of the hearth. "Before my, ah, Calling, lord baron, I had in Rome some training in matters of the law. Those old habits compel me yet to review events until

my heart is satisfied that they are as they appear to be, or
as they have been presented."

A rattle of cups announced Fricca's return. "Wine, my
lord."

"What kept you? Give it here!" The baron poured and
drank. "So. What of it, man? Go on."

Guillemo resumed his pacing. "A young girl drinks too
much, is escorted from the hall by a handsome captain. A
while later, she is found by her chambermaid, sprawled on
the floor, her garment a ruin."

"Only stained, my lord," Fricca ventured. "A good soak-
ing might save it. And she wasn't sprawled. She'd fainted,
poor lamb."

"Go on, Brother," said the baron tightly.

"Well, my lord, as a protector of God's Laws and as your
friend, this is the thing I must ask: what about this boy-
soldier of yours? Do you trust him?"

"With my life," the baron growled.

"Ah, well, perhaps. But with your daughter?"

Erde heard Fricca's soft gasp, then nothing but the flames
and the sound of her father drinking.

Finally the baron said, "They were raised together. He's
like a brother to her."

"Reassuring, I agree, though that could put her more at
ease with such men than might be proper for a young girl."

"She's an innocent, Guillemo. She knows nothing of
men. She walks alone in the forest without thinking what
might happen. She . . ." The baron cut himself short. "She's
an innocent."

"Yes," the priest replied and Erde heard in his voice the
soft rasp of a dagger being drawn. Why did her father keep
listening? Why didn't he tell this awful man to go away
and let her sleep? She knew she should leap up and defend
herself, or run away down the halls to Alla who could handle both her father and the priest. But it was like hearing
someone else's story. She was frozen in horrified fascination, and Guillemo was moving in for the kill. "Innocent,
exotically beautiful, ripe on the edge of womanhood . . ."

"The boy's as much an innocent as she is."

"Ah, but a man nonetheless. And what young man
doesn't harbor a bit of the Devil in his heart?"

Something, a wine cup, fell to the floor and shattered.

"My lord, don't you listen to him!" Fricca exclaimed. "It's a shame! A man of God, saying such foul things!"

A brisk knock at the door silenced her.

"Ah," said Guillemo. "Your patience for a moment, my lord."

Erde heard him whisk to the door for a murmured conference. She prayed he'd be called away on urgent business.

"My lord," he said finally. "If you'll indulge me, some further evidence has been uncovered."

The baron only grunted. Someone, Fricca perhaps, gathered up the shards of the wine cup.

"Bring her in," called the priest. There was a shifting of booted feet and slippers. "Now, my girl. Don't be afraid. You've done nothing wrong. Just tell my lord baron what you saw."

It was only whimpering at first, but Erde's gifted ear recognized the voice of the third floor laundry maid.

"Speak, girl. The truth serves both your lord on this earth and the One in heaven."

"I'm making up beds, your reverence, and I . . . I seen them coming down the hall."

"Who did you see, child?"

"The captain, and my lady Erde. He was carrying her and they was laughing."

The priest cleared his throat again. "Carrying her . . . as in holding her against himself bodily?"

"Um, well, yes, sir, you could call it that."

"And what else?"

"Oh, nothing else, your reverence. They just passed by like they never seen me at all."

"But there's nothing unusual in that, is there? I mean, in being ignored by your betters?"

The servant girl hesitated. Erde heard some sniffling, so well-orchestrated that she would have laughed, were she not already so horrified. She could not imagine what she'd done to make this girl betray her so readily.

"Would it be unusual?" prompted the priest.

"No sir, I mean . . . well, yes, sir, with the captain, sir . . . I mean, after all he's said, sir . . . well, I mean he could have given me a look, you know? Like he even knew I was there!"

"All he's said? Promises? Has he made promises, in return for . . . ah, favors?"

The sniffles dissolved into loud weeping.

"That'll do," the priest snapped. "Return her to her quarters."

The door thudded shut. In the silence, Erde heard Guillemo moving about. She could picture him, pacing deliberately, his dark face a mask of righteous concern.

"Well, my lord baron. It appears the boy is not as innocent as you thought."

Wood and leather groaned as the baron heaved his bulk out of the chair. "Wake her up, then!"

Fricca found her tongue. "My lord, how can you listen to such tales? That laundry wench is a famous flirt! She's made eyes at every soldier in the barracks. Let the child sleep, she's feeling so poorly . . . !"

"Wake her up! We'll hear it from her."

"Calm, my lord," Guillemo urged, and Erde ground her teeth in rage. As if it were not he who was responsible for the baron's intemperance! "We are only considering the possibility. The word of a servant should not carry much weight, and we have a better option. The truth can be ascertained by a simple examination, to be performed here and now in your presence, and the matter be done with."

"Wake her up," the baron snarled. "Or I will!"

"No!" Fricca wailed. "Leave the poor child alone! With you too drunk to know what truth is!"

There was a sharp crack, Fricca's muffled squeal, and the thud and clatter of her soft weight falling amid the metal fire tongs and the ash bucket. Erde was relieved to hear her weeping. Silence would have been more terrifying. Then the baron ripped aside the bed curtains and stood staring down at her, breathing hard. "Get up, Daughter."

Erde gathered the quilt around her, saw Fricca huddled on the floor in the firelight. Her father's eyes on her were like a hunter's. She fought to keep her voice steady. "Yes, Papa."

"Been listening, hah?"

"Yes, Papa."

"Well?"

A knock at the door, Rainer's knock. Erde could not help it. Her eyes darted toward the sound.

"Get it," the baron barked. Fricca had scrambled up and was already there.

"It's Alla, my lord."

Alla pushed past the half-open door. "What's this, Josef? The girl's not so deathly ill that you've need of a priest! Come, this is women's business. Clear out now, both of you. Let me do my work." She flashed Guillemo an unedited look of dislike and shoved at the door to swing it wide. "Bring that in, lad, and set it by the hearth."

Rainer hesitated in the doorway. He held a steaming crock by thick, oversized handles, and his face was soft with concern. Erde could not have known that the look passing between them would suggest so much to a man of the world like her father.

"Bring it in, lad," he mimicked. "Set it down."

"Oh, Josef," said Alla, beckoning Rainer in. "Too much wine. What would your mother say?"

"My mother, as you may have noticed, is no longer about to tell me what to do."

Alla raised an eyebrow. "So much the worse for you. Go to bed before you embarrass yourself. Where's that crock, lad?"

Rainer eased in, eyes tight to his burden. He set the crock down, shot his lord an empathetic glance intended to be of the sort shared between men in the midst of female matters, and turned to go. He found Brother Guillemo between himself and the door.

"Please stay a while, Captain," said the baron pleasantly.

Rainer came to attention. "My lord."

The baron took him by the shoulder and turned him slowly to face Erde. "Now, Daughter, can you answer the good brother satisfactorily? Have you anything to tell me about what went on earlier this evening?"

"No, Papa. Nothing went on." But her bewilderment was disingenuous. She had overheard too much. "It's not what you think."

Rainer's eyes widened, flew to Erde, and the baron caught the glance before each looked away.

"Not what I think, eh? What was it, then?"

"Nothing, Papa! Nothing! I was sick, you know I was sick, and he was helping me like you asked, that's all." He stared at her as if she was suddenly covered in mud. Erde knew she should weep, but she was afraid, so afraid, and could not manage it.

Alla moved past the baron, bringing Erde a cupful of hot liquid. "What is this nonsense, Josef? What poison has this priest been spilling? Don't you know what's happened here?"

"Do you, Alla? Do you really know what goes on in this house? Or are you in on this, too? Am I a fool? I see the way she looks at him!" The baron glared as if Rainer's very presence enraged him beyond bearing. His grip tightened until the young man winced. "I see it now. You're the one she's been meeting out in the forest!"

"Never, my lord! Erde, tell him!"

The baron shoved him backward and slapped him as he might a dog. "My lady, to you, boy!"

Rainer hunched in shame. "Yes, my lord."

Baron Josef grabbed him again. "How long, hah? How long without my knowing?"

"Papa, listen to me! You never listen!"

"I told you she met no one!" Fricca yelped.

Alla faced the baron calmly, hands on hips. "Stop this right now. Send this priest away, and we'll settle this when you're sober enough to think rationally."

"I marvel, my lord," remarked Guillemo from the fireplace, "that your household treats you with such ill respect. Do you not honor God, woman?"

"Shut up, priest!" The baron's face was flushed as deep as his burgundy velvet. "Get me some help."

Alla laid her small hands on his arm to quiet him and to loose Rainer from his rigid grasp. He brushed her aside. "Go!" he growled over her head.

Guillemo bowed and whispered from the room.

"Now we'll see . . ." He twisted Rainer away from him until the guardsman's sword was within reach. With his free hand, he jerked it from its sheath and set the point to Rainer's throat. "You ungrateful pup! I made you and this is how you thank me? You think I'm so gullible? Like some foolish woman you can fool me with an innocent face? I ought to gut you here and now!"

Rainer found his strangled voice. "But what have I done?"

"He did nothing," said Alla. "Didn't you hear her say he did nothing?"

"She's protecting her lover, old woman! Can a priest see that better than you?"

"Papa! You're drunk!"

Rainer dropped to one knee at the baron's feet. "My lord, on my life, I never . . . how could you even think . . . ?"

"Couldn't content yourself with the serving girls, hah? No, they're not good enough for the son of a King's Knight! It had to be my daughter! My precious daughter! MINE!"

Rainer reached out in protest. The baron recoiled. "So that's your game! Think you can take the old man in a fight!"

"My lord, no!" But he rose instinctively to defend himself.

Baron Josef threw the sword aside. It nearly sliced Alla's shin, skittering past her. The baron swung an arm back and slammed Rainer sidelong, sending him sprawling on the stone floor. Erde shoved her quilt aside and ran at her father like a lunatic, snatching at his arm, screeching at him to stop. He staggered but knocked her away and lunged after Rainer, hauling him up with one hand. As the young man stared at him in disbelief, the baron hit him full in the face, then rammed a knee into his stomach as he went down.

"No! Oh, no!" Erde scrambled to the fallen guardsman, her bare legs scraping across the splintered boards. She fell on him to cover his head with her own body. Now the blood on her garment was his.

"See?" roared her father, swaying above them drunkenly. "You see how she protects him?"

"You are a madman!" Erde screamed. Rainer coughed and groaned beneath her.

Brother Guillemo returned. Swords and white-robes filled the doorway. "My lord?"

The baron wiped his mouth on his sleeve and pointed. "That one."

"Josef," Alla begged. "Think what you're doing! Stop this while you're still able!"

The baron turned slowly to glare at her. His eyes glittered like small unseeing jewels. "Go to your room, old woman, if you know what's good for you."

Brother Guillemo gestured sharply. Two white-robes dragged Erde away from Rainer and tossed her like a sack of grain onto her bed. When Alla tried to go to her, another hustled the protesting midwife from the room. Two more jerked the young man to his feet. Hanging stunned and bleeding in their grasp, he looked to Erde, who could only shake her head in disbelieving horror. Then he raised his bruised eyes to meet the baron's.

"What did I say about being used, my lord? Look around you. I have never lied to you or abused your trust. You'll never have a more loyal man than me."

The baron spat in his face. "Get him out of here."

Erde saw only a bearded death's head as Brother Guillemo smiled his self-righteous smile and signaled to his men to take Rainer away. With the room emptying and no antagonist left, the baron seemed to lose focus. He looked for his wine cup, and not finding it, drank from the pitcher. Guillemo offered his own cup from the mantle, then bowed to him deeply. "You should rest, my lord. From the shock."

Baron Josef frowned distractedly, then merely nodded and turned toward the door, the pitcher still clutched firmly in one hand.

CHAPTER FIVE

Erde was locked in her bedchamber. No visitors came, no one with food or water or even fuel for the fire. *This will be over soon,* she thought, and then when it was not over, she cried for hours, curled up in her nest of bed linens. When she had wept herself dry, she got up and paced, feeling her own rage stir like acid in the pit of her stomach.

She hated him. She hated this so-called father who could listen to a man he'd known less than a day, over his most trusted bodyguard, over the word of his own and only daughter. How could such a thing be?

The window rattled and the drafts howled in the ceiling vaults. The wind hurled sleet and ice against the shivering panes of glass. Winter crept into the room, and still no one came. Erde imagined her father still raging drunkenly around the castle, and the servants too frightened to come to her aid. She made tasks for herself, to ward off the cold and her sense of drifting unmoored in an alien sea. She rationed the remaining firewood. She tore up the white gown and fed the pieces to the flames. She drank the stale water in the pitcher by her washbasin. She moved her chamber pot to the farthest corner to avoid the stink.

She understood nothing that had happened. Her father was always a dangerous drunk, but his rages had never been this violent before. Still, there was a chance it would all be over when he finally sobered up.

The next evening, someone came at last, an older guardsman she did not recognize. He admitted Fricca with a pail of cold water and orders to make Erde presentable.

"It's cold!" Erde complained, "Doesn't he think I've been punished enough?"

Fricca said nothing. The guard stood by the open door and watched until Fricca insisted he turn his back. Erde was outraged. Did the man not know his place? She begged for news, for something to eat.

Fricca shook her head, weeping as she sponged Erde's shivering arms. "Oh, such goings on, my lady!" Her pale murmur was nearly drowned out by the splash of the water into the pail. "Your father is in a mad drunken fury like I've never seen! Who knows where we'd be if the Holy Brother'd not been there to soothe him and read Scripture to him and be responsible until he's himself again."

The notion of Guillemo in charge made Erde shiver all the more. "My father needs a healer, not a priest. Where's Alla?"

Fricca laid a finger to her lips. "They'll not let her see him, for fear she'll enrage him further."

"Then what of Rainer?" Erde whispered. "How's Rainer?"

"Locked away, my lady. Oh, the poor foolish lad!"

"Foolish?" Erde pulled away. "Don't tell me now you believe these lies? You know better than that!"

"Oh, my dearest lady-child, I know what *seems,* but in black times like these . . . I mean, what can we know about such things?"

"What things?"

"Well, the holy brother says . . ."

"The holy brother knows nothing!" Erde yelled. But she could see he did, that he was in fact fiendishly clever, for he was keeping her father from the very people who might coax him back to sanity. What she didn't understand was why.

At her yell, the guard snapped around and ordered them to silence, bidding Fricca to hurry. She wept and wept, but would not speak another word.

When she was done and had departed, still weeping, the guard took Erde to the great-hall, where her father sat on the baronial throne in near-darkness. The assembled court stood grimly silent. Erde thought they looked frightened, a bit confused. Guillemo's robed entourage lined the walls, where Rainer's men should have been. Torches flared here and there, and a few people carried lanterns, but the great twin hearths were still and cold, and no candles burned. When her eyes adjusted to the dim light, Erde understood the courtiers' dismay. The baron, always so concerned with protocol and a pristine public image, was unshaven, slumped carelessly in his chair, and still wearing his feast robe, which a day later was badly wrinkled and wine-stained. One hand balanced a goblet on his knee. In the shadows behind the throne stood Brother Guillemo.

Erde awaited the stern, perhaps even slightly raving lecture about her behavior, a humiliation she could probably live through. But her father did not even seem to notice her. The guard pushed her to her knees before him, and the Baron glanced unsteadily aside and raised his goblet. A white-robe hurried to fill it. Erde was hauled up and led to a stool to one side of the dais. Her guard stood near. Erde's eyes sought the carved dragon capitals for comfort.

Two of the white-robes dragged Rainer in. His wounds had not been washed or dressed, and his torn black tunic was gray and slick with mud. When Erde rose to her feet in shocked protest, her guard shoved her back down again. Now the court murmured covertly. She could hear a few of the women praying. Rainer could hardly stand, but he shrugged off his escort to face the throne alone, where the baron had now drawn himself up with a drunken glare of hatred. Rainer did not look Erde's way, and she resolved to avoid even a glance, lest it harm his cause.

Brother Guillemo stepped forward to present the charges. Rainer was not allowed to speak in his own defense. Erde tried several times and was silenced, first by Guillemo's command, finally by the callused palm of her guard. Both were made to sit and listen while Guillemo detailed his own twisted version of the events, to listen while the sniveling laundry-maid described what she'd seen in even more lurid detail, to listen while silly helpless Fricca admitted, yes, she had found the baron's daughter weeping and distraught after the captain had left her. It wasn't until the priest had nearly completed his case that Erde understood that only Rainer was on trial. An actual trial, no mere public scolding or wrist-slapping. Sitting rigid on her stool, Erde felt real fear creep into her heart. She noticed that the von Alte dragon tapestries, which had hung on these walls for a hundred years, had been taken down, exposing the pale cold stone. Surely if her father was sober, he would not let all this go on. She sought again the dragons in the upper shadows, but they could offer only silent comfort.

The only voice raised on Rainer's behalf was Alla's, blunt and indignant, and so very sane. Guillemo heard her out without comment, did not even question her testimony, and Erde wondered why he had let her speak at all. His motive surfaced when Alla had said her piece and limped proudly from the hall. Then the priest shook his head warningly. "Satan's wings have brushed us, oh my people. Clearly what this old witch-woman says can never be taken as truth. My lord, she must be looked into. I fear some deeper plot here."

Not long thereafter, Brother Guillemo asked for a verdict, and Erde heard her father slur even the few words required to condemn Rainer to death by hanging, sentence to be carried out the next morning.

She began to scream and did not stop, even when one of Guillemo's white-robes clamped a fist over her mouth and dragged her from the hall.

CHAPTER SIX

Erde knew now what caused a caged animal to go mad and gnaw at its own flesh. Mere tears were not desperate enough for such a catastrophe.

She stood all night on the high sill of her window. She began in the chill silence of thought. After a while, thought became fantasy, and she called on the Mage-Queen to appear and carry Rainer and herself far away to safety. But the fantasy did not sustain her and the early hours of dawn found her rocking and moaning. She had determined that there was no conceivable way she could free Rainer from his cell, and so she went to work on building up the courage to fling herself onto the cobblestones sixty feet below. Maybe then the baron would set Rainer free out of remorse. In truth, her life experience thus far did not include a world in which, when the time came, her father would actually execute his favorite guardsman.

But what finally kept her frozen to the sill was the sight of the chicken-crone sitting on the well-head in the middle of the storm, grinning up at her toothlessly and beckoning.

Then there was a muffled thump outside her door and the scrape of a key in the lock. Erde stayed where she was. If it was her father or the priest come to make her watch Rainer hang, it would be all the excuse she'd need to throw herself from the windowsill.

But it was Alla who eased open the door, stuck her head in, then ducked back, grunting and breathing hard, hauling on something heavy. Erde ran to help her.

"Alla, Alla, thank God! Oh, Alla, what are we to do?"

"Help me, child! Those white-robes of his are everywhere!" The heavy weight was the guard who'd been posted outside. Together, they dragged him into the room.

"Alla, we have to help Rainer! We have to . . . !"

"No time, I can't . . . I've done what I can," Alla panted. "Now it's up to . . ." Her breath failed her briefly. Two bright spots blazed on her cheeks. Her white hair was loose and tangled. She unslung a leather satchel from her back and pressed it into Erde's hands. "Hide this, quickly! Take the key and lock the door behind me!"

"No!" Erde snatched at her sleeve. "You can't leave me!"

"Have to. They can't know I've been here. Your father is . . ."

"Still drunk? No! Is he still drunk? Alla, what's the matter with him? He's never been this bad before!"

The old woman hugged Erde tightly, kissed her, then held her at arm's length. "I know, child, but he's never met his evil genius before. Now, listen, my dearest girl. It's all out of hand. I can't protect you any more. That vicious priest . . . he's after my skin. It's gone way beyond just plying your father with drink and flattery. He and Josef . . . they encourage each other's madness. You should have seen the two of them, hauling the tapestries from the great-hall onto the fire."

"Burned? The von Alte tapestries?" Erde felt a hole grow in her heart.

Alla stroked her cheek. "Yes, kidling. As evil totems of dragon worship. Can you believe the folly of it? Built a raging pyre in the upper courtyard and tossed them in, all the time laughing like boys, while the foolish court all stood about like scared dumb sheep! There's no telling what . . . the priest's talking now about taking you 'in hand' . . . exactly what I fear he means to do, the lecherous bastard, even as he pours evil into Josef's ear about you and the lad. You must get away. You must! Hide yourself in the villages until the priest is gone, or go to the king. No time to send word, just go!"

Shouts from the courtyard blew up the stairwell with the icy drafts. Alla patted her pockets, glanced swiftly around. "Fare ye well, light of my heart."

"But what about Rainer?"

"Don't think of him, child."

"How can I not think of him?" Erde wailed.

"You're best to never think of him again." Alla held their four hands together in a knot. "Be brave, hawkling! Your dragon awaits you!"

"My . . . what dragon?"

Alla ducked away. The clamor from below spread to the upper corridor, men running, boots and swords clanging against the stone. Erde swung the heavy door closed and locked it, then remembered the guard lying near the hearth and worried that he might wake up. Bending closer, she discovered he was not just unconscious. His jaw gaped, his eyes stared. A small stiletto puncture bled at his neck. Erde recoiled with a squeal, then hushed herself, feeling her world turn over. How serious some games became, and how suddenly. *Your father's evil genius,* Alla had said. No one had understood how unstable his balance was until the coming of the priest had tipped it. By dawn, Rainer would be as dead as this poor man, because of her childishness, because she had insisted on an innocent stupid kiss.

Erde cried out as guilt and grief and rage surged over her, spilling strength into her limbs. She grabbed the corpse by the heels and dragged it under her bed, then ran to stash the leather satchel behind her stinking chamber pot. Out in the hall, armor clanked. More men raced past. Someone tried her latch, then pounded on her door. Erde sat down by the dim hearth, easing her breath and her heart so that she could remain calm when the key arrived to let her father into the room.

The baron stared at her from the doorway, weaving a bit, taking in her strange stillness. His hair was matted as if he'd just awakened, yet he was as richly dressed as he would be for a ceremony. He was pale and exhausted, with shadowed fragile eyes, as if his mad rage had held him unwilling prisoner and he was unsure of where it had left him, or when it might seize him again.

"The priest insisted he ought to examine you himself, but I wouldn't allow it. I have to let him have his way with lesser matters, or . . ." He trailed off. His narrowed glance seemed to demand thanks or congratulations. He moved toward her unsteadily and reached to stroke her hair just once, and smooth his finger across her cheek and down along the line of her jaw, like a worm crawling so slowly that Erde thought she would scream with revulsion. His voice was scratchy and weak, but his gaze fixed her intently. "I don't care, you know, that he . . . it doesn't matter, it's nothing. He's nothing, a boy. Not worthy of my little girl anyway, my soon-to-be young woman. A few hours, it will be over, we can forget him and move on. Everything will be as it was, no, it will be better. Matters are changing hereabouts. Tor Alte is not the end of the earth, or won't be for long. Wealth and power lies before us . . . and so much more." His hand was on her hair again, stroking. "But how could you understand such things? When the priest has proved his worth, you'll see. You'll see it was all for your own good."

He leaned over, hesitating for what seemed to Erde an eternity, poised above her, his breath sour with wine. Then he bent and kissed her roughly, his stiff tongue prying open her mouth.

Erde jerked away, shuddering, and hid her face in her hands.

"I know, I know, but you'll see how it will be. I have so much to teach you." He leaned his body against the curve of her back and was about to say something more when an urgent shout down the hall distracted him. He glanced vaguely around the empty room and turned away, closing the door, oh, so very gently as if Erde were still asleep.

Soon Fricca brought a tray with breakfast, and fresh water for the kettle on the hearth. When she spotted the bucket, Erde raced over to splash her face, rubbing her lips over and over until Fricca stared.

A yard servant appeared with an armload of firewood. Bundled in her bed quilt, Erde watched silently, listening for the grim roll of drums in the courtyard. As the room warmed up again, she wondered if the dead soldier underneath her bed would begin to smell, thus giving Alla's mortal deed away.

"Oh, I haven't ceased crying a minute since your grandmother's funeral!" Fricca's hands shook as she filled the kettle. "Who'd have thought we'd have harbored such witchery, right here in our very own nest! No wonder we have summer snow and ravens."

"Who is it, the chicken-crone?"

"What? Lord, no, that's a pure Christian woman. No, I'm not to mention the name, on peril of my immortal soul. But it's that eastern blood of hers, surely, that gives her the power. Isn't the holy Brother right about keeping ourselves ever vigilant? Came along just in time, when we sorely needed the strong right arm of Heaven to protect us!"

Has the whole world gone insane, Erde wondered. Fricca swung the kettle over the fire and came to sit beside her on the bed. "And you, too, poor lamb! Such a time of it! It's no good way to start out your life as a woman, but there's plenty of men will have you for your other qualities, so you must try to put it behind you. It was none of the poor lad's fault but his own weakness, and we're all best just to move on, now he's gone."

Erde knew her heart had stopped. "Gone?"

Fricca sniffed, wiped her eyes. "Oh, yes, dear. Didn't they tell you? Some of the men were trying to tend to his wounds, but he'd found himself a little knife somewhere and laid right into them. He was killed trying to escape."

Killed?

What was that awful stillness? Had all the air been sucked out of the room? Erde tried to cry out Rainer's name, but the sounds stalled in her throat. Surely she would choke on them.

Fricca mistook her wide-eyed struggle to breathe, to speak. "Yes, and very nearly made it, so the men say. Saved himself from the disgrace of the scaffold and died like the brave lad he was. Oh, you'd be proud! There's blood all over the stable yard." Fricca daubed at her cheeks with her apron. "But there's to be no funeral allowed. The baron's in such a rage—taking it very hard, 'cause he trusted the boy so—wouldn't let anyone near but his own Guard. Ordered the poor broken body hauled up the mountain and left for the wolves!"

Killed? Erde stumbled to the washbasin and emptied herself of all the fresh bread and fruit she had just eaten.

Thinking he was going to die had been the worst pain Erde could have imagined. Hearing he was dead left her without any feeling at all.

Frightened, Fricca brought the baron. "She won't eat, my lord. Won't say a word. Just sits there like a stone."

The baron approached her bedside. Erde noticed he was actually steady on his feet again, brushed and clean but wan, like a man recovering from an illness. He leaned over to look her in the face but did not come too close. "Daughter?"

She let her eyes focus somewhere twenty miles beyond him.

"This won't do any good, you know."

She was on Glasswind, with Rainer beside her, flying in the service of the Mage-Queen.

"I'll not indulge this behavior! What's done is done, and the boy's dead for his treason. It's fit punishment, better than he deserved, and sulking won't bring him back again."

Sulking? Did he think it so minor as a sulk?

Fricca fluttered about, keeping a fearful distance. "Let the holy brother come to her, my lord, to ease her soul with prayer."

"No!" The baron snapped upright. "None but you or I sets a foot in this room, do you hear?" He took a breath, as if shaken by his own vehemence. "A father can deal with his own child."

"Yes, my lord, but she won't talk, I promise you." Fricca wrung her hands. "I've been asking myself, what if she *can't?* You know what they say about the Devil stealing your tongue!" She forgot herself and came near to grab the baron's velvet sleeve. "Oh, my lord, with all else that's gone on, what if Alla has witched her, too, like she did our poor dead Rainer?"

And thus Erde heard the new gospel according to Brother Guillemo, how the unwitting guardsman took the baron's daughter while under the vile influence of a witch's spell, which made the girl forget the whole encounter, though the cries of her unwholesome pleasure had been overheard by the laundry-maid. Later, the witch made a glowing bloody sword appear in the prisoner's hand, and sent demons to unman his guards. This time, the blessed faith of the priest and his brothers weakened the witch's power. The escape failed, but Tor Alte was under dread attack by the forces of Satan. Their souls were in peril. The witch must be discovered and routed out. Invoking the authority of the Church, Guillemo interrogated Alla and declared her to be the very witch in question. He advised her immediate arrest, ordering his brothers to lock her in a cell and guard her closely.

These lies were more than Erde could stand, and she fixed her father with her dark eyes and meant to tell him so, but nothing came out. Her mouth worked soundlessly. Fricca whimpered and cringed.

The baron stepped back stiff-legged, like a dog with its hackles raised. "God's holy angels! Fricca! Not a word of this to anyone! He'll want to burn her, too!"

"My lord, I beg you! Consider the holy brother's offer! He's our only salvation in this time of peril!" She slipped her hands around his arm and clung to him. "My dear, good lord! Give her into his keeping like he says, for her own sweet soul's sake!"

The baron's face twisted. He gazed at Erde as if it were his own soul in torment. "No. Not with Guillemo, woman, I could never . . ."

"Your pardon, lord baron . . ."

The baron spun on the man in the open doorway, who clearly did not relish being the bearer of one more piece of bad news.

"Well, man? Out with it!"

"It's the witch, my lord . . ."

"What? . . . escaped? More spells and visions?"

"Well, no, sir. Dead in her cell. Hanged herself, my lord."

The baron's shoulders sagged. "Oh, brave woman," he muttered.

Erde stared straight ahead, rocking silently, and felt nothing.

Soon she was alone again, and forced to think about what was happening to her.

She pondered the question of being unable to speak. Perhaps she *was* cursed. Perhaps by the chicken-crone, to her thinking the most obvious candidate for witchery. Certainly not by Alla.

Alla.

Rainer dead. Now Alla dead as well. How strange it felt to form those words in her mind. Erde knew she should feel grief but could not remember how to do it. She remembered feeling grief for her grandmother. Was it a skill one could forget? She discovered quickly that she could still grow bored of sitting still, and so considered her narrowing choices. She could lose herself in her fantasies, fly again with the Mage-Queen and her dragons, or . . . or she could do something. She stirred herself suddenly, raced across the room and pulled Alla's satchel out from behind her chamber pot. She spread its contents on the floor.

Several candles wrapped in a boy's linen shirt. A sleeveless leather tunic, worn but serviceable. Loose woolen breeches and low, cuffed leather boots. A gray knitted prentice cap. A small tinderbox. A thin sharp dagger with leather sheath and belt. A loaf of bread, four apples, and a hunk of hard cheese wrapped in oilcloth. A dark carved box. The objects were real, material, comforting.

Erde opened the box. Inside were a rolled strip of parchment covered with script in a language she could not read, and a large brooch such as one might use to fasten a cloak: a worn rust-colored stone set in silver. Cut into the stone was a tiny figure of a dragon. Erde turned it in the firelight, remembering. She'd often seen her grandmother wear this brooch. Here, then, was the dragon that Alla had said awaited her. She pressed it gently to her lips, surprised at how live and warm the red stone felt in the chill room. She replaced it carefully in the box. She devoured one of the apples, repacked everything into the satchel, and returned it to its malodorous hiding place. Alla had indeed meant her to leave Tor Alte, and had provided the means of escape.

Erde sat down to think.

CHAPTER SEVEN

The dagger's keen edge sliced through it easily. Erde gathered up the shorn dark mass of her hair and threw it on the dying embers. The sudden flare seared her eyes, and her nose wrinkled at the odor. The new lightness of her head, with the hair just short of her earlobes, made every motion feel unhinged.

Well past midnight, and outside, the wind still howled. In the cooling room, she stripped to her shift by dim firelight, tucked the hem into the woolen men's leggings. Rainer had let her try on his leggings once, when they were much younger, and Erde had never forgotten the sense of freedom and power such clothing provided. She was grateful that this first time of her bleeding had been short. She needed no womanly inconveniences now.

The linen shirt, worn soft and patched at the elbows, went over her shift and hung past her knees. Erde cinched it up with the dagger belt and sheathed the knife. After all, any boy might wear his older brother's cast-off shirt.

She laced up the leather tunic, then slid on the boots and walked around in them a bit, amazed that Alla could have fit her so well simply by guesswork. She emptied Fricca's latest hopeful offering of bread, cheese, and apples into the satchel, then added her own thick cloak. It made the pack uncomfortably bulky, but strapping it to her back the way Alla had always done on their herb-gathering forays made the burden manageable.

She thought of the nighttime forest, and felt only relief. She pulled the gray prentice cap over her shorn hair, settled the dagger more comfortably on her hip and stood gazing about the darkening room, at the old tapestries billowing in the draft, with their tales of dragons woven in faded hues, the minor cousins of those her father and the priest had burned. She'd no doubt these would be next. She peered into the shadows beneath her costly bed dressings, at the firelit marble mantle carved in the shapes of two trees meeting in an arch, into the recesses of the vaulting above her head where bats sometimes slept off the daylight hours.

There was nothing here that she would miss. No one left that she cared about or did not fear.

Erde took a quick breath and went to drag the dead guard out from under the bed. She was glad for darkness and tried to look at him as little as possible. He was beginning to smell a bit, and she hoped he would forgive her for postponing his last rites for so long. She prayed the poor man wouldn't burn in hell as long as she probably would.

She heard metal scrape as she yanked him by his boot heels, and saw a faint glimmer in the shadows beneath the bed. Reluctantly, she took a closer look. His jerkin was snagged with the blade of a sword.

Rainer's sword! The one her father had tossed away in the heat of his madness. Erde pounced on it, hugging it to her chest as if it were Rainer himself. If she'd had any tears left, she would have shed them then. Instead, she floated in numbness. Something inside her, some gear or mainspring, had broken. She could not feel, she could only act. But action at least offered some sense of forward motion, of being still alive. So she grasped the sword by its hilt and tried to level the blade in front of her. The strain of its weight pulled on her untrained wrist. She could not carry it, but she could not leave it behind. She tore one of her sheets into strips, bound up the sword to blunt its razor edge, and tied it to her own body with more of the sheeting, so that it nestled against her back like a steel spine.

She laid the guard out in the middle of the room, where he would be most visible from the doorway. She drew the bed curtains shut, opened the high casement window and knotted the torn sheet around the handle, draping it artfully over the sill. She took the pitcher, the washbasin, the kettle, anything that would break or make noise. She had planned to scream and tried, but could not. She prayed there was only the one man guarding her chamber so late at night.

She stationed herself against the wall just to the side of the door and began flinging things to the floor.

The door cracked open. The young duty-guard peered in cautiously, not wishing to follow his captain's fate with regard to the baron's daughter. He saw a large body sprawled in the darkened room, then the open casement with the sheet ruffled by the draft. Shouting, he shoved the door wide and sprang in.

When he had bent over the corpse and his back was to her, Erde ducked silently around the doorjamb and ran for her life.

She used all the old back stairs, the narrowest unlit corridors learned in her childhood, where the wind whistled through the chinks in the stone and the people who worked the longest days slept the hardest. The sword at her back set her posture unnaturally straight, the way Fricca had always nagged her to stand. With no clear idea of where she was heading other than somewhere down the mountain toward the villages, she slipped through the dark warmth of the kitchens, past the yawning bakers already beginning their day. The herbal talisman that always hung over the bread ovens to bless the rising had been replaced by a large wooden crucifix. Erde let herself out the scullery entrance. The wind and damp cold hit her full in the face.

How can it really be August, she wondered, wrapping her arms about her against the chill. *Surely I have slept, and in my daze, it has become November.*

The thin dogs sleeping in the lee of the wood yard raised their heads with interest as she approached, but Erde spoke to them in the language of hands and put their minds at rest. She unpacked her cloak and wrapped it shawllike about her head and shoulders, as she'd seen the prentice boys do, then struck out boldly across the cobbled rear court toward the inner gate.

The guards there were throwing dice and arguing. A mere passing prentice was hardly worth their notice when a month's salary hung on the toss. Erde descended into the mud and ruts of the armory yard, head bent, her walk purposeful. Escape was beginning to seem ridiculously easy, when she rounded the corner of the forge and came face-to-face with the chicken-crone, hauling her basket of corn to the bird pen. The ragged ancient peered at her and waved her irritably out of the path. Erde drew her cloak closer and stepped aside to pass. Suddenly the crone snatched at the cloak, spilling corn into the icy mud and raising a piercing squawk as if wolves were in the hen coop.

"Witch! Witch! Witch!" Her mad shriek echoed off the armory walls like a call to battle.

Erde jerked herself free and ran, doubling back toward the stables. She still had a few moments of grace before anyone thought to take the cries of the chicken-crone seriously. She let herself into the long wooden shed nestled against the middle ring wall. Most times, she knew, the horse gate leading from the stables into the outer ring was left unguarded, the animals themselves being touchy enough to give alarm. But the great shadowy forms flared their velvet nostrils and let Erde pass. She found her own horse Micha, bade him farewell, and hurried on.

Now there were the beginnings of commotion in the inner yard, and one gate left to pass, the massive Dragon Gate with its iron portcullis that was lowered every day at dusk. The wheel crank that raised it was inside the guardhouse, windowless but for an arrow slit that looked out on the gate. Its low entrance was barred by a door of rough planks. Erde put her eye to a crack.

Three men on duty: two fast asleep, the third huddled by the smoking firepit, drinking and staring into the coals. Erde knew this one—Georg, a lank and flat-faced fellow who was often on duty when she took an early walk. He'd stall the morning raising of the portcullis in order to hold her in conversation, going on about the long night and his sad lot and the abuses of his superiors. He smiled at Erde a lot, though this did not tell her whether he was her friend.

Back in the inner court, the dogs were barking. Soon the search would be on. Erde had no choice but to try and bluff it out. She gathered the cloak around her head, leaving as much of her boy's clothing showing as seemed reasonable, then rapped manfully on the planks and stood back waiting by the gate.

Inside, Georg fumbled about, rose, and looked out the door. Erde gestured to him casually to open up. He nodded grumpily and turned back inside. The crank rope groaned as the gate inched up. Past the folds of her hood, Erde could see George squinting at her through the arrow slit. A foot off the ground, the iron grille stopped.

"Hey, boy, where you headed in this devil's weather?"

Erde was unsure whether it was better or worse that she could not answer him. She waved.

He left the crank and came out toward her. "You might have a civil reply for your elder!"

Erde shrugged, trying to look shy, even when he reached and grabbed a fold of her cloak. He frowned, rubbing the soft fabric between his fingers. "Who'd you steal this from, eh?" He snatched her hood back, stared a moment, then recognition came. "Well, well. If it ain't the captain's highborn whore. You don't look so good without your hair."

He might as well have slapped her. Erde blinked back tears and set her jaw. She inclined her head proudly at the gate.

Georg snorted. "You want out, your little ladyship? Little late for a walk isn't it? What is it, a lovers' tryst? The captain ain't dead half a day and you're lifting your skirts for another? Got used to getting a little, did you? My, I like a girl with spirit."

Erde scowled at him indignantly and put her finger to her lips.

"Ssh, ssh, I know, don't wake the castle!" He grinned, then seemed to get an idea, and moved closer. "Tell you what, missy. I'm happy to accommodate you if you do the same for me."

Erde made the mistake of letting hope show in her eyes.

"Oh, that priest may say you're hell-bait, but I ain't afraid. I've always thought it'd be just fine to have a hot little witch-girl to snuggle up into when I come home. What d'ya say? You just give me some of what you gave the captain, and I'll let you go wherever you want." Georg folded his arms and smiled. "What d'ya say? It's cold out here, so cold, and I got a joint needs warming."

Erde finally understood. She shrank back instinctively and tried to bolt. Georg lunged and pinned her against the iron gate. His heavy wine-breath reminded Erde sickeningly of her father. The alarm raised in the inner yard had moved on to the stables. Horses neighed and stomped, and guardsmen shouted orders. But Georg was too intent on pressing his hips into her and working his hands through the layers of her clothing. Erde had no voice to reason with him. She tried to shove him away.

"Oh, like it rough, do you?" He grunted nastily, sucking at her neck and tearing at her breeches. "Is this how the captain gave it to you? Did he give it to you hard?"

As his fingers groped for parts of her body that no man had ever touched, Erde knew another game had turned deadly serious. She hadn't a chance of fighting him off. His weight pushing at her outlined the chill of Rainer's sword against her back, and the shape of Alla's dagger against her side. The reminder of Alla and what Alla had done to save her calmed Erde and told her what to do.

She forced herself to relax against Georg's body, to let his rough hands find her skin and thrust themselves impatiently between her legs. While he sighed and groaned and fumbled to loose his own ties, she eased the dagger out of its sheath, slid her arms up as if to embrace him, and rammed the slim blade into him as hard as she could.

She felt the blood spurt, hot and reeking, and was glad it was too dark to see his face as he reeled back from her, clutching his neck, his thick hose sagging around his naked thighs. She held tight to the dagger until his spasms jerked it free, then shrugged her own clothes up around her and dropped to the ground to wedge herself into the cold mud until she could roll through the narrow space beneath the gate.

Free of the mud and iron spikes, she stood shaking, fighting nausea but determined not to give up an ounce of precious nourishment. She could not flee to the villages now. She had just murdered one of their own.

The wind tore up the mountain to stiffen her sodden clothing and hurl razor-edged sleet in her face. But to Erde, stumbling up the rocky path toward the uncertain shelter of the forest, it seemed only fitting that her body should be as numb as her heart.

PART TWO

EARTH

The Journey into Peril

CHAPTER EIGHT

She ran until she was well out of the dim light cast by the gateway lanterns, ran until she could blend with the trees. Her feet found their way by memory. She knew every pothole and rock ledge between the castle walls and the forest. But the mud was deep and treacherous, and the windblown sleet like a barrage of tiny needles. Her boots were full of icy water by the time she reached the first dark firs.

She halted there, gasping more from fear than lack of breath, and resettled her pack to ride her back more securely. A disorderly pursuit was forming in the stable yard. She heard men shouting and dogs barking, eager for the chase. The horses neighed and stomped, fearful of the wind and the dark. She had to think; she had to decide, and she had to do it quickly. Tor Alte's half-dozen dependent villages were scattered among the alpine meadows a little way down the mountain. The biggest had its own parish church, and briefly she considered seeking sanctuary there. But she feared the long reach of Fra Guill. To take refuge in a church would be like walking right into his arms. She could not risk the villages now.

Then where could she go? She had food and warm clothing, but she was wet through with rain and the guardsman's blood. Her feet were already numb. Without shelter, she would freeze before morning. Time enough to worry about the long term when she'd found a place where she could light a fire without being discovered. Rainer's sword was a weight on her back but a goad as well, and Erde would not abandon it on the mountainside the way his poor body had been.

The baying and shouting in the castle yard grew louder
and more organized. Numb as she was, Erde felt panic stir
beneath her skin, like a torrent swirling below a fragile
layer of ice. Only Alla's instructions, murmured over and
over in a soothing litany, kept her from bolting headlong
into the night probably to brain herself on a low-hanging
branch or fall off the nearest cliff. She guessed the riders
would go first to the villages, so she headed upward into
the trees, away from the path, away from the settled val-
leys, toward the caves above the tree line. Winter bears
sometimes went to ground there but right then, she'd rather
negotiate with a sleepy bear than with her father or Fra
Guill.

She recalled a cave she'd found with Rainer when they
were children. Or perhaps the baroness had showed it to
them, on one of the long hikes she'd favored in their company. It lay deep in a barren jumble of rock. Its narrow
crack of an entrance seemed to lead nowhere, but actually
it camouflaged a descent into a system of tunnels and caverns that burrowed much deeper into the mountain rock
than they'd had the courage to explore. Erde struck out
bravely in that direction. When the sounds of pursuit
passed below her on the road and receded downward, she
slowed a bit and began gathering bits of deadwood as she
climbed, as much as she had strength to carry, bundling it
under her sodden cloak in the hope it would be dry enough
to burn by the time she reached her hiding place.

It was near dawn when she got there, the thin gray light
coming as sullen and cold as a morning in mid-December.
It was oddly still, as if even the weather disdained this bare,
unlovely height. The wind had died, and snow as fine as
frost dusted the air. The cave was there as she remembered
it, a jagged fissure like a sideways smile in a wind-smoothed
rock that turned its back on Tor Alte and faced east.
Toward the Russias, Erde thought, *the home poor Alla will
never see again.* Suddenly her exhaustion seemed a weight
too great to bear. She staggered through the slitted cave
mouth and leaned against the rock wall to catch her breath.
So easy to drop the load of wood that cramped her arms
and bent her back, so easy to collapse right there in the
entrance, cold and wet and shivering, where any pursuer
could find her. But while Rainer's sword lay cool and rigid

along her spine, she could not even sit. Moving like a sleep-walker, she dug out one of Alla's candles, then crept farther into the cave to take a look around.

She passed through shallow chambers musty with old leaves and animal dung. She listened for the whisper of bats. Her small candle wavered fitfully, but without it throwing shadows all about, she would not have found the second narrow cleft hidden by an edge of rock. Pitch-black, with a cool stony draft that stirred her short-cropped hair and raised goose bumps on her skin. Her candle flickered, and she put up a hand to shield it. Her only refuge lay in that unexplored dark. Erde eased through the crack.

The tunnel led downward, sharply at first and slippery with rubble. Erde followed it haltingly, hand to the rough wall, and felt rather than saw it level out, just before the wall beside her ended and the flickering circle of her candle flame vanished into darkness. She knew she had come into some sort of cavern. The long dying echo of her step told her the cavern was enormous. Raising the candle like a beacon as high as she could did not reveal a ceiling. But it tossed long shadows across treelike pillars of rock that reminded her of the great-hall of Tor Alte. Ahead in the darkness, something glimmered, like the flash of light off a living eye. Erde froze, then let herself breathe again. A still pool spread over the cavern floor. She had spied the reflection of her candle dancing across the dark water like a sprite. She would have stumbled right into its depths, had she not stopped short, fearing the approach of some one-eyed cave demon. When her heart ceased racing, she bent to touch the glassy surface. The water was numbingly cold and tasted earthy, like the fresh dirt of her grandmother's grave. But she palmed it up eagerly, then walked around its shore and lit her fire in a dry high-vaulted side-chamber, where a tiny shard of gray daylight showed far above when she extinguished her candle.

She unslung her pack and laid out her cloak. The dark stains of the guardsman's blood drew a mottled map of her crime across the fine wool. It was cold in the cave, but Erde kicked the cloak away, unable to wear his death a moment longer. She unstrapped the sword and sank to the ground at last, holding it in her lap. She wasn't ready to think about how deep in the earth she was now, how alone and how completely without a plan. She did allow herself to wonder if she'd been rash to run away, if the known evil was, finally, preferable to the unknown. But Alla had wanted her to go, had said she *must* go, to the king, yes, why not? As good a destination as any. But the king was in Erfurt, two hundred miles to the west, down in the lowlands.

The thought of walking two hundred miles made Erde's head ache. She let it loll back against the cavern wall and closed her eyes, her chill hands still cradling Rainer's sword. She found herself imagining that the hilt was warm to her touch, as if someone else had been holding it. Warm enough to ease her shivering. She told herself it was Rainer himself, watching over her in spirit. She knew if she thought about it long enough, she could convince herself that he was actually there in the cave, and this was too eerie even for her, so she pushed the notion from her mind and accepted the uncanny warmth as an omen of his approval that his sword was with her. She built up the fire and steamed most of the damp from her shirt and leggings, but could get no more than halfway through a single apple before exhaustion finally claimed her.

She woke suddenly, as if from a tap on her shoulder, out of a restless sleep colored by vivid nightmares. She was stiff and sore and could not understand why her bed felt so sharp and hard. Then she remembered where she was, and why.

Her small fire had burned out. The cavern was cold and no comforting sliver of daylight from above penetrated the hovering darkness. It was night, then, outside. She had slept through the entire day. Shivering, Erde felt for her cloak and wrapped it around herself, grateful just to be awake.

Her father had raged through her dreams, touching her where a father shouldn't and calling her by her mother's name. Alla had died in flames again and again, and Erde saw Rainer bloodily cut down by the guardsmen's blades, all the while staring at her with stunned, accusing eyes. Fra Guill had stalked her dreams as well, and the man she had murdered.

Murdered. She let the realization settle in. She'd traded a man's life for her own. She held herself very still, feeling the bloodied cloak close around her like a shroud, bringing her no warmth. She'd been better off before she'd slept, while numbness still dulled her conscience. It was always possible she hadn't killed him, she told herself, but she knew she had. A man could not bleed such torrents and survive. She felt her stomach turn. This wasn't right. Too many people were dying for her sake.

Erde threw her head back to moan, and produced only raspy breath. Her voice. She'd forgotten. She pushed her breath up against her throat in frustrated gasps. If only she could howl her anguish, like the lunatic boy who lived in the stable yard, she'd never ask to speak human words again.

As she struggled vainly to be heard, sounds from the outer cavern invaded her unwilling silence. Guilt and grief fled as Erde stilled to listen. She had not imagined it: soft steady splashes, and breathing. Something big was moving slowly through the shallow water, shuffling and snuffling, as a bear might do if it had been stirred from early hibernation by the smoke of her fire.

Erde felt no surge of terror. She had already used up her supply. She gripped Alla's little dagger, then left it in its sheath. It was sufficient to kill a man, as she knew too well, but small defense against an angry bear. She thought of Rainer's sword, but couldn't bear to bloody its pure shining blade. Her sudden calm astonished and confused her, but one thing she was sure of was that she didn't want to kill anything, or even try. She'd had enough death and killing, and if the proper punishment for her crime was to be eaten alive, then let one of God's creatures be His avenging angel.

The snuffling neared the entrance to her cave and stopped.

Its presence was more than sound. Erde could *feel* it out there, its questing like a touch on her skin, the anticipation of it an invisible hand pressing on her brain. The bear, or whatever it was, tried the entrance, with the unmistakable scrape of claws on stone. It seemed to struggle, as if it couldn't easily fit through. Briefly, Erde was relieved. Then she realized what this meant about the size of the bear. The passage into her cave was tall and not particularly narrow. This must be a bear out of all natural proportion, not

God's bear at all but some terrible demon sent by the Devil
to drag her to Hell for her crimes.

A demon. Mere stone would not keep a demon out, and
sure enough, in it came. The sound as it squeezed through
the opening was the metallic hiss of a sword being drawn.
A smell like a snake pit invaded the cavern as the demon
dragged itself across the floor.

Some vague terror began to penetrate. Erde clutched the
sword to her, rolled herself into a knot beneath her cloak,
and waited for fangs and claws and oblivion. The acrid
snake smell enveloped her. She sensed the demon hovering
above her, heard the creak of bones and scales and a vast
hollow rasp of breathing as it lowered its head.

The demon nudged her. Its snout was hard and felt as
big as her entire body. It pushed at her gently, snuffled a
little, then eased its great weight down beside her, sighed,
and began to snore.

Erde didn't move a muscle. The demon had decided to
rest, and was saving her for breakfast. Somewhere inside,
a voice screamed at her to get up and run while she had
the chance. She knew she should. But she was so cold, and
this demon was so pleasantly warm. The deep rhythm of
its breathing soothed her. After a long while of listening to
it snore, Erde decided that either it had put a spell on her
or she was still dreaming. She gave up waiting to die and
drifted off to sleep.

She dreamed of her father again, and poor dead Rainer,
fighting. Cruelly they slashed at each other with shining
swords much bigger than the one she'd carried away into
exile. Their dueling ground was not the familiar battlements
or castle yard of Tor Alte. It was flat, a perfect horizon-
stretching flatness such as she had never seen, having grown
up in a mountain kingdom. It was as flat as she imagined
the ocean to be, with no visible end to it. The surface of
this plain was unnaturally dark, like earth seared by fire,
and so hard that the men's boots rang against it as if it
were hollow, a plain of stone. In the distance behind rose
a tall line of towers, shrouded in smoke. A cold wind stung
the back of her throat, leaving behind the taste of metal.
After a long while watching the terrible battle, unable to

turn away, Erde became aware that someone beside her was speaking her name.

She woke again, the dream call still whispering in her ear. She stirred and looked up into a pair of round windows, side by side, glowing amber with the rising sun.

Erde blinked and reconsidered. She was inside a cave. These could not be windows but . . . She remembered the demon. Eyes. The demon's eyes! Eyes as big as windows, and lit with their own inner fire. She could not scream, but her body convulsed into a protective ball beneath the folds of her cloak. Breathing shallowly, she waited, but the demon made no move. After a while, she found herself wondering why it didn't just eat her and be done with it.

With a careful finger, Erde drew away a corner of fabric from her eyes. The glowing windows were gone. Dawn had returned to the mountain and the faint light filtering down from above outlined a great horned head set on a long muscular neck, powerful forearms and chest tapering past strong short haunches to a stubby tail that lay curled partly around her. It looked like . . . Erde decided the demon meant to trick her, looking like that, so like a . . .

A dragon?

She suppressed her sudden thrill of joy. Of course it could not be a dragon, not here in this tiny dark cave. And joy in her situation was not logical. A murderess about to be eaten should not feel joyful. It was the dream still possessing her, or the demon's spell. But the trouble with dreams and spells was, even if you knew you were in one, it was hard to know how to get yourself out. The joy within her demanded recognition, even if it was a demon's illusion. Besides, why couldn't it be a dragon?

Erde considered further. If it was a dragon, it might be just as hungry as a demon. Perhaps Alla had been wrong about dragons not eating people. Perhaps a dragon and a demon were the same, like Fra Guill said, and she'd be no better off than if it was a demon pretending to be a dragon.

The demon opened his eyes again and blinked at her slowly. Its transparent lids glided crossways like shimmering curtains of rain. Erde sighed. Their beauty took her breath away.

Could she really be dreaming? Would she, raised in the rich legacy of her grandmother's dragon-tales, have ever dreamed a dragon with no wings? And if it was demon-sent, wouldn't it be a bit more terrifying? This creature seemed big enough when crammed into a hole in the ground with you, but looking it over, she saw it was no match at all for the fantasy dragons of her childhood. Glasswind's back alone had been the size of her whole bedchamber. This dragon, if it was one, was closer to the size of her bed.

And what would a dream-dragon, or even a demon, expect of her, for the oddest thing about this creature was that it seemed to want something of her rather immediately. It only stared and blinked, very slowly, but Erde could *feel* its expectation. Strangely, she felt no threat, though beyond the expectation was hunger, hunger like a longing, like the sharp attention of the dogs in the wood yard when she passed them on her way for a walk: demanding looks, as if it was her responsibility to take them with her and tell them what to do.

Erde stirred in her nest of damp wool and clothing. One could not sit forever, waiting to be eaten. The stiffness in her limbs and a desperate need to relieve herself made it seem very likely that she was not dreaming this dragon after all. She needed to see it more clearly. Perhaps then she would know. She sat up slowly and felt for her satchel, found a candle, flint and tinder, and struck a spark. The dragon drew back in surprise, then lowered its big head again to regard the candle flame with something resembling professional interest.

Erde rose, stretching carefully. The luminous eyes followed her. Logic told her this scaly creature might snap her up at any moment, yet she felt inexplicably calm. She faced it bravely, holding the candle high to study it. It definitely looked like a dragon, or at least a sort of dragon. Staring into its eyes was like standing at the top of a tower, wind-blown and vertiginous, with voices calling you from a distance.

She was seized by a need to touch it. Amazed by her own boldness, she laid her palm on the bony ridge of the dragon's snout. It felt hard and very rough, like worn granite, but suddenly the joy inside her swelled, as if something warm and needy were pouring into her from outside. The surge abated as soon as she jerked her hand away.

My goodness. Erde sat down again to think.

In her fantasies, she had never bothered about how one communicated with a dragon. She had simply endowed them with human speech. But nose-to-nose with this creature, even an ardent fantast such as herself could not imagine its blunt crocodilian jaw producing comprehensible German. Even if it did by some magic find its tongue, she would not now be able to answer it.

But Erde knew well enough that men's words are not the only medium of communication. A dragon was, after all, an animal of sorts, and she'd never had any trouble talking with animals. She knew to put her hands on them—dogs liked their heads held and horses preferred an arm slung about their shoulders—while thinking about whatever it was she wanted them to know. Somehow, the messages got through. But dogs had relatively simple agendas and were familiar to her. A dragon was another matter entirely.

As she contemplated it, the dragon began to shift its bulk from one forearm to the other and back again. *It's getting impatient,* Erde concluded. *If I can't figure out what it wants, perhaps it will eat me after all, no matter what Alla said.*

She decided to test whether it would allow her freedom of movement. Holding her candle high, she stepped over the thick scaled curve of its tail and marched slowly across the cavern. It made no move to stop her. But as she neared the entrance, she was nearly brought to her knees by a piercing sense of loss welling up inside, as if from the depths of her soul. Erde cringed in pain and hugged herself, spilling hot wax on her jerkin. The dragon wrenched its bulk around in the narrow space and came trailing after her, making soft mewling noises like a puppy. When it reached her and she did not back away, it quieted. The sharp pang in her heart receded and she could stand up straight again. She stared at it, breathing hard. It stared back, beseechingly.

Erde knew then that this creature was not going to eat her, that in fact it was going to attach itself to her and did not want her to leave without it. Cautiously, she let herself feel a little of that joy inside. After all her years of dreaming and fantasizing, here was an actual living dragon, and it had chosen her. However remarkable that might be, Erde felt there was nothing in her life so far that she was as well prepared for. She put her hand on the dragon's nose and bade it follow, and it did.

She retraced her path around the edge of the underground pool with no destination in mind, wandering for the sheer delight of watching the dragon trudge after her like a worried and faithful hound. It waded through the pool, sending huge dark ripples coursing across the cavern to reflect the candle flame in bright, ever widening circles. It followed her willingly enough through connecting tunnels and caves up toward the surface, but Erde felt its anxiety build with the steady increase of gray light seeping down from the entrance. Where the tunnel began its final ascent, the dragon stopped.

Erde blew out her candle and stowed it in her jerkin. The light from above was just bright enough to see by. She decided to make a quick search for more firewood, and started up the crumbled slope. The dragon swayed uneasily from side to side and broadcast its alarm until Erde put her hands to her ears and begged it to stop. She turned and looked back at it, its head down between its claws like the Devil's hunting dog, a dog of living rock, all gray and dusty in the dim light.

I will be back, she thought at it carefully, in simple words, as if speaking to a small child. It lay there listlessly, with a dog's tragic gaze, and she was sure it had not understood.

But it was not just firewood she needed. She needed to be up top under open sky, for a moment at least. The more she thought about it, the more urgent the need became. She headed upward again, her boots skittering across the brittle surface. Small cascades of broken rock rattled down behind her. She knew she was not being careful, but caution came too late. She did not hear the bear entering from above, or see him until he had already seen her, blocking the passage to his winter den.

It was a large bear, and very touchy. His eyes squinted. He could not see well, but smelled her out instantly. He snarled, and one huge paw slashed out warningly. Erde slid backward down the slope and shrank against the wall, but mere retreat did not satisfy the bear. His roar echoed through the tunnel like thunder as he launched himself down the slope. She fumbled uselessly for her dagger, caught in the folds of her shirt, then lost her footing and fell sliding backward.

Dragon! she thought blindly as she plummeted downward in a hail of gravel and angry brown bear. She hit bottom and rolled into a ball, awaiting the crush of rough fur and the terrible rake of claws. Her last tumble brought her face up, in time to see the dragon snatch up the bear, the whole head in its mouth as if that great hairy bulk weighed nothing. While Erde scrambled up, backing against the cavern wall, the dragon shook the big bear once, very hard. It held the limp corpse dangling in its jaws for a moment, then shambled over to lay it down with delicate formality at Erde's feet.

The baron's daughter had found a new champion.

CHAPTER NINE

Your dragon awaits you.

And indeed the dragon was waiting, with an expectant look in its eyes, glancing from the pile of dead bear to Erde and back again. The bear was beginning to leak blood from its mouth. Sickened, Erde backed away. When the dragon snatched it up once more and dragged it off into a corner, she understood it was only waiting for a sign, for her permission. Turning away while the dragon noisily devoured its meal, Erde recalled Alla's words again, and wondered how the old woman had known.

Perhaps Alla had been a witch after all. Erde knew that she'd put no spell on Rainer, but she'd had many unusual skills and knew many mysterious things. If being a witch meant being like Alla, Erde didn't see why people thought it was such a bad thing.

She risked a glance over her shoulder. Each time she looked at the dragon, she felt that same surge of wonder and joy. But this time she was glad for the faintness of the light, as faint as her heart became at such a sight. The loud crunching and rending was bad enough. This dragon was not a tidy eater and it was ravenous, as one might expect a newly awakened dragon to be if one knew one's dragon-lore, and Erde considered herself a bit of a lay expert.

She was glad to learn that the dragon had spared her not because it was sated or an herbivore or even particularly mild-mannered. It was hungry and possessed a proper dragon-like appetite, yet it had left her alone. Whatever torturous pathways of thought she followed, she reached the same conclusion in the end: her sense of connection with this implausible creature was a true one.

Your dragon awaits you. She wished Alla had given her just the smallest clue as to what it awaited her for. Dragons, like all magical beings, had a distinct reason for being. You didn't just acquire one out of simple good fortune.

The Mage-Queen was dragon-bound, but the Mage-Queen, a benevolent power, had been Erde's own fantasy, even if she did sometimes wish she was real, or sometimes forget that she wasn't. In the true dragon-lore, such connections with dragons were spell-wrought. They were generally sought by evil mage-lords, who sacrificed their firstborn or sold their soul to the Devil for the privilege. Erde was fairly sure that killing a man in self-defense, though surely an awful crime, was not quite the equivalent in black magic terms, so this small bit of knowledge left her no more enlightened than before.

The dragon finished bolting its meal. Erde sensed this by the expectant silence that settled in behind her and she knew, just *knew,* that the dragon was waiting for more. Her fleeting concern that once its appetite was whetted, it might move on to her was dispelled by the supplicant quality of its waiting, like a giant nestling, mouth slightly agape, helpless but demanding to be fed. The demanding part she could accept. All dragons expect service from humankind. But helpless?

It thinks I brought it the bear, she realized. *And it wants another.* Erde shook her head. Service was all very well and good, but she was going to have to disabuse this creature of the notion that a fourteen-year-old girl, a fugitive at that, could provide it with a steady supply of dragon-sized dinners. She was just coming to grips with the problem of hiding out alone in a cold cave and feeding herself. The little bits of food she'd brought with her wouldn't last more than a day. Feeding a dragon would require entire barnyards. Why couldn't it feed itself?

Overwhelmed, Erde sank to the cave floor in despair and put her head in her hands.

Oh, Alla, what have I done? What can I do now?

Alla had said, hide out until the priest leaves or go to the king. But Alla had not expected her high-born nursling to effect her escape in blood. Erde could not ask even temporary shelter of the villagers now, or for their help in getting to the king. The man she'd murdered had three children, one of whom was sickly. She would have to remain in the caves, sneaking out only at night to steal whatever food she could find, until life returned to normal at Tor Alte. She was sure her father would be less bothered about her having killed a common soldier in defense of her honor. But then, it seemed her father did not believe she had any honor left. Womanly honor, at least. She wasn't sure he valued any other kind, since he'd shown himself so spendthrift with Rainer's.

Ah, Rainer. In the distraction of the dragon, she'd all but forgotten. How could she? No, she'd never forget. Erde called once more to mind the surprise of his kiss and wrapped the memory deep inside where it would always be safe.

The dragon shifted about in its heavy-limbed dance of impatience. Erde lifted her head and signed in its direction. It had left the bear's head and claws uneaten. She would have to clean up the mess before it began to smell and attract other dangerous wildlife. The dragon moved a step closer and resettled itself doglike on its haunches. It could not lick its chops—its tongue was not flat and so easily manipulated. It was more like a lizard's tongue, thick and oval, tapering to a blunt point. But Erde had noticed that it often let the slender tip hang out of the side of its mouth, where a space was left between its big canines and its double rows of bicuspids. However endearing, this habit was not dignified, and Erde had always believed dragons to be deeply concerned with their dignity. Apparently not this dragon.

As she sat there staring at her new companion, she found herself thinking of sheep, seeing them rather, fat sheep on a soft green hill, like a daydream, only clearer. Very real in her mind's eye. Oddly, these particular sheep were large and brown and very shaggy, not at all like the thin, gray ewes kept by local herdsmen. Yet they were there in her head and she knew they were sheep. Odder still, the landscape surrounding these strange sheep wasn't familiar either. The hills were much too low and gently rolling, the meadows far too green. There was too much sky. Yet this image in her head was as clear and present as one of her own memories.

Erde peered at the dragon speculatively. Was it the source of these alien visions? Could it conjure and send them at will? Even better, could it receive?

Erde cast about for a way to test her hypothesis, and her eye fell on the grisly bear's head. It was easier to look at now that it had given her an idea. She watched the dragon closely and called to mind, as quickly and forcefully as she could, her last sight of the bear before she had covered her eyes, all fangs and claws hurtling down on top of her. The dragon's head jerked toward the upward tunnel. A fleshy crest that Erde had not noticed before raised up along the curve of its head and neck like the hackles on a dog. When no bear appeared, the dragon looked back to find itself being studied and seemed to understand that Erde had been testing it. It lowered its crest, shook its great head and let its tongue-tip loll out the side as if ready and willing to play this new game. But the only thing that came to Erde's mind were more images of sheep.

Erde's shoulders sagged. The dragon was either stubborn or stupid, or her theory was incorrect. Or perhaps it was so obsessed with its hunger, it could not think of anything else. She wondered how long it had lain asleep deep inside this mountain, working up an appetite.

Despair overwhelmed her again. But Alla had always said that action was the antidote to despair, so Erde decided to follow her original upward urge. She did need more firewood, and maybe some dry grass for bedding. She sent the dragon an image of herself returning to the cave with her arms laden, though she was careful not to promise it food. She didn't wish to face a dragon's disappointment. She laid a reassuring hand on its snout, still full of wonder that she was actually touching a real dragon, then headed for the surface.

She listened at the cave mouth for a long time, but heard nothing stirring, not even an early hawk or raven. The mountain was shrouded in dense fog. Except for its clinging chill, Erde was grateful for the cover it provided. A wind during the night had swept the rock ledges clear of snow, though it had gathered in the nooks and crannies to remind her once again of the unnatural state of the weather, snow

in August. For several hours, she clambered back and forth
from her cave to the tree line, gathering up every loose
branch or fallen sapling that she could carry.

By midmorning, the fog was clearing. Erde stowed a final
armload of twigs inside the cave, then climbed to the top
of an old rock slide. From there, hiding behind a large
boulder, she could see safely down the other side of the
mountain.

A half mile away, the towers of Tor Alte crouched on
their own lesser summit, like a lost city rising out of the
gray mist that filled the valley in between. It did not look
at all like home to her. The massive walls were faceless
and bleak under the lowering sky. Erde gazed at it for a
long time, searching for a sign of life other than the black
and green flag of the von Altes, wind-whipped on the highest tower. She sensed she was waiting for an omen of some
sort or a feeling from inside, just the faintest homesickness
or longing, enough to tell her she should give up her mad
flight and throw herself back on her father's mercy. Nothing
came. Only the submerged razor edge of the pain she was
running from. Only the memory of Rainer's breathless grin
as he glanced up at her from the practice yard. She couldn't
think of it. She wouldn't. If a memory was too painful to
bear, she would put it aside. That dark pile of stone was
someone else's childhood home. Every thing that Erde von
Alte longed for there was dead. Now she was glad for the
numbness, which had returned as soon as she'd set her eyes
on those grim towers and grim walls.

So she could not go home, since she had no home to go
to. Besides, to return would imply acceptance of Alla's
death and Rainer's murder. But knowing she could not go
home did not tell her where to go instead, or whether she
should leave the dragon where it had found her. Sneaking
away without it would surely improve her own chances of
escaping undetected, but the notion came and went as if it
did not even bear considering. Just when she'd lost everything, the dragon had appeared. This was certainly the sign
she was looking for.

Yet she waited, staring down at the fog-wreathed for-
tress, so still that the arm she leaned on went to sleep. She
woke with a tingle when movement below caught her eye
and she jerked upright.

A party of several dozen riders appeared outside the Dragon Gate, milling and dodging, no standard raised to identify them. The hounds were no more than a crowd of tiny dancing blurs, but their excited baying carried easily through the mountain quiet. Erde knew the hungry cry of the Baron's Hunt.

Erde flattened herself against the boulder, then scrambled back down the rock slide. Her panic didn't loose its grip until she was well inside the cave, far from searching eye of daylight, where finally she let reason take hold. She laid her cloak out on the floor, piled on as much of the firewood as it would hold and dragged it down the inner tunnel toward her hideout and the dragon. *Her* dragon.

CHAPTER TEN

She scrubbed the blood from her cloak as best she could, and steamed it dry. She tended the fire. She spent an hour retrimming her shorn hair. She tried to keep too busy to eat, but by nightfall she had finished all her food. It had seemed like so much more when it was heavy in her pack. Now it barely filled her, and the dragon too was hungry, so hungry it could not keep still. It paced in the outer caverns like a caged lion, and she wondered why it didn't go forage for itself the way dragons were supposed to do. Of course, its not having any wings might make that difficult. Dragons were supposed to be able to drop out of the air and scoop up their unsuspecting victims. She'd also assumed all dragons were created fully formed, but perhaps this one was young and still developing its wings. Meanwhile, it would have to sneak up on its prey and drag it away like any other large carnivore.

Listening to it pace and snuffle in the outer darkness, Erde knew that the dragon would drive her back into the open even before her own hunger and growing claustrophobia got the better of her. Up there it could surely feed itself—she hoped then it would cease its steady barrage of sheep images, crowding up her brain when she was desperate for a clear head to make her plans.

Two things she was sure of: she was not going back to Tor Alte now—maybe not ever—and she had to get the dragon out of the caves. She had seen it move fast when it felt motivated, but could it move fast enough to elude the Baron's Hunt, which would surely track them down before long? She had to get it away, down the mountain into the lowlands, where her face wasn't known, where the farmers were sure to have fatter sheep in their meadows and where she wasn't on a first-name basis with practically every deer in the forest. And better to do it sooner than later, while they were both still strong, or before the half-starved dragon devoured her in desperation. Perhaps just down and away was enough of a destination for the time being. If she knew she was heading in the general direction of Erfurt and the king's court, she could learn the way as she went along.

At last the time came when drinking the cold earthy water of the underground pool no longer slaked her hunger pangs. Erde brushed rock dust from her shirtfront, put on all her clothes, and packed up her meager possessions. She made a sling for Rainer's sword from strips of the sheeting that had bound its blade. Now it rested at an angle across her back, with the hilt by her right ear. She settled it comfortably and shouldered her satchel. She sent a *follow-me* image to the dragon and led it to the surface.

The snow and mists had cleared. The temperature was chilly but a little more like a normal mountain night in August. Erde was sure the Hunt had been at the cave mouth at some time during the day. The bits of bare ground seemed more scuffed than she remembered and she smelled horse dung. The Hunt never ranged this high because neither did the deer, which confirmed her assumption that the baron had sent his huntsman after his daughter. She wondered if it was dragon-scent that had kept the hounds outside the cave.

A clear half-moon lit their way, scudding through broken clouds, but the journey down was slow and perilous, slippery with leaves that were already beginning to fall from the trees. Erde knew every trail and the dragon appeared to have remarkable night vision, but she had never traveled these steep-sided woods with a pack and a man's sword strapped to her back. Plus the dragon was curious about everything and a little clumsy. Its horns, matched arcs of shining ivory, caught in overhanging branches. Its claws slid on the rock. It had a pronounced tendency to go crashing through the noisiest brush or to send cascades of loose stones rattling down the mountainside. It was like fleeing through the forest with a very large, dusty child. Erde was forced constantly to impress on it the need for silence, while urging it ever onward.

She rested as often as she dared. She had thought her mountain walks fairly strenuous until now, when she could no longer go home to food and a warm fire after a few hours. But fear kept her moving past her first exhaustion, and later she found new strength for the dragon's sake.

She stayed well away from the mountain villages so that the dragon would have no cause to become interested in them. She wanted it to forage on its own, but in the forests. Mysteriously missing livestock so close to Tor Alte would alert the Hunt. The countryside was aroused enough already, and she didn't want *her* dragon made a target for Fra Guill's dragon hatred. Yet the dragon didn't show much inclination to hunt, despite its hunger. It did halt once, on a hill above an isolated farmstead, at the sound of a dog barking. It raised its huge nostrils to the wind and would not be lured forward. The image invading Erde's mind was finally a new one, a kind of aggressive blank that shoved aside all her own thoughts, rather like blundering into a blinding snowstorm inside your head. Erde suffered a few astonished moments of panic before she could assure herself she wasn't going mad and her brain hadn't broken. She noticed that her face was pressed into a questioning frown, and decided that the blankness was the dragon's way of demanding information.

She conjured the sleeping farmstead in her mind, its muddy rutted yard, its stubby slate-roofed cottage, every detail but its barns and herd stock. She did add in the dog for verisimilitude, but made it a small thin mongrel not worthy of a dragon's attention, too irritating to be bothered with. Finally, the dragon moved on, and Erde learned that its pride was vulnerable and could be played upon to advantage. But she was not cheered by the fact that she had barely yet learned to communicate with the creature and she was lying to it already.

Just before dawn, it began to rain lightly, blown into a chill mist by gusty breezes more reminiscent of October than August. Erde's route, half-knowing, half-random, took them above the village of Tubin, where the richest of the local merchants lived. Erde had visited it many times with her father. One of the merchants there sold the baron all his silks and velvets. Taking shelter in a pine grove where she could look down at Tubin's dark, once fertile valley, she recalled that merchant's elaborately paneled shop, with its crackling hearth fire, and the small supper he laid out for his best customers. She nearly wept. She had never been so cold and hungry in her life.

Tubin was practically a town. It had several main streets and a stout gated wall protecting its market district. Inside the wall, the cobbled church square was lined with the merchants' two-storied stone houses. But most of the town lived outside the wall, among the fields and farmyards. Erde resolved to find dinner here for her dragon and later, for herself, before her strength failed her completely.

She searched out a forest gorge where the dragon could hide, on a dry ledge overhung by tall dark pines clinging to the vertical rock. She rested briefly, then left the sword and her pack in his care. The rain had stopped but not the biting wind. Erde hugged her cloak closely and shivered. She thought it odd, as she trudged through the dark sodden meadows outlying the farmsteads, to hear the bell in the church tower tolling before any sign of daylight, not the quick peals of celebration or the hard-edged clang of alarm but slow and steady like the drumbeat of a marching army.

She heard dogs barking from the cottages closest to the road. Keeping tightly to the deeper shadow of hedges and fence lines, Erde spotted lanterns moving along the road, a group of farm folk murmuring among themselves as they walked into town. She smeared mud on her cheeks and, reluctantly, on her cloak whose fine wool had already once betrayed her identity. She shrugged it high around her shoulders, leaving the prentice cap showing. Nervous about going in among people again but driven by the fever of her hunger, she fell in behind the group on the road, then realized there were others behind them, and more behind them. She saw she was caught up in a moving throng, and nearly bolted. But away from the dim flare of the lanterns, it was dark enough and no one took any special notice of her. She struggled to walk steadily, not to show her abnormal exhaustion in any obvious way. The road was muddy and slick. Cold rainwater lay deep in the wheel ruts and soaked into her boots. But Erde was relieved to be among people again, especially people who weren't chasing her. And she was curious to know what would make the entire country-side head into town in the small hours before dawn. She quickened her pace to catch up with the two men directly in front of her, to eavesdrop on their subdued conversation.

". . . rode into my yard and walked right into the smoke-house," muttered the tall one on the right. "Started cutting down hams. Said the baron ordered it."

"That priest is eating well enough," his companion growled.

"Better than we are."

"Wasn't no surprise though, when he pointed that one out," the stouter man declared. "And she standing right there in the crowd like she'd lived in the village all her life, same as the rest of us."

Erde could not hear the tall man's reply, muttered beneath the woolen blanket he'd wrapped around him for warmth. But the stout man seemed to feel the need to prove his great foresight further. "Sure, remember Podi's cow, after she visited his wife that time? And the smith's cousin, who lost her gold ring in the well? She'd had some dealings with her."

The tall man muttered again. Erde strained and still could not hear him. The stout man's voice only got louder.

"She was *your* neighbor, Deit. You'd better be keeping a closer eye out. What about all this god-forsaken rain and cold? Business so bad all around and you don't wonder why?"

"Don't talk to me!" The tall man's chin finally emerged from its cocoon. "We lived side by side for years with little more than a how-de-do. It was you always tagging after the woman, so even your wife could notice."

The stout man glanced around fearfully, in case someone might have overheard. "Well, hell, a young widow woman usually likes a little company. If I'd have known then . . ."

"You didn't know nothing till she turned you down. Now, my wife was friendly to her. Said she had a healer's gift. Saved my boy from the agues that time. I had nothing against her. Just looks to me like she turned down one man too many."

"Here, now, what're you saying?"

"Nothing, nothing."

"Your trouble is, Deit, you're always saying something."

"I said, I ain't saying nothing."

"Well, I wouldn't, if I were you, not out loud where the holy brothers can hear you or you'll end up in one his visions. You're lucky we're such old friends."

Erde nearly turned and fled. But hunger spoke more eloquently than panic. If there was a crowd in town, there might be food sellers, and if the crowd got excited, it might be easier to lift a loaf or a pie during a distraction. She promised herself that if she spotted so much as the sleeve of a white-robe, she'd be gone in a flash. She let the crowd carry her through the town gates and toward the main square, following the ceaseless grim summons of the church bell.

It was warmer inside the gates, out of the cold ceaseless wind. The streets were narrow, walled in by tall stone houses and shops, overhung with wooden signs that dripped rainwater into Erde's face. The traffic thickened as they neared the square, and she avoided anyone carrying a lighted lantern. She had been in this town before as her father's daughter. Someone might recognize her.

People poured in from the side streets, men and women, old people hobbling along on canes, sleepy-eyed children in their parents' arms. Among adults again, Erde was once more a child, yet she knew her childhood was over, however prematurely. She felt her first tinge of homesickness, of nostalgia for the security of having adults to care for her and tell her what to do. Though their parents' faces were reserved and serious as they moved through the dark wet streets, the young boys darted wildly in and out of the crowd, splashing through puddles, snatching at each other's tunics and hooting as if it were a feast-day celebration. Erde envied their ruthless innocence. Those boys suffered no shame over the sweet-cake they stole from the neighbor's kitchen window, or the dead mouse on their sister's pillow. But then, they had no cause for *real* shame, not like she did.

The memory of Georg flailing backward seized her, filling her nostrils with the sweet-sour smell of his blood. Erde stumbled, her empty stomach turning, and nearly fell. She wrapped her arms around her chest and grasped herself hard for a moment, leaning weakly against the rough wall of a boot-maker's shop, gasping and fighting for balance while the throng flowed past unawares.

Except the hand that caught her elbow. "All right there, lad?"

She was alert in an instant, sure she'd been discovered. She nodded without looking up.

"Sure, are you? You look a bit peaked." The voice was gruff and matter-of-fact. "Look like you slept in a mud puddle."

Erde ventured an upward glance. The man's face was solid, seamy and blessedly unfamiliar. He was quite tall but carried himself with a diffident stoop, in the way of tall people who do not favor always relating downward to the rest of the world. Or, she thought next, in the way of people who wish not to be noticed. His damp, close-cropped hair and beard were silvery gray, but the arm supporting her was strong, his grip on her elbow secure. His cheeks were weather-hardened but somewhat puffy. Erde thought she recognized the signs. But if this man was a drinker, he was certainly sober now. The most striking thing about him was his leather jerkin, worn and sturdy but dyed a deep red. Erde couldn't imagine choosing to wear the color of blood. Still, something about the garment seemed oddly familiar, though she was sure she had never seen this man before.

"Well, can you walk?"

She tried a quick smile and a nod. If he was from town, he would know that she wasn't. She did not want him getting too friendly or inquisitive.

"Speak up, lad. Are your parents about?"

A stranger. She was safe for a while, then. Erde shrugged, shook her head and, inspired at last, put her fingers to her throat in the time-honored explanatory gesture of mutes.

"Oh. That's how it is. I see."

She nodded again, trying now to slip invisibly out of his grasp.

"Well, I'm sorry for that, boy." The man frowned, not without pity but as if the very idea stood in for all the world's other evils as well. "Let me guess . . . when was the last time you ate something?"

Her eyes flicked at him and away so fast that he chuckled

out loud. "No need to be ashamed. We're all a little short these days." He dug into the wide studded belt that banded his peculiar red jerkin, and brought out a coin. He flipped it to her, and Erde, untrained in such maneuvers, fumbled it and nearly dropped it on the cobbles before managing a firm grip. She shot him a look of gratitude, even as she wondered why he should bother to help an unknown prentice lad.

Now the man was studying her speculatively, as if he regretted the coin already. Fearing he might ask for it back or demand some service in return, Erde saluted him quickly with her clenched fist and ducked away. He called after her, but she managed to lose herself in the crowd. It wasn't until she was well away from him that she sneaked a glance at the coin. She nearly dropped it again. It was a silver mark, stamped with the king's portrait on one side and the royal coat-of-arms on the other. It conjured a sudden image of festival market days and her grandmother's long-fingered hands, so like her own, counting out in the king's own currency her careful payment for a bolt of Italian velvet or a bushel of exotic citrus.

Erde could hardly believe her good fortune. She held in her hand money enough to buy food for a month, or maybe, several sheep.

CHAPTER ELEVEN

She nearly ran after the man in the red jerkin to thank him properly. But the impulse quickly passed. It was only her upbringing talking, appropriate for a baron's daughter but not for a fugitive murderess. Besides, the man must have some ulterior motive to go about giving silver marks to beggar boys. Either that or he was so very rich that having one mark less would mean little to him.

The excitement of this windfall infused her with new energy. She could actually buy her dinner now, like a normal honest citizen. Clutching the coin in her palm as if it were a religious relic, she fell in with the crowd again, streaming along the main thoroughfare that led to the church square. The many lanterns swinging in people's hands made the chill puddled street seem warm and festive. Most of the single-story shops were still shuttered, but here and there, lamps gleamed behind wrinkled glass as the hungrier shopkeepers prepared to open early. The food sellers would bring their wares along on carts and set up at the big event, wherever the crowd was headed. Erde was greatly cheered by the prospect of a hot meal. She strode along in her most boylike gait, just on the verge of enjoying herself.

The market square was already packed with people, with crowds pouring in from all directions. Erde had never seen it so full, even on market days, especially so early in the morning. She thought back through the church calendar, wondering if in the recent chaos of her life, she'd forgotten some major religious festival.

Her own throng arrived at the far end of the broad windy rectangle, opposite the church. Tubin's church was the largest in the baronage, and Erde thought it a proper model for all churches, even though the two-towered sandstone edifice was as yet uncompleted and she had never known it without scaffolding veiling its tall facade. Standing on tiptoe, she could see the top few tiers of scaffolding over the heads of the crowd, the maze of rain-heavy canvas windshields and the ramps and cross-bracing dripping water. Behind it all, like an unfinished sun, rose the outline of the huge round window that the monsignor claimed to be the latest in church design, which he said would surely convince the Bishop of Ulm to elevate it from church to cathedral, and thus bring visitors and pilgrims from far and wide into Tubin's marketplace. Come dawn, the masons would return to continue mortaring the delicate curved mullions. When completed, the window was to be fitted with the finest colored glass imported all the way from Venezia.

She was distracted from her reverie by the aroma of roasted meat, drowning out even the heavy odors of farmer's boots and unlaundered clothing. Searching frantically above the heads of the milling townspeople, Erde spotted the iron braziers burning on sturdy flatbed wagons parked along one side of the square. Flame shadows danced across the painted signs and multipaned windows of the craft guild halls behind. Prentice boys dodged about, dark shapes bobbing against firelight, tossing on armloads of wood, turning the spit-cranks. The spitted carcasses were thinner and stringier than the fare that had always graced the baron's table. Once she'd have thought them too scrawny to be worth cooking. Now she thought differently. Her mouth watered. She thought of the dragon with its tongue-tip hanging out, and laughed in anticipation, except that what came out of her mouth could hardly be called a laugh, being all breath and no sound. It was the first time she'd even attempted a laugh in the three days since she'd lost her voice. Remembering why drained the breath and joy right out of her, leaving only hunger, now honed to a knife's edge of determination. Her whole body tightened like a fist. She had to restrain herself from pushing through the crowd. She had an inkling now of why a person might kill in order to eat.

The first food seller she approached was a thin, quiet woman who glanced at the coin on Erde's palm and shook her head. "You could buy the whole stock and stall with that coin, dearie, and what would I have left to give you in change? Tell your master you need something smaller next time."

Erde nodded her thanks and moved on. The next man wouldn't even look at her. He was too busy fawning over a large party of richly dressed men who seemed intent on devouring the entire scrawny lamb turning on his spit, before it was even cooked. Erde ducked away, wanting to avoid any local landowners who might know her father. She passed by a baker's boy unpacking a small basket of loaves and meat pies onto a portable tray. The pies smelled delicious, but she was sure he wouldn't have change for her silver mark. At the next stall, thin chickens dripped over glowing coals. Erde showed her coin to the red-faced owner, pointing and nodding at the biggest hen.

The food seller squinted at the coin. "What's that you've got, boy?"

Erde held it into the light of his pole-lantern. The man snatched at it, narrowly missing it. Erde sprang back a step, but pointed again at the sizzling bird.

The man grinned. "Oh, *that* one? Now *that* one'll cost you all of it." He held out his hand.

Erde shook her head, amazed that she was even tempted.

"You don't think I know where you got that?" the meat-seller hissed. He began to wave his arms and shout at her. "What do you think I am! Get away from me, you little thief!"

Erde backed away from him, appalled. The prentices had stopped their fueling and cranking to stare in sullen hope of an interesting fight. Erde turned and fled into the crowd, reconsidering the value of Red-jerkin's gift. Maybe he'd meant to get her caught. She might be forced to steal her meal after all.

There was a stir in the market square. Something was going on in front of the church. The throng was lining up now, in disorderly rows three and four deep. Small children were being lifted up to sit on their fathers' shoulders. They blocked Erde's view of the square, but food was more important to her right then than whatever ceremony was about to begin. She made her way along the back row toward the end of the line of food stalls to try her luck again. Suddenly, the crowd in front of her parted in a wave and regrouped to open a passage from a side street into the square. A hush fell over them. Even the children lowered their voices. Necks craned in the direction of a muffled drumbeat and the creak of wagon wheels. Erde peered around the plump shoulder of the woman in front of her, and shrank back immediately.

White-robes!

Marching to solemn cadence in their all-too-familiar double-file formation came Fra Guill's thirty acolytes, heads bowed, deeply cowled. Two of them walked a pace ahead, beating small hand drums. The rest pulled a slat-sided wooden cart, leaning into the ropes as if the burden were greater than any mere mortal could bear. Yet the cart was small and it carried only a solitary woman.

Slim torches burned at the cart's four corners. The woman stood tall, gripping the thigh-high side rails, shivering visibly but staring straight ahead. She wore only a rough muslin shift, wet through from the rain, so that her full, handsome breasts and smooth hips were plain for all to see. Erde found herself blushing for the woman's sake. She had never seen a person in such a state of public undress. How could she hold her head so high? Had she no modesty?

Among the watchers, the wives muttered their fear and disapproval, which only barely hid their envy, for the woman was very beautiful. The men shifted about and hiked up their clothing at the crotch.

Then Erde noticed that the woman's wrists were tightly bound to the rails, and she felt her stomach drop away from her backbone and every hair on her body thrill with horror. Now she understood the conversation she had overheard on the road into town. She had stumbled onto a witch-trial. She was unsure why this complete stranger's predicament should compel her so, except that it reminded her of Alla. And it was confusing to sense a faint stirring of pride that the woman could look so strong and beautiful, even when wet and shivering and obviously terrified. Erde had promised to flee at the very scent of a white-robe, but now she found she could not.

When the grim procession had passed and the last white-robe had put his back to her, she stole a glance after them.

In the square, at the bottom of the church steps, prentice boys hauled canvas tarps off of a stack of twigs and branches wrapped with grass into thirteen bundles. The canvas had kept the grass pale and dry. The twigs were dark with a coating of pine tar. Inside each bundle was a stack of logs. Erde's horror increased. This was not a trial at all, it was a burning. The white-robes had found a victim. *Run, run,* urged her voice of reason, but morbid fascination held her rooted to the spot.

Her grandmother, the baroness, had a dislike of witch-burnings which many considered peculiar, so they had not been common around Tor Alte during her reign. She would not allow them on her own lands and discouraged her household from attending them elsewhere. Yet it seemed to Erde that she'd heard almost every woman she knew over child-bearing age accused of being a witch at some point or another, particularly if they did something out of the ordinary. The baroness herself came under suspicion as often as any. Erde had never thought much about it. Not that she didn't believe in witches. She'd heard the stories of witches' spells and curses. Sometimes she'd even seen the results. But she couldn't take such talk seriously about people she knew—except maybe the chicken-crone.

But the chicken-crone was old and impossibly ugly. The woman in the church square was still young and lovely, most likely a mother of young children. She must have done something very awful indeed to deserve the stake at her age. But then, Brother Guillemo had passed over the chicken-crone and tried to burn Alla. Erde knew Alla hadn't deserved burning, whether she was a witch or not.

The cart pulled up at the base of the church steps and the white-robes halted with a resounding slap of sandals against stone. She looked for Guillemo among them, but as usual, their faces were deep in the shadow of their hoods. The drumming stopped, the bell ceased its tolling. The sudden hush was deafening, as if everyone in the square had caught their breath. The torches on the cart danced and snapped, the only sound but for a child crying somewhere in the crowd. Their bright heat spilled across the wet paving stones as if the pyre was lighted already. Erde recalled the reflection of herself afire in her father's cold eyes, and wished she'd fled when she could have done it unnoticed. Only by a supreme exertion of will did she keep herself from rushing in blind panic from the square. The witch-woman's frozen stare was like the eyes of the deer before the huntsman's grace stroke, calm with the understanding that struggle was useless and in the end, degrading.

When the silence had stretched almost to the breaking point, one of the drummers threw back his hood, set down his drum, and mounted the steps. Guillemo. Of course. Playing the crowd as usual. Erde shrank farther back into the press of bodies, fearful of his searching gaze, which had proved so adept at picking her out, perhaps even in so large a throng as this where he could not possibly expect to find her. One of the brothers held out a torch to him. The others began piling the bundled wood and twigs inside the cart, ringing the witch-woman's feet. Guillemo accepted the torch with elaborate humility. At the top of the steps, he crossed the entry porch and swung up the nearest ladder to the masons' scaffold. He climbed briskly, torch in hand, to the second, then the third level, where he set the torch into a workman's brazier and spread his arms for attention.

Which he already had. Every eye in the square had been fixed on him breathlessly from the instant he'd grabbed the torch and started up the scaffold.

"Oh my people! I call you to witness!" The priest's deep voice carried to the back of the crowd, echoing like cannon fire off the stone facades of the merchants' houses and guild halls, like the thunder of avalanches rolling down from the surrounding mountains. "The Time of Plague is upon us! As the dawn brings light today, the Light of God will enter this mortal place as we make a bold stroke against Satan, our mortal enemy. But ridding ourselves of one viper does not clean out the whole deadly hidden nest!"

At his gesture to the brothers below, the drums rolled again. A black-garbed priest of the parish ushered two children from inside to stand on the church steps. They had been dressed in white, in clothes obviously not their own. Bitterly, Erde decided Guillemo had missed his proper calling. He should have been an actor, or a creator of theatricals. At least then his madness would have remained relatively benign.

One of the children was a girl nearly Erde's age. The

younger, a boy, tried to break free and run to the woman standing in the cart, but the priest held him firm. Guillemo began his harangue, pacing up and down the scaffold platform just as he had on the bench in the baron's eating hall, as if it were a pulpit.

"See here, oh my people, the corruption of Innocence! See here how the Devil hides himself in alluring disguise . . ."

Erde stopped listening. She felt a sob working its way up from deep in her gut. She could not press her hands to her ears or sing hymns to drown him out, as she'd once seen villagers do to a priest who bored them with his sermon. She eased herself backward, letting heads and shoulders screen her view, then turned away as if to canvas the food stalls. To her horror, there behind the baker's boy was the man in the red jerkin, his glance casually taking in the crowd as if he was looking for someone who might not want to be found. Erde feared it might be her, for Red-jerkin was probably one of Guillemo's civilian searchers, or even a white-robe in disguise! She hunched into her cloak and drew up the hood, as if against the rain, which had stopped a while ago. She was trapped. What a bold and reckless notion it had been to come into town!

Fighting for calm enough to consider her options, Erde decided she had a better chance getting past Red-jerkin than the combined forces in front of the church. She observed him covertly for a while from beneath the fold of her hood, and because she was watching him so carefully, she noticed the change in his attention when Guillemo threw into his rant something about the king, some not-so-veiled insult. The crowd pressed forward, murmuring their approval. A few clenched fists were raised. And Erde saw the anger that flushed Red-jerkin's face, his glare at Guillemo as quick and venomous as a snake-strike and as quickly hidden again behind his former businesslike manner.

Perhaps not the priest's man after all. What sort of man, then, to care so much for the honor of the king? Erde knew she was confused about this issue. Tor Alte was too rugged, too far away and too unimportant to be on the aging monarch's visiting schedule. The king was at most an ideal to her, since her grandmother while she ruled had offered all due fealty and respect to this distant sovereign, insisting that a central absolute authority helped keep civilization together. But her son disagreed, and since her death, Josef von Alte had been increasingly vocal about the king's incompetence and irresponsibility, as well as his presumption in claiming sovereignty over so many far-flung baronetcies, especially when his own family lands weren't much to speak of. Her father even spoke positively of the widening split between the old king and his barons.

So Erde thought it peculiar that an obvious man of the world such as Red-jerkin would take a common complaint so much to heart. She felt that she knew a secret about him, and that she was somehow obscurely privileged, even though she hoped never to lay eyes on him again. She wondered if he served any of her father's vassal barons. At least she could see he had no love in his heart for Guillemo.

She meant to sneak past him while his attention was engaged, but then she heard Tor Alte's name flung against the stone facades to echo around the square. A spontaneous roar rose from the crowd, then died away into a darkening murmur. She saw Guillemo pause, high on the scaffolding, waiting them out, quieting them with little waves of his hands until he could be heard again.

"And lo! You've all heard rumor of the trouble at Tor Alte! Now let me tell you the truth of it! Your own, your very own valiant and pious lord cannot keep the Devil from his door! Consider that, oh my people! If the most high cannot protect themselves, woe be upon the lowly! Woe indeed!

"Your own baron's immortal soul was in deepest peril when I arrived, and he never suspecting it! God help *him,* had I not found him in time to root out the Evil that dwelt in that stronghold, poised as it was to seize control!

"But all glory be to God and all his saints, who protected me from evil and put the strength of righteousness in my hand! The witch of Tor Alte is dead and her spells and demons could not harm me!" Fra Guill's right arm shot up, fist clenched as if it held a flaming sword. The crowd roared again and shook their own raised fists. "She claimed innocence like this one here, and like this one here, she was put to the test by the holy office of the Church. Oh my people, that you'd been there to witness it! The fire of His

Righteous Wrath shriveled her into cinders right as she stood there, spewing out her pernicious lies!''

You lie! Erde was grateful she had no voice to betray her now when she'd have been unable to keep from screaming her outrage. *Alla took her own life to keep it from your hands!*

"A sacred day!" the priest howled, "A holy day, oh my people! The witch is dead, and her warlock minion!" Again, another growling roar, and again Guillemo waited for quiet.

"But wait, oh my people, but wait . . ." He dropped his arms as if in defeat and hung his dark head as he paced back and forth in an eloquent posture of shame and torment. Then he turned to face the square, palms spread in entreaty. "It is not all good news I bring you this day. We had one holy victory at Tor Alte, and will have another here today. But, oh my people, here is the sad tiding I bring you: though your good baron was saved by God's Will, working through His most humble servant, I did not come to Tor Alte in time to save the baron's only daughter! The black evil that lodged in her grew desperate at my advance, supported by the strength of my good brothers, God's holy champions. It stole away the innocent child's voice to prevent her from speaking its name in exorcism! It corrupted her sweet obedient womanhood!''

The crowd moaned as one. This time Guillemo did not wait for quiet. He let the horrified murmur swell, then raised his own voice over theirs until the very air shrilled with it. Erde's skin prickled with the eerie power he possessed. "That blackest Evil put the sword of Darkness in her hand and raised up her child's arm against an innocent man so that she slew him and then another and another until no man was left to stand against her and she escaped! Escaped, oh my people! This demon incarnate walks abroad among us!''

Erde felt his eyes sweep the crowd, felt his searching glance, felt despair and terror close around her like a vise. She backed up blindly, bumping the spectators behind her. But they were too inflamed with the priest's rhetoric to notice. What soul would believe her now, in the face of such convincing lies? She almost believed him herself, staring at him up there, seeing him as the crowd saw him: a militant saint or angel, larger than life, with the torch blazing behind him and the new dawn bleaching the shadowed tint of his robe to silver.

"And here is my revelation!" cried the man on the scaffold. "Another piece has been revealed to me of the mysterious dream-omen that stalks me every hour I lay down in sleep, my God-sent holy vision of the witch-child and the Devil's Paladin! This is the child, oh my people! The witch-child is come among us and she is a child you all have known, become an agent of Satan who seeks the destruction of your immortal souls! We must call on our God to protect us! THE DAYS OF PLAGUE ARE AT HAND!"

The priest fell to his knees on the swaying scaffold. In the square below, four of the white-robes grabbed the torches that burned at the corners of the witch-cart and stood with them at the ready. Guillemo tore open his robe, spread his arms wide and bared his naked hairy chest to the heavens. "Rise up in flame against the powers of darkness, o my people! Set the holy and cleansing fire of righteousness! Burn this evil from the land . . . and . . . from . . . our . . . SOULS!!!"

The four white-robes flung their torches at the witch-cart. The grass bindings on the bundles caught in a rush, speeding their eager blaze to the tar-soaked twigs. On the church steps, the little boy began to wail and beat his fists against the priest who held him. The girl-child just stared ahead, seeing nothing. Flame and dark smoke exploded around the witch-woman faster than a gasp of breath. At first she coughed and tried to turn her head away. The useless poignant gesture tore at Erde's heart. Then the woman's brave composure deserted her. She struggled senselessly against her bindings until her wrists tore and bled. Erde's hands worked at her own wrists. She feared the poor woman might tear her arms from their sockets, like a wild animal pinned in a snare. When at last the fire licked at the hem of her shift, the crowd sighed and leaned forward. The woman began to scream.

Erde spun away through the press of eager spectators, blind and nauseous, seeing herself burning, breathing that black acrid smoke, with those same soul-rending shrieks tearing the life from her own lungs. This would be her fate, if Fra Guill ever got his hands on her.

Around her, children sobbed and the women crossed themselves, weeping and fainting. Erde shoved through the confusion unheeding. When she broke free of the crowd, she found herself two steps from the baker's tray, where the boy had left it to climb up one of the brazier carts for a better view. There, he danced up and down, his small fists clenched and his eyes riveted to the spectacle.

Erde learned then that hunger is a strong instinct. Like a rush of cold water, cunning cleared her head. She dropped the silver mark into the heel of her boot, then quickly doubled up the flap of her cloak to make a pocket. She darted a glance up and down the line of food stalls. No one watching. Like the baker's boy, the entire throng was rapt by the witch-woman's death throes.

Except Red-jerkin. He had spotted her from the far end near the church. Her movement counter to the crowd had drawn his attention. Erde froze like a wild animal, and their eyes met. He raised his arm a bit, as if to signal her covertly, then started to work his way through the throng in her direction. It seemed that he too was seeking to avoid notice, and this terrified her all the more. What unknown pursuers lay in wait for her in addition to the known?

Erde let instinct take hold. She stepped up to the baker's tray, cleared the entire surface into her cloak with one sweep of her arm. Then for the second time in three days, she turned and ran for her life.

The streets of Tubin were deserted as the unwelcome dawn lightened the narrow band of sky between the rooftops to the color of pewter. The wet cobbles and stone walls shone dully as if the entire world had turned to metal, slick, cold, and gleaming with malice. Clutching her laden cloak against her breast as if it were her life and not mere bread that she carried, Erde ran with the last of her strength. She ran for the dragon. If she could only reach the dragon, she would be safe. Even when her breath threatened to fail her, she would not stop, could not even think of stopping, sure that the echo of her own footfall in the narrow wet streets was the clack of Red-jerkin's booted heels on the paving behind her.

But she cleared the town gates safely and swerved off the main road into the maze of cottages and yards and kitchen gardens. There, she hid gasping behind a hayrick for long enough to assure herself that there was no pursuit, and long enough to gobble one of the meat pies she had stolen without inhaling the bulk of it into her lungs.

When her breathing had steadied, she chose a more concertedly circuitous retreat through the emptied farmsteads. There was no one about, but she was weak and shaking with exhaustion. She had no more flight in her. But the food did help. In one unguarded cottage yard, she found a small flock of goats penned in a muddy thornbrush corral. Erde halted, considering, while she wolfed down another pie. She spotted a coil of rope abandoned atop a barrel, and this somehow decided her. She dug the silver mark out of her boot, then searched out two especially long curving thorns from the brush fence. At the cottage door, she stuck the thorns crosswise into the soft, worn planking to form a tiny cradle, into which she slid the silver coin. The side stamped with the King's Arms was facing out, and she noticed that a horned and rampant dragon supported the shield. An omen of good favor, she decided, pressing at it to be sure it would rest there safely until discovered.

She ate another meat pie. Then she returned to the corral to collect her dragon's dinner.

CHAPTER TWELVE

Erde's dragon-lore suggested that once well fed, a dragon could go several weeks before eating again. She hoped this proved to be true. She'd had enough cause already to wonder if much of the lore in her grandmother's stories was out of date.

The outlook was promising at the moment, with the dragon sated and drowsy beside her on the ledge and three goats out of ten remaining, currently grazing away with surprising equanimity in the gorge below. One was a sturdy black and white spotted milker, taller and sleeker than the rest, evidently due to sheer force of personality. If there was any food to be found, this ewe would claim it for her own. After all, she had stared the dragon down.

Erde had assumed that the violent devouring of the bear was the dragon's only way of dealing with a meal. She'd anticipated the worst sort of bleating and mayhem when she drove the little flock into the gorge and informed the dragon they were his. But the goats seemed almost not to notice the dragon lumbering among them, except for the big spotted ewe. She stamped at it and presented her horns. The dragon regarded her a moment, then lowered its own great horns in imitation. Erde would have sworn that goat and dragon were bowing to one another. Then the dragon turned away and delicately picked up one of the other goats by the scruff of its neck, like a cat with a kitten. The goat hung there placidly while the dragon carried it off to a hidden corner of the gorge. It returned six times and each time, ewe and dragon matched their unequal horns, and the dragon took another. After the fifth, Erde shook her head in astonishment. *At least I'll have milk to drink,* she told herself and promptly fell asleep.

When she awoke, the dragon was curled up beside her. Erde lay still, grateful to be warm and fed and dry, and glad of the chance to study her remarkable traveling companion, to look it over at leisure and in daylight, if the gray afternoon sinking through the dark pine boughs could be called daylight. She thought about the summer that had never really come, and wondered if she would ever see the sun again.

The dragon was muddy from its travels, and its long sleep inside the mountain had left a coating of earth so hard and caked even the constant rain had not managed to wash it off completely. But in the gray half-light, Erde saw that its dull, dust-colored "scales" were actually a richly tapestried hide of grays and browns, ranging from the warm russet deep in the joints between the big concentrically-textured plates on its back that resembled a flexible tortoiseshell, to the smooth and glowing sienna of its belly or the luminous ivory of its razor-tipped horns and claws. The richness was subtle, and brown was the overall impression, but the details were various and stunning. Erde was relieved. She'd been avoiding the conclusion that her dragon was ugly.

Her dragon. How could she call it hers? She didn't even know its name. But it did seem to need her, or think it did, and this was both novel and flattering. It gave her purpose at a time when she could not have imagined one on her own. But now that the dragon was hopefully no longer so obsessed with its stomach, perhaps it was time to talk to it about something other than food. Erde settled herself squarely opposite its snoozing head and composed her interrogative in her mind.

—*Dragon?*

Very quickly, she saw in her mind's eye a dragon yawning and settling into sleep.

—*Dragon?*

The dragon in her mind stretched, yawned more widely, and turned its back on her. Erde's eyes narrowed in pique.

—*DRAGON!*

The dragon in front of her raised its enormous head with

a low growl. Erde swallowed. It heard and understood her
at least.

—*Did I not find you a fine dinner, Dragon?*

The dragon resettled its jaws comfortably and blinked.

—*So will you talk to me a while?*

She read assent in its mind but resignation in its eyes.

—*If you please then, Dragon, may I know your name?*

She did not ask if it had one. All dragons had names.
Her grandmother had said they were extremely proud of
them, and that you must be particularly polite when re-
questing an introduction. Usually their names were unpro-
nounceable and had to be translated into some poetic but
inadequate German equivalent.

The dragon did not answer immediately. Perhaps it did
not trust her yet. Erde waited. She sensed a struggle and
the beginnings of distress. A great blankness filled her
mind. Sadness gripped her throat. Not reluctance at all, but
a huge, heaving effort to . . . remember.

—*What? You can't remember your own name?*

She had meant to ask more gently. Her own shock and
surprise had gotten the better of her. A dragon that didn't
know its name? The poor creature's sigh was like a great
sob of shame, and Erde gathered every wit she possessed
to try to soothe it.

—*You'll remember. Of course you'll remember. You've
been asleep too long, that's all. Try this: when I'm trying to
remember something, I concentrate on the very first thought
I had when I woke up.*

The dragon's struggle felt like muscles toiling in her
mind, like men rolling heavy stones uphill or dragging laden
carts through the mud. It remembered waking slowly, being
drawn as though to a voice . . . suddenly, the memory dam
burst. A torrent of images surged through Erde faster than
she could grasp: soft green hills, a buried vein of shining
metal, farmer's plow breaking the fresh sod, mountains
shuddering with inner fire, bright young shoots pushing up
through dark humus. Sand and hills and trees and rock
and soil.

Earth.

—*But that's* my *name.*

The dragon looked at her as if she had foolishly stated
the obvious.

—We have the same name?

Again, assent.

Erde had never heard of a dragon having the same name as a person, but it did show an unorthodox kind of logic, if it—*he,* she now sensed—if he was to be her dragon.

—There! You see? I told you you could remember!

But she sensed continuing distress. He had remembered his name, but not who he was or why he was there. Abruptly, she was deluged with doubt. Nothing seemed certain and nothing made sense. The value of life itself was in question. But Erde knew she was not given to such imponderables. It must be the dragon who was desperate for such answers. She tried again to soothe him.

—Maybe we don't all need to know our purpose right off.

Earth flooded her with images of stalwart, all-knowing dragonkind, proper dragons who knew their purpose. It was a terrible disaster that he'd forgotten his.

—You'll remember. Just give yourself time.

But the dragon would not be consoled. Feeding upon itself, his distress increased until it filled Erde's entire head and brought tears to her eyes and great racking sobs to her throat.

—Dragon! Earth! Please!

Surprise, a grasping at self-control, then a grumbling kind of apology. The dragon rose morosely and moved off down the ledge.

—Wait! Don't go!

He sent back an image of goats.

—Oh. Um. Will you . . . ?

Cautiously, she pictured a question of him eating the spotted ewe.

Emphatic negative. Offense that she should think such a thing, when the she-goat had not yet given him permission.

Permission? Nonplussed, Erde sent back gratitude, which Earth did not seem to understand until she imaged herself milking the goat and drinking the milk. He responded with agreement, then slid down from the ledge to accept graciously the self-sacrifice of any goat except the spotted ewe.

Watching him lumber away into the gorge, Erde had a stark sense of having failed him. But how could he expect a mere human girl to provide answers to such deep questions? Even if you did think of a possible answer, it only led right into another question. Such as, if Earth, being a dragon, had a specific purpose in life, it followed that she also had a purpose in being with him, and what might that be? She doubted it was anything so simple as feeding him and offering him moral support.

But meanwhile, he did have to eat, and because of what Alla had said and because her grandmother would surely have wanted her to, Erde accepted feeding the dragon and keeping him safe as her responsibility. This gorge would not shelter them forever. It was nearing September and even if the weather suddenly became seasonable again, one could expect the fall snowstorms relatively soon. Her near disaster in Tubin told Erde she had to move on and quickly, away from the inhospitable weather, away from her father's huntsmen, away from the murderous reach of Brother Guillemo Gotti, far from this perilous neighborhood where everyone knew her face and name and took her for a witch.

CHAPTER THIRTEEN

They traveled by nights and slept out the days in whatever deep thicket or rock shelter they could find. Each
day, Erde was less tired when she lay down than she'd been
the dawn before, and less painfully sore when she awoke.
The burden of her pack and Rainer's sword lightened as
the long miles passed.

Earth learned to travel more quietly and with less interest in the countryside. Though the food-flock was soon reduced to the she-goat, he showed no interest in eating her.
After a while, since the goat was agile, traveled well, and
seemed content in their company, Erde did not even bother
to tether her. She followed of her own accord.

As they put a safer distance between them and Tor Alte,
Erde encouraged the dragon to hunt, especially as the time
since his last meal lengthened and he continued to show
little inclination to do so on his own. She began to wonder
if he knew how. At dawn, their quiet time between travel
and sleep, she conjured hunting images for him, graphic
and colorful enough to inform an idiot, drawn from the
days before she'd refused to ride with her father's hunt.
Earth responded with his unflinching golden stare and an
aura of eager incomprehension. Eventually, Erde stopped
their night's travel early and banished him to the woods,
insisting that he stay out there until dawn. For the first few
days of this new regime, he slunk off reluctantly, only to
return as soon as she'd let him. But one morning he was
gone until the day was bright and Erde began to worry.
Only a day ago, he'd come hurrying back to report that a
hunting farmer had discovered him in the woods and run
off shrieking. Earth did not understand the man's terror.

Erde thought it had even hurt his feelings. But this time, she sensed his satisfaction even before she heard him rustling back through the underbrush. He'd heard a doe calling, mortally wounded, and she had begged him to end her misery. Erde thought he was more pleased at having eased the doe's pain than for the meal she'd afforded him.

The weather stayed dank and gray and unseasonable, but Erde did not suffer as long as the dragon was near. Earth, it turned out, was no cold-blooded reptile. To sleep pressed against his golden belly was like sleeping inside the hearth. Erde often woke in a sweat, dreaming of hot coals, and was forced to move some distance away from him in order to sleep comfortably.

Each dawn, before giving in to her exhaustion, Erde unwrapped Rainer's sword and laid it out beside her, to shine in the early light. Then later, wrapped in heat and fever, she dreamed of him and her father fighting at Tor Alte. Her memory of Rainer's face was more elusive with each dream. She fought to preserve it, but was always distracted. There were stranger things than that entering her dreams: bleak scorched landscapes she didn't recognize and voices whispering words she couldn't understand but knew were full of grim foreboding. These dreams were always plagued by wildfire and torn by harsh clangings and roars she could not identify. They were thick with the odors that hung over the smithy's forge, metal and smoke and acid. Erde could not recall having dreamed in odors before.

One cold gray noon, she woke up screaming, or thought she'd been screaming. She knew it was impossible, only part of the awful dream, but her throat was raw and the dragon was awake, staring in concern.

—*A dream. Only a dream.*

It took some explaining, but finally Earth seemed to understand, and he allowed as how there were places he also went when he was sleeping. They were not very nice either, but he did not seem to have any choice in the matter. She asked him to show her some. The first image that rose up in her mind told her that she and her dragon were sharing the same dreams, or rather, their dreams were mixing, but increasingly, she was dreaming his.

Like the Summoning. Erde called it that for lack of a better name. Often, as she shared Earth's dreams, came the distinct sensation that someone was calling them. Sometimes she actually heard a voice, but then it was Alla's voice or her grandmother's, and she could never understand what they were saying. Sometimes the summons was as vague as Earth's insistent expectation during their first night in the cave. Earth still looked to her for explanation, but she had nothing to offer him. Certainly she could not admit that each evening, she awoke more certain that there was some duty they were meant to be performing, and were failing at. She wished it *was* Alla's voice she was hearing. Alla would know how to answer a dragon.

This distress and their broken sleep plagued them and slowed their progress, but their biggest problem was always food. Erde presumed, as they journeyed south by two, seven, now ten days, that conditions would improve, that at some point, a decent harvest would appear and fields with fatter, healthier livestock. But the bad news that the fake-Guillemo had brought to her father's banquet table was not exaggerated. Unending rain flooded the fields and the kitchen gardens. Blight and mildew and damp-loving snails claimed a huge portion of the crop wherever they went. Erde became an adept sneak-thief and stole, guiltily, what little she could from outlying hen yards and storehouses. But people do not leave much lying about in times of famine. She could not feed herself by thievery. She survived on the she-goat's milk, and on the dragon's foraging. For all his reluctance to take advantage of any but the most willing hot-blooded meals, he did show real talent for sniffing out a mushroom or berry patch, and seemed to know what was safe to eat and what was deadly. Erde's only problem was to remind him to leave her some.

After Tubin, she'd carefully avoided any village larger than a few houses. But on the eleventh night, approaching the outskirts of a town, Erde decided they must by now have passed out of the sphere of von Alte, into some other baron's domain. It was a very small town on a thinly-traveled road, surrounded by small rocky farms. Erde didn't know where she was or exactly how far they'd traveled, only that each dawn, the sun still rose more or less in the direction they'd come. It was time, come daylight, to risk venturing into town again, for news and information, and the chance of finding real food.

In town, it was market day, a good day for one wanting to eavesdrop in the anonymity of a crowd. A weak and uncertain sun was struggling through the clouds for the first time in several days, and the muddy town square was busy with carts and pigs and people. But as Erde wandered about trying to appear purposeful, she could see that though it was nearly September, well after time for the early harvest, the wood and canvas stalls were only half-stocked and the produce was bug-eaten and scrawny. The farm wives stood behind their canopied trestles and flatwagons with their arms folded, grim and irritable with guilt as they refused over and over to barter food they might soon have to eat themselves for a broken crock or an old robe they didn't need and couldn't resell.

Listening to their restless chatter, Erde learned it wasn't just the poor harvest that threatened these farmers' livelihoods.

"Had little enough as it was and he took the best," a thin and drawn woman complained to a nodding neighbor. "The very best, wouldn't you know! And then the baron came after and took his share!"

"Mine, too." The neighbor was plumper but pale and tired-looking. She jostled a basket of runty misshapen potatoes for emphasis. "Every one worth a prayer, he said. We must each serve God in our own way. Then he promised a mass for a better harvest."

The first woman grunted and looked away, staring past Erde as she paused a few paces away to lean against a wagon wheel and fuss with her boot. "Does a man deserve more food because he wears a priest's robe?" the woman muttered. "Does he deserve better?"

Her companion clucked warningly and resettled her potato basket, neatening this and that on her table unnecessarily. Two men walked by, haggling over the price of a thin donkey limping after them at the end of a frayed rope. When the men had passed, the plump woman leaned over to her neighbor and hissed, "We must all remember Tubin!"

The other woman crossed herself and nodded.

"Did you hear Mag's baby died suddenly?" the plump woman began. "Seems there's reason to believe . . ."

Chilled, Erde moved on to another row of stalls. She did better than many in the market that day. Pretending to be too shy to speak, she bartered a capful of berries and the two dozen mushrooms she had carried in the hood of her cloak for a loaf of dark bread and a salted fish. No one looked at her with any more suspicion than a solitary prentice boy might usually arouse, but everywhere she heard talk of ill omens and Fra Guill and his doom-ridden prophecies. The warning of Tubin was on every other tongue, and the farmer who'd stumbled across Earth in the forest had already become famous for miles around.

"Albrecht wouldn't know a dragon if he fell on one," a grizzled farmer remarked between hammer blows at the smithy's portable forge.

"A bear, most likely," agreed the smith's customer. "He's been listening to the priest too hard."

The smith let fall a final stroke, then held up the crooked rake tine to squint at his repair. "Don't be too hasty. What those trappers from the high hills came across didn't sound like bearshit to me."

His scrawny apprentice nodded, eyes wide, all bones and Adam's apple. "Dragon sign! My da's keeping our cow inside the barn all the time now, 'cept when he leads her out himself . . ."

Completing the circuit of the market, Erde heard a lot more dragon talk. Dragons had eaten this man's sheep or that man's dog. Dragons were gathering among the mountaintops, awaiting only the foul signal of their Dark Lord to launch themselves upon the countryside. There was no talk that day of raising dragon-hunts, but plenty of witch-rumor and threats of witch-hunt, and finally Erde overheard a rumor of an army that the Baron of Tor Alte (a distant and mysterious figure to these lowland farmers) was raising to vanquish the forces of evil and get his stolen daughter back so her soul could be saved by the Holy Brother Guillemo Gotti.

An army? Calmly munching her bread, Erde strolled out of the village when what she really wanted to do was flee headlong. This last rumor was just stupid enough to be true. With a touch of the graveyard humor that was becoming her defense against fear and loneliness and her increasing sense that the world had gone mad, she totaled up the evils her father's supposed army would face: a small dream-haunted dragon, a girl, and a spotted she-goat.

Earth found no willing victim in his hunting that day, but reported being nearly spotted twice by shepherds foraging for decent grass for their sheep. He was learning to conceal himself, but the land was becoming more populated as they left the high mountains behind. In the late afternoon, he and Erde lay down in a thicket to nap and slept through nearly till midnight, when both of them bolted up out of a shared nightmare. They had been pressed into a long, narrow, smelly room full of faceless bodies. They could barely breathe from the closeness and the stench. The noise was ear-splitting, and they seemed to be moving somewhere at breakneck speed. The dream upset Earth so much that he nearly forgot his promise to the she-goat.

Desperate for a way to calm him, Erde offered the thing that would have calmed her. She said what they really needed was a wise person with knowledge of magical things such as dragons and dream-visions, a person like her friend Alla. If there had been one such person, there had to be another. She conjured her childhood favorite, the Mage-Queen, who in her fantasies so resembled her grandmother. Inventing as she went along, she imagined a Mage City for the dragon, with many tall white towers gleaming in the sun. Into the early morning, when they should have been sleeping, she told him all the tales she could remember, until she had almost convinced herself that there was such a power in the world, and that the real purpose of their journey must be to find her. Heartened, Earth himself proposed the idea that it might be the Mage-Queen who was summoning him. Out of compassion and a remaining shred of childish hope, Erde did not discourage him. She agreed that the next day would be the first day of their search. Earth then ceased his pacing and moaning to regard her with those expectant dog eyes. *Now?* he seemed to ask. *Can we go now?*

And so they moved on, traveling for the remaining hours until dawn, then slept through the day in a sweet-smelling pine grove, so that Earth could take the next night to hunt. It was almost dry, deep among the pine boughs, where the cold wind was only a sighing in the upper branches. Erde stuffed her cloak with needles and could not remember the last time she had been so comfortable. Sharing Earth's constant nightmares left her eager for the possibility of a length of sleep without them. She barely stirred when the dragon left for the deeper forest.

But she woke to the crackle of fire anyway, and the smells of smoke and charred flesh burning the darkness. She sat up to shake the nightmare from her head but it was not a dream. The fire was there, right in front of her. A small fire, of twigs and pine cones. On the far side of it sat the man in the red jerkin, grilling a small bird carcass on a stick and watching her placidly.

Erde recoiled into her pine bed with a breathy gasp. Feebly, she felt for Rainer's sword where she had left it beside her.

Red-jerkin reached a hand to one side and lifted the sword out of the shadow. "Is this what you're looking for?"

Erde stared at him like a cornered rabbit.

"Easy, now. I haven't followed you all this way to do you harm." He laid the sword down and patted it gently. "In fact, I had just the opposite in mind. You want to learn how to use this thing?"

He waited for her to say something. Erde's return gaze was unblinking. She no longer believed the promises of men who said they were not going to hurt you. Besides, she could not comprehend how this man had sneaked up on her, lit a fire, and actually started cooking a meal without waking her. She'd have been speechless even if she'd had her voice. He was some baron's footpad, or a thief who preyed on travelers in the forest. Where was the dragon when she needed him?

Red-jerkin mistook her quick glance sideways. "Don't worry, I'm alone. Oh, except for the Mule, that is." He saw he'd piqued her interest, or perhaps her concern. His grin was lopsided and sly. " 'Course the Mule eats little children for breakfast, so maybe you should be worried." He leaned back from the fire and called softly over his shoulder. "Come on out, Mule. Introduce yourself."

Erde steeled herself for some exotic ogre of a man, this

cool thief's monstrous partner. But it was indeed a mule that stepped up to the fire, a white lop-eared ordinary mule. It stood over her and stretched its neck down to study her with jaded, intelligent eyes. Not quite ordinary. Distracted, Erde smiled at it and stroked its soft gray nose.

"Later he'll eat you," remarked Red-jerkin.

Erde's eyes flicked back to him and her smile faded.

"Does this really need to be a one-way conversation?" She nodded.

"You mean, you can't . . . or you won't?"

Erde shook her head, obscurely irritated that a common thief should accuse her of guile.

Red-jerkin frowned. "Really? I was sure it was just a ploy . . . how'd it happen? Right, right, you can't tell me. Well, let's assume I believe you. So, yes and no answers only for now. Later maybe we'll manage something more complicated. I don't suppose you can read and write?"

Her prideful instinct betrayed her, sat her up straight in protest. She didn't think to be surprised by the implication that he could.

"That so? Well, good for you. I'd assumed otherwise, you being Iron Joe's daughter and all . . ."

Erde froze. He knew. Now she understood. He was some baron's man, after all. He had found her out and now he meant to kidnap her and hold her for ransom. She shrugged and tried to look blank.

"But then," he continued as if she had agreed with him, "you are also Meriah's granddaughter." He read the soft crease of Erde's brow, and smiled. "Will you please believe I don't mean to harm you? Meriah would see to it I burned in hell. She's sure to be a favorite with the Recording Angel already."

Erde felt the first stirrings of doubt. Would a thief have given up a silver mark? It could be what Red-jerkin himself had called a ploy, but very few people had called her grandmother by her given name. In the firelight, his eyes were kind. She narrowed her own eyes in what she hoped was a steely glare.

Watching her, the man's grin turned rueful. "I see her in you. She was captivating, you know—in her youth and long, long after. As you will be, milady, if we can keep you alive long enough." He lifted the bird out of the fire, tore off one of the leg joints, and held it out to her. "Hungry?"

Erde felt as if she had come into a conversation that had been going on for a long time without her. Too confused to pretend otherwise, she accepted the leg gingerly. If he meant to hold her for ransom, he'd be unlikely to poison her. And he didn't look so well fed himself, for all his silver marks. Though his eyes were bright, his cheeks were gaunt, and the hand that held the spit was ropy with starved muscle. She guessed he was as hungry as she was. Meanwhile, the bird was hot and delicious. Trying not to gobble too noisily, she waited for Red-jerkin to surprise her some more.

He tore off the other leg and stuck the spit upright in the ground beside him, then ate nearly half the joint before he spoke again.

"Now, introductions, yes? I know who you are, though you are welcome to continue pretending otherwise. I am, or was, Heinrich Peder von Engle, Knight of the Realm in service to His Majesty the King, and at your service, milady." He bowed deeply over his crossed legs like some prostrating mystic, then sank back into his comfortable slouch with a fleeting mirthless grin. "Now I'm mainly Hal Engle, or Sir Hal, when I need to impress a few villagers who don't know any better. Although these days, a King's Knight gets very little respect . . ." He glanced away as if to toss aside his chicken bone, and Erde believed he was what he claimed, seeing that same twist of righteous anger catch his face, then pass him by. He had, she could tell, the rare gift of storytelling, for she was already drawn into his tale. She tried harder not to appear so interested.

"I had once upon a time and not so very long ago," he continued, "land and estates to the north of here, maybe two weeks' hard ride, like Tor Alte about as far as you can get from court and still be His Majesty's subject. And I was very much his subject. My duties as a Knight of the Realm kept me in Erfurt a lot of the time. But I left my lands in the charge of my two grown sons, which proved to be such a workable arrangement that I grew farther and farther away from the everyday workings of the domain. I felt free, in my, ah . . . maturity, to pursue in between my court duties a special interest of mine, the collection and study of legend and lore relating to the existence of dragons."

Erde's composure nearly deserted her. A dragon-hunter! She had heard of such men, and this one had caught her unawares as he must have hoped he would, for sure enough, he was studying her much too carefully. For the dragon's sake, she must appear unconcerned.

"Are you interested in dragons, milady?"

Erde shrugged, but it was more a convulsive twitch, and Red-jerkin read her nervousness clearly. But he surprised her again. He leaned forward over the dying fire with a barely restrained eagerness totally at odds with his hard-bitten manner. "Oh, lady," he murmured. "Please tell me you have the knowledge that I seek."

Erde snatched at impassivity and held it tight.

"Ah, well," he said, sitting back. "Such knowledge is not easily won. I of all men have learned this, a dubious privilege of advancing age. Pray permit me, milady, to continue my tale."

Erde could not help it. She nodded graciously, as a baron's daughter should.

Red-jerkin took a deep breath. "As the seasons passed, so did the times of plenty in our lands to the west. His Majesty's vassal lords grew restless. Traveling as much as I was, either on the king's business negotiating with some malignant baron or other, or when I could, following up some report of dragon-sign . . . I was unaware that the worsening condition of my estates exceeded anyone else's. The whole kingdom was suffering, after all, but . . . oh, yes, my dear lady, I see that look. *Meriah's* look. You might properly call my distraction negligence—I'll bear that guilt fully. But I was also kept in ignorance by my two wastrel sons, who were covering up a profligacy of habit that had not been so evident while the harvests were rich but as soon as . . . well, I'm sure a daughter of Iron Joe can well imagine."

Is my father profligate? Did he mean not all high lords considered feasting and velvet robes a critical expenditure? Erde considered the new and revealing notion that her own instinctive scruples might have been more proper in this matter.

Noting her pensiveness, Red-jerkin nodded. "Indeed,

your grandmother and I share the misfortune of our sons. Perhaps it is the price of being dedicated to something other than heir-raising. Perhaps if we'd had them together, as I intended . . . well, I suppose that might have been even worse, though I can't conceive of how. But I'm wandering, aren't I? Bear with me, milady. Another privilege of age."

Erde was surprised he spoke so self-consciously of his age. Her impression of him was one of strength and great vitality.

"So one gray fall day, a wandering friar begged the hospitality of the household, and managed to find excuses to keep himself there all winter. Meanwhile, the king's relations with his barons were disintegrating, as you recall . . . no, perhaps you were too young to be aware of such matters lo these two long winters ago, but I assure you I was extremely busy trying to maintain the King's Peace . . . a futile effort, as it turned out, in that winter of the silent revolt. But once or twice between my frantic comings and goings, I met this so-called priest who'd taken up residence in my home, then the deep snows isolated me at court until the spring. He seemed an inoffensive sort, this cleric, if rather given to hysterical prophecies and an obsession with the supposedly divine dominion of men over women and the natural world."

Their eyes met over the fire, and Red-jerkin smiled sourly. "Ah, yes, you are Meriah's get, bless you indeed . . . you're at the mark before I've even loosed my arrow." He leaned forward so that the flames lit his face eerily. "It was Fra Guill who sent you running from Tor Alte, wasn't it? He turned your father against you somehow."

Erde nodded, transfixed.

"Nay, don't look so amazed. I'm no mind-seer. Any man who's dealt with that hell-fiend of a priest and not been cozened by him would see the truth of it. But not the baron your father, I take it?"

Erde shivered, hung her head.

"And not my sons," he admitted softly. "The priest's lust for power gives him a damnable nose for weakness. He ferrets it out like a truffle hound and moves right in to woo and devour." He stirred up the fire, tossed on a few twigs, then neatly sectioned the remaining bird and passed half

over the flames to Erde. She took it gratefully and without
pretense. This was her first hot meal in nearly two weeks.
Red-jerkin—or Sir Hal, as she was finding enough sympathy to think of him—ate for a while with deep concentration, allowing her to do likewise. They passed a
companionable silence together, cleaning every morsel
from the scrawny bird bones. Finally the knight unslung a
leather wineskin and raised it to his lips, then lowered it
just before drinking and held it out across the fire.

"Your pardon, milady, for my lapse of manners. I've gotten so used to solitude, I quite forgot I had company." He
jerked his head at the mule, who appeared to have dozed
off standing by the fire. "He doesn't drink."

Erde wished she was not so easily charmed by his courtier's ease, however out of practice he might claim to be,
but the familiarity of it was reassuring, and his dry humor
a relief after the rough conditions she'd been enduring. She
took the wineskin and sipped from it delicately. She could
not help the face she made.

Hal laughed. "Awful, isn't it?"

His laugh was generous and open. Erde smiled with him
just a little as she passed the offending wine back to him.
He took quite a long drink of it for a man who'd just
complained of its quality, then dug a rag out of his jerkin
to carefully wipe his beard and hands, folded the rag, and
put it away.

"But what did you do to become the unwelcome focus
of his deranged and self-serving visions?" Hal peered hard
at her, then waved a hand. "No matter. We'll get to that
later." But he continued a little reluctantly, "So, as you
have already guessed, milady, with a wisdom far advanced
of your youth, after that winter's undeclared rebellion of
the vassal-lords against their king, I returned home at first
thaw to find that in the same way that His Majesty had
become king in name only, I was no longer master of my
own lands. My sons had become willing puppets of the hell-
priest, who had used the long winter to good effect, spreading his lies and paranoia throughout the domain, turning
family, friends, and sworn vassals against me on the
grounds of my 'unholy practices.' My fault, my fault, all of
it, the cause of the bad weather and failing harvests. My
practices, if allowed to persist, would soon bring the final

wrath of God down upon them all. And as the tide turned against the king, my neighbors were none too eager to stand up for an avowed royalist."

Erde could not mask her surprise.

"Ah, milady, when I say a *silent* revolt, I do mean that loyal subjects of the king such as your grandmother would not have been included in the secret barons' cabal, or even kept informed. But you can be sure this was one song Fra Guill sang to your father in his siren's voice!"

Hal paused, blew some of his anger away in a long exhalation. "Another task that devil's spawn had dedicated the winter to was gathering around him an elite band of 'followers,' fellow fanatics who were coincidentally well-versed in the martial arts." He sighed, then inclined his head in pained resignation. "You see how, even before he had need of protection from the world, he planned for it and carried it out so smoothly that I'd wager even the brothers themselves aren't aware they were recruited to serve as Fra Guill's personal bodyguard."

Hal looked up from his study of the coals. The rage and loss in his eyes were as fresh as an open wound. "Milady, he drove me from my lands by force, he and his white-robed henchmen. Friends turned me away from their gates with arrows and exorcisms. Word spread to the court, and I could not turn to the king without disgracing him, thereby eroding what little power he had left. The final blow was a rumor, the priest's own invention I've no doubt, that the King's Knights were plotting a coup of their own. All seven of us." His mouth twisted but his rage had run its course. He sighed and spread his hands. "Coup de grace. So here I am. Wanderer. Knight-errant, if you will. Not exactly a public enemy, but certainly suspect to any revolting baron. The perfect candidate, if I may modestly point out, to take up the task of protecting the Lady Erde von Alte, so recently gone errant herself in the eyes of the law, her father, and the hell-spawned Fra Guill." Hal raised his eyebrows and gazed at her down the length of his nose. "That is, if milady will have me. . . ."

Erde regarded him uneasily. Even if she could speak, she would not have known what to say to him. He knew who and what she was, and did not call her a witch. His tale, if all true—and he was a convincing teller—touched her heart and made him her natural ally. If they joined forces, she could probably stop worrying about starving. But could she really trust him? What of the dragon? Did he mean it help or harm?

Hal could read her doubt. He shrugged, like the merchant who's been told that the price is too high. "Let an old soldier convince you, lady, that he found you much too easily. You've been very very lucky so far. Luck such as yours cannot be expected to hold out. You need a little guidance."

Erde returned his gaze steadily.

"Oh, my, but Meriah would be proud of you." He grinned at her admiringly. "True, you've no reason to trust me or my story, and yes, you've guessed it. I have an ulterior motive that I see no point in concealing further. Perhaps you are wondering what particular practice the heathen brother found most unholy? Something so unthinkable that he could use it to turn my neighbors against me? Well, please believe it was not gluttony or drunkenness, though I have drunk too much in my time, Lord knows, and probably will again. Nor was it lechery, at which Fra Guill himself could beat any man's record." He paused abruptly, flicked a glance at her, and then looked away. "Your pardon, lady, if I touch on anything you may have painful firsthand knowledge of."

Erde shook her head emphatically, frowning.

He let a breath out through his teeth. "Thank God for that. No, I'm sure none of us has heard the real story. But we'll leave yours for another time, hah? The finale of mine, the grand debacle, is that what Fra Guill seized upon to turn my people against me was, of course, my dragon-study, which I had never been secret about and certainly could not deny. He twisted an honest scientific and scholarly inquiry into a pact with Satan himself." He fixed her with an indignant glare. "Can you imagine? He accused me of attempting to raise dragons out of the Fiery Pit to lay waste to the countryside—further waste than I'd already caused, though why I would do this to my own lands he never did explain satisfactorily. I told anyone who'd listen, and there were damned few by that time, believe me, that despite my knowing as much as any man alive about dragons, I had never yet laid eyes on one and was not even sure I believed in them anymore."

Hal reached into his jerkin as he talked, digging out two small round objects that glinted in the firelight. He jiggled them pensively in his closed hand. "But I made the profound mistake of declaring to the brother one sunny and innocent day, out of the depths of my enthusiasm and before I was truly aware of his power and my peril, that there was very little in this world I would treasure more than to stand face-to-face with an actual dragon. With that casual remark, he ruined me."

Now he fixed his bright gaze on Erde intently, his voice rough with passion. "Ruined or not, lady, the remark still holds true. Having little else to direct my life toward but survival, my dragon-quest continues. We live in dark times, perhaps the darkest, but you know, milady, dragonkind are the purest of God's creations, the elemental embodiment of the life-force, of anything that has meaning. They could be our salvation. The hell-priest has vowed to destroy dragonkind. I cannot let that happen."

Erde's breath came a bit more easily. She could see he was a man obsessed. And that she had wrongly assumed that dragon-hunter meant dragon-slayer.

"I have become expert over the years at reading hidden signs." Hal cleared his throat. "That is, at interpreting rumor, at hearing what they are really saying in the countryside and what they are not. I've followed many trails and most of them are cold long before I get there. One is not. The one that intersects with you."

He gave her a moment to react. When she did not, he held up between thumb and forefinger the silver mark, or one like it, twisting it back and forth so that it flashed firelight into Erde's eyes. "You know, there're many won't accept this as legal tender anymore." Suddenly he flipped the coin at her. Once again she fumbled the catch.

Hal chortled, satisfied. "Young girls probably don't throw things at each other as much as young boys. Well, so much for your disguise. I might not have given you a second thought, back there in the town. But then my curiosity was aroused . . . I heard there was a search on. So now, tell me, lady, what need you had for ten goats in the town of Tubin when a mere week later I find you with only one?"

The mule, who had wakened from his nap to nose quietly for grass along the edge of the firelight, raised his head suddenly to stare off into the forest, his nostrils flaring.

"Next, the long-term evidence," Hal continued. "The token of an ageless history I'll wager you have no inkling of. Or do you?" He slipped the mark back into his belt and in its place, held up a ruddy cut-stone brooch. "How much did she tell you?"

Erde gasped voicelessly.

"Your pardon for my inexcusable liberties with your luggage, dearest lady. But you cannot know what this means to me. My whole life I have . . ." He leaned forward. "Lady, I beg you, tell me if you know. Are you the Dragon Guide? If you are, I lay my life and my sword at your feet forever."

Erde felt Earth's return well before the mule, who knew it sooner than Hal. He snorted, wickered a warning, and moved to stand protectively at the knight's back.

Hal rose into a crouch, still watching Erde as if his salvation depended on it. "Who comes? Is it he?" Seeing joy and anxiety bloom simultaneously across her unguarded face, he shivered and slid to his knees. "Oh, lady, what will you tell him?"

Erde's only hope, as the dragon's great horned head loomed up out of the forest darkness behind them, was that Hal would not be too disappointed.

PART THREE

EARTH

The Call to the Quest

CHAPTER FOURTEEN

Hal rose and turned toward the dragon. His hand was tight on the hilt of his sword, but his face glowed with a tender expectation that touched Erde in a place normally reserved for younger children and small animals. She sent Earth hope and reassurance and her preference that he not greet this stranger as he had the attacking bear.

But Earth seemed to have sensed an Occasion. He drew himself up at the edge of the firelight, as august as royalty. Bright flickers played across his leathery snout and his sharp-tipped ivory horns. His body vanished behind him into darkness. In the small clearing, he seemed enormous and terrifying, and his huge eyes shone brighter than the fire. Erde saw a new Earth, or at least a side of him that was more *dragon* in its aspect, a creature out of myth such as the dragon-seeker wished to see. The mule, she noticed, had backed off into the shadow in a posture of submission and respect.

Dragon and man stared at each other for a long moment. Then the knight grasped his sword and unsheathed it in a gallant sweeping arc. With shaking hands, he knelt and laid the sword hilt-first at the dragon's feet. Earth watched majestically, his golden eyes unblinking. To Erde's surprise, he raised his right foot and placed it down with great deliberation so that the tip of one massive claw rested on the sword's worn and silvered hilt, which Erde noticed was shaped like a winged dragon wound around a tree, its wings creating the cross-guard. *Like a panel from a story tapestry,* Erde thought, *knight and dragon in some old history of heroes and sorcerers.* Her last doubts about the man's motives and sincerity faded, for he had forgotten her entirely.

His head thrown back, his gaze fixed on the great head hovering above him, Heinrich Peder von Engle, late of Winterstrasse, wept unashamed tears of joy.

Earth lifted his claw and eased the knight's sword toward him across the mat of pine needles. Hal leaped to his feet. He swept up the sword with one hand, palming moisture from his cheeks and beard with the other. He stepped back, stood tall, and raised the sword in a courtly salute, then sheathed it smartly.

"My lord," he offered the dragon gravely, "I am ever at your service."

Watching, Erde wondered about the history of men and dragons, of fighting men in particular, of their ancient traditions of faith and enmity. Earth had neither offered nor required such formality of her when they'd met. Of course, she told herself, formality would be fairly silly when the dragon can read your mind. Even in her daydreaming, she'd had a very personal relationship with her dragons. Yet Earth had understood Hal's offer of fealty, and had known exactly how to satisfy a King's Knight that his oath had been officially accepted.

Hal had not forgotten her after all. He turned with a slight bow. "Milady, if you will, ask him what he . . . I must know my duty . . . what he requires of me." He paused, visibly confounded. "But how will you speak for him, Dragon Guide, if you have no voice?"

Erde was flattered by this tone of reverence from a man old enough to be her grandfather, but she had no wish to be taken as a mere mouthpiece for anyone, even a dragon. Her chin lifted, she mimed writing. After all, she had a few questions of her own to ask someone who had spent his life studying dragons. The first one would be: what is a Dragon Guide?

It took a while to work out the mechanics, but a cleared patch in the dirt, a built-up fire and a sturdy pointed stick accomplished wonders. Hal crouched over their earthy slate with the distracted intensity of an expert who has waited a long time to ask his questions and is not quite sure where to start, fearful of losing the chance to ask them all. When not directly engaged, his attention wandered inevitably back to the dragon, who lay in a dark pile under the pine boughs, snoozing after a successful hunt.

"I suppose this will do . . . nothing is ever what you . . . Well, ah, let's see . . . what is he called?"

EARTH, she wrote.

He raised an eyebrow, both wondering and amused. "How appropriate. Was it your grandmother who named you?"

Erde nodded.

"Of course," he mused. "She hoped. Or perhaps she even knew." He smiled, but Erde sensed some disappointment that his brisk manner was meant to cover. "Then you are Dragon Guide indeed. Not that I doubted. How do you speak with him?"

PICTURES.

"Pictures? Where?"

Erde put a fingertip to her forehead, between her eyes.

"Right there? Really?" The knight peered at her as if he hoped to discover a third eye. "No language? No . . . words?"

She shook her head.

"Interesting. I'd always imagined it would be like a voice just inside my ear, sort of a . . . well, it doesn't matter now." He turned on the dragon a more scholarly gaze. "Has he told you why he's come?"

HE DOESN'T KNOW.

Hal frowned at the scratches on the ground, cocking his head to make sure he'd read them right. "Perhaps you've misunderstood," he reproved gently.

Erde's headshake was emphatic.

"How can he not know? He's a . . . a dragon." He hadn't said the word aloud yet and the reality of it clearly gave him pause. For good measure, he whispered it again. "A *dragon.*"

Erde added a firm underline beneath her scratchings.

"But, milady, you know of course that dragons are the source of all knowledge. Perhaps he doesn't wish to tell you . . . yet?"

Erde was further encouraged. Other people might have said dragons are evil and eat virgin princesses. She smoothed the dirt and began again. HE TELLS ME HE DOESN'T REMEMBER.

Hal massaged his eyes with one hand.

HE HAS DREAMS. She left out "bad," hoping to ease the knight's distress.

"He tells you his dreams?"

I SHARE THEM.

The envy on the knight's face was poignant. "Milady, may I dare to ask? What does a dragon dream?"

THAT SOMEONE . . . she rubbed out "one" and wrote in "thing" . . . IS CALLING HIM.

Hal brightened. "Right! Of course. That's why he's here. He would only come to a Summoning. But he doesn't know who or why?"

HE KNOWS HE SHOULD. HE CAN'T REMEMBER. Erde cleared more pine needles. She would need real room if this conversation got much more complicated. HE IS UPSET.

"I'm not surprised," replied Hal dryly, finally seeing the humor in the situation.

I SAID IT MIGHT BE THE MAGE-QUEEN. CALLING HIM.

"The who?"

She shrugged. JUST TO GIVE AN ANSWER.

"Oh. Well." He nodded. "It's as good as any, under the circumstances. I mean, I always assumed . . . but what good are assumptions?"

She knew what he couldn't bring himself to say. She felt the same helplessness. A dragon was supposed to be omniscient, all-powerful, the closest thing to perfect outside of God's angels. A dragon was supposed to be a lot of things that this dragon clearly wasn't.

Hal let the reality sink in a while, gnawing pensively on his lower lip as he watched the slow rise and fall of the dragon's dusty flanks. Finally he sighed, shrugged, and spread his hands. "Then we must help him. That must be why I am here."

Erde nodded eagerly. BUT HOW?

"Well, he's a dragon, therefore he has a Purpose. We must help him discover it. Earth. It's an odd name for a dragon, but the name often tells you . . . well, obviously I lack the proper knowledge, but someone must . . . someone will be able to read the signs." He seemed relieved to have fastened on something he could be sure of again. "There are no arbitrary dragons."

She didn't really understand what he was talking about, but his conviction, even in sentence fragments, was reassuring.

He rose to pace before the fire with renewed energy, one hand tugging fitfully at his beard. "First find out who or what is doing the summoning. That should be easiest to trace since it will issue from some sort of directional source . . ." He stopped, finding himself even with the dome of the reclining dragon's head. He hesitated, looked to Erde with the suddenly wide eyes of a little boy. "Will he . . . may I touch him?"

Erde nodded. She didn't really know if the dragon would mind.

Hal laid one, then both hands tentatively on the fleshy folds of the dragon's crest, and the dragon opened one giant eye. "Earth," said Hal, a long breathy whisper. He slid his hands forward to the base of the dragon's horns and wrapped his fists gently around them. His fingers and thumbs did not quite meet. "All my life . . ." he murmured. He looked to Erde again, and she smiled. Some things just did not need to be said out loud.

"Without a routine, you get sloppy," remarked Hal later as he banked up the fire and laid out his bedroll. "Routine and discipline will get us through the hard times, when we haven't found food or the search has been unproductive for too long."

Erde sensed the knight's entire recent history packed into that simple declaration.

"So here's what we'll do. You've been right to travel at night, even in this godforsaken weather. We'll keep after that. But we'll know exactly where we're going each day and how far we have to travel. We'll eat if there's food and wash if there's water, even if we're too tired to want to. And at dusk when we wake, we'll take an hour with these." He patted his sword hilt, then nodded at Rainer's blade shimmering where she had reclaimed it beside her. "Practice."

Erde managed to look both dubious and incredulous.

"Why not? Why bring it if you're not going to use it?"
He reached around the fire for the sword and hefted it
casually. "Maybe a little heavy for you to learn on, but . . .
was it your father's?" Her offended look puzzled him. He
returned the blade to her side. "Well, anyway, no dead
weight. You shouldn't carry what you can't use."

Erde wondered briefly if he'd forgotten she was a girl.

"I taught your grandmother to use a sword, when we
were . . . keeping company." Hal smiled at her a little too
brightly, as if the memory held more pain than comfort.
She was delighted to hear that the baroness had encouraged the courtship of a mere knight. It sounded very romantic and sad, and reminded her of Rainer. But the
notion of her grandmother wielding a sword was another
thing entirely.

"Really. I did. So you see, we were fated to meet, you
and I. There are no coincidences. She was built just like
you, and many a man's no taller or stronger. But Meriah
didn't practice."

He became very involved in smoothing out the wrinkles
in his bedroll for a moment, then settled on it with a sigh.
"When I heard she'd . . . passed on, I almost came to the
funeral. But that hell-priest would have burned me on the
spot, so . . ." He shook his head. "Meriah inherited so
young. She didn't have time for 'such frivolities,' as she
said. Ha. She didn't have time for me much after that. She
made a marriage that was 'good for the domain.' She said
I lacked a proper ruler's sense of purpose. I . . ." He
laughed bitterly. "Am I boring you?"

Erde had never thought of her grandmother's life before
marriage. Couldn't he see she was fascinated?

Hal went on as if compelled by her waiting silence.
"Well, I never could make her understand my notion of
service, you see. She said the king was all very well and
good but shouldn't I be seeing to my own lands as she was
to hers?" He shrugged, smiling at Erde crookedly, though
his eyes were serious. "Perhaps she was right. She ruled
well and gave her people security in her own time. But she
didn't teach her son so well, did she? She knew he was
weak. I hoped she'd send him to me for training, but . . .
well, my guess is, she was pinning her real hopes on you."
He turned his gaze again on the dragon. "But your duty is

not with lands or stronghold. It lies here before you, and I surely know my part in it, which is to pick up where Meriah left off. Why else would I be here? *You* will practice!"

Erde grasped Rainer's sword and mimed being barely able to lift it.

"Now it's difficult," he agreed. "But that's what practice is about. An hour a day. I hope you're not one of those spoiled high-borns."

His tone suggested that he would know how to deal with her if she was, but Erde smiled at him anyway, liking him. So what if he was a minor lord. She wished her own father had been more like this man, and wondered how close he had really come to being her grandfather.

Hal's eyes were back on the dragon. "He'll be after us, you know, that hell-spawned priest, especially now he's decided you're the witch-child of his prophecies."

WITH MY FATHER'S ARMY? Erde scrawled.

Hal snorted. "I heard that rumor, too. Who could feed an army in these times? No, I doubt an army, but there will be pursuit, and if I am killed, you must be able to protect yourself . . . and him."

A new notion. Erde had thought the dragon was protecting her. Why else return to her fire, now that he'd proven he could hunt successfully on his own? YOU DON'T THINK I'M A WITCH?

"What if I did?"

Her eyes widened.

Hal grinned at her. "Never fear, milady. I've known a few witches in my time."

She stared at him expectantly.

"Well, let's say they're like dragons. Never what you expect them to be."

LIKE ME?

"I think that remains to be seen," he replied cheerfully. "After all, we don't know each other very well yet."

His sudden evasiveness gave Erde a chill. Was he suggesting she *was* a witch? She decided to pursue the subject in another way.

WHAT, she wrote, IS A DRAGON GUIDE?

Hal peered at her thoughtfully. "It really must pass down in the blood, for you to be here with him and yet so unknowing. How did you ever find each other? No, wait, first

tell me this." He again produced the dragon brooch out of
his jerkin and handed it to her as if he'd rather not let it
out of his keeping but knew he must. "Does it warm to
your touch?"

Erde frowned at it, then laid it to her lips, recalling how
she had done so before. The stone was warm, body temperature, as if it were alive. Superstition chilled her. She nearly
threw the brooch down but caught hold of herself and
merely nodded. Together they stared at it, lying there on
her open palm: deftly wrought silver, finely carved red
stone, a tiny dragon rampant.

IT HAS NO WINGS, she scratched in the dust.

Hal nodded, and they both turned to regard the dragon
asleep in the shadows. After a while, he sighed and took
the brooch from her hand, holding it up to the fire.

"Yes, girl, there is magic in the world." He twisted the
carved stone in the ruddy light. "Carnelian, I'd say. The
setting, oh, probably a hundred years old at most, from
the working of it. The stone, well . . . I always suspected
Meriah was . . ."

A witch? Erde glanced at him questioningly. He took
her hand and wrapped her fingers around the brooch, then
enveloped her fist gently with both his own as if she was
something rare and precious. "Listen, dearest child, whatever we may think in the here and now, whatever our questions and confusions, our . . . disappointments or
misfortunes, the truth is that longer ago than either of us
can imagine, an eternal promise was made. This stone is
the sure token of it. You are its fulfillment. Can you understand any of that?"

She shook her head worriedly.

"It will come, with time." Hal squeezed her hand and let
it go. "The token was passed down and down and down in
secret, most of its bearers as unaware as you of the responsibility carried in their blood. Only through exhaustive
study such as mine would you . . ." He turned his head
away but it was less a negative than a warding off. Erde
could read his ache and his effort to accept the evidence
of his ears and eyes. Whatever this Dragon Guide was
meant to do, Heinrich von Engle felt he was better suited
to it than an ignorant fourteen-year-old girl. But acceptance
of meanings deeper than he could perceive was part of his

scholar's burden. She understood why he focused so heavily on the random luck of lineage.

"No one could know when the time would come," he was explaining, "for the dragon to wake, for the promise to be called upon. The Dragon Guide must guide the dragon through the world of men while he carries out the purpose he's been awakened for. The very purpose, milady, that we must set our lives to discerning." Hal watched her hopefully, as if waiting for some light of revelation in her eyes. Erde could not offer him any, but the knight did appear to have achieved some pragmatic measure of resignation. He waved an arm unnecessarily. "But look, it's dawn already, and a foolish old man with too much talk has robbed you of your necessary rest. Sleep now. The Mule will stand guard."

Erde nodded her good night and lay down. Her stomach was full and her brain was bursting. She'd need many nights of lying awake to sort out the confusion that the knight's arrival had added to an already muddled and complex picture. But tired as she was, this night would not be one of them.

An eternal promise? What if I cannot fulfill it?
She fell asleep listening to the dragon snore.

CHAPTER FIFTEEN

Erde woke from a dream-struggle with a real hand clamped firmly over her mouth. She was sure her father had found her. But it was the stranger knight's voice close to her ear, begging her to lie still. Her first clear thought was to regret that she'd misjudged him after all, then to wonder why the dragon did not come to her rescue.

"Hush, milady, you must be still! You must be still!" Hal's quiet persistence finally got her full attention. She stopped fighting him, and he let her go.

"That's better." He sat back on his heels. "Are you awake?"

Erde looked about. Gray light filtered through the pine boughs, hazed with pale floating ash from the dead fire, which she had kicked up in her troubled sleep. She had no idea what time of day it was.

"You cry out in your sleep, did you know?" Hal whispered hoarsely. "Out loud."

Erde stared at him.

"Truth, milady."

She tried her voice. Perhaps it had come back while she wasn't noticing.

Hal watched her strangled efforts. "Well, there's nothing wrong with your workings, I swear it. But it's a providence you woke me. Listen."

Erde heard, in the distance, the baying of hounds.

"Picked up your scent, damn their well-bred noses. I'd hoped the rain would . . . well, no matter. We'll have to move in full light for a few hours. Pack up, now. Time we were leaving. *Quickly.*" He held her attention a moment with a hand on her shoulder. "Was it one of . . . *his* dreams that frightened you so?"

Erde shrugged. She remembered nothing but a sense of being unable to breathe.

"Well, try to remember it. Whatever it was, it gave you your voice again for a while."

She had no time to think about dreams. It should have been easier traveling by daylight, even as it began to fade into steely dusk, but now speed was essential and the thick pine needle mat was as slippery as a slope of glass. The low-hung branches whipped at her face as Hal urged them swiftly upward through the forest, searching for drier, rockier terrain where their passage would leave a less obvious trace. He set a punishing pace, flanked easily by the she-goat, who had taken a liking to him as a stray dog might. Though the mule now carried her pack and sword, Erde managed a mere short hour before flagging. The knight did everything but drag her along to keep her going, and finally, it was the dragon who lagged behind, as if he didn't really understand the need for all this urgency.

Hal stopped at the top of a rise when it was almost dark. A black sky whipped with clouds showed through the thinning trees. He seemed hardly winded, and the mule, who had followed behind the dragon as if herding him, was cool and dry.

"They'll have us within the hour if we can't move faster." Hal looked up, sucking at his teeth. A bright full moon was rising past the dark branches. "I did think he would have wings . . . ."

Catching her breath, Erde let her head loll back to stare at the clearing sky. She could not recall ever seeing such brilliant stars, as thick as daisies in a meadow. Even the moon did not diminish their sparkle, and the sharp music of the hounds cut through the night air like trumpet alarms. The pack was gaining.

"At least we'll be able to see where we're going," Hal remarked. He pointed ahead down the hillside, where a narrow stony valley split the forest with a sudden gash of moonlight on weathered rock. A rush of water fell away in a twisted course among man-sized boulders. "No cover, but we might lose them in the creekbed."

He led them down the rock-strewn slope toward the surging water, past waist-high stones that gleamed as white as teeth rising from the cold dark ground. At the river's edge, the she-goat knelt for a long drink while Hal called the mule to him.

"He is very surefooted, milady. If you ride, we're more likely to elude the pack." He smiled as if it were a Sunday jaunt. "And you will keep your feet dry."

Erde did not argue. The mule was narrow and bony, but her legs were twisted with cramp and the knight's worn saddle looked very inviting. She had no strength left. Only her fear of capture kept her upright and moving. Hal had been right to say she'd been lucky so far. She let him boost her up. Feeling about for the reins, she realized there weren't any.

Hal rested a hand on the mule's dappled neck. "Oh, we did away with those quite a while ago, he and I. Can you manage without? Believe me, he knows better than we which road to choose." He stroked the mule's nose. "Swift as you can now, Mule."

The mule tossed his head as if he hadn't needed to be told, then moved briskly into the shallow, fast-moving water, picking a delicate sure path among the rocks. The she-goat followed, bounding from stone to stone with weightless precision. Hal waited for the dragon to precede him, but Earth stalled at the edge and would not step into the rushing water. He stretched his neck toward Erde and swayed back and forth in misery and confusion.

"My lord, you must," muttered the knight, with the air of a man who senses his rhetoric to be out of date, but has no acceptable substitute.

Clinging to the mule as it tottered precipitously downstream, Erde saw in her mind the dragon's panic, so like a child's—lurid, distorted images of vast horizons, of dark and rolling waves, of falling water, wrenching currents and suffocating undertow, all foreign and terrifying to her own landlocked imagination. She'd seen Earth walk into water before, but then it had been shallow and still and comfortably (for him) confined by cavern walls. She tried to project calm and reassurance, but he would have none of it, perhaps because she was as frightened as he was. She didn't know how to swim. Court ladies were not taught how to swim. In desperation, she imaged the Mage City for him, his new goal, for which all fears must be overcome, and this convinced him at least to follow along the bank as fast as he could, slithering snakelike up and down among the boulders. Hal waded in behind, a dark silhouette against moonlit stone.

The pack was so close now that Erde could distinguish the voices of individual dogs and hear the occasional spooked scream of a horse being spurred against its better judgment through a strange nighttime forest. Her own fear encouraged the dragon's. Together, their terrors built to a fevered pitch until she felt she was actually drowning in the nightmare ocean of Earth's imaginings. She knew this could not be, yet felt the deep wet chill and the water rushing into her mouth. She welded her body to the mule's saddle and gave up all other awareness in order to picture herself swimming, somehow swimming, holding the dragon's great head above the torrent.

The creek deepened as they moved downstream, gathering in wide fast-moving pools between steepening rapids. The piled boulders lining the banks grew higher and higher until they fused into the broken walls of a gorge that rose straight up from the rushing water. The dragon was forced to climb the cuts and ledges to keep abreast of Erde and the mule. The rising sides threw the streambed into deep moon-shadow and the roiling of the water filled the air with noise. They came to the edge of a pool, a smooth oily surface spanning the width of the gorge. The mule hesitated, then launched himself into the frigid darkness.

The real water was colder and wetter than the imagined ocean. It shocked Erde's awareness back to her own predicament. The air was dank and roaring. The mule was a strong swimmer but hidden currents in the pool drew them crosswise, toward the source of the noise, toward a black misted horizon where the river plunged into a gap between two huge upright stones.

A falls! Erde could only stare ahead as she was drawn toward the thundering void. The mule struggled valiantly, and the dragon's anguished call filled her head. This was what he had feared. This was what he had seen, before any of them had been aware of it.

Suddenly, a pale form materialized in the shadows alongside, the she-goat dancing on a flat rock that jutted at a slant into the deep water. Her little hooves beat a staccato on her water-smoothed landing and the mule swerved toward her. Hope strengthened his breathless, groaning strokes. He gained momentum against the current, found footing at last. The current tore at stirrups and saddle and Erde's numbed legs, but he heaved himself out of the water with a wrenching grunt and scrambled onto the she-goat's rock.

Over the roar of the falls, Erde heard the baying of the hounds.

The goat danced back and away, seeming to vanish unaccountably. The mule plunged after her, into a slanting fault that formed a narrow ramp up the wall, hemmed in by an old rock slide from above, so narrow that Erde's legs scraped the stone. The cut climbed toward the top of the gorge, then doglegged away abruptly in an open ledge. Below, the river plummeted into blackness with a sound like mountains falling.

Erde clung to the mule, shivering in the mist-drenched up-draft. Past the crumbling edge of the ledge, she could see nothing but a curve of moonlit hills softening the dark and distant horizon. Around the dogleg, the ledge widened, cutting back into the rock to form a shallow cave. The she-goat backed into the overhang and immediately lay down. The mule glanced about, turned himself around gingerly to face the void, then twisted his head around to nudge Erde's knees.

She slid off the mule without thinking, then sank to her hands and knees to crawl back along the ledge. The racketing of the dragon's terror in her brain left her blind to all but a need to rush to his aid. She felt along the wall to the corner where the cut descended and the rock slide closed around it. Scaling a low boulder, she could see across the falls to the far wall of the gorge. Bright moonlight spilled across, outlining the dark bulk of the dragon trapped on a high dead-end ledge in full view of anyone upstream. In full view and well within range of her father's archers, once they reached the edge of the pool. Now Erde could hear the shouts of the men as well as the baying of the hounds.

Oblivious to all but the dragon's peril, she began to

scramble up the rock slide toward him, heedless of the precipitous gap and the thundering falls that separated them. The first of the dogs bounded into sight at the head of the gorge.

"NO!" Hal grabbed her roughly about the waist and hauled her backward off the rock. He was soaked through, as if he had swum the pool. "Stay down! You can't help him now! Where's the Mule?"

Erde pointed up the ledge.

"Don't move!" Hal sidled away, then returned with his longbow and quiver from the mule's saddle.

On the far side of the pool, the dogs swooped downstream in a rush. Discovering an impassable depth, they circled and whined at the edge, and made little dashes up into the surrounding rocks and back again. Clattering and shouting, the huntsmen arrived behind them as if already on the attack, several on foot with their crossbows loaded, the rest still mounted, their horses slipping and stumbling on the water-slick stone.

"Nervous, aren't they?" Hal notched an arrow. "Keep still until we know we're seen."

Erde pressed her forehead to the cold rock. The arrival of the hunt was terrifying when seen through the dragon's eyes, far more so than it was in reality—the awful baying of the dog pack, their evil smell filling his nostrils, the vicious sinewy curve of a bow, the steel tip of an arrow gleaming in the moonlight. She could not push reason to the surface past his panic. Her heart raced. Her breath came in silent gasps. Every muscle strained with Earth's helpless need to flee. She gripped the rock with both hands to stay herself from leaping up again.

In a blink, the horrific visions were gone. Erde saw nothing but the backs of her eyelids, felt nothing but the chill grit of the rock beneath her grasping fingers. It was as if the dragon had winked out of existence, leaving her with only her own eyes and ears, and her own more familiar terrors. She looked up. Earth was there as before, clinging to his narrow ledge.

She heard Hal gasp softly, saw him squint in amazement, staring across the gorge. At the pool's edge, the archers milled about, pointing this way and that, cursing and cuffing the whining, confounded hounds, never noticing the hulking creature perched on a ledge in plain view in front of them.

"This is some magic of his," Hal murmured wonderingly.

Erde frowned at him questioningly. She gestured at Earth's dark profile, so clearly etched against the pale moon-washed stone.

"You see him still?"

She nodded.

"Not I. He was there as clear as day, and now only a chunk of the natural rock."

Erde worried about the knight's eyesight, but up till this moment, it had proven exceptionally sharp for a man his age. And the skilled huntsmen below were not the sort to miss so large a target, even at night. Apparently they couldn't see the dragon either. She stared at Earth, trying to separate her awareness from his until he flickered a bit, then actually did blend with the wall behind him. When she blinked, he was there again. She sent him a view of himself as she'd seen him, an innocent chunk of rock on the wall of a gorge. Once he believed her, they both understood he'd done something to save himself without being aware of it. He could not tell her how it had come about.

There was much arm-waving down in the gorge as the hunt-master summoned his men for a conference.

Hal tugged her sleeve. "Recognize any of them?"

Erde nodded. The leader was a stout braggart named Otto, another of her father's recent appointments. Watching him posture before his men, she realized how the new baron had chosen to surround himself with men weaker than himself. Even Rainer, she noted guiltily, but only because he'd been so young. This man Otto was blustery and stupid. Erde scratched his name in the dust with abrupt strokes.

"Who's the best shot?" asked Hal.

Erde pointed out another man, shorter and grizzled, with a large hound tagging his knee. An old pro, this man, who had served her grandmother long and well. It seemed strange to be hunted by men she'd known all her life, even though she'd considered them the enemy since she'd begun leading the deer away from them.

GRIFF, she wrote.

"Griff. Ah, yes." Hal adjusted the aim of his bow. "I

recall that man from my days with Meriah. He's much aged . . . but then, so am I."

Otto's sharp voice carried easily over the roar of the falls. "She must have crossed over way back! If we double back fast, we're sure to catch her."

"I thought witches don't cross over water," returned a voice.

"Gave us the slip in the rocks, then. You can bet she didn't go over the falls."

Griff stood apart, studying the walls of the gorge. The dog beside him did not mill and whine with the others. Erde strained to hear his reply. "You know, a girl alone could hide herself anywhere in a spot like this. Some of us ought to stay behind and wait her out."

"Wait here? Are you kidding?"

"A witch can make herself invisible. She might be standing right next to you!"

Hal grinned. "See how jumpy you've made them?" he whispered. "Hunching about like they expect to be spell-struck? Good thing the dogs can't tell him everything they smell out there on the ground."

A good thing also, thought Erde, *that Otto is too insecure in his position to listen to anyone, even a more experienced man who had been hunt-master when the baroness was alive.* It had not been easy leading the deer away from Griff. But her father had demoted the old huntsman, saying he was not "respectful," and replaced him with a lesser man, who was now turning his sensible advice into an argument.

"You're dog-man now, Griff, remember? You'll do what you're told! We've wasted enough time here already! That damned bitch of yours has lost her nose! I've a mind to do her in right now!"

Griff looked up at Otto, then away. So did the dog lying at his feet. "You would have some explaining to do to his lordship."

"Well, he's a fool and so are you!"

The other men shifted uneasily, but Griff only smiled sourly, then gathered up the rest of the dogs and led them back upstream.

Hal unnotched his arrow. "We're safe for now, I think."

* * *

Earth withdrew into himself on the ledge above the pool, and stayed that way long after the baron's men and dogs were gone from the gorge. Hal would not let Erde risk the pool and the falls to go to him.

"Is he still there? What's the matter with him?"

Erde looked away from the dragon long enough to scrawl a reply.

THINKING. WON'T TALK TO ME.

"Thinking?"

HOW HE DID IT.

"How he went invisible?"

Erde nodded, keeping her eyes fixed on Earth.

"Yes, well, that will be interesting to hear. Now, no moving about until I've made sure friend Otto hasn't left an archer or two behind just to hedge his bet." Hal called the mule to him. "Keep an eye on milady, a close watch, you hear?"

He took his longbow and quiver, and slipped away among the rocks. The mule stationed himself in the path and gave Erde the same concentrated attention she was giving the dragon. One glance told Erde there'd be no sneaking past him. So she put all her energy for mental persuasion into drawing Earth off his ledge. She felt the loss of him in her mind as a vague but persistent anxiety, a potential for unbearable grief. Shivering in her still-damp clothes, she sent him pleas of love and encouragement, and very specific how-to pictures of himself climbing down into the gorge. The dragon did not respond. He was too busy thinking.

Hal returned before Earth did, with a small deer over his shoulder. The mule woke Erde from her doze with a gentle nudge.

"They've camped a mile or so up out of the gorge along the streambed. With luck, we'll be able to slip past them." He shrugged the deer carcass onto the mule's withers. "Don't know about you, I'm starving, but we should move out of this dead end before it gets light." Hal nodded across the falls. "Any luck with him?"

Erde shook her head, as much to clear it as to answer him. Anxiety had dulled her hunger, but she wanted more than anything to be warm and dry again.

"At least I can see him now."

Erde looked, then eased back against the rock as the dragon's presence returned to her in full flood. Hal's concern faded to relief tinged with envy as he watched the joy spread across her face.

"Is he all right? Will he come down now?"

Erde nodded, eagerly clearing space in the dirt.

HE THINKS HE REMEMBERS.

Hal waited.

NOT MAGIC, she wrote. SKILL.

The knight looked dubious.

STILLNESS = INVISIBILITY.

Hal frowned, reading her words several times over. "That would be a very profound stillness indeed . . ."

DEER IN THICKETS.

"But . . ." Hal rubbed his eyes. "Ah, why should I expect to understand him anyway. What's important is, can he do it again?"

HE DOESN'T KNOW YET.

Hal nodded wearily. "Well, I hope he'll let us know when he finds out. Brush those letters away, eh?" He turned back to the mule. "We've got to get moving before we freeze."

Earth clambered down from his perch with a modestly self-satisfied air. He awaited them in the gorge, but still would not cross the stream.

"Can't he explain about the water?"

IT'S MOVING, she scratched in a sandy spot.

"There's a clue in that," muttered Hal. "Somewhere." He let the she-goat find a drier path around the pool, and they rejoined the dragon where the stream narrowed. Earth seemed surprised and gratified when Erde threw herself at him and hugged him joyously.

"Well, I've had a thought as well," Hal announced. "I know our next destination. It's a short week's travel from here. Not exactly this whatever Mage-Queen you've promised him, and we may not exactly be welcome, but it's as good a place as any to start unraveling this mystery."

CHAPTER SIXTEEN

They sneaked past the Hunt's encampment well down-wind, threading precariously through a high tumble of rocks that had once fallen just short of the gravel beach where the huntsmen slept. Down in the shadow of the boulders, the coals of a hastily built cook fire sputtered amidst a scatter of snoring bodies. No watch had been posted, but Hal pointed out a ring of crude crosses, fastened out of twigs and stuck into the sand around the sleepers.

"They'd do better to fear the living," he murmured in Erde's ear.

As they passed by above, the dogs below stirred and whined but did not raise an alarm.

Hal led his party around the crest of the mountain. By dawn, they had descended into the evergreen forests on the far side and felt safe enough to build a small fire of their own in the lee of a rock shelf, just as the sun glanced pinkly off the tall thin spikes of the firs. Erde envied those trees. She would risk a good deal just to stand quietly out in the open sun.

"Exercises tomorrow," declared Hal. "This morning, we rest. It's an advantage that they still think you're out here alone. They'll underestimate your food supply, the water you can carry, the distance you might travel, everything about us."

He cut venison to cook for Erde and himself, then apologetically offered the rest of the deer to the dragon. Earth sniffed at it curiously, then curled up like a vast scaly dog and went to sleep.

"Too dead for him. Dragons are not scavengers," the knight explained as he skewered chunks of venison with lengths of green sapling. He seemed pleased that at least one bit of his hard-won dragon-lore had proven correct. Erde did not offer to explain Earth's bizarre relationship to his living meals. It seemed far too complicated a subject for the limitations of sand scratchings. "But he's eaten recently, has he not? He'll be all right for a while." Hal offered a filled skewer to Erde, who sat huddled in her cloak against the rock wall. "Come on, girl! Work for your supper!"

She roused herself for the skewer, then settled by the fire with eyes downcast. Their narrow escape from the Hunt had left her drained and feeling newly vulnerable.

"You're looking rather sad and thoughtful just now, milady." Hal lowered his own heavily laden skewer into the flames. "I'd rather you ate that up and got some rest, but if there's a tale you wish to tell, I'll stay awake for it."

If only I could *tell it,* Erde mused. But even if she'd had her voice, the tale she had to tell of events connected only by chronology, not by any logic or meaning that she could perceive. Not like Alla, or the court bard, whose stories always made sense. Events were not random in their tales as they seemed to have become in hers.

She was beginning to understand that the weight dragging down her feet and her eyelids by the end of each night's travel was not just exhaustion. There was also the pain she hadn't faced yet, the true depths of the grief she'd shoved aside in her struggle to survive. Hal's arrival had eased the struggle. He was a resourceful male adult, and she trusted him. Under his protection, she could be a child again, the child she still was inside. She could feel free to grieve.

She let the skewer drift close to the fire as she brooded, until a log shifted. Sparks flew up around her wrist and the raw meat sizzled. Erde jerked her hand back, aware that her other hand gripped the hilt of Rainer's sword so hard that it had gone numb. She lifted it out of the cloak folds and dragged it into her lap.

"How 'bout you start by telling me about that?" Hal pulled his meat out of the fire and blew on it delicately.

Erde regarded him with big eyes and shook her head. She wished she could, but it was still too painful. Even in her dreams, her mind shied away from it. Besides, she knew

she could not tell the story of Rainer's death to anyone,
not even the dragon, until she understood what he had
meant to her.

"Then let me tell you what a fighting man can tell from
this stranger's weapon." He spread his wiping cloth on the
pine needles and laid out his too-hot dinner, then extended
his hand. Reluctantly, she placed the hilt in his palm. Free-
ing it from its linen wrappings, he stood, groaning and complaining of stiffness though he settled into his fighting
stance with the grace of long experience. Erde gathered up
the wrappings possessively, resisting the urge to snatch back
the sword and cover its nakedness. Hal held it level, first
balanced on one palm, then gripped and held out in front
of him. His eyes narrowed in concentration. He swung it a
few times, a long sideways arc, then overhand. Satisfied, he
resettled himself in a dappled fall of early sunlight to study
the hilt and shaft in detail.

"A well-made blade but plainly presented. A skilled armorer, a day-to-day purpose. A working blade, not a courtier's, definitely not your father's, I see that now. Iron Joe
would never stoop to such an honest blade." He turned it
in the light like a chirurgeon with an old bone. "A newish
blade, not too heavy but on the long side. A tall man,
lightly built, probably young. A blade not often bloodied
but scrupulously maintained. A responsible young man, a
little insecure yet but proud enough of his ability to spend
several months' salary on a better than average weapon,
and unpretentious enough to avoid needless decoration."
Hal lowered the tip of the sword until it just touched the
ground. "I hope this wasn't the man they say you struck
dead with a witch's spell at the castle gate. I could use the
man who carried this blade. I'd make a fine soldier out of
him. Don't go killing them off, milady—there are few
enough around as it is."

He glanced over at her, grinning, and found her face
twisted with grief. He had described Rainer so accurately
that it left her breathless. She could almost see him just
beyond the fire, sword in hand, fresh from the practice
yard, his favorite place, smiling in welcome. For a moment,
she hated the elder knight. It should be Rainer sitting
across from her now. Why couldn't he have kept himself

alive? At last, the tears came freely. She could no longer hold them back.

Hal knelt quickly and set the sword aside. "Ah, child, you can't mind the self-serving inventions of a power-mad cleric. I know you have killed no one."

Erde shook her head frantically, then both her hands, then buried her face in them and wept as she had not been able to since she'd been told of Rainer's death. Brother or lover, whatever he was, it didn't matter, she wept for him anyway, and for Alla, her only other friend, and for her grandmother, whose counsel and company and strength she did not feel whole without. And she even wept for Georg, whose life she'd been forced to take, so that her own might continue.

Hal reached across the fire and patted her shoulder once, then let her cry.

She wept long after the knight had banked the fire and gone to sleep. She was unable to stop herself. She crawled over to the dragon's side, curling up next to him for warmth, but could not keep the sobs from coming. Wave after wave until her brain was dulled with it. Only when the afternoon gloom deepened under the thick pines and the dragon stirred and woke, filling her mind with his curiosity, needing her attention, demanding her response, did she get hold of herself and dry her eyes. Her grief remained as sharp as ever but having finally given in to it, she could put it in its place. She had to. She could not be dragging about like a stone, weighed down by painful memory. She had to be fit and alert. She was the Dragon Guide, and she knew where her duty lay.

CHAPTER SEVENTEEN

Erde had thought it was just the usual man-talk, but Hal really did mean her to learn to use the weapon she had carried into exile. He rushed her through their meager breakfast and, while there was still light enough to see clearly, he found an opening among the tree trunks and began shoving the pine mat aside with the edge of his boot.

He waved Erde into action. "Help me with this! Good footing is crucial!" When he was sure she'd keep at it, he trotted away into the woods and came back with two stout sticks that he'd cut, each the length of one of their swords. She was almost disappointed. Now that the mule was packing Rainer's sword, she missed it, as if the time she spent with it was what kept the memory of him alive in her mind. But the stick that Hal handed her was plenty heavy enough.

The dragon watched Erde swing the stick about for a while, then wandered off to hunt. Hal inspected the circle of cleared ground.

"Good enough. Let's get to work."

As he raised his own stick and took up his stance, Erde felt a sudden panic. What if he attacked? What if he humiliated her? But the knight drew her over beside him, a few paces apart, both facing a shared audience of one very jaded mule and a puzzled she-goat.

"Now. Watch my movements and repeat them exactly. No, I said *exactly!*"

The movements seemed neither difficult nor complicated. Erde's confidence soared with her relief. But Hal made her repeat each one until she had managed ten perfect repetitions in a row with no rest in between, and after the fourth simple ready, step, and swing exercise, she was heated up and breathing hard. Her right arm ached in places she hadn't even known she had a muscle.

As soon as he saw her growing clumsy, Hal stopped the lesson.

"Enough for today." He took her stick and tied both of them to the mule's saddle. "Now. Here's how you stretch that arm out so it won't tighten up on you."

And so it went, for many nights' travel through the unbroken forest. They were spared rain for a while, and the temperature warmed slightly as they descended from rock ledges and tall pines through dense stands of birch and golden-leaved aspen, down into maple and wide-spreading oak touched with a blush of early fall color. For a while, the shared nightmares ceased, perhaps because both Erde and the dragon felt safer in Hal's company, perhaps because they were eating more regularly, or simply because he pushed them hard and they were too tired. They would stop at dawn, exercise, eat, and sleep, then wake at dusk, exercise and move on, night after night.

They kept to the cover of forest, staying clear of the towns, skirting the occasional farmstead cut out of the wilderness, avoiding a woodcutter's cottage or two. Finally, when Hal was confident that he could detect no pursuit, he left Erde to sleep one day while the dragon hunted, and rode the mule into a charcoal burners' camp to trade news for bread and cheese.

He found his news was already stale, but being able to offer an eye-witness account of the Tubin burning gave him his choice of supper tables and a full pack to speed him on his journey.

"Came in from the north, like I was headed from Tubin the long way," he explained to Erde later. "Left to the south and cut back east soon as I could. You know what the latest story is?"

She shook her head, her mouth gloriously full of fresh bread and cheese.

"That the Baron's Hunt cornered you where two rivers crossed, and were just about to bind you when you called up a demon in a blinding flash of light to carry you away to safety." He cocked his head at her. "There's just no end to your powers, milady."

Erde smiled back at him, trying to take the witch tales

as casually as he did. But they weighed on her increasingly, because she was sure that someday she was going to be made accountable for them.

During the first nights of travel, Hal talked to her as they walked, about the countryside, the route he was taking, where they might camp for the day. But after the first few, he ceased trying to keep up both ends of this one-way conversation. Soon they were traveling in silence, but it was a companionable silence.

"I've traveled alone for two years now." They were setting up camp by a streambed. "There's many out in the countryside that don't know or understand the details of the king's troubles with his barons. Some'll still show a King's Knight some respect, and there are things I can do to help out here and there, so I get along." Hal brushed bread crumbs from his jerkin. "I still wear the Red as you can see, out of respect for His Majesty—only took it off once or twice sneaking into Erfurt to check up on the situation at court. I'm best off staying unobtrusive, so some baron doesn't get a notion to try me for invented treasons. So I'm used to silence. I talk to the Mule sometimes, but I never let myself talk to myself. That way madness lies. . . ."

Erde was not sure of that. She'd talked to herself quite a bit when she'd had her voice. She'd never thought she was going mad until she could no longer speak her mind out loud. Besides, Alla had talked to herself nonstop, sometimes even when you were there in the room with her, and Alla was the sanest person Erde had ever known. Except for her grandmother, although, to Erde's mind, the baroness' dedication to duty and power did occasionally put her sanity at risk. Suddenly the purpose of this line of reasoning became clear: if she dedicated herself to the dragon as it seemed she had been born to do, what would she become? Would she give up love for the sake of duty, as her grandmother had apparently done? Would she give up her lands for the sake of an obsession, as Hal had done? She brooded over this until she remembered she had neither lands nor lover anymore, so what did it matter?

Even so, she woke the knight out of an after-dinner doze by the fire to discuss the issue.

DID MY GRANDMOTHER LOVE POWER TOO MUCH? She formed the letters very carefully in the soft ash layer, as if to render her question more comprehensible.

Hal blinked, yawning. "Hmmm. Well. Yes. Now that's a hell of a question to come out of a young girl."

Erde frowned at him sharply.

"Yes, yes, just let me think. That was a sound sleep you woke me out of. Let's see . . . it depends on who you ask, you know?" He sat up, rubbing at his beard as if it might help him to think more clearly. "If you ask me, which you did, I'd say yes, of course, since she loved power more than she loved me. But ask the crofter whose survival depended on her honesty and diligence in running the estates, and he'd like as not say no. At least your grandmother, unlike your father, was capable of wielding power's responsibilities and thinking of someone other than herself. Does that answer your question?"

Erde nodded pensively. She'd thought of power as a license to take what you needed and push other people around. That was what her father did. But not her grandmother? Power as a responsibility was a new concept, yet it made sense in the pragmatic context Hal had offered. She understood she'd been frivolous all those times she'd vexed her grandmother with airy insistences that she didn't care about power. She was troubled by his suggestion that the baroness had considered her to be Tor Alte's proper heir. Had she failed her grandmother without knowing it? Would events have fallen out differently if she'd been a more diligent student in the baroness' unofficial course of study?

At least her grandmother had never spoken of power with personal relish, the way her father did. Yet in following the priest's lead, the baron had given up power to him. Why give it up so readily, if he loved it so much?

Hal was dozing again. She nudged him with her foot. WHY DID PAPA GIVE OVER TO FRA GUILL?

"What has gotten into you, girl? Was it the fish for supper?" Hal struggled up again, groaning as if the effort were enormous. "I know you won't rest till I answer."

Erde nodded, offering an eager placating smile.

"You want the long or the short version?"

SHORT.

"Good, that's easy, assuming your father to have no

greater fear for his immortal soul man the next man. So—what does your father want more than anything else?"

TO BE IMPORTANT.

"And what will make him important?"

POWER?

Hal nodded approvingly. "He to whom power is important is vulnerable to anyone who wields it more cleverly than he does. The hell-priest is damnably rich in power just now. I assume he promised your father a share of it."

Erde's mouth worked in instinctive protest. Nothing came out but a puff of frustrated breath.

"But how could he trade his only daughter for the promised share? Well now, that's either a true measure of his obsession or something a bit more complicated. I suspect it's a bit of both. But that's the long answer."

Erde did not want complications. Her mind was drawing long loops, seeking simple connections. Complications could come later.

WHAT ABOUT THE KING?

"How's that?"

THE BARONS LOVED POWER MORE?

"No, he . . ." Hal paused, sucking his teeth morosely. "Well, maybe so. What the king values most is peace. He had power enough to establish it in good times, but not enough to maintain it through times like these. So for now, he sits in Erfurt at their convenience, ruling in name only."

FOR NOW?

"Of course, for now," he replied indignantly, "You think I wear the Red for sentiment? His Majesty is still king by the grace of God, and what other duty could a King's Knight claim but to see his monarch securely on his throne once again?"

For that, Erde had no answer. She sat back, pulling the folds of her cloak up around her shoulders. She had enough to chew on for one day, and finally she let the knight sleep. She hoped it was not too late to become her grandmother's faithful student.

Meanwhile, the dragon practiced becoming invisible.

CHAPTER EIGHTEEN

Of course, Earth could only be invisible while he was standing still. This meant he must practice while his companions rested, or be left behind. Or so he thought. The dragon had not yet understood that he was the glue that held this oddling band together.

"Don't ever tell him we'd each die before leaving him behind," Hal warned quietly. "He's slow enough as it is."

How quickly men become impatient, Erde marveled, *even with the things they claim to worship.*

"I hope you'll pardon my presumption, milady, but . . . can't you get him to move along a little faster?"

Erde shrugged, shook her head. Being unable to speak did offer relief from having to explain herself—or the dragon. The truth was, she hated hurrying him unless he was in danger. Hal was fairly sure that they'd eluded their pursuers for the time being, and she thought what Earth was learning was too important to rush. He seemed so encouraged by having discovered he had at least one skill. Let him practice at his own pace.

"He's getting the idea, at least," Hal conceded. "And I suppose if you're as old as he is, an hour or two of human time seems like the blink of an eye. What can 'hurry up' possibly mean to a dragon?"

Erde steered him toward a bare patch of ground. She now carried a short pointed stick in her vest to use as a stylus.

HOW OLD?

Hal chuckled. "Oh, old, you can be sure. Older than me, even. Can you believe that?" Then he grew grave and drew himself up out of his stoop as he did whenever he talked of dragon-lore. "There are conflicting opinions as to the exact day and hour of the creation of dragonkind. I myself favor those who place it on the First Day. Others are of the mind that dragons were created first among the creatures of the air, which would make it, of course, the Fifth Day. The hell-priest would place them with the fall of Lucifer and the birth of heresy in the world. Now, this *particular* dragon . . ."

The peevish look he turned on Earth, who was once again struggling to catch up, made Erde laugh. The sound was all breath but so unaccustomed that they stared at each other in surprise. Hal's mouth tightened against a grin. "Well, look at him! Does he look like something you'd expect the Good Lord to come up with on the First and Holiest Day? He's ignorant, he's clumsy, he's . . . ah!" His grin bloomed ingenuously. "Is it a disguise?"

Erde shook her head.

"Well, it was just an idea. It's just hard to accept that he's so . . . so like a child."

Erde nodded emphatically.

"Oh, you think that's good, do you? Surely, it takes one to know one." Hal made a sour face, then slowed, chewing on a thumbnail. She imagined him stalking the aisles of his library in just that posture, that is, when he'd had a library. He scratched his beard thoughtfully. "Now, you know, there are a few truly renegade minds who consider dragons to be creatures of nature that are born, grow old, and die like the rest of us. It's a radical notion, very eccentric, but their idea is that dragons mate and reproduce by the laying of great leathery eggs. Of course, I'd never given this theory much credence but . . ." He glanced back at Earth, but the dragon had again pulled to a halt and vanished. "Confounded beast!"

Erde clapped her hands in breathy voiceless mirth.

"Always happy to provide comic relief," the elder knight growled, but his eyes smiled. "Ah, well. Laughter is a healing thing, milady, and you deserve a little, after all you've been through. Maybe we both do."

A week's nights of travel brought them to the edge of a big lake. Erde had never seen a lake so broad. She ran down to the slim, graveled beach to stare out across the dark water, wondering if this was the ocean that the minstrel tales so often sang of, where great sea monsters devoured ships and all the men on them in a single gulp. The waning moon shimmered on ranks of white-capped wavelets driven toward shore in the brisk chill wind.

The dragon snorted at the nearness of all that deep moving water. He refused to share Erde's wonder. He rocked from side to side and would not follow. He pelted her with water terror until his fear overwhelmed her wonder, and she could not help but draw back nervously into the shelter of the trees with him, even though a moment before she had hoped that Hal meant to take them out on this marvelous ocean to dance with the waves.

Fortunately for the dragon, the lake itself was not Hal's destination. He led them along the shore to the lee-side of a sheltered cove where the trees hung low and close over still water, and the moonlight did not penetrate. He chose a weedy bluff back from the edge and called the mule over to unload.

"We'll rest here until morning," he declared, though they'd accomplished only half their usual distance since sunset. "He'll be awake, for sure, but we're better off not bothering him after dark."

Erde touched his sleeve inquiringly. Did he mean *safer,* she wondered. The knight pointed to a curving shadow of land across the cove. She saw a glow that came and went as the trees swayed in the wind off the lake, like a faint winking eye. The scent of wood smoke tickled her nostrils. Hidden among the trees, the dragon sneezed and sent an inquiry about white sun-tipped towers rising above green hills.

—*Soon,* Erde promised him.

She tugged Hal's sleeve a little harder.

"Answers tomorrow," he said, gathering leaves into a pile and laying out his bedroll. "And no fire tonight. Bad enough we're upwind of his expert nose, but it can't be helped. Get the sticks. Time for practice."

At dawn, the cove was sunk deep in mist. The opposite shore was as invisible in the pale light as it had been in darkness. Hal stirred and went to the edge to splash water on his face.

"Arrgh! Cold!" He stood, beard and eyebrows dripping, and stared across the cove. "Huh. Well, let him get some breakfast into him first."

Whoever "he" was, Erde was convinced she would find him terrifying, if he made the knight so uneasy. She joined him on the misty beach, mouthing a silent WHO?

Hal considered, then shook his head. "No use my trying to explain. You'll see soon enough. If he'll even talk to us, that is." His stare shifted to the dragon, who had spent the night huddled as far into the trees as he could go without losing sight of Erde. "My hope is, Earth will win him over."

After their own meager breakfast, they packed up and started single-file around the cove. There was no path to follow. The woods were a mossy tangle of low branches and downed trees. Hal's mysterious quarry preferred living inaccessibly. In some places, they were forced into the water, and only because it was still and shallow could Erde convince Earth to follow. The underbrush was dense all the way to the shore and very damp, as the mist rose and left the weight of its moisture behind. Behind the Mule, in front of the she-goat, Erde wrapped her cloak tightly around her, but her boyishly cropped hair was drenched by the time they broke through a final curtain of bramble and saplings into a dim swampy clearing sheltered by a dozen or so tall and spreading firs. A low arm of land projected into the lake, its narrow neck protected by a barrier of thicket. Erde could see pale water past the tree trunks on three sides.

"Tell the dragon to stay back in the brush," said Hal. "Even better if he can be invisible. We'll go on to the cottage alone."

Cottage? Erde could see only a pile of forest rubble, lurking like a shadow amid the darker fir trunks. Rubble, or at most, the lodge of a very large beaver. It wasn't much taller than she, but it was set as if by design in the exact center of the clearing. A delicate wisp of smoke curled up from the top of the pile, so she supposed it was the cottage Hal meant. There was even a thick slab of bark at ground level that might be a door.

"Well, here goes," Hal muttered. He marched resolutely up to the bark slab and knocked on it with courtly restraint. If it was a door, he was going to have to stoop mightily to pass through it.

There was no reply.

Hal knocked louder, and then again, with a big stone he'd picked up from beside the door. He waited, pointing to a mutilated area in the center of the slab. "See that? He makes everybody do this! You'd think a fellow living this far away from the civilized world would want a visitor every now and then!" Hal banged on the slab again, then threw the stone at it in disgust. "Come on, Gerrasch, I know you're in there!"

"QUIET!"

Erde held herself in place by sheer will as the pile spoke, or rather, screeched. The voice was harsh and broken, as if long out of practice.

"Quiet, quiet, quiet, QUIET!"

The door flew open and out stormed the pile's occupant. For a moment, Erde feared this Gerrasch actually was a giant beaver. He was short and round and lumpy, with a great mane of curly hair covering his face. He wore what seemed to be a tunic of dark fur, overlaid with a vest of leaves, and he waddled much as a four-legged creature might if forced to walk upright. Seeing no sign of a beaver's large flat tail, Erde breathed a sigh of relief.

Gerrasch planted his stubby feet and spread his arms to grip either side of the doorway. "QUIET!"

"I hear you, Gerrasch," Hal replied.

The creature lifted his moplike head to stare at Hal with veiled but beady eyes. "Then be it." He turned, vanished into the darkness of his hovel and slammed the door behind him.

The knight sighed profoundly, one arm propped against the rubble pile, slowly shaking his head. Erde relaxed a little. It was not fear that made him wary of this exasperating personage.

Hal threw her a rueful shrug. "You'd never know we've been friends for years." He knocked again, softly. "I've brought you a dragon," he crooned.

After a long moment of wind coughing in the pine trees, the door cracked open. "I knew that," said an invisible Gerrasch.

"You know everything."

"Everything, yes."

Behind his back, Hal's fingers drummed a silent staccato.

"If that weren't so close to true, I wouldn't put up with you."

Gerrasch remained in shadow. "A minor dragon, yours."

"Oh, really? Then am I to take it you're not interested?"

"Am, am, am, am, am."

"You've a damn funny way of showing it." Now Hal winked at Erde. "Maybe I won't show him to you after all."

"Where?"

"I thought you knew everything."

The door edged closed.

"He wants to meet you . . ."

The door stilled. Bright eyes peered out of the darkness.

". . . when he's sure that your knowledge is worth his bother."

The bark door swung wide. Beckoning Erde to follow, Hal ducked inside.

The inner gloom was thick with smoke and musty animal odor. The twig and rush ceiling curved so low that Hal could not stand fully upright. A circular hearth burned in the center of a dirt floor which was littered with containers of all shapes and sizes: an astonishing variety of earthenware bowls and jugs and wavy glass jars with ceramic tops, brown clay bottles and metal pails, wooden buckets, reed and wicker and woven grass baskets, even a crudely wrought barrel or two, all jumbled together, precariously stacked and piled, and all full of indeterminate substances. As Erde struggled to take it all in, Gerrasch shut the door behind her, plunging them into further darkness.

"Pull up a keg," Hal advised her comfortably.

Erde waited for her sight to adjust to the dim red glow from the hearth, then settled herself on a low cask near the door that looked the least likely to tip over. At her feet lay a basket of broken eggshells, another of pine cones, another of twigs and dirt, plus a box of assorted turtle shells. The rough-hewn walls of the hut formed an octagon, lined floor to ceiling with shelves, each bowing under the weight of more jars, jugs, bowls, and bottles.

The knight lounged silently on his keg. Erde watched him carefully for an indication of what to do next, while Gerrasch shuffled about among the jars and baskets showing only his round back, as if he had forgotten them entirely.

"So here's this dragon," offered Hal finally. "And . . . he comes with a mystery."

Still puttering with his containers, Gerrasch snorted. "No mystery to me."

"Good. Excellent. Exactly why we came."

Suddenly Gerrasch spun around to stare at Erde as if he had just noticed she was there. "Boy or girl?"

"Hard to tell, if you don't see many of either," replied Hal dryly. He resisted reminding the creature of his claim to know everything. "Gerrasch of Eiderbloom, may I present the Lady Erde von Alte."

Gerrasch lurched across the dark room toward her. Erde cried out voicelessly and recoiled off her cask, backing up against the overflowing shelves. Jars rattled. Dried branches crackled beside her head.

"Easy, girl," the knight murmured.

Gerrasch pursued her. He shoved his nose close to hers, blocking her sight entirely so that she saw only a huge halo of hair backlit by the embers and a faint reflection glimmering in his eyes. She turned her head aside, repulsed by Gerrasch's strong musky odor. She looked to Hal for support. But the knight watched impassively, as if from a great distance, his arms folded across his chest.

Gerrasch placed furry, pawlike hands on Erde's cheeks and turned her to face him. His palms were smooth and oddly cool. He sniffed at her, as a dog might inspect a stranger, then pulled his hands away and snatched up one of hers. He pressed it flat like a gypsy fortuneteller and bent his head over it, though the room was much too dark for reading anything. Erde could feel his warm breath on her skin. He sniffed again, muttering, then licked her palm. The hot wet touch of his tongue frightened her. She tried to pull her hand away, wishing to be out of this close, lightless hovel, and away from this malodorous creature who held her fast, staring as if he could see through her in the gloom. Her anxiety roused the dragon. His concern rushed into her head, his loud complaint at being left outside with only the Mule and the she-goat for company. Erde calmed herself and him, and made him promise to stay hidden in his thicket.

"A dragon. Yes. Will be." Gerrasch gave a satisfied grunt and dropped her hand. He shuffled away from her briskly and settled himself in front of the dying fire, opposite Hal. He stirred the coals, tossing on a few twigs. Hal watched him. Erde realized she had suddenly become irrelevant.

"How much?" Hal asked finally.

"Ten," came the gruff reply.

"One."

"Ha."

"Two."

"Ten."

"Three."

"Ten, ten, ten, ten, ten."

Hal unfolded his arms, dusted his palms together. "Forget it. I'm sorry I bothered." Erde was astonished that the knight thought this creature could know anything worth paying for. And if he was so mercenary, maybe it was dangerous to have come here at all. He would likely sell his knowledge of her whereabouts to the highest bidder, who would of course be her father, or perhaps the priest.

Gerrasch clicked his teeth together. "Eight. Eight, eight."

"Four," said Hal. "Not a mark more."

"Five."

"Done."

Gerrasch stuck out his hand. Tiny new flames licked up from the hearth, and Erde could see that his palm was as smooth as a baby's, fresh and pink, emerging from a dark cocoon of fur and rags. As she watched in disbelief, Hal dug into his belt and counted five silver marks into Gerrasch's soft, pink palm. The creature prodded them gently, crooning like a mother, then closed his fist around them. Shining silver vanished into darkness.

Hal looked to Erde. "He'll take it because the king's silver is still the purest."

"Five questions," the creature announced.

"Someday, Gerrasch, your greed will get the better of you."

"Ask. Time is short."

Hal scoffed. "Out here, you've got nothing but time."

"I, yes. You, no. Ask." His beady gaze shifted, then fixed on Erde. "Maybe she ask better."

"Fine with me," said Hal.

Erde frowned at him. She did not understand the game.

Either he was playing with her or with Gerrasch, for surely he did not expect this half-man, half-animal to be able to read. But the knight just smiled back at her expectantly. Erde shook her head.

"The Lady Erde declines," Hal declared, "to speak with one so rude and selfish with his knowledge."

It was Gerrasch's turn to look disgusted. He turned his back on Hal with a wave of his pink-skinned paw, and peered at Erde harder. "Ask!"

His intent stare riveted her, and she felt she must answer him somehow. She patted her throat and shook her head.

Gerrasch snatched her hand away. "Ask! Ask, ask, ask, ask!"

She let out an explosion of breath and effort, and felt tears well up hot in her eyes. Gerrasch cocked his curly head, then pressed his soft palm to her throat. "Ah. Oh. Aww. Humm. Yes." His fingers probed her neck. "Word stuck."

"The lady has lost her voice," offered Hal quietly.

"No. No. Voice there. Word stuck." His touch was surprisingly gentle. "Yes, yes. Feel it right . . . there."

Erde knew a word had no substance. It could not be lodged in your throat like some kind of fish bone. But it did feel like that when she tried to speak, and Gerrasch had focused on the exact spot she would have chosen, had she been asked to pinpoint the problem. She even had the sense she'd once known what the word was. She had only to remember it and her voice would be restored. Gerrasch pressed and sniffed and she found herself smiling at him. Suddenly the hovel did not feel so hot and close. She put her fingers on top of his and nodded. She thought he smiled back, but in the dim light she could not be sure, and too quickly he pulled his hand away and stepped back, no longer looking at her.

"One answer. Four more. Next?"

"Now, wait a minute," Hal protested.

"True answer, true. Only, she must find right word."

Hal stood, hunched up under the smoke-stained ceiling. "Come on, Gerrasch. I paid good King's Coin for useful information, not the hocus-pocus you cheat the locals with."

"Not hocus-pocus!"

"Oh? Then why can't you—who knows everything—just tell her what the word is?"

Gerrasch whirled away, shaking his stubby arms and head so violently that his curls battered his eyes. "She. She, she must find it!"

"He doesn't mean a real word, of course. It's a metaphor, for finding your own cure."

Erde put out a staying hand, begging him not to harass the creature further. Gerrasch's explanation was oddly satisfying, however whimsical. It made her feel less damaged and she wanted to believe him, though she had no idea how he could know such things.

Hal backed off. "All right. Besides, the questions we came to ask are about the dragon."

"Dirt."

Hal stared at him, then frowned reprovingly. "Earth."

"Dirt. Stone. Sand. Dirt."

Erde recalled how Earth had used these words in image-form to identify himself.

"I wouldn't call him Dirt when you meet him," replied Hal. "He might decide you look good to eat. You know how dragons feel about their naming."

Erde was sure she saw Gerrasch's hair-veiled eyes dart apprehensively toward the door. She wanted to reassure him that dragons don't eat people, but she wasn't entirely sure he was a person. Did being able to speak make you human, no matter what body you wore?

"Dirt, dirt, dirt," muttered Gerrasch. He lifted his heavy chin, sniffing distractedly. "Can't stay here," he hissed suddenly.

"You don't want to see the dragon?" asked Hal.

"Don't need to see."

"Smell him, then. Close up, in person."

Gerrasch was agitated again. "Can't, can't, can't." He grabbed Erde's hand, pulled her to her feet. "Dragon, you, all must go now."

"Our questions, Gerrasch. You owe us four."

Gerrasch whirled on the knight, an outraged bulk of flying curls. "You ask, then! Quick, quick, quick! You are followed."

Hal stilled. "No."

"Yes!" Gerrasch sniffed again, a long intake of breath with his stubby neck extended. "Yes, yes, yes, yes."

"Damn! I was sure . . . how many? Can you tell?"

"One, one."

Erde heard a dog baying, faint with distance.

"One? One man?"

"One, one. That is all." Gerrasch shuffled away from the hearth to pull a canvas pouch from one of the shelves. He hung it over his shoulders crosswise, then went from shelf to shelf, grabbing a pinch of this, a handful of that, and stuffing it all into the pouch. "Next question. Quick, quick. Three left."

"Damn!" growled Hal again. "All right, fast then. This is important, Gerrasch, or I wouldn't have bothered you, you know that."

"Yes, yes! Hurry!"

"Here are our questions—they're all related. Milady, if you will alert the Dragon that we are followed, he'll pass it on to the Mule."

No need. The dragon had heard the baying from his hiding place. Erde had to use all her powers of persuasion to keep him from bolting without them.

"Question One," said Hal. "The dragon claims to have forgotten his mission: why has he been called? Two, he dreams of an unnamed Summoner: who has called him? Three, where do we go to find the one who calls?"

As Hal said this, an image of shining white towers rose up in Erde's mind. Where indeed?

"This dragon sleeps still." Gerrasch's entire interest seemed to be in filling his pouch.

"Yes, yes, but how can we wake him?"

"You cannot. He must. He, he, he must. Now you go."

Hal scraped stiff fingers through his thinning hair. "Come on, Gerrasch! For five marks, I could have supplied that answer. We need your help!"

"No help, no, no, no! Can't!" Gerrasch dug in his leafy vest and flung three silver coins at the knight's feet. "You go now!"

Erde listened. The baying was still far away, still only one voice. Could Gerrasch's "one" have meant one dog? The dragon was relaying pictures of huge packs, many hundreds of monstrous hounds with gleaming razored teeth, but she knew by now that fear made him exaggerate. Meanwhile she wondered, why only one?

Hal had gathered up the coins. He held them out in his open palm. "You agreed, Gerrasch. One cast, then. We have time for one cast."

Gerrasch's pouch was full. With a sharp glare at Hal, he jerked it around to lie against his back, then scuttled away and bent among the kegs and ceramic jugs, muttering furiously. Returning to the hearth, he cleared twigs and stones and a bowl of mushrooms from a patch of dirt floor with one sweep of his wide, flat foot. He lowered himself in front of it and tossed a fistful of objects on the ground: dark, round pebbles, pearly shells, and tiny pinecones, a bone or two, and some strange seed pods, furry and sickle-shaped. Gerrasch stared at the scattering he'd made.

"Well?" prompted Hal. "Anything?"

"One: the purpose is to fix what's broken."

"Broken," Hal repeated softly. "Does it say what it is?"

Gerrasch shook his head. "Two: the Summoner is not here."

"Of course he's not here. If he was, we wouldn't be looking for him!"

"Her."

"He . . . oh. Her." Hal nodded. "Well, that's something. So where is she?"

"Three: don't know. Don't. Not here."

"Obviously!" Hal snapped. "Like I said, if . . ."

"Not *here!*" Gerrasch swept a broad arm through the pebbles and shells, destroying whatever coherence had been apparent to him. "I tell what I see! Go away! Get out now! You want more, go to the women!"

"The women know more than you?" Hal prodded mockingly.

"Sometimes. Yes. Different things. Go there!"

"Fine. I was headed there anyway."

"Good! Ask them about the City!"

Hal laid hands on Gerrasch for the first time, grabbing him by the shoulders and staring him in the eye. "WHAT CITY?"

The City. Erde felt an absurd surge of hope, and the white towers shimmered again in her mind. The City. Just the word itself had a magical ring. She didn't know any cities. She'd only heard the word used to refer to places in the Bible, ancient places, places of miracles. Or to the City of Rome, which was the City of Heaven on Earth and was far enough away to seem ancient and miraculous.

"What city, Gerrasch?"

Erde prayed he meant her city. *Ask him where,* she thought desperately, ask him where we should go.

Gerrasch would not be intimidated further. He shoved Hal's hands away. "Ask them. Them, them, them, them."

Hal looked to Erde. "We've gotten all we're going to. Best be off, like he says. Not right to bring our hell-hounds down on his head."

Erde was torn. She had no desire to stand around waiting for her father's Hunt to arrive bows-at-the-ready in Gerrasch's little clearing, but what if he had the knowledge they needed?

Hal read her hesitation accurately. "We'll get no more here. When he's done, he's done."

So Erde nodded and Gerrasch nodded with her.

"Yes, yes, yes, yes. Must go. Quick, quick, quick." He pulled his shoulder pouch around to the front again and began kneading it frantically. A dry crunching sound and the odor of crushed herbs filled the hut, sharp enough to cover even his own musky scent. "Good. Now, come."

He waddled toward the door, snatching up a small woven-grass basket as he went. He dumped its contents on the floor and shoved it into Erde's hands as she followed behind him. At the door, he stopped short and turned.

"No Dirt," he rasped at her. "No Dirt, no, no."

Erde spread her hands in confusion.

"He doesn't want to see the dragon," Hal translated. "I think he doesn't want any knowledge that could be taken from him by force."

"Force, no fear," Gerrasch grumbled. "Bigger magic."

Hal nodded darkly. "We should respect that. Tell Earth to stay well hidden."

Only when Erde had agreed did Gerrasch open the door. He stepped cautiously into the cool dappled light, blinking as if rushing into sudden sun. The distant baying had stopped. He made Erde hold out her little basket, then filled it with his herb mixture. "For later, yes?" The rest he scattered on the ground, circling his hut in a precise and ever widening spiral.

"Covering our tracks," murmured Hal. "He'll want us to do likewise on the way out."

"Good-bye, good-bye, good-bye," Gerrasch sang hoarsely as he broadcast his herbs like a farmer sowing corn.

Hal took Erde's arm and drew her toward the dragon's thicket "A pleasure as always, Gerrasch. I hope I haven't spent the good king's silver for nothing."

Much closer man before, the baying began again.

CHAPTER NINETEEN

A watery sun shone through the thinning mist. Hal hustled them to the lakeshore, avoiding the thorny tangle that barriered the land access to Gerrasch's clearing. There was not a breath of wind. The lake stretched southward like a clouded mirror.

"It's shallow. He'll have to dare it," Hal insisted as, with a snort, the dragon pulled up short at the water's edge.

When the hound sounded again, Earth waded in with the rest of them.

"He's getting braver," the knight approved. But Erde knew it was because the water was still. Earth could see the sandy bottom and knew it held no terrors for him. He was like a child in many ways, yet he was waking up, slowly but surely. She recalled Gerrasch's comment and wondered, *what will he be like when he's finally, fully awake?*

Hal set a stiff pace through the shallows, following the curve of the shore until a strip of graveled beach appeared. The gravel was coarse and tightly packed. They could move fast with hardly a sign left behind. He kept to the beach for a half mile or so, then turned abruptly inland where the underbrush thinned between the trees and the land rose away from the beach.

"Remember how Gerrasch tossed that stuff around? Follow me and do the same across our trail. The Mule can show Earth what to do."

Erde didn't need to tell the dragon anything. He was already watching the mule carefully, learning about animal stealth. The two of them slipped into the undergrowth without leaving a sign. The she-goat followed closely, and Erde fell in at the end of the line with her basket of herbs, scattering them carefully behind until she ran out. Hal climbed the rise along the shore and halted in the cover of a stand of branchy young pines perched on the edge of a low sandy cliff. He gestured them to silence and listened.

"Odd, isn't it. Still only the one dog."

Erde nodded. She thought the dog sounded hoarse and tired. Through the dense velvet of the pine boughs, the beach was just visible below. She felt Earth's anticipation in her mind. He was unsure, but his fear was tempered with a new sense of readiness.

"Perfect spot for an ambush," Hal murmured. "Or at least to discover what's following us." He whistled the mule to him, unstrapped his bow and quiver, then his sword. He set them carefully on the pine mat beside him like a carpenter laying out his tools. "The Mule can take you ahead while I reconnoiter."

Erde shook her head.

"I know, girl, but it's better than exhausting ourselves running to keep ahead of them."

She nodded as sagely as she knew how.

"Oh, no, you don't. You're not a fighting man just yet."

She unsheathed Alla's slim but deadly dagger. She had cleaned the blade scrupulously out on the moonless slopes of Tor Alte, and used it many times since as a cutting edge. But now as she looked at it, she was sure some of Georg's blood still stained the shining steel.

Hal saw her face twist and misunderstood. "But you'll be fine with the Mule. The Dragon will take care of you."

Even if she could speak, how could she explain? Tell him that guilt, not fear, weakened her? Fear was simple, men understood fear. Fear only needed to be overcome. But guilt? Most men would be proud to have killed in self-defense. Hal would lose his faith in her spirit, in her grand-mother's indomitable, supposedly inheritable spirit, and maybe so would she. Well, it didn't matter whether he un-derstood or not, she refused to be sent ahead into hiding with the dragon. He wouldn't have sent her grandmother into hiding. Erde caught hold of herself, grasped the knife with a firm hand, and struck a menacing pose.

Hal hid a wry smile. "Fine. You're not scared. I still can't allow it. Off with you, quickly!"

Erde planted her feet. It was the first time since the

knight had appointed himself her guardian that she'd thought to oppose him. He gazed back at her confounded, as if he'd just realized it wasn't actually his right to order her around.

"Milady, be sensible, please. For the Dragon's sake."

Erde felt Earth shuffle closer and settle down, his new readiness like a wall behind her, though the cry of the hound was nearing rapidly. Suddenly the baying stopped. The she-goat, forgotten in her self-made nest of pine needles, rose up and bounded out of the grove and down the steep slope toward the water. At the bottom, she slowed, then lowered her horned head to graze in slow casual circles along the beach.

"Well!" exclaimed the knight softly. "A full-blown mutiny! What's got into you all?"

Tired of running, Erde would have replied. She was not sure what the dragon had in mind. His nose was to the wind. He imaged one dog to her, and one man.

"Promise you'll sit down and keep still?" Hal went to the mule and quickly stripped off the rest of the packs.

Erde knew he would not debate Earth in serious matters. Complain as he might, the dragon's will was still this knight's command. He even looked pleased as he shrugged and settled himself to wait and watch for movement back the way they'd come. Minutes passed, silent but for the soft lapping of the lake and the drone of insects stirred by the pallid sun. Then, sporadic barking, a confused hound's query.

"He's lost the scent. Probably reached Gerrasch's clearing."

With a yelp of triumph, the baying began again. Unperturbed, the she-goat grazed a beach barren of anything that could have been of real interest to her.

"Here we go." Hal notched an arrow.

A large hound, of the brown and black long-eared breed common to Tor Alte's pack, burst through the trees at the far end of the beach. It flew along, nose to the ground and tail erect, singing its rhythmic song of encouragement to the hunter. Suddenly the breeze brought a distraction. The dog halted, looked about, spotted the she-goat, then cried out happily and charged. The she-goat drew herself into fighting posture and presented her horns. The hound neared, slowed, then ran back and forth before the goat, whining piteously.

Erde nudged Hal with a smile. Tor Alte's hunt pack was trained not to attack domestic animals. And she knew this dog. This dog had been one of her father's favorites, a strong bitch that ran well and produced fine litters. But she was no longer young, and as she paced closer, Erde saw she was exhausted and sweat-slathered, her short coat raked with brambles. Still she would pace and whine, until the Man arrived.

It's wrong to run a dog that hard. Erde started up from her crouch in protest.

Hal jerked her down reflexively, his eye fixed on the beach. "Where's the rest of the pack?"

Finally, a lone man armed with a crossbow detached himself from the trees along the shore, having decided no doubt that it was silly to conceal himself so carefully from someone's stray she-goat. One dog, as Earth had told her, and one man by himself. The dragon was learning that he possessed a remarkable nose. The man disarmed his crossbow and called to the dog, signaling her to circle and pick up the trail again. But the goat had walked her pattern over the trail, and Gerrasch's herbs had done the rest. The dog ran about, barking in frustration until the huntsman yelled at her to lie down and wait. She sank to the ground, panting.

The man approached slowly, and Erde saw it was the huntsman Griff, who'd served her grandmother so long and well.

"We know this one," remarked Hal.

Erde nodded. She did not recall Griff having a limp, but he was surely favoring his left leg, and looked as worn out as the dog. The two of them alone was odd enough, then she remembered that Griff was a fine horseman and always rode, even in deep forest or the worst terrain. She wondered what had become of his horse.

"One man, like Gerrasch said. Perhaps a conference is in order." Hal rose slowly, lowering his bow with the arrow still notched, and made a circling gesture to the mule. Erde caught his sleeve and indicated that she could deal with the hound. "All right, but keep at least ten paces apart from me at all times. Multiple targets." He jerked his chin at the dragon. "He stays hidden."

Erde sent stern visions to Earth, who was happy to stay put, once he'd spotted the huntsman's crossbow. *I guess you can't smell out a man's armaments,* she reasoned. She gripped her dagger and hauled her cloak up around her cheeks. While the mule approached noisily from the other direction, Hal and Erde crept down along the lowering cliff until it rejoined the beach. The huntsman was distracted by the mule. Before he could decide that there was something unnatural in this assemblage of farm animals alongside a deserted lake, Hal was within range behind him. Instinct made the huntsman turn, but Hal put an arrow in the sand between his feet and reloaded before he could set his crossbow. The hound growled and charged. Erde whistled, the way Rainer had taught her, and the dog slowed, whining, then swerved toward her and was soon dancing at her feet. She sheathed her dagger and knelt to greet it.

The huntsman, breathing hard, lowered his unarmed bow. His narrowed eyes flicked from Hal to Erde and back again.

"Are you alone, friend, as you appear to be?" asked Hal companionably.

"Appearances aren't everything. Who wants to know?" The man could not turn his attention from the odd behavior of his dog.

"We can have your army against my army," Hal replied, "or we can talk, like civilized men."

The huntsman searched the empty beach. The tree line was too far away for a limping, winded man to reach before the tall stranger's bow stopped him. Plus there was his dog, leaning happily against the smaller stranger's knee. "Alone," he conceded.

"And a little the worse for wear, I'd say."

The man stiffened proudly, though his breath was still labored. The side of his jaw was bruised and there was a fresh cut over his right eye. "I'm well enough, and I'll be on my way if you've no cause to detain me. I've nothing worth your while."

"I meant no offense. And we're no thieves, either."

The huntsman squinted into the pale sun, which Hal had put behind him. "What are you, then? What do you want?"

"Your name would be an excellent start."

The huntsman shrugged. He was shorter than Hal, though they were matched in age, and the knight was armed. "I travel from Tor Alte, with Baron Josef's Hunt."

"Tor Alte. A fair distance. East, as I recall? Does lack of game bring you so far? There's little enough to spare here as it is."

The man shook his head. "Answers for answers."

"Fair enough." Hal circled slowly until his face was no longer in shadow. "Of late, I come from Erfurt."

"Erfurt." Interest flickered in the huntsman's eyes, and was as quickly hidden.

"A friend to His Majesty."

Now the man's brow shot up. "A brave admission to a stranger in these days."

"Then judge me by it."

Erde absorbed this exchange intently, noting its ritualistic formality and how Hal had leaned on the word "friend," as if it meant more than it appeared to mean. The mention of the king seemed to raise a subtext far beyond the usual male sparring for position, as if Griff now saw this stranger as something more than the steely tip of an arrow pointed at his throat.

"You wear the King's Red," he noted.

"Aye."

Griff wet his lips, then said carefully, "A little the worse for wear, I'd say."

Finally, Hal grinned. "And what King's Knight would not be, in these days?"

"None who serves him truly."

"As did your lady, the Baroness Meriah."

The huntsman cocked his head, as if hearing a far-off bell. "Ah. I do know you, sir," he said slowly, "from long ago."

"Yes, you do." Hal lowered his bow. "Heinrich Engle."

"Griffen Hesse." The huntsman stepped forward to take the hand offered him, then stopped, recalling further. "No, it was . . . ." He stepped back, bowing. "Your pardon, sir. Wasn't it *von* Engle? Baron Weisstrasse?"

Erde threw Hal a look. He'd never said he was a *baron.*

"Aye, Griffen Hesse, but who can call himself baron, who's lost his lands and stronghold?" Hal kept his hand outstretched until the huntsman gave in to common courtesy and shook it. Erde recalled her father with this man, how he'd treated him like a stable hand. She admired Hal's more generous nature.

Griff found it admirable as well. The look he gave the knight was nostalgic. "That is the news in the marketplace, my lord, though there's some who'd rather not believe it. Some who'd prefer matters to be otherwise, even at Tor Alte itself."

Hal studied the huntsman speculatively, and Griff, perhaps worrying that he'd said too much, shifted and nodded at Erde. "Your lad there is good with a dog."

Hal barely spared her a glance. "Yes. He is. Have you left Tor Alte's service, then, Griff?"

The huntsman started. "No, my lord, I . . ." He faltered, frowning, then lowered his gaze to the sand. "Well, sir, it's possible they may take it that way. I haven't been too careful with my mouth."

"I know how that is." Hal nodded and whistled the mule over. "Have you eaten, Griff? Will you share a meager meal with us?"

Seated on a rotting log at the top of the beach, Hal doled out chunks of bread, then unwrapped their dwindling block of hard cheese. Its pungent odor made Erde's mouth water. She took her share and sat apart, as a proper prentice lad should do, but within listening range.

"No wine, I regret." Hal unstoppered his waterskin and offered it. "Where are you headed now?"

Griff glanced over at the hound, now folded in a pile by Erde's side. "Following the dog. On the trail of Baron Josef's daughter, who's run away."

Hal chuckled. "Eloped, you mean? Who's the lucky man?"

"No, my lord, it's nothing like that. My lady's but a child still, and the new hunt-master was sure we'd lost the scent. But I'd an inclination to follow my instincts. And my old Bet's nose."

"So there was, ah . . . ?"

"A parting of the ways, yes, there surely was, my lord." Griff's rueful grin was curtailed by his cuts and bruises.

"But the men didn't mix in, so I had the best of it, and off I went."

"You'll have made an enemy there, I fear."

"True enough. But it was that way anyway, my lord. Guess I'm just too old to start taking my orders from a fool whose only skill is telling young Baron Josef what he wants to hear."

Erde couldn't think of her father as young, but she understood how a loyal man like Griff would think anyone an upstart who presumed to succeed Baroness Meriah.

"So the girl just up and ran away?" asked Hal casually.

"Well, they say she was lured away by a witch's spell."

"Witches!"

"There's talk of witches all over east, sir."

"You sound skeptical, Griff."

"Oh, I'm as good a churchgoer as the next man, my lord. It's just that, well . . ." Griff fell silent a while, chewing his bread, then seemed to come to a decision. "Well, my lord baron, here's the truth of it, and I hope you'll pardon the mention. Young Josef's in the thrall of that same priest who they say turned you wrongly out of house and home. It's Fra Guill who's stirring up all this terror of witches and burning everyone he can get his hands on, and I just can't believe there's as many lurking about as he'd like us to think. But there's plenty who swear by his every word as if it were gospel. Now we're to be looking out for dragons as well."

"Dragons."

Griff eyed him carefully. "Yes, sir. In fact, I do believe your name's been mentioned in that regard, now that I think about it."

"Yes, that's how he usurped me. I'm suspect because of my innocent scholar's interest."

"It's worse than that now, sir. Dragons have been sighted, so they say. You're in league with Satan himself."

"Am I really? How interesting." Hal brushed dirt off his knees and straightened his jerkin. "The Prince of Darkness should take better care of his minions."

The huntsman laughed, a quick bark that spoke of a deep reservoir of anger. "The problem is, some fools will believe him."

Hal's jaw tightened. "My sword awaits him, priest or no."

"I'd do it myself, if I could get in range. He never goes anywhere without four stout men with him, his so-called brothers with short-swords beneath their robes. Does a true man of God need such protection?" Griff stretched legs and arms, warming to his complaint. "And young Josef—the baron, I mean—sits still for all this witch-talk that the baroness would never have allowed. He gives the priest the run of the castle, and takes him around to the other domains where the priest preaches hellfire to the people, then all the high-born sit up late carousing and plotting."

"Carousing and plotting." Hal sucked his teeth disconsolately. "At least that's nothing new."

"Aye, but usually they're plotting against each other." Having given rein to his tongue, Griff seemed in no mood to stop. "Now it seems there's an army being raised, my lord."

"An army?" Hal contrived to look skeptical, but this man's information was sure to be more than rumor. "What for?"

"The priest and the young baron call it a crusade of believers, gathering to rescue the kidnapped child from the Legions of Satan. And the countryside is in a terror, with no better explanation for their bad luck and misery. But, my lord . . ." Griff leaned closer and dropped his voice, despite their obvious solitude. "I could easily see how this 'crusade' might be aimed somewhere else. When we lost the girl's scent and the new hunt-master was so ready to turn back, the men thought it was fear of her witch-powers. But I had to wonder if he was under orders not to drift too far from Tor Alte, where the Hunt might be called upon to provision the kind of army whose loyalty depends on how well you feed them."

"To many, a full belly is reason enough to offer one's sword in service these days."

"There are not deer enough in the forests for that kind of army."

Hal leaned in closer, elbows on knees. "Aimed where else, Griff?"

"I think you can guess, my lord."

Hal's fists clenched. "At the king! Of course! Times are bad and the throne is now truly vulnerable. That hell-priest has allied himself with the barons' cabal, or they with him.

I wonder who's using who. Where is this army? Who else is involved?"

"So far, the army is only a few hundred men marching about under Baron Josef's command, rousting out sinners and witches, and emptying out the peasants' larders in the process. But word is, others are preparing, may even be on the road already. The cabal, as you say, flocking to the priest's crusade." He cleared stones with a sweep of his hand and sketched a rough map in the sand. "Stürn, Dubek and Zittau in the east, Rathenow and Schoenbeck in the north, and then Köthen, your old neighbor."

Hal started. "Köthen? The old man?"

"The elder lord is dead, sir, just last year."

"Not *young* Köthen? In arms against the king?"

"That's not what they call it, my lord."

"Yes, yes. A 'crusade.' Is there any resistance? I must get to the king. Does no one call them traitors?"

"Who'd dare oppose the word of the Church? A mere whisper of disapproval and there's a white-robe in your courtyard, sniffing out witch-plots."

"Stürn and Rathenow I'd expect, but Köthen! The king's own nephew, who fostered the crown prince! I can't . . . I must . . . I've wandered enough!" Hal's outrage forced him upward into motion. He paced the sand in broad, abrupt strides. "Isn't it enough that they hold the real power? Now they want the throne for themselves?"

Griff glanced up and down the beach before nodding once. "And I'll have none of it. But I'm outnumbered at Tor Alte right now, so off I came, after the girl. If she really has been witched, so much the worse for me, but a man's got to have a purpose in life, and the trail's old but not yet dead." He ran a scarred hand through his thinning hair and smiled slyly. "Like ourselves, sir, you know what I mean?"

Hal snorted, then laughed outright, his rage deflected as an idea came to him. "Indeed I do." He sat down again and passed along the last of the bread, together with another thin slice of the cheese. "Suppose I was to suggest to you another purpose?"

Griff studied his food thoughtfully. "I might find myself listening, my lord."

"Go back. Be the king's eye at Tor Alte, or if possible,

with Baron Josef's army. You could start by spreading word that the baron's daughter is dead."

The huntsman chewed on a curl of crust. "How do you figure that, my lord?"

"Well, if the witch-child is dead, what further excuse for a crusade?"

"They'll say dragons, or the weather. They'll not back off now. It's gone too far."

"Then let it go farther!" Hal's eyes took fire again. His back straightened. "Force them to show their colors! Call it what it already is, what it's been for the last two years! A full-fledged baron's revolt!"

Griff eyed him with wary respect.

"We're not the only ones getting old, Griff. But His Majesty is not dead yet, and his son's a fool whose only asset is his legitimacy. No, don't look scandalized. You know it's true, and so does the king. He takes his help where he can find it."

The huntsman considered this, taking the time to finish off his bread and savor the last of his cheese. "The people do cry out for a leader, sir. Oh, I mean, not where a peer or a white-robe can hear them, but there's hope and desperation enough out there to stoke the wildest rumors. I've heard a few already."

"I'm sure." Hal shook his head warningly. "But when people look for messiahs, they end up with Fra Guill. We must be our own salvation, I fear."

"Yes, sir. But now, what of the girl? I feel . . . well, the baroness' own granddaughter—shouldn't someone be looking for her?"

"The girl is safe."

"Ah." The huntsman nodded slowly.

"She's suffered greatly and needs more than anything else to be free of pursuit."

"Hmmm. Well."

"I cannot tell you where she is or how I know this, but you can take it to be true, upon my honor. So, will you do it? Will you carry the lie back to Tor Alte?"

Griff grinned at him. "I suppose if you were a warlock like the priest is saying, you could just witch me into doing your bidding."

"I'd prefer that the king's name had that power."

"And so it does, my lord. So it does."

*   *   *

By midday, the beach was swept clear of their traces and the huntsman had begun his journey back to Tor Alte to spread Hal's "righteous lie."

TO THE WOMEN NOW? Erde scrawled on the sand as the knight checked the fastenings of the mule's packs.

"To the Women, yes. You listen well."

WHAT WOMEN?

"Oh, some friends of mine."

AND GERRASCH.

Hal cocked an eyebrow. "Yes, his also, and you could learn from the old bast— . . . your pardon, my lady. You play the squire so well, I keep forgetting . . . the old *gentleman's* example: the less you know, the less you can betray."

I WOULDN'T TELL.

"No, not if you could help it." He tightened a final knot with an unnecessarily abrupt jerk. The mule glanced around in surprise. "If Fra Guill will burn innocent women, don't you think he'd relish getting his hands on someone like Gerrasch? Someone truly unconventional, someone 'unnatural' who roots around in the forest gathering herbs and dabbling in magic? I can feel the heat of the stake already. It wouldn't be pretty."

IS GERRASCH A WITCH?

"Milady, please!" Hal quickly obliterated her words with his foot. "Gerrasch is one of God's Holy Innocents, though I doubt the hell-priest would see it that way. So remember, his safety depends on our discretion."

Erde took his cue and carefully scuffed away the rest of her scribblings. Hal seemed to have a lot of friends who required this special secrecy. Erde knew she must honor that need as long as she continued to accept his protection and advice, which she must until she got where she was going. But she could see she was not always going to agree with him.

For instance, she was not entirely comfortable with the notion of the "righteous" lie. She pondered this during their long hours heading southwest into the hills at the far end of the lake. At first she'd thought it would serve her father right to hear the gruesome tale that Hal and Griff had concocted between them, her tragic death by drowning in an icy torrent, her broken body swept away over the falls. She conjured satisfying visions of a remorseful baron, too grief-stricken to leave his rooms. But picturing Tor Alte as she trudged along yet another rocky and unknown road made her homesick for the castle and the life she'd known. Even though her rational self knew that life was ended forever, the child in her longed for it anyway. She began to feel a bit sorry for her father, to regret that she had allowed such a terrible lie to be sent to him. It seemed the burden of her guilt would never lighten, only increase in this inexorable fashion.

YOU WERE GOOD WITH GRIFF, she wrote during a hasty break for a meal. Though they'd been traveling for several hours already, the huntsman's news had made Hal as impatient as the hound had been. He worried aloud about the king, and cursed himself for not staying in Erfurt, under cover, to be there when his sovereign needed him. He talked of armies and strategies and the various possibilities of alliance as he saw them. He muttered about where one could hide something as big as a dragon. He felt they were rested enough and ought to press onward through the night. She had to jog his elbow to bring his attention to her dusty scrawl.

"Good? You mean I was nice to him?"

CLEVER.

Hal studied the letters in the sand as if they might rearrange themselves to read something different. "You're implying manipulation, aren't you." When she gazed back at him noncommittally, he laughed out loud. "Ha! I do perceive Meriah's steel in you! Of course I manipulated him, but not as in playing with him or using him without his knowledge—I merely turned his head so he could view the situation clearly." Hal swept his arm in a wide arc as if the valley behind them with its gray lake and dark trees were the only kind of view he meant. "So he could see where his interests might intersect with ours. That's called diplomacy."

CRAFT.

"Ha! *States*craft!" he declared. "Well, that's what I'm good at—my gift, you might say. For twenty years I've put it at the service of our king, an itinerant manner of service your grandmother never really understood either, but a crucial one to monarchs nonetheless."

HOW CAN A LIE BE RIGHTEOUS? Erde scrawled stubbornly.

"When it will forward the righteous cause." The knight watched her consider this, then added, "Perhaps expedient is more accurate, the *expedient* lie. Does that rest better with your conscience, my lady?"

Erde shook her head.

"You see no difference between our little lie that might save your life and the great big lie Fra Guill is using to raise up an army against you? An army, child! An *army!*"

F.G. IS NOT RIGHTEOUS.

"And I am? Well, thank you for that, at least. I do consider myself a righteous man, imperfect but at least trying to do what's right."

WHAT IS RIGHT?

"Phew! You need a priest, not an old soldier! I mean, a real priest." Hal looked so confounded that Erde finally had an inkling of how the dragon must feel when she could offer nothing profound enough to answer one of his all-encompassing questions. With a look of apology, she wiped the dirt smooth and rephrased her thought.

I AM NOT RIGHTEOUS.

He smiled. "Why ever not? Did you steal a few too many sweets or mumble your prayers at Sunday mass?"

His gentle condescension provoked her pride and a scowl. Impulsively, she wrote, I KILLED A MAN.

Hal read, then glanced up at her quickly. "You did? When?"

ESCAPING.

"Killed? Not just wounded or . . ."

She underlined 'killed,' and lifted Alla's dagger briefly from its sheath.

"So it's not all tall tales they're spreading."

Erde placed her palm over the offending word. She was surprised what a relief it was to tell him at last, to admit her dreadful crime, the crime that burdened her so that each day she trudged along carrying the weight of two. Three, if she counted Alla. Three deaths? Was it three deaths on her conscience? Erde shook her head to clear a sudden fog of confusion. Why did she think it was three when she could only remember Georg and Alla?

"Would this man you . . . killed have prevented your escape?"

She nodded, still distracted.

"Was escape necessary to your survival?"

Erde made herself focus on him. She could tell where his argument was going and did not want him rationalizing for her. She'd hoped he would scold her, or at least glare at her disapprovingly, this "righteous" man. Then she could feel somewhat punished for her sin. But he was taking it ever so calmly. She tried to imagine what penance Tor Alte's chaplain would have exacted in response to such a confession.

"Would this man you killed have hurt you to prevent your escape?"

Erde shuddered at the memory of what he would have done, his invasive touching and clutching, which brought back vividly the memory of what she *had* done. Hal saw tears well in her eyes. He picked a bit of brush to sweep her confession into blank forgiving dust.

Then he said, "Dear girl, just as there can be a righteous lie, there can be a righteous killing. Not a mere expedient, but the only right choice given the circumstances. Self-defense. What would the Dragon have done if his Guide had died before finding him? These are choices we must make, and there will be many such. Then we live with the burden that righteousness has placed on us for acting for its sake. I wish I could tell you that my own experience has been otherwise. Meanwhile . . ." He reached over and clasped her shoulder warmly. "Congratulations. We'll make a soldier out of you yet!"

And Erde thought, *I should have known he'd take it that way.* Even so, she knew his answer, however practical, was one she would never be entirely comfortable with.

CHAPTER TWENTY

They traveled through the night, a long shallow climb into lightly wooded hills where narrow streams fell back along curving lowland glens toward the lake. Despite all indications that Griff meant what he said and could be trusted, Hal wanted to put as much distance as possible between them and the baron's disaffected huntsman. Once he made them freeze, like deer in torchlight, thinking he'd heard the rattle of harness and armor moving past in a valley below them. Skittish, he skirted the open meadows, where the grass was tall and damp, taking the time to go the long way around within the deeper shadow of the tree line. He was not happy that the she-goat lagged so far behind, catching up on her grazing while there was good grass to be had.

"But I'd sure like a moon tomorrow to see our way by, when the going really gets rough," he remarked as they rested beneath a large oak, the biggest Erde had ever seen. In the darkness, she could only guess at its true size from the great girth of its trunk. Hal laughed as she stretched her arms around it.

"I can tell you're a mountain girl. This tree's a midget compared to some of the oldsters along the river near Erfurt."

Erde was content with just the sighing sound of it. She wandered around trying to reach a lower branch. She thought its leaves must be huge, in scale with the trunk, for it to make so heavy and melancholic a rustling.

The hills got steeper as they went on, and the trees closer together. It also got colder. When they finally made camp at first-light, Hal insisted on their weapons practice, and Erde was willing to give up the last of her strength to it because she stayed warmer when she was moving than when she sat still. Afterward, she was too tired to struggle with the stale bread and dried venison that was all that remained of their food supplies. She fell asleep propped up against the dragon's side, with a cup of goat's milk in her hand. Hal eased the chased silver out of her grip and drained the milk himself, then laid her wool cloak over her and let her sleep.

He retired to his bedroll and sat staring at the little cup, letting the gray morning light swell until he could make out the Weissstrasse coat-of-arms embossed on its side. He traced the emblem with his fingertip, then sighed and tossed the cup back in his pack.

Earth dreamed again that sleep-time, more vividly than he had since Hal had joined them. The dream seemed as real to Erde as her own life, and the Summoning took on a new urgency. Later, she recalled an endless enclosing maze of corridors, and knew it was a city, though unlike any city she had ever imagined. The walls were hard and cold and shining dully like the blade of a knife. Where the passages turned, the corners were as sharp as broken glass. The floor was a grid of metal strips, laid with spaces between, like rows and rows of tiny windows, so that Erde could see through them into the vast and roaring distance below. As always, there was the bitter smell, and the smoke and clang of the forge or something like it, so much more acrid and more deafening than the forge she knew at home.

For the first time, she saw herself and the dragon in the dream together, as if she were watching it from outside, yet still hurrying down the corridors, her lungs aching, the metallic air sharp on her tongue, desperate to get Somewhere, only they didn't know where. The voice of the Summoner rang in their ears like a cry of pain.

Ahead, another razor-edged corner, then the corridor darkened and stretched away for an endless distance, as straight as a stone mason's plumb line. They knew that the Summoner was at the end of that distance, and the dragon began to run, so fast that Erde could not keep up. She snatched at him, caught hold of the end of his stubby tail, and was jerked off her feet to be carried aloft behind him, like a battle pennant.

In the nearer distance, the corridor bloomed with sudden brightness. A man of light on a horse of fire, an armored knight with a shining silvered lance, wreathed in glowing smoke. He wore a golden circlet on his helmet, a crown. His visor was down. She was grateful that she could not see his face, for rays of incandescence leaked through the ventings and she knew his face would blind her. His shield, a perfect circle, bore a strange emblem, rather like a spi-raled compass rose, dividing it into four nested arcs like the bowls of spoons lying one against the other. Again, these spaces were like separate window openings. Through one, Erde saw trees and rolling meadows; through another, green water and foam-crested waves. The third arc showed a dark mountain ablaze with a fountain of fire, and beyond the fourth was only air, as blue and empty as the sky.

She urged the dragon onward, to get a closer look. But as they sped toward the unknown knight, he seemed to get farther away, shrinking like a dying flame until he was only a pinpoint, as tiny and brilliant as a star. The bright circle of his crown persisted momentarily, and then he was gone. As his light faded in the darkening corridor, the Summoner shrieked and moaned like a mad thing, and the walls trem-bled with her grief.

Erde woke to the rending cries of the woman she'd seen burned at the stake. Half in, half out of dream, she real-ized it was the she-goat, bleating in terror. Across the clearing, Hal swung upright on his bedroll with a shouted oath of surprise. A harsh red dusk was falling. The trees thrashed violently, though there was no wind. Erde thought the big oak would uproot itself. The ground heaved beneath them.

The dragon was still deep in his dreaming. Erde shouted him awake with a barrage of thought. He stirred, lifted his head, and the ground quieted.

Hal continued swearing until he'd gotten hold of himself, then he and Erde stared at each other across the strewn contents of the mule packs, scattered by the rolling of the ground.

"Terra is suddenly not so firma," he remarked at length.

"Is it over?" He groaned to his feet, dusting himself off unnecessarily. He looked around, noted the she-goat struggling up on wobbly knees by the base of the big oak. "Earthquake. Must be." He coughed, then shrugged. "I've heard of them happening farther south, but here . . . ? Where's the Mule, I wonder?"

Erde rolled over and hugged the dragon's rough-skinned foreleg. His golden eyes were as wide as she'd ever seen them, and he was shaking.

—*Earth, you were dreaming again.*

His brain still racked with nightmare, Earth relayed an apology.

—*No, it's all right, only . . . the ground moved.*

Earth agreed that it had.

Erde sat back on her heels, studying him pensively. The obvious, sensible explanation was that the agitation of the ground had sparked the trembling in the dragon's dream. But she'd been sure when she awoke that it was the other way around. She cleared a patch of dirt and tried the idea out on Hal.

"Yeah, he was dreaming . . . And?"

THE GROUND MOVED.

"So?" He looked around, whistling for the mule.

Erde added HE DREAMED at the beginning of the phrase.

Hal licked his lips, looked at the dragon, looked at her. "What are you saying?"

She shrugged, then put a period after HE DREAMED.

"Oh, no. No, no, no. Not possible. The earth does not move to any command but God's, not even for dragons."

NAMED EARTH, Erde scrawled, unable to stop herself. Then to keep from feeling completely crazy, she added a question mark.

"Earth . . . quake. Hmm." Hal grew thoughtful, then with a flick of his eyebrows, dismissed the notion as insane. "What does *he* say?"

HE DOESN'T REMEMBER. HE WAS

Hal stayed her hand. "I know, I know—he was asleep."

Erde nodded.

The knight rolled his eyes and went off in search of his mule.

*   *   *

Earth was skittish that evening. First he wanted to stay in the oak clearing and not move until they'd discussed his dream in lengthy detail. When Hal insisted it was perfectly normal to walk and discuss at the same time, the dragon came along, but he stuck very close to Erde, crowding her sometimes dangerously as they moved into the dense and rocky woodlands of the upper hills.

Erde took extra care to avoid getting stepped on, and did not scold him. She knew how anxious the dream and its aftermath had made him. It had made her anxious, too. She wondered if the sudden sharp chill in the air, like the first tang of winter, had anything to do with the earthquake. Hal was more than usually pensive as well. He had not been granted the moon he'd wished for, and the climb was getting steeper and rockier, their footing increasingly treacherous, with roots and loose stones hidden beneath a slippery layer of leaves. He let the mule lead the way, and they stumbled upward in near blackness, each wrapped in the separate silences of concentration.

But eventually, Hal could contain himself no longer.

"How could he make the ground move?"

His question was rhetorical, since Erde had no way in the darkness to provide an answer, even if she'd had one to offer. She wondered why this latest surprise bothered him particularly, when he was so ready to believe the dragon capable of all sorts of miracles. In fact, expected him to be. Erde wished the knight would stop focusing on what a dragon *should* do, and concentrate on what this dragon *could* do, especially while Earth was struggling so hard to discover what his skills were. Hal was like a stern parent disapproving of a brilliant child because its gifts were not as orderly or predictable as he'd like them to be.

Erde suspected that magic was neither orderly nor predictable. She thought it peculiar that the knight seemed to divide the miraculous into categories: this is possible, this isn't. But she had to keep in mind Hal's long years studying dragon-lore. When a man has devoted himself that passionately to something, he's bound to want to see it proven right. Perhaps he just needed enough time with each new bit of information to fit it into his own scheme of things.

Sure enough, half a mile later, he cleared his throat tentatively. "Well. Let's say it's possible. Maybe it is. If it is, is it something he can control?"

She did not know, and neither did the dragon.

And later, she could hear the ghost of a smile in his voice. "You think he'll be practicing moving the earth over and over again, like he does with becoming invisible?"

Erde did know the answer to that one. The quake had terrified Earth. He had no desire to feel the ground move again just yet, or even to attempt doing it on purpose. Mostly, he wanted to think about it and what it meant and, to Erde's dismay, ask her a million other questions that she couldn't answer.

After a rest and a meal break, their ascent grew so sharp that in places Erde had to haul herself upward with her hands. But the trees thinned and the moon at last made a fitful appearance, slipping in and out of slow-drifting veils of cloud. Their route lay over solid rock now, pale ledges each the size of a castle yard, like a vast staircase aspiring to be a mountain. Small trees huddled in hollows where soil had gathered. Tufts of brush bunched in the seams and cracks, and here and there thin grass softened the weathered granite.

The dragon hated the climbing. His thick-limbed body was not built for hauling its own great weight straight upward for hour after hour. His gleaming ivory claws were not meant for gripping stone. He gave Erde to understand that he was sure there was a better way to travel, if only he could remember what it was. She urged him to try, but he could only picture himself first in one place and then in another, with no idea of how he might actually accomplish getting there. Erde worried that he might be feeling bad about his lack of wings—he'd heard Hal complain about it often enough. It occurred to her as she urged him up a particularly steep ledge that each of them were defective in some vital way: Earth had no wings, she had no voice. It was probably why they had ended up together.

The thought made her sigh, and she was tired of sighing. A sigh was an irritatingly melancholy sound but the only one besides a cough or a sneeze that she could still produce. She decided she would ask the knight to teach her how to whistle, something even her grandmother had not allowed her to do.

"Ladies do not whistle," the baroness had always insisted when Erde expressed envy of the stable boys. They could hear a tune once, then whistle it again whenever they wanted to. Erde understood that it might not be appropriate for ladies to whistle in public, but wouldn't it be a good thing to know how to do, to amuse yourself when you were alone? Not that she'd spent much time alone growing up in Tor Alte. That was another thing ladies did not do. If she wasn't with Alla or the baroness, there was Fricca, or some chambermaid. There was always somebody watching, telling her what to do and what not to do.

She thought about all this as they topped a particularly barren rise. The way they'd come spread out behind them in an endless march of nighttime hills glazed with moonlight. Far off, the ghostly shimmer of the lake—and beyond . . . ? Now that Gerrasch had mentioned a city, she was coming to believe that there might actually be such a gathering place for mages. Idly, she conjured the slim spires of her fantasy, to glow like a mirage on the horizon. She felt the dragon in her mind, imaging it with her, and saw its towers grow more real before her very eyes under the power of his belief in it. The breeze gusting across the ledge was damp and raw with chill, but Erde was conscious of how deeply she could breathe, of the sense of lift and freedom that came from being surrounded by all that open space. She felt hopeful. Like a bird must feel, just before taking wing. There were advantages to leaving home, she realized, beyond the obvious one of her survival. She doubted if Hal would ever say, "Ladies do not whistle." Most ladies did not learn to use a sword, either.

From the crags ahead came a sudden distant yowl. The mule's long ears flicked, and the she-goat glanced up sharply from the bush she was eating. The mirage towers vanished, leaving only a darkly crenelated, threatening horizon.

"Wildcat," noted Hal. "Best stick close from now on. We're not the only hungry creatures out prowling these hills tonight."

Erde shrugged her cloak more tightly about her shoulders. Free or not, she wondered if she would ever be warm again.

The intemperate yowl of the cat seemed to follow them, fading in and out with the rush of the wind as they struggled over ledge and through gorge. The mountain brush was as rough as the rock. Erde's cheeks and lips were chapped from the icy gusts. Her hands stung with scrapes and scratches and the brittle ends of thorns. She had thought she was hardened to travel, but her knees and ankles ached from the constant up and down. Hal had never pushed them this punishingly before. For the dragon's sake as well as for her own, Erde insisted they stop more often than Hal was willing to. Always he would offer a courtly apology for tiring them, then want to be off again the next moment.

"Not much farther," he'd promise, already in motion up the slope. "Not much farther." He was tireless, eager, driven, a man with a real destination finally in mind.

She knew they were descending when the wind stopped screaming in her ears, but it still felt as much up as down, and the going did not get any easier. It clouded up again and they lost the little bit of light the moon had offered. Then it began to sleet, a fine blowing frozen mist that invaded Erde's eyes and nose like needles and melted into the layers of her clothing. Twice she lost her footing in a slide of ice and loose gravel, and went tumbling to the bottom of a slope with Hal shouting after her to grab on to something, anything she could, and the dragon wailing in her brain not to leave him out there alone in the darkness. Each time, after Hal had made his way down to help her up, he reminded her how lucky it was she hadn't slipped beside the edge of a cliff, and she began to have some notion of how infuriating, even heartless a man can be when in the throes of some particular obsession.

The dragon had begun to mutter, at least Erde had come to think of it as muttering, the peculiar grunting sound he made when he was fretting about something. This time it was a scent his clever nose had caught but could not identify. He tried relaying it to Erde in the same way he sent images, and she recalled how vivid the odors always were when she shared the dragon's nightmares. But awake, her mental nose was no more sensitive or sophisticated than her anatomical one, so she was no help to him. Earth kept muttering. Obviously the smell was not going away.

The rain tapered off as the clouds thinned again. Ahead of them rose a rank of tall stones, standing almost upright like a slightly drunken army at attention. The mule disappeared among them and the rest followed. Erde heard Hal cursing under his breath as they threaded almost by feel the narrow alley between towering walls of rock. Then a screech and a bleat behind them stopped him cold.

"It's that cat! It's got the goat!"

He whirled to race back to the aid of the she-goat, but the dragon blocked his path. As the goat's outrage escalated into shrieks of panic, Earth struggled to turn himself around, wrenching his bulk from side to side, his claws grinding uselessly against the rock. The shadowy shape of him bucked and swayed, and for a moment, Erde was convinced she saw him blur and fade, blur and fade, then grow substantial once again. She blinked hard, several times. Perhaps she had stared too long, trying to make him out clearly in the darkness, or perhaps . . .

—*This is no time to go invisible,* she warned him. All she sensed in return was a wall of desperation that also danced in and out of substance, as if Earth's existence itself was wavering.

Then new pandemonium broke out behind him. The cat yowled in fury. A moment later, the she-goat came scrambling over the dragon's back, nearly bowling Erde over as she bolted past and collapsed against Hal's legs. The cat did not follow.

Hal knelt over the goat, feeling for damage. "Bit of a mess here . . . that's quite a gash there. Be all right if the bleeding stops." He tried to get her up on her feet but she kept sinking back against him. "Come on now, girl, I can't be carrying you."

Earth crowded in, his great head wedged between Erde and the rock wall. Hal stood back, offering what little room he could. The dragon nosed at the goat, sniffing and muttering. In the dark, Erde could not quite tell what he was up to. She worried that he might at last be considering a meal, if only to put the wounded goat out of her misery.

But listening carefully, Erde realized that he was licking her, his huge rough tongue making great doglike swipes across her back, nearly enveloping her horned head and her stick-thin legs. He did not stop until he had licked her all over at least once, and her fur was damp with his saliva. Then he scooped her up in his jaws and stood there, holding her delicately, waiting for the humans to proceed.

"He exhibits a most generous nature," noted Hal. "Unusual in a dragon to be so sensitive to the needs of lesser creatures."

Erde knew he was alluding to Earth's peculiar hunting habits, which were inconvenient if, like the knight, you wished to keep your dragon well fed. But she thought that if dragons were, as Hal claimed, the most perfect of God's creations on Earth, they very well ought to have generous natures. Unlike Man, or most men anyway, who were—judging from her recent experience—the most imperfect. She did notice that whenever Hal expounded on the nature of a "proper" dragon, even speaking in the arcane language of the dragon-lore, it sounded more like what he'd want a leader of men to be, for instance, the king he served so loyally. High expectations indeed. But a man could not be a dragon, nor a dragon a man. No wonder the knight was so often disappointed in both.

They came down out of the standing stones without further mishap, beyond a few additional scrapes and bruises. The icy rain had stopped. The moon had set, but the sky seemed to be clearing at last. In between the scudding shadows of clouds, a few stars could be seen. They reached level ground, a broad grassy ledge, and Hal whistled to call back the mule. Erde heard water falling over rock somewhere in the darkness.

"We'll stop here for the rest of the night." Hal tossed down his shoulder pack and stretched. "We need to get warm, so we'll risk building a fire, if we can find anything up here to burn."

Earth lumbered about with the goat suspended in his mouth until he found a spot to his liking. Erde heard him scratching up grass and dirt into a sort of nest to lay her in. When he was done, the goat curled up in it immediately and went to sleep as if drugged.

Erde helped Hal search out stray twigs and branches for
the fire, then walked carefully to the edge of the ledge,
where the rock sheered away sharply as if cut with a knife.
Beyond, she could see nothing but the deepest night, but
she sensed a large volume of space just past this pale,
white-veined border, and was intrigued by the current of
distinctly warmer air rising up out of the void.

When Hal had managed a small fire, she went over and
cleared her usual pallet-in-the-dirt.

WARM! she wrote, inscribing an arrow in the direction
of the edge.

"Yes," Hal agreed. "It's quite remarkable, really." And
then, despite every strategy she could muster, all during the
parceling out of their meager meal and until she finally
gave in to her exhaustion, he refused to elaborate further.

Erde woke in daylight, curled up between the she-goat
and the dragon, conscious of the sound of birds and an
unusual sense of well-being. Frost lay white in the hollows
of the ledge, but the sun on her shoulder was actually
warm. She sat up carefully, to avoid jostling the injured
animal. The goat stirred with her and rose easily to her
feet. Her eyes were bright and her carriage erect and lively.
Her spotted coat gleamed like new-spun wool, with no sign
of blood or wounds anywhere. She shook herself like a dog
and trotted off toward the sound of falling water.

Erde glanced around for Hal, to bring this new amazement to his attention. Then she caught sight of the view.
Scrambling up, she ran to the edge of the ledge to stare in
wonder. The dragon roused himself and followed.

A valley spread out beneath them, all green and golden
in the softly angled rays of the mid-afternoon sun. Like the
valley in her dreams, not the rank nightmares she now
shared with the dragon, but from her childhood, her dreams
of the "safe place," the holy landscape, what her grandmother always called Arcadia.

The valley was long and narrow, embraced by a high
palisade of rugged hills such as she had just endured. From
the rolling prairie far below, sheer cliffs rose abruptly on
all sides, to a point level with Erde's ledge, as if the entire
valley had broken free at once and dropped away into the
earth. Thin white cataracts plummeted down the cliff face,

then snaked in shining ribbons to meet the river that wound and sparkled between velvety patches of forest dotting the bottom land. Huge flocks of birds rose in arching coordinated flight. Above, a pair of hawks circled. Erde heard their screeching blown on the breeze, but nowhere could she spot a sign of human habitation.

And then there was the warmth, a soft draft like a breath from below, carrying the scents of summer. Earth hunkered down to arch his long neck over the edge. He inhaled deep inquiring breaths. The old image of fat white sheep ghosted into Erde's head and made her laugh, a soundless explosion of spontaneous joy.

—It isn't the Mage City yet, but it's almost as good.

Daydreaming succulent sheep, the dragon agreed.

"Ready for a little exercise?" Hal appeared beside them with the practice swords, his hair and beard dripping from a dunk in the waterfall. He waved an arm at the valley, grinning from ear to ear. She had never seen him so pleased. But he still would not tell her where they were or what they'd find, once they'd braved the final precipitous descent.

Erde remembered the goat and dragged him over for a look. Hal's solicitous inspection grew more amazed and deliberate as he discovered no fresh wounds anywhere, only the occasional pink glow of scar tissue.

"Maybe the cat never actually broke skin. Maybe she was just wet from all that mud and ice."

But Erde shook her head vehemently. She had seen the dark blood glimmer the night before and felt it, slick and hot, turning cold on her hands.

"Well, it was the cat's blood, then," Hal protested. "No wound heals that fast! Unless she's magic." This thought made him laugh for some reason, and he put the mystery aside for the time, sending the goat on her way with a bemused slap on her rump. "The Mule's gone on ahead— our 'magic' goat can lead us down this time."

CHAPTER TWENTY-ONE

Erde shed her thick woolen cloak after the first few switchbacks of the long descent. Though it was still damp from the rain, she stuffed it unceremoniously into her shoulder pack and wished the mule was there to carry it for her. Next she found herself loosening the collar tie of her linen shirt. For the first time since leaving Tor Alte, there were too many layers, her clothes felt too heavy. She was actually hot.

She'd forgotten what it was like to be free of rain and mud and sleet, free of the confining weight of wool and padding. She inhaled the perfumed air and felt as light as a feather floating on it. She flapped her arms experimentally, like a dark-headed stork considering flight. Earth picked up this image from her as he lowered himself step by ponderous step behind her. He sent back panicked entreaties of caution. Erde giggled voicelessly, giddy with heat and her newfound sense of freedom. Then a stone rolled beneath her heel and nearly sent her cascading over the edge into oblivion.

Hal heard the clatter of pebbles and glanced around sharply. "Do not, I repeat, do NOT hurry. The way is treacherous."

The dragon echoed this sentiment.

Yes, it's treacherous, thought Erde, *but so was every place we've come from, and at least this has a path.* She was eager to get down it. It was narrow, slippery and steep, but appeared to be a used thoroughfare. Mostly by animals, perhaps, being too precipitous to be satisfactory to any but the truly surefooted. Still, it gave her hope that they might actually be going somewhere, not just wandering about in the wilderness, as she'd sometimes begun to think. If they were getting somewhere, she reassured the dragon, they might actually find their Mage City. To please him, she conjured the familiar cluster of tall towers gleaming at the end of a long white road. She breathed in the sweet warm scent of the rising air and watched the elegant dance of the hawks wheeling in the sun. She could feel the sun and sudden warmth working on the dragon as well. He, too, watched the birds, with wonder and longing. She tried picturing him with wings, vast gossamer webs like Glasswind's, all the colors of the rainbow. It wasn't right, somehow. It didn't fit. But she could imagine him in flight, the two of them together, not soaring like the hawks, but . . . *traveling*.

"Milady, pay attention!" Hal warned again as she stumbled into him with her eyes fixed on the sky.

They came down off the cliff through an old fall of boulders that spilled out across the bottomland like a stone archipelago in a sea of waving green, a green so rich it seemed to vibrate before Erde's eyes. The soft air was pungent with odors. It went to her head, as if she'd inhaled a sweet young wine. Ahead, the trail vanished beneath waist-tall grass. The she-goat stopped immediately to graze. Hal stripped to his jerkin, tossed his cloak over his shoulder, and struck out confidently across the plain toward a grove of trees in the near distance. The swish of the grass against their boots was like the breathing of large animals. Erde followed dreamily, dazed with sun and heat and sweetness, and the suddenness of the change.

The grove was a large circle of oak trees, thick-trunked and ancient. Their broad outer limbs arched high, then swooped nearly to the ground, enclosing a leafy cavern within their shade, paved with moss and rounded stones like river rock. A peaceful stillness hovered there, a sense of refuge and contentment. Erde was reminded of the great-hall of Tor Alte, with its treelike columns and branching rafters. This grove had the same grace but lacked its chill solemnity. Small creatures busied themselves everywhere, among the leaf piles and in the burrows between the spreading roots. In the center of this shadowed whispering space, where the branches thinned, a shaft of sunlight filtered in onto a small still pond. On the grassy shore, a cairn of rocks stood guard over a herd of drinking deer. Nearby lingered one or two very thick and shaggy brown creatures that Erde decided must be cattle of some wild variety. As they approached the cairn, she saw the flat top stone was piled with wildflowers as fresh and bright as if they'd just been picked. The deer lifted their heads, muzzles dripping sparkling beads of water. They seemed merely curious, breathing in man-scent and dragon-scent as if both were simply information, then moving away slowly to graze or lie down in the deeper shade.

Erde sensed Earth's quickening interest and his hunger, and felt both consciously set aside. He raised his own great head, deerlike, testing the air, and promptly vanished.

Hal knelt for a drink at the pond. "He's getting very good at that, but why . . . ?"

A voice hailed them, a cheery greeting from the far side of the copse. Out of the shadows trotted the mule. In place of his pack and harness, he bore a smiling woman, sitting astride his bare back, at ease and waving gaily. Erde pulled her prentice cap down over her ears and tried to think herself back into her disguise. As the mule shambled to a halt in front of them, the woman slid off gracefully, planted her sandaled feet, and spread her arms wide.

She was small, a head shorter than Erde, with delicate ankles visible below the shin-length hem of her loose-fitting garment. The soft white fabric was dye-printed in shades of blue, birds in flight. Erde could see that the full skirt was split, like baggy leggings. She was instantly envious. This was exactly the sort of garment she had always wanted. She was equally envious of the woman's brilliant infectious smile and the dark cloud of hair that danced around her shoulders as if it was alive. Erde thought she had never seen anyone so beautiful.

"Hello, Raven," said Hal. Erde watched openmouthed as the knight snatched the woman up in a hearty embrace.

When he'd set her down again, Raven held him at arm's length for serious study. "A sight for sore eyes! You're looking well, Heinrich."

He offered a courtly bow. "And you, my heart's desire, as always. How are you all keeping?"

Raven's fine mouth tightened, a brief shrug in her gaiety. "Oh. Well enough, all things considered." She gripped both his hands, then released him gently. "More of that later. What have you brought us this time?" She turned to smile at Erde. "Forgive us. His visits here are so rare and so welcome."

"Of course. Permit me." Hal looked too happy to be embarrassed. He snatched Erde's cap off her head and fluffed up her cropped hair playfully. "Raven of Deep Moor, may I present the Lady Erde von Alte."

Raven laughed and clapped her hands as if at a feat of magic. "Traveling incognito! How exciting!"

Erde was unsure of Raven's social standing or what ceremony might be appropriate. She certainly did not dress like a lady, or as Erde had been taught a lady should dress, or behave like one either, riding about bareback and flinging herself into men's arms. But Erde wished neither to presume nor condescend with one who called the Baron Weisstrasse by his given name and was so familiar with his person. She bobbed shyly, and looked to Hal for a further hint. Her hesitation was not lost on him.

"Raven," he offered slyly, "is Queen of All She Surveys."

"Oh, my lord, you are too kind!" Raven dropped into a ground-sweeping curtsy, then rose out of it with a giggle and hooked Erde's arm within her own. "Welcome, my dear. Erde, is it? Are you hungry? Thirsty? Has he exhausted you with his mad trekking about? Well, no mind, we'll feed you here and rest you and pamper you like you must be used to!"

A flush of pride made Erde wish she could point out to this woman that if she'd been your usual petted high-born, she'd never have made it this far. She also thought it peculiar that Raven spoke in collective pronouns and went about touching or holding everyone she talked to, even a perfect stranger.

"We could all use a little pampering," remarked Hal.

Raven threw him a dark smiling glance. "Oh, you'll get it. When do you ever not?"

He laughed, and stretched luxuriously. "It is very nice to be here. Do you have any idea what it's like out there?"

Raven sobered. "We hear, and none of the news is good. Tell me, which way did you come? Did you meet Lily and Margit on the road?"

"No, but we weren't ever on the road. Are they coming or going?"

"Coming, we hope. From Erfurt. They've been out quite a while. Too long, actually, and we're worried, since Doritt said they shouldn't go at all. But Rose has heard nothing, so . . ." She shrugged as if all this made sense, then cocked her head. "But wait . . . the Mule said three?"

Erde wondered if she actually meant *said.*

"Three, indeed," replied Hal as if he'd heard nothing unusual. "Four, with the goat. He never counts himself, you know."

The she-goat had wandered into the shadows to graze, but Erde could feel the dragon waiting nearby.

Raven gave her musical laugh. "Then someone is hiding . . ."

Hal dipped his head gravely. "My lady Erde, will you make the introductions?"

Erde tried to smooth the doubt from her forehead. Her own identity was revealed, and now she had to trust Hal's judgment that the dragon would be safe. She asked Earth to make himself visible.

He appeared gradually, like a memory returning. A shaft of sunlight rippled across him in waves as the branches shifted in the breeze. Was it a trick of the light, Erde asked herself, that made his color so newly rich? She thought of him as, well, rather dull and dirt-colored—but now he was vibrant with sienna, ocher, and olive. Had his crest always been the dark blue-green of winter spruce? Suddenly, he almost seemed the hero's vision of a dragon, his great amber eyes shining like beacons out of the mossy shade.

"Oh!" Raven's hands flew to her cheeks. Bright tears started in her eyes. "Oh, Heinrich! Oh, wonderful! You finally found one!"

"My lady Erde found him," Hal corrected, looking Earth over with approving surprise. "I found her."

Raven's awe did not include a moment's fear. Nor did she complain that this was small for a dragon, and wingless. She went straight to him and laid her hands on him, petting and murmuring as if to a lover, telling him how beautiful he was and how welcome. She flirted with him, just as she seemed to with everyone she met, and Earth blossomed in the bright warmth of her praise. He stood up straighter and arched his massive neck, then tried to curl his stubby tail. Erde was caught between jealousy and laughter. She'd never seen him preen before, and she could sense a spark of self-confidence waking in him. But then, she hadn't told him he was beautiful all that often. She hadn't thought he was, until now.

"A living dragon," Raven cooed adoringly. "And just this morning, Rose said she thought something remarkable was about to happen."

"He is called Earth," said Hal. "And he needs your help."

Finally, Erde understood. Raven was not just any woman, she was one of *the* women, of whom Gerrasch had spoken.

"Then he shall have it," she replied. "Of course he shall."

Raven led them out of the oak grove and along a faint track that undulated across the rolling grassland toward a darker line of forest crowning a distant rise. While Hal told their story, Raven strolled next to him, her opposite arm slung over the mule's withers, her loose linen sleeve pushed up past her elbow. The arm was slim and brown, as smoothly muscled as a young boy's. Erde felt herself weak and pallid by comparison. She dropped back a few paces, then several dragon lengths, unsurprised when Hal and Raven didn't notice her absence, too absorbed in news and gossip and each other.

Under the full gaze of the sun, Earth was reduced to more mortal dragonkind, though still no longer "dirt-colored." It was as if one filmy obscuring layer had fallen away but others remained, still cloaking the full beauty waiting underneath. Erde sent him an image of a snake shedding its skin, then a butterfly climbing out of its cocoon.

—*I think you're changing. But it's all right, you know. It's like growing up.*

Earth took the notion away with him into his mind to think about.

That same bold valley sun told Erde that Raven, though beautiful, was no longer a girl. Beyond that, her age was mysterious. She behaved so much like a girl, or perhaps,

so unlike a grown woman, at least the grown women that
Erde had known. She thought Raven was one of the lucky
few who can act however they please *because* they are
beautiful. People think anything they do must be beautiful
also. If someone ugly puts their hands all over you without
asking, you're insulted. If a person is as beautiful as Raven,
it's no longer an affront. It becomes flattery.

Erde knew she would never be that beautiful. She had
also thought she didn't care, but now—watching the inviting curve of Raven's neck as she inclined toward Hal like
a flower to the sun, listening to the low, gay music of her
voice—Erde knew that she did care, and the understanding
made her inexpressibly sad. It reminded her that someone
had once told her she was beautiful, but it must have been
a long time ago because she could no longer recall who it
was. She worried that her memory was fading. No matter
how hard she tried to hold onto them, certain details softened, others remained bright. Alla. Her dear grandmama.
She felt the loss of them all over again, sharp enough to
bring tears to her eyes.

Earth snorted behind her. She felt a clumsy prodding at
her back, as if a vast weight was bumping her ever so gently, which it was, the weight of a dragon snout.

She turned, distracted. He had not shown an awareness
of her mood before, being too submerged in his own dilemma. Or was it just that, in the unaccustomed sun and
open space, he was finally feeling playful? As she faced
him, he stopped and dropped back on his haunches to stare
at her with his tongue lolling. Erde had to smile, and laugh
her breathy silent laugh. How could she do otherwise, with
such a great and silly creature as her devoted companion?

They saw scattered groupings of the ragged long-haired
cattle in the fields along the trail and later, a large herd of
sheep guarded by a slim black and white dog. The sheep
barely noticed them. The dog glanced their way, alert,
looked at the dragon and then to Raven as they passed,
but did not budge from its post.

Bypassing the sheep was hard for the dragon, whose hunger was beginning to preoccupy him. Erde knew this from
the constant thoughts of eating in her own head. She was
amazed that all these animals took the reality of a dragon

in their midst more or less for granted. They seemed curious but unamazed, even though Erde was sure they couldn't have ever seen a dragon before. Almost as if they'd expected him, or rather, since Raven had shown no evidence of prior knowledge, as if they'd *always been* expecting him.

Erde wasn't sure what she meant by that. She considered Earth's peculiar hunting practices. A notion was forming in the deeper part of her brain, not yet whole or coherent, about the nature of the dragon's presence in the world. That somehow, no matter how terrifying he might look, he knew how to "be" without causing distress or even very much notice. Her image of it was the huge bulk of him crossing a beach of smoothed sand without leaving footprints.

Her own thought process mystified her just as much as Earth did. Often of late, while trudging through the forest or struggling up some stony hill, she'd found herself in the grip of an idea she couldn't quite make out the logic of. Like holding a knitted garment that's come unraveled, a pile of half-sleeves and tangled yarn and loose ends. You search out this end, then that, and tie together the ones that match, but still the shape or size of the garment is unfathomable. Erde had begun to suspect this was because the garment—or the idea—was much bigger than she was.

The grassy trail led over a low hill and down beside a sand-bottomed creek that curled off around the foot of a bigger hill dotted with trees and thickly wooded at its crest. A flock of small birds danced in the bramble hedge along the bank, arguing over the last of the blackberry crop, though there were plenty left for all, dark and glistening on the vine. Erde could have filled her cap twice over, but even better, there were apples on the trees farther up the hill, and here and there a few late cherries glistened among dark green leaves. And pears! She counted half a dozen trees filled with little brown teardrop fruit. She had never seen a pear tree growing wild, only the scraggly seedlings her grandmother had imported year after year from the South in sympathy with the castle gardener, who each spring would swear he'd found just the right spot to help them thrive. As far as Erde knew, there'd never yet been an edible pear produced at Tor Alte. She ran to catch up

with Hal and Raven, pointing out this fruity cornucopia
that was making her mouth water for something other than
stale bread and dried venison.

"Amazing," Hal observed. "As always."

"It's a fine harvest this year," Raven agreed. Erde wondered how she found the energy to smile so much.

"You've heard how it is out east?" he asked.

"Every time Esther goes to market. It's even worse up
north, and the west is hardly better. We've sent what we
could to our sisters in the villages, and Esther sells at the
lowest price she can without, you know, calling attention."

"Umm. Attention like that you don't need, right now."

Raven nodded. "We've had a few close calls of late."

"It's that scourge of a priest," said Hal. "His ravings
encourage others to say and do things they'd go to confession for ordinarily."

"These dark times do likewise. People want an explanation for their misery. He gives it to them."

Hal merely grunted in reply and then, their cheer damp-
ened, they paced along in silence, until Raven slipped her
arm through his and hugged him warmly. "But we're so
glad you've come. We're way overdue for a serious discussion of strategy. Many of us think it's time to pull our heads
out of the sand."

Hal frowned. "Let's not get reckless, now. You're most
useful here and safe where you are."

"We've always thought that. Now we're not so sure."
Then she let him go and waved. "Look! Here's Doritt come
to meet us!"

Ahead of them, the path filled suddenly with black,
lop-eared goats. A tall woman dressed in brown urged
them forward with the help of another black and white
dog.

"I'm not coming to meet you," the woman declared as
she drew abreast of them, and the herd flowed around them
like black silk. "I'm clearing these damn goats out of the
yard. Every baking day they come crowding in, thinking
they're going to get some. Ha! Dreamers! Well, there, Hal,
how are you?"

Hal grinned. "Well enough, Doritt. And you?"

Doritt grasped the hand he offered. "Did she ask about Lily and Margit?"

"She did. I didn't see them."

Doritt frowned. "Pity. Well, here you are anyway." She peered at Erde with frank curiosity. "This lad belong to you?"

"The lad's a lady, can't you tell?" laughed Raven, leaning comfortably into Doritt's side. "Her name's Erde."

Doritt stuck her hand out again. "So much the better."

Erde did not have much experience with handshakes. She was surprised at the vehemence involved. Doritt's hand was as large as Hal's, long and strong like the rest of her. It engulfed Erde's own strong hand completely and made her feel satisfyingly small. Doritt had a plain oval face and the largest, darkest eyes Erde had ever seen on a human being, deep and liquid with intelligence, like a dog's eyes. Her wavy brown hair was caught in an untidy knot at the back of her neck. She fussed with it, tucking in strands that immediately shook loose again with the abrupt motions of her head as she talked.

"Now the Mule says you've brought me another one!"

Erde had quite forgotten the she-goat, who came trotting up now to mingle with the herd.

"I guess I did," agreed Hal. "And I'd like you to take a good look at her. She was mauled by a cat last night."

"It's Linden should have the look, then."

"No, that's just it, the goat is fine. Just absolutely fine."

Doritt peered at him suspiciously. "You're confusing me."

"Well, I'd just like to know how she got so fine, this soon after a mauling."

"There's a tale needs telling here," remarked Raven.

"It will be mostly *his* tale, I suppose." Doritt nodded at the dragon as if noticing him for the first time. Like Raven, she showed no fear, and even less surprise. "Yours?" she demanded of Erde.

Taken aback, Erde could only nod.

Doritt turned to Hal, arms flailing in the air. "You're not planning on leaving *that* with us as well? He'll eat us out of house and home!"

"Oh, Doritt," reproved Raven. "Think of it! A dragon!"

"Well, yes," said Doritt. "Exactly."

Hal glanced back at Earth. "I don't expect he'll be staying long. He's on a Quest. But he could use a good solid meal, if you could see your way to it."

Doritt sighed. "I knew it. Dropping in out of nowhere as usual, telling me I got to round up the old folks and give 'em the ax."

"I think you'll find he has his own very civilized methods."

Doritt fussed with her rebellious hair. "Does he want to eat now?"

Hal looked to Erde, who nodded without even asking Earth.

"We can't refuse a dragon," declared Raven softly.

Tall Doritt shrugged. "Oh, hell, give him the run of the valley. He's a dragon, after all. He's got to eat."

When Earth had wandered off on his own, with dubious backward glances and requests that Erde accompany him, Doritt sent the goats in another direction with the dog, and fell in alongside. By the time they reached the first signs of habitation, Erde knew the good and bad of every creature in Doritt's care. She wasn't sure if the other woman even noticed that she hadn't said a word.

But for its verdant productivity, which would have been astonishing in any place, in any season, the farm was not impressive at first glance. Erde saw no fortifications, no walls, no defining gates to announce where pasture ended and yard began. They were well inside before she recognized that the brash and unkempt foliage threatening the path for at least the last quarter mile was an endless vegetable garden. Everywhere she looked, she saw something edible. She stopped to inspect a bushy plant as tall as her chest and found a dozen fat green squashes lurking beneath its broad prickly leaves. How unfortunate, she mourned, that farmers who grow this well couldn't find enough time for a proper patchwork of garden plots, with their reassuring squared corners and neat rows. Just past the squash, a fruit tree had been left to grow in the middle of a lettuce patch. Erde couldn't imagine Tor Alte's gardener standing for such disorder.

Even the buildings, good sturdy stone structures, were

scattered here and there at odd angles, hidden within a clump of trees or half-buried in the side of the hill, their walls choked by some overgrown sage bush or fruity bramble, and their roofs submerged beneath trailing bean vines, looking in sorry need of maintenance.

And where was the center of this chaos of plenty and disrepair? Erde found it too disorienting. You could stroll through this entire farm and never know it was there. Except, of course, for the animals, who created a chaos all their own.

Erde could not spot a single henhouse or hog pen. Animals wandered loose everywhere: chickens, turkeys, and ducks pecking about underfoot; a brown pig rooting with her seven fat children; gray rabbits rustling in the hedges; a small horse dozing beneath a nut tree; huge lazy cats lounging in the dust of the path; and the occasional elderly dog taking the sun. A flock of black geese spotted Doritt from afar and streaked to meet her with much flapping and honking, pressing around her feet and nibbling at her clothes. She scolded and complained, but gave each one of them a moment of her full attention.

Hal halted in a grassy clearing ringed with big old maples just starting to turn orange. With his arm around Raven's waist, he inhaled deeply. "Ah. Paradise found."

Erde joined him with an experimental sniff. The aroma of fresh bread mixed with barn smells and the perfume of fall roses. She wondered where among all these trees a bakery might reside.

Doritt kept walking, turning back midstride at the edge of the clearing with a belated wave. "See you at dinner!" The black geese followed noisily behind.

When their honking had faded into the trees, Hal cleared his throat. "Well, where is she?" For the first time since entering the valley, he seemed not quite sure of his welcome.

"Working." Raven arched her brows prettily. "Did you expect all of us to drop everything the moment you arrived?"

"Um," said Hal. "Well, no. Of course not."

"She went right in as soon as she'd talked with the Mule. Something's been on her mind all day."

Hal laughed nervously. "Maybe she knew I was coming."

"Oh, yes. Well, naturally that would upset her." Raven glanced up to see if he knew she was teasing, then added seriously, "It's something in addition to that."

"Ah. Well then, will she . . . should I . . . ?"

Having made him truly uneasy, Raven smiled and touched his arm reassuringly. "Of course you should. She's waiting for you."

Hal beckoned Erde to him. Resting a hand on her shoulder, he guided her toward the trees. And there, hidden in the shade of the branches, was a shallow flight of neat stone steps leading to a flagged terrace roofed with thatch. The rafters and cross-beams were slender trees with the bark still on them. Crickets and small birds chirped in the straw. A wide wood-framed doorway set in a rough stone wall led into a low shadowy room. Groups of chairs and tables were scattered about, but in here, the disorder was human and comfortable. The furniture was tightly made and the smooth-planked floor was worn to a satiny luster. At one end towered a darkened fieldstone fireplace. At the other, a row of tall windows had been set very close together to let cool light into the room through a break in the trees.

In front of the windows, a woman sat at a spinning wheel easily as tall as she was, surrounded by piles of carded wool. The light filtering in behind touched her pale hair, her white garment, and the soft white wool with the same hazy gleam. She raised a hand from the wheel in greeting, then bent back to her work. Raven came in behind them and went to sit beside her.

"That's Linden," Hal whispered, and Erde agreed that there was a special serenity in the room, a kind of living stillness that made you loath to break the spinner's concentration, that compelled you either to sit down and beg to be put to work, or to pass on through without disturbance.

Hal led her across the room, out onto a narrow covered walkway that framed the four sides of an open, stone-paved court. The roof of the walkway was the overhang of a second story, the first real indication of the building's size. Above a final, pitched slate roof, the maple grove loomed and swayed, so that light dropped into the court like sun through water, shifting and diffuse. In some more shadowy corner, a fountain played delicate music to a birdsong accompaniment. Erde was reminded of the peaceful cloister at the little convent in the valley below Tor Alte, where she had accompanied the baroness each Christmas with food and gifts for the nuns.

Out of this tranquil bird-sung dimness, a spot of color glowed. In the steadiest shaft of sunlight, a woman dressed in a warm riot of color sat reading at a stone table. Erde could not tell her shape or the shape of her garment, only that it seemed comprised of many layers, each one a different shade of red or orange or lavender or brown.

Hal stopped at the edge of the walkway, smoothing back his hair and beard, straightening his worn red jerkin. Silently, he waited.

The woman kept reading. One hand traced her careful progress through the text. The other toyed with an assortment of small stone tiles lying on the table. Finally she raised her head, without urgency, as if she'd heard a faint noise or wondered what time it was. She glanced their way but her eyes seemed to stare past them into the distance. For a moment, Erde thought the woman was blind.

Then her gaze focused, and she smiled. "Ah, Heinrich. There you are."

The slight pressure of his hand bade Erde wait. Hal stepped into the court, crossed the mossy flagstones with measured strides, and dropped to one knee as if the woman sat on a golden throne instead of an old three-legged stool. She gave him her hand, and he held it reverently to his lips. Then he rose, leaned over, and kissed her lingeringly on the mouth.

Waiting in the shadows, Erde blushed. Hal's familiarities with Raven now seemed merely playful by comparison. She'd seen the soldiers stealing lusty kisses from the pantry maids, but true earnest tenderness such as this ought to be kept private. It made her feel funny inside.

Hal leaned against the stone table, his arms to either side of the woman's shoulders, and gazed down into her eyes. "Rose. I've missed you."

Her voice was low and so resonant that Erde felt it sing through her own body like lute music. "Then you should find your way to us more often."

"If only I could."

The woman raised a reproving finger. "And you could even come when there isn't something you want from us."

Hal's soft laugh honored this old debate between them, but refused the challenge. Erde recalled how ardently he'd spoken of her grandmother that first night by the campfire, of lovers separated by duty and distance. Was it always to be so for this loyal King's Knight?

"Meanwhile," said Hal, "there is something, and here it is." He straightened away from Rose and gestured Erde into the light. She approached shyly. Seated, the woman appeared to be of trim, middling stature. Her curly auburn hair was shot with gray and, to Erde's delight, cut short as a boy's. She had thick brows over bright blue eyes and a strong jaw, a compelling face. Though she was not as old, perhaps closer to Hal's age, something about her reminded Erde of Alla, something that made her want to kneel at the woman's feet as Hal had done.

"Rose of Deep Moor," Hal announced, "Erde von Alte."

Erde noticed he'd left off her title for the first time and wondered why, not that such things mattered to her. When the woman stood, beads and little bells chimed faintly in her long, loose sleeves and in the deep folds of her skirt.

"And if that weren't remarkable enough," supplied Rose, "she comes with a dragon."

"Yes."

She smiled without looking at him. "How wonderful for you, Heinrich. After all these years."

"Yes."

Rose grasped Erde's hands, looking her over. They were not quite matched in height. The commanding blue eyes gazed up at her and still Erde felt diminished by her presence.

"So this is the witch-child." Rose turned to level that same deep stare on Hal. "And her Paladin."

Hal snorted. "What? Me?"

Rose nodded.

"Oh, hardly, Rose. Not me."

"Oh, yes, my dear. Did you think you'd escape Fra Guill so easily, simply by backing out of his view? I hate it when he's right, don't you?"

"Rose, I'm not exactly the ravening image of Dark Power he conjures up for his witch-child's champion."

Rose drew Erde left, then right, as if showing her off. "Nor is she his nightmare vision of a witch."

He smiled. "But then, who is?"

Rose dipped her head. "Yet here she is, and here you are. Besides, I said her Paladin, not her Champion. But we'll speak of that later. Meanwhile . . ."

"Rose, there's no way Guillemo could have known."

"Heinrich, Heinrich."

"All right, so he got lucky."

Rose shook her head warningly. "You let your hatred blind you to the man's real power. He's a hound on a scent. If a pattern exists, he'll sniff it out. It's a true prophetic gift, tragically turned to evil ends."

"You haven't seen him in action. I have. He's a lunatic, Rose."

"Yes, and his madness springs from being unable to control what he sees so clearly."

This exchange and the long dark glance that passed between them filled Erde with unaccountable dread. She missed the dragon's comforting presence and hoped he'd finish with his hunting soon.

Hal sucked his teeth and turned aside abruptly. "Then we can't stay here." He paced away, then came back and drew Rose into his arms. "Forgive me. I've endangered you thoughtlessly."

Rose smoothed the stained red leather hugging his chest. "Not thoughtlessly. A still-sleeping dragon and a dream-reader who's lost her voice? Where else could you go for the sort of help you need?"

Erde waited for Rose to mention how she'd come by all this information, but she did not, and Hal seemed to require no explanation.

"Now, food and rest and a good hot bath for both of you. Of course you'll stay, long enough to see what help we can actually provide." Rose looked up and touched a finger to Hal's jaw. "And long enough to remind this old woman what a man looks like."

He hugged her to him, laughing. "Why, Rose, you'll embarrass the young lady."

CHAPTER TWENTY-TWO

The denizens of Deep Moor gathered for the evening meal in the communal dining area at one end of a huge kitchen. Brick ovens and grills and spits lined the opposite wall. Windows let in amber dusk light along both sides. Two rows of sturdy worktables dominated the center, and the smoke-darkened beams were a hanging forest of herbs and onions in braided lengths and garlic and dried peppers and delicate nets bulging with winter squashes and potatoes.

Erde had napped and then been introduced to the pleasures of a hot bath. She'd always hated bathing, except sometimes in the summer. Now she realized that the water had never been warm enough, or smelled so fragrant with herbs and the softening oils that Raven poured on so liberally. In some obscure way, it felt sinful. She spelled this out for Raven, primly, shyly, in the dew gathering on the red floor tiles, but Raven only laughed and tossed her a square of fine knitted wool to rub the oils into her skin. She came down to the kitchen feeling reborn, wearing a clean linen shirt from the household stores and one of Raven's block-printed shifts with the divided skirts. Hal, who was lounging with his feet up on a table and a mug of ale in one hand, sat up in surprise.

"Milady, you look radiant!" He put down his ale and stood, handing her into a seat beside him with courtly formality while Erde blushed and stared at her feet.

Earth had still not returned from his hunt, so while Hal explained about the dragon and his unknown quest, and told the tale of her escape and their journey so far, Erde watched the dinner preparations. She wished Hal had not been so intentionally uninformative about the circumstances at Deep Moor, about who these people were and why Rose knew what she knew. But she could not ask him now, so she settled in to be patient and to observe. It did not occur to her to try to make herself useful until Doritt plunked down a basket of apples and a knife on the table in front of her.

"Well, I'm sure this dragon's Purpose isn't to stay and eat up my herd. Here, slice these up. I'll find a bowl to put them in."

She sailed off to the far end of the kitchen. Erde stared at the gleaming red fruit. She had never sliced apples in her life, though her grandmother had taught her the proper way for a lady to section a small apple for eating. This knife was much too large for delicacy, but she gave it a game try. Doritt returned, watched her struggles for a moment, then grabbed a stool and drew it alongside.

"Tell you what: I'll peel and quarter, then you just cut 'em up any old which way, all right?"

Erde observed carefully, admiring Doritt's deft skill with the knife, and learned the preparation of apples for pie. Meanwhile, she counted: five, ten, twelve women drifting in and out of the kitchen, bringing fresh milk, washing vegetables, slicing bread, stirring the pots. A pair of lithe red-haired twins in their late teens did a lot of the heavy hauling. A chunky laughing woman was clearly the chief cook. Two elderly women wandered in rather vaguely. They were fussed over and treated with great deference by the others, but did not sit by idly. They went right to work slicing up whatever was set in front of them with concentration and efficiency. Erde heard Lily and Margit mentioned often, as one woman or another stepped in to do a task usually assigned to one of the absentees. She sensed in this a fond sort of ritual, as if the frequent naming of the missing women would keep them safer and bring them back sooner. She had also been waiting all afternoon to learn where the men and the servants were. Now she discovered there weren't any. There were no young children either.

A community made up entirely of women, which wasn't fortified or walled in any way, and wasn't a nunnery. Erde had never heard of such a thing. And no help but themselves. In a way, it reminded her of Tor Alte while her grandmother was alive. Of course, there were plenty of men at Tor Alte, but the women had felt easier about themselves under the baroness' rule. And though they were not at all similar physically, Rose did have the baroness' same sure authority.

Yet at dinner, she watched Raven tease Hal as she laid steaming platters on the table, flirting with him outrageously, and all the while Rose smiled benignly, nestled into the curve of his arm. Her grandmother would never have stood for that. Erde asked herself again how these women protected themselves. She surmised that there was a lot going on here she did not understand.

The long refectory-style table was as well-worn and shining as the floor. The food was fresh, plentiful, and delicious. There was clear springwater to drink and a pale, dry ale that made Erde feel refreshed rather than light-headed. The conversation was not quite boisterous, but it was lively and certainly informative.

"The honey is from our hives, of course," Linden was explaining in the mild precise way that seemed to characterize her. "And the candles as well. Raven makes the most beautiful candles, don't you think?"

Erde nodded. The many candles burning on the table were amazingly tall and thin, and even more astonishingly, they were pink, the blushed color of a wild rose. She thought to ask how one made a colored candle, and readied quill, ink, and the little pile of paper that Raven had supplied her with, rejects from the Deep Moor paper press. But Linden was busy being very serious about the bees and how sensitive they were to mistreatment or neglect. Erde wiped her quill and laid it aside.

Linden, whom she had seen at the spinning wheel earlier, was as pale and dry as the ale, but with its same hidden sweetness. Pale jaw-length hair, pale gray eyes, pale flawless skin, with flush-spots on her cheekbones so distinct they might have been painted there by a rather wobbly hand. Her color bloomed whenever she spoke, especially when she was speaking to Hal, as if the very act itself put her in mortal danger of exposure or embarrassment. It took Erde some time to learn that Linden was Deep Moor's healer, for she would never boast of such a thing herself. But she had spent the late afternoon examining the she-goat and now, as Raven and a slim older woman named Esther cleared the dishes to make room for the sweets, Rose asked for her report.

Linden placed both hands before her to grip the edge of the table and cleared her throat. "She is fully healed."

"Healed," repeated Rose, and Erde wondered how you could pack so much mystery and meaning into a single word.

"So I didn't imagine all that blood and gore," said Hal.

Linden focused carefully on the smooth plank in front of her. "There is clear evidence of serious injury, long tears and deep claw punctures. But this must have been at least three weeks ago, from the amount of healing already completed."

"Last night," said Hal. "It was just last night, was if not, my lady?"

Erde nodded.

"I don't see how that's . . ." began Linden.

"Well, it is. It happened." With a grin, Hal leaned forward and replenished his mug of ale from an earthenware pitcher. "We have a magic goat." He eyed Doritt mischievously. "I'll bet you don't have one."

Linden frowned at the tabletop, shaking her head ever so slightly.

"What else occurred," asked Rose, "between the attack and when you noticed her healed?"

Hal shrugged, then decided to stop pretending that he wasn't taking this seriously. "We made camp, we ate, we slept. The goat slept very deeply."

"All right. Yes." Linden bobbed her head, staring at her thumbs. "Animals do often go into a kind of trance state when they're badly injured. But that's usually to ease their dying."

"What else?" Rose prodded. "Any other detail?"

Erde reviewed the previous evening moment by moment: the cat screeching and the attack, Earth struggling to turn around within the walls of rock, then the goat streaking in over his back and the dark blood on Hal's hands. Then what? Then . . .

She grabbed for her quill and paper, and wrote carefully: EARTH WASHED HER.

She was amazed that the ink did not sink deeply into the

thin pliant sheet and bleed her letters out of recognition.
Apparently, Raven made very fine paper as well as candles.

Linden peered at her message, then read it aloud. The
women murmured thoughtfully. The two elderly women at
the far end of the table put their heads together in lively
muttered discussion.

Then Hal swore softly and slapped his head. "Of course!
Where is my mind? It's very common in the lore to claim
that a dragon's tongue has healing properties!"

The two old women nodded approvingly, though one of
them frowned when Doritt said, "I thought their jaws
dripped acid and stuff."

"No, no, that's just fairy tales . . . or if you listen to what
the Church says. The *lore* says . . . ah, why didn't I think
of it sooner?"

"It will be just so lovely to have a real dragon to study,"
ventured one of the old ladies. Her voice reminded Erde
of butterfly wings.

Hal bent his head to her. "I plan many hours in your
excellent library, Helena, while you're off dragon-
watching." He offered Erde a crooked apologetic smile.
"Won't he be relieved to know there's something else he
can do."

"That's a fine way to talk about a dragon," Doritt
snorted.

Gentle laughter rippled around the table.

"But isn't it typical?" chided Rose. "A man finds what
he's been searching for all his life, and right away he's
complaining that it doesn't fulfill his expectations."

"Well, he doesn't," Hal retorted. "Does he yours?"

"I've not yet met him," replied Rose sweetly.

"Don't worry, he won't. Maybe someday, but now . . ."

"I think he's a very nice sort of dragon," said Raven.

"Nice?" Hal was peevish. "He's not meant to be *nice.*"

"Why not?"

"He's meant to be powerful, magnificent, omnipotent,
and . . ."

Rose smiled. "Perhaps he could be all those, and nice,
too."

"What a concept," remarked Doritt.

HE IS STILL LEARNING, Erde wrote, in a broad ad-
monitory hand. Briskly, Linden passed the paper to Hal.

"True," he conceded. "I only hope he can discover himself in time."

"In time for what?" asked Rose.

Hal drained his mug and pushed his plate away with a definitive gesture. "In time to save us from the apocalypse according to Guillemo Gotti. I can't imagine what else he would have been sent for. Have you heard the priest is raising an army?"

"Oh, yes. To cleanse the world of the likes of us. That's why we sent Lily and Margit to Erfurt, to find out all they could." Leaning into his shoulder, Rose turned the thin wooden stem of her goblet between two fingers. "But what if Fra Guill is not the dragon's purpose?"

"Not? What do you mean?" He sat up straighter in order to gaze down at her sternly. "Are you saying it isn't? Do you know what his Purpose is?"

"Without talking to him? Of course not. What am I, a fortune-teller?"

Brighter laughter drifted around the table. Raven snapped her fingers rhythmically and hissed, "Gypsies!" Erde wondered what was so amusing.

Hal caught her eye over his shoulder. "This is my punishment, you see. Rank mockery, because I don't show up to pay homage often enough."

This drew hoots and catcalls, echoing about the warm candlelit room. Erde had never heard such raucous laughter from women.

"Oh. Homage, is it?" laughed Raven.

"Well?" he challenged. "That is what you want. Isn't that what you all want?"

"We want a lot more than that." She ran her finger around Hal's ear and pinched his earlobe. Hal brushed her hand away, glancing self-consciously at Erde.

Across the table, Linden was giggling, and blushing furiously. The older woman Esther paused behind her with an armload of empty platters, her grin expectant. Rose tickled Hal's arm. "Don't get them started, my dear. You know you'll only be sorry."

Raven leaned in, her lips soft against his temple. "Sorry? Oh, I don't think so. I don't remember you ever being sorry." Hal's breath caught as her tongue snaked out and licked his ear.

"Raven," Doritt murmured. "We have a guest."

"Oh, pooh," said Raven, but she eased away from Hal to gather up a final stack of dishes.

A guest. Erde had heard the singular and knew it meant her. Heinrich Engle was no guest here, that much was clear. But neither was he a member of the household. Erde was confused. She did not understand these women's behavior. She knew her grandmother would have had a name for it, and it would not have been flattering. And yet, Erde could see nothing overtly wrong with it . . . only if you thought about what you'd been *told* was right and proper.

Hal cleared his throat, then went on as if nothing had happened. "But why do you question the dragon's Purpose?"

"Not that he has one," Rose replied, equally unfazed. "Only that it might be other than what you expect."

"Some Larger Purpose, you mean. Beyond my ken."

The knight's deeply humble expression made Rose smile. "Not necessarily *beyond*, my dear. Just different."

"Well, Gerrasch said the Purpose was 'to fix what's broken.' A bit cryptic, I thought."

"No more than you'd expect."

"From a badger," muttered Doritt.

Rose smothered a grin. "But what I was referring to is that another candidate has arisen for the job you have in mind."

"What?" Hal came bolt upright. He looked almost frightened. "Another dragon?"

Raven laughed loudly from the sink. "Well, that got to him!"

"Of course not another dragon!" said Rose.

"Hal, Hal, where have you been?" Doritt leaned forward on her elbows. "Haven't you heard about the Friend?"

"Whose friend?"

"That's what people call him."

"Just . . . the Friend?" He glanced at Rose. "Interesting coincidence. What about him?"

Doritt noted Erde's puzzlement. "Loyalist code," she explained. Then Erde recalled Griff's response to the word.

"Delicious rumors." Raven waltzed back to her seat beside Hal. She twirled one finger in his bristly hair. "You know how women are."

Hal scowled and batted her hand away, causing another trill of general laughter.

"They come in from the west," Linden put in kindly, without looking at him. "The rumors. If you've come from the east, they may not have reached you yet."

"From widespread parts of the west," Raven added more seriously. "Even as far as Köln. Some claim that's where he's from."

"City boy," noted Doritt.

"No, that can't be right."

"Why not?" asked Linden.

Raven smiled and shrugged. "He just doesn't sound like a city boy to me."

Doritt frowned. "What does it matter? You don't believe in him anyway!"

Erde recalled her grandmother talking of Köln. Köln was a true city. It was said to contain at least twenty thousand people. She had no image of it except that it must be very crowded, but then, she had no image of any city at all besides her fantasy one.

Hal asked, "So why do they call him the Friend, if not . . . ?"

"Supposedly, it's because he does all kinds of reckless acts of goodness."

"Reckless and random," added Raven. "So they say."

"Remember that random is in the eye of the beholder," murmured Linden. "I mean, random is simply whatever you weren't expecting."

Raven wagged a playful finger at her. "Oh-oh, Linnie, you'd like to meet this Friend, wouldn't you?"

"Leave her alone." Esther came back from depositing her pile of platters in a corner washtub. "It's me bringing these tales in, mostly. I hear them when I go Outside to the markets."

"Ah." Hal sat back. Erde thought he seemed relieved. "The idle gossip of farmwives."

Esther raised a sharply pointed brow. "And farm men as well, and traveling merchants and big, bully convoy men. The best I had was from a troupe of actors. Their leader said he liked the tale so much and heard it so often, he was working up a play about it."

"Lily and Margit were to look into it," said Rose. "Perhaps even try to contact him if such a thing seemed possible."

Hal grunted, crossed his arms. "But who, if he even exists, is this so-called Friend supposed to be?"

Raven giggled and nuzzled his shoulder. "Poor Heinrich. You'd really prefer to save the world single-handedly, wouldn't you?"

Hal ignored her, leaning forward to hear Esther's tale.

"Well." Esther shoved back her sleeves. She found room on the bench between Linden and Erde, and prepared herself self-consciously, much like the actor she had just spoken of. "The stories tell of a mysterious young man—he is always young and always nameless . . ."

"Because they don't know his name, or he won't tell it?"

"Sometimes one, sometimes the other. But nameless anyhow, and thus always referred to as the Friend or simply "he," and in the markets these days, they know who you're talking about." Esther's long slender hands illustrated her words as gracefully as a dancer's. "Sometimes he's a poor farm lad, sometimes, yes, a city boy. Sometimes he's even a prince. Last week, he was a *foreign* prince!"

"A *gypsy* prince!" crowed Raven, getting up to fill her mug.

"It's been suggested. Or Frankish, if he's really from the west. He's said to be well spoken and handsome, of course. Not dark, not light. Everything about him seems to be the middle road."

"Where's his shining armor, and his golden helm that he never takes off?" Hal scoffed. "Clearly we're dealing with fantasy here."

Esther stared him down. "Perhaps. Anyway, an anonymous young knight of indeterminate breeding who travels about the countryside warning the farm folk against the evils of Fra Guill."

Now Hal looked interested. "Hunh."

Rose nodded. "He's brave, if nothing else."

"A rabble-rouser!" exclaimed Doritt appreciatively.

"A handsome gypsy rabble-rouser!" Raven twirled and stomped, her arms entwined to support a pitcher of ale above her head. "Better and better!"

Rose held out her goblet to be refilled. "They say Fra Guill flies into a mad rage at anyone who takes the Friend seriously because he has no place in the Prophecy. That's enough to make him very interesting, as far as I'm concerned."

"If he exists," said Hal.

Esther planted both long palms on the tabletop. "Do I get to tell this story or not?"

Raven slunk back to her seat, gripping her mug to her chest in mock-contrition.

"Tell it, then!" Doritt whooped.

"Well, you haven't left me much." She continued over a chorus of sighs and groans. "Only that he's supposedly gathering followers as he goes along, and that although his route is rambling and slow, in general he seems to be headed east, toward Erfurt."

"And toward us," Hal noted. "With his own little army behind him."

"Around him, actually. And if they're armed, it's only with knives and pitchforks." Esther folded her hands pensively beneath her chin, suddenly reminding Erde of the elderly monk who had taught her reading and writing much against his own better judgment. "This is where it gets interesting. There appears to be some confusion about the exact nature of this gathering. They're not spoken of as an army."

"Then they're a mob."

"Those who don't like the idea call it a mob. Either way, the Friend apparently refuses the usual privileges of leadership. He sleeps among his followers—some even call them disciples, but for most this comes too close to blasphemy. He marches among them and defers to their counsel. He dresses as they do and shares their food, which is happily supplied from the countryside, the same food that people out east are hiding away from Fra Guill at great risk to their lives."

"And he's particularly outspoken against Fra Guill's witch-hunting," noted Rose quietly. Erde decided that each time she spoke, it was like a phrase of a song being dropped into the conversation.

"Well, no wonder you're all so in love with this chimera," Hal declared. "But have you thought this out? What if it's some new kind of peasant rebellion? 'Friend' or not, the last thing His Majesty needs is a new enemy."

"If you'd just let me finish." Esther caught his eye and held it. "The name may not be coincidental. Those who claim to have seen him say he carries the King's Banner."

"The King's Banner? Openly?"

Esther nodded. "And beside it, the emblem of a dragon."

For the first time since the meal began, silence prevailed. Then Rose said, "I hadn't heard that part."

"New, as of yesterday." Esther preened, pleased by the stir she'd created.

Hal blew out a long breath between his teeth. "King and dragon together. The people actually favor that connection?"

"There's a lot of debate, but mostly, they do."

"Hmmm. And the barons?"

"As you'd expect. They're denying he exists."

"And he's heading toward Erfurt." Hal looked down at Rose. "What truth to it all, do you think?"

"I don't get Out. I'd only be going on hearsay. Esther?"

Esther's shrug was that of a skeptic still willing to be convinced. "We'll know more when Lily and Margit get back, but in the markets, tales of the Friend are accepted as news, that is, as true as any word that comes from so far away."

"So what are they really saying?" mused Hal.

"It could be the country folks' way of expressing their dislike of Fra Guill, by inventing a hopefully invincible enemy for him."

Raven sighed. "Or that the people dream of a hero to rescue them from bad harvests and early winters and rumors of war. Who can blame them? It feels like the end of the world."

"But what if there really is some man on his way east with an army?" proposed Doritt reasonably.

"Indeed. What if? And carrying the King's Banner . . ." Hal was slumped in thought. "I wonder . . . could it . . . ?" He sat up slowly. "What if it's *him,* Rose? What if it's Ludolf? It could be, you know . . . ?"

Rose gazed into her goblet as if she wished he wouldn't get started on this matter. "There's been no word, Heinrich."

Raven rolled her eyes. "And you call us romantics!"

"But it could be. Why not?" Brightening, he faced Erde

across the table. "This is going to sound like another tall tale, but it's true, I was there at the beginning of it. The king had another son, Ludolf, two years younger than Prince Carl."

Erde nodded. Everyone knew Prince Ludolf had died when just a boy. The king had produced no other children since then.

"I know what you're thinking, but that's just the story we gave out. Because His Majesty's relations with the barons were becoming treacherous, the lad was fostered out in secret for his own protection, so secretly in fact that his whereabouts are unknown, even to the king."

Hal had been right. It did sound like a tall tale, but Erde thought it very romantic indeed.

"Most of us assume he really did die," Esther put in sadly. "Both of them in some accident or killed by brigands on the road or in some betrayal we never got wind of."

"Only this one . . ." Doritt jerked her thumb at Hal. ". . . persists in the folly of believing the boy's still alive."

"A boy no longer. A young man now, nearly twenty. And I'm not alone in this so-called folly. The king himself agrees with me."

"Of course. A father would," said Esther.

"A leap of faith," said Rose.

"Admittedly."

Esther laughed. "Dear Hal. Your endless capacity for belief is one of your most endearing qualities. May you never lose your faith."

"If I can maintain my faith while I'm in this household, nothing can shake it." Hal leaned forward onto the table as if over a map, suddenly businesslike. "Now. How big is it supposed to be, this unarmed army?"

Esther flicked her hands pointedly, a comment either on her sources of information or on Hal's shift of subject. "One story will say fifty, another will say a thousand. It depends on the teller."

"No surprise in that. I fear he will get them all killed and himself hung in the bargain . . . if he exists." Hal sucked his teeth, his characteristic gesture of doubt. "Come on, surely you have some feelings about this, Rosie."

But Rose had noticed Erde's abstracted gaze. "What is it, child?"

Slowly, Erde wrote: IS THE FRIEND EVER A KNIGHT?

Esther laughed. "Not this particular Friend."

"Why, dear?" asked Rose.

EARTH DREAMED A KNIGHT. Erde passed her scrawl to Rose.

Hal read over Rose's shoulder. "He did? You didn't tell me that. It wasn't . . . who was it?"

Erde met his eye sympathetically. She hadn't mentioned it, to save his feelings. He'd want it to be him, and she knew it wasn't.

HE WORE A CROWN.

At this, even Raven gave a small gasp of surprise.

Rose arched her brows. "What did the knight do in his dream?"

NOTHING. HE WAS THERE AND THEN HE FADED AWAY.

"When was this?" asked Hal.

Erde erased and scribbled. THE NIGHT OF THE EARTHQUAKE.

The candles were burning low on the table. Raven snubbed two of them. Linden held Erde's scrap of paper up to the nearest guttering flare and read it aloud. The women exchanged glances.

"Earthquake?" Rose asked. "Where?"

"That's something you read about in the Bible," scoffed Doritt.

"No," said Esther, "I think they've actually happened. There are stories."

"Well, they don't happen around here."

"One did," said Hal. "Two nights ago, only a day's travel north of here."

EARTH DREAMED THE EARTHQUAKE, Erde wrote.

"Right. I forgot to mention that." Hal scratched his beard uncomfortably. "Apparently, the Dragon dreamed that the earth moved, and it did. Woke us up out of a sound sleep."

"*Earth*quakes!" Raven snatched up Erde's paper and waved it triumphantly in front of Hal's nose. "How can you be disappointed in this dragon?"

Rose nodded thoughtfully. "I've never heard of a dragon

making earthquakes. That is a very rare and ancient skill. Of course there is the undeniable coincidence of his name." She turned an approving eye on Erde. "And yours. Well. Earthquakes. An unknown knight. An undisclosed purpose. Is it time for us to take a Look?" She glanced around the table, inviting consensus.

Hal relaxed back into his chair, arms loosely folded but eyes watchful. One hand drummed a faint staccato on his elbow.

Linden nudged Erde. "This is what he's come for, you see. But we must all agree to it, 'cause there's always danger in a Seeing, especially to Rose." She lowered her voice to the barest whisper. "And he knows some of us do not respond well to being pressured."

Erde thought to ask who, but had already noted Esther's jaw tightening and Doritt's dubiously pursed lips. But Linden was hiding a girlish grin behind her hand.

"We'd do it anyway, for your sake, but it doesn't do to let him know that."

Covertly, Erde wrote: WHY?

Linden's giggle was as soft as water over moss. " 'Cause no matter how much you'd like to, you can't give them everything they want just right off. They're too spoiled with getting already."

THEY? scrawled Erde.

Linden nudged her again, her cheeks crimson. "Men, of course."

Erde nodded sagely. This was an interesting notion. Certainly all the women she'd known, except maybe Alla and her grandmother, spent their lives waiting for things to come to them—a meal, a new gown, a husband back from the hunt or from the wars—and by waiting, often did not get what they waited for. Men, however, just went out and took what they wanted. Like Fra Guill. Or her father. She remembered Alla complaining about how spoiled the baron was. Yet he had called his daughter spoiled for wanting something so simple as to walk in the woods by herself. She recalled his sudden dark scowl, his peremptory tone. Of course the alone part had bothered him. But not because he feared she was meeting some boy. He'd never let her meet any boys. What he really couldn't stand was the idea of her managing on her own outside of the walls, outside his protective embrace. She decided that those unlady-like walks were preparation for her escape, and was grateful for them. They'd kept her first act of real rebellion from becoming a total disaster.

She looked at Hal, an impatient man waiting with all the patience he could muster. She had no problem conjuring the tantrum her father would have thrown in such a situation, and she loved this good and earnest knight the more for not being so spoiled after all, no matter what the women of Deep Moor might think.

"Any discussion?" asked Rose. "Dissenting views?"

The women shook their heads, even Esther, and Doritt, last of all but emphatically, as if it had simply taken her that long to clear her mind of any lingering doubt.

"Then we're agreed." Rose brought her palms together soundlessly in front of her, then pushed them apart. The stilled table erupted into activity.

CHAPTER TWENTY-THREE

The meal was cleared and the dishes washed and stacked with dizzying speed. Erde sat with the old women to dry the plates and bowls. Even Hal was pressed into labor, hauling brimming buckets from well to kettle, then kettle to basin. The sight of a red-leathered King's Knight, a baron at that, tipping a steaming kettle over the big tin washbasin was a memory Erde would treasure. Whatever this Seeing was, Hal wanted it very much indeed.

When the kitchen was tidied and all the candles snuffed but one, Raven took up the single flame and led them through the dim lamp-lit rooms of the farmhouse, out into the fresh and temperate night. The women grabbed lanterns from the stone porch, lighting them one by one from Raven's candle. The young twins pulled a low, brightly painted dogcart out from under the branches beside the steps. They helped the two elderly ladies in, settled them comfortably, and stepped into the traces themselves.

"Treasures, those old ones," murmured Hal in Erde's ear. "Keepers of the knowledge, scholars, librarians. They collect the books and write down all the spoken traditions. I've spent many fruitful hours consulting them. They're sure to have a useful notion or two about our dragon's Purpose."

Watching the lore ladies and the gentle attention the twins lavished on them, Erde mourned once more for Alla. Tor Alte had not shown that wise old woman the respect she'd deserved, not ever.

Then, lanterns in hand, the whole party set off along the meandering roadway through the farm, looping past the murmuring darkness of the sties and barns, raising the occa-

sional sleeping duck or dog from the path. Several of the
dogs decided to come along. Doritt's flock of black geese
discovered her and fell in behind, mere shadows bobbing
through the grass, uncharacteristically mute. The cart rattled along and the twins began to sing softly to the rhythm
of their stride. The other women laughed and chattered as
if off to some midnight festivity. Their joy and energy was
contagious. Erde felt it expand inside her chest, like the
soap bubbles Alla had taught her to blow within the loop
of her fingers, luminous and big and so fragile that it hurt
her heart to think of not being with these women forever,
on balmy moonlit nights like this, filled to bursting with
laughter and singing and belonging.

The path forked beside the apple orchard. Raven led
them over the stone bridge that crossed the narrowest waist
of the stream, then up the hill among the fruit trees. Doritt
and Linden joined the twins in the traces to draw the cart
up the steeper incline.

Near the top of the hill, the trees thinned, leaving a
grassy rounded crest exposed to the night like the dome of
a man's head left without a hat. The women gathered at
the very apex of the curve, eased the two old women onto
the grass, then joined them without ceremony in a circle
that took the highest point of the hill as its center. Rose
pressed Erde's hand and sat her down between Linden and
Esther. She seated Hal next to herself on the opposite side,
so that Erde faced her directly across the crest of the hill.
The black geese nested into the grass at Doritt's back with
a minimum of fuss, and over Hal's rather self-consciously
hunched shoulders, the moonlight drew a familiar silhouette, the mule with his head down to graze but his long
ears flicking about, alert to the night. A rustling behind
Erde announced the arrival of the she-goat and a spotted
dog she'd taken up with. Their coats and coloring were so
similar that Erde wondered if one knew the other was a
goat, or a dog. Or perhaps it didn't matter on such a night,
when the very air vibrated with fellowship. Erde shivered
deliciously. Only in the forests had she ever felt like this.
Surely this was what the presence of magic felt like. She
had heard no incantations and seen no casting of spells,
and this was only a bunch of women and animals on top

of a hill together. Even so, every nerve in her body thrilled with expectation.

Perhaps it was only the stillness that settled over the circle, waiting yet content. The women set their lanterns on the ground in front of them. Erde noticed that the grass inside the circle was cropped short, as if grazed down to a velvet brush by very careful sheep. She thought suddenly of the Mage City. Wouldn't it have lawns this soft and manicured? She became convinced that if anyone could tell her how to get there, it would be these women.

Rose rested her elbows on her knees, her hands making a nest for her chin. She spoke to the circle at large and formally, but her voice strummed inside Erde's chest. Listening to her was like breathing in sound.

"Our sister Erde comes to us haunted with dragon dreams. If she will share them with us, perhaps we can offer some insight as to their meaning."

Erde glanced at Hal for a clue to what to do next. She'd left behind her pen and paper. Besides, you couldn't read out here in the darkness anyway. But Hal's smile only encouraged. He was eager, nervous, like a young boy finally allowed to stay up late with the adults. He tipped his head toward Rose.

"We'll need no words," said Rose. "But understand, my child. I can only See what is, and of that, only what is open to me, and my sisters here like a lens provide the focus, with the hope that Seeing will bring enlightenment, about what is to be, about how to act. So now, gather up these dreams in your mind as if you were picking flowers. Hold them there until your memory is secure. Then think of offering them to us, to all of us, generously, as you would give a gift."

It was not going to be like speaking with the dragon. With the dragon, he was just *there,* in her mind. This would apparently take some effort. Erde hadn't given many gifts in her life. She was more used to receiving them. But she thought and then remembered a small silk pillow she had embroidered when she was six or seven, for her grandmother's birthday. She'd always lacked patience for the fussy detail work of sewing, but this one task she worked at night after chilly night, head and hands gathered close in the candle's dim light, long after Fricca had fallen asleep by the cooling hearth. And not just because it was a gift for her grandmother. For once, she'd been allowed to choose the design she was to embroider, and she'd rejected the usual ladylike basket of fruit or floral bouquet. Over Fricca's protests, she had sewn a dragon for the baroness.

Erde hadn't thought about that pillow for a very long time, but now its image flashed into her mind, as clear as a painted miniature, minute silken stitches all green and gold and brown against soft beige linen. She recalled her grandmother's delight when the gift was revealed within its brocaded birthday wrappings, how her long forefinger, heavy with the baronial ring, had lovingly traced the dragon's tiny shape.

"A fat little dragon," she'd exclaimed with satisfaction. Then she'd caught Erde's eye. "But he looks a bit shy. Why is that?"

Erde couldn't remember her reply, only that she hadn't intended the dragon to look shy. The stitches had just come out that way. She knew she hadn't told her grandmother that. It might sound like she hadn't worked on it hard enough.

And then the baroness had said, "And he has no wings. How interesting."

Erde reeled in a moment of vertigo.

Beside her, Linden gasped softly and caught her elbow. "Are you all right?"

"Why, that's lovely," murmured Rose. "Is that what he looks like?"

Erde stared across the circle, but she was hardly seeing Rose at all. Instead she saw Earth's thick arching neck, his short muscular lizard-body, his stubby pointed tail and curving ivory horns. And especially his humble demeanor. It was all there. She had embroidered him exactly, seven or was it eight years ago?

"What is it?" Hal whispered urgently, glancing from Rose to Erde and back again.

"A carnelian jewel . . ."

"Yes! Meriah's brooch!"

Rose's gaze on Erde was distant. "Does it warm to your touch?"

Erde nodded. No one but Hal knew that, not even the dragon.

"What about it, Rose? What do you See?"

Raven nudged Hal reprovingly but Rose nodded, as if his impatience was only to be expected. "Destiny," she replied.

"Whose? Hers? The Dragon's?"

"They are intertwined. I see lines of force, not where they will lead. I can confirm, Heinrich. I cannot predict."

I should. not be surprised, thought Erde. But she was. And frightened. No one had ever read her mind before. Oh, there'd been those winter parlor games with walnut shells and playing cards, where coincidence and body language occasionally conspired to produce a delicious whiff of the uncanny. But this was so direct and unambiguous. It was like the Mage-Queen would have done, in her fantasies. But the Mage-Queen was haughty and magical, and always wore white. Rose was so . . . normal.

"Perhaps his Purpose can be Read from his dreams," murmured Rose. "Tell us a little of them."

But the little embroidered Earth would not leave Erde's mind. The image and its implications crowded her consciousness. She recalled what Hal had said about the carnelian brooch and its "ageless history," and was suddenly overcome by the responsibility. All those ages of history devolving down to her, and she hadn't the slightest idea what she was supposed to do about it.

Rose's deep voice vibrated through her paralysis. "Think of taking hold of something and setting it carefully aside."

This offered a distraction, and with some effort, Erde complied. The little dragon image faded and, dutifully, she turned her mind to Earth's most recent dream. At first it was easy to conjure up, like looking at a mural on a wall, the hard gleaming surfaces and sharp planes of the nightmare landscape, with its constant overlay of cacophony and stench. She pictured the knight fading away in the corridor and heard again the ringing call of the Summoner. But she couldn't hold onto the image. The details quickly went soft, as if the artist's elbow had smeared the still-wet paint. Some other din distracted her. Erde concentrated harder, but the clash of steel was drowning out all thought.

"Ah, yes. Now I see them," said Rose. "The two swordsmen."

The blurred painting fell away like an evaporating fog and Erde saw the source of the noise: her father, in pitched battle with a much younger man. The young man was tall and slim, more agile than the baron. His face, handsome even while distorted by fear and rage, was familiar to her, but she could not recall his name or who he was to her. For some reason, this filled her with despair. She remembered a sword, but not a name, could not conjure it to fit his image, no matter how desperately she tried. She would have wept but for the comfort of Rose's steady voice filling her ears.

"There, there, child, not all can be Known at once . . ."

But I did know it once, Erde told herself. *I know I did.* Perhaps she really was damaged after all.

"What? What is it?" Hal begged. "Rosie, please."

"I see Josef von Alte," Rose reported. "Overmatched, fighting his final battle." Then, to Erde, she said, "As for this other, his truth is still hidden from you. When you can name him, you will be free of him."

Erde shook her head. Was Earth dreaming her father's murderer?

"Try to speak his name," Rose urged.

Hal made a sound of protest. Rose laid a staying hand on his knee. To Erde, she urged, "Speak it. You can, you know."

But she couldn't speak and didn't know the name, and if that's what speaking it would mean, she was glad. She didn't want to be free of this young man, whoever he was.

"Well, perhaps it's not time to face that truth yet," said Rose. "But these are not dragon dreams?"

Erde frowned. Indeed. How would the dragon know her father? Her own dreams, then, mixing with Earth's, getting in the way. For the first time, she considered the source of dreams. Where did a dream come from, and how did you tell one to go away?

"Your dreaming is not like the dragon's," said Rose. "He hears the voices of Power. Yours come from within. Human dreams are our inner voices begging to be heard."

Erde vowed to silence these importunate voices. She must allow the dragon to be heard.

"But you must listen to your own dreams as well," said Rose. "Self-sacrifice is rarely the answer."

"Some sacrifice is inevitable," Hal put in sharply.

"She is a child. A child must have her dreams in order to grow."

"She is the Dragon Guide."

Rose glared at him. "And you are the Paladin, who will keep her always to her mark."

He took a breath, then set his jaw. "If I must. If that is my destiny."

"Your destiny. *Your* destiny!" Rose stood abruptly and walked away through the long grass to the edge of the lantern light, raking her hands through her cropped graying hair. "Your destiny!"

"Rose . . ."

The other women relaxed. The tightly drawn circle eased into a ragged arc of casual arms and legs, listening.

"Rose, you saw it yourself. She is the Dragon Guide. If I walked away from this today she'd still have no choice."

"No. You are assuring that she'll have no choice."

"The Dragon assures that."

Rose paced away from Hal's reasonable tone. Erde did not understand this sudden irritable concern. Surely if Rose could read minds, she knew no other choice was wanted. Erde would always choose for the dragon, and willingly.

"Rose, you said it yourself," Hal repeated. "You said you saw Destiny."

From the edge of the shadows, Rose replied, "I saw it, but I don't have to like it."

"You shouldn't judge the . . ."

"Don't tell me what I can and cannot do!"

"Rose!" Hal threw up his hands. "I mean, is this useful? Does this offer us a single bloody clue about what to do next?"

"You take what you get with a Seeing, you know that! You can't control it like one of your household servants!" Rose stalked off into the darkness.

Hal leaped up to shout after her, "I don't have any servants! I don't even have a household!"

Esther leaned over to murmur in Erde's ear, "He would have, if the two of them could get along for longer than an evening's meal."

"They have, they do," protested Linden softly. "It's just that he's always leaving, from the moment he gets here."

Raven wrapped an arm around Hal's legs, hushing him.
"Sit down. Let her come to it her own way."

Hal sat. His long back curled over his crossed knees, he
massaged his forehead. "Sorry," he mumbled.

Raven patted his arm.

Erde was disturbed by being a cause for disagreement,
but thought that if Rose and Hal really loved each other,
they wouldn't fight so often. She was sure that when she
fell in love, she'd never disagree with her beloved. She
remembered the handsome young man in her dream and
wondered again who he might be.

Hal straightened with a sigh. "Rose, please come back.
The child needs your help."

And Rose returned out of the darkness and sat down beside him as if all was forgiven. The women resettled themselves alertly. Hal sighed again, his face shuttered with relief.

Rose gazed across at Erde without apology. "There is
also a white city in your dreams. At the end of a long
white road."

Erde nodded, her heart suddenly in her throat. The white
towers swam in brilliant light before her eyes. Was this the
moment she found out her true destination?

Carefully, Hal murmured, "Gerrasch did mention a
city . . ."

Rose ignored him. The lanterns gathered their deepest
shadows beneath her brow but threw off a reflected glimmer within. "That white road is longer than you can presently conceive of."

"What the hell does that mean?" Hal growled.

Raven elbowed him, sharply this time. "If she knew, she
would say so."

"But what city is it? Can you see where it is?"

"Please!" Rose shaded her eyes with her palm, as if
blinded by some bright sun. "I don't . . . it's odd. I can't
tell. The image is so very clear, yet I have no sense of
where." She paused for a moment, then added slowly, "Not
even of *when*."

"The when must be now, Rose," Raven reminded her.
"You only See the now."

"Yes, but . . ." Rose frowned at Erde distractedly. "You
think that it isn't, but it is."

"Is what, isn't what?" Hal fumed.

But Erde thought she knew what Rose meant. The city was *real*. But how could it be?

Rose met her puzzled gaze. "I don't understand it either."

"Is this city our destination?" asked Hal.

"Yes." Rose bowed her head, as if there were something else she found even harder to believe.

"How can I take them there if we don't know where it is?"

"I don't know." She spoke with sudden gentleness, though still without looking at him. "You will take them to the gates."

"To the . . ." Hal blinked at her, absorbing her meaning. Erde had never seen a man's hopes collapse visibly before. She had to restrain herself from scrambling up to comfort him. Finally Hal licked his lips, cleared his throat. "Only to the gates."

"You will be needed outside."

"Outside what? I don't want to be outside! Because I don't share his dreams, I have to be left outside?"

Erde stared at her knees. Hal's dragon-envy was a swift and treacherous current flowing within him. Occasionally, it surged free and flooded them both with its tides of guilt and longing.

Rose raised her head as if surfacing from a deep pool. The shadows had faded from her eyes and moved into the hollows of her cheeks. She looked exhausted. "You ask to know Destiny, Heinrich, but what you really want is to be able to choose the one you prefer."

"Wouldn't any man?"

"This is not given to mortals, man or woman. Not even to dragons is it given."

A breeze sprang up, setting the lanterns aflicker. For a moment, their light dimmed and the night flowed into the circle like dark water into a pit. Erde shivered. She had taken it for granted that the knight would be there to protect her for the full length of her journey, wherever it was leading, which appeared to be into some place of her own dreaming. She could not imagine how to get to such a place, but how else might she understand Rose's Seeing?

At length, Hal answered softly, with bleak humility, "I know. And therefore, so be it."

And the breeze died, the lamps flared, and the pain and tension was drawn away out of the circle, along with the darkness.

"The Seeing is over," said Rose.

"Now let us offer our love and silence to the night," Esther intoned ritualistically.

The women sat quietly, and Erde thought to fill the time appropriately by chanting various little benedictions she'd learned from the nuns. But she was too distracted for prayer. Sometime soon, she had to admit to Earth that the Mage City was only a fantasy she'd let run out of control to soothe him, to offer him—no, both of them—a goal, a hope when there'd been so little. Now that the aura of power was gone from the circle, Erde was sure Rose must have misunderstood her Seeing, to suggest that they could actually go to such a place. She vowed never to lie to the dragon again.

As she sat, restless and uncertain, a certain stillness came to her after a while, alive with the night breeze and the scents it carried of grass and earth and ripening fruit, and the sounds of insects and owls and the noisy brook at the bottom of the hill. She felt so welcome among these women and content, and as it had on the road out, this sense of well-being filled her chest like a great intake of breath. She felt her ribs expand with it, and her back straighten. It grew until it was so big she knew she could not contain it. She felt she might burst, and began to think of letting a little of it go, letting it flow out of her into the night like warm water, like milk, releasing the pressure of joy inside her.

Around her, the women sighed and smiled. Rose smiled also, but glanced at Hal to see if he had sensed this invasion of warmth. She was answered when he leaned over and kissed her quickly, sweetly, then grinned like a boy who'd just gotten away with something.

"When this child finds her voice," Rose murmured, "she will be dangerously charismatic."

Poised for another kiss, Hal raised a brow. "When? Then you know she will?"

"Oh, yes. This much is certain."

"I thought maybe Linden could . . ."

"No healer can cure this. She must find it herself."

Erde heard, yet didn't hear. The joy in her was drawing

together into a presence. Finally she understood it was the dragon returning from his hunt. It disturbed her that she hadn't recognized him immediately. There was something different about him, something . . . bigger. She sensed his same plodding gait as he toiled up the hill, the same distracted curious air, nosing her out yet knowing exactly where to go. But there was an aura of bigness, a new sense of resolve. He had come in search of her and he had something on his mind. Clearly, the dragon had eaten well.

Across the circle, the mule leaned in to nudge Hal's shoulder. The dogs stirred and the she-goat stood up and shook herself. Erde thought Earth's image at Rose as hard as she could, but only caught the edges of her attention. Rose frowned vaguely and glanced her way as if she'd mumbled something incomprehensible.

But by that time, the dragon's approach was audible, the rhythmic swish of his bulk pushing through the tall grass, the sigh of his breath, so like the sighing of the wind in the berry bushes. All around the circle, the women drew up into postures of expectation. Those with their backs to him turned in place but the arc remained unbroken, a circle of lamps inside a circle of women. The solitary man leaned back on one arm and tried to look casual, but his waiting was as poignant as the rest.

Earth gained the top of the hill and halted when he saw the lantern light. He had expected to find Erde, but not the rest. He paused a moment in confusion, puffing slightly, then regained his dignity. Erde noted with a shock that he did seem bigger, even brighter. Another trick of the light? She would swear the dragon had grown substantially since noontime, when she'd sent him off to hunt. Even his color was bigger, more luminous. The moss greens and dirt browns were brighter and shone with highlights of bronze and gold. Admiring murmurs ran around the circle, and the dragon stretched and preened.

Erde was overjoyed to see him, and felt his own welcome rush through her like a fever. She gathered herself to leap up, but he sent her an image of waiting. So she held back, while Earth came forward to offer his formal greeting, a deep bow to the circle with ivory horns presented, gleaming like arcs of light in the reflected lamp glow.

But once he'd completed what he considered to be the

necessary formalities, he was all over the inside of her head
like a puppy dog. Images raced past too fast for Erde to
grasp.

   —*Earth! Slow down!*

   She was stunned to see Rose clap her hands to her ears
as if she'd shouted out loud. She offered a look of apology,
hoping Rose would understand that sometimes she just had
to yell at the dragon, or he wouldn't listen. But Rose continued to hold her head, curling over her knees as if in
real pain.

   Hal leaned in. "Rose? Rosie? What is it?"

   "It's . . . him!" Rose gasped.

   "What's happening?" Hal turned to Erde. "What's he
doing?"

   Frightened, she shook her head.

   "Whatever it is, tell him to stop!"

   She tried to get the dragon's attention, but he was too
caught up in what he wanted to tell her. Pictures flashed
in and out of her head like the colors on a spinning top,
all blending into incoherency. Erde considered more drastic
measures. She built a detailed image of an open door, held
it in her mind and with all her strength, slammed it shut.

   The dragon started and blinked. His torrent of images
stopped dead in astonishment.

   —*You were hurting this woman here.*

   Earth dismissed the possibility. He'd been nowhere
near her.

   —*She can hear you. Sometimes when you think too fast,
it's like . . . like that waterfall we nearly went over.*

   The mention of the waterfall seemed to impress him. He
went very quiet for a while.

   Rose uncurled, massaging her temples in relief. "Is he
always like that? How do you listen without burning your
brain out?"

   "You can hear him? You can hear the dragon? You can
hear what he . . . ?" Hal foundered midway between pride
and hopeless envy.

   "Not very well." Rose shook her head as if clearing it.
"Not very well at all. Mostly his enormous power. It was
how I imagine a god would speak." She regarded Erde with
new respect. "Child, you have a remarkable gift."

   "She is the Dragon Guide," Hal reminded her simply.

"Will you introduce me?" Rose asked Erde. "Perhaps we can learn a way to talk together in a less painful fashion."

The new deference in Rose's rich and wonderful voice made Erde self-conscious. She wasn't sure she deserved it. After all, it was the dragon who was remarkable, not she. But it was interesting to think about what it meant to be able to do something other people couldn't do. There was a kind of power in that, especially if it was something other people wanted to be able to do.

—*Dragon, this is Rose of Deep Moor. She has a great hearing gift. I think if you think very small and quietly, she might be able to understand you. This might be useful right now, since she has a working voice, and could translate for you.*

Earth blinked again and turned his huge eyes on Rose in a deeply speculative gaze. Erde saw faint flickers in her mind, little whispers of image, but Rose smiled and sighed as if she'd been given the most wonderful treasure.

"Can you hear him?" Hal demanded. "What does he say?"

"He doesn't exactly *say* . . . anything."

Hal nodded sagely, fighting to keep his envy in check. "No words. That's what she told me."

"He greets me, and you, the women of the circle. He's very polite. But there is something he's eager to tell us . . ."

New images ghosted into Erde's mind, appearing slowly like the sun through a mist. The scale was small, the colors were bland, but she recognized the Mage City, a pale echo of itself.

Rose inhaled sharply. "It's the city, the one you showed me! He says he knows where it is!"

The women exclaimed softly. Doritt let out a small cheer. Then Esther said, "Listen!"

On the night wind came an insistent clanging, from the direction of the farmstead.

"The alarm bell!" breathed Doritt.

"It must be Lily and Margit come home," said Raven, "wondering where we are."

Rose raised her face to the breeze like a wary animal. "Oh, this is the darkness I've felt all day. It's Lily, and she brings us bad news."

The circle broke instantly. Raven and Doritt scrambled

up and took off down the dark hill at a run. The twins
made quick arrangements for the return of the dogcart, and
sped after them.

"Margit is the twins' birth-mother," Linden told Erde
nervously as she helped the old lore-keepers into the cart.
Hal had promised to pull them home so the others could
hurry ahead. Rose thanked him gravely, then moved into
his arms for the offered embrace.

His lips brushed her forehead. "All will be well, Rosie."

"No, my love, it won't. Not any more." Rose pressed her
face briefly into his chest. "Deep Moor's grace time is over,
I feel it. The world has come to our doorstep. I only hope
we've not waited too long to act."

CHAPTER TWENTY-FOUR

Earth spent the whole trip down the hill babbling to Erde about his discovery. It wasn't exactly true that he knew where the Mage City was—Rose had misunderstood some of the finer details. But lying out in the meadow enjoying himself after a satisfying meal, he had heard the Summoner's voice for the first time while he was awake, in his head, not like a real sound, but the voice was now directional. It drew him like a lodestone. He was sure he could follow it to its source which, of course, was the city.

Erde told him what Rose had said about the city. He took this as further proof, which she would have been inclined to do also, were the Mage City not her own invention. She felt too deeply mired in her "righteous lie" to see a way out of it. Besides, she did have to wonder about what Rose had seen. Perhaps she had not made it up. Perhaps the image of the Mage City had come into her mind from somewhere else, from some*one* else. Once again, she decided to say nothing of this to the dragon. Even a fantasy destination was better than no destination at all.

The yard in front of the house was deserted when Hal and Erde reached the farmstead. The lanterns burned in scattered groups on the porch where they'd been hastily abandoned. The lore-keepers looked grim.

"All inside, I suspect," said one. The other hung a lantern to either side of the door, then blew the rest out and replaced them neatly in their rack. Erde left the dragon pacing impatiently in the yard. She followed Hal into the house.

Inside, oil lamps flared around the stone hearth, where

the women were gathered. A young woman lay bleeding in Raven's arms, struggling to speak while Linden sponged her wounds. Her clothing was torn and mud-spattered. Rose knelt alongside, holding the woman's limp hand and bending close to hear her broken whisper.

Doritt caught Hal's arm as he came up beside her. Her big dark eyes glimmered with unshed tears. "Margit's been taken!"

"What! Where?"

"Erfurt," she hissed. "Lily's run back all the way alone."

"How's she doing?"

"She'll be all right."

"Who got Margit?"

"Adolphus of Köthen."

"Of . . . Köthen? *Köthen?*"

Doritt nodded. "I'm sorry, Hal."

"Köthen in Erfurt?"

"He's leading the barons' army."

Hal seemed to wish he hadn't heard her right. "What about the king?"

"The king has fled."

His only response was a soft moan.

"Toward Nürnburg, with a few of his household. Prince Carl stayed with Köthen."

"Willingly?"

"Willingly."

Erde watched the knight's entire body reel under this last piece of news. In their month together, she had never seen his manner go so hard and cold, and yet somehow so sad. "Köthen always did have an abnormal influence over the boy. Is Margit alive?"

Doritt's mouth tightened. "So far. We don't have a lot of details yet, but Lily's afraid that Baron Köthen will use Margit to prove his loyalty when Fra Guill arrives next week to give his blessing to the barons' coup."

"The hell-priest in Erfurt, too? Oh, too close, Doritt, too close for comfort. I hope Lily covered her trail."

Doritt looked offended. "Lily's our most gifted Seeker. Of course she covered her trail."

"Erfurt taken. The king's own seat." Hal glanced about furtively as if he were being held against his will. "I must get to Nürnburg. I must get to His Majesty."

"What about Margit? You know he'll burn her, Hal."

"She knew the risk, as we all do. My duty is with the king."

Doritt looked away, frowning, then nodded. "And Margit would surely agree. Will you leave the girl and her creature with us?"

His nod was businesslike. "They're safer here than anywhere."

Erde grabbed his sleeve and shook her head.

"Milady, please understand. Speed is essential now."

She was sure from his posture that he was about to explain how this was men's work ahead of him. She searched about, found a scrap of Raven's paper in her pocket. EARTH WILL NOT STAY. HE IS CALLED.

"Ah, yes," agreed Doritt. "He's on his own quest, after all. They'll just go off on their own without you."

"And Fra Guill will have them in a blink of an eye. Ah, sweet Mother, help me. What do I do?" Hal paced away and back. "King or Dragon? Must I choose?"

Erde wrote: WE'LL ALL GO TO NÜRNBURG.

"Milady, our little walk in the woods has just become infinitely more dangerous."

She nodded, once and briskly.

"Rose's Seeing proves you've still a ways to go together," Doritt pointed out.

"He moves too slowly! He's like a snail!"

HE'LL MOVE FASTER, Erde promised.

Because the knight did not refuse her outright, she knew that the session up on the hill had changed something fundamental in his thinking about her and the dragon, a change she sensed in her own thinking as well. New sensations of confidence and potential were spreading through her like slow warmth, a growing need to act, to stand against the evil tide of events rather than be swept along by it. She had fallen in with this loose network of royalists by accident, if there was any such thing as accident (which she was beginning to doubt), but they were her natural allies. Her enemies were their enemies. Most importantly, she had a notion that the dragon was also readying himself to act. She had no idea what form his action might take, but as Dragon Guide, she might well influence his choice.

She had a strange moment of self-awareness, as if she

were standing across the room looking back. She saw a tall young woman with a ruddy boyish face and determined jaw, strong and lean from travel and the knight's training exercises, clothed in a man's pragmatic garb. The sallow longhaired child in slippers and velvet dresses was a fading memory. Her mouth twisted with reflective irony. She'd become what she'd always pretended to be in her fantasies, what her father had always feared and despised. Interesting that it had required the sacrifice of her entire life as she'd known it to accomplish the transformation.

Possessed by this new self as if by some benign but reckless demon, Erde grinned at Hal and scrawled: WE'LL SAVE THE KING TOGETHER.

Hal squeezed his eyes shut once, then nodded helplessly.

PART FOUR

EARTH

The Meeting with Destiny

CHAPTER TWENTY-FIVE

She promised him haste, and he got it. With twelve women bending their efforts to it, the provisioning was quickly accomplished. Food, a skin of wine, a new linen shirt for Erde and her old one clean. Presents, too, casually produced and packed away as if they'd been hers all along. There were warm gloves and new stockings from the fine wool of Doritt's sheep. Rose gave her a thin rectangle of slate pierced by a thong, and a soft pointed stick that made bright letters on the gray stone. This gift Erde hung gratefully around her neck, but not before scrawling THANK YOU on it in large letters.

Hal hunted up a leather breastplate and greaves that he'd left behind on some past visit. He stowed them in the mule packs along with a borrowed supply of extra woolens. Erde touched his arm in question as he was stuffing them into an already full pouch.

"Rose says we'll need these." He closed the pack briskly and tied the thongs. Then he went to draw Rose aside from the women crowding around the loaded mule. He said his good-byes and Erde said hers. They were on the road before the moon had set.

Raven and Doritt came out with them as far as the oak grove. They walked arm in arm beside Hal, their mood somber. The dragon did not share their foreboding. He was as eager as if the Summoner awaited him right outside the valley. He forged off like a happy hunting dog through the tall grasses to the right and left of the track, vanishing into the darkness and then returning to report to Erde on the beauty of the night and the interesting smells to be had out in the meadow.

Meanwhile, under the steady pressure of Raven's persuasion, Hal reconsidered his itinerary.

"Nürnburg is a week's hard ride," he grumbled, "Never mind what it will take with this group. The king on the road, exposed and vulnerable . . . what if Köthen's sent men in pursuit?"

"But Erfurt's on the way," she reminded him. "A swing up there won't add more than a day."

"If all goes well." Hal sighed as if bullied and overmatched. "Well, let's say we do it. Four or five days to Erfurt, then I slip in quickly by night. We must still have a loyal source or two who could help me find Margit. All right. If I'm not too late, I'll do what I can."

"It wouldn't be the first time."

"No," he admitted gloomily. "It wouldn't."

Raven put her arm around his waist and leaned into him gratefully. Doritt's brisk, serious nod said she didn't hold out too much hope, but she was relieved that he would try.

"I hope they won't have taken her crucifix," murmured Raven. Doritt muttered sympathetic agreement but Hal shook his head.

"Pray she'll not endanger her soul with that."

"Don't be so disapproving," Raven chided. "You know the same Church that makes such prohibitions is the Church that's burning innocent women. Would you begrudge our Margit a quick and comfortable passing?"

"Pray there'll be no need," Hal repeated primly.

Raven released her arm and stood away from him. "Heinrich, are you really a man to whom the law means more than human life?"

"Not man's law. I'd deliver the grace stroke myself, were murder the only way to save her the agony of the stake. But we're talking here of God's Law." He shrugged delicately, as if embarrassed by his own obstinance. "I do truly believe it's a sin to take one's own life."

"It's men who've decided what God's Law is," Raven returned. "What if they were about to burn you?"

Erde, who'd been listening mystified, saw it all in a bright and sickening rush: some fast-acting poison from Linden's stores of herbs and elixirs, a tiny lethal reservoir inside the crucifix. She'd heard of such things in the bard tales. It was a once remote and romantic notion that now seemed pragmatic and humane. Surely it was not a sin to save yourself from suffering a prolonged torture? She wished the witch-woman in Tubin had had such an option. She was surprised that Hal could be dogmatic about suffering, especially when he had seen so much of it.

But on the other hand, Raven's reply did amount to outright heresy. Every good Christian knew that God had decided God's Laws.

The birds were just stirring in the oak trees as they reached the grove. Their early songs hung crystalline in the still air. The heady sweet scents of fern and wet leaves were like fairy voices begging Erde to stay. She knew she would, were it not for the dragon. She was probably mad, having found such a wonderful place, to be leaving it so quickly.

Hal squinted through the branches toward the lightening sky. "We'll travel till dawn, then rest until dark. I want to get well clear of this valley in case we're noticed."

Raven took the late rose she'd worn in her hair and laid it on the stone cairn by the pool in the middle of the grove. "For your safety this day and those to come," she intoned. She took Hal's hands. "Find our Margit." Then she kissed him and embraced Erde, turning away briskly with tears in her eyes. Erde found her own suddenly wet.

"Come, Doritt. Let them be on their way."

"Yes, yes, soon enough." Doritt shook hands around, finishing with a firm pat on Erde's shoulder. "We've not seen the last of you, girl. Don't fret."

Raven was already lost in the shadows. "Is that a true notion, Doritt?" she called.

The tall woman nodded. "You can count on it."

"Well, that's encouraging," remarked Hal as they approached the steep switchbacks leading out of the valley. "Doritt's notions are her gift. She gets them about how things will turn out. Not like Rose's Seeing what *is,* much vaguer and long-term. She doesn't get them very often and she can't call them up—they just arrive, or they don't. But Deep Moor swears by her."

They found the dragon at the foot of the cliff, stock-still, staring upward. When Erde asked him what he was looking at, she received his blank-mind state, the same as she did when he was being invisible. Several times, he glanced at the base of the trail, then back at the top of the cliff, a good half-mile above.

Erde pulled out her new writing slate. HE WON'T TALK TO ME.

Hal laughed. "You know how he hates to climb. He's wishing he had wings, like a proper dragon."

As they stood watching the dragon stare intently upward, the first pink of dawn flushed the mountain range to the west. Hal sent the mule and the she-goat up the trail.

"We must be moving. If you go ahead, he'll follow."

Which he did, but with a puzzled, distracted air. Erde sent him a wistful image of himself with sleek reptilian wings, soaring toward the cliff top. His response was the closest thing to a chuckle she'd heard out of him yet: a vision of himself with his tongue lolling ridiculously. It was her first clue that he knew what humor was.

—*You thought I was making a joke?*

He returned assent and a new image: himself decked out with giant bird wings, flapping and panting, but unable to lift his massive body off the ground. Then he showed her how wings large enough to lift his weight would be too cumbersome to carry around on the ground. Erde thought this was unimaginative thinking for a mythic creature such as a dragon. She wrote out the conversation laboriously for Hal on her slate.

"Dragons," he offered seriously, "er . . . *winged* dragons are said to have hollow bones made of magical substances that cause them to weigh nothing at all."

Erde made a face. NOT THIS DRAGON.

"No," the knight mourned. "Apparently not."

Earth had more to say on the subject of travel. He'd been thinking about it a lot, but the results were hard to express in visual images. He'd become convinced that knowledge of an easier way lurked just beyond the edges of his memory. Because she knew how miserable and inadequate he felt when his memory failed him, Erde concentrated on soothing his frustration, simply to keep him going up the hill. She asked about the Summoner. Earth told her the voice came and went. It was not as constant in his waking existence as it was in the dream, but he was confident he would hear it soon again, and know which way to go. Erde hoped it would be in the direction of Erfurt and Nürnburg.

The air cooled noticeably as they climbed. Erde recalled the torn but heavy layers of clothing that Lily had arrived in, and the woolens that Rose had made Hal bring along. She thought of the mud and chill of her journey from Tor Alte, and stole many backward yearning glances at the receding valley. She'd hoped to stay a while, to sleep in a warm soft bed again and wake rested to the sound of birdsong and the comfortable chatter of women.

When they gained the top of the cliff after an hour's hard climbing, it was like walking out of a warm house into winter. A stiff cold wind rushed down off the mountains, as lung-searing as a torrent of ice water. Just past dawn and the sky already glowered with dark and shifting layers of cloud. Panting from his climb, Earth perched on the edge, his snout raised to the gusts as if the wind itself might bring a message.

Hal had not looked back once since starting the ascent, but now he settled on a rock to catch his breath and faced the valley, his red-leathered back to the gale. "Rose swears it's a coincidence of geography that keeps Deep Moor so temperate when the rest of the world's halfway to winter. It's like a place set apart, where the usual rules just don't apply, where the society is humane, and nature's always in balance. A religious man would say it's God's grace. A superstitious one would call it sorcery. I don't know what I believe. But of all the places I go, Deep Moor is the only place I ever really *want* to be. I just . . . my life . . . well . . ." He shrugged, gave up, and rose from his rock. "We'll unpack those woolens now. Put 'em on soon as the sweat dries. Damn unseasonable weather."

They retraced their steps up through the gray army of standing stones, where the she-goat had nearly met her end, and back across the barren ridges that hid the valley from the world of men. The wind stayed gusty and biting. The summer foliage was black and slimy with frost. Along the way, Hal covered their tracks obsessively, searching for any sign that Lily might have left in her panicked homeward flight. Finally he had to admit how astonishingly careful she'd been for an injured fugitive at the very end of her strength.

"Somehow, they always keep it hidden. You ask around at the nearest market town? People never know where Esther comes from. It's as if they never think to ask. Yet there she is, with vegetables twice the size of theirs, and crockery and weaving that bring the farmwives from all around. Remarkable, these Deep Moor women. Remarkable, every one of them."

Witches, thought Erde, *real ones,* and knew it to be true.

They camped at noon deep in the woods on the downward slope. The animals lay down as soon as Hal called a halt. Even the dragon, despite his eagerness to be following his Voice, recognized limits to a day's travel that the knight seemed to have forgotten. Hal's impatience made him restive. He talked of the king as they set up camp, told stories of their better days together. He insisted on a rigorous sword practice before their meal and bed.

"Twice a day now. You're strong enough. Just at the point where you can start actually learning something. Here." He tossed her the practice stick. Erde snatched it out of the air with one hand and did not fumble it. "See? Now, present your weapon."

Erde took her stance, gripped her stick, and held it out in front of her. Hal turned to face her, his own stick laid across hers for the first time. Erde felt a twinge of nervousness, but it was performance anxiety, not fear. She had been looking forward to the moment of actual engagement, to see if all this effort would amount to any real skill.

"Now, watch. This third move we've been practicing becomes a right cross-parry. Try it. It's a standard parry for swordsmen who can't count on superior strength. Good. Now use it when I come at you like this. One and two and . . ."

He came at her slowly, in the speed and rhythm of their usual practice routine. Erde cocked her wrists, straightened the appropriate arm, and his stick slid neatly off hers toward the ground. She knew he had relaxed into the parry, but the move still felt right and it gave her a most unwholesome sort of satisfaction. She grinned wickedly. Hal grinned back, winked, and sobered. "Now, again! Faster! One and two and . . ."

*   *   *

They rested, and awoke at dusk to move along again. The terrain became rocky and broken beneath stands of young trees thick with thorny undergrowth. The going was slow. Even the goat and the surefooted mule found it treacherous.

"I know I'll be breaking my own rules of safety," Hal said on the second night out, "but a little north of here, we'll come up on the road west toward Erfurt. I'd like to chance it for a while, till we get free of these hills." He daubed at the raw scrapes and scratches on Erde's palms with a salve Linden had sent along. "We've made maybe eight to ten miles a day this way. It's too slow. On the road, we could make twelve to fifteen, and turn five or six days to Erfurt into four. What do you think?"

Erde sent back a tired grin. Surely he wasn't actually asking her advice?

"What would you do if you were out here alone?" he pursued.

He wanted an answer. Erde considered, then wrote on her slate: MOVE MORE SLOWLY.

He laughed. "What if you had to move faster?"

I WOULDN'T. HE CAN'T.

"Ah. But what if you were without the dragon?"

THE ROAD.

He nodded. "Good. Then that's what we'll do."

Had he only wanted her agreement, or was he insisting that she begin to take part in the decision-making? Now they knew Hal would not always be there to guide her. Their paths had nearly divided in Deep Moor. Erde had an inkling of some new aspect being added to her training, and vowed to pay more attention to such things. She had no sense of how fast or how far they'd traveled. Hal had told Rose that she and the dragon had covered some two hundred miles in the month since she'd left Tor Alte. Two hundred miles seemed an enormous distance, yet she was not halfway across the east-west stretch of the kingdom, Tor Alte being on its extreme eastern border. She was beginning to understand why a kingdom was so hard to rule and keep together, why it could be so easily split apart by the machinations of a few dissident vassal lords.

"It'll be risky, but a lot easier on him." Hal jerked his head at the dragon, who was nursing a deep gouge in his flank from a broken limb he'd tumbled into. All his injuries healed with miraculous speed, but the forest had become so dense he often could not squeeze between the trunks. He'd have to cut a wide arc around to find a way back to them. "To say nothing of easier on us," Hal added ruefully. "And it might improve our chances of getting to Margit in time."

He got no argument, so the next dusk found them hunkered down in the trees above a rough track cut through the forest, wide enough for four men to ride abreast without their helms and standards being snagged in the overhanging branches. Earth eyed the open roadway with approval. Hal studied the muddied wheel ruts.

"Well, it's in use all right, and by more than just a few local farmers. Horses carrying men and armor. Mostly heading west. West . . ." Hal blew air through his teeth. "Ah, would I could fly like a bird. Would I were with His Majesty."

He didn't say, would this dragon had wings. Erde laid a sympathetic hand on his arm.

"Right. Here's what we'll do. Pack up the Mule more farm-style, hide the swords, but keep them handy. Tether the goat, if she's willing to be led. You'll be the idiot goatboy, should anyone come along. Earth will have to be invisible, which in the dark, shouldn't tax him too much."

They climbed down to the road as a peasant widower and his unfortunate son journeying to visit relatives outside of Erfurt. Hal embellished the tale as they strode along, both to tighten their cover in case they had to use it and to keep his mind off his concern for the king's welfare. The road was deep in mud and standing puddles of icy water, but it was easier going than the woods.

"Another good night like this and we'll be within striking distance of Erfurt," Hal remarked as they bedded down for the day high in the pine woods above the road. He would not allow a fire. Some traveler on the road might scent the smoke. But before they went to bed, he roused Erde for practice. This time, he untied the pack bundle that held the real swords, and freed them from their wrappings. His own was sheathed and he buckled it on with evident satisfaction, as if he'd missed the weight of it, companionable against his hip. The other, naked blade he passed to Erde hilt-first.

She took it confidently, then felt suddenly thrown off balance. It wasn't the weight. She could lift it well enough. But she'd taken it in hand assuming it was his, a spare he carried. Then holding it, she'd realized it somehow belonged to her. What was she doing with a sword? There was resistance as she tried to remember, as if that information was locked away in a shadowy place where her brain didn't want her to look. With great effort she recalled finding the sword under her bed at Tor Alte. But no straining would tell her how it came to be there. Another blank spot, another lapse. She thought of the dragon's dilemma and wondered if she was losing her memory as he regained his.

Hal read her stricken look and sudden paralysis as novice's nerves. "Oh, now. Just take a good grip on it, go ahead, like you would your stick. It's no different, really."

Being given a task to focus on broke Erde's daze. She did as he said, and found the hilt fitted well into her palm. She flexed her fingers around it, frowning. Perhaps it was hers after all.

"Good hands," approved Hal. "Strong hands."

She'd always been self-conscious about her hands. Too big and rangy for a girl, not frail and soft and white. Fricca had once advised her to sit on them in public. She gripped the hilt and found it warm as if from someone else's hand, though Hal had held it only by its linen wrappings and by the incised base of the blade. The uncanny warmth sparked a flare of memory that fled almost before she was aware it had been there—a face, a smile, then gone, leaving only an ache inside. Fending off this unidentifiable pain, Erde raised the sword with both hands out in front of her. Automatically, her body corrected for the weight. Her stance widened, her back uncurled, her hips tucked. She felt a transition into balance, into harmony with the shining length of steel. She twisted the blade back and forth, letting it catch the dapplings of dawn falling through the trees. The flash of light was powerful, mesmerizing.

Hal laughed softly. "See? You can lift it easily now. Don't look so thunderstruck. I told you I was a good teacher. Now let's run the whole routine. Face forward, blade down. Ready? And one, and two . . . ."

*　　*　　*

It rained during the day, drenching them in their sleep, then it cleared and became cold and dry. But the next night, the road was ankle-deep in stiff black ooze, iced over in the shallows. It had narrowed considerably to wind through a steep-sided glen lined with dense stands of birches, as slim and white in the moonlight as old bones and set as close as prison bars. A grown man could scarcely pass between them to scale the darker slopes.

Hal was in a black complaining mood from loss of sleep and damp clothing and not being with the king, where his duty lay. He was so intent on hurrying his party along that he didn't hear the men approaching until they were nearly around the bend. He stopped dead in the middle of a complaint. "Christ Almighty!" he breathed. "Listen!"

Ahead, the creak of harness and the quiet splash of many hooves through the mud.

Hal shoved Erde toward one side of the road, the mule toward the other. "Scatter!"

Erde had reached the thicket of birch trunks and was scrambling up the slope when the horsemen came into view. They were moving slowly, cautiously, wary of the forest night. Helmets and lance tips gleamed in the moonlight. Erde dropped to her belly. The she-goat was a flicker of motion freezing into silence farther up the hill. Erde guessed that Hal had split to the other side with the mule, and the dragon was . . .

Still visible in the middle of the road. The close-packed birches might as well have been a stout palisade to him, and the road was too narrow for the horsemen to pass him by without touching. Invisibility would not conceal him. Earth was trapped, with a dozen armed and armored men coming straight for him, still unaware that they were about to run into anything unusual. The dragon, who could have done serious damage to them before they'd have time to strike a blow, was terrified. His fear clanged deafening alarms in Erde's head as he charged the trees like a battering ram, rolling all his weight against the trunks. The smallest gave way and cracked rendingly, the thickest swayed and held. He backed up and rushed them again, creating a barrier of splintered wood rather than a passageway. The armed men were closing in. The leader raised a hand and called a halt, peering down the darkened road.

He was jumpy, unsure. He gestured to two of his men to investigate the strange racket. Glancing at each other nervously, they set their lances and eased their horses forward.

Earth saw the steel-tipped shafts moving toward him through patches of shadow and moonlight. He panicked. He threw himself again and again against a tangle of broken branches scarcely less sharp than the lances themselves. Sure that he'd impale himself, Erde leaped up out of hiding and tumbled back down the slope to stop him. One of the lancers spied her. He shouted a warning, the shrill cry of a man frightened of what might be lurking deep in a forest at night.

A sudden curve of flame arced through the darkness and into the mud at the lancers' feet. Another followed. Their horses neighed and backed. The riders fought for control, their lances colliding, nearly unseating them. The rest of the party spurred forward at the leader's sharp command. Another burning arrow thunked into the mud, then another. A bright line of flame separated the lancers from their unknown quarry. The leader shouted. The horses shied and would not cross.

Erde reached the panicked dragon, her mind yelling at him with all her strength to be still. He saw her dancing around him, felt her too close, ducking his flailing limbs, risking the crush of his plunging bulk. He froze. She laid her palms on his neck and climbed up on his foreleg to grip his head with both hands and stare into his eyes. Desperate to calm him, to get him still and invisible, she sent him the safest, most soothing image she could conjure. His mind leaped at it and clung to it eagerly. He knew that place, knew it well. He wanted to be there, longed to be there, not in a muddy dark forest pursued by sharp points and cold steel. Not here but . . .

Erde felt her stomach turn over. Her mind went suddenly numb. She squeezed her eyes shut. He was falling or she was going to faint, from fear or . . .

The dizziness passed. The dragon relaxed beneath her, and she risked a breath, a deep breath of warm, moist air smelling of grass and flowers. *Familiar* smells. The shrilling of Earth's inner alarm bells ceased. In its place, an astonished but gratified sense of satisfaction. Still clinging to him, Erde opened her eyes.

They were back in the meadows of Deep Moor. Not even attempting an explanation, she let go of the dragon and climbed down into the tall, sweet-smelling grass. She walked around a bit, dampening her hands with night dew. It was not a dream. She stared around the moonlit valley, then back at the dragon.

—*You did this. How?*

He sent her an image of a shrug, a notion she had taught him and now wished she hadn't. It only encouraged his childishness.

—*Think how it happened! You must!*

His smugness unappreciated, he put his mind to remembering. It had actually been very simple. She had made him think of Deep Moor and he'd wanted to go there desperately, to the valley where he'd be safe, right here on this spot that he recalled so clearly, and so he just *was.*

—*And me. You brought me with you.*

Assent. Earth did not see anything particularly remarkable about that. She had been there in his mind, after all. What he marveled at was being safe again.

—*But it's a miracle! Can you do it again?*

Assent. He reminded her that the only good thing about this snail-paced process of regaining his memory was that once he remembered part of a thing, he remembered all of it, like unlocking a door gave access to everything behind it. This was the better way to travel that he'd been struggling to recall. If he could image a place accurately enough, he could quite simply *be* there.

Erde laughed in soundless delight, then stopped short with a gasp as she remembered Hal, alone, bearing the brunt and the mystery of their sudden disappearance. The flaming arrows were a stroke of genius, but they would have given his position away.

—*We have to go back!*

?????

She imaged Hal defending himself single-handedly against a dozen armed warriors. Earth countered with visions of lances and steel.

—*We must go back! We can't desert him! He'd fight to the death to protect you.*

The dragon moved away from her, pacing and circling anxiously, sending up rich aromas of dirt and crushed grass.

—Earth, please! We have to help him! What about the Mule and the goat?

He sent back horrific images of her being sliced and dismembered, of himself having to kill soldiers in order to save her. It was wrong to take a life without permission. He didn't want to do that.

—You won't have to. We can go back, grab Hal and the others, and bring them back here. You can do that, can't you?

Earth considered. He could go back, he knew that, and he could retrieve anyone or anything he could picture well enough to hold in his mind as a separate entity. Finally, he could not find an honest reason, besides his own fear, to deny her.

—Then we'll do it. Umm, how do we do it?

He pictured her drawing close to him, helping him remember the place they had come from, though his image of it was far more vividly recalled than hers could ever have been. Hers was night-dark and vague, distorted by the emotional state she'd been in, but he remembered everything because he noticed everything, despite his fear, in all the sensual dimensions, sight, sound, touch, and especially smell. What she could help him with was the motivation to take himself and her to a place he had no wish to return to, and since wanting a place, desiring to *be* there, was crucial to his new method of transport, she had to convince him. She urged and encouraged, she shamed him and pleaded with him and finally, she reminded him that he had accepted an oath of fealty which brought certain responsibilities in return.

Responsibility turned out to be the key. She felt him sigh and gather himself, then go very still. Then the same sudden dizziness and blankness of mind assaulted her, and she was back on the cold muddy road in the forest. Sound exploded around her like a bomb, the cries of men and horses, the clash of steel. Earth had returned them a neat hundred paces down the road from where they'd left. His accuracy astonished her. Ahead, the men and horses were caught in a melee. The arrows still burned in the mud. Someone was trying to light a torch. It looked like the men were fighting each other.

—How will we find him in this mess?

Earth imaged himself signaling the mule and the she-goat. His low bugled cry was barely audible over the neighing of the frightened horses. The torch finally burst into flame, illuminating a man dancing in and out among the others, whacking a horse here or a man there with his fist or the flat of his sword. The sudden light revealed him to the men as a stranger, and to Erde as Hal. The lancers howled their rage and humiliation, and turned on him as one. Hal ducked away from the horsemen to find himself confronting a man on foot with a sword raised to strike. Slewing his own blade around to parry, Hal lost his footing in the mud. He staggered, then dropped and rolled sideways as the other's sword sliced downward into the black ooze. The man was young and fast and recovered quickly for another chop while Hal struggled to regain his balance. Just before his downstroke, the man cried out and erupted forward, back arched and eyes wide. His sword went flying, nearly decapitating the man racing to help him finish the stranger off. Hal stared for a split second, uncomprehending, then scrambled to his feet as the she-goat rocketed past. She saw him, skidded to a halt, and raced back again, butting and nudging him away from the fray. He swatted at her in astonishment, readying his sword again and turning, but then the mule was there with her, much more persuasive with a hank of the knight's sleeve between his big teeth and his broad chest pressed hard against Hal's ribs.

The lancers were recovering. A few more torches had been lit. A foot soldier spotted the stranger being dragged off into the dark by two animals that had appeared out of nowhere. The man muttered, crossed himself, then squeaked out a warning. His fellows stared. Some hesitated, a few retreated. Several of the bravest shouted a victory cry and charged, torches flaring. Hal shook the mule off and began to run.

And there, looming up before him, huge and menacing in the flickering torchlight, was every reason that the soldiers had feared going into the forest at night. They stopped dead to take in the horned head and reptilian neck, the raking claws and burning eyes of the creature that the priest had warned them about.

A dragon.

Frantically conjuring Deep Moor in her mind, Erde saw

terror and dread drain all expression from the lancers' faces. Stock-still, bathed in torchlight, they watched the stranger-warlock sprint to meet his dragon steed, his animal familiars racing by his side. At the edge of the darkness, the demons slowed, gathered, and disappeared.

CHAPTER TWENTY-SIX

"**Y**ou mean he could do that all along? All those miles on foot when we could have been traveling like that? We could be in Erfurt now. We could be in Nürnburg!" Hal was a tall shadow stalking around the dragon and waving his arms, simultaneously apoplectic and elated. "Can he take us to Erfurt? How many can he take? Could he take a whole army?"

"Heinrich," said Rose patiently. "You don't have an army."

Erde sat cross-legged on the velvet grass of the clearing in front of the farmhouse, leaning back against Raven's shoulder, busy with her writing slate. Beside her, a lantern gave off soft, comfortable light.

HE NEEDS TO KNOW WHO HE'S TAKING, she scrawled.

She could hear the she-goat and the mule grazing serenely in the darkness along the edge of the trees. The breeze was soft and Erde was warm again. She was overjoyed to be back in this magical place, and wished she could stay this time.

Raven read her message aloud.

"He needs to know them personally?" Hal demanded.

"I understand, I think," Rose supplied. "He needs to feel them in his mind. Each person separately. It's like a conversation."

Beside Erde, Doritt muttered, "I knew they'd be back, but I didn't figure it'd be this soon . . ." She'd been talking with Raven on the porch when the dragon materialized in the clearing. She said it had sounded like music coming out of the air. At the very same moment, Rose had woken up out of a sound sleep. She'd heard a bell ringing, one clear ethereal tone, and knew they had returned.

"Well, then we'll just appear in the market square and snatch Margit from the stake, right out from under Fra Guill's pointy little nose!" Hal faced Rose, hands on hips, giddy with the potential of the dragon's latest gift. "We could do that." He turned to Erde. "Couldn't we?"

Rose tilted her head in disbelief. "And reveal Earth's presence to all his worst enemies?"

"But he can escape them now. Just picture it!" Hal did a boyish clenched-fist dance of anticipation. "It'll scare the piss out of that priest!"

"No, it'll only give him satisfaction to see his prophecies proven true. It will add to his power."

"It will save a life." Hal folded his arms. "The girl offered his help—now I'm calling on it."

"Rose, if it'll save Margit . . ." Raven murmured. "How else can we do it?"

Erde didn't want to seem recalcitrant. She understood the knight was challenging her to make good on her reckless promise, or be left behind for sure this time—with the rest of the women. But she had to make sure the circumstances favored success. She held her slate into the light of the lantern for Raven to read.

"She says he's never been to Erfurt."

"So? Does he have to have been someplace already to be able to go there? That could be awkward."

HE NEEDS TO KNOW WHERE HE'S GOING.

Hal stared back with one eyebrow raised. Raven giggled and he glared at her.

Erde tried again, writing very small to fit it all on the slate.

HE NEEDS AN IMAGE IN HIS MIND.

"Ah." Hal turned away, deflated.

"Can he take an image from someone else's mind?" asked Rose.

Erde smiled at her, then erased and scribbled briefly.

"She says, ask him," Raven supplied.

Erde did not feel possessive about the dragon. It was actually a relief to have someone else who could talk to

him for a while. She reminded him to speak to Rose very
gently, and while he was at it, to get a sense of Margit from
her, to fix in his mind.

Earth was willing to try, now that the danger to his
friends' friend had been explained to him. He was nowhere
near as phobic about fire as he was about water, but the
idea of burning to death horrified him.

"If I can put an image into his head," Rose reported,
"he will know if it's good enough."

Hal cleared his throat. "I have no army, Rose, and you
haven't been to Erfurt in thirty years."

"No, it confuses my Sight to go out into the world. But
Esther has, and Lily, and I can read both of them fairly
well."

"Lily's in no shape to do anything," said Raven.

"Linden says Lily's fine," Doritt countered. "She's just
bruised and tired out."

"And terrified and grief-stricken and . . ."

"Oh, well, yes. I thought you meant . . ."

Rose raised both palms in a warding gesture, and the
younger women fell silent. The lamp glare caught in Rose's
short hair to make a fiery halo around her shadowed face.
Out of the light came her voice, that voice that could not
be disobeyed. "We'll let Lily sleep, as Linden has pre-
scribed and as she deserves. Raven, would you go wake
Esther?"

"Lily would want to be here if she thought she could do
anything to help Margit," Doritt mumbled, a parting shot
as Raven hastened toward the house.

"We'll see how we do with Esther," said Rose.

"You see, Esther's our tale-teller," Doritt told Erde.
"She has the real eye for detail."

Erde could feel the dragon basking in all their approval,
and was glad for him. He was so proud of having done
something right.

"Who was it on the road?" asked Rose.

"A party of Köthen's men, coming out from Erfurt to
hunt down royalists, no doubt." Hal spat into the grass.
"He's so unashamed of his treason, his henchmen wear his
colors openly. Rose, is there any chance Köthen's holding
the prince against his will?"

"You know far better than I, Heinrich, to what depths Köthen will stoop."

"Thought I did," Hal muttered. "Guess I don't."

"Well, there's one piece of news Lily brought that might cheer you." Rose waited until he'd stopped pacing to listen. "The Friend is secretly arming his followers."

"What?"

She nodded. "And the forges in the villages are hot day and night, though there's not a weapon to be seen when the soldiers come around."

"Lily *saw* the Friend?"

"No, but she spoke to people who had. His existence is no longer in doubt. He was three days west of Erfurt when Köthen's coup took place. The Friend halted his progress, which Köthen took as a sign either of acquiescence or cowardice. Apparently he doesn't take the Friend or his notions any more seriously than you do."

"Or he's afraid if he does, Fra Guill will get after him," remarked Doritt.

"I took the idea of him seriously. I just wasn't sure I believed it."

"Now you must. Lily's source claims he's got three thousand men out there and the number's growing now that Köthen's made his move." Rose mimicked Hal's stance, hands on hips, and her small straight body seemed more than a match for him. "Heinrich, the Friend has your army, waiting within striking distance of Erfurt and Nürnburg."

The knight let out a snort of dismissal. "Peasants armed with sharpened rakes and plowshares."

"But three thousand of them."

"Three hundred, more likely, and every one an idealist who'll turn tail the moment he's faced with a trained fighting man."

"You don't know that." Rose cocked her head at him. "Are you afraid of actually being able to take action, Heinrich? Do you prefer hopeless causes?"

Hal winced and scowled. "Of course not!"

"Besides, what if he is the lost prince you still believe in? Don't you want to find out?"

"Of course I do!"

"Well?"

Erde scrawled on her slate, then got up and handed it to him.

Hal turned it toward the lantern, squinting. "Hmm, well, I guess I did, didn't I."

"Did what?" asked Rose.

Hal's grin was sour. "Milady reminds me I told her I could make a soldier out of anybody." He kicked at the grass irritably, paced around a bit, and stopped at Earth's snout to grasp his horns as if for moral support. "If he really has taken the Dragon as his sigil . . . why would he do that?"

"Oh, one more coincidence, I'm sure," teased Rose.

"It is significant," Hal agreed, as if he'd thought of it all himself in the first place. "I'll search him out, at least. See what he's really about."

Raven hurried quietly from the house with Esther stumbling in tow. "I put tea on. Doritt, would you . . . ?"

Doritt nodded, got up, and padded into the house.

Esther rubbed her long face with both palms. "Hello, Hal. Pardon my nightdress. I thought you'd left." She smiled at Earth sleepily. "Hello, Dragon."

Rose was brisk. "Sorry to get you up. Are you awake? We need your help with something."

"So Raven told me. Erfurt. I don't know. Think it'll work, Rose?"

Rose took her hands. "Remember the time I needed to know what a certain person looked like who you'd seen only once?"

"I remember you had to get me very drunk before I could relax enough to be useful to you."

"But it worked."

Esther laughed. "I thought you were making it up. Or I was."

Hal untied the plump wineskin from the mule packs and held it out with a serious grin. "Well? Let's get down to business."

CHAPTER TWENTY-SEVEN

Esther recalled the location perfectly. Rose translated, and the dragon took them there. Erde was amazed at how easy it was.

The place was the back courtyard of a brick maker's, on the edge of town. Hal knew it also. It was a royalist contact site. They had settled on it, after some discussion, as a relatively safe destination, likely to be deserted in the early hours of the morning, and large enough for the dragon to shelter comfortably while the others were reconnoitering.

The courtyard was cold and dark when they arrived, with the tall cones of the brick kilns along one side and hard packed ground underfoot. After so long in the open, Erde felt immediately penned in by the brick and stone of a town. The air smelled like smoke and snow. Frigid gusts of wind tore the grit off the brick piles and flung it in her face. Hal found a straw-filled corner of a storage barn for the dragon to wait out the hours behind the brick stacks, until his skills were needed. They stowed their packs in an empty feed bin and covered them with old hay. Hal left the mule outside the door. He said when the brick makers arrived at dawn, they'd recognize him and avoid the barn without questions.

They slipped into the unlit streets with the she-goat in tow, the peasant laborer and his goat-boy once more. The town was not entirely asleep. Erde guessed that a town this big, nearly a city, probably never was. It was big enough that she could imagine getting lost in its narrow twisting streets. She wished Earth could be along to see it. Instead, she stored up images to bring back to him. Erfurt was the king's seat, the Royal City, she reminded herself, though she didn't think it very grand at the moment. It looked closed up and in retreat, the aftermath of Baron Köthen's coup. But now and then, a loaded cart passed by, and behind glazed windows, the bakers were already hard at work. And down some narrow alley or at the end of a darkened court, lamps burned and voices murmured around the thin warmth of dying embers. Men sat hunched over mugs of ale and argued. Hal left Erde crouched at the door of a few of these establishments, mostly the ones with no fancy painted sign overhead. Men came and went, quietly, paying no heed to the boy dozing with his arm slung across his goat's withers while his father got drunk inside. A few times, despite the cold, she did actually fall asleep, and then she'd feel Hal's hand on her shoulder, rousing her to move on.

"Not so many faces I recognize any more," he complained finally. "Or who'll admit they recognize me. About half the population either fled with the king or have sneaked away to the Friend's encampment. No further details about him, since none who made it out have come back to report. They could be alive or dead, for all I know. Only the barest bones of the underground are still in place." He shook his head irritably. "Come on. Let's see what all the noise is."

They followed the sound of sawing and hammering to Erfurt's huge market square. Erde halted in astonishment as they cleared the corner and faced the giant twin-towered cathedral and the ranks of fine houses to either side. Hal pushed her onward. "Don't stare. Supposedly you see this square every day." But he did let them pause to watch the joiners work by torchlight. His face was grim.

"My sources say Köthen's got the town surrounded, extra men at every gate, checking everyone who goes in or out. Noon today is the appointed hour, and no one can tell me where they're keeping her. In the church, is my guess. Köthen's declared a general holiday to welcome Fra Guill and your father, who are camped two miles out of town with an army of five hundred fighting men that the townsfolk are calling, at his own suggestion, the Scourge of God. Guillemo always did have a neat turn of phrase."

Her father and Fra Guill, at this very moment, merely two miles away. Erde shivered and pulled her cloak up around her nose. She hadn't realized how much comfort she'd derived from putting all that distance between herself and those two men.

She followed Hal along the long side of the square, past the shuttered four-story houses of merchants and guildsmen, away from the bustle of men and fresh-sawed wood in front of the cathedral, and away from the three or four white-robes who stalked among the workmen, barking orders and keeping up the pace.

"A very fancy affair Köthen has planned," Hal growled. "The stake raised on a scaffold, altarlike. That ought to appeal to Fra Guill. A viewing stand on the cathedral steps for the privileged guests. I wonder if he'll be serving refreshments? The last dregs of the town's larders." His face twisted. "Isn't it a lovely burning? Do you like the quality of the screams? Louder? You want louder? Can I offer you some wine and cheese?"

Erde slipped her hand into his and squeezed it tightly. He put an arm around her shoulder and held her close.

"Well, we'll do what we can." He sighed, letting his glance trail slowly around the big square, searching the doorways and balconies of the tall expensive houses where the king's court had so recently lived. "We need a place to wait, a launching point as it were, where we can see but not be seen."

Erde found herself searching the rooftops, recalling how the dragon had eyed the height of the cliff. But most were sharply peaked to shed rain and the weight of winter snow. One particularly tall one, however, seemed to have partly burned or collapsed, exposing the attic floor beneath. Builder's canvas hung from the skeletal rafters, billowing and snapping in the chill wind.

Hal followed her line of sight. "That was a beauty. Old Baron Schwarzchilde's house. One of the best wine cellars on the square. He would have stayed loyal. I hope he made it out alive."

Impatient with his nostalgia, Erde pointed to themselves and then at the roof.

He understood quickly. "Ah! Good idea. If it's a holiday, the repairmen won't come to work. Besides, all the joiners in town are working on Fra Guill's little celebration. We'll have the roof all to ourselves. Study it carefully, milady.

Memorize each and every detail. You'll have to bring the dragon up there and then right to the base of the scaffold if we're to have a chance at getting away with this." He grinned nastily. "And ah, if we do, I don't care what Rose says, I hope the hell-priest is standing next to me when we land, so I can spit in his face!"

At dawn, they returned to the brickyard. A few workers sat yawning around a smoldering firepit in the yard, sharing a jug and a loaf of bread, and rubbing their hands briskly over the fire's dim heat. They nodded as Hal passed. The oldest looked him straight in the eye and touched his cap respectfully, then made as if he was only adjusting the fit.

Hal left Erde in the barn and returned to the streets, saying there was something he'd sensed, something stirring that even his few sources wouldn't talk about. He promised to be back soon with more news and breakfast. The dragon welcomed her gladly, complaining of particularly vivid nightmares. When she lay down with him to rest, the voice of the Summoner was immediately ringing in her ears.

She woke at mid-morning to the sound of Hal sharpening his sword. When he heard her stir, he laid his weapon down and went out, returning with fresh bread and a small bowl of soup still hot from the brick makers' fire. "It's all they could spare—there wasn't much to go around, but at least it'll warm your stomach." He'd stripped down to his red jerkin and buckled over it the leather breastplate he'd brought from Deep Moor. Beads of moisture dotted his shoulders. "Dress warmly, milady. It's snowing out there."

She blinked at him, but actually, the mad weather had ceased to surprise her. It had come to seem an appropriate metaphor for the state of the world. The broth was watery and its contents well past their prime but she wolfed it down appreciatively, meanwhile rehearsing her memory of the broken rooftop and the market square.

"Not much other news to be had, bad or good, though I swear there's something going on that they're not telling me." Hal went back to work on his sword, his tense aura of anticipation touched with dry amusement "I'm glad you're not one of those anxious types who can't eat before a battle."

A battle. She hadn't thought about it that way, but then,

it was not for nothing that the knight was honing the edge of his already well-sharpened blade. They were about to drop into the middle of a town square full of white-robes and soldiers, and snatch away the reason for the gathering. Erde decided to get nervous.

The first leg of the journey went well, though Erde worried for the strength of the joists as the dragon's full weight settled onto the attic floor. The roof was deserted, dusted with a fine layer of wet snow. Earth stilled immediately and vanished. Hal and Erde ducked behind the charred front facade and peered over the edge of the stone parapet.

Their view of the square and the scaffold was unobstructed.

"You'd think it was May Festival," grumbled Hal disgustedly. "Pennants and banners, silk drapings on the viewing stand, everyone decked out in their most colorful best. But then there's this snow." He glanced at the lowering sky. Huge black clouds were bundling on the western horizon. "Or maybe something worse."

The square was full—men, women, and children, thickly wrapped against the sudden cold—but strangely hushed for so great a number crowded into one space. Even at a distance, Erde could see their faces were pale and tired, their mouths tight, their eyes narrow and anxious. A few stragglers were still arriving, escorted by small parties of foot-soldiers.

"A command performance," Hal noted bitterly. "Every able body left in town." He canvased the crowd, chewing his lip. "Not a lot of swords out there, though. A few of Köthen's personal guard on foot, the rest holding the gates. I guess he's feeling confident. Fine. So much the better for us. Though if I were him, I wouldn't bring Fra Guill into my town without the men to stand against him. I wonder if he's actually yet met the man face-to-face. He might not be so eager to . . . Ah, here we go!" He pointed diagonally across the square. "Speak of the Devil, and lo . . ."

Brother Guillemo made his entrance from the side of the square opposite the cathedral, a long stately progress on foot through the crowd with his phalanx of hooded white-robes in lock-step behind him. The throng drew away from him as he approached, like the Red Sea parting. As he drew near the scaffold, he glanced up at the sky, and Erde saw him brush snow from his robe. In his wake came a small party of armed horsemen wearing the black and gold of Tor Alte. To see her family crest and colors again was like a shock of ice water thrown full in her face. Erde ducked behind the parapet as she recognized the rider in the lead, her father decked out in his baronial finest.

My father! My father is here in Erfurt! She didn't want him there, didn't want to see him. Seeing him made her feel like a child again, yet she had to stare at him, his broad velvet-swathed chest, his ruddy face and prematurely silver hair. Perhaps seeing him would repair the gaps in her memory of those last days at Tor Alte. But there came no lightning bolt or revelation. It was only him, her father as she remembered him, though seeming a bit thinner, less robust. But perhaps that was only the effect of distance, diminishing him in her eyes. She was sure that no one else in the square could see beneath his show and swagger to the anxiety beneath. Josef von Alte. Her father. She had thought she would never see him again, yet here he was in Erfurt, her past and present lives commingling for the first time. Her old self-image, the one he'd helped form with his rage and his constant challenge, bubbled to the surface like air out of melting ice. Her newfound confidence drained away. She cringed against Hal's side, shaking uncontrollably.

"Easy, girl," Hal murmured. "They're only men. As mortal as any of us."

Erde wished she could snap back at him: *But one of them is my father!*

"Can't let them rattle you." The knight had put his nerves aside. The nearer it was to the moment of truth, the cooler he became. Erde drank up his calm like a draught of wine and let it soothe her. Then she felt his body tighten. "Here now, girl. Get up and pay attention. Here comes Margit."

The witch-cart came from the opposite corner, drawn by four foot-soldiers, blazoned in blue and yellow. They followed a single rider, a stocky bearded man, blond and bareheaded but wearing darkly glimmering mail beneath his tunic. He wore no other ornament but his own blue and yellow crest. His sheathed sword hung on the pommel of his cloth-draped saddle. He carried his feathered helm in the crook of his arm, clasped in his mailed fist.

Hal pointed. "That's Köthen in the lead, looking the fine figure of a man as usual and doing his humble act."

She thought Hal stared at Köthen with a particular intensity, perhaps giving him special study as the one clearly in charge. And this in itself was interesting, because Baron Köthen was much younger than she'd expected, barely into his thirties, making him at least ten years her father's junior, which she knew must be particularly annoying to Josef von Alte. Plus, Köthen was impressive, even handsome in a coarse, worldly sort of way. Square-jawed and serious, he *looked* like a leader. Erde decided that for all his youth, Köthen could easily eat her father alive. She worried for Josef, despite all he'd done to her. And despite the way he stared so obviously at the woman in the witch-cart. Köthen hardly gave her a glance, though she wore the usual clinging white shift, sure to arouse the lust and envy of the men, and the pity and envy of the women. Erde recognized the twins' red hair and slim, muscular build. She wondered if these witch-hunting men ever considered it worthwhile to burn a woman who wasn't beautiful.

Köthen and Brother Guillemo met in the middle of the square, in front of the scaffold. Josef von Alte reined in some yards away. Both riders dismounted and bowed to the white-robed priest, then submitted to having their hands joined by him with great ceremony. Köthen stood back as soon as his hand was released.

"Ah, good." Hal's grin was feral. "They hate each other. That may prove useful. Now. We should get her while they're taking her up the steps, which could be any minute now. Are you ready?"

Erde nodded, though there seemed to be a lot of men and horses in the way. Plus her father, so close . . .

"Alert the Dragon, then."

She tore her eyes away from the square to concentrate on the dragon, but Earth was already prepared. He'd found a hiding place that provided a view of the scaffold. One corner of it was obscured by a charred rafter slung with canvas, but Erde could offer detail where it was lacking. And this time, she did not have to provide motivation. For the moment, not a thought was in his mind about the Summoner or his own particular quest. A subtle outrage was brewing in the dragon's depths. His sense of justice was awakening.

"Köthen's signaled his men to take her out of the cart." Hal drew his sword and reached for Erde's hand. "Listen carefully, girl, and do exactly as I say. Stay close to the Dragon. If they get me, don't worry about Margit. You get out of there. You have more important things to do, you and him. Go back to Deep Moor. They'll understand." His grip tightened, then released. "All right. Ready?"

Erde gathered the image in her mind and joined forces with the dragon. Poised together, they awaited Hal's signal.

"And . . . WAIT! Wait. Don't do anything yet."

There was a commotion in the square. Shouts and the sharp ringing of hooves on the paving stones. Erde heard voices crying Köthen's name. She whirled back to the parapet. Hal had risen to his feet and she hauled him back down again. He shook her free but stayed low, peering over the edge, shivering oddly. Erde worried until she realized he was laughing. "I think . . . yes! It's our friends from the forest! Come hightailing back to report there's a dragon on the loose! You've got to see this!"

Erde looked. Baron Köthen was surrounded by frantic horsemen, all talking at once and jabbing their fingers in the direction from which they'd come. Brother Guillemo listened from the bottom step of the scaffold. His expression, even from fifty yards away, was a visible contest between terror and unholy glee.

Köthen bellowed for silence. The horsemen shut up immediately, but for one tardy one, whose last words floated like an echo into the hush that fell over the square.

". . . dragon, my lord!"

The crowd leaned forward as if pulled by a string.

The men dismounted and made a try at being orderly. Josef von Alte stalked over to Köthen to hear the details, but Brother Guillemo whirled and raced to the top of the scaffold.

"A sign!" he shouted. "A sign, oh my people! These men have brought us a true sign!"

Half in, half out of the witch-cart, Margit also listened. She stood nearly forgotten, watched by one guard and bound only by the cord that tied her hands in front of her. The throng was riveted on Guillemo as he pounded back and forth across the platform, warming to his tirade. The pale noon light dimmed as the dark clouds bunching at the horizon broke loose and sped closer. Guillemo took his cue.

"See how the heavens darken! The sun itself, God's given holy light, will be swallowed up! This is no natural occurrence! The forces of evil are gathering, oh my people, gathering around us now!"

"Now would really be the time to do it," muttered Hal.

And then the priest, who possessed a panoramic view over the heads of the crowd, stopped dead in the middle of a shouted sentence and stared, his face gone slack and pale.

Hal elbowed Erde hard and pointed. "Look! Over there!"

A new horseman had entered the square, a lone armored knight on a huge golden horse. His helm and breastplate gleamed with gold chasing. A closed visor concealed his face. The crowd gasped and murmured and opened a wide path for him as if expecting some new report of sorcery, perhaps even the sorcerer himself. And he did look magical, Erde thought. As he bore down on the center of the square, his sword raised above his head, she saw that his pure white tunic was blazoned in brilliant red, in the sign of a dragon.

"It's him!" Hal exclaimed. "I'll bet it's him! Who else could it be? He's decided to make the challenge official, the reckless sonofabitch! Got a real taste for theatrics! Esther didn't say her Friend was lunatic as well as idealistic!"

Erde stared as the golden knight galloped across the square, scattering what little resistance stood in his way. She was remembering the visored, shining knight in Earth's dream on the night of the earthquake. Could the dragon have dreamed of the Friend?

On the scaffold, the priest screamed "No! No! No!" and waved his arms as if he could make this sudden and inconvenient apparition disappear.

Hal gripped Erde's shoulder. "Wait, Jesus, he's coming for Margit! The man's insane. How did he get in, with Köthen blocking the gates?" He paused for breath, considering. "And how the hell is he going to get out?"

Before the men at the scaffold knew what was happen-

ing, the horseman had thundered into their midst. The soldiers were dumbstruck. Cursing, Baron Köthen dove at the
man nearest him to grab his sword and shove him aside.
Josef van Alte ran for his horse, shouting at his men to
attack. Above, the apoplectic priest finally found words
other than his helpless repeated denial of what was clearly
a reality. He called for a sword. He raced about on the
platform but did not venture down the stairs. The white-
robes racing to respond and protect him blocked both von
Alte's path and Köthen's. The two barons bellowed in frustration as the golden knight pulled up at the witch-cart,
sliced the ropes binding Margit's ready, outstretched wrists,
sheathed his sword, and scooped her up and onto the back
of his saddle in a single unbroken motion.

"Bravo, lad!" whispered Hal. "Done before Köthen had
a weapon to hand! I like this madman!"

The knight spurred his horse forward with a victorious
whoop. The crowd's roar was ambiguous, but they cleared
an escape route straight out of the square, then closed behind him, a few of them seeming to give chase.

"Bar the gates!" Köthen's shout echoed like drumbeats
around the square, though he already had men posted everywhere. "Not a soul in or out!"

Still alone on the scaffold, Brother Guillemo ceased his
screeching and fell to his knees, his arms outstretched in
an apparent trance of prayer. The white-robes finally reaching him stood back in chagrin, then formed a circle around
him, their swords at ready.

Hal leaped to his feet, not caring who spotted him.
"There he goes, out of the square! And the crowd's
blocking the pursuit! But can they get him past the gates?"
He snatched at Erde's arm, already on the move. "Quick!
Back to the barn! He may need our help!"

Help? The streets would be crawling with Köthen's men,
and her father's. Erde had no idea what help Hal thought
they could be, or how he even planned to find Margit's
miraculous rescuer. Maybe he didn't need their help. If
dragons could exist, why not magical knights? But she was
eager enough to be away from their vulnerable position on
the rooftop. She alerted the dragon and helped him image
the brickyard.

* * *

The dragon was precise. He materialized within the same square footage in the barn from which he had left. The she-goat emerged from hiding in the straw and did her grave little dance of welcome. Erde made sure to praise the dragon effusively. Praise so improved his mood and his confidence, especially now that he was hinting at being hungry again, after all this work. She told him a meal was a hopeless notion for a while, and the best thing to do was to take a nap and not think about it. He agreed, but not happily.

Hal sped off into the courtyard the moment his head cleared. The wind gusted through the open doors, delivering little flurries of snow. Shivering, Erde went to close the doors, then peered through the center crack. Hal was slumped at the firepit with the old man who'd shown him such respect, warming his hands over the dying embers. Their conversation was slow, unanimated, like two habituated cronies. She thought how casual it would look to the idle passerby, if there was such a person left in Erfurt. The old man had a dusting of snow on his cap and shoulders. She wondered why he hadn't retreated indoors or, more curious still, why he wasn't with the crowd in the market square. But watching him with Hal, she understood he'd been keeping an unofficial eye on the barn. Soon Hal rose, nodding, from his crouch and headed her way. He slowed as the sound of horsemen approached. From the barn, Erde could not see the passage under a second story that allowed access to the courtyard from the street, but she heard the clatter pass by in a hurry and breathed a sigh of relief. Hal sprinted for the doors.

"It's as I suspected," he whispered hastily as he shut the doors behind him. "The partisans got him in, and they plan to get him out . . . with Margit. I told old Ralf they didn't stand a chance with all that combined force after them, but that I did." He paced over to the sleeping dragon and regarded him with avid satisfaction. "I said if they'd bring the pair of them to me, I could get them out." He came back and sat down beside her. "I don't know if he believed me, or why he even should, but he said he'd carry the message. Of course I didn't want to tell him exactly *how* I could get them out, so we'll see. It depends on how desperate they get." He looked down, pushing straw around with

the toe of his boot. "And on how much faith these diminishing royalists still have in an old King's Knight."

They waited, and no message came. Out in the street,
horsemen came and went. Hal sharpened his sword some
more, halting abruptly to listen each time the mule made
an unusual sound outside the door. He replayed the events
in the market square over and over, musing on the identity
of the mysterious knight.

"He has the king's own stature, I'll say that much," he
muttered at one point.

Erde didn't know how he could tell what the man looked
like, under all that concealing armor. But he knew the king,
and she didn't. Plus she supposed that men of war understood such things.

Growing restive after a while, Hal went out again to talk
to the old man he'd called Ralf. He came back dispiritedly.
"He says he passed the word along. He also says Köthen's
men are searching the town door by door, and that we
ought to look to our own safety, as they'll no doubt be
here before long." Hal slapped his hand irritably against
his thigh. "I didn't want to leave without her."

Outside, the mule came alert with a snort and a single
loud kick against the wall of the barn. Hal sped to the door
and barred it as the sudden racket of men and horses invaded the courtyard. Erde woke the dragon from his nap.

"Five, six, eight, damn!" Hal counted, squinting through
the crack between the doors. "Two searching the sheds,
two heading this way, three at the fire questioning Ralf . . .
no!" He spun around, reaching for his sword. "Cowards!
Beating a defenseless old man!"

Erde ran for him, snatched at his arm. Outside, the soldiers slapped the mule away from the doors and threw their
weight against the bar. Quickly, the blade of a sword was
shoved through the crack to pry the bar loose. Erde pulled
Hal toward the dragon. In a dizzying split-second, they
were back on the rooftop overlooking the square. Hal
looked momentarily dazed and frustrated, then got his
bearings and clapped Erde on the back manfully. "Good
thinking!"

Ducking, he sheathed the sword still naked in his hand
and scrambled toward the parapet. Erde stayed to praise
the dragon for his quick response and share his palpable

excitement. To him, this spiriting around town was like a
game of hide and seek. His confidence bloomed with each
successful trip, and with it, his pride. It didn't matter that
he was clumsy on the ground. He was no longer a useless,
wingless burden. He was the secret weapon.

But there was also a nagging worry. After the first time,
escaping from the soldiers in the forest, he'd noticed that
he was hungry, but he'd been recently so well fed that it
hardly mattered. But after the second and third, he found
himself growing steadily ravenous. This most recent trip
had left him famished and weak, so much that he was unsure if he had the strength to transport anyone anywhere
without refueling. Finally, hiding out on the burned-out
rooftop, he laid out his predicament with irrefutable clarity.

—But can you get us out of here?

Earth thought he could, but as his weakness increased,
so did his concern. Being able to think of nothing but his
hunger was distracting. He worried about maintaining the
concentration necessary to transport accurately.

Erde's own mind was crowding already with the dragon's
thoughts of food. Now that he'd begun to awaken to his
true power, she found it increasingly difficult to keep his
images from dominating her brain, difficult even to separate
her own thoughts from his. She didn't really know whose
idea it had been to return to the rooftop. Earth did not
consider this a problem. To him, *our* thought was a perfectly acceptable alternative to *yours* or *mine*. Perhaps even
a superior one. Erde was not sure.

"It isn't a sight fit for a lady," hissed Hal from the parapet, "but you ought to take a look at this anyway."

Erde joined him at the edge. Brother Guillemo's white-
robes, with their short thick swords now in full view, had
blocked off all the streets leading out of the square. The
townsfolk had been herded against the grandstand on the
cathedral steps, and Josef von Alte's horsemen stood guard
over them as if they were criminals. The wailing of children
was blown upward by a biting wind thickening with huge
wet flakes of snow. Men stamped and hugged their arms,
having given their cloaks to the women to wrap themselves
and the babies in. Hal touched Erde's arm and nodded
toward the western end of the square, where the barrier of
white-robes had parted to admit a stumbling group of el-

derly citizens, driven faster than they could walk by several
of Baron Köthen's horsemen.

"Now it's the sick and the infirm!" Hal exclaimed. "Not
enough he's hauled the poor nursing mothers away from
their hearths in this churlish weather! This is Fra Guill's
order, not Köthen's, surely. That priest'll have the whole
town dead of ague before he's satisfied." Now he pointed
toward the empty scaffold, crowned by its tall stake and
unlit pyre. Beside the steps, so freshly built that the wood
still leaked its sap, Josef von Alte stood barking questions
at a young man pinned roughly against the stair by two
von Alte foot-soldiers. The sight of him sent a surge of
memory coursing through Erde's head, too quick and elusive to hold on to. Something about her father and the
priest and . . . what? She wanted to look away and could
not. On the scaffold, Brother Guillemo was now prostrate,
flat on his face in prayer, watched over by a stout quartet
of his brethren.

Köthen sat to one side, receiving the reports of the
search from a velvet cushioned chair. A brazier burned
nearby. His men came and went briskly. Köthen listened
carefully, rubbed his hands in the heat of the flame, and
every now and then, glanced at the sky, palming snowflakes
from his brow.

"There's the only sensible man among them," observed
Hal. "But he's at a loss, for once. He's thinking it can't get
any damn darker for just after noon. He's thinking maybe
the priest is right after all, something devilish is going on,
and here he'd signed on just to take advantage of a
power grab."

Erde wondered why Hal thought he could speak so as-
suredly of what was in Baron Köthen's mind. She pulled
her slate out from under her jerkin. LIKE MY FATHER?

"Surely. Except Köthen's smarter and abler than your
father, if you'll pardon my saying so, milady." He grinned
at her crookedly. "D'you think intelligence is like twins . . .
it skips a generation?"

She showed him her slate again. EARTH NEEDS TO
EAT.

"What, again?"

Painstakingly, she explained how the transporting process
was draining the dragon's strength.

"How much more can he manage without eating?"

HE DOESN'T KNOW.

Hal chewed his lip. "Suddenly I don't feel so glib about this anymore."

Erde nodded a tense agreement.

"Can he get us back to the barn?"

HE THINKS SO.

"Then he'd better do it now. Köthen's men should be done turning the place inside out. Then you'll wait there in case Margit and the wonder lad show up, and I'll go search up something for himself to eat. There must be some hog or lamb left about that the soldiers haven't yet confiscated." He glanced over his shoulder. "Hello, what now?"

A dead hush had settled upon the square again, as heavy and soft as the snow that was blanketing the paving stones. Stirring at last from his prayer trance on the scaffold, Brother Guillemo rose to his feet with his arms still outstretched, as if drawn up by an invisible wire. Strange sounds spewed from his gaping mouth, deep animal growls and yelps that coalesced finally into harsh but human syllables and then into words. His astonished brothers deserted their guard duty to gather at the foot of the scaffold and kneel in awe. Guillemo's words became exotic names, names that Erde recalled from her Bible studies.

"Oh Hamaliel and Auriel! Ah! Ah! Raphael! Come, Asmodel and Zedekiel!"

Hal listened with alert suspicion. "He's calling on the angels, and not all of them from the official Word. That's a little close to the edge for a man of the Church."

"Ah, Gabriel! Come, Khamael! Come with your swords of light and your flaming brows! Descend and protect us from what is nigh! See how the sky darkens and the sun is taken from us! Come, Melchidael! Descend to us now! Save us from the coming of dragons! Oh great archangel Michael, hear our cries! Take pity on us as you would on little children!"

"How dare he ask for pity," growled Hal. "He who's never shown any in his life!"

"Come, holy ones, holiest of holies! Dragons befoul the land and today, this very day, we have seen Satan himself take human form to appear among us and snatch his hand-maiden from our righteous grasp!"

The priest's ranting was familiar, playing through the full range of vocal possibilities. But beneath the pyrotechnics, Erde heard something new, some hint of genuine terror, some faint loss of control.

Hal heard it, too. "It's really gotten to him, having Margit stolen out from under his nose so spectacularly. He hadn't planned on that, and he doesn't like one bit what it implies about his precious prophecies. If ever he gets his hands on her again, he'll exact the worst revenge he can think of. Though what could be worse than being burned alive, I can't imagine."

BUT HE CAN, Erde scrawled.

Hal's mouth tightened. "You're right. Enough of this poison. Let's see if our steed has the strength to bring us home again."

CHAPTER TWENTY-EIGHT

The trip back to the brickyard was momentarily terrifying. For Erde, it was a nightmare of drowning, a struggle in darkness with limbs too heavy, a desperate longing for the surface and for breath. Then for the split-second that she was conscious enough to think about it, she was suspended in a void without hope of escape. The arrival was like being flung down from a height. Erde gasped for air and wondered if she'd broken a rib.

Hal staggered to his feet, his chest heaving. "Christ Almighty! Don't want to do that again until he's eaten!"

The big double doors of the barn had been pushed open. The beam that had barred them lay askew on the floor. Past the dark rectangle of the opening, the snow-covered yard was scarred with muddy footprints and the signs of a fight. A man lay by the firepit, the thick white flakes dusting him like ash. From around the corner of the barn came the squeals of the mule and the bleating of the goat.

Hal made sure Erde was standing. "Check for our packs!" He prodded her toward the feed bin, then drew his sword and bolted for the yard. Erde ran to the bin and found their possessions still intact. She let the heavy lid drop and raced after Hal.

The searchers were gone from the courtyard but had left one of their own behind to confiscate the animals. He had tied the she-goat to a post and was fighting for control of the mule. The hapless man was thin and young, and the mule was lashing out with teeth and hooves, showing him little mercy. Hal showed him even less. He sprinted up behind the man, slashing the rope that held the goat as he passed. He wrapped his arm around the man's throat and yanked him back hard. The man flailed and went limp. Hal dropped him like a stone. Without a second glance, he ran over to the fallen man at the firepit and eased him over onto his back.

Erde met him there, her eyes full of what she had just seen him do. The man on the ground was old Ralf, unconscious and bleeding from a gash across his cheek and from others as well, judging from the amount of red staining the snow. The knight glared about the yard. He seemed to Erde a dangerous stranger, not at all the kindly elder gentleman she had been traveling with. His movements were hard and clean and fast, and he'd disposed of the would-be mule thief with such unthinking despatch that it left her breathless. She knew she should feel safer in his company, but mostly it unnerved her to see him transformed so suddenly and so entirely. She kept her distance, eyeing him warily.

But he was gentleness itself as he drew the old man's head and shoulders into his lap. "Still breathing, but he's lost a lot of blood. Ah. Here it is. Stab wound in the back. Cowards! Bring the wineskin, milady, from the pack."

Erde ran back to the feed bin and struggled the heavy packs out onto the floor. By the time she'd freed the wineskin, Hal was at the door with the old man in his arms, looking for a soft spot to lay him down. The mule and the she-goat followed close behind. Erde hurriedly gathered up loose straw to make a bed. Seeing the she-goat so nimble on her feet reminded her of what the dragon had done the night of the cat attack. She grabbed her slate.

EARTH CAN HEAL HIM.

Hal's scowl eased. "Right you are, girl! Quickly, close the doors!"

The dragon was curled up at the back of the barn, in the very darkest corner. Hal carried the old man over and settled him on his side in front of the great horned head. He looked to Erde. "You'll ask him?"

She did. Earth's response was sluggish. Erde hoped an attempt at healing would not exhaust him further. Yet he must try. He opened one slow eye, then tilted his head ponderously to sniff at the old man's injuries. Three long swipes of his huge tongue cleaned the stab wound and staunched the flow of blood. Earth sighed and went back to sleep.

Hal sat back on his heels. "Amazing." Gently, he hauled the old man's unconscious weight to the hay mound Erde had gathered. He swabbed blood from the gashed cheek with a snow-dampened rag. "Good, this one's shallow. The rest, mostly bruises. He was knocked fairly senseless, but look! He's coming around already!" He raised the old man's head and put the spout of the wineskin to his lips. "Never knew you to refuse a sip, Ralf. Can you take a little now?"

Ralf coughed and sputtered, but managed a gulp.

"Good man." Hal patted his shoulder and propped his head up for another swallow. He was careful to place his own body between the old man and the dragon. "How do you feel?"

"Dizzy," the old man muttered.

"Well, this was my fault and I'm sorry for it, but grateful just the same."

"Glad to see you . . . in one piece, my lord. They were . . . Köthen's men were . . ." Ralf paused to cough again, and take another sip of wine. ". . . very surprised to find the barn empty."

"But you were right to try to prevent them, Ralf."

Ralf's grin was crooked, as if from an old injury. Erde thought it made him look sly but could see that Hal trusted him implicitly. "If they'd known it was you, they'd have sure feared for sorcery."

"Still that old canard? I swear, a false reputation's the hardest kind to lose."

Again, the sly grin. "I never thought you did much to discourage it, my lord. Never hurts to put that extra fear into them, eh?"

Hal scratched his beard. "Well, thing is, Ralf, sometimes a man stumbles on magic without even trying. Do you believe that?"

Ralf shrugged but his eyes narrowed a bit. He tried to sit up. Hal caught him and eased him up against a stack of bricks.

"What I mean is, I guess, are you feeling strong enough to meet what you were protecting?"

Erde tried to stop him. She was sure he shouldn't be so free about revealing Earth's existence. But she'd purposely moved away when Ralf awoke, and couldn't get to him in time. She had to watch helplessly as the knight stood and removed himself from the line of sight between the old man and the dragon. Old Ralf's head may have been spinning but his eyes were sharp. He let out a sharp yowl and tried to crab sideways toward the door on his hands and feet.

Hal knelt at his side, his hands soothing. "Easy, old man, easy. Don't be afraid."

"But my lord baron . . . !"

"You're safe, I promise you."

Ralf quieted, but it was more like obedience than true calm. He stared hard into the shadows, his jaw dropping open like a door on a rusted hinge. He blinked several times, then shook his head and crossed himself hastily. "Was it the blow to my brain?"

"No, you're seeing truly."

"But is it . . . no . . . is it . . . a dragon?"

"A dragon it is indeed," replied Hal gladly.

"Angels defend us!" Ralf cringed behind Hal in a new surge of terror.

"There's no cause for fear. He's been working hard and he's tired. Right now, he's asleep. Besides, this dragon saved your life."

"How's that?"

"You'd a bad wound in your back. His healing gift kept you from bleeding to death. I promise you, my friend—this is none of Fra Guill's devil's spawn. This is a King's Dragon."

But the King's Dragon was not just tired. He was unwell. Erde realized that her head had been strangely vacant since the rough return from the rooftop. She sent him images of concern and got no answer. She cursed herself for letting mere events distract her, and ran to him. He lay inert. His hide was dull again, faded to the same color of windblown dust that it had been when she'd first met him, ravenous from his long sleep. There was no handy bear now for him to devour. The rise and fall of his breath was so slow and shallow as to be imperceptible. Appalled, Erde dropped to her knees and laid her head against his neck.

"What is it?" Hal called from the front of the barn.

Erde rocked back and forth in panic.

The knight left Ralf to recover from his shock, and joined her at the dragon's side. "Is he all right?"

Erde shook her head helplessly.

Hal dropped beside her, his face ashen. "What's wrong with him?"

NEEDS FOOD. FUEL. She underlined the last word several times.

"Then he shall have it." Hal placed a palm gravely on the dragon's snout. "Your pardon, my lord. I didn't understand that this weakness could threaten you so suddenly."

IT'S THE EFFORT OF THE TRAVEL, Erde reminded him. AND THEN THE HEALING.

"Yes, yes, I understand. I'll go immediately." He rose, and found the old man on his knees, still gawking and shaky but willing to crawl a few brave inches nearer.

"Saved my life, did he?" He touched the livid bruise on his face as though it was his real cause for concern.

"Yes."

"Awful quiet. Don't a dragon snore when he sleeps?"

"He's . . . unwell. Usually he's very sociable."

Ralf gazed slowly from dragon to knight and back again. "If you say so, my lord. But now he's sick?"

"Starving. Needs a meal very badly."

Still on his knees, the old man backed up a step. "You'll find naught left in Erfurt to feed a dragon. The soldiers have seen to that."

"Oh, come now, Ralf. You have an eye for these things. No one you can think of likely to have one or two stashed away somewhere?"

Ralf peered back at him oddly. Erde thought he suddenly did not look so respectful. "I hardly think, milord, that you should ask a man to give up his children, King's Dragon or no."

"His *children?* Sweet Jesus, man, what is it you think he eats?"

"He, is it? Ah." Ralf watched as the she-goat approached the dragon and lay down deliberately between ivory claws the length and breadth of a strong man's arm. "Well, milord, isn't it young virgins a dragons makes his meal on?"

In other circumstances, Hal might have laughed off this

time-honored misperception and launched into a lecture
about the feeding habits of dragons. But Earth was in trouble, so the knight was not amused. "Not this dragon!" he
snapped. He waved an abrupt hand. "See there? A goat
and a boy within easy reach and he makes nary a move,
though he's fainting with hunger."

"Maybe he prefers an older meal . . ."

Hal was outraged. "He saved your life, man! Would he
do that if he was going to eat you?"

Ralf raised a defensive palm. "Well, they say, my
lord . . ."

"Well, they're wrong!"

Erde tossed a glare Hal's way. This was no time to argue
the interpretation of lore. Earth was not entirely inert after
all. He was engaged in some kind of discussion with the
she-goat that he would not let her be privy to. She went
to work trying to convince him otherwise. She told him
she could not be his guide if he was going to keep secrets
from her.

Hal blunted the edge on his voice. He helped Ralf rise
shakily to his feet. "Forgive me, old man. I've had much
longer to get used to him. Of course you were scared, of
course you made the wrong assumptions. How is anyone
to know, if they haven't met a real dragon? Believe me, all
he needs are a few fat sheep, or even a few scrawny ones.
Or maybe you know of someone with an old milch cow
hidden away?"

Ralf tested his balance, then shook his head. "Everything
on four legs was rounded up days ago, by Baron Köthen's order."

"Is there no food anywhere in Erfurt?"

The old man shrugged. "An army travels on its
stomach."

"Then I'll take what I need from Köthen!" the knight
declared angrily. "Where's he keeping it all?"

"The king's stronghold, milord." Eyeing Hal's worn red
leather jerkin, Ralf awaited the expected response.

Predictably, Hal started to pace. "The king's . . . how
dare he! That pup! That treasonous cur! Wait till I get my
hands on him! Does he wear the king's crown as well?"

Ralf's bruised mouth twisted. "Not yet, milord. Though
I imagine he tries it on now and then before he goes to

bed nights." He peered again at the dragon, limping around to the side to study him, careful to keep a healthy distance. "A dragon, it is indeed. I never thought to have the privilege."

Hal calmed and joined the old man so that the two of them gazed at the dragon side by side. "Nor did I."

"Not and walk away from it, I mean. Pardon my asking, milord, but . . . well, a big thing like that . . . How did you ever get it in here?"

Hal caught his eye and held it solemnly. "Magic. Dragon magic, and if we find him something to eat, you can see that magic for yourself. This dragon can take us safely out of here, out of Erfurt entirely, along with the woman I spoke of and the stranger-knight."

"All of us?"

"All of us, safe and sound. If he can eat, and if you can bring them to me."

Ralf nodded, then turned away. "I'll go, then."

"You? You can hardly walk, and the streets are crawling with Köthen's swordsmen. Tell me where and I'll go for them."

Ralf cracked a real smile for the first time, showing pink and empty gums. "Each of us has our secrets to keep, milord."

Hal dipped his head. "Of course. Your discretion does you credit."

"Only way I know of to get to be as old as we are."

Hal chuckled. "Indeed. Go then, and Ralf . . ."

The old man stopped, glanced back.

"Remember me to His Majesty if you see him before I do."

Ralf laughed soundlessly, and slipped around the door. Almost immediately, he was back. "You might want to remove the evidence, milord, before they come looking for him."

"Ah. Right. I'd quite forgot."

Erde made sure the old man had gone before she showed Hal her slate. IS HE DEAD, THE MAN OUTSIDE?

"Oh, yes. Very."

A NECESSARY SACRIFICE?

"Um, well . . . yes."

She knew and he knew it had not been truly necessary,

but she nodded, erased, and wrote again. THE GOAT HAS GIVEN PERMISSION.

He didn't understand at first, and then he did. "What? No! He can't do that!"

Erde underlined the whole sentence brusquely and held it up in front of his face.

"But she's his friend!"

She'd known he'd react like this. She recalled his argument with Raven about Margit's suicide device. But how could he be so self-righteous about a willing sacrifice when he was ready to die at any moment in the service of his king, or when he'd just killed a man he didn't even know because it was—there was that word again—expedient. She rubbed the slate briskly against her sleeve.

SHE KNOWS HE'LL DIE OTHERWISE.

"Die? No, I think he'll only go back to sleep. Dragons are immortal, milady."

She glared at him. MY ANCESTORS SLEW DRAGONS.

"Of course. Mine, too, the fools. A dragon can be destroyed with a weapon or a spell. But they don't just up and die on you."

HE WON'T TALK TO ME!

"He's hungry and tired."

HE SAID HE WAS DYING!

Erde didn't care what Hal's lore told him. Earth had told her he was dying. It was the only thing he'd had the strength to say to her, and now she felt him receding from her mind like an ebb tide. She would miss the goat, but she knew she could not live without the dragon. She erased the slate, scrawled DYING! in the largest letters that would fit, then grabbed Hal's arm and propelled him toward the door. Finally, to calm her, he gave in and let himself be led outside, granting the she-goat and the dragon the privacy appropriate to the gravity of their task. Just outside the door, Erde turned back. She ran to the goat and kissed her on the head. Then she followed Hal out into the snow.

CHAPTER TWENTY-NINE

Outside, the wind had dropped. The snowfall was finer and steadier. Though the yard was a stretch of solid white, Erde saw no trace of Ralf's path of retreat. She wondered how he'd managed to cross without leaving any prints. The dead soldier was a long white lump beside the brick kilns. Erde regarded the body uneasily.

Hal had not expected to be scolded for doing what he considered to be his duty, especially when he'd accomplished it so cleanly and efficiently. "Leave him there a little longer, he'll look like just another dirt pile," he remarked sourly. Erde frowned and he shook his head. "I suppose you want me to give him last rites and bury him."

She kept her eyes steady on him, the way she remembered her grandmother looking when she'd done something wrong.

"Are you to be my conscience now? You don't think my own is active enough already?" He got very still, his jaw tight. "I thought you understood, milady, when you insisted on coming along, that this is war." He gestured sharply toward the yard. "That man was my enemy. He'd have killed me without a thought. You, too, though if what Ralf says is true and he'd seen you're a woman, he'd have had another use for you first!" He turned and stalked away to retrieve the soldier's body, brushing the snow off his red jerkin as it fell, as if loath to let it gather for even a moment.

He might as well have slapped her, and finally, Erde decided she deserved it. She had insulted him deeply with her naive disapproval of a skill he'd spent a lifetime perfecting. But she wasn't sure she wanted to be anything else but naive, if being worldly required an acceptance of murder as a common expedient. She wondered if it had anything to do with being a woman. Was this why women retreated into convents, or why Rose and her companions had withdrawn to the seclusion of Deep Moor, despite their self-sufficiency and their obvious relish for the more sensual aspects of life?

She turned her musings to the dragon in the barn. There he was, devouring—though with the greatest possible grace and mercy—a fellow creature he'd spent the last month traveling with. He was probably in the midst of it now, for as she reached out to him, his mind was shut to her. And in his case, it really was an issue of survival. Hal could have shown the soldier mercy, but the only mercy the dragon could afford right now was to do it quickly. Erde sank into a huddle in the snow against the wall of the barn. She felt as confused and alone as she ever had since the night of her flight from Tor Alte. Brushing tears from her eyes, she watched Hal grasp the dead soldier by the armpits and drag him toward the nearest of the brick kilns.

She owed him at least a gesture of apology. She'd started across the yard to help him when she heard the horsemen on the street. The snowfall had muffled their approach and they were clattering through the archway into the yard before either Hal or Erde had time to react.

Hal did not even try for his sword. He backed against the kiln, gesturing Erde to him. "Get behind me, lad!"

As she ran, she called to the dragon. He was still not answering. Across the yard, the mule shuffled into a less conspicuous position and began working his way around the perimeter.

There were six of them. The first three men were off their horses with their swords drawn before the others had pulled up inside the yard. They formed a quick semicircle around Hal, then looked to the fourth, a pudgy young man who remained astride his stout gray. He was not wearing Baron Köthen's yellow and blue, but some more garish colors of his own. A younger son of some minor lord, Erde decided, gone into service with Köthen for lack of any more promising future. Reading the insecurity in him, she had a moment of pity. She had known someone in service once . . . or so she thought. But the faint wisp of memory faded before she could identify it.

The last two men dismounted to see to the body. "Dead, my lord."

The lordling regarded Hal worriedly. His small, defensive eyes took in Hal's venerable red leathers and the well-used soldier's sword swinging easily at his hip. Hal drew himself to his full height and faced the young man calmly, as if he had every right in the world to be where he was, hauling around the corpse of their comrade.

"Your name, sir!" barked the younger son, playing at confidence but not taking the risk of forsaking his manners.

"That honor is for your superiors," Hal returned, not so politely. "Who are you?"

The other men murmured and made gestures with their swords that suggested they didn't care a whit about manners.

"I must ask you to surrender your weapon," said the lordling.

"Am I taken prisoner? If so, what is my offense? I demand the privilege of rank."

"You are not on the battlefield, sir knight." He pointed at the body. "That is your offense, just to begin with."

"Him?" Hal shrugged at the corpse as if it had just appeared in front of him. "Poor man, he was all stiff with the cold. I was helping him to a bit of shelter. Devilish weather, isn't it?"

The lordling scowled belligerently. "He's dead. You killed him. Are you claiming you did not?"

Hal shrugged again, a calculated annoyance. Would he have lied, Erde wondered, if he felt himself in any real danger?

"Your sword, sir, or I will have it taken from you."

Hal gave up his sword, as if it hardly mattered to him.

The lordling beckoned one of his men over and whispered briefly. The man swung up on his horse and cantered out of the yard. Then the lordling crossed his wrists on the pommel of his saddle and leaned in with a trace of bravado. "So tell me. What is a King's Knight doing in this town?"

Hal let his eyes widen. "Are we not in Erfurt? Am I mistaken? I thought the king ruled in Erfurt."

"Very funny."

"It was not intended as a joke." Hal grinned at him.

"Your king is the only joke."

Hal's grin died. "What would you know about such things?" He looked away and very deliberately, spat into the snow.

The lordling reached blindly to regain the advantage. "For all I know, it might have been you who snatched the witchwoman. I wouldn't have thought a man your age would be capable. Did she magic you?"

"Speak in comprehensible sentences, lad. What are you talking about?"

Erde was grateful for the anonymity of servants. She huddled behind Hal, observing the details of his performance. Meanwhile, she isolated careful images of the events for the dragon and sent them off into the ether, not knowing whether he received them or not. She worried that the she-goat alone might not be enough of a meal to restore his strength. She begged him for a sign.

The lordling brushed snow from the fringe of blond hair cutting straight across his brow. "Yes, I think it must have been you. Where is she? Where have you hidden her?"

Hal spread his arms. "There are no women here about, my boy, much to my regret. Is she good-looking, your witchy-woman? If so, send her my way, I do implore you." He threw a fraternal glance at the men surrounding him. "I've been a long time out in the East, you see, where cold as it is, the women have no need of clothing, so thick is the pelt on them."

One man suppressed a smile, another snorted. All three relaxed their sword arms a trifle.

"In fact, you wouldn't believe. One time I . . ." Hal continued, and the soldiers leaned in to listen.

"Quiet! This is not a tavern!" The men smirked and the lordling stiffened his jaw. "The barn. She's probably in the barn. You and you, search that barn!"

The two idle men took off at a trot. They found a recalcitrant mule between them and the doors.

Hal relaxed back against the brick kiln, looking unconcerned. "Is he any better yet?" he murmured to Erde. "I'll give him every second I can manage."

Imperceptibly, she shrugged, shook her head.

He bent to dig snow out of his boot. "Perhaps he should reconsider his prohibition against eating human flesh. Like right now."

The mule squealed and lashed out, striking the sword from one of the soldier's hands. The man swore in pain and hugged his wrist.

Hal straightened, suddenly smiling and helpful. "Oh, he's a real killer, that one. My boy here can't even handle him. I don't know why I keep him. Here, I'll do what I can." He went toward the mule, dragging Erde with him. He made a lengthy show of being unable to calm the spooked and violent animal while Erde stood in the snow silently pleading with the dragon to listen, to respond, to give her just one sign that he was alive and well and aware of what was happening.

But the lordling soon lost patience. "Quiet him down or he's a dead animal, never mind the baron's order!" He signaled his men. "Get those doors open!"

The mule allowed himself to be driven off to one side, but would let no one touch him. The soldiers hauled open the heavy doors and rushed inside. Erde heard them thrashing about, slamming bin lids and rustling through the straw. She heard no exclamations of horror or surprise. She exchanged a quick glance with Hal and as soon as both could casually do so, they peered around the edge of the doorway. The soldiers stood at a loss in the middle of an apparently deserted barn. One of them was searching the mule packs. All he came up with that interested him was a second sword wrapped in linen. He tore off the bindings, examined it possessively, then set it aside. Alla's little carved box he opened and tossed back in the pack when he found it contained only a strip of paper. Erde was glad she wore the dragon brooch pinned to the inside of her shirt. She sent praise to Earth, even though he never responded when he was being invisible. At least he'd found the strength to do that.

The lordling rode his horse into the barn and looked around. "You've hidden her well, sir knight."

"I've hidden no one," Hal replied truthfully.

"Perhaps she's hidden herself. A vanishing spell. A witch can do such things."

Erde shuddered to think how close to reality he'd stumbled.

Hal rolled his eyes as if the young man were raving. "So I'm told. But then, why would she hide out in a barn? She could simply vanish and walk right out of town."

The lordling drew himself up in his saddle. "She wouldn't get past. The holy brother has an acolyte at every gate to sniff out any unholy witchcraft."

"Is that so?" replied Hal, as one might to soothe a lunatic.

"Besides, you are her loyal minion who saved her from the stake. She will come back for you, and we will be waiting. You there! Bind his hands!"

One man scurried for rope. Another yanked Hal's arms around his back and held them ready as his companion tied them tightly.

Hal looked up at the man on the horse. "Are you sure you're ready to face the Powers of Darkness all by yourself?" When the young man blanched, he returned an avuncular chuckle. "Really, lad, there is no 'she.' I've got no woman hidden. I'm hungry, you're probably thirsty, we're all of us freezing our asses off, and what you should really do is take me to Baron Köthen right away. I'm sure his hospitality will prove superior to this drafty old barn."

"Superior, no doubt, and a lot more secure," said a dry voice behind them.

The lordling slid quickly off his horse.

"Ah. At last." Hal turned easily. "Still so light on your feet, Dolph."

Baron Köthen stood in the doorway, snow melting on his bared blond head. His arms folded and his stance hipslung, he looked both edgy and satisfied. "Well . . . I learned from the best."

"Just searching about town on your own, eh?"

"Oh, please, I came as soon as I heard. How many King's Knights are there left running about loose, after all?" Behind him, a large party of soldiers swooped into the yard amidst the multiple clinkings of harness and armor. Köthen moved in from the doorway, casually but in full enjoyment of his authority. His clothing was plain but well-cut, with just the right amount of swagger. His beard was neatly trimmed. His eyes, Erde noted, were dark, belying his lighter coloring. He spotted Hal's peculiarly stiff posture, bent to glance behind him, then turned on the lordling in a rage. "What? You've bound him? Fool, where are your manners? Release him immediately!"

The lordling himself jumped to untie the ropes. Hal rubbed his wrists ceremonially. "So. You come to me, Dolph? I'm honored."

"With all the respect possible, my knight, under the circumstances."

Something like pain shadowed Hal's eyes momentarily. The two men stared at each other, then Köthen took a step forward and held out his hand. Hal moved at the same instant to meet him. They clasped hands eagerly, with visible affection. The lordling stood by, astonished.

"You're looking well, Dolph."

"And you, considering. What brings you to Erfurt?"

Hal regarded the younger man steadily. "I came to visit a friend, but I gather he's left town."

Köthen laughed softly. The smile turned his rugged face briefly boyish. He reached out to pinch the red leather of Hal's jerkin between two fingers. "I hope you'll tell me, my knight, that you wear this still because the impoverished circumstances of your life deny you the luxury of a new wardrobe."

Hal looked down, spreading his arms to survey himself better. "What? You don't like the cut? Or perhaps it's the color. Yes, the color, no doubt. But I rather think it flatters me. I always hoped you'd grow to favor it yourself."

"There are more fashionable colors now in Erfurt."

"Ah, yes." Hal sucked his teeth noisily. "The blue and yellow, perhaps? But you know me better, Dolph. Never one to change my color at the whim of fashion."

When Köthen made as if to turn away, Hal grasped his wrist and pulled him nearer. Swords rattled all around the barn but Köthen held up a hand and waved them away. "Give us some privacy here, for Christ's sake!"

The soldiers backed out of the barn. The lordling remained in the doorway, feeling suddenly irrelevant.

"So, Dolph. What is this you're up to?" Hal demanded quietly. "Conniving with your fellow peers is one thing. It's what a baron does. But to take up your sword against His Majesty? Didn't I teach you better than *treason?*"

Köthen's head dipped. Erde saw his eyes squeeze shut
briefly. He took a breath and when he spoke, she could
barely hear him. "You taught me everything I know that's
worth anything, but your most vivid lesson was one you
never intended, and that was about the futility of devoting
your life and loyalty to a weakling monarch." He looked up
at Hal intently. "We live in woeful times, Heinrich, listen to
me. I will be a better master to our people. I will keep
them safe. I will hold the barons in control. I will make the
kingdom prosper again."

"You could do all that, Dolph—and I don't doubt you
could—and still do it in the service of your king. Come
wear the Red with me. Make it honorable again. Are you
so hungry for a crown?"

Köthen shook him off with a snort of anguish. "You'll
force me to make an enemy of you."

"Your deeds here have done that for you already.
Though it doesn't mean I love you any less."

Köthen's laugh was harsh this time. "Well, I'd rather you
hated me!"

"If I were to hate you, I'd have to give up hope of changing your mind."

"Hate me, then. Show me some human foible, Heinrich!
Cut yourself down to life size in my eyes, so I can bear the
pain of disappointing you."

"Ah, Dolph, I'm a foolish old man still unfashionably
loyal to his king. Is that not disappointing enough?"

"You're not that old, and you're certainly not foolish."
Köthen stared at him resignedly. "Which means you're still
dangerous, and my unwilling guest no matter what." He
turned away to walk farther into the barn, stretching. The
fine dark links of his mail jingled musically along his arms.
"Well, I'll try to keep you alive as long as I can, though
with this mad priest, there's no telling . . ." He searched
about vaguely as if at a loss for further conversation, then
rounded again on the lordling. "Here! A seat for Baron
Weisstrasse! For me, too, if you can find more than one."
He noticed Erde finally and seized on her as possibly neutral subject matter. "So, is this your latest? Starting them
awfully young now, Heinrich. Looks hardly old enough to
lift a blade."

"As old as you were, when you came to me."

Köthen's shoulders hunched, then he shook off the memory. "What's your name, boy? Speak up! What household are you from?"

"He can't, Dolph, and he's not from any household. What lord would give their sons to me to train nowadays? He's a mute orphan lad I saved from starvation, and he serves me well enough."

"Well, I'm sure he's a worthy lad and I'll try to keep him alive as well. Though you don't make it easy for me, my knight."

Hal eyed him satirically. "If I gave up my principles at my age, what would I have left?"

Köthen turned back to grip Hal with both hands and shake him gently. "A comfortable rest of your life in my service, as my most valued counselor. Heinrich, I beg you, listen to reason."

"What is comfort without honor?" returned Hal recklessly, but his eyes over his grin were serious.

"What is honor without power?" Köthen replied.

"Ha. I should know never to debate the fine points with you. My sword was superior, but you were always the better politician."

"As events have proven."

"Perhaps. Though we haven't seen the end of this yet. What of the prince? Have you left him alive?"

Köthen flushed. "Of course! Did you think . . . ?"

"I think you won't actually claim a throne while it has a living heir."

"Carl is safe!" Köthen returned hotly. "Fool that he is."

Hal looked glum. "I won't disagree with you there."

"I'll rule as regent."

"The king still reigns."

"Where? You tell me where!" Köthen jabbed a finger at Hal like an angry schoolmaster. "You find me one corner of this land still loyal to that weak old man and I'll go there and clean it out with my own hands! My own bare hands, Heinrich. I swear! This kingdom is dying and it needs a leader, a *real* leader, to make it whole again!"

Into the chill silence that fell between them then came new sounds, from out on the street. Men's deep voices booming out a liturgical chant. Listening a moment longer, Erde knew her worst fears had been realized.

"Damn!" Köthen muttered, grinding the heels of his hands into his eyes.

"My lord baron," began the lordling from the door. "It's . . ."

"I know who it is, idiot! Why now? Maybe it's coincidence. Maybe he'll just pass by."

Fighting a panic so visceral that it nearly froze her to the spot, Erde glanced wildly around the barn for some sign of where the dragon was hiding himself. She found nothing, and began to doubt if he was there at all. She clutched at the dragon brooch inside her shirt for comfort. It provided her none. The smooth stone was icy to her touch, as frigid as the wind outside, as chilled as her doubting heart. What if Earth had gone off without them? What if the she-goat had provided just enough strength to take him to Deep Moor, and he'd gone back to feed? He'd have no way of knowing he'd be leaving her to the grotesque mercies of the white-robed priest. The chanting grew louder as it neared.

"They're singing an exorcism," noted Hal. Erde watched suspicion bloom across his face.

"Are they really," Köthen replied without a shred of interest. "Only you would know such a thing."

The singers rounded the corner and passed under the arch into the brickyard. Erde pulled her hood up and her cap down, and edged backward toward the darkest recesses of the barn. She knew it was hopeless. If the priest came in, he would sniff her out somehow. He had that gift.

Köthen sighed and started for the door. "If only he'd keep his mind on his own business!"

Hastily, Hal put himself in the way. "Dolph, don't let him in here. Keep him away from me."

"I'd as soon keep him away from all of us."

Hal lowered his voice. "No joke, Dolph. I mean it. You don't know what you're into here. Keep him out. You won't like what will come of it, even you."

"*Even* me. Ha. Spare me your contempt, Heinrich."

"Dolph, I'm warning you. He'll have me on the stake."

Erde knew who the knight was really worried about, and she was grateful. But she doubted that his offering himself up as a distraction would fool the priest for very long.

Köthen of course could not understand as she did. He laughed. "Is that old reputation still dogging you? Come now, my knight. What is this unmanly terror of a mere cleric?"

"You already know better than that."

"Well, all right, yes, I do. It doesn't take very long, it's true. But relax, he only burns witches and warlocks."

Hal nodded. "Precisely."

Köthen paused, eyes narrowing. "Heinrich, no one who knows you takes any of that old sorcery stuff seriously. You may die on the block, like a man, but at the stake? Not while I'm in charge."

"If you let him in here, you may not have the choice."

"I see." Köthen eased back onto his heels, studying him. "You tell me, then, my knight: just what am I into that I don't know about?"

As Hal quickly weighed how much was safe to tell him, too soon there was someone at the door. The lordling stood aside with a bow. Erde shrank further into the shadows, burrowing into the straw and screaming in her mind for the dragon to come and save her. But the man who entered was not Brother Guillemo. It was Josef von Alte. Köthen stiffened, then moved a long step away from Hal. Von Alte blinked, his eyes adjusting to the relative darkness of the barn. His silver hair brought in an icy glint from outside. He saw Köthen, then Hal. He squinted, then frowned.

"Weissstrasse? Is that you? What the hell are you doing here?"

Hal bowed deeply. "Your servant as always, my lord of Alte."

Köthen snickered. "Don't pick on him, Heinrich. He's had a hard day, too. No, come to think of it, pick on him all you like. Save me the trouble."

Erde wished that, like the dragon, she could become invisible. But for the moment, these three rival barons were too busy jockeying for position to notice a mere prentice boy. She watched her father covertly, breathless at being thrust into his presence like this, without warning. From the rooftop, he'd looked all right. She remembered how he used to fill doorways. She thought his slimmer shape suited him. But close up, his eyes were pouchy and his skin sallow. It wasn't just age. Hal was probably twenty years older and looked far more fit. She saw her father was ill at ease. At Tor Alte, she'd thought him a model of the worldly, mod-

ern courtier, even when she didn't agree with him. But
here, shown up against the likes of Köthen and Hal Engle,
he seemed provincial, a bit pretentious, and painfully aware
of it. It wasn't his clothing or his accent, but his lack of
confidence, as if somewhere in the journey between Tor
Alte and Erfurt, his will had been shattered. (How ironic,
that during the very same journey, her own had been
forged.) Only cunning and bravado kept Baron Josef from
complete collapse. Erde blamed it on the priest and his
promises of glory. If her father had stayed at home to mind
his own lands, like his mother the baroness had insisted on
doing, Erde thought he could have learned to rule properly.
Now he was working very hard to be bully and likable,
which was not really in his nature, especially when faced
with Köthen's unconcealed disdain. There was also the dis-
advantage of not understanding why these two men before
him now, who ought to have been blood enemies, met him
with an unidentifiable solidarity and identical expressions.
A sharp rise in the volume of the chanting saved him from
having to respond to Köthen's gibe.

"What is he doing out there?" Köthen was irritable, as
if von Alte was responsible for the existence of the priest
as an obstacle in his life. Which in a way, he was.

Baron Josef looked faintly embarrassed. "Performing
an exorcism."

"Told you," murmured Hal.

"But why is he *here?*"

"My lord Köthen, he came on the word of your
messenger."

"I sent him no messenger."

"Then one who claimed to be your messenger. An old
man with a limp. Looked like he'd just been in a fight."

"Say again?" Hal came up beside him. "An old man?
With a limp? Did he have a fresh gash on his cheek right
here?"

"You describe him exactly. Perhaps he was your messenger, Weisstrasse?"

"Hardly."

"But you know the man? He didn't mention you."

"Well, that's something at least."

Von Alte frowned at him suspiciously.

"I mean, I was mistaken. I only thought I knew him."

Hal turned away with a stunned and sickly look. "Alas for the world. Treason is everywhere." He wandered over to the nail keg that the lordling had pulled up for him moments ago. He sat down on it heavily and buried his head in his hands. Erde understood his anguish. You save someone's life, or teach them everything they know, and still they betray you.

Köthen stared after Hal curiously, then returned his attention to von Alte. "What did this messenger say to bring Guillemo so quickly and so . . . noisily?"

"The usual. I only heard part of it. Something about the witch-woman and a dragon." Josef chose this first opportunity of being alone with Köthen to make a play for his sympathy. "He's obsessed, you know. You saw his reaction to your men's dragon scare. He sees them under every rock. But there's never any truth to it. My whole time with him has been one long chase after specters and will-o-the-wisps."

"Then why do you stay with him if he's such a burden?"

"Why do you welcome him into your town? My lord Köthen, our reasons are the same."

"Why do either of you have anything to do with the man?" cried Hal from his nail keg. "He's not just inconvenient, he's unclean. Unclean! Filth spews from his mind and blasphemy from his mouth! He corrupts everything he touches!"

"Of course, Heinrich," soothed Köthen reasonably. "We all know he's mad, but the people believe in him. The man who brought you the message, von Alte, was he in earnest?"

"Oh, quite. The man was obviously terrified."

"You see, my knight? The people want to be saved— from hunger, from disorder, and especially from dragons. You don't understand this because if you see a disorder, you try to fix it yourself, and if you ever met a dragon, you'd welcome it into your library for closer study. But not everyone is so equal to the world. They want to be taken care of."

Erde was sure Köthen was right. Though Old Ralf had been told that Earth had saved his life, he'd only pretended to accept the idea of him for as long as he considered himself at risk in the dragon's presence. Once he was safely 'out of range, the old fear and superstition went back to work on him. Either that, or he'd been a spy for the king's enemies all along, but she thought the fact that he'd reported the dragon and not the King's Knight proved it was abiding terror that had driven him to it. Of course, the result was the same in the long run.

Outside, the chanting ceased.

Her moment of grace had ended, her brief idyll while time stopped for politics and manly posturing among three men whose decency had been sorely tried, but who still retained their basic humanity. Outside, the real evil lurked, and it was coming in to join them. With Hal no longer standing between her and her father, Erde's last illusion of safety evaporated. She burrowed deeper into the hay, hoping to back imperceptibly behind the feed bin.

When he appeared in the doorway, Erde recognized instantly that Brother Guillemo was no longer sane. Despite the biting cold, he wore his rough robe open to his waist, where the belt was cinched in so tightly that it left long red chafe marks on his belly. Snowflakes caught in the thick black hair matting his chest. His feet were also bare. The hard and blackened look of them suggested that he'd gone shoeless for quite a while. His hood was thrown back, revealing his bald head which, before, he had taken such trouble to conceal when not in one of his transports of prayer. But all this could have been detail for one more role, assumed like the others to fit his current purpose, except for the terror deep within his eyes. He looked like a man standing naked in a gale.

Erde wondered why it should be that she could read this man so truly, this one man whom she hated and feared above all others. She'd been able to from the moment she set eyes on him—even before, when in Tor Alte's greathall she'd seen through the lie of the white-robe claiming to be Guillemo Gotti. She felt connected to him in some awful, inexplicable way, and recalled Rose's insistence with Hal about the priest's real gift for prophecy. She wished she'd had more time to discuss it and its relationship to her own future, before she had to face him again.

But here he was, waiting just within the door frame, rocking slightly, as if getting his bearings, the one thing she knew he would never quite have again. Köthen and von Alte moved instinctively to triangulate the priest, making Hal the third corner, unarmed though he was and with his head still buried in his hands. No one said a word. The lordling reached behind him for his horse's reins and backed out of the barn, grateful to leave Guillemo to his superiors.

In the silence, Guillemo's wild expression calmed a bit and became crafty. He glanced from von Alte to Köthen and back again. "Where is it? Is it here? Is it gone? Did it leave any sign?"

Köthen cleared his throat. "Do join us, Brother. What were you expecting to find?"

Guillemo squinted at him. "Ah. Then it's gone. Again, I'm too late."

"What is gone?"

"The witch's minion. The Devil-beast your messenger spoke of."

"Not my messenger, good Brother."

"Not?" Guillemo frowned and looked to Josef von Alte, who shrugged defensively. The priest's hands clenched, then brushed the air as if shooing flies. "Ah, I see it now. Some demon mocks me. I am being tested . . . no!" His restless movements stilled. He sniffed carefully and peered around into the shadows. "No, the dark clouds roil and gather. He was here. He's gone now, but he will return for her. No. He's here. I feel him near." He paced in a small circle, taking in all corners of the barn. "I *feel* him."

"He? Who?"

"The dragon, my lord baron."

Köthen rolled his eyes, but Erde shivered. Was it possible? Could he actually sense the dragon's presence, even when she couldn't? She wouldn't put it past him.

Guillemo walked his rapid little circle and halted in front of Hal. "Who's this?" He grabbed the short-cropped nap at Hal's temples and jerked his head back to see his face. Hal did not resist. He stared up at the priest with a vengeful death's head grin. Guillemo stared back for a breathless second, then let go and sprang backward with a bone-chilling screech. His continued wails brought three of his brothers crowding to the door.

"Out!" Köthen snapped. "You, out! All of you! This is a gentlemen's discussion, Guillemo. I want them out of here!"

Guillemo got hold of himself enough to cease his shrieking, but continued to stare and point, his whole arm outstretched as if reaching to touch the knight while keeping as far away from him as possible. "How did you get here? You're not supposed to be here!"

"What's the matter, Guillemo? Did you hope I'd died or something?" Hal rose from the nail keg and walked to the door to glance purposefully up at the glowering sky. The three white-robes backed away into the snow.

The priest balled his fist and dropped it to his side like a hammer. "I should have known it would be you!"

"I see you two are acquainted," noted Köthen dryly.

Hal turned smoldering eyes on him.

Köthen spread his hands. "What, what?"

"Christ Almighty, Dolph. If you're going to come charging in to steal a crown, you ought to at least take time to find out what goes on in the kingdom." The extremity of Hal's anger gave him strength to hold it in check. "Surely you're the only man left in God's Creation who doesn't know it's this so-called priest who made me a homeless wanderer!"

"Him? Thought it was your sons."

"He put the weapon in their hands."

Under the heat of Köthen's glare, Guillemo glanced aside but raised his chin. "He is the Anti-Christ."

"Who is?"

Guillemo jutted his chin in Hal's direction. "Him. Him."

"Hal Engle is the Anti-Christ? You've got to be kidding."

"He has converse with dragons."

"Ah, yes. Dragons." Köthen eyed Hal sympathetically. "You see what comes from too much study? It's that old reputation, getting you in trouble again."

"Mock, mock, my lord, on peril of your soul!" The priest was pointing again. "He brings the ice in summer! He brings dragons to lie in wait!"

Hal smirked at Köthen with sour satisfaction. "And you said nobody took it seriously."

Guillemo saw his advantage slipping away. He collected

himself with effort. He tightened his robe a bit and smoothed its folds across his chest. "You may well mock, my lord baron, but do you consider it mere coincidence that finds us all here together at this moment?"

"What should I consider it?"

"Destiny, my lord of Köthen."

Erde absorbed the loaded word with a shudder and wished with every nerve in her body that she was back in Deep Moor. She'd used the distraction of Guillemo's screeching to gain the cover of the feed bin, but she still felt completely visible to him, sure that it was only a question of when he would choose to notice her.

"Destiny." Hal made a rude sound.

"Yes! The forces of Destiny have drawn us together! He should not be here now, and yet he is, with all that he can summon from the cold depths of Hell! It is not on the battlefield but in this humble unmarked place that the true contest will be won or lost!"

Köthen had no answer for that. He shrugged. "A battle of the spirit, then, good Brother, which I as a mere soldier can leave to your superior knowledge and experience. Heinrich, gather your kit and your boy. I'm afraid you'll have to leave your dragons behind. Let's find someplace warm and get some food in our bellies. Damned unseasonable weather, isn't it?"

Erde knew it would not be that easy.

"You leave at the peril of your immortal soul, Baron Köthen." The priest's voice was suddenly flat and sane, more like the Guillemo that she remembered.

"Ah, but I stay at the peril of my health and my stomach," Köthen returned with scant civility. "What a dilemma."

Erde's father watched this exchange avidly, as if to see if Köthen had any better luck mastering the priest than he'd had.

"You do not fear God or the Devil?" Guillemo gathered himself a little more. It was like watching a man rein himself in on a leash. "Then perhaps a threat to your newly acquired scepter will concern you more."

Köthen hesitated, and Josef von Alte smiled knowingly.

"Not acquired yet," Hal threw in uselessly.

"What is it, priest? Can't you ever just say what you

mean?" Köthen crossed his arms. He knew he'd been snared and wasn't happy about it.

"I have, my lord. I am. I always do." Guillemo took up his diffident advocate's stance, though it remained a bit stiff and artificial, his brain demanding a posture his mad heart could no longer support. But his insinuating tone of voice sent another hot surge of memory through Erde's skull, a face again and blood, a young man's body flying through the air, then nothing. But now she knew it was only in hiding. She felt it lurking, just out of reach, the entire memory, awaiting its cue. Guillemo took up a slow back and forth pacing, and Erde heard the slap of sandals on stone, even though the floor was dirt and the priest was barefoot. "Perhaps the meaning is sometimes obscure to you, my lord Köthen, but I say it nonetheless, without concealment. And what I am saying now is that your soul is in danger and your power is threatened. I will leave it to you to decide which peril concerns you more, but how much clearer do you need me to be?" He turned to face Köthen with elaborate politesse

"Go on," said Köthen.

"There is a conspiracy at work here, my lord, and it is both treasonous and unholy. My own heaven-sent visions are explained and proven out by the information I had from a man who I thought was your messenger but who now I see had fled to me in righteous terror to bare his soul of what he'd witnessed."

Guillemo turned to point at Hal again, a bit too fast, a bit too avidly, and jerked himself back into a more reasonable stance. "I'd thought, my lord, that I had prevented this, months ago, but alas, the Fiend has found a way around me to do his foul work. Tonight, the poor man told me, this devil's minion will tryst with the escaped witch and her rescuer, whom some call the Friend. But he is no friend to the godly. You will notice, my lord, how the name becomes 'fiend' with the subtraction of a mere letter. So then, when they are all met, this one here will summon his dragon familiar and spirit them away to the un-Friend's encampment so that the accursed witch can do her black magic with his godless mob. This I have seen in my visions over and over, though I did not at first comprehend it. The witch will render the mob into an invincible army, which

will march on Erfurt in the name of the deposed king."
Guillemo paused, lowered his pointing arm. "Does that stir
your interest at all, my lord Köthen?"

"Do we know it was the Friend who rescued her?"

"I say it was."

The younger man stared thoughtfully at the floor, toed
some broken straw around with his boot, then sighed and
looked at Hal.

Hal chuckled. "I'd do it if I could, you know that."

"Except for the dragon part, my knight, it all sounds too
plausible to be ignored."

"Ah, but the dragon part seems fairly essential. How am
I to spirit them away otherwise?"

"How about the dragon part as a metaphor for the royalist underground? I know the town's riddled with . . .
'friends.' This place in particular." Köthen nodded toward
the shadowed corners of the barn. "I've had my eye on it
for weeks. Haven't been able to catch anyone in the act . . .
before now."

"An unlikely spot for secret meetings." Hal waved a dubious hand around the room. "Too public. Look how just
anyone can drop on by."

"Exactly. Who would suspect the odd coming and going?
How else could a King's Knight be standing here before
me within my own closely guarded walls? How else could
Guillemo's witch and her rescuer have already evaded me
for several hours? The royalists may have gotten them out
by now, for all I know." He watched Hal closely for a
betraying sign.

"I'd much prefer a real dragon," said Hal.

Köthen tried and failed to suppress a laugh.

"No, it's not true! They're not gone!" barked Guillemo,
a little too loudly. He jabbed an agitated finger at the straw-
dusted floor. "The specific persons may be obscured in my
visions, but the force lines definitely meet here. They will
be joined. It must be! There is . . . there is . . . here. It
must be here!"

The priest began to pace his tight circle again, faster and
faster. The three barons looked on with varying degrees of
incredulity, concern, and contempt. Cringing behind the
feed bin, flattened against its splintery slats, Erde knew not
a whisper of contempt. She took in the priest's circling as

the mouse blindly senses the hawk above and freezes in primal, animal terror. She called again to the dragon, a final attempt, a desperate yearning fling of her mind into the void that was still, unbelievably, dragonless.

And the priest, circling, also froze, and listened. "It . . . ? Or she . . . ? She. *She!* She is here! Here! Now I understand it! Now I see it all!" He lunged back into motion, circling still but even wider, brushing unseeing past the men who watched dumbfounded, shoving Hal aside as the knight stepped deliberately into his path.

"Really, Dolph, can't you do something with the man?"

Josef von Alte moved aside warily.

Köthen said, "Guillemo . . ." and reached for him.

"No!" The priest swerved, batting his arm away. "She. You. Didn't believe me. I knew. Here now. Right . . ." He circled toward the feed bin. Hal moved to intercept him, but Köthen stopped him short with a broad arm across his chest.

"It's the lad. He'll . . ."

"Easy. He'll come to no harm."

"Dolph, you don't know . . ."

"You keep saying that."

"Here!" shrieked Guillemo like a malicious child in a game of tag. He reached behind the bin, grabbed Erde by the back of her jerkin and hauled her into view. He snatched off her prentice cap and shoved her roughly forward so that she stumbled and went sprawling facedown on the dirty straw. The mud-stained boots she saw a short yard from her nose were not Baron Köthen's, but her father's.

"Behold the witch-child!" Guillemo bellowed in triumph. "Ha, Josef! I told you she lived still!"

CHAPTER THIRTY

Erde pressed her face into the straw and prayed for dragons.

Josef von Alte stared. He glanced at Brother Guillemo uncertainly, then back at the person sprawled at his feet. "Witch-child? I thought . . ."

"You thought! You're a fool, Josef! You listened to rumor and the words of inferiors! But I told you what the truth was!" The priest jabbed both arms toward Erde, his hands as stiff as blades. "Now you will have faith! Now you will believe me!"

Von Alte did not move. Erde wished and did not wish that she could see his face. Would it be rage or joy that she'd find there? Slowly, she drew in her limbs beneath her, until she was curled in a turtlelike posture of retreat and submission. She wished she'd tried to learn the dragon's skill of invisibility. She was sure she could make herself still enough to vanish. She heard Baron Köthen murmur to Hal, but did not catch the older man's reply. Soon Hal stepped forward with a sigh and a rustle of straw, and bent down to grasp her arm and ease her ceremoniously to her feet.

"The granddaughter of Meriah von Alte need bow to no one." He brushed dry wisps from her cloak and hair, then backed away to Köthen's side.

Erde understood his unspoken message. She made herself stand tall and proud, the focus of all attention. It was easy to pretend to ignore the priest. Raising her eyes to meet her father's was the thing she could not manage.

"A woman?" Köthen marveled.

"A girl," amended Hal.

"His daughter? The one who was kidnapped?"

"No! Bewitched!" yelped Guillemo, beginning an agitated dance. "Corrupted! Suborned by the agents of Satan!"

"A child fleeing for her life," Hal countered. "The only evil she knows is the one she escaped." He looked to the priest. "Him."

"Liar!" Guillemo shrieked. He danced toward Hal but skittered sideways when Köthen did not move from his path. "Ha! I know! I see it now! It was you, wasn't it, all along? The signs were there but I . . . I misread them! I should have seen, when my visions perplexed me, that it was you, the knight in my dreams. The Devil's Paladin!"

The knight in his dreams. Erde shivered. Too much coincidence with Guillemo. But she knew that the knight in her own dream, the dragon's dream, was not Hal Engle.

"It was you who thwarted me at Tor Alte! It was your spells that broke the locks and put the weapons in their hands! You . . ."

"I wasn't even in the neighborhood," Hal said sourly.

"What proof is that? The Eye of Darkness sees farther than . . ."

Köthen's patience ran dry at last. "Brother Guillemo, stop your ranting! You disgrace your holy office!" To Erde's surprise, the priest subsided, though he continued to mutter and wave his arms. Köthen shook his head. "Well, you're right, Heinrich. This complication I would not have guessed. Von Alte's lost daughter. Where did you find her?"

"Starving in the forest. But my usefulness is ended now. You must give her your protection, Dolph."

"I? It's her father should do that, not me."

"He didn't the first time. Please, Dolph, she's too young for politics. Take her in. Does a young girl flee into the wilderness unless she's truly desperate?"

"Or very brave," mused Köthen. "Or both. Well, what about it, von Alte? Does the father say nothing?"

When her father did not reply, Erde could finally muster the courage to meet his tongue-tied stare. The eyes she looked into were distant and horrified. They rebounded from hers as if she had struck him a blow. They flew to the priest, then back again like frightened birds to look her up and down, taking in the details of her shorn hair and her travel-stained man's garb. At last they slid upward to meet hers furtively as if, Erde thought, he was peering at her from behind a shutter, or through a veil.

He's scared, she realized. *He sees someone he recognizes but does not know. It frightens him how much I've changed.* She watched her father run his tongue along dry lips and gather himself to speak.

"Is this truly my daughter Erde?"

She didn't believe that he could really doubt it. Without thinking, she opened her mouth to answer him. Her breathy wordless rasp made him recoil and glance away, first at the priest—who had ceased his dancing and circling to watch this exchange with his predator's eye—and then at the open doorway, where the grim gray light of day was already waning.

"See!" hissed Guillemo. "Beware, Josef, for your soul's sake. What was your daughter is no longer."

"He knows nothing of souls—don't listen to him," Hal warned. "She's your own flesh, von Alte. Meriah's dear blood."

"Ah!" murmured Köthen beside him. "Now it comes clear. I'd quite forgotten."

Baron Josef shifted his weight a few times, regarding the snow-drifted doorsill with elaborate interest. At length, he wagged his head slowly back and forth, without looking at anybody. "No, this cannot be her. This is not my daughter."

Erde started toward him instinctively, hands outstretched to deny his denial. Only then did he meet her straight and square, his eyes warning her off with a stare that said, *I know you and I reject what you are, what you have become.*

Erde felt a binding loosen within her, a constriction she'd hardly known was there. Though his denial could mean death for her, she breathed more easily. Her spine straightened of its own accord, as if its burden had lifted. She thought: *But I'm proud of what I am.* In her mind's eye, she saw a great gray sea from which Tor Alte stood up as a lonely island, and herself drifting away from a diminished and diminishing father who stood at the gate as if it were a dock. She was a boat cast off from its mooring, drawn swiftly away by the tide that was Life. Then the current eddied, leaving her without momentum, without identity. If she was not von Alte's daughter, who was she?

Yet despite her confusion, the moment had a certain inevitability to it. She'd chosen a new mooring, more like a sea anchor, that stabilized without denying movement and change. Her new identity would be forged with the dragon. Erde did not permit herself to wonder if Earth's silence was permanent. She wished her father would act on his doorward impulse and simply walk away, thus ennobling this family rupture with a clean and dignified break.

But Josef von Alte was plagued with the weak man's need to justify. He took a step back, gesturing dismissively. "Not her. You're right, Guillemo. My Erde is a lady and an innocent, not some broken-down knight's whore and camp follower."

Hal growled deep in his throat and lunged. Köthen caught him, pulled the older man back again. "If your concern is for her virtue, von Alte, you've never known this particular knight very well." His dry chuckle held little humor, only scorn. "Might have been better for you if you had."

Hal eased himself free and brushed at his sleeves needlessly. "If she wouldn't marry me, she'd hardly have asked me to foster her son."

Köthen shrugged. "That's two bad decisions."

Brother Guillemo grew restless with being a mere audience to confrontation. He clapped both palms to his face and cried out, "Ah! I see! The vision clears! I should not fear the witch-woman's escape. It was trivial and temporary. It was a sign, to remind me of my true Mission! Oh, glory be to God who lends me such iotas of his omniscience!" He dropped his hands to his sides, palms outward in prayerful reverence, and beamed at the three uncomprehending barons. "Don't you see? It's so clear! It must be obvious, even to the likes of you!"

"And what 'like' is that, good Brother," asked Köthen darkly.

"The unenlightened, my lord baron, but it's no fault of yours. We cannot all be conduits of the Will of Heaven."

Hal spat loudly into the straw.

"Please enlighten us, good Brother."

"Oh my lord of Köthen, it's perfect! It's sublime! Our ceremony and great preparations were not wasted!" Guillemo began to circle again, as if he could not speak and be still at the same time. "It was all to make us ready for *this* moment, for *this* inevitability. But we were impatient. We were willing to be satisfied by a trivial burning. We tried to deny Destiny. So the Lord took us in hand and swept away our mistake, so that our holy pyre could await the true cleansing fire!" He halted suddenly and whirled to face Erde, his eyes glittering with lust and anticipation. "It will be the pinnacle of glory! God's Will be done at last! We will burn the witch-child! We will burn them all, and the Devil's Paladin, too!" He reached for Erde, his fingers like a claw fisting in the folds of her garment.

Quickly, Köthen stepped between them. He pulled the priest off her firmly but gently, as a chirurgeon would a leech. "Not so fast, good Brother. I think we must hear more of this before we put some innocent peeress to the torch."

"Innocent?" the priest yelped.

Köthen put him at arm's length and pushed him away. He turned Erde to face him and took a long moment to study her, long enough so that Erde tired of staring at her feet and raised her eyes to his out of mere curiosity. She tried to follow Hal's example: stand easy but strong. Köthen's gaze was frankly appraising. His dark eyes were surprisingly warm and she saw in them something that from a man, she had known only from Hal: respect.

"So, my lady . . . Erde, is it? . . . can you speak or no?"

Erde shook her head. She was trying to understand what it was about Adolphus of Köthen that made her feel so girlish and awkward.

"Ah. A pity. I should very much like to hear your side of this story."

Then Köthen smiled at her, a brief, almost intimate flash of complicity, and for a moment she couldn't breathe. Heat flushed her cheeks, every nerve focusing on the pressure of his hand on her arm. Erde dropped her eyes, grateful for the afternoon gloom already settling into the barn.

Köthen let her go, as if reluctantly, and turned back toward Hal. "Well, I'll do what I can for her."

"No, you shall not!" bellowed the priest. "She is mine!

Mine! The prophecy must be fulfilled, and then we will be saved! The sun will return and the flocks will fatten in the fields—but only if the witch-child burns!"

A burly white-robe ducked in breathlessly at the doorway, his brows beetled with expectation. "Holy Brother, there's motion in the street."

Guillemo started, then collected himself visibly. He drew in his shoulders and his flailing arms. He stilled, became rodlike with purpose. "Go. Tell them to prepare as we agreed. The moment is now. The final coincidence of forces. Go." He turned to von Alte, then Köthen, formally in turn, pulling up to his tallest and putting on his deepest voice. "My lord barons, ready your men. What we thought lost to us returns. Destiny approaches."

Von Alte was relieved to be released into action. He strode to the doorway and signaled his men to hide their horses and take cover. Turning back, he drew his sword. "The witch-woman and her rescuer. Now we'll see, my lord of Köthen, won't we?"

"I guess we will." Dubious but never a man to be caught unready, Köthen unsheathed his own weapon. His own half-dozen soldiers had appeared in the doorway, awaiting orders. Hal caught Erde's eye, questioning. She shook her head. No, she had not yet heard from the dragon. She followed his straying glance toward the sword the searchers had discarded from their packs, still lying in the straw beside the feed bin. The dull hidden glint of its blade was like a last faint ray of hope.

Köthen directed two of his men to clear the yard of any sign betraying their presence. He told the others to prepare torches. "Or lanterns, if they can be found. It'll be dark soon. What should I expect here, Heinrich? What plot have you mastered this time?"

"You know as much as I, Dolph. Once I had the illusion of control, but these days, events just seem to happen to me."

"Try that on von Alte, my knight, but not on me."

"No plot, Dolph, I swear. The gifted plotter here is not me."

Köthen frowned, a quick flare of rage that lit his eyes with fire. "Careful, careful . . ." He turned away abruptly, flexing his sword arm. "Then we'll lie in wait as the good brother advises, and see for ourselves. Von Alte, take the left side, why don't you. And keep your lady daughter well out of sight."

Baron Josef wagged his head bearlike and slow. "Not mine, my lord. Let the priest manage the witch."

Two of the white-robes had returned to take up guard around Guillemo. He shoved them aside to come at her. Erde slewed her gaze around to fasten on Köthen, pleading. Again Köthen moved between them. He caught Erde in the arc of his sword arm. The sweep of his blade sliced the air at the priest's knees. Guillemo sprang backward with an outraged howl. Köthen drew Erde aside toward Hal. "Your responsibility still, Heinrich. Swear you'll make no sound to raise alarm and I won't have you bound."

"On my honor."

"Over here, then. We'll take the right."

"Is that divine or otherwise?" Hal quipped.

"Heinrich, I warned you . . ." Köthen split his remaining men to either side of the door. "Take straw. Brush the snow there. Too many footprints. Where are those torches? Quickly!"

Von Alte stared. "You'll trust a King's Knight, Köthen?"

"More than I would a fellow baron, my lord of Alte."

"On your head be it. He'll betray us all."

"He will!" raged the priest. "See how he works on you! Bind him! Gag him tight! Beware, Adolphus! He woos away your soul! You must stop his voice so he cannot lay his spells! He is the Anti-Christ!"

"To your place, Guillemo! Your voice alone will give us away."

Köthen set up a signal relay between his men outside and those inside the barn. He motioned to Hal and Erde to conceal themselves behind the high wooden partition of a stall. Erde could see the doorway clearly through the hand's width spacing between the slats. Across the barn, her father and the priest crouched behind the tallest stack of stored bricks, two white-robed bodyguards hovering at their backs.

Erde called again for the dragon. For the first time, real doubt assailed her. Perhaps he would not return. Perhaps her duty as Dragon Guide was past, just as Hal had remarked about his own usefulness to her. Perhaps Earth had

already learned enough to be able to manage on his own.
Perhaps he'd tired of following other people's quests and
had decided to focus on his own. What would she do then?
She did not think of the stake. She could not. Such thoughts
were made too vivid by what she'd witnessed in Tubin. She
did not want to panic and lose her newfound dignity. Instead, she thought about the Friend and felt badly for him,
traveling all those miles from the West, giving hope to the
people and gathering up so much support, accomplishing a
daring and miraculous rescue—all this, only to die in a
brickyard, betrayed by a false promise of escape. The promise had been Hal's and it had been rashly made, before the
mechanics of the dragon's gift were fully comprehended.
Still, Erde felt responsible. Another needless death on her
conscience—two, with Margit counted, and possibly Hal's
as well, if Köthen could not save him. The only solace was
that she would not have to live with this guilt, for if they
died, she most certainly would die with them. She was not
sure she minded very much, if the dragon was really gone
from her life.

She stole a sidelong look at Köthen, so intent on the
open empty doorway. There was a very sturdy feel to him.
Her nose came to his shoulder. His profile was like the
rock face of a mountain, though the skin over those crags
was smooth and clear. His blond hair was thick and strong
and tended to clump in bunches like the tines of a feather.
Erde decided she liked looking at him. She was astonished
and a bit ashamed to find herself thinking such thoughts
when she should be preparing herself to die. She should
be praying.

She glanced across the darkening barn. Between the
rough-hewn support posts, she could see her father staring
at her. When he saw he was discovered, he looked away.

As the light failed, Köthen kept his gaze tight to his man
inside the left of the doorway, who in turn watched a man
outside to the right. Hiding behind a brick kiln, Erde
guessed.

After a few long moments of waiting, Hal leaned across
her back to murmur, "They may have spooked already.
You should have brought the old messenger man along to
serve as bait."

Köthen would not shift his eyes from the door. "I would

have, except you forget, my knight—this is the priest's game. I knew nothing of it. It was word of you that brought me here."

"Ah. Well."

"But I see you still feel the need to advise me."

"Old habits die hard."

"They needn't. You've still time to accept my offer."

"Dolph . . ."

The soldier at the door raised his hand. Hal and Köthen straightened and stilled, paired motions taken at a matched rate. If only they shared political alliances as they did so much else, Erde mourned. What a magnificent team they'd make. It should be them running the kingdom together. Then she realized this was exactly what Köthen was offering. She wondered just what would it take to convince Hal Engle to redefine such long-held loyalties. She almost wished he would. It'd be a sure way to wreak sweet revenge on Brother Guillemo.

But what of the king, and young Prince Carl? What of the hidden second son that rumor claimed? Erde put a stop to her treasonous train of thought, and turned her own attention to the waiting doorway, now a black rectangle framing lighter gray, the faintly luminous snowfield of the yard, and beyond, the darker brick of the enclosing walls. The silence was unnatural, missing even the mundane unremarked noises of a town. As if the whole world awaited this arrival. Erde prayed that the very abnormality might warn Margit and the Friend away. She prayed that it wasn't them coming at all, but someone else, some innocent citizen who could be justly enraged by rough handling at the hands of the barons' men.

For someone *was* coming, there was no doubt now. She could hear the moist crunch of their steps crossing the snowy yard, cautious but still in a bit of a hurry. As they approached the doorway, Köthen brought his sword around behind her and set its point to the small of Hal's back. Waiting, every muscle and sinew rigid, Erde swayed with sudden dizziness. She caught herself with one hand pressed hard against the slats, willing the sharp edge to prod her back to clarity. A soft ringing filled her ears. She gasped for the breath that she'd been holding back, but the ringing did not go away. She had no time to think about it. Kö-

then's arm slid up along her back as the tip of his sword
rose toward Hal's neck. Someone was in the doorway.

At first it was only a silhouette against the gray, a tall
man dressed in the loose, layered clothing of a laborer. He
hesitated in the opening, listening, and once again Erde
stopped breathing. There was something familiar in the tilt
of his chin and his square, broad shoulders. Before she
could absorb this mystery, a second silhouette joined him,
a woman. When Hal's hand tightened on her shoulder, she
was sure the woman was Margit.

They stood side by side in the doorway, uncertain, then
moved into the dimness of the barn. The ringing in Erde's
ears swelled to a buzzing inside her head. The dragon
brooch was a point of hot light against her skin. What was
it saying to her now? The man entering pulled up abruptly
as his boot stuck something in the straw, something that
clanged like metal. He bent quickly to search in the near
dark around his feet. Erde heard his soft grunt of satisfaction as he rose slowly with the object in his hand. Hal's
grip signaled again, and she understood. The stranger had
stumbled across the discarded sword, the sword she'd carried all the way from Tor Alte without ever really knowing
why. Now she was glad she had, if only for this single moment, to offer one last chance to an enemy of Fra Guill.

The man grasped the sword and tested its weight. He
swung it a couple of times, back and forth with little pauses
between, as if something about it perplexed him. Erde was
struck again by the familiarity of his stance. She wished for
a bit more light, to see him better, and then Baron Köthen
answered her wish.

"Now!" he barked. His blade was inches from Hal's
jugular.

The barn doors swung out and around and slammed shut
heavily. The new arrivals were caught like deer in a flare
as torches bloomed in the near corners of the barn. Erde
herself was momentarily blinded, then she could see that
the woman was indeed Margit, her red hair hidden beneath
a soft-brimmed fanner's hat. The man had whirled away
toward the door at Köthen's cry. His back was to her, but
Erde's body responded before her brain was able to process
the notion that there could be two such backs in God's
universe. She bolted. Her head was full of noise and her

lungs washed with heat. She tried to climb the stall partition. Hal grabbed her around the waist and hauled her backward. She fastened herself to the slats with hands like grappling hooks and fought him wildly.

"Keep her back!" Köthen warned, arcing his sword up over their heads to meet the tall stranger rounding toward the sound of his voice.

He was young and scared and ready. Erde froze as recognition jolted through her, palpable anguish, a torrent of fire racing upward from her heels. The face she knew, the bronze-gold hair, shorn though it was to near invisibility. The name she could not yet grasp, but she could feel it surging through her with the fire, searing her soul, rising to her lips with the memory, all the memories, of a young man she'd loved and thought was dead.

She didn't stop to ask how he could be dead, yet still alive. Out of the corner of her eye, she saw the priest leap up from his hidden crouch to grab the short-sword of the white-robe behind him. The young man was intent on Köthen's leveled blade, with Margit close behind him, a small dagger in her hand. Guillemo sprinted forward, his snatched weapon raised to strike. Erde shook Hal off in a sudden ferocious seizure of strength and threw herself up the chest-high barricade. Hal caught her legs. Her chest slammed against the top slat. She would not reach him in time. Her jaw worked soundlessly, like a fish gasping in the open air, and then—

"RAINER!!! Behind you!"

The young man started, openmouthed, but glanced behind, in time to bring the sword he held around to meet Guillemo's charge. The priest, though bulkier, was no match for him. The short-sword clattered to the floor. Guillemo sprang back, his wrists pressed against his chest, then dove for the sword again.

But suddenly the earth roared and bucked and tossed him aside. He flung his hands over his head and rolled. The barn shook. The rafters groaned. Soldiers and weapons went flying and skittering across the heaving floor like leaves caught in a gale.

Erde tumbled backward into Hal's arms. He grabbed her and leaned hard into the corner of the wall, fighting for balance like a sailor on the plunging deck of a ship. Her

brain was full of the same shrieking and roaring. She could
not clear it, and yet she must, for what was coming. She
felt it coming. She felt—

His return.

At last! Ah, the joy of it, the wholeness once again. She
had not really realized how incomplete she'd felt without
him until he was there again.

—*Dragon! Is it you? Are you doing this?*

Pride at his accomplishment, his first intentional
earthquake.

—*Where have you been?*

He showed her the green meadows of Deep Moor.

—*You've eaten?*

Assent. The she-goat had lent her strength to get him
there.

—*You're nearly too late! I thought we were lost!*

Great need. Nothing in his head but the call of the
Summoner.

—*I know, but I need first, and others of your friends.
Once more, and then it will be only you, I promise.*

The call is unceasing now. He feels only the need to
follow.

—*Dragon, I beg you, take us out of here!*

She formed the constellation of identities in her mind:
Hal, Margit, and herself he had a fix on already. The fourth
she gave him from her memory and hoped it would do.
She wondered briefly if it would be clever and strategic to
kidnap Köthen, but decided that it would not be wise to
offer such a man, however interesting he might be, the secret of Deep Moor.

—*These four, Dragon, and then no more. Will you do it?*

Assent. Reluctant but . . . *Yes.*

She heard him then in her mind, speaking. The voice was
deep but querulous, the voice of an overgrown child.

In honor of the she-goat. Besides, Rose said I must.

—*Language, Dragon! Words and sentences!*

Pride again. **So am I learning.**

—*You've been teasing me! Let's go!*

Yes.

The ground stilled. In the seconds after, the silence was
broken only by the moaning of terrified soldiers. Köthen
was the first to recover, then Josef von Alte. Both scram-

bled to their feet and snatched up their swords to bully
their men back into action, ordering them to take Rainer
and Margit, who'd managed to remain standing and were
now back to back, Margit with her dagger at ready, Rainer
with the sword, his sword, Erde remembered, his very own.
She wondered if he recognized it, then watching him, was
sure he did. The priest crawled about in the straw, raving
about the wrath of God. His white-robes hovered around
him, helpless and frightened. Köthen moved into the fray,
his blond beard burnished to flickering gold by torchlight.
Erde filled her eyes with him, with his strength and his
intriguing otherness, stored him away inside her and let
him go. She stirred in Hal's grasp.

"Milady? Are you well?"

"He's here," she croaked. "Get ready."

His grin was transfiguring. "And I'd thought I was hearing things . . ."

Erde gave Earth an internal nod. In the torchlit barn,
where the shadows leaped about them like a legion of
demons, the soldiers were terrified to find themselves suddenly grasping at air.

CHAPTER THIRTY-ONE

Their arrival was as smooth as silk, dead center in the farmhouse clearing. A circle of women awaited them.

Margit blinked, saw where she was, and then the dragon in front of her. "Oh wonderful!" she cried. Then her knees buckled. She sank to the ground in exhaustion and relief, and began to weep the tears she had not been able to all the time she'd been expecting to die. The twins raced to her side and the three of them rocked and wept, while the other women gathered around them.

Rose pulled away first. She hugged Erde quickly, then pressed herself into Hal's arms. "When he turned up alone, I thought . . . I was sure . . . I couldn't SEE you anywhere!"

Hal stroked her hair, kissed her temples. "There, there, Rosie. There, there."

Separated from Erde by Earth's stubby tail, Rainer pulled himself slowly to his feet and gazed about him with the alert but jaded air of a man who's seen too much in his short life already to be astonished by anything. He'd carried the sword with him but dropped it on arrival, upon finding himself so suddenly translated. Erde restrained the impulse to throw herself at him, weeping her own tears of relief and joy. Her father's harsh rejection had made her self-conscious about her altered appearance. She considered ducking quickly into the farmhouse. Surely Raven or Linden could lend her a proper dress to wear. But by then it was too late. He'd spotted her standing at the dragon's side, and was staring at her guardedly. So she approached him with all the self-possession she could muster, picking up the fallen sword from the grass as she passed. Where to start? There was so much to tell, so many lessons learned and crises passed. She wanted him to hear it all, to know everything at once. And so she said nothing. The wonder of her voice returning seemed petty and uninteresting compared to the miracle of seeing him alive again. When they were face-to-face, she handed the sword to him, hilt-first.

For a moment, he just looked at her. Then he ran his tongue quickly across his lips. "I hadn't heard that name in a long while."

She smiled ruefully. "It's not been so long, really."

"What happened to your hair?"

"Oh, I . . . cut it."

"You look really different."

"So do you." Less of a boy, more of a man. She hadn't really thought of him as a boy before, though now she could see that he had been. Not anymore.

Gingerly, he took the sword. "How did it get here?"

He sounded merely curious, as if there was nothing much more important to talk about. Probably he didn't know where to start either. She decided to let him set the pace. She matched his casual tone. "I thought I might need a weapon when I left Tor Alte, and there it was . . ."

"You left with . . ." Now his jaw tightened. ". . . your father?"

"Not exactly. I ran away."

"Ah." He gazed past her into an immense distance, then gestured at the dragon. "He's yours, isn't he."

"It's more like I'm his. His name is Earth."

"Earth. Hmmm. Where did you find him?"

"He found me, in the caves above the castle." She felt the need to boast. "He made the earthquake that saved us. He brought us here."

Rainer nodded, impressed as she had wanted him to be. "So Alla was right, little sister. She told me you were destined for something strange and wonderful."

Little sister. He had never called her that, even when they were children together. Erde heard the distance in his voice and took a half-step backward as if he'd pushed her. No warmer welcome? Not even a hug for her? How could so much change so fast? She vowed not to pressure him. It was her impulsive gesture that had gotten them in trouble to begin with, those few months ago that seemed like years. "How did you escape from the priest and my father?"

"Alla. Didn't she tell you?"

"Alla's dead. She didn't have time to tell me anything."

"Dead? How?" For the first time, he looked shaken.

"Took her own life, before they could put her to the stake."

"Oh, no. Poor old woman. Well, you know she'd be proud of you. She had the Power in her, too."

The Power? Was that what he saw, looking at her from so far away? "I thought . . . I couldn't speak. I thought you'd been killed."

"You did? Well, I'm sorry, I . . ." He shook his head without looking at her. "I wouldn't have wanted you to worry."

What did you think I'd do? she nearly screamed at him. Impassive. That's what he was, as if he'd felt too much and gone numb from it. Erde remembered what that was like. "My father said you were dead."

"Your father!" Now a shadow of rage bloomed in Rainer's eyes. "He would, if only to save his face. Lucky for me, he even convinced the priest. If Fra Guill had known who the Friend really was, he'd have reached out and squashed me like a bug!"

Erde doubted that. She was losing faith in the priest's supernormal powers. Except his predictions. But she didn't want to talk about Fra Guill, and she didn't want to talk about her father. She wanted her moment of joyous reunion. She thought she deserved it, after all she'd been through. She thought they both deserved it. Perhaps Rainer was just waiting for permission. Erde remembered the shyness that had come upon him as she'd begun to mature. She reached to touch his arm, to bridge the gap, and then having gone that far, felt her own restraints slipping. If changes had happened, it was time to admit to them. She was a grown woman, and not answerable to her father anymore. She threw caution to the winds and hurled herself into Rainer's arms. "I thought you were dead and you're alive, you're alive! It's such a miracle!"

He caught her awkwardly. She could tell he was working hard not to recoil. Willfully, she misunderstood and hugged him harder. He reached behind and grabbed her wrists, bringing her arms around between them, pushing them apart.

"Oh, it's all right!" she giggled. "We're in Deep Moor! Nobody here is going to mind at all!"

"Well. Even so." He eased her away from him and stepped back. "You know, I . . . it's been a while, you know? A lot has happened. I never meant to . . ."

Indeed. Finally she began to understand how it was.

She felt a calm settle over her, like a protective veil. She recalled the very moment of hearing that he'd been killed, how the ice had formed in her heart and the grief had lodged in her throat. How she'd carried that grief and guilt with her into exile until she couldn't bear the burden of it any longer, and one day, had simply abandoned it along with all memory of the event, so that she could get along with her life. She could see now that Rainer would never understand any of this. The fateful kiss in the halls of her father's castle had been a lark to him, a curiosity, a dare. The great love she'd fantasized about and broken her heart over was exactly that: a tale spun of her own heated girlish imaginings. Somewhere deep within her was a sigh that was going to shake her very being when she got around to it. For now, it would have to wait. There was her promise to the dragon to consider. Surprising herself with her own poise, Erde turned away, beckoning to him over her shoulder. "Come, meet my new friends."

Hal met them coming, with Rose on his arm. He swooped up Erde's hand and kissed it victoriously. "A bit close for comfort, milady, but well done anyway!" He bowed to Rainer. "Heinrich von Engle."

Erde eyed him sideways. What happened to just plain Hal Engle? She felt politics closing in on her.

Rainer shook the hand offered him. "Rainer of Duchen. I'm honored, my lord baron. The name of Weisstrasse is spoken often among those loyal to the king."

Hal looked gratified. "We'll have a lot to talk about on that subject."

Rainer nodded. Erde saw how he aligned himself instantly with the knight. She pressed close to him. "Hal found me in the woods—Oh. Is it all right? May I call you Hal?"

"Milady, now that you've your voice again, you can call me anything you please."

"Hal saved my life, Rainer, and the dragon's, too. We were starving!" Erde thought her voice sounded disappointingly thin and childish, as if it hadn't yet caught up with her new self. Nothing had really changed. She was still just the little girl he grew up with. And now she could hear the dragon in her head, reminding her of her promise and his own impatience. "Rainer is my dear, dear friend. We grew up together."

"A Friend indeed, and a more than interesting coincidence." Hal had his own agenda. He eased his lady forward. "May I present Rose of Deep Moor."

Rainer bowed to Rose, who was studying his face as if there were paragraphs written there.

"What d'you think, Rosie?" asked Hal.

"Possible, Heinrich. Now that I see him, I'll have to say it's possible."

Rainer smiled in puzzled inquiry, and Erde decided what was most changed about him: on the surface, he retained all his former habits of interest and concern but there was no substance to them. Of who or what he had become, behind that pleasant manner, he gave no indication.

Hal was not so guarded. "We wish to ask you, lad, what you know of your parentage."

Rainer's chin lifted in surprise, his first real sign of discomfiture. "You've heard the rumors, then, even here."

"We have," said Rose. Her rich voice brought Rainer's attention around to her. "Are they true?"

"I don't know. I can't remember back that far."

Hal wanted a more definitive answer. "If your claim could be proved legitimate, with what you've already done for the people . . ."

"My lord baron, I make no such claim. The intent of my campaign was only to stop the priest's evil from destroying others as it nearly destroyed me."

"But if you did make a claim . . . if you could . . . the people would flock to you, and to your . . . to the king, if they could know his heir was no traitorous weak tool of the barons like Prince Carl. I knew the man who escorted young Prince Ludolf into hiding, a King's Knight like myself. He was from Duchen."

Rainer was silent a moment. He glanced at Rose, and when she smiled at him warmly, looked away. "Well. I can only say what the old woman told me just before I fled Tor Alte . . ."

"You mean Alla?" Erde gripped his elbow eagerly. She hadn't been able to talk about Alla since losing her, and needed to. "What did Alla tell you? Oh, don't you miss her, Rainer? I miss her so much!"

"Easy, lass, easy," Hal drew her back, jovial but firm, to Rainer's evident relief. "It's a joy your voice is back, but do let the man speak."

Rose intervened. "The man will speak, Heinrich, when he's had some rest and sustenance. All of you, in fact. Come inside first, and then we'll talk."

The other women were helping Margit into the house. Rose took Hal's elbow and urged him after them. Rainer followed a few paces, then stopped to glance over his shoulder. "Are you coming?"

Erde had not moved. "I'll just stay with Earth a while."

He either did not hear or avoided her invitation. "See you later, then."

"Yes. Later." But she knew already that she wouldn't.

She watched him walk away across the velvet grass, into the farmhouse where the lamps were being lit and pots were clanging in the kitchen, where animated conversation had already begun. They would talk long into the night about the king and the barons and their various armies and strengths and strategic positions. And Hal would start making plans for how to use the dragon to get the throne back into the hands of its rightful owner.

But the dragon had his own mission to fulfill, and therefore, so did she. Erde gazed at the empty darkening porch for a long long time, feeling that sigh still deep inside her, unable to be sighed. Then she turned to the dragon.

His great head rested on his claws, the very image of ageless patience. He could have been carved of stone, but for the fires of eternity burning in his golden eyes. He blinked at her gravely.

—*Thank you, Dragon, for saving my friends.*

You're welcome. Is it my time now?

—*It's your time. What do we do?*

Follow the Call.

There was no hesitation in him, no doubt. No talk of Mage Cities and Mage-Queens. Only pure hard purpose. She felt the dragon brooch warming beneath her shirt. Hal would be sorry to be left behind, but he had his own business to attend to.

—*We should go now, before they can stop us. Is it far? You know which way to go?*

I will take us there.

—*You mean, take us? It's someplace you've been before?*

Only in our dreams.

—*Our dreams? But . . .*

I must! I am called! Are you ready?

Erde laid her hand on the hard curve of the dragon's snout and thought of Rainer's receding back. There went one dream that would never be fulfilled. "Yes. I am ready," she replied aloud.

Well, she'd miss Hal and she'd certainly miss Deep Moor, but if she survived this quest, she'd head right back here. Oddly, the last image in her mind, as the reality of Deep Moor faded, as the sparkling whirling dizziness claimed her, was Adolphus of Köthen, smiling at her as if he knew something she didn't.

CHAPTER THIRTY-TWO

When consciousness returned, Erde took a deep breath to clear her head, and was seized by a terrible coughing fit. It was hot and dry and the wind was full of dust. It smelled of . . . she wasn't sure. An acrid smell, thick and pervasive. Erde thought *There's something wrong with the air.* She opened her eyes.

She stood on a stretch of sand, pale and vast. The heat rose around her in visible waves, as if the sand itself was on fire, giving off transparent smoke. The sky was gray and lowering, tinged with yellow. To her right, the sand ended several stone's throws away in a wall of dirty green foliage. To her left, it fell in soft, debris-strewn mounds toward the widest horizon she had ever seen, a horizon of vivid turquoise that raced up to meet the sand in roaring, foaming curls. Water, in a torrent repeating itself, over and over and over.

—*Dragon? Where are we?*

I have no idea.

Earth did not bother with his usual curious survey of the new surroundings. He stared expectantly at the place where the sand met the foam.

There! She comes!

—*Who?*

The one who Calls me.

Erde squinted at the line of dirty froth, expecting to find someone walking along the shore. Then she spotted movement, a narrow head on a long neck lifted snakelike above the cresting waves.

Another dragon was rising from the water.

END OF VOLUME ONE

THE BOOK OF WATER

FOR SHEILA

editor, friend, soul of patience
. . . and the one who got me into all this in the first place.

And many thanks to the usual suspects and a few new ones, all of them more generous with their time, advice, and encouragement than any author has the right to hope for:

Lynne Kemen and Bill Rossow
Barbara Newman and Stephen Morris
Antonia Bryan
Martin Beadle
Kenny Leon
Charlotte Zoe Walker
and the dedicated organizers and supporters of **Oneonta Outloud,** where portions of this book were first read.

The Creation

IN THE BEGINNING,
AND A LITTLE AFTER . . .

In the Beginning, four mighty dragons raised of elemental energies were put to work creating the World. They were called Earth, Water, Fire, and Air. No one of them had power greater than another, and no one of them was mighty alone.

When the work was completed and the World set in motion, the four went to ground, expecting to sleep out this World's particular history and not rise again until World's End.

The first to awaken was Earth.

He woke in darkness, as innocent as a babe, with only the fleeting shadows of dreams to hint at his former magnificence. But one bright flame of knowledge drove him forth: He was Called to Work again, if only he could remember what the Work was.

He found the World grown damp and chill, overrun by the puniest of creatures, Creation's afterthought, the ones called Men. Earth soon learned that Men, too, had forgotten their Origin. They had abandoned their own intended Work in the World and thrived instead on superstition, violence, and self-righteous oppression of their fellows. They had forgotten as well their primordial relationship with dragons—all, that is, but a few.

One in particular awaited Earth's coming, though she had no awareness of the secret duty carried down through the countless generations of her blood. But this young girl knew her destiny, when she faced a living dragon and was not afraid.

Thereafter, Earth's Quest became her own, and together they searched her World for answers to his questions. Some they found and slowly, with his memory, Earth's powers reawakened. But the girl's World was dark and dangerous and ignorant, and the mysterious Caller who summed Earth could not be found within it. One day, blindly following the Call, Earth took them Somewhere Else.

That Somewhere Else would prove stranger than either of them could have imagined . . . except in their dreams.

PART ONE

The Summoning of the Hero

CHAPTER ONE

He thinks he's safely away, then he hears the rubble shift behind him, and again, to the right. He shrinks into the hot shadow of the shuttered doorway, thinking fast. His hands are wet, his breath too loud for comfort. He has not expected pursuit.

N'Doch quiets his breathing and awaits their next move. He considers his alternatives. Deeper into town would provide the most cover, but no strategic advantage. His pursuers—her brothers, no doubt—know the maze of alleys and junk lots as well as he does, maybe better, and though he thinks he has the advantage of speed, they're sure to have the advantage of numbers. He tries to recall how many brothers the silly girl has still living. He stops counting at four and wonders instead how likely it is that all of them are out of work at the same time and therefore at home, too bored and idle to sleep soundly through the midday heat like everyone else in town. He can't remember if she'd said. He was too busy being charming.

Now he also wonders if it was a setup. Too easy, maybe, those five plump globes glowing in the sun on the girl's unguarded windowsill, their green-orange ripening toward red, their warm tart juice almost a sure thing in his parched mouth. N'Doch cannot remember the last time he's eaten a ripe tomato. Especially a safe one. He feels them now, inside his T-shirt, bunched up against the waistband of his shorts, as smooth against his skin as the girl's firm brown breasts. N'Doch grins, feeling her again in his hands. Silly, but pretty. She'd almost distracted him from his purpose. Maybe he should have taken her first and *then* the tomatoes. Maybe she wouldn't have set her brothers after him so fast.

Around him, the quiet is unnatural. Even the flies and crawlies are waiting to see who'll break the stalemate first. N'Doch squints into the hazed white glare at the end of the street. The market square wavers and dips, intoxicated with the heat, reminding him of his mama's old video in a brownout. He decides that if he actually escapes with the tomatoes, he'll bring her one. Maybe the promise will bring him luck. For now, he'll head for the market and hope for the best. Lately, the stalls are shutting down during the day, to open again in the faint cool of dusk. Still, some shelter might be found among the thicket of carts and canopies, enough at least for him to double back and lose his tail.

Across the hot street, a skintight alley cuts between two crumbling stucco facades. The windows are high and barred, boarded with corrugated plastic, pairs of faded green squares in a bleached flamingo wall that's shedding old campaign posters like dying skin. No entry there, but the alley is shaded and promising. A few sharp bars of sunlight drop through the dust to spotlight piles of litter scattered along the left-hand wall. Briefly, N'Doch is speared with envy. It should be him in that hard bright spot, singing his songs for the eager multitude. He catches himself surrendering to the familiar reverie and hauls his attention back to the alley. Halfway down its length, some squared-off bulk makes the narrow darkness darker. But N'Doch counts no obstacle as impassable. He is younger than most of Malimba's brothers—taller, but thinner and lighter. He's got no one at home raising safe food to fatten him up, no walled and locked courtyard in which to grow it. For once, he'll consider that an advantage. He'll go around that darkness, or over it.

He shifts his weight soundlessly. Wedged into the shallow doorway, he has no view of the street behind him. He leans forward, his head cocked sideways like a wary bird. His bare arm scrapes the peeling shutters, and chips of dry blue paint tickle his toes. He's sure it's a rat, probably a sick one if it's out in broad daylight. He doesn't flinch, but his reflex gasp sounds to him like a vast sigh across the white-hot silence. Up the street, the rubble stirs again. N'Doch readies himself. He'd gladly wait forever in the safety of this doorway, eating his tomatoes in peace like he'd planned. But he

can't risk a rat bite. Besides, his pursuers won't wait out
there in the rubble forever. He must gain that crucial survi-
vor's one step ahead.

He coils his muscles, then springs across the street into
the alley. The sun is a breath of flame across his back as he
sprints sideways into the shadow. The brothers erupt from
hiding, but they lose a step or two, blocking each other's
way, so eager to be after him down the narrow passage.

N'Doch risks a lightning backward glance. Four of them,
no, five—yes, indeed there are, one for each tomato. They
are thick and muscled. They wear only the light briefs they
sprang out of bed in when roused by their sister's outraged
squeals. The dark obstacle midway down the alley is a pile
of discarded plastic crates. N'Doch leaps, grabs, and climbs
like a cat. The crates sway, threatening to buckle, and a
voice squawks vague curses at him from inside. He slaps
the tops and sides as he scrambles over. Maybe he can roust
out the denizen of the boxes to slow down his pursuers.
With luck, there's a whole family in there. He doesn't wait
to find out. He leaps to the ground on the other side and
pounds away down the alley. No point in stealth now. Almost more than fear, hunger propels him. He bursts into
the glare of the market square, scattering a flock of scrawny
hens that rise up around him in a flurry of grit and feathers.
Heat and sun engulf him. He cuts sideways down an aisle
of bread stalls into the gauzy shade of the canopies. The
smells make his mouth water, but every stall has its razor-
edged grillwork locked down tight. Halfway to the end, he
swerves left, hoping his pursuers won't see him turn. Next,
it's a hard right past the software carts. The vendors doze
behind tinted plexiglass shields, only their bright arrays of
solar collectors left open to the air. Normally, N'Doch
would linger here, longingly, trying to bargain for what he
cannot afford. But not today. He makes a few more sharp
zigs and zags, and then he's across the square, free of the
stalls and racing down the wide main boulevard toward the
town gates. The black tar is soft and steaming. The heat is
like a weight. It doesn't occur to him until he's well out
into the open to wonder if the brothers took the time to
grab their guns. He's seen no flash of sun on metal in his
quick looks backward, but a big enough hand can conceal

all the firepower necessary to blow a grown man away. The thought makes him shiver. The drab blighted trees that line the boulevard are his only possible cover.

But no spray of bullets comes after him, only the steady rhythm of multiple bare feet slapping against pavement, still a ways behind him but gaining. N'Doch speeds past the tall steel mesh gates. He wishes they still worked, so he could slam them in the brothers' faces. But no one bothers to fix anything anymore, especially something in public use. Now the scorched peanut fields spread white and brown to either side of him. Ahead, the red laterite road snakes through the palm grove toward the port. Tall trunks are down everywhere, uprooted or snapped off by the last big storm. There've been a lot of those coming through lately. The TV guys blame it on global warming and try to tell you what to do about it, but N'Doch zaps the channel when the weather comes on. He doesn't see how you could fix anything that big, and he's got more important things to worry about, like right now, saving his skin. He stretches his rangy legs like a thoroughbred and runs for all he's worth. But he notices the pressure inside his ribs, the merest hint of a cramp in his side. He begins to think maybe he won't get to eat any of these tomatoes after all. But that can't be, all this risk and effort for nothing. Still, if he drops them now, the brothers might let him go. He wonders if they've counted them, decides to take the chance. He yanks his shirt out of his shorts, lets the round red fruit roll free but catches the reddest, the ripest one as they fall. The soft thud of tomatoes hitting the dust behind him is the saddest sound he's ever heard.

The road through the grove is as dry and slick as flour, and danger hides in the ankle-deep red silt—shards of metal, rigid scraps of plastic waiting to slice up the unwary foot. N'Doch follows the track of a dune buggy, wishing such a vehicle would come along right this moment and spirit him off to safety. But he's managed to pick the only time of day or night when the road is empty, another in what seems to be a series of miscalculations. The *bidonville* under the palms is mute and motionless, everyone napping out the worst of the heat except a mangy young dog who bounds from the shade of an oil drum, sure that N'Doch has come to play with her. She springs up noisily, tangling in his legs.

N'Doch does not kick her away. He had a puppy he loved, back when he was a kid in the City, and he knows it won't be long before this one, too, is somebody's dinner.

But her leaping and yapping gets in his way, so he snatches up a twig from the road and tosses it behind him. With luck, she'll chase after it and tangle in the brothers' legs instead of his own. Through the scythe-curves of the palm trunks, he sees the smoky glare of the water, drawn up against the yellow sky in a fuzzed line of haze. He thinks if he can make it to the beach, he's safe. Malimba's brothers don't hang out at the beach. They won't know their way around the wrecks like he does. He can lose them there.

But he is slowing, and the cramp in his side is harder to ignore. He risks another backward glance. The brothers are slowing, too. One has dropped back to rescue the lost tomatoes from the dust. The other four pound after N'Doch, fists clenched, blinking sweat and grit from their eyes, and snarling. The brother in the lead trips over the panting eager dog as she scrambles to retrieve the stick. He lashes out, kicks her sideways. She tumbles, yelping, into the red gravel along the verge and lies there, stunned.

N'Doch feels his soul rebel, the way his stomach would against rotten food. He'd pull up short to help the pup, could he do so and live. He's had nothing against Malimba's brothers so far, except their understandable urge to chase down the thief who stole their supper. But the pup's only crime is being innocent enough to think that humans are her friends. N'Doch's nostrils flare. He surrenders up his luscious vision of eating the remaining tomato slowly and with great ceremony once he's gone to ground. Instead, he'll eat it *now*, while the brothers watch, while the sweat pours salt into their angry eyes, and their bodies strain to match his stride. And then, his final act of revenge, when he's safe and alone again: he'll make up a funny song about it and sing it all around the neighborhood, about the pup and the tomatoes and the stupid mindless viciousness of Malimba's brothers.

Anticipation makes him grin, and the notes are already stringing themselves together in his head. Sure, his friends will think he's weird, singing about dogs and tomatoes, but hell, they already do. N'Doch wipes the tomato on his shirt as he runs, then takes a bite. The skin is taut and hot but the juice is cooler than his tongue and so tart-sweet that he groans with pleasure and forgets to savor it. Between gasps for breath, he devours it in great gnashing gulps. His mouth and throat vibrate with sensation, and then the precious fruit is gone and all he can do is taste the sour regret that he dropped the other four along the road.

He's past the last shanties and lean-tos of the *bidonville*. The palm grove is thinning. Ahead, he sees the gray stretch of water and the long bright arc of sand, littered with the black hulks of the wrecks. N'Doch is glad he's eaten the tomato, though it sits like a cold acidic lump in his empty belly. He can afford no distractions now, for the beach is even more treacherous than the road. Shoals, entire reefs of debris lie submerged in its deeper sands, ready to cut off a toe or slice through a tendon, leaving you hamstrung. N'Doch thinks the beach is like life, full of hazard. He negotiates it very carefully. He's written a bunch of songs about it, like the fact that there's less of it each time he comes here, as the sea level rises. As he breaks out onto open sand, he hears one of the brothers curse and fall behind, hopping on one foot, stopping short. N'Doch crows silently. Score one for the mangy pup. He dodges right and left, his eyes fixed on the pocked ground. The first wreck southward is a burned-out sea tug. N'Doch knows the family living in the aft section above the high water mark. He's sung at their hearth on more than one occasion. It's low tide now, so he chooses the farthest-away path through the pieces of the wreck, right along the water's edge. The old man is just up from his siesta, taking a piss from the rusted rail of the mess deck. He waves.

"Yo! Waterboy!"

N'Doch grins breathlessly and returns the wave as he passes. He doesn't mind the nickname. Water seems to him a fine and precious thing to be named after. Had he been named "safe water" or "pure water" or even "cold water" instead of merely "water," he'd have liked it even better. But his mama preferred names that could be yelled quickly and easily, so "N'Doch" it is, or "Waterboy" to the old geezer who lives in the tug wreck.

Now, Malimba's brothers haven't heard this nickname before, and when they pick up on it, it doesn't sound so fond or playful. It's mockery pure and simple.

"Water boy!" they screech in coarse falsetto. "Waaa-ter boyh! Come heah, boyuh! Yah, boy, yah, yah, yah!"

N'Doch knows what they're up to, trying to rile him, slow him down with a little extra burden of rage, maybe even goad him into turning and standing for a fight. But N'Doch has learned to be slow to anger. He's never been much of a fighter. His speed is his strength. As for Malimba's brothers, let them ask their silly sister if he's a *boy* or not.

Already he thinks of the girl with the same regret as the lost tomatoes. Silly, perhaps, but pretty enough, clean and healthy and a virgin, he's sure of it. Not so many of those around, though at almost twenty, N'Doch has had his share. It would have been nicer to lie down with her a while instead of just snatching the fruit and bolting. Then she might have *given* him one, if he'd pleased her well enough, and there'd be no need for all this sweating and racing about. N'Doch knows he has a gift for pleasing women, even those he doesn't take to bed. It's one reason he hasn't had to fight so much. Whatever trouble he gets into, he can always find a woman or two to take his side. In groups, he has found, women can be very powerful allies. This is maybe his worst miscalculation this time—to attempt such a serious snatch when the aunties and grandmothers and the satisfied widows who might have hidden and protected him are all shut up in the shade of their houses, fast asleep.

He clears the last chunk of the sea tug and cuts shoreward to skirt the sand-filled hulks of two landing craft left unclaimed after the most recent failed coup. Together, they form a solid wall of rust and bullet holes and peeling camo paint, half in, half out of the water at low tide. N'Doch considers whipping around the hind end and climbing the far side to drop down onto the wash of wet sand inside. But the brothers are too close behind to fall for this ruse. They're sure to see him fling himself over the top, and then he'll be trapped and done for. But he can use the great bulk of the landing craft to cover his sprint to the next wreck down, one of the really big ones, a storm-grounded supertanker whose half-submerged stern juts into the water for the length of several soccer fields. N'Doch has a long run over open sand, but if he can reach the tanker before the brothers pass the landing craft, he'll be home free. He can hide himself forever in the dark and complex bowels of that derelict giant.

But as he rounds the end of the landing craft, his next disastrous miscalculation is revealed. This time, N'Doch curses himself out loud. The fishing fleet is in, as he'd have known it would be, if he'd given it a moment's clear thought. Hauled up on the sand between him and his refuge are thirty high-sided, high-prowed, brightly painted boats shaped like hollowed-out melon slices, heavy old wooden boats with galley-sized oars pulled by four men each. They're as tightly packed as a school of tuna. N'Doch can see no alley through them. A path around will take too long. Over the top, then, it has to be, though even at midships, they're half again his height. He races at the nearest, leaping to grab for the gunwales. He misses, catches a strand of fishnet instead, then flails and falls back, pulling the load of netting and floaters over on top of himself. By the time he's struggled free of the web of slimy, stinking rope, the brothers have made it around the landing craft. They slow and walk toward him, with nasty grins on their faces.

"Hey, water boy . . ."

"D'ja eat good, water boy?"

"Time to pay up now . . ."

They fan out in a semicircle as they approach, cutting off his chance of a last minute end run. The shortest and lightest-skinned of them has picked up a ragged scrap of metal. He swings it casually, like a baseball bat, but there is nothing casual in his eyes. N'Doch shakes off the last of the netting and backs toward the water. Maybe he can outswim them. He knows this is folly. He has hardly a full breath left in his body. His chest is heaving like a bellows, but then, so are theirs.

The surf pounds. A long wave foams up around his ankles. He hopes there's nothing too lethal hiding in the sand behind him, or in the water. The beach slants sharply. It drops off fast here, so the waves crest and break close to shore. The undertow is already pulling at his calves, sucking the gravel from beneath his heels, tipping his balance. He feels not so much driven backward into the water by the brothers' approach, as drawn inexorably into its depths, like he's being inhaled by the ocean, as if the water itself was alive. It's a peculiar sensation. It makes him light-headed, and now he's thinking he hears music in the crashing roar of the surf. He thinks maybe this is how you feel when you know you're about to die. He doesn't understand why he isn't terrified.

A particularly big wave breaks loudly behind him. The spray flings needles at his back. He braces himself against the hard swirl of water, the boil of foam around his knees. Another big wave coils and crashes, then throws itself at his thighs. And another. N'Doch backs deeper into the water, wondering if there's a new storm offshore that he hasn't heard about. Two of the brothers are wading in after him now. The short one is in the lead, brandishing his metal club. He lashes out suddenly. N'Doch ducks. It's a near miss. The short guy has very long arms. Another monster wave breaks. N'Doch knows he'll have to swim for it soon. He can't back out much farther in this high rough surf and keep his footing. The very next wave knocks him off-balance, and the club-wielder lunges after him with such a splashing and buffeting of metal and limbs and water that it isn't until the swell is pulling back and N'Doch has his feet under him again that he feels the sear along his upper arm. A thin trail of blood slips out with the wave like a coil of brown kelp. He claps his hand to his bicep. The bastard's cut him!

Finally N'Doch begins to feel afraid. An open wound in *this* water? Any number of nasty things he could pick up. And then there are the sharks that cruise the beaches, for lack of prey farther out. The merest whiff of blood will bring them in, and a starving shark is more fearsome than any number of Malimba's brothers.

The biggest wave so far thunders into its curl behind him. N'Doch waits to be engulfed. No, he'll dunk fast just before it hits and let it pummel *them* into the gravel. He scans the brothers' faces for a measure of the wave's size and sees instead a stark and uncomprehending terror. The short one has dropped his club. Suddenly, all three of them are back-stepping through the surging water as fast as they can, heading for shore. N'Doch is sure the sharks have come in with the wave, but he cannot bear to look. He throws himself after the brothers, paddling frantically with his hands. Briefly he worries that it might be a ruse to draw him within range, but he doesn't believe they're *that* gifted as actors.

Their terror is pretty convincing. The minute they're out of the water, they're pounding away up the beach. They seem to have forgotten him entirely.

N'Doch struggles against the pull of the undertow. He expects jaws lined with razors to clamp onto his thigh and haul him back again. As he stumbles into ankle-deep water and regains his balance, two of the brothers halt, high up on the beach. The short one is yanking on the taller one's arm. The tall one shrugs him off. He's yelling, and pointing toward the water. With his feet safely under him, N'Doch can resist no longer. He turns, and he sees a thing beyond his wildest imaginings.

It's not a shark. At first he thinks, *Damn, that's a really big porpoise.* Then he thinks, *No, it has legs. It's a giant crocodile.* No, the head's too small, neck's too long, it's . . . like something he's seen in the movies. The only word he can come up with is *dinosaur.* Right. Okay. A dinosaur. It can't be, but there is it. And now he's sure he's hearing music. Very strange music, like, inside his head. Maybe that tomato wasn't so safe after all. *It's poisoned me,* he thinks. *I'm hallucinating.*

And then, for a moment, he stops thinking anything at all.

With a flash of wet blue-gray and silver, the creature rises out of the waves in front of him. It has four mammalian legs and a sleek, close-eared head set on a sinuous muscular neck. It stands motionless in waist-deep water but he can *feel* its liquid grace. He thinks of a big cat inside the skin of a seal. He's never seen anything so beautiful. Though it seems to tower over him, it's actually no bigger than a large horse. Its eyes are dark and round, almost level with his own, and they are staring straight at him.

N'Doch takes the obvious step backward but that odd absence of fear has taken hold of him again. He feels no need to run. The music fills his inner ears and mostly he's thinking how absolutely fucking weird this whole thing is, and could the brothers have poisoned the tomato on purpose? Were they only chasing him to be there watching and laughing when he freaked out? Well, he isn't going to give them the satisfaction. Besides, they're the ones who're freaking out. Which means either they're pretending to see something terrifying, or they really *are* seeing something terrifying, which means . . .

N'Doch notices his legs have given up supporting him. He sits down hard on the sand and stares dumbfounded into a pair of round, dark eyes that are beginning to show signs of impatience.

Behind him, he hears someone coughing.

CHAPTER TWO

At first she was sure he'd landed them in the middle of a fire. The hot light was so hazed and the air so thick with soot and fetid odor. She shrank against him, pressing her shoulder to the dragon's side to take comfort from his girth and solidity, from the hard geometry of his leathery hide, retreating into his shadow from the glare of this sun, this searing angry red-faced sun so unlike the sun she knew. Even in the dragon's shade, she felt heat radiating upward from the scorched sand. Her nose tickled and her lungs hurt. She coughed, tried not breathing, then realized why that couldn't work, so drew a breath and coughed again.

—*Dragon? Where are we?*
—*I have no idea. But . . . look!*

Abandoning the language of words that he'd only recently learned, he poured into her head a quick reminder, images culled from the dark and noisome dreams they'd shared of late. Erde had to agree this could be the very place, the landscape of their recurrent nightmares, a place of horror. There was the same burnt yellow sky striated with gray, the same acid smells, the constant roll of thunder. Despite the heat, Erde shivered. It had been night when they'd left Deep Moor, mere seconds before. Here, everything was suddenly too bright. Her eyes burned. She squeezed them shut. She didn't want to see this place anyway.

—*Look!*
—*I don't want to look! It's ugly! Why have you brought us here?*

She hoped her voice in his head did not sound as querulous as it did in her own. Yet maybe he would reconsider, and spirit her back to the meadows of Deep Moor where she could breathe again.

—Here am I Called. Here the Quest will truly begin.

He sounded very sure, but Erde could detect in his formality just the faintest hint of false bravado. This place they'd come to wasn't exactly what the dragon had hoped for either.

Which meant he would need her to be strong. No time for girlish hearts or a lady's refined sensibilities. Not that she was ever very refined. Erde thought of Hal, who had yearned so to be a part of the dragon's Quest. He hadn't even minded that the dragon could not identify the object of that Quest. She wished the elder knight was with them now, to apply his skills and discipline to this unfamiliar situation, and all the equally unforeseen ones likely to come out of it. But he was back at Deep Moor with Rose and the others, up to his elbows once more in the game of king-making. Of course, he didn't consider it a game, and Erde knew she shouldn't either. No more a game than the dragon's Quest, which she'd taken seriously from the moment she'd been faced with it. Therefore, she must follow Sir Hal's example. If he was not there to tell her what to do, she must imagine his advice and be guided by it. The child in her complained that she was too young to shoulder such a burden, too exhausted from the upheaval of the past two months of fear and constant flight to face an even greater uncertainty. The adult, so recently come to consciousness, reminded her she had no choice.

—So, Dragon. What shall we do?

—Wait. Watch.

The dragon eased himself down on his great haunches, claws and head forward like an alert guard dog, and evidently just as willing to sit still forever until what he waited for came to him.

Watch. Erde remembered Hal's habit of observation. Wherever they'd camped on their long journey from Tor Alte, his first task before any was to take careful stock of the area, not only to search out ambush or pursuit, but to learn which local resources were available and which were not. Water, firewood, food perhaps. Shelter from the weather, cover from their enemies. There were always enemies.

At least, Erde thought, *we've escaped from them this time.*
To this dry landscape, alien yet familiar, not just from the
dragon's dreams but her own as well, she realized. The
dreams where her father and Rainer fought, and their
swords clashed and sparked in a harsh and smoky place
was more like this place than the one she'd left behind.

Rainer. Ah, Rainer. But it did not do to think of Rainer,
not in any way except as lost, as she'd thought he was until
mere hours ago, hours that now seemed like years. He was
lost again anyhow, even before she'd left Deep Moor. Erde
raised her head from her crouch at the dragon's side and
turned her mind to her surroundings.

She'd felt the hot sand underfoot but had not realized
there was so much of it, more than she'd ever seen in one
place. It stretched behind her like a dry riverbed toward a
long line of trees, impossible trees with tall, curving trunks
as slim as needles and a pincushion of leafy branches sticking out on top. There was lots of stuff in the sand, broken
stuff. Some of it was wood, sun-bleached and weatherworn,
but most of it was shiny or glittery, materials she couldn't
identify. Erde pushed off the dragon's shoulder for a better
look, teetering along his forearm and grasping one long
ivory horn for support. Balanced on his right paw, her eyes
were level with his own golden orbs, each one as big as her
head. She peered over his stubby snout.

First she saw a mass of huge bright boats crowding the
sand off to the left. They were nothing like the flat-bot-
tomed scows that plied the rivers of the lowlands back
home but they were surely boats, none the less. She'd seen
such boats sewn into the tapestries that softened the stone
walls of Tor Alte. But she could put no label to the square
dark hulks looming to the right like a range of hills. They
could be buildings, she supposed, but she saw no doors or
windows, only seams and slits in the rusted metal. Fortifications of some sort, she decided. And then, between that
grim and faceless wall and the rainbowed hulls of the boats,
there was the water. So much water! Now Erde understood
the source of the continuous rolling sound of thunder. She
knew without being told that she was looking at the sea.

The sight of it lifted her spirits. She had always dreamed
of visiting the sea. But the dragon regarded the roaring,
tumbling water with evident trepidation. Erde patted his

bony nose reassuringly. Moving water was not his favorite thing. She thought this odd, since in the bard tales, it was the uncharted seas from which the dragons of legend arose to swallow unfortunate sailing ships and their crews. But Erde had learned to think differently about dragons since meeting this one. Her dragon was definitely earthbound, and unlikely to swallow up anything without first asking its permission.

Then, over the din of the waves, she heard shouting. Male voices, several of them. She couldn't make out the words, but there was no mistaking the high-pitched tone of derision. Around the end of the dark unknown hulk, a man came running. At least, she thought it was a man. It was shaped like one, though he ran with the rangy sure grace of a young colt. But there was something wrong with his skin. It was unnaturally dark, darker than a farmer's after a summer in the fields, darker even than the gypsies who sometimes pulled their wagons up to Tor Alte's gates to barter for food and shelter with their exotic trinkets.

The dark man pulled up short when he spotted the bright fleet hauled up in front of him on the sand. Even from a distance, his dismay was obvious. Beside Erde, the dragon tensed. She could feel him stilling, preparing to make himself invisible. He sent her an image of hiding behind the nearest boat. But it wasn't the running man who was shouting. It was the three others behind him, as dark as he but shorter and thicker. When they spotted the first man, one stooped to snatch up a club. Erde thought they looked terrifying.

—*Now, Dragon! Before they see us!*

Erde prepared to dash for cover among the boats. But the dragon was no longer watching the events unfolding on the beach. He sat up very tall, intent on the churning water. A sort of thrumming sang through his body, like the vibrations of lute strings after the music has ended.

—*Dragon, what is it?*

—*There! She comes!*

—*Who?*

—*The one who Calls me!*

Erde squinted at the line of dirty froth. Was there someone else approaching along this crowded shore? Then she saw it, the snakelike neck and narrow head, lifting above the cresting waves. The body was slim and streamlined and surprisingly small, but Erde had grown up with legends. She had no trouble recognizing one when she saw it.

Another dragon was rising out of the waves.

CHAPTER THREE

N'Doch decides he can't be hallucinating. Instead of the usual speed buzz, there's music in his head. And it's pretty interesting music, too. He's tempted just to give in and listen, when suddenly, he figures it out. He laughs with relief, and right away starts looking around for the hidden lights and camera crews.

A dinosaur on the beach. Yeah, sure.

He knows what's going on. This is no poisoned-tomato vision, it's a special effect, got to be.

Of course the vid people won't know they've stumbled on a veteran. Usually they want amateurs for these "true-life" guerrilla shoots, so N'Doch won't tell them about playing background last year in *War Zone*. He'll let them see him do his stuff first.

Meanwhile, the special effect continues to stare at him like it wants something important. He's impressed. It's very realistic. Not your ordinary robot, then, but some new kind of cybercritter, maybe, or even . . . a cleverly engineered mutant! That means the vid company must have money, lots of it. N'Doch sees this might be his big break. If they're rolling tape now and he plays his part well, they'll keep it in and he could be famous. He'll have to guess what he's supposed to do. They never tell you in advance, or it wouldn't be a "true-life" pic. And if he can figure out a way to work in a song, he'll really have it made.

He springs to his feet, but his legs are still shaky. They don't really want to carry him the several steps it would take to come within arm's length of the critter. It, no, *she*—somehow he knows this—shifts her feet restlessly but does not approach. N'Doch wonders idly, if she isn't a robot, how the wranglers give the creature her cues.

A deep wave recedes across a stretch of wet sand, revealing the critter's long flat tail: a blade of muscular flesh, which she coils neatly around her webbed feet as she eases onto her haunches in front of him. N'Doch looks her over, calmer now that he's settled on a logical explanation for her presence. His legs decided to hold him up, and once again, he is taken by the creature's beauty.

What seemed from a distance to be shiny fish scales is actually a fine silvery fur as silky as the richest velvet. N'Doch has never touched real velvet, but he's seen it on TV. Immediately, he longs to touch it. What he covets most are its strange electric-blue highlights. He wonders if it grew this way, or if they've somehow wired her for it. And probably she's bred small so they can fit her into the frame with human actors. Otherwise, they'd need a long shot to see all of her.

Her head, which he'd taken for naked but for her large dark eyes and little seallike ears, is set with a ruff and crest of gauzy iridescent flesh. It lifts lightly as it dries in the sun, softening her sleek profile with curls and complications. The crest trails down her slim neck and along her spine. N'Doch thinks of the gossamer-finned carp he saw once in a rich woman's backyard pool—the first (and last) time he's ever been confronted with food just too beautiful to eat.

He can't settle on any one of the current vid series to connect with this particular situation. It's been a few days since he's caught up on his TV-watching. It could be a new story line in an old show, or a pilot for a whole new program. Maybe they don't even know the story yet, and they're waiting for it to develop naturally out of the Precipitating Event—how 'bout it?—**a man meets a dinosaur on the beach.** N'Doch wishes he'd been at *that* story conference. But this must be why the creature looks so impatient. She's waiting for him to get on with the action.

Since the ball's apparently in his court, he tries imagining the song he'd write about such a meeting. He decides the first thing he should do is *touch* the creature. They're sure to love that, him looking like he's totally amazed and trying to prove what he's seeing is real. No problem playing it, either, since it's exactly where he's at. But it's a hard thing, he discovers, to make himself cross the narrow but infinite space of sand between him and the critter, and lay a palm to that blue-lit silver velvet.

Still, his career's at stake. He manages it. The first impossible step is all it takes to draw him swiftly the next three or four. He reaches out, trying not to look too tentative. The critter's fur is the softest thing he has ever felt. As he smooths his hand from shoulder to ribcage, he feels a rush of heat and embarrassment because the touch is so oddly intimate. Bemused, N'Doch retreats a step. Again he hears coughing behind him, but now he cannot look away. The creature fixes him once more with her liquid gaze, then opens her wide mouth and sings to him.

It is the music N'Doch has waited for all his life. He doesn't realize he's been waiting until he hears it, but there it is, and his first response is tragic: the only *right* music has already been written, and by someone else. His next is relief that it has no lyric. At least it has waited for him to put words to it. He begins to hum along. The melody comes into his head just as it is leaving her throat. He knows already the words he will write, words of awakening and discovery and of a great task to be accomplished, notions he's never concerned himself with in his music so far, but N'Doch knows better than to argue with inspiration. He slips into harmony. They are a perfect duet. They build a crescendo together, append a short coda and finish on the same drawn-out high note. They stare at each other in silence. Even the surf has quieted to a rolling caress.

N'Doch thinks: *Wow. This is even better than sex.*

Then the creature lifts her gaze above his head and sings again. The bulged reply is so harsh and unmusical that N'Doch whips around, offended.

What he sees first is a white girl standing beside a big rock. He's perplexed by the white girl, who is very strangely dressed, but mostly by the rock, which is the size of a semi. He can't remember a rock that big on this part of the beach and it's not exactly the sort of thing you'd miss. Just as he's deciding the white girl is part of the production crew and the rock is a piece of scenery, the rock moves. In that instant, it is no longer a rock, but a bronze-and-green beast, also the size of a semi, and looking even more like a dinosaur than the one that came out of the water. This one even has horns, and claws each the length of a scimitar.

Two of them. Wow. N'Doch grins. Now he's *sure* the producers have money. He smiles at the white girl, in case she's one of them, even though she does seem kind of young. But he knows the media are run by young people. He's been worried about being over the hill at twenty.

When she doesn't smile back, only stares at him wide-eyed, he sees she must be an actress—she's thin enough, maybe a little too tall—and the director has told her to be afraid of him. N'Doch thinks she's doing a pretty good job. He gives her a brief nod which he hopes looks professional. He's a bit jealous that she seems to know the script and he doesn't. Her costume is weird, like something out of a gladiator epic. Well, maybe not gladiators, but something with swords, from a much colder part of the world than this one. He tries to figure what country she's meant to be from. No place is *that* cold anymore, except maybe Antarctica in the winter. The dumb girl's wearing leather and long sleeves and heavy woven trouser-things and boots, more clothes on her back than N'Doch's ever owned in his life, and she looks like she hasn't washed in months. Plus, her hair's all choppy. N'Doch admits he doesn't know much about white girl's hair but he does know a bad 'do when he sees one. He likes the neatly sheathed dagger at her belt, but can't help thinking how she must be dying of the heat under all that stuff. Right now she's not doing much but staring at him, but he can see she's beginning to sweat.

The two cybercritters are staring, too—at each other. N'Doch wonders if they're supposed to fight. That would account for the strange tension he senses in the air between them. Some kind of communicating going on, he decides, so they *must* be machines, remote controlled by the technicians.

The big brownish one rises from his couch. He takes a few big steps down the beach. The smaller silvery one goes to meet him. She's quicker, more lithe. Her greater grace makes N'Doch feel proud, though he can't imagine why, particularly since she moves right past him like she's never seen him before in her life. And after all that music and touching. He stands aside, miffed. He's really hoped this part would be more than a walk-on. Then he notices the white girl is sticking right by her beast as he moves. N'Doch thinks, *Hey, you can just accept what you're given or you can try to make the most of it*. He turns and follows the silver one up the beach.

The two creatures meet halfway. N'Doch waits, or rather, hopes for sparks to fly. Instead, they halt a few paces apart and bend their long necks in simultaneous bows. The brown one towers over the silver one. His curving ivory horns pass like scythe blades to either side of her blunt, sleek head. The formality of it raises the hair on the back of N'Doch's neck. It seems so proper somehow, so . . . *ancient*, even if it is all for the camera.

The big brown one twists his golden gaze back at the white girl. She comes immediately to his side, her hand sliding familiarly up his rough cheek. She smiles shyly at the silver beast, then dips and rises in a gesture of greeting that looks awkward in leather and pants. N'Doch guesses it would look all right if she were wearing some kind of ball gown. He tries picturing her in fancy dress, lots of makeup and jewels, a little less hair or a whole lot more. The effect is not unpleasing. Maybe they're planning something like that for the finale.

But next, all three of them are staring in his direction. To N'Doch, it feels like an assault. He just knows someone is expecting something of him. At a loss, he spreads his arms and grins, and again his head is full of music, sounds he's sure he's been on the point of imagining. It crowds his thoughts, drowns all awareness, of the beach around him, of the thick heat and the subdued crashing of the surf, all this fades before a rush of tone and rhythm and harmony. N'Doch struggles to keep his cool. He's had his moments of mad musical inspiration, but it's never come to him like this, fully orchestrated, damping his other senses as it demands his immediate and total attention. His body is actually vibrating like a drumhead. He thinks maybe they're beaming the sound track directly into his brain. Last he'd checked, this wasn't possible, but there it is inside him, this sound, this music that's like someone else's voice singing in his head. He is helpless to do anything but surrender and listen to it.

Then it becomes clear to him—he doesn't know how—

that the source of the music is the silver beast herself. It's like the music she was singing aloud a moment ago, a further development of the same theme, only this time less of a declaration . . . more of a demand. N'Doch gazes at her in wonder.

"How are you doing that?" He's just gotta ask. She's probably not programmed to answer questions, but if she can sing, maybe she can also speak. He does not ask, "What do you want with me?" That would be like asking, "Um, what's the next line?" It sounds wimpy, and it'd spoil the take.

So he moves in closer to join the group, trying to look like he knows what he's doing. The girl retreats from him a bit, into the shadow of her beast like a child into its mother's skirts. She's definitely on the tall side, he sees now, and her eyes, studying him so carefully, are very dark for a white girl's, almost black. Her skin is a fine pale olive roughened by sun or wind or maybe, though N'Doch cannot truly imagine it, by actual cold. And it looks real, now that he sees her close, like she's not even wearing makeup. He guesses her to be about fourteen.

The brown beast shrugs gently, a slow earthquake that jostles the girl sideways off her perch on his forearm. She regains her balance easily on the sand. N'Doch can see she's no stranger to exercise. She tosses the beast what N'Doch reads as a dirty look, the first sign of spirit he's seen in her. Then she squares her shoulders as if preparing for some onerous task, and turns to face him.

"Mein Name ist Erde," she announces. *"Erde Katerina Meriah von Alte."*

"Ummm," says N'Doch. He recognizes the harsh gutturals of one of those white northern European languages, but does not understand a word. He can't recall the last time he saw a vid in anything but French. Even the American ones are mostly dubbed. Are they trying to trip him up? Okay, it's gonna be a scene about communication. He smiles. *"Comment ça va?"*

Her dark eyes narrow. She doesn't understand him either. N'Doch is surprised. Most Europeans speak French. Will the viewers buy that she can't? Maybe she's supposed to be from some boondock isolationist principality. He's heard of such things. He's sure now she won't speak Wolof, so he switches to English, which he's learned only from vids. "Hey there, how ya doin', kid?"

She still doesn't get it. N'Doch gets ready to try sign language. So far, he doesn't think much of this script. He thumps his bare chest, like some guy in a bad jungle movie. "N'Doch," he says, "N'Doch."

The girl gives the big brown guy a quick sidelong glance, as if he's said something she didn't quite hear. But next she looks back at N'Doch with a gleam of understanding. She points at him and forms the sounds carefully.

"En-doche."

He nods encouragingly. "N'Doch," he repeats, correcting her pronunciation. He points back at her and cocks his head.

She taps her own leather-clad chest. *"Erde. Mien Name ist Erde."*

N'Doch tries it out. "Airda?"

"Erde."

"Right. Airda." They both nod, but N'Doch is thinking, *God, this is stupid.* He's never met anyone he didn't share at least one language with before.

Then he notices how the two beasts are regarding them with patient indulgence, like parents whose toddlers are meeting for the first time. He relaxes a little. *Well then,* he thinks, *I guess it's okay. Must be I've kept to the script so far.*

CHAPTER FOUR

In her eagerness to follow the dragon's Quest, Erde had
expected to travel a goodly distance, but she hadn't
counted on finding herself in a country that was so hot and
where people didn't speak German. Never mind that she'd
only recently gotten her own voice back: Just what did you
do if somebody couldn't speak your language? But she was
fairly sure language would be the least of her problems—
the dragons would figure it out between them. Certainly
the two of them were having no problem understanding
one another. She felt Earth's relief and excitement hum-
ming through his body like a murmur of gratitude. Not
since he'd woken up in that deep cold cave above Tor Alte
had he been able to communicate with another being so
fast and so fully, too fast for Erde to keep up. But she had
snagged one astonishing revelation as it flashed by her: This
new dragon from the sea was apparently Earth's relative.
She'd actually heard him call her his sister.

Erde recalled how she'd felt when Rose of Deep Moor
had proved able to sense and decipher Earth's image signals in her head. Not as clearly or as easily as Erde, certainly—the dragon had to be gentle with his sending to
avoid burning Rose out. But she'd been the first since Erde
and Earth had found each other and learned that they
could speak in a way that did not (at first) include language.
It helped that Rose was Sir Hal's longtime beloved, and a
truly remarkably power in her own right. But mostly, instead of feeling the expected jealousy, Erde was glad to
have someone to share the burden of communicating with
the dragon's ferociously curious and demanding intellect.

And, even better, another dragon to help answer Earth's

difficult questions. It wasn't that Earth considered her ignorant or inadequate. His generous nature was not given to
that sort of harsh judgment. She was still his boon companion, his Dragon Guide, and forever would be. But Erde
sensed she had come to the end of her useful knowledge,
at least as far as helping Earth discover the reasons for his
recent reawakening. And just when she'd needed help, help
had arrived. It occurred to Erde that she and the dragon
had been lucky that way. Sir Hal, too, had appeared out
of nowhere to aid their escape just as she was about to fall
into the clutches of Fra Guill's army of monks. It must
mean that, like it or not, this hot, ugly, scary beach was
exactly where they were meant to be to continue the dragon's Quest.

Which also meant that this dark young man—he seemed
younger now than he had from a distance—this "Endoch"
was meant to be also. If he was here with this sea dragon,
he must be her dragon guide. But what Earth seemed to
take for granted, Erde had a harder time accepting. He just
didn't look like a dragon guide, running abut half-naked
and grinning, so full of himself, yet at the same time a bit
too eager to please, as if there was something he thought
she might give him if only he was charming enough.

Well, thought Erde, *I have nothing, and I wouldn't give
him anything even if I had. Besides, he must have done
something wrong, to have people chasing him so furiously.*

At the back of her mind, she felt the pressure of the
dragon's censure. He was not too involved with his newfound relative to remind her that people had been chasing
her very recently. And what, after all, does a dragon guide
look like? The image he showed her was like a mirror held
up in her mind. Did a scrawny, wide-eyed, wind-roughened
fourteen-year-old girl inspire any greater confidence?

Chastened, Erde reconsidered her inner tirade. The
dragon was right. It wasn't proper to take on so against an
innocent stranger. It was just that, well, he was so strange.
But judging from the men who'd been pursuing him, dark
skin and no clothing was the way things went in this smelly,
steamy country. Erde had a sudden sense of reversal, like
being tossed head over heels in a torrent. The sense of it
was so physical, she grabbed Earth's neck crest for support.
In this place, it could be her own pale skin and heavy cloth-

ing that seemed unnatural. As the thick heat wore on her, she was already prepared to shed a few inappropriate layers.

So she'd better give this young man a second chance. If the sea dragon was Earth's sister, it then followed that this Endoch should be, in a way, her brother. Erde found she could warm to that idea. She'd always wanted a brother or a sister. Someone nearer her own age to talk to. Her life in her father's castle had been filled with adults twice her age or older. Except for Rainer. Well, Rainer had been sort of her brother, until he grew up so tall and handsome and she was dumb enough to fall in love with him. She wasn't going to do that again. Tentatively, she smiled at Endoch and he grinned back, revealing the whitest, evenest teeth she'd ever seen, set in a round mobile face as smooth and fine as polished walnut. His grin asked, Well, what's next? Erde hoped Earth would have an answer.

She tapped at him mentally to get his attention.

—*Has she said, Dragon, why she's Called you?*

A flood of images burst into her head, tumbling, crowding, flashing past too fast to be made sense of. Erde slammed up a barrier of protest and sent back an image of herself drowning. Earth relayed apologies and braked reluctantly to the snail-pace of language.

—*Oh, wonder! Oh, devastation!*

—*What? Dragon, what is it?*

—*Wonder that I have found my sister again!*

Again? Erde puzzled at that but there was first a more pressing concern.

—*What could be bad about that?*

—*Devastation that it is not she who Called!*

—*Not? How do you know?*

—*She, too, has heard the Call, from the depths of the sea, and has waked to answer it.*

Erde conjured images of comfort and reassurance.

—*It is another who Calls. She thinks she knows who.*

—*Can she tell you your Purpose?*

—*She's hardly sure of her own. But she remembers more than I.*

—*What is her name?*

Erde hoped she did not offend by asking. She knew how

sensitive dragons could be about their naming. But Earth seemed to find great joy in the announcement.

—*Her name is Water.*

Water. Earth and Water. A notion began in Erde's brain that slid away forgotten as Endoch stilled suddenly, losing his grin. He turned to stare at the narrow space of sand between the dark rusting wall and the impossible pincushion trees. Erde listened as he was listening, hard with bated breath.

"Uh-oh," he said, and she had no trouble understanding his meaning.

CHAPTER FIVE

N'Doch hears it now, an approaching throng. He'd have heard it a lot sooner if he'd been paying less attention to his chances for stardom and more to his personal safety. He can even hear the clang of the weapons—hoes, rakes, tire irons. They've brought whatever was to hand, and probably a raggedly lethal assortment of firearms. This'll really give the cameras something to focus on. He's surprised the brothers didn't recognize a vid-shoot when they saw it, but he knows they could never have roused the *bidonville* with a complaint about stolen tomatoes. The bunch of them must have charged in hollering about mutant monsters attacking the beach. It's mostly fishermen who live in the shantytown, a hard life and getting harder. They'll be worried about their boats, and these days, they'll believe anything bad about the water.

N'Doch has to laugh at that. If they think his own little silver-blue critter could do damage to one of those old hard-built boats, wait till they see this big brown guy. Then he wonders if the fishermen are in on it, too. Maybe the whole town knew about the shoot except him.

Doesn't matter. He's deep into it now. For at least the fifth time that day, he ponders his routes of escape. He can see the white girl has the same idea. She's casing the nearest fishing boat with obvious intent to board.

"Can't hide there," he cautions. "First place they'll look."

She gazes at him uncomprehendingly.

"Damn. Forgot." He'd felt like they were communicating pretty well until he'd had to fall back on words. Then he gets excited all over again. This has got to be it, his big moment, where he gets to rescue the girl from the ravening horde and be the hero. He wishes he'd found more to eat today. One tomato is hardly an energy-builder. He's not sure yet how the cybercritters fit in. The brown one, at least, is much too big for the hidey-hole N'Doch is contemplating. He thinks the blue one will just make it, but probably they're meant to face down the crowd first as a diversion while he makes a run for it with the girl. He finds he's not very happy about that. It means one or both of the critters will likely be torn apart by the mob, to rouse the viewer's blood lust a little and create more sympathy for the hapless escapees. He hopes it's not the little blue one, though her size and beauty make her the prime candidate. But he reminds himself she's only a prop. He shouldn't be thinking of her as *his*.

Anyhow, he knows what he should do. The only question is, whether he should wait until the crowd comes into view around the landing craft, to help build suspense and give the cameras a dramatic long shot. By now, the critters have their heads high and searching. The girl is looking this way and that, especially at him. Her eyes are very clearly demanding help. He remembers she knows at least some version of the story line—probably she's trying to cue him that it's time to make his move. Besides, he's hearing that weird music in his head again.

"Okay, let's go!" N'Doch beckons hugely, then recalls how, when he did his walk-on, the director singled him out of the whole crowd of extras and told him to stop acting so hard.

"*Act*ing!" she'd said, as if it was some kind of dirty word.

So N'Doch backs off his mugging and gesturing and trots up the beach to cut around the end of the fishing fleet. He expects the girl to follow, but beside the last boat he looks back and she hasn't, though the silver-blue critter is close behind, tailing him like a big long-necked dog. Her manner isn't doglike, however. She seems to be urging him to hurry. The mob is so close, he can distinguish individual voices and words. Any moment, they'll be in sight. N'Doch sprints back down the beach and grabs the girl's hand to haul her into action. She resists only briefly. Now the brown guy is moving, too. They both get the idea and hurry after N'Doch. He gestures at them to watch where they step.

On the other side of the fishing fleet, the super-tanker

awaits them, as long and high as a city block, its bow broken and sunk so deep into the sand that it looks like it grew there. Gaping holes smile darkly, scars of the harbor mines that took it out when it blundered into them during the storm. The girl stares at it horrified, as if she has no idea what she's looking at. Even the critters seem to hesitate. N'Doch takes the girl's hand again and races for the largest gap, but when they get there and he's pulled her into its shadow, it's plain the big guy will never fit.

The one from the water, *his* one, checks out the ragged opening. It's close. She's wider than he's guessed and the metal edges are nasty. But she heads right in. N'Doch winces, worried for her fine silky fur or her delicate fleshy crest, then blinks as she seems to thin and elongate, and slip through easily. N'Doch is sure his eyes have given out for a moment, as if his vision blurred, just for an instant, then the moment passes and the sea critter is there inside the hold with him and the girl, looking very self-satisfied. He shakes his head, wondering, but he can't spend time on it now. The big guy is still outside in the hot sun, nosing around the sharp edges of the gap. His curving horns clank against the rusted metal, then he withdraws. N'Doch goes to help him, in case he's been wrong about this one's size as well.

When he steps out into the sun, he can hear the mob just about to spill, foaming at the mouth, from behind the fishing fleet. He glances swiftly about. No sign of the big cybercritter. The wide stretch of sand is empty, but for scattered rubble and a big rock halfway toward the water. A big brown rock that wasn't there before.

N'Doch squints at it, frowning. For the barest instant, he can see it as the cybercritter, settling in to wait out the battle. Then it's a rock again, and he knows the mob will also see a rock, and ignore it.

Man, he marvels *that is one amazing piece of equipment.* Then the girl is behind him, pulling him out of the sunlight.

"*Gehen wir,*" she whispers urgently.

N'Doch holds back, pointing to the new brown boulder, but she only nods and yanks on him some more.

"*Ja, ha, gehen wir! Schnell!*"

Finally he gets it. This miracle is nothing new to her at

all. Probably she does lots of these high-tech vids. Feeling obscurely put down, N'Doch shrugs and brushes past her with a sharp gesture. "This way."

The blue beast is waiting in the shadows. She chirps at him briskly as he nears. It sounds as much like an order as like encouragement, but for her sake, N'Doch chooses the widest passage into the bowels of the downed ship-giant. He leads them toward the stern, the seaward end, where the lowest holds are filled with water and hung with sea-weed and barnacles and mutant starfish with too many arms. The fishermen don't like the tanker. Not even the most destitute will live in it, though the upper decks are mostly intact and dry, above the high water mark. They claim that the rotting bodies of dead sailors wash about in the holds to rise at night and walk the shredded decks. N'Doch has found a bone or two, nothing more. After all, the fish visit the wrecks at high tide, and with food as scarce as it is, they're not likely to leave much behind. As for any lurking ghosts, he's grateful to them if they keep unwanted visitors from penetrating as deeply into the tanker's wet gloom as he dares to go.

This girl, he guesses, would side with the fishermen. She looks near to panic in the close dim passages. At the raised sill of a door hatch, N'Doch puts on the charm to urge her forward. She returns him a look of offended bravado but takes his offered hand anyway, sticking close behind him as he negotiates a section of collapsed decking. The hole is filled with surging black water. N'Doch isn't worried about his footing. He knows every nook and cranny. What's both-ering him is the cameras, now he's disappeared inside the ship. Then he figures the girl must carry a camera with her, maybe one of those micro-implants that uses her eyes as the lens. He's seen an infoshow about the r & d on that but he's surprised to see it's already in commercial use. Of course, the Media get all the good tech before anyone. They're the ones with the real money in this world, after all.

Past another hatch, he reaches a dry level spot where light drops through a blown-out exhaust stack. The girl looks up, as if light alone could save her life. She hugs the dank wall, breathing hard and shallow, but ready to continue. N'Doch checks back for the blue cybercritter. She's just stepping daintily through the hatchway behind them, and

again he finds himself blinking at her and staring, because
she seems so much shorter and longer than she did outside,
almost an entirely different shape. And if she was human,
he'd say she's preening a bit, to be sure he's noticed. He
thinks of the big guy's gift for looking like a rock and begins
to suspect this one of harboring other equally mysterious
skills.

Then he hears banging and raucous shouts echoing from
the gap amidships. The mob'll be in after them soon,
worked up enough to dare coming inside a ways. He's got
to get moving again, now the girl has caught her breath.
The hardest part's still ahead of them.

He signals the girl and moves on down the slanted passage. He wishes he could tell her how he thinks of this huge
vessel as a man lying dead in the water. They'd been threading through his stove-in rib cage, and now they've reached
his broken, sunken spine. N'Doch eases around a mass of
wreckage, some vast engine or turbine hurled upward by
the blast, only to fall back, crushing everything in its path.
When he's in here, N'Doch can't help picturing the ship's
gallant last moments. He's written songs about it, but none
yet that's satisfied him. The mammoth scale of the event as
he imagines it is beyond the range of his ancient keyboard
and amps. One of the reasons he wants so badly to be
famous is so he can afford better equipment.

He slows a bit, knowing what's just ahead. They creep
around a particularly dark corner—even N'Doch has his
hand to the wall, feeling his way. Then, in front of them,
the dark gets darker and the floor falls away. There were
stairs here once. Now water laps along the base of the walls
where they end in blackness. This hold was breached only
below the waterline. It is lightless and vast, and the moist
air is close with rank sea smells. The ebb and flow of water
makes the stressed and rusting metal creak and groan. It's
this part of the ship that gives rise to tales of the walking
dead.

"And here's the bad news," murmurs N'Doch from the
edge. "We gotta swim across." He doesn't mention that the
local shark herd likes to hang out in this cooler, darker
water. As his eyes adjust, he sees the whites of the girl's
eyes shift. She's staring at him as if she suspects his meaning.

He nods, making broad swimming motions he hopes she and her camera can pick up in the faint light.

"*Ich kann nicht.*" She backs up sharply, shaking her head.

N'Doch doesn't blame her really. This part couldn't have been in the script she read 'cause he's just written it in. But she's getting good pay for this, so he shrugs and jabs a thumb behind them, where the shouts and banging make it sound like the ship is being torn apart for salvage. He tries to sound tough and heroic.

"No choice, babe. Sorry."

The girl eyes him owlishly. N'Doch likes her little glower. It makes her look brave, even if she isn't. Except really, she is, to have come this far past the scripted action. He wonders if the story includes a big love scene where she gives herself to him in gratitude for being so manfully rescued. Usually, he'd be up for that, as it were, even on camera, though he's never tried *that* before. But somehow, this is different. *She* is different. First, she's so young. He knows all the hot sexpot vid stars are around her age, but somehow, she seems even younger. He can't bring himself to undress her in his mind. He's embarrassed to think that "innocent" might be the word he's looking for, but there it is. He doesn't have a sister, but this is probably what it's like. He feels more like protecting her than making love to her.

And it's weird, feeling so responsible. N'Doch figures he's really getting into the role now. In which case, he'd better set a strong example. He crouches at the edge, then shoves off lightly into the water with hardly a splash. No use announcing your presence to the damn sharks. If they're here, they'll find you soon enough. Reciting private incantations against all sea vermin, he beckons encouragingly and treads water to give the girl a moment to work up her nerve.

But she's still shaking her head and making big warding gestures with both her arms.

"*Nein! Nein! Ich kann nicht schwimmen!*"

She seems to be trying to explain her reluctance. N'Doch is glad she's smart enough to keep her voice down despite her panic. He's not too hot on strange dark places either, but all he wants right now is to see her in the water. The sooner she's in, the sooner they're both out. He'd like to tell her to stop acting so hard, like the director did to him. Instead, he frowns at her fiercely. She just glares right back at him.

Suddenly there is motion in the darkness. N'Doch makes for the edge, sure it's the sharks. But it's the blue cybercritter, barely visible, sliding silently into the water. She glides over, nudging him insistently. She doesn't give up until he wraps an arm around her neck to keep from being swamped. He feels like he's just been boarded by the Harbor Patrol. Dragging him with her, the critter eases sideways against the edge of the drop-off, warbling calming music to the girl.

"*Gott sei Dank!*" the girl murmurs. To N'Doch's amazement, she starts stripping off her tall leather boots and vest. She bundles them up and, clutching them to her thin chest with one arm, she lowers herself into the water to hang on to the edge for dear life while the cybercritter coasts along beside her. With a desperate lurch and grab, the girl flings herself astride the critter's back and holds tight with her free arm. In the dim reflected murmur of light sifting through random cracks and punctures, N'Doch sees both terror and determination sculpting her face into something as steady as stone. She doesn't seem to care that she's gotten wet, just that there's something solid underneath her.

Now N'Doch gets it at last. He's thought it was the sharks she's afraid of, not the *water*. He's a little embarrassed, hopes he hasn't messed up the script. But hey, how was he to know a grown-up girl like her wouldn't know how to swim?

But now the cybercritter is singing an impatient demand for directions. He can tell she's not too interested in hanging out in a shark tank either. N'Doch pulls himself together and points, and the blue beast bears them secretly into darkness.

CHAPTER SIX

Dragons are certainly the world's cleverest creatures, thought Erde gratefully as she clung to Water's long silky neck and struggled to keep her boot bundle dry. She understood that Endoch wasn't being cruel or stupid, trying to force her into the water. He didn't know she was a baron's daughter and lucky to have been taught how to read, never mind a skill so unladylike as swimming. Indeed, she envied his ease with it—to be able to glide over this fathomless black without fear of sinking would put an entire category of nightmares to rest. Hal had promised to teach her, but they'd never found the time. Besides, it had been so cold up there—she thought of home now as "up" because she knew it got warmer as you traveled farther south and surely the Germanies must be very far north of any place as hot as this. But the cold hadn't been normal. Right in the middle of August, it had snowed. The smaller ponds had even iced over. And terrible storms and hail and too much rain. Just thinking of it made her shiver. That weird, unseasonable weather had roused the villagers to go out hunting the witch responsible for the curse. She would have been their victim, had Fra Guill had his way.

Meanwhile, here she was, running from another howling mob, hiding in another cave. Erde recalled the peace and pleasure of Deep Moor and nearly wept. She'd had such a short time in that magical valley, with Rose and the other women who guarded and nurtured its secrets, yet somehow she had come to think of it as home. She had no other, certainly not Tor Alte, not as long as her father remained under the priest's evil sway. And now she didn't even have

Deep Moor—she had a dark and noisy pit filled with salty, smelly water.

She caught herself whining, and didn't at all like the sound of it. At least the water was cooler than the fetid air. And how dare she whine when they'd found another dragon, one who could understand her, even if its dragon guide could not? Erde did not feel Water in her head like she did her own dragon. Water responded via a fast relay to Earth and back again. This dragon-to-dragon communication seemed virtually instantaneous, as real magic should be. It was as good as having an interpreter standing right at your ear.

What did not seem to be so clear or instantaneous was Water's communication with Endoch. But Erde remembered that it had taken her a while, several days in fact, to learn how to "talk" properly with Earth. Endoch was probably "hearing" more than he realized. It had been that way for her, and then understanding had arrived rather suddenly, like a morning fog lifting off the mountains. From then on, it had been as natural as breathing.

For now, Endoch had fallen into nodding and pointing a lot, rather like she'd had to do when she'd lost her voice. But she guessed he had met a lot of people who didn't speak his language, since he acted as if it was nothing odd, merely inconvenient.

And so, with broad gestures and murmured incoherencies, he led them far across the dark lagoon to an equally dark shore. Finally, Erde heard rather than saw him let go of Water's neck and swim several long strokes to clamber up on a bank that rang softly under the weight of his step. Water slid alongside this shore while Erde felt for stone or sand, anything solid to stand on. Instead, she found Endoch's hand, hauling her out of the water. He drew her quickly away from the groaning edge, which was hard as stone but smelled like a smithy's rubbish pile.

"Come on," he said quietly. "This way."

Erde's alert ear detected familiar syllables. "*Kommen*?" She felt him stop short and turn in the darkness.

"Yeah," he said with slow surprise. "That's right, come on."

"*Ja*," said Erde. "*Ich komme.*"

"Yeah?" He gave a little laugh of disbelief.

"Ja."

"Ja," he repeated experimentally, mimicking her with an actor's precision. Then he slapped his forehead. "Of course! It's German. You're speaking German. It sounds a little different, y'know? I didn't recognize it at first."

Erde was sorry to disappoint him, but her silence told all.

"No, huh? Okay, lemesee . . . German . . . I know that one. It's all over those big trucks we scavenge. It's, um . . . Deutschland!"

"Jawohl. Deutsch." Erde almost giggled. He was close, but how funny that he had turned a mere language into an entire kingdom. Deutsch*land*? Didn't he know that a whole lot of kingdoms and duchies spoke German?

"Deutsch," he repeated. "That's right, Deutsch."

Water announced herself with a wet nudge at Erde's shoulder. There were lanterns or torchlight flickering along the walls of the opposite shore.

"Sei ist hier," Erde whispered anxiously. *"Gehen wir, ja?"* But Endoch had spotted the approaching light and was already drawing them away from the water. Erde sensed the tunnel closing in around them again. She put out a hand and immediately jerked it back, suppressing a squeal. The wall was slimy. Cold strings of stuff gave damply under her fingers. Probably the same stuff so soft and slippery beneath her feet. A childish horror rose up in her gullet. Surely, like Jonah in the Bible, she was being swallowed alive!

But Water was there at her back to nudge her along when she froze. The dragon's breath was like a warm breeze beside her ear. Erde thought of her beloved horse Micha. Her terror eased, and she was able to move on. Only for the dragons' sake would she set foot in such a terrible place.

Soon she realized she could see again, mostly faint shapes of gray and grayer, but at least now she could make out Endoch's tall, slim form moving along the passage ahead of her. The ground slanted upward, which Erde took as a fair and welcome sign that she might soon see the light of day again.

At the bottom of a flight of steps, Endoch paused and glanced back. "Everyone okay so far?"

Erde understood only his tone of concern. She nodded and picked up her pace a bit.

"Almost there."

She heard anticipation in his voice now, and a hint of pride. She climbed the steps behind him thoughtfully. This place he was taking them must be something special, maybe his family stronghold, and this was the hidden entrance. Erde was surprised by his generosity. She wasn't sure she'd reveal such a secret to someone she'd just met. But after all, it was his own skin he was saving, as well as hers.

A thin shaft of light from above lit the top of the steps. A glow down the passage promised a lot more beyond. Erde gazed about as details rose into visibility, like riders appearing out of a mist. She saw a long narrow corridor with a flat floor and a low, absolutely flat ceiling. She'd never encountered a place so rigorously rectangular or even imagined such a thing was possible. Yet, for all the apparent right angles, there was not a sharp edge anywhere. The walls were very light-colored and entirely smooth, without a crack or mortar line, only a seam every so often, flanked by rows of close-set little knobs, either decorative or some kind of fastener. Cautiously, she put a fingertip, then her entire palm to the surface. It was dry and faintly cool to the touch. Clearly, they had left the cave without her noticing, and climbed up into a strange sort of building. Endoch's family must be very powerful if this was the castle they lived in.

She was so busy studying the odd walls as she moved along them that she was unprepared for the space beyond. Passing through a doorway, she stopped short, letting her boot bundle slide unnoticed to the floor.

A great-hall, she thought, *or even a cathedral.*

But there was no altar or throne to be seen, no choir stalls or banqueting table. She stood in a tall, square room with rows of huge, many-paned windows set high up on three of the four pale walls. The ceiling above was lost behind the bright glare through the glass. Many of the panes were cracked or missing, letting currents of air into the room to swirl dust and insects about in the long thick pillars of light falling past shadowed corners toward the floor.

The floor made her nervous. It seemed to be floating.

Erde bent and laid a hand to it. It felt and looked like wood but was as seamless and smooth as pond water at dawn.

Endoch appeared out of the shadows, grinning boyishly. "Isn't it great? Isn't it just mega?"

Erde hated to dampen such luminous pride, but how long should she go on pretending she understood what he was saying? Water slipped in behind her and padded into the sunlight and smoky air. Erde watched her slim and lengthen toward the high bank of windows, and knew her for a shape-shifter. Quite astonishing to observe for the first time, really, but nothing surprising. Shape-shifting was an attribute of dragons often mentioned in the lore, one that Earth, being tied to soil and stone, did not possess. Erde hoped he would not be jealous.

She glanced at Endoch, and found him watching the she-dragon with a narrowed eye. He, too, had noticed the shape change, but he seemed puzzled by it, as if unsure that he'd actually seen it. She wondered if his study of the dragon lore had been as complete as her own. She knew that much of a young man's time must be spent in the armorer's practice yard or out with the Hunt, but surely he could have picked up the basic essentials just by paying good attention to the bard tales or the old songs sung at the village festivals. If he didn't know the lore, he'd have no idea what his duty was as Water's dragon guide. She could certainly tell him, but Erde wondered if he'd even listen to advice from someone so much younger, and a girl.

Whatever conclusion he'd reached, Endoch finally pulled out of his stare with a quick doglike shake of his head and went back to the entrance to yank on a piece of the wall beside it. When it began to swing forward, Erde realized it was a door, huge and rounded at the corners. Endoch pivoted it carefully into place so it settled against the opening with a heavy muffled clang. He twisted some kind of latch that squealed as he turned it, then came away, dusting his palms together with a satisfied air.

"That'll keep 'em guessing. No one's ever got past the shark tank so far, but you never know. . . ."

Erde nodded helpfully, which she thought was more polite than shrugging or pointing. The newly relaxed tilt of his shoulders did suggest that he felt they'd finally escaped their pursuers. Taking her first easy breath in a while, Erde rolled up her dripping legging and began to worry about Earth.

She had no sense of how far they were from where they'd left him on the sand beside the ocean. Since finding each other two months before, she and the dragon had hardly been separated. The void his absence left inside her was an almost physical pain. When he used his gift of stillness to become rocklike, or to still even further to virtual invisibility, it took all of his energy and concentration, or at least that was his explanation for why they could not communicate while he was being invisible. Erde had been sending him a stream of images just in case, ever since following Endoch into the cave. Now that they were in a more dragon-sized room, Earth could join them if only she could send him a good image of it, for he was able to transport himself to any place he could picture clearly in his mind.

Just as she was pondering what to do next, there he was, winking into existence beside Water in the middle of the room. Erde ran to him joyfully.

—*Dragon! How did you get here?*

—*My sister! She showed me and I came.*

Like an excited child returned from a great adventure, he began filling her head with views of the mob milling and shouting while he'd been hiding in plain view on he beach.

—*Water can be with you even when you're invisible?*

Assent. A proud dragon nod inside her head.

—*How wonderful.*

—*Yes, she is wonderful. She is my sister.*

—*I know, I know.*

Then Erde felt ashamed, for she knew she'd sounded snappish. He was still so caught up in the wonder of acquiring a sibling. She didn't blame him, particularly since the sibling's gifts seemed to dovetail so conveniently with his own. But she worried now that she, not he, might be the jealous one. She would just try to think of it as having two dragons instead of one. She was eager to question Water about who she thought the Caller was, and about what else she might know that Earth did not. But first, there was the question of Endoch.

—*Dragon, is Water sure this dark man is her dragon guide?*

Assent, query, puzzlement.

—Well, I mean, he . . . I don't think he knows very much about dragons.

Earth looked at her, then looked across the room at Endoch, who had frozen in mid-stride and stood staring at them with his mouth open.

—Hmmm. My sister says maybe you are right.

CHAPTER SEVEN

N'Doch knows what he's seen. He's been watching the silver one since she did her growing taller thing right in front of him, and then—in a moment shorter than an eye blink—the big guy is there beside her. Three-D and substantial. Definitely not a hologram. N'Doch notes that the white girl can actually lean her whole weight against the critter's scaly brown shoulder.

The problem is, he can't believe it. He wants to, but he just can't. He's always told himself those vid people can do anything. Hire *them* to put men on Mars, he's always said. They'd get it done soon enough, and make a good show out of it, too.

But here, in the dusty shadow and light of his favorite hiding place, his own secret kingdom, this officers' gymnasium, his credulity is tempered by the still, sane presence of the space. Here—safe, relaxed, clearheaded—he finally has to admit that he's been making up most of his explanations for the events of the last half hour, or at least stretching what he's heard to fit what he's been seeing. He's never seen a real cybercritter, only the infoshows about the cutting edge developments in special effects, shows he realizes are no more reliable than your everyday newscast. Because he *wants* them to be true, somehow they become true when he needs them to. But right now, in this calm room, away from the constant hype and hustle of his daily life, those stories are no longer working.

But he's never been without a story, so what should the new story be? The big guy was on the beach, and now he's here. Apparently translated through steel and plastic and wood within the space of a breath. Not an easy thing to explain in the world as N'Doch knows it. In fact, it's a bigger stretch than cybercritters.

And then there's the silver one with her head-invading music. The right music. *His* music.

N'Doch finds himself weak at the knees again. He's dimly aware that his arm is hurting where the short brother slashed him. He knows he should be paying more attention to the wound, getting it cleaned and covered before any one of a billion bugs take up residence. But this other matter has him too distracted.

"This is all a setup, right?" he asks the girl, one last chance at a rational explanation. "You know, for the vid?" If she's not an actress, if she's making this up as she goes along, just like he is—and her look of innocent bewilderment is almost enough to convince him she is—then what are these critters?

If not a vid-tech special effect, then . . . what?

To stave off the upswelling panic, he resorts to an exercise of logic. Either they're real, these critters, or they're not. Fine. If they're not real, he's seeing things. If he's seeing things, he's either sick or crazy. Or—he remembers the tomato—he's been drugged.

But he doesn't think he's crazy, and he doesn't feel drugged, at least not the usual way. And except for the growing heat in his arm, he feels healthy enough. He'd managed not to drink any of the sea water drenching him, and he'd spotted both critters within moments of being cut. No bug goes to work *that* quick. Anyhow, the brothers saw them, too. That's what saved his life.

Which means they're real, the conclusion he'd already reached and explained away with invented technology. But if they're real and *not* cybercritters, then what the hell are they?

This time the panic will not be kept down. Rising up with it comes a notion that defies all his attempts at logic. N'Doch tries to ignore it, but he knows where it comes from. It's the same part of him he goes to when he writes his music, where the answers have nothing to do with logic, they just appear out of his soul like magic.

Appear like magic. That was it. That was the notion he was trying to avoid. *Magic.*

N'Doch meets the great golden gaze of the larger critter and gives in. His knees buckle.

*   *   *

Erde saw the fear rush into his eyes just before he collapsed. It was like watching black water flood a ditch. Earth's sudden arrival must have frightened him. The dragon was big, after all, though not nearly as big as she'd thought a dragon should be. And he could look terrifying if you didn't know him. But why was Endoch scared now, when he hadn't been before, back on the beach? Must be he was better at covering it up than she was.

Then she noticed there was blood on the floor where he'd fallen, and recalled the vicious swipe the man with the club had delivered. She relayed the reminder to Earth, but it was Water who went to him, lowering her sleek head to nose at him, crooning gently. Endoch yelped and scrambled backward on ankles and elbows as if terrified. Erde thought Water was the least sort of dragon to be frightened of, but Endoch's terror rang in the air like a hammered bell. Erde found herself gripping Earth's neck crest in sympathy. She could sense the dragon's bemused surprise.

—*He is frightened. He does not know what she is.*

Erde nodded, remembering.

—*I didn't know who you were either, when I first saw you. I thought you were going to eat me.*

A graver negative than usual washed across her mind.

—*What, not who. He does not know what a dragon is.*

This, Erde could not imagine.

—*You mean, he doesn't believe in dragons?*

She'd met people like that, though they were rare. They usually didn't believe in witchcraft either, until someone laid a proper spell on them. But most people thought witches and dragons were the minions of Satan, which was why Fra Guill's campaign against them roused such fervor throughout the countryside. But Erde knew better, about both dragons and witches.

The question was, how to convince Endoch?

N'Doch's whole world is turning upside down.

He's too old to believe in magic, or maybe too young. His weird grandfather believes in magic, for God's sake, and he's so uncool and old-fashioned, it's an embarrassment to have him in the family. Not that you ever saw anything of him, living all alone out in the bush like he does. The old man once told him towns were bad for his health. *Well, yeah,* N'Doch recalls replying, *but so is being a hermit.*

N'Doch's fear retreats a bit before a vivid rush of childhood memories, rising like a flight of birds to distract him: the heat and red dust of the bush, the stillness at midday, the scent of parched vegetation. His mama often sent him out to stay with Papa Djawara after his father took off and she was so busy working. Jeez, the man was old even then. And weird. N'Doch feels his mouth curl in an involuntary grin. The old man did tell great stories. Sang them, really. *Probably what got me started,* N'Doch realizes, listening to all those long songs that went on verse after verse, late into the night, unbelievable yarns about powerful shamans and evil curses and spirits of the dead that enter the bodies of men and animals in order to work their will among the living. The usual old tribal stuff.

But there was that one long tale, N'Doch recalls, one that was different from the rest and the old man's special favorite. He always reworked it so it was about the adventures of a young man named Water. As N'Doch roots around trying to retrieve it from faded memory, he finds himself gazing up into a pair of liquid dark eyes that are focused on him with alarming intensity. He reads concern there, yes, but also rebuke and impatience. He remembers the song now, and the memory takes his breath away: a young man named Water meets up with a monster from the sea. Only she's not a monster, she's a magical creature, a dragon, and the whole long song is about the quest they embark on to save the world. He doesn't recall ever hearing the ending. He always fell asleep first.

A dragon?

No.

The silvery-blue critter nudges him, showing just the faintest trace of irritation. N'Doch backs away in horror.

A *dragon?*

He blinks, he coughs, he shakes his head. He does all the requisite things, even pinches himself, but he's been looking at this critter for over an hour and he knows she's not going away that easy. He's not dreaming, he's wide awake, his arm hurts like hell and there's a dragon in his hidey-hole.

Two dragons. And a weird white girl who acts like she's

dropped in from some other planet. Who knows? Maybe she has. Why should things start getting any saner? Meanwhile, he's flat on his ass and elbows, and bleeding all over his beautiful wooden floor, the only thing in his life that's whole and perfect. N'Doch grasps at logic again: what do you do when something you can't believe is happening, actually is? Hey, you go with it. Like the first bars of a new melody, you just follow it out, see where it leads you.

So he tries to get up, but his legs won't work. And it's hot in the gym, so much hotter than usual. He's bathed in sweat and slipping in his own blood as he struggles to rise. The blue critter puts her forehead to his chest and presses him back to the floor. He's surprised how gentle she is, since she's looking so irascible. There's music in his head again, and N'Doch decides to lie there and listen, while the blue critter noses at his arm. Her inspection hurts despite her gentleness, but the pain is somehow past the edge of his current awareness, which is filled with the music. He understands now that the bugs are in his wound, the worst bugs, the really fast-acting kind, and that means he's got to act even faster. He's got to get serious about moving to his stash of antibiotics, though who knows if he's got anything here that's recent enough to kill this bug—they all mutate so fast and his pill source is not exactly over-the-counter yesterday's formula.

His breath is getting short, a bad sign. He draws his knees up to his chest and turns over onto his side. Again, the blue critter stops him. N'Doch is amazed by the strength in that seemingly delicate neck. He struggles a bit, but the music swells in his head and then he can't recall why he's resisting so hard. Her voice is so soothing, her warm breath on his cheek so familiar, his mama's of course, why didn't he see that? She'll take him into her arms and make his hurt go away. His grip on consciousness is tenuous. N'Doch forgets why he's holding on at all, and lets go.

CHAPTER EIGHT

His fever had risen so suddenly, she hadn't seen it for what it was. He'd seemed so hale while leading them to safety, as if his wound didn't bother him at all.

Cautiously, Erde joined Water at the dark boy's side. She shouldn't think of him as a boy, he was clearly several years older than she was. But on his back and so feverish, he looked young and vulnerable. She wondered suddenly if his fever was contagious. The only sickness she knew that rose so fast was the plague. Chilled, she retreated a few steps. She saw no rashes or boils, the outward signs of plague, but she did not want to have come all this way simply to be felled by disease.

Earth lumbered up beside her. She wrapped a hand around his nearest horn for comfort as he lowered his big head thoughtfully over the stricken youth. Then she recalled how the dragon had healed the old man in the barn at Erfurt. He'd been beaten senseless and was bleeding to death from a sword cut to his side, but when Earth was through with him, he got up and walked away. And the she-goat. Earth had healed her, too, by washing her awful wounds with his big cowlike tongue.

Erde wasn't sure she should remind Earth of the she-goat, whom he'd been later forced to devour to keep himself from starving. The noble goat, of course, had given her permission. Instead, Erde imaged the old man, though he'd proved far less noble, an ungrateful coward who'd revealed their hiding place to Brother Guillemo himself.

—*Dragon! Do you remember? Can you help this one too?*
There was doubt and diffidence in the dragon's reply.

—The wound I can close and make well, but he already burns from within. . . .

—The fever? You can't heal the fever?

An immense sigh, like the ground shifting, then sadness, failure, a sense of inadequacy.

Water raised her head from her scrutiny of Endoch's condition. She fixed Erde with her demanding stare, and an image formed in Erde's head, which she saw exactly mirrored in the broad expanse of Earth's mind. She knew immediately that the thought came from the she-dragon. The quality of the communication differed so from Earth's blunt, honest imaging. It slid into her consciousness—not surprisingly—like water, rushing here, a trickle there, not to be denied. Insistently flowing into cracks, following the contours of her thoughts, shimmering like the ruffled surface of a lake. At times two images, or three or several, layered one over another, adding depth and richness.

Erde was delighted. With Earth as a conduit, she could speak with Water almost directly, if she could but learn to read her imaging coherently. Right now, the layering and shimmering obscured the meaning of the image. There seemed to be several narratives playing at once: one of Earth washing the dark youth's wound, one of the four of them huddling together in an earnest, conversing fashion. But surely Water did not intend the topmost layer the way it seemed, for it showed Erde with her dagger in hand, stabbing into the soft fur of the sea dragon's neck, then catching the flowing blood in cupped palms.

—Dragon! What is she saying?

Earth's horror was as profound as her own. But after consultation with the sea dragon, it faded to wonder and admiration.

—Her blood will heal the fire inside. You must give it to him.

—I? Me?

Vigorous assent.

She has shown you how. Quickly, she says. You must do it now!

Dragon's blood. The most magical substance of all, according to the lore.

Erde gripped her dagger dutifully but was stopped by the

sinuous beauty of Water's beckoning head and neck. Earth shoved at her with his snout.

—*Quickly!*

—*Oh, Dragon, I can't!*

—*She says you must, or he will die.*

Erde forced herself the few steps to Water's side and slid her dagger from its sheath. Alla's dagger. The old woman's parting gift. Lying on Erde's palm, the fine tapered blade seemed to drink in the broken sunlight and return a steadier glow of its own. Water arched her neck to expose the most delicate underside. Clenching her jaw, Erde laid the razor edge against fine silver fur. The dragon drew away sharply, startling her. She shot a doubting glance back at Earth.

—*The point. You must use the dagger's point.*

"Ohh," replied Erde faintly. She could not imagine. Sir Hal would be better at this. He would know the appropriate ceremony. But at Earth's insistent urging, she gathered herself again and set the dagger point-first. This time, when she applied a bit of pressure, Water did not recoil. Rather, she leaned into the blade, and Erde took a breath and drove it in, then jerked it right out again with a cry of remorse.

The blood did not spurt from the wound. It pooled at the opening, glistening, waiting. Water curled her slim head around to regard Erde expectantly. Erde stared, then quickly sheathed her blade and offered cupped and shaking hands to the wound. Like water from a mountain spring, the blood flowed neatly into her palms. It ceased flowing when the hand-made basin was full. Light-headed with wonder, Erde carried the precious liquid to the unconscious youth.

But he couldn't have been entirely unconscious, for when she let a few red drops leak into his half-open mouth, he roused himself enough to drink in the entire handful, swallowing as greedily as if he sucked in life itself. The blood ran out of Erde's hands as cleanly as water, leaving no stain behind. With the last drop, Endoch lay back again, smiling, and fell into a deep calm sleep.

Dragon's blood.

Erde had always wondered how one acquired dragon's

blood to do magic with, without hurting the dragon. Oh, if only Hal were here to see this. She stared at her pristine hands, still cupped and shaking, then back at Water.

Earth was washing the sea dragon's neck, gently closing the wound.

CHAPTER NINE

When he wakes up, N'Doch feels better than he has in a very long time. He knows right off that something amazing has happened.

He's got no idea how long he's been out. He's lying on one of the exercise mats—he can tell from the unexpected comfort beneath him and the slightly musty smell. He inventories his body parts carefully. There is no pain anywhere, not even in his left arm, which he recalls was slashed wide open last time he checked.

Shouldn't move, he decides, better not reveal his return to the living before he's cased the situation. He listens to the ship, the way he's learned to, for any noise he doesn't recognize that might be the mob banging about inside, searching. He hears nothing, only the gulls outside and the slap of the sea against the hull, removed by the distance of six decks between. A cautiously raised eyelid reveals even less. At first he's sure he's gone blind. Then he realizes it's night, and he's facing a wall. He has to turn somehow, at least his head. He rolls it back soundlessly and sees, in the broad, bright squares of moonlight falling from the windows, the two cybercritters crouched head to head.

Not cybercritters, he reminds himself.

Dragons.

He's still having trouble taking that one in. But he's decided it is the only explanation left, if you can call magic an explanation. He wonders what they're up to out there in the middle of the basketball court, so still and silent but looking so at ease with each other. Having some sort of dragon confab, he's pretty sure, whatever dragons confab about.

He twists his head a centimeter farther and, past them, he can make out a flat darkness in the opposite corner: the girl, asleep on another gym mat. N'Doch almost laughs out loud. She couldn't have gotten farther away from him unless she'd left the room. But then he thinks, *Well, that's good.* She's safer that way. She looks innocent, but she isn't.

He realizes that accepting the notion of dragons still doesn't give him a clue about what to do next. He's pretty sure the fishermen won't venture into this "haunted" boat at night when the dead might walk, so he's got till dawn to decide. If he got up real quick and quiet and just slid out through the locker room just to his right, he could slip past the mob alone and be away, free of all this crazy business in a flash. He wouldn't have to worry about how there could be dragons and girls from Mars. Or wherever. But then he'd never have the whole story. And think of the songs in it. It might just be his big chance in a whole other way. He's got to play it out for a little while, or he'll wonder about it for the rest of his life.

But he can't just lie there waiting for whatever's due to happen next. He's never been much for lying in bed, which is what's got him in this trouble in the first place—like, if he'd plopped down for the midday snooze with everyone else instead of going out prospecting for supper, he'd be the same old N'Doch he was this morning. But now—and this is what really concerns him, 'cause he knows it like he always knew when the first winter rains would come: inexplicably, in his gut—he knows that since the silver dragon swam into his life, his life's never gonna be the same.

N'Doch contemplates that one for a while. He's always thought he wanted his life to change. Now he finds himself hoping the longer he lies there, the longer he can keep this new life from starting. It was okay when he thought he was acting. Eventually everyone'd pack up the cameras and go home, and his life would be still his life, only better. But now that it seems that he really does have a dragon on his hands, it's another thing altogether. Because, hey, what do you do with a dragon? You don't exactly take it home with you like a stray dog. Feeding a dog is hard enough, or keeping it from being someone else's dinner . . . but a *dragon?*

On the other hand, who's to say his old life was anything worth holding on to?

This thought makes him roll over in involuntary revolt. He's surprised by the depths of rage he suddenly feels about his lot in life. He's not sure where it's come from. He thought he was getting along okay these days, apart from wanting so bad to be famous and not be hungry so much of the time.

But the rage is real, and so strong that it propels him to his feet before he can stop himself, and across the floor to glare belligerently at the communing dragons, without a clue why he feels he should challenge them with it. The abrupt motion reminds him of his arm. While he stares at the dragons, he sneaks his right hand around to check out the gash.

It's gone. He looks, steps sideways into a patch of moon, and looks again. His skin is smooth. No blood, no scab, not even a scratch.

N'Doch clenches his eyes shut, raking his memory. Did the short brother miss after all? Was he so scared, he just thought he'd been hit? No, no. He remembers the hot sear of pain, his panic about infection and the bright blood messing up his precious gym floor. He *remembers* this.

When N'Doch looks up again, the dragons are staring at him, taking no notice of his rage and confusion. The big one is a horned tower of shadow with a luminous glance. The little one is silver with moonlight and her eyes are dark. N'Doch hears a note start—long, soft, an oboe, he'd say, if he was hearing it outright instead of in his head. But it's impossibly sustained, which is why it holds him. He's waiting for the next one, for the pattern to develop, for the melody to show itself.

Instead he gets pictures, and this is where he decides he must be still asleep or maybe delirious. Either way, he's dreaming. No wonder his arm is healed and he feels so good. Well, it's been a nice dream so far, why not go with it? The pictures are like his own private video, playing in his head.

It starts with a landscape of cold, fog-shrouded mountains. N'Doch likes how the chill of it actually seems to penetrate the sodden heat of the gymnasium, cooling the sweat on his brow and the small of his back. Next he sees a big old castle, perched on a high rocky spur of these mountains, gray and forbidding, with little slit windows and lots of towers like in one of those King Arthur vids. N'Doch has no interest in white guys wearing tin suits—though his mama tunes them in whenever they're on—so he can't imagine why he'd be dreaming castles. But then this long-shot p.o.v. changes, zooming in fast on the tall front gate. He's expecting a moat and piranhas, crocodiles at least, but there's only dry rock, falling away sheer from the base of the walls and crossed by a built-up stone causeway. A stout iron grille stands between two round towers of stone. There's carving over the gate, animals of some sort fighting, but he doesn't spend time on the details because now he sees the girl, the Mars girl. She's there in his dream, on her belly in the icy mud, squeezing through a narrow slot between the iron gate and the ground. The oboe note slips behind a muffled wash of percussion, and a solo cello appears, low, grinding, urgent. When the girl struggles to her feet, N'Doch can see she is half-frozen, terrified . . . and running away.

Next thing he knows, he's in a big dark space, like a cave. He's never been in a real cave, but he's seen the pix. This dream is like some virtual reality tour where it's not his hand on the controls. The girl is there again, still terrified, and this time there's something sneaking up on her, something really huge and nasty. Only it turns out to be the big brown dragon, and N'Doch thinks he's looking kind of scared and lost himself. The cello accompaniment turns decidedly plaintive. In the way of dreams, N'Doch understands that the big guy has lost something, and the girl's supposed to help him find it. He can see how she takes to the critter right off, despite his being a dragon. He sees the awe and dedication in her eyes, as if a dragon is what she's been waiting for all her life. Like he felt about the blue critter's music, first time he heard it.

Then, in a moment of dizzying coincident vision, N'Doch sees himself at the same time he's seeing the girl. He *is* the girl, and yet he's himself, staring at the little silver dragon with the same awe and dedication. The vision is too much. The sweetness of it pierces him. It catches in his throat and he has to look away. He's not used to sweetness, or beauty that shortens his breath. He stands there, shaking in the moonlight, staring at the patterns of bright and dark cutting in such sharp angles across the floor.

He understands that he has not been dreaming.

Suddenly there's an entire story in his head: the girl's escape from her drunken father's boondocks castle, the perils of her flight into the countryside with the dragon, the hot pursuit by priests and armies, like something out of a costume drama. Is it true? Has he made it up? He doesn't know where it came from or what to do with it.

And still, there's more. The images keep unraveling. He sees the brown dragon waking to his magic gifts and understands he's being told it was magic that sealed up his wound as if it had never been. But it's too devastating to believe such things, or to believe anything with the kind of conviction N'Doch senses is lying in wait inside the silver dragon's dark stare. In his world, people die when they believe in things. People who might be related to you. They're gunned down on their doorsteps, or they vanish into prisons and are never heard from again. N'Doch has spent his nearly twenty years learning to stay fast and loose, with ties to nothing and no one. He'll do what he can to help his mama, but she pretty much takes care of herself. The only thing he believes in, really, is his music, and that he carries safely inside him. It's sustained him through the hard times like no person ever could or would.

Of course, a dragon is not exactly a person.

The images stop, leaving him bathed in a waiting silence. N'Doch looks up finally, meeting the silver dragon's gaze.

All right, he concedes. *This is really happening.*

Her music, their music, swells in his head, and the next thing he asks himself is *Why me?*

CHAPTER TEN

Erde dreamed that the dragon was nudging her shoulder. When she stirred, she saw him crouched beside Water across the room. The floor beneath her was still shuddering gently. Ah, she thought. One of his baby-quakes.

She allowed herself a proud smile. He was using his gifts without having to be endlessly petted and encouraged beforehand, which meant he was finally gaining some self-confidence. Despite the mob outside and the peril of their situation, she decided she could tease him a little.

—I am awake, O Great One, and at your service.

Earth turned from his huddle and stared at her. He blinked slowly, twice. In her head, Erde saw only an embarrassed blank. She giggled, and for a moment, the dragon let his big tongue loll from the corner of his mouth, as he used to in comic puzzlement. But Erde sensed it was self-parody this time, Earth recalling his former self for her amusement as well as his own, and sharing a bit of pride in his maturing. But not too much pride.

—I am not great yet, not until I have learned what Purpose I am to be great for.

Erde thought his logic a trifle circuitous and literal-minded, but she knew what he meant.

—Will you still talk to me, then, and wake me with earthquakes?

She had meant it fondly and in jest, but he blinked again, regarding her gravely.

—I will, for you will be great with me.

—I am already great. I am a baron's daughter.

It was lovely to be able to joust with him verbally. His

grasp of language had grown dizzyingly. Erde mused that if human children learned so fast, there'd be no keeping up with them.

Then Water was there, flowing into Earth's consciousness, eddying busily in his mind, diverting both their thoughts like a guild master calling a meeting to order, reminding them both that they had a crisis to deal with by pelting them with images of a howling armed mob tearing an unseen something limb from limb. Earth returned his attention to her so obediently that Erde found herself wondering if the sea dragon was perhaps his older sister, since he deferred to her so readily. Or was it that, despite her having waked more recently into the world, she had more confidence than he did? She was graceful and she was beautiful, and Erde knew Earth thought himself dull, brown, and clumsy. But the sea dragon was also turning out to be a little bit bossy. Now that she'd gotten their attention, she was flooding them with images of Endoch.

Erde tried stopping up her mental ears.

—*Shouldn't you ask her about the Caller, who she thinks it is?*

—*Her first concern is the boy, to wake him to his duty,* Earth relayed. *And she needs your help. She wants you to explain things to him. She says you must use your words to help him understand.*

—*My words? I don't do words very well. I only just got them back.*

—*You must try. Please, you must. He knows how to hear the meaning in words.*

—*But, Dragon, he doesn't speak my language, and I don't speak his.*

She could feel his puzzlement, like an itch inside her brain. A hurried conference with the sea dragon eventually produced the understanding that the sounds Erde heard Earth speak in her head were an illusion of words he had learned to create in order to accommodate her human habits of communication. Earth was surprised (and interested) to learn that the sounds Erde made when she spoke did not convey meaning to the boy, and vice versa.

—*My sister hears what he means. You must teach him to listen to her.*

—*How will she know what I mean?*

—I will tell her.
—Who will tell him?

N'Doch senses the shifting of attention away from him.
Then, suddenly, the girl gets up from her mat in the corner,
out of what he'd thought was a dead sleep. She comes
straight for him, padding on bare feet, her face purposeful.
She takes his hand awkwardly—he can tell she's not too
keen on the idea—and leads him to the silvery dragon's side,
pressing him to sit there on the floor. The girl sits down
opposite, cross-legged. He worries she's going to make him
play one of those girly hand-clapping games he thinks are
so dumb. Instead, she lays a feather touch on both his eyelids, closing them, holding them shut very gently. N'Doch
gets the idea. He keeps them shut when she takes her hands
away, figuring he can't see much in the dark anyway.

"*Sehr gut,*" she says. Next she lightly pinches his earlobes
and pulls them outward. "*Hören sie.*"

"I got it," nods N'Doch. "You want me to listen."

She speaks slowly and carefully, as if she thinks that'll
make him understand German all of a sudden, which he
doesn't and won't, but he goes along with it anyway. He's
glad she doesn't shout, like some people do when they don't
speak your language. She keeps her voice quiet, intense.

After a while, he can tell she's repeating the same sets of
words over and over. He's getting a little bored, so he
shakes his head, but she reaches out again and presses rough
palms flat against his temples to hold him still, then talks
at him some more. When the music video starts in his head
again, N'Doch realizes she's not doing this on her own. He's
in for another dose of force-fed information and credibil-
ity testing.

But when he gives in and pays attention, just for the hell
of it, he notices that the video and the music are repeating
themselves just like the girl, at pretty much the same
rhythm. An image of himself and the silver-blue dragon
comes with a certain musical phrase and a certain string of
the girl's now familiar but incomprehensible syllables. An
image of her and the big dragon brings up different words,
different music.

N'Doch has always liked the cartoon of the lightbulb
clicking on in someone's head. It's exactly what happens to

him now, as he puts two and two together: Brilliant light floods his brain. It's the light off the vast glowing landscape of understanding that opens up as comprehension dawns: the girl is not the only one talking to him.

"Wow," he breathes.

His eyes pop open from the shock. The girl is smiling at him in the moonlight. He hasn't seen her smile before. He's momentarily charmed by the warmth of it softening her delicate somber face. But she makes him shut his eyes again, and continues talking. N'Doch tries putting words to the images visiting his brain and as he does, he hears the girl's spoken German echoed by his own French, English or Wolof, like she's being overdubbed, with a slight delay. It's a messy, echoing effect but the delay keeps shrinking, until the overlap is a match, not perfect, but if he manages to shut out the sounds she's actually *speaking*, what he hears in his head are words he can mostly understand, though in no way fathom the source of.

"*Sei ist* your dragon," says the girl. "*Du ist* hers. You hear her when she sings?"

He nods. He's reluctant to admit it.

"You must listen to her in your head. Then you will understand everything."

That music has meaning is no mystery to N'Doch. He's just never thought of it as literal language before, and suddenly, the possibilities seem endless.

"Too cool," he tells the girl. He stops worrying about what's real and what isn't. Now all he wants to do is sit here in the dark with this blue dragon she calls *his*, and learn how to talk in music.

But first he has to ask: "What's her name?"

"Water," says the girl, as clear as daylight.

His eyes pop open again. He looks at her. "But that's my name."

She smiles knowingly. "Of course it is."

Erde recalled so well the thrill that had shot through her when the dragon informed her that its name was the same as her own. She had not for an instant considered it a mater of mere coincidence and neither, she could see, did Endoch. But instead of looking thrilled, he looked trapped and wary.

"Why do we have the same name?" he demanded, and a few echoes and relays and image-layers later, Erde understood his words, though not how to answer them. A proper metaphysical answer required someone like Sir Hal, a lifelong scholar of dragon lore. Erde thought she'd best limit herself to the practical aspects.

"You are her Guide. There are matters in the world of men that a dragon will not know about. Therefore we are here to help them."

Endoch eyed her skeptically. "Help them do what?"

He's so suspicious, Erde noted. Probably he'd been taught bad things about dragons, like the people at home. She would have been, too, but for her grandmother and her nursemaid, Alla. She felt both worldly-wise and totally inadequate to this task the dragons had laid on her. If Endoch had grown up without anyone to prepare him for his destiny, she would have to fill him in on the crucial details. It would not be easy. She was sure it was going to be a bit of a shock.

"We must help them carry out their Purpose," she replied.

He frowned. "What purpose?"

"Well, the Thing they're supposed to do."

"What are they supposed to do?"

Erde licked her lips, suddenly aware of a vast, not entirely physical thirst. Because, of course, this was the hardest part of the explanation. "They don't know yet."

"They don't . . ." Endoch rolled his eyes. "Are you for real? Is this thing some kind of gimmick after all?"

"Gi-mic?"

Neither dragon could translate these syllables. Earth couldn't recognize the image, Water couldn't put a sound to it.

"Yeah, you know, a stunt of some kind? If so, what's in it for me? Why should I go 'round risking my life for you guys? I don't even know you!"

Erde was momentarily stymied. Earth interposed his analysis.

—He does not yet wish to accept his destiny.

Erde sighed, sucked in a deep breath and prepared to settle in for the long haul. "Is there a well in this stronghold?"

"A well? This is a boat, girl. There's no well in here. Don't you have boats where you come from?"

A boat? Erde glanced at Earth. Had one of them misunderstood? *No*, insisted the dragon. Scanning the darkness around her, Erde tried matching the bright-hulled craft on the beach with this cavernous square-walled room.

"Then it is a very big boat," she marveled. "Your liege lord must be very rich and powerful. Is he a king?"

Endoch furrowed his brow, then shook his head. "Man, I guess you're from Mars after all. But you know what? You're in luck." He stood up, stretching, checking his arm again as if to make sure it really was healed. "I got some okay water stashed away here."

He strode off into the darkness. Both dragons watched him go somewhat anxiously. But Erde saw in the young man's doubt and resistance something that dragons, who always knew what was real and what wasn't, never could.

—*He won't leave. But he can't let himself value a thing he fears will be taken away from him.*

—**What thing?**

—*His dragon. If she is not real, he will lose her.*

—**Of course she is real.**

—*He doesn't know that yet. I think he has led a very hard life.*

Endoch came back with a squarish, white jug hooked onto one thumb. He twisted its neck to remove some kind of stopper, then set it to his mouth and drank deeply. Then he placed it on the floor and slid it toward her. "Help yourself."

Erde grasped the milk-white handle. The jug wasn't as heavy as she'd expected. Its sides gave easily as she pressed her palms against them, but did not break. She lifted it gingerly and took a cautious sip, followed by a long grateful series of gulps when she found the water to be warm, brackish but potable. She set the jug down and tapped the side of it with her fingernail. It was hard like clayware, pliant like oiled leather and, now that she studied it in the moonlight, translucent like glass. But glass could never be so sturdy or so flexible.

"What ware is this?" she asked.

"What what?"

"What is it fashioned from?"

Endoch snorted. "You sure do talk funny. I hope you sound better in German—I mean, to someone really hearing German. 'What ware' . . . well, I guess it's Tupperware."

He seemed to think he'd said something clever. Erde looked blank.

"Plastic, girl. What'd you think it was?"

She fingered the parchment-thin edge of the jug's mouth. "We do not have this at Tor Alte."

"Come on! You're from Germany, right? They make all kinds of plastic in Germany. Mostly the expensive kinds."

Erde did not wish to argue with him and further expose her ignorance. Perhaps her father's provincial mountain domain was more backward than she'd realized. "I have some bread and some cheese," she offered instead.

Endoch's eyes lit up. "You do? Outstanding!"

She took that as approval and went to retrieve her pack from the cloth pallet she'd been resting on in the corner. The small loaf was nearly stale—it was hard to imagine, after all that had happened, that it had come from Deep Moor's bake ovens only a day ago. But the pungent scent of the cheese, as she unwrapped the stained oilskin, made her mouth water. She split both neatly in half and handed Endoch his portion.

He took it quickly and wolfed down half his chunk of bread before sniffing more carefully at the cheese. "You make this stuff yourself?"

Her mouth full, Erde shook her head.

"But you know it's safe?"

She returned him a puzzled frown. Did he think she would poison him?

"You know, all the hormones and drugs, and the stuff the animals pick up in their feed . . . ?"

She hadn't the faintest idea what he meant, and neither did the dragons.

Endoch looked at her, back at the cheese, and shrugged. "Well, what the hell. You're eating it. I'm too hungry not to." And he did, slowly this time and with great deliberation. "Not bad," he concluded. "Tasty." He let his gaze swing about casually, then settle finally on her pack. Before she could stop him, he'd reached, grabbed it into his lap. "What else you got in here?"

*   *   *

The taste of the cheese is what gets his mind working. It's like nothing he's ever eaten before, a deep sharp rich taste that lingers on his tongue like a fading chord in his ears. He thinks, *This cheese came from somewhere else.* Fancy imported stuff. Just enough to get him *really* hungry. He wishes he had more.

It's habit that makes him snatch her pack. Normally he'd be on his feet and out of there, with the pack his spoils of the day. But he's not going to steal from this girl. He can't even seem to consider it. It would be like stealing from the dragons. But he'll take food if she's got it, and he does want some answers, better than the ones she's been giving him. Maybe the pack has some of them inside.

He dumps it out on the floor, waiting for the girl to squeal and pummel him, like the girl this morning—was it this morning?—with the tomatoes. But this one just watches. Her silence chastises but she makes no move to stop him. N'Doch unfolds the inner bundle and lays out the contents. The wrapping is a thick blanket of some kind. He shakes it out. It's a cloak, dense and gray. He holds it up to his nose. The smell is strong but indefinable, until he decides it's what he imagines sheep would smell like. Real wool, then. Amazing. There's more real wool in the bundle: a knitted cap that looks homemade. It also looks small. He does not try it on. He picks up the leather vest she'd been wearing, now neatly folded. He thinks that might actually fit him, but he lays it aside with the cloak and the cap. Next, a small metal rectangle with a lid. He opens it. Inside, a couple of flat rocks and a bunch of crackly wood shavings. N'Doch holds it up and cocks his head.

"To make fire," the girl says, as if it should be obvious.

"Why not just carry matches?" Even more obvious. "Or a lighter. Take up less room." He fingers the flinty rock restlessly. The taste of the cheese is still in his mouth, and the musky smell of the wool. Some things about this girl are beginning to fall into a pattern. He puts the tinderbox down. "Hey, look—are you from one of those nature-freak communes where they don't allow technology? Where they, like, you know, live in the past?"

He can see she's thinking it over, which probably means he's got that one wrong. Finally, she says, 'Why would one wish to live in the past?"

"Well, yeah, good question." In fact, he wonders if he can answer it. "A lotta people think it was better then."

This time she nods. "When I was little, I always wanted to live back when my ancestors fought with dragons."

She says it with such conviction, he has to grin and shake his head. "Mars," he murmurs. "For sure."

"Then I met Earth."

"That's his name, the big guy? Earth?"

She nods.

"Tell me yours again?"

"Earth."

He remembers he's hearing it in translation. "Right. Gotcha. Like you said, of course it is."

He picks up the final object in the pile, a dark box of carved wood. The girls' eyes flick down at it and away, too quickly, and he thinks, *Okay, the prize is in here, maybe her money or her credit cards.* He studies it at eye level. He'd say the style is old, but the box itself seems pretty new. It looks like a prop from the costume vids his mama watches, but he knows what vid props are like and this box is too well made. The carving is skilled and elaborate, leaves and flowers and the faces of men and women, and on the top—somehow, he is not surprised—is a small figure of a dragon.

N'Doch shakes the box gently. It rattles. "Whadja do, rob a museum?"

When she just keeps watching, he twists the little latch, raises the lid, and pokes at the contents, an old scrap of paper wrapped around something round and hard. He takes it out and the paper unravels neatly on his palm, offering up its contents as if to say, *voila!* N'Doch is taken aback, both by the uncanny presentation and by the beauty of the object exposed. It's a big red stone, set in silver. Even in the cool flat light of the moon, the stone looks like a drop of blood with a flame shining through it. On top it has, sure enough, another tiny dragon cut into the curving surface. N'Doch stares, astonished by the fineness of the detail. It's not a sparkling sort of jewel like he's used to. He can tell it's old. The weight and warmth of it are heavy on his palm. "Man," he breathes, with newfound respect. "This is some heist you pulled off, girl."

"It was my grandmother's brooch, the dragon brooch of the von Altes. She had it from her father and he from his."

"Yeah, right."

She blinks at him. "You do not believe me? Why should you think I would lie to you, Endoch?"

It's the first time she's actually used his name, or at least an attempt at it. She's probably trying to manipulate him. "N'Doch," he corrects irritably, "And I think so because anybody would and everyone does."

"No," she says back, straight as a bullet, as if she expects that'll clear it up, just like that.

"You think I'm a fool, right?"

"Of course not."

What's weird is that N'Doch does believe her, but he can't let her see that. "Like for instance, you'd lie to me if you stole it."

Now she looks perplexed. "But I wouldn't have to steal it. It's mine. It was in my family. Besides, it wouldn't let itself be stolen. It belongs to the Dragon Guide."

"The what?"

"The Dragon Guide. That's me. You. *Us.* Like I told you." She peers at him. "You really don't know, do you."

And that's what finally riles him, her sympathy so close to condescension. He tosses the big stone down and springs to his feet. "No! I don't! And you know what? I don't care! I've had enough of this shit!"

The girl looks down at her hands while his snarled words ricochet around the room. He feels rather than hears the dragons stirring behind him.

"I am sorry, Endoch. It is difficult at first," she concedes softly, "But you get used to it."

"I don't have to get used to anything!"

"But you do, Endoch. It's your destiny."

"There's no such thing! My life is what I make it! No rich girl with family jewels tells me what to do! I do what I want, you hear?"

N'Doch's pacing brings him face-to-face with the sea dragon, shimmering blue and silver in the moonlight. Her calm, intent stare stops him cold, fills him with dread. Actually, he does believe in Destiny, but he's always said his destiny is to sing songs and be famous. This dragon business would put a serious crimp in his plans. The beast wants him, wants everything he has or is to be put to her service. He'll be a slave to her. He sees a lifetime of being bonded in some weird-ass mystical way he doesn't understand to a creature he doesn't want to believe in, pursuing some mysterious "purpose" that sounds like a wild goose chase with a crazy white girl he has the misfortune to feel protective about. If anything is proof that this dragon stuff is dangerous, that is. If he was his normal self, he'd have seduced this girl long ago. It scares him that he can't even bring himself to fantasize about taking off all those layers she's wearing and laying her down on one of the gym mats. The thought stirs nothing down there, only a chill nausea in his belly. He feels like a stranger to himself and it frightens him, more than hunger or the mob, even the sharks off the beach. More than anything. He can think of only one way out, and in his panic, he takes it.

He whirls, snatches up the red jewel from where he's tossed it down in front of her. He's at the door in a second, through it in two, and is racing down the corridors to freedom.

escape through the tanker's far side. But first he decides he'd better scope out the beach.

From a broken-out porthole a few decks above the big gap on the port side, he can survey the sand below. He peers out carefully. To his disgust, the mob is still there. In fact there seem to be even more of them. They've built a bonfire out of palm fronds and turned his pursuit into a party. A few of the men are roasting fish over the blaze. One idiot's using his precious gas ration to power a vid set with a portable generator so no one'll miss the soccer match. Jugs of home brew are being surreptitiously passed. Even out there, far from the imam's watchful gaze, the men are cautious. N'Doch's mouth waters. The thing about being a fisherman is you can just go out and catch something more or less edible, as long as you avoid the bottom feeders. He'd have learned the trade himself if they'd let him, but he didn't have the family connections. These days, you can't even surf cast on a Saturday without them getting after you, protecting their territory. N'Doch doesn't blame them, really. There's so few fish left to catch. *I'd protect mine, too,* he muses, *if I had any.*

Now there are voices raised around the fire, over the yells and catcalls from the soccer game. He hears his name being tossed about, so he settles in to listen. It seems the fishermen are annoyed. They haven't yet laid eyes on these sea monsters supposedly in the act of gobbling up their boats. Where's all the excitement they were promised? Some are calling the brothers liars. Others had clearly reached N'Doch's first conclusion, that the whole thing was a vid shoot, so they'd rushed off to the beach to take part and are sullen about missing their chance to be on camera.

The brothers—all five of them now (one has his foot heavily bandaged and keeps checking it worriedly)—are busy tapdancing, tossing out this tale and that excuse to keep the mob from turning on them. They have to shout to be heard over the game, and must have been doing this for a while, 'cause they're all going hoarse. N'Doch would enjoy this drunken spectacle, were it not that their most successful tactic seems to be exaggerating the heinousness of his own crime and hyping him into a threat big enough to throw the mob's rage back in his direction. So now, in

the short brother's mouth, N'Doch the tomato thief becomes N'Doch the vandalizer, the armed looter and hostage-
taker, N'Doch the violator of innocent young women.

Violator? N'Doch swells up with outrage. He grips the
ragged sides of the porthole and almost yells out in his
own defense. He'd *never* take a woman against her will!
Most of the pleasure is wooing them and winning them
over.

But the fishermen are buying it, hook, line, and sinker.
They are shaking their fists and roaring because, N'Doch
thinks, it's probably what they'd like to do to at least one
woman of their acquaintance, and they're pissed that he got
there first. He tells himself he'll get even, in the way he
always has: when this nonsense is over, there'll be a whole
new repertoire of nasty songs about drunken fishermen
going around town.

When it's *over.* . . .

He realizes he's thinking about the blue dragon, holed up
forward in the gym. He has been all along, with a part of
his brain that won't set her aside. It keeps asking, will she
be safe in the ship? Will this stupid mob get bored and go
home, or will they keep at their drinking and roaring until
they've worked up enough courage of numbers to invade
his sanctuary? What will the dragons do then? Eat them?

For a moment, he thinks how much he'd like to be there
to see that. Then he reminds himself forcibly that he doesn't
care what happens to the blue dragon, or the brown one
with the girl. But he doesn't need to check his pocket for
the jewel he's stolen. It lies warm and heavy against his
thigh, weighing inexplicably more than a thing its size reasonably should. Small as it is, for a jewel, it's big enough.
Finding a fence for it will be tricky. N'Doch has never dealt
with the Big Guys before.

Meanwhile, it's time to be out of range of the mob before
its outrage whips up from passive to active. N'Doch crosses
back to starboard and skins through the thin gap between
two in-bent metal plates. Between the inner hull and the
outer, he has stashed a tarred length of rope for just such
an emergency, looped around a cross-tie. He drops the loose
ends through the outer hole and lowers himself hand over
hand to the sand. He jerks the rope free, coils it quickly

and tosses it deftly up into the hole. He's racing away before he's sure if it's landed correctly.

He speeds along the beach without really knowing where he's heading. His brain is full, too full to think. He puts himself on autopilot, his eyes squinting to scan for debris. The moon has set, and a predawn glow is creeping across the sky. N'Doch feels vulnerable, too visible, dark against the lightening sand. The damp night air is thick with fish stink. He wonders about it until he feels the first few dead ones under his feet. Another kill, washed in with the tide. Getting to be commonplace. He shifts his trajectory, avoiding the water's edge, and slows. He skirts two small inhabited wrecks, people he knows. He sees the elder son of one family pacing the deck with a shotgun, probably anxious about all the shouting and firelight down the beach. N'Doch stays out of sight and cuts inland at the next path through the palm brake.

He spots the thicket of old vid antennas and satellite dishes sprouting from the *bidonville,* and slows when he reaches the first tents and lean-tos. A runner always looks guilty, he reasons, even if running for help. People in the camp are just stirring, the women mostly, starting their morning duties in the dull, slow way of the unwillingly awakened. Maybe the mob back at the tanker will go straight to their boats when dawn comes. Wait till they see the beach already littered with their day's catch. But they'll go out anyway, and maybe this morning, their wives will get to eat some of the breakfast they cook.

Several campfires are already burning. The starchy hot scent of boiling rice reminds N'Doch that he's now as hungry as he's ever been. The girl's little morsels of bread and cheese were just a tease. He decides he'd better head home. Whatever little food his mama might have, she's sure to give him some.

It's full dawn when he reaches her house, a cinderblock box lined up with a thousand others along a dusty road on the far side of town. The houses are small and dark, having been thrown up several governments ago during a rare moment of social oratory convincing enough to lure foreign aid. The mortar between the cinder blocks is already crumbling and the corrugated plastic roofing is brittle and cracking from the heavy, steady dose of UV in the sunlight. But it's a house and his mama is lucky to have it. She knows this. She's so aware of it that she hardly ever leaves it for fear some squatter will move in and take possession while she's out at the market. It's the only thing she has, the house and her vid set, which is as old as she is but like herself, still functional.

She's up and talking to it when N'Doch steps in the open doorway, a tall woman in a once-bright print moving slowly around her one small room, scraping up last night's cold rice from the bottom of the pot. Surreal color flickers along the cement-gray walls. His mama is shaking her head.

"I told you yesterday if you let him do that to you, you'd sure be sorry," she's scolding. On the pinched old screen, a lovely woman is weeping while an angry man throws crockery around a perfectly appointed room. It looks like no room N'Doch has ever seen.

"Ma," he says. He's sorry now that he has nothing to bring her. But wait. He has. The stone in his pocket. *She* could fence it, maybe. Say she found it somewhere in the rubble.

His mother clucks her tongue. "Anybody could have told you that, girl."

N'Doch tries again. "Ma." He does not move from the doorway.

Her eyes are fixed on the vid, reflecting the dancing image and brimming with knowledge and empathy. She turns her long back to N'Doch as she shakes the used tea leaves loose in her cup and pours in boiling water. "Well, don't just stand there like a lump, boy. Get on in and sit down."

N'Doch thinks it's weird that his mama never calls anyone by their name. A lot of the time he calls her by *her* name, which is Fâtime, mostly to get her attention. He slouches in and drops down at the scarred metal table under the window next to the door. The window's too high and narrow to see out of, but it's the only one and it does let in some light and air, to add to the breeze provided by the man-sized hole his father pickaxed through the back wall just before he took off. To cover it, N'Doch salvaged an old Venetian blind as soon as he was old enough to carry something that big. He gazes around the room, taking stock. The pocked cement floor is gritty under his feet.

"You sold the couch?"

She nods, spooning the cold rice into a plastic tub. Her eyes on the vid, she sets the tub in front of him. "Ayeesha's third is too old to be sleeping with her now. She took it. I told her she'd have to come get it herself, 'cause I wasn't gonna be dragging it all the way 'cross the street, so she did."

N'Doch pouts irritably, knowing Fâtime won't turn away from the screen long enough to notice. Now the table and the two folding chairs beside it, plus the TV on its plastic crate, are the only furniture in the house besides the loom in the corner and the broken-down cot behind the sheet on a rope that offers Fâtime a measure of privacy. The sofa was hers, after all, and it's true he hasn't been home in a while, but where's she think he's going to sleep?

"She pay for it?" he demands through a sticky mouthful. He sees the finished weave on the loom is still short, a long way until her next sale. His mama's generosity worries him sometimes.

"'A sack of relief rice, near full. Ten cans of beans, two melons, and the promise of a dozen of those big yams she's growing up right."

He sits up, impressed. "Got any melon left?" He can't think of anything that would taste better right now.

Fâtime rolls her eyes back at him briefly. "Finished the first two weeks ago. She'll bring the second when her next crop comes in."

Two weeks?' It's been longer than he realized since he's visited. He should come by more often, he knows he should. He's all she has left, 'cept that crazy old man out in the bush, his grandfather. But he hears no reproach in her voice. His mama, he knows, gave up a long time ago expecting much out of the men in her life. They're always dying or leaving.

He reaches for another fistful of rice and discovers he's cleaned the bowl out already. Impossible! He's just started eating! He tips it toward him. Sure enough, he hasn't left her so much as a grain. He sets the bowl down and flattens his palms on the table. But maybe he won't show her the jewel just yet. In fact, he can't really bring himself to take it out of his pocket, to reveal such a lovely thing in the drear light of this house.

"Ma, I didn't bring you anything this time. I was . . ." How can he begin to explain? ". . . kinda in a rush."

Fâtime shrugs, points at the screen. The lovely woman has changed one sparkling gown for another and redone her makeup. "Not a brain in her head, this one with the nails. Now that other one, with the head of hair, look, here she comes now, see her? She's a smart one. She don't let anybody by her."

N'Doch looks. The woman in the French-style gowns has been replaced by another slim beauty wearing bright festival robes and a high, elaborate hairdo, corn-rowed and braided and strung with glittering glass beads. Her skin is dark silk, flawless. She is breathtaking. Normally N'Doch would use this occasion to drift off into a fantasy about himself and this woman in a soft bed somewhere. Perversely, he finds himself staring at her hundreds of beads and tiny braids, thinking that both he and his mama could eat for a year on what that hairdo cost. Probably the jewel he's stolen wouldn't bring as much. A single hairdo!

This is an odd thought for him, not that he hasn't counted such things out before, but odd that he should feel *angry* about it, rather than merely envious. The equation is somehow shifting in his mind. He used to be glad that at least his mama had the vid and its constant diet of fantasy to distract her from being so hungry most of the time. Now there's this vague, undeveloped notion that if the hairdo wasn't eating up so much of the world's money, there'd be more of it around to feed his mother and himself. The idea sighs into his head like a night breeze and out again as he loses his grasp on it, unable to apply it in any pragmatic way to his own life.

But it leaves him looking at his mother from a new angle, actually *looking* at her, for the first time. She's his mama, but she's also a stranger, a rangy, sloppy woman who happens to resemble him, as if someone else's skin had been wrapped around his skeleton. A woman afraid to leave her house. A woman starting to put on weight, who weaves and watches the vid and expects no more out of life. A woman who's finished.

It's the resemblance that catches in N'Doch's throat. Suddenly he sees himself, a fat old man glued to the tube. It's the starch that puts the pounds on and stretches out the skin, swelling it up, then leaving it slack in the endless cycle of gain and loss. When the food comes, you eat as much as you can, storing up for the times when there is none. Rice, bread, yam. The relief people never send anything fresh like a vegetable, and who knows what brew of chemicals are laced into his mama's favorite, their instant mashed potatoes? Only N'Doch's music and the chance of fame stand between him and this horrifying vision, this endless . . . sameness. Only his music, and now the . . .

His hand has slipped unnoticed into his pocket. The red jewel is a hard, hot lump on his palm. When he closes his fist around it, the heat is nearly unbearable. Yet it draws him, like the flame tongues of a bonfire beckoning in the darkness, and he understands he'll never sell it. Could never. Not this, the dragon stone. He'll keep it, then. It'll be his secret talisman. He holds it tightly, suffering the biting heat as best he can, and hears . . .

MUSIC.

N'Doch's head whips around. Where? But it's not the television and it's not his mother singing to him, though that's what it sounds like, her low tuneless lullaby that soothed him when he was too hungry to sleep. He knows who it is, of course. It's the one he's just tried to leave behind, the other Big Chance he doesn't want to think about, the one who's gonna ask so much in return for what she'll give. It frightens him that she can touch him even here.

He stares at his mother while she stares at the vid. She's totally absorbed. How can she not hear this music, so like her own? She's lost to it, and probably lost to her own as well. N'Doch doubts she could sing to him now the way she used to. And suddenly, he can't sit like this any longer, not speaking, with her locked up in her vid world. If he'd talked to her more in his life, maybe she'd be talking back. But he hasn't, and she isn't. He has to leave, just like he always does. But this time, he isn't off to meet up with his boys or chase after some girl or pursue any one of the many scams he's usually juggling.

This time, he doesn't know where he's going. In town, the brothers will be after him. On the beach, there's the mob. They won't leave him alone as long as his supposed villainy offers them entertainment at his expense. So he doesn't know where he's headed and he's not sure when he'll be back. Abruptly, he's tired of the runaround. It doesn't seem as glamorous as it did when he was a kid, first getting into gangs. But he should tell Fâtime something if he's going to be away for a while, make up a story at least, so she doesn't worry. He opens his mouth with the beginnings of an excuse.

"Ma . . ." He stops, stumped.

She turns to him. She looks at him directly, for the first time since he came in, yet her gaze is fuzzed, like she's watching something just a fraction past him, like where the back of his head might be if she could see right through him.

She says, "If you're in trouble again, go visit Grandpa Djawara."

Then she turns back to the vid, and it's like she'd never said a thing. It's like smooth water closing over a sunken boat.

N'Doch is chilled. It's been years since she's tried to pawn him off on his grandfather. It's also the third time in twenty-four hours that the old man's come to mind. Weird. And three is a mystical number. N'Doch reminds himself he doesn't believe in omens or signs or any of that superstitious stuff. On the other hand, he didn't believe in dragons either, until yesterday. And Papa Djawara's *would* be a good place to lay low for a while.

It would also be a good place to hide a dragon.

The thought is in his mind before he can stop it. Once there, it digs in and will not be evicted, even though he opens his fist to let the jewel go, then snatches his hand out of his pocket. The stone is like hot lava against his thigh. N'Doch stares at his palm, amazed that it is not scorched and bubbling.

Her eyes on the screen, tracking the woman with the exquisite hair as she weeps over a dying child, Fâtime says, "Go to Papa Djawara."

"Ma. How would I get there?"

"Walk, if you must."

"Walk? You're kidding, right?"

"Just go. He will explain everything."

And then, the vid claims her attention entirely. Try as he might, N'Doch can get no more out of her.

CHAPTER TWELVE

Erde stirred on her mat, sensing a change in the hot stillness of the room. She sat up in bright sunlight, even though she'd shoved her pallet into a corner. The low early rays had searched out her spot exactly, as if trying to wake her. She'd been dreaming of darkness and cold, dreaming of home and horses and men marching in snow and rain. It had been very real, her dream. As real as life. The surprise of sun was disorienting.

She glanced about groggily. What had changed? She listened for the howls and clanking of the mob outside, and heard nothing but the cries of the big white birds that wheeled in the air outside the high windows.

She peered into the far corners of the room. Empty. Then the dragons had not yet returned from their fishing expedition. Clever Water had gone first, down and out through the great hole in the middle of what Erde now accepted to be a ship but could not yet picture in its entirety. Earth had transported after her, once she'd searched out an empty stretch of beach and imaged it back to him. Both dragons had been starving. Erde wished Water good hunting, wondering if she'd been aware from the first that she'd have to deliver Earth's share of the catch directly to his landlocked feet. He wouldn't venture so much as the tip of a claw into such deep and turbulent water.

Erde sighed and stretched. After the confusion of the night and the anguish of the boy fleeing, stealing the dragon brooch, Water had sung to her and she'd slept well, except for the dreaming. She wondered if Water's singing her into so deep a sleep had somehow prompted her dream. It didn't matter. She felt infinitely more clearheaded. But her stomach was rumbling. She drank a little water from the strange jug that the boy had left behind. Keeping Hal's training in mind, she rationed it carefully. Who knew when she'd find drinkable water again, in this strange country of so much water but all of it seemingly salt.

She wondered if it was only the sun that had waked her. And the heat, though she had by now shed every layer of clothing that modesty allowed. Her woolen men's leggings and leather tunic, plus her own linen stockings, lay neatly folded inside her pack. She'd taken off her oversized linen shirt but kept it beside her while she slept. From what she'd seen so far, clothing was not very important in this country. Still, Erde doubted she could bring herself to parade around in only her shift. At least it was adequate for sleeping in.

She scanned the room again, peering into the sun-hazed shadows in the corners and under the balcony that ran along the far side. She saw nothing she hadn't seen in her careful search before she'd gone to bed.

Then someone spoke.

She recognized the voice, but not the oddly strangled tone of it. Without the dragons, she understood not a word. She reached to touch her dagger, belted neatly against the small of her back, but felt no real fear. The dragons had said he would be back and that she must try to be patient with him, and understanding. Mostly Earth had said this. Water understood it and agreed, but found the necessary patience somewhat harder to achieve.

She turned toward the voice. "Endoch! You're back!"

"N'Doch," he grumped. "N'Doch. Can't you get it right?"

Now his tone was very clear. Erde tried again. "Nnnndochh."

He snorted from the shadows. "A little better."

Annoyed, she sat up straight on her mat and pointed to herself. "Erde."

"Yeah, I know."

She set her jaw, squinting hard through the bright shafts into the darkness beyond. "Erde."

"Okay, okay. Jeez. Airda."

She shook her head. "Erde. Erde."

The shadows fell silent. Then the boy stepped out into

the sunlight, one fist raised stiffly in front of him. Erde read
it not as a threat but as a warding gesture. Though he
was scowling ferociously, he seemed reluctant to come any
nearer. He glared at her for a long frozen moment, then
tossed the thing in his fist at her. The dragon brooch fell
into her lap. "Erde," he growled.

She took up the brooch gratefully and gave him her most
brilliant smile. "N'Doch. Thank you."

N'Doch grunted and looked away, around the room, then
back again, turning his palms up in a demanding shrug.

Erde knew who he'd come back to see. "They're out
hunting."

When he frowned at her, not understanding, she made
exaggerated eating gestures, which seemed to satisfy him
partly. Still, he did seem to need to pace, back and forth,
back and forth. She wanted to tell him he needn't feel
anxious, or ashamed for having bolted. The dragons understood, perhaps better than he did. But she couldn't, until
the dragons returned to translate, so she sat quietly on her
mat and smiled at him encouragingly.

He paced past her and stopped. "They're still out there,
you know. Sleeping off all of that rotgut. But they'll be up
with the heat, and mad as piss. You can't stay here."

He glared at her as if he expected a reply. All Erde
could offer was an apologetic shrug. N'Doch scowled and
withdrew into the shadows to pace, refusing to even look
at her.

She was relieved finally to feel the familiar quickening in
her head, the sense of a void being filled, that announced
the dragons' return, both of them together this time, with
Earth using his gift to bring his sister along with him. Erde
jumped up to meet him, wondering at the smug satisfaction
he was projecting, until he opened his jaw and spilled a
slippery, silvery mass of fish onto the floor.

Raw fish, some still living. Erde thanked him, effusively
enough (she hoped) to conceal her dismay. She wished not
for the first time that Earth and his sister were more con-
ventional dragons. Then she'd be able to roast this pile of
fish in the flames of their fiery breath.

Fire. She remembered the line of thought that Water's
arrival had sparked. The dragons' names, Earth and Water,
had suggested a familiar sequence which followed with Fire

and Air. The four Elements. Was it significant or just a coincidental word association?

But once again, the matter of N'Doch was more pressing than her own mind ramblings, and the thought slipped away as her attention was called for. Both Earth and Water had settled down facing the darkened end of the room where the young man stood, stilled with renewed awe at the dragons' sudden reappearance.

They'd done it again, damn it. He'd been all collected and ready to face the shit they'd no doubt deal him for snatching the jewel and bolting, ready to take it quietly, ready even to try to explain, ready for anything but being knocked off his feet again by his own wonder.

Dragons. Real dragons, out of thin air. What else might the world hold in store, if dragons are possible?

N'Doch thinks it'd be easier if they were pissed at him. It's what he's expected, but what he gets instead is a welcome.

The feeling inside him is not a comfortable one. His head aches with unsung music. His heart feels too big for his chest. Again, he badly wants to run away, but this time he knows that he can't run fast enough or far enough to escape this silver-blue inevitability, what the girl calls his *destiny*.

It's not just that he has nothing better to do. It's that he can't seem to do anything else. He's tried it and failed. Returning to the tanker was like being hauled back by an invisible leash. All he can do is resent it furiously, which he does, but that too is getting old. He's getting tired of himself.

Destiny. An impossible, old-fashioned notion, like magic. In N'Doch's world, chaos is the rule, the randomness of life and events. But in N'Doch's world, the impossible has recently become possible, and the only thing he can see to do now is go with it. Think of it as just another random event. Follow the melody out. See where it leads.

Once again that first step is the hardest, but then he's easily across the floor and facing the blue dragon directly, flattening his palm on her velvet brow, letting her music flow into him like water.

Water.

A dragon.

His dragon.

PART TWO

The Journey
into Peril

CHAPTER THIRTEEN

She's almost caught him this time.

N'Doch considers himself pretty much in touch with himself. He's an artist, after all, and a good song must come from the heart. But after a few moments of feeling turned inside out and displayed raw, he lets his hand slide from the blue dragon's brow. It's one thing to pour all your emotion into a song—where it's neatly packaged, safely contained by the melody. But even his sloppiest, mushiest, written-after-a-bottle-of-cheap-wine ballads never made him feel as flayed, as vulnerable, as weak-kneed in the grip of it as he feels staring into the dragon's eyes. Is this how it's always gonna be with her? He averts his eyes, backs away. He's not sure he likes it very much.

The fish are an easier thing to deal with. Remembering the dead fish on the beach, N'Doch hunkers down and paws through them expertly, to sort out the ones with parasites or diseases. To his astonishment, he finds none. This has never happened. The usual ratio is one more-or-less healthy fish to three sick ones. The fishermen toss fifty percent of their catch back to the sharks and you have to check out the ones they do sell pretty carefully. But this, N'Doch can't believe: right in front of him, dripping their salt damp and scales onto his precious polished floor, are at least two dozen fat and perfect fish.

He says, "We got an hour, maybe two, before those guys outside come to their senses. Let's eat!" He yanks his switchblade out of his gym shorts and sets to work gutting and cleaning.

After the first three, it occurs to him what a mess of fish guts he's going to have all over the place. He wipes his hands on his thighs and pads off to his stash in the gym's wood-paneled locker room. He's had many occasions already to be grateful that the Toe Bone Gang didn't bother with mundane objects like kitchenware and janitorial supplies when they stripped the ship. Returning with a four-liter bucket and a plastic tarp, he finds the girl crouched over the pile of fish with her big knife in her hand. It's the first time N'Doch has seen it out of its sheath, and he studies it with interest. It's longer and heavier than he's expected. In fact, he's thought it might be just a prop, but the bright gleam along each edge tells him this blade means business. A *man's* weapon, despite its prissy antique facade. Puts his own beloved blade to shame. He wonders if the girl knows how to use it.

He lays out the tarp, scoops the fish guts into the bucket and sets it between him and the girl. He lines up the three cleaned fish in a neat row on the blue plastic, then squats and reaches for the next one, watching the girl while pretending not to. With care and some obvious experience, she scales the fish, then slits it open and scrapes the guts into the bucket. N'Doch nods in grudging approval and picks up his pace. He'd hate to be outdone by a mere girl. Soon the tarp is covered with fresh fish fillets and N'Doch's stomach is rumbling. The dragons have retired to the far corner of the gym. He gives them a covert look as he returns to the locker room for the two-burner stove he's cobbled together from parts of the ship's galley. He's been careful to use it only when he has to, so for now it still runs on gas. He loves the little castered frame he rigged for the meter-and-a-half-tall propane tank, and his favorite find was a magnetized matchbox that stores right on the cylinder.

Well, that's not true, he decides, blowing grit out of his one dented frying pan. *My favorite is really the flipper.*

He hefts the only slightly bent aluminum spatula. It's bright and smooth, with the satisfying weight and balance of expensive cutlery. The only reason it's in his hands is that it had fallen down behind a row of cabinets. He shows it off to the girl, but she offers only a blank expectant look, so he shrugs and gets down to work. He extracts a single kitchen match from the rusted box. When he lights it, the girl gasps and recoils. He sees her doing that crisscrossy hand thing that Catholics do when they're upset. *From*

Mars, he thinks again. He puts the match to the burner and turns on the gas. Thin blue flame erupts and settles soothingly as he adjusts the flow. He's proud of this stove, proud that he could make it work without blowing up himself and everything else. He turns to the girl to soak in her admiration and finds her staring at the lighted burner like she's never seen one before in her life. Now he's sure he's right about the no-tech commune. He turns the burner up and down a few times to watch her eyes widen, then scolds himself for wasting gas. He bends away to load his pan with fish and, out of the corner of his eye, he sees the girl stretch her fingers toward the flame. He grabs her wrist just in time.

"Are you nuts? You'll burn yourself!"

She stares at him, then sit back on her haunches with a puzzled, considering scowl. She twists her head slightly, as if listening, toward the dragons in the corner. "Hot," she says distinctly, in French.

N'Doch blinks. "Well, yeah. Hot." Then he says, "You gotta understand, the worst thing is not having the choice."

He's got to give her one thing, she's not stupid. She makes the leap. "Yes, N'Doch, I do understand. But you see, that's exactly what I like about it."

"Hunh," he says. "Well, different strokes . . ."

He turns away and settles the pan on the burner.

Erde watched the dark-skinned youth lay two large fillets in the flat metal dish. She knew now that she had misjudged him. Why had the dragons not mentioned, when she'd questioned his qualifications as a Dragon Guide, that this Endoch was a magician?

N'Doch, she corrected, rehearsing his name silently. She rolled the foreign sounds along her tongue and thought of the mage she'd promised to find for Earth those two long months ago, the one who'd help him remember his Quest. Maybe she'd found him after all. She knew N'Doch was a mage because he'd just exhibited a mage's most basic skill: he'd conjured fire in his bare hands, and had not been burned by it. Plus the flame burned blue, the color of magic. Now he was preparing his pots and potions. Erde settled down to observe what further alchemy this unlikely mage might produce. Soon the crispy scent of frying fish

informed her that this particularly alchemy was going to be
culinary, that N'Doch was *cooking* in that odd metal dish
with the handle. Erde was not disappointed. She was hungry enough right then to prefer food to any kind of magic.

N'Doch climbs the tall fire ladder to the high windows,
laying the uneaten fish out on the wide sills to dry in the
sun. When he climbs down again, the girl and the dragons
are gathered in the center of the gym, facing him with identical expectant stares. He's amazed that a dragon can make
the same expression as a human, that look the girl has that
says, "Well, now that we've all eaten, it's time for you to
get on with solving the rest of our problems."

Or that's the way N'Doch reads it, and rebellion rises
within him, swift and hot as lava, mostly for being caught
up in inescapable forces that he doesn't understand—except
for knowing there's something he's supposed to do. But accepting the reality of this so-called destiny doesn't mean he
has to like it. He'll go along, for a while at least, but it's
gotta be on *his* terms.

From the bottom of the ladder, he glares back at the
dragon huddle, then slouches over and hunkers down. He
is careful not to look directly at the dragon Water. He can
feel her anyway, hear her inquisitive background music invading his head, but if he doesn't meet her glance, at least
he can avoid losing himself once more in her scary blue
stare. He doesn't worry about what language he's speaking.
He knows now that somehow his meaning will get through
to all parties. He says, "I think . . ." then stops himself. He
traces obscure patterns on the gleaming floor and starts
again. "My mother says hide out at my grandfather's. I
think maybe we all could."

Silence settles into the room along with the pale dust
motes falling through the sunlight from the clerestory, and
N'Doch hears sounds he shouldn't be hearing yet.

"Someone's in the corridor!" he hisses.

The dragons understand right off, and the girl gets it a
second later. N'Doch leaps up and sprints for the door to
make sure the lock is still in place. He puts his ear to the
surface and listens for a moment, then pads deliberately
back to the huddle.

"We are in deep shit," he says quietly. "There's at least

ten, maybe fifteen guys on the other side of that door. It'll take 'em a while to get through, unless they send for a cutting torch, but we can't go anywhere either. Sooner or later, they'll get smart and start climbing in the windows. So we're trapped, unless . . ." He pauses, then guesses wildly, glancing up at the dragon Earth. "Unless you can get us out of here."

More silence, and the banging and clanking out in the corridor gets a lot more aggressive. Then the girl says, *"Ja. Sei kann."*

N'Doch shakes his head, but this is no time to argue the terms of the agreement. He shuts his eyes with a grimace and wills himself to allow the dragon music into his head.

"He can," the girl repeats, "but he needs to be able to see where he's going."

"What?"

"Just listen! He will explain."

N'Doch is amazed how simple and instantaneous comprehension can be when you have the right interpreter.

CHAPTER FOURTEEN

Even so, when they actually make the move, N'Doch is not really prepared.

They have to move quickly, so they agree that Water should image an interim destination. N'Doch's first experience traveling with Earth should not be from the driver's seat. He pouts, thinking they don't trust him, but he's glad enough when the time comes. Any lingering doubts he's allowed himself about the reality of dragon magic are blown to bits when he shakes the dizzying tingle out of his limbs and looks around.

He's back on the beach. But not the port beach, where the broken supertanker lay, where he'd been a split fraction of a moment ago. This is a different beach, and N'Doch knows it well, recognizes its diamond-bright sand and the smooth blue water of its protected inlet even though he's never seen it like this, in broad daylight. He doesn't take the time to wonder how he's ended up there. That could be a fatal luxury. Instinctively, he ducks, then glancing up and seeing the girl just standing there, snatches her down beside him.

"Why'd he bring us *here?*"

They're out of sync again. The girl frowns. N'Doch grits his teeth, looks to Water and repeats himself.

The girl is puzzled. "She showed him and he went there."

"Then she's gotta show him somewhere else! Fast!" He's whispering, though he knows it's pointless. The spy ears are sensitive enough to hear an ant walking. "Back to the boat! Anywhere! Just get us outta here!" Better a mob of irate drunken fishermen than Baraga's bionic dogs and the men they'll bring with them. The girl wouldn't stand a chance. And the dragons . . .

N'Doch sees it, a horrifying flash. His beautiful silver-blue monster boxed up in a high-tech cage for Baraga's video zoo. Just the sort of prize the Big Man would pay top bucks for. In his former life, mere hours ago, N'Doch would've already opened negotiations, might still if his life depends on it, which it might, he recalls, if he doesn't quick-wise explain to the dragons why this apparently deserted, picturesque, and pristine beach is the worst possible place to drop in on. He grasps the girl by both shoulders, like his brother Sedou used to do when he was supposed to really pay attention. He guesses this means he's the big brother now. He only hopes he lasts longer.

"There's this rich guy lives here, you got me? I mean, *really* rich. You can't imagine how rich." He circles his arms, encompassing the miles of unbroken white curling to the north and south—not even a footprint—and the mani-cured grove of royal crown palms embracing the curve of the beach like a green-armed lover. He wishes he could point out something obvious, like razor wire or guard towers, or mega laser emplacements, but that's not the Big Man's style. "And this is his private beach estate, that he doesn't like just anybody wandering around on."

If the girl weren't from Mars or wherever, the sheer un-touched beauty of the place would ring her alarm bells im-mediately. But N'Doch sees she has no problem understanding the perils of trespassing at least, so that anti-tech commune of hers must have taught her something about the standard division of wealth out in the world. He's wondering if they impressed upon her just how far some folks will go to preserve that division, when he hears the dogs. The girl's eyes widen.

"Knew it," N'Doch groans. For a wildly optimistic mo-ment, he'd hoped dragons and girls from Mars are invisible to Baraga's blanket of sensors.

The sound is literally bloodcurdling. He could explain to the girl how the dogs have been genetically engineered to produce the loudest, scariest howl a mammalian throat can produce, so that their victims will have plenty of time, while the dogs approach, to regret their trespass. But explanations wouldn't be too reassuring, since their bodies have been engineered as well. At least she's listening, and the buzz of image and music in his head says the dragons are, too. In fact, the images are getting kind of frantic. N'Doch clenches his eyes and shakes his head uselessly against the surge of mental static.

"He doesn't like dogs," the girl says apologetically.

"These aren't your normal dogs."

"This was her fishing place . . ."

He's just figured that out. Where else could you come up with a pile of hundred percent healthy fish? Baraga stocks the bay from his own hatcheries. "Fine, fine. Now tell them to get us out of here."

The girl smiles at him. Does he detect condescension? She's not as worried about this as she should be. "She hears you, N'Doch. That's why you hear me."

"I know that," he growls. "We got no time for lessons now."

"We have to have time." Her smile hardly wavers. "Here's what you must do: recall a place that you know in every detail."

He's looking over his shoulder, monitoring the dogs' approach. "Most of those kind of places are right here in town."

"A *safe* place. You spoke of your grandfather's . . . ?"

He shouldn't have said anything. What if he can't remember well enough? "I don't know . . . it's been a while."

"Think, N'Doch! If you can really *see* it in your mind, Earth can take us there."

She'd said this back on the tanker, but he didn't truly absorb it until the reality of instantaneous transport was finally incontestable, when he found himself on Baraga's beach. He gets it now: kind of like the old Star Trek vids without all the fuzzy lights and music. The blue dragon aimed them at the one deserted spot she could image, and there they went. Pretty neat. Not her fault it wasn't a real smart choice, but he's got to do better.

He bears down on his brain, digging after old memories of the bush. Concentrating is hard, with that uncanny howling tearing at his ears. And now, behind the dogs, he hears the resonant hum of the sleek sand sleds that give Baraga's patrols their own kind of instant transport. N'Doch tastes a bitter surge of envy, like he always does when he's reminded of the Big Man, the so-called Media King, and of what a man can buy with all that money. There's no one he hates with such purity, such simple fervor. But it's not so simple, really. He hates Baraga because the man's got everything and can do what he likes. But N'Doch knows that if the Media King chose to smile on him, say, sign him to even a minor recording contract, he knows he'd be bought as fast as the next poor kid with a keyboard. And this makes him hate Baraga even more.

But this is an old old rage and he hasn't got time for it now. The primal yowl of the dogs is maybe five hundred yards away. The girl looks nervous. The blue dragon is pinning him to the sand with her gimlet glare.

"Someplace safe . . ." he mutters. "Don't you know what you're asking?" Things will have changed in the bush, though maybe not so much, that far out. He can recall well enough the endless miles of scorched peanut fields, and the scattered, hard-baked villages. Familiar, yes, but in his mind, there's a sameness to all those miles. Can he remember one specific field or place along the road? If they could wait until dark, it'd be a lot easier to avoid detection.

But no such luck. He can make out the individual drones of the sleds now. There are four of them coming, and these are the two-man sleds. Probably Baraga's spy-eyes have them on visual, so they already know what a prize awaits them. N'Doch doesn't want to stick around to find out, though it would be fun and a rare taste of power, however fleeting, to wait until the sleds and dogs and whatever have pulled up around them, then vanish right out from under their noses.

He lets the image dance through his mind and abruptly, the background dragon music he's almost forgotten about turns sharp and urgent. Not even his fantasies are his own any more. Dogs or no, he'd like to sulk, but the dragon will not indulge him. Hard music, a storm of music in his head presses for action. He feels like a child being punished, and it turns out that's just what he's needed to vividly recall his time in the bush.

"Okay, I got one!" The dogs are in sight. "How do I do this?"

The sensation is painless, but he feels like his brain is being vacuumed.

*   *   *

It's an odd little place, just a thicket of rocks and an old baobab tree out in the middle of nowhere. *Nowhere is good right now,* he thinks. He'd recalled it at the last minute, mainly because it's where he escaped to when he missed his mama, or his grandfather was mad at him. Uncannily, the rocks themselves—pale, wind-smoothed boulders—are piled up in the shape of a dragon. As a kid, he'd called it the dinosaur. Now he sees it differently.

He's impressed by the big guy's accuracy. First, he's brought them nearly a hundred klicks in less than a heartbeat. On these roads, that's a long day's ride on a crowded, rickety bush taxi, not counting breakdowns or hijackings. Second, N'Doch had envisioned the rock pile from a bit of a distance, trying to fit the whole of it within his mind's eye, and that's exactly where he finds himself, once again breathless and queasy, a short walk away from this almost forgotten shrine of his childhood.

"Cosmic," he murmurs. He scans the horizon, notes that the girl does, too, only he doubts she'll know what to look for. He's glad she's held tight to the water bottle he gave her. She does seem to grasp that you gotta carry everything you need if you mean to survive.

So far, the horizon is empty, just the dry unplanted fields and scrub. He remembers there used to be some untilled land out this far, but that's long gone. It's the bush in name only these days. The scrub is gray and limp, and the sky's got that sickish yellow tinge to it even here.

But he sees no telltale rise of dust, no thin trail of smoke from some midday cookfire too close for comfort. 'Course maybe nobody's got much left to cook. Still, he's pretty sure the nearest village is at least two miles past his grandpapa's. He feels the old twinge of agoraphobia that the bush always brought on but, right now, anywhere but Baraga's beach is okay with him. Once he gets everyone into the rocks, where they can't be spotted from the air, they'll be safe—for a while, at least.

Erde sensed the true isolation of this new place he'd brought them to and let herself relax a little. True, it was hot as a smithy's forge and the air was full of red dust, but as N'Doch herded them toward the rock pile, she could see shade there. The crevices between the biggest boulders were as deep as caves, and, mercifully, dragon-sized. Nobody would be chasing them for a while. She mentioned this to Earth and he agreed it would be a novelty, at least in their own recent lives. Time to settle in, time to finally question Water, and then, plan the next leg of their Quest.

N'Doch seemed to share this need, once he had the dragons under cover. Erde thought him overly concerned about the view from above—did he suspect the very birds might give them away? But she smiled benignly to see him fuss so over Water, when a few hours ago he would scarcely acknowledge her. These wise and ancient creatures bound you by making you feel responsible for them. How silly, to think that great and magical dragons might have need of mere mortals, yet there it was. She remembered well how helpless Earth had seemed when she'd first found him—or rather, when he'd found her, at a time when her life had collapsed in ruins around her. The only thing that kept her sane and moving forward was the dragon's obvious need of her. Perhaps N'Doch's life was in a similar crisis, or was it just coincidence that they'd both been on the run when their dragons found them?

With a final upward glance, N'Doch shrugged, apparently satisfied. He took a long drink from his white water jug—Erde had been honored when he delivered one of these magical objects into her care—then he dropped down cross-legged to face her with the air of a man with a billion questions and no idea where to begin. He glanced furtively at Water, dozing behind him. He hadn't learned yet that his connection with the dragon wasn't directional and did not require eye contact. Only awareness, an inner listening. "Okay," he began. "Now let me get this straight . . ."

"These are real dragons," he states propositionally. It's getting familiar now, almost comfortable, this simultaneous translation thing. Like talking with the vid playing. "And somehow I'm hooked up with one of them."

The girl nods. So far, so good. He knows this sounds like kindergarten, but he's got to get all this weird shit out on the table where he can see it. Maybe saying it in words will give it logic or structure, like writing a song makes sense of messed up emotions.

"Like you're tied up with the big guy."

"Earth."

"Yah. Earth." He's not sure why he avoids calling the dragons by name, except that it feels like giving in. If you name a thing, it's for sure real, but at least you retain the power of the naming, which is a kind of power over the thing. If a thing *tells* you its name and you accept it, you also accept that the thing has a power in its own right: self-determination. If he had a dog or a monkey, he'd pick a name and that would be that: The dog or monkey would be his. He studies the silver-blue dragon thoughtfully.

"And she's Water."

"Yes. Water. She's Earth's sister."

Though he hears musical agreement in the background, he makes a face. "Nah. Can't be. I mean, look at 'em. They don't look anything alike."

Instead of snapping back at him like usual when he doubts her, she seems to go off on a thought of her own. "I know. Isn't it peculiar?"

N'Doch laughs. Does this mean the girl has a sense of humor? "It's all pretty damn peculiar, I'd say."

She nods, serious again. "But you get used to it."

"Okay. So there's these two dragons . . ."

He's interrupted by a bugle of music, not urgent or angry this time, but eager, as if the sea dragon's just thought of something she'd meant to tell them all along. The girl's deadpan face blooms with amazement and delight.

"She says there are more! She remembers four! Oh, a wonder! Isn't it, N'Doch?"

"I'm having enough trouble with one."

"Oh, but *four!*" She turns to Water. "Where are they? Do you know?" The sea dragon looks glum. The girl turns back. "She doesn't know."

"You're a one-woman conversation." N'Doch wants to get back on track. "Now listen up, okay? There's these two dragons—and maybe more—and then there's you and me, and we're supposed to help them do something, only no one knows what it is."

She resettles herself, but she's having a hard time restraining her glee. "It's their Purpose. We have to help discover it. Four!"

"Yeah, okay, four. But couldn't they just, you know, *be* here, like on vacation?"

She frowns. He can see she doesn't appreciate his levity. "All dragons have a Purpose. They wouldn't be here otherwise."

"Hah," he mutters before he can stop himself. "Wish I could say the same."

Her sudden smile dazzles him. "You can, now."

"Yeah, well . . ."

She spreads her hands, palms down, like she's calming a riot. N'Doch notices how they're large and long-fingered like his own. He wonders if she plays an instrument. Maybe he could teach her one. "Earth woke from his long sleep under the mountain because Someone was Calling him to his Purpose."

"Oh, yeah? Who?"

"That's what I keep telling you! We don't know!"

N'Doch hears for the first time the big dragon speaking in his head, and understands that a further level of connection has been achieved, probably because he hasn't been fighting it so hard. The big guy's voice is not the *basso profundo* rumble you'd expect from a dragon. It's more like a young voice that will be deep when it grows up. And N'Doch can hear humor in it, a wry, self-deprecation that matches the sad-sack expression the big guy often wears. It's almost playful. Nonetheless it shakes N'Doch to his very bones and sinews to hear someone else's words forming between his own ears.

—I did not even know my name when I woke.

—I knew mine. Water chimes in busily, like the mezzo making her entrance late into the quartet. *—But I am older.*

"Gaaaghhh . . ." is all N'Doch can manage. His brain rocks with sound, words, music, meaning. He thinks he might just pass out.

"We tried to figure out who was Calling him," continues the girl, like nothing out of the ordinary is happening, "I told Earth we'd find a Mage to tell us, but we were having these awful dreams and being chased all over by my father and the terrible priest, and the Summoner was calling him all the while! If it wasn't for Sir Hal . . ." She's stopped by the look in N'Doch's eyes. Even she can tell overload when she sees it.

He's grateful for the momentary silence, but he wants to look like he's up to the challenge. He can keep up with a girl from Mars, even though she's got a lot more words in her than he'd thought. He takes a long steadying breath. "Sir Hal?"

And she's off again. "Yes! He found us. Saved us. Taught us how to get along in the wilderness. He's a famous scholar of dragon lore, well *in*famous, really—most people don't approve of dragons, you know. And he's a King's Knight, one of the few still loyal to His Majesty."

"His majesty who?"

"Otto, High King of all the Germanies." She looks crest-fallen. "Have we come so far south that you haven't heard of King Otto? Oh dear! Have you even heard of the Germanies?"

"Well, *Germany,* yeah. A way while back, there was East and West, but now there's just one. Germany." He's always amazed by how thoroughly these regression cults indoctrinate their members. "I'm no history geek or anything, but I'm pretty sure they haven't had a King of Germany for at least two hundred years."

He watches the girl absorb this one. When no trace of guile shows through her confusion and dismay, he asks her casually as he can, "So, tell me something. What year do you think it is?"

Her chin lifts, hardens. "Think? I am no ignorant peasant! I am a baron's daughter. I can read and write and tell the hours. The year is 913 and it's September." She squints out into the sun. "But I can't really tell what time it is. It's different here, somehow."

"I'll say it is." N'Doch sucks his teeth. "Well, here's the thing: You got the September part right. And you're in the People's so-called Democratic Republic of Maligambia. That's in Africa, which *is* pretty far south of Germany. But, girl, let me break it to you gently. The year is 2013."

"It is?"

"Uh-huh."

To her credit, she doesn't launch right off into one of those twisty rationalizations the cultists always trot out to shore up their most ridiculous beliefs, like how God put the fossils in the rock to test the faith of Christians. She just stares at him, and the music in his head starts sounding more like bees swarming. She's having a silent confab with the scaly duo—no, not fair—neither of them are scaly, certainly not his silky blue monster, his lovely Water. Another cliché down the drain. N'Doch scolds himself. He knows he's just feeling miffed at being left out of a conversation moving too fast for him to handle.

"Hey," he says. "Can I get into this discussion?"

The girl turns a long, long gaze on him. He can see the years themselves in her eyes. "2013? Then we have traveled far indeed."

The future was something Erde had few thoughts about, other than the most immediate variety such as, "What's for dinner?" or "What can I possibly make for Grandmother's Name-Day?" Occasionally she would wonder which baron's son her father would marry her off to or what castle she'd live in when she grew up, but such thoughts never bore the weight of reality. Not like actually *being* there, feeling the truth of it all around you.

She had no problem believing that she was indeed in the future. Magic can make anything possible. She just wished the dragon had warned her. But perhaps he hadn't known either. Dragon time was less linear than her own, she was learning. Her sense of it was that time began *now* and ended *then*. After all, didn't you live one day, then another, and so on? But for the dragons, it seemed, time just *was,* and you could go anywhere in it you wanted to if you had the right directions.

Which of course for Earth meant the right *image.*

Which meant that if, in transporting to the place they'd seen in their nightmares, he'd brought them to the future, then they'd been dreaming the future all along. Erde decided not to tackle the mystery of how you could dream something that hadn't happened yet. She supposed it was something like the gypsy women and their picture cards, or Hal's lady Rose and her Seeings. Rose claimed to be able only to See what was now, but the dragons said all of time was now, happening all at once, which would explain why Rose occasionally seemed to See the future. Erde couldn't quite get her mind around it, but the dragons were magic and they knew best, so she'd just have to take their word for it.

The notion that she couldn't ignore was that the world might not go on as it was—as she knew it—forever and ever, that the passage of time might automatically equal change. Therefore, the difference of N'Doch's world might not be due simply to her having traveled far, far south into exotic lands. Instead, the whole world, from north to south, might have changed, might be like it was here in what he called Afrika: hot, dry, dusty . . . unrecognizable. So if she went back north, there might be nothing familiar there either. This was more frightening than any breakdown in her definitions of Time. She'd always been proud to be able to say that Tor Alte and its surrounding lands had been held in the von Alte name for three hundred years. But *eleven* hundred? Suddenly she wanted more than anything to go there and see.

N'Doch was watching her carefully, as if he'd expected some desperate reaction to his news. But even if she did feel desperate, she'd try not to show it.

"Is . . . uhm . . . German-y . . . like this now?" She gestured around vaguely. She didn't want to seem to be judging his world too harshly.

"Now? As opposed to when?"

She thought they'd been through that, but maybe he wasn't listening while she discussed it with the dragons. If he didn't start making a habit of listening, it was going to be hard to keep track of who understood what.

"As opposed to when I come from." She liked the sound of that, how easily it came out. Not "where I come from" but "when."

N'Doch sighed explosively. "All right, look—enough is enough. It's none of my business but somebody's got to clue you in sometime, might as well be me. So listen: whoever's told you the year's 913, your parents, this King Otto, whoever, they're just pretending you all live in the past, 'cause they can't deal with the present. You get it? It's all a big fat lie. I'm telling you that here and now, and you just gotta accept it. Okay?"

She let him finish and then calm down a bit, for he was getting rather heated about it. She guessed that the fact that, as young as she was, she'd been born eleven hundred years ago was a hard one to swallow.

"I don't mean I've lived that long," she reassured him patiently. "That would be impossible. Only dragons and the Wandering Jew live that long. I mean I just came from there yesterday."

She says it with such simple conviction, it makes his hair stand up on end. Not from Mars after all, but from the past. A time-traveler. And she's so sure about it, he can't think of a way to refute her. Especially when he's asking himself: If dragons can move through Space, why not through Time?

Abruptly, he's tired of it, all of it. Tired of having his brain crowded with other people's thoughts and voices and concepts, of having his reality stretched beyond all reasoning. And no wonder. He hasn't slept in twenty-four hours, except for being down for the count while they cured his fever, and that can hardly count as rest. It's only that he's eaten better than usual that's kept him going. It doesn't really matter, he realizes, if she's from now or whenever. She's here and so are the dragons, and somehow, he's got to deal with them.

"Okay, I got it. You're from the past. Fine. I'm gonna get some sleep now." He lies back and folds his elbow over his eyes, sealing out girl and dragons, the whole preposterous vision. "When it's dark, I'll go talk to Papa Dja."

CHAPTER FIFTEEN

Erde told Earth that she'd never in her life met anyone so badly brought up.

—*Ending a conversation without so much as a by-your-leave!*

—**He's tired. He's had a lot to think about today.**

Water stirred from her doze.

—**I think we could all use some rest.**

—*But he was so rude! And we were actually talking about something for the first time ever!*

—**Remember, you're not a baron's daughter here. He owes you no fealty.**

—*What about simple courtesy?*

—**His definitions are different from yours.**

—**Rest now, child. I feel great things are about to happen here.**

—*You do?*

—**Rest.**

The dragons were the ones who really wanted to rest, Erde decided, so she'd better let them. Forcing her petulance away, she studied N'Doch as he plunged into sleep beside her. He didn't ever seem to worry about how he *should* behave. He did whatever he felt like at the moment. Erde found this both enviable and infuriating. Did everyone just do what they felt like in this world of 2013? How did they get anything done without fighting about it?

She resisted sleep for a while. She thought she should stay awake and keep watch. But the hot close air in the shadow of the rocks made her drowsy, and neither N'Doch or the dragons seemed concerned any longer about the possibility of attack. She stared out at the brushy horizon until her eyelids drooped. Then she seated her dagger more comfortably against her waist, laid her head on her pack and fell asleep.

When the dream came this time, it was not like the old ones. It was not on alien ground, or wracked with deafening noise and odious smells. She was home again, not a specifically known location but an easily comprehended one: a wide, frost-seared grassland backed by fog-shrouded mountains, a dark forest of pine and fir flowing over the waves of foothills down to the edge of the plain, a chill, thin river. It was early morning, just coming light, of a dull wet day. Along the meeting line of grass and trees, an army was camped.

Erde found she could approach the camp, slowly, at eye level, as if riding along the rutted path and in among the silent tents on horseback. The illusion was so real that she started in fright, in the dream, when the door flap of a nearby tent was suddenly thrown aside and a man stepped out, not ten feet in front of her.

He was solid and blond, with the hard-muscled body of a warrior but sporting a courtier's close-cropped beard. His breath made smoke in the icy air, a chill Erde could not feel. The man stretched and shivered, shrugging his wool cloak more tightly around his naked chest. He tested the wind, listening intently, then frowned and looked toward Erde. She recognized Adolphus of Köthen, and wondered if he would remember her. But instead, he stared past her, as if surprised by not seeing the something or someone he'd expected. He turned away, then glanced back again, quickly, as if trying to catch that someone in the act of being there after all. Erde knew in her dream that he could sense a presence, maybe even her own specific presence, and that this puzzled him. It puzzled her, too, since they hardly knew each other, and why should she be dreaming about Adolphus of Köthen? But she was glad it was only a dream because this formidable, intelligent man was officially her enemy, the ally of her father and the terrible priest. She wouldn't want to be this close to him if he could actually see her.

And yet she lingered, because the dream gave her the

power and because, she realized guiltily, she liked looking at him, liked his interesting combination of toughness and reserve, liked how his thick, straw-gold hair bunched along his neck like pinfeathers, liked even his oddly dark brows and eyes. His alert scowl reminded her of her father's favorite peregrine, Quick, except Köthen carried himself with an easy confidence unlike the posture of any bird of prey. Much else about Köthen reminded Erde of Hal, though this was no surprise since Hal had fostered him as a lad, and by Kothen's own admission, taught him everything he knew. Erde thought it a great human tragedy that Baron Köthen felt called upon to go to war to usurp the King, thereby pitting himself against his beloved mentor. For there never was a more loyal servant to His Majesty than Heinrich Peder von Engle, Baron Weistrasse, known to his friends as Hal. Except, now that she thought of it, Köthen had invariably called him Heinrich. A mark of respect, or a way of distancing a man whom he honored far more than was convenient for him?

Now Köthen looked the other way. Armor clanked. There was a stirring of men and horses outside a black-and-green tent flying the von Alte battle standard. Her father's tent. Past it were a quartet of white pavilions, each guarded by a stout, white-robed monk. Other monks were lugging heavy pails of heated water into the largest pavilion.

Erde felt a chill at last, and a sudden urge to scurry away, as if some roving eye searching a crowd had picked her out with evil intent. She stared with Köthen, then after him, as he turned abruptly, his scowl deepening, and stalked past her, away from her father's awakening and the tents of the priest, away from the camp and the new smoke rising from cook fires, into the morning darkness under the trees.

When she woke in the thick heat of a far century, she knew it was not precisely a dream that she'd had. A profound sense of home lingered. Somehow she had *been* there, had returned to the preternaturally early winter of 913, and been privy to a true event, however insignificant . . . or probably not. Only time would tell that. But why Köthen? She scanned her mind for the dragon to tell him the news, but he was still sleeping off his bellyful of fish. She opened her eyes, slitted against the late-afternoon glare, so bright even in the deepest shadow of the rocks. Once again, N'Doch was gone.

CHAPTER SIXTEEN

On the way to Papa Dja's, N'Doch rehearses his explanation for showing up out of the blue after all these years of ignoring his grandpapa entirely. How long?—he counts backward—eight years, it has to be, and five since Sedou's funeral, when the old man walked all the way in from the bush to sing the ancient death rituals behind the imam's back. He wouldn't take a bush taxi. Wouldn't even take the public bus.

N'Doch would never admit it out loud, but he misses his older brother. More than, say, his little brother Jéjé who died so young the family hardly had time to get used to him being there. Or Mammoud, the eldest, who was out of the house and into the army at fourteen, when N'Doch was just learning to walk, and dead a year later. With Sedou, he'd actually had a sort of relationship, a rocky one for sure, with Sey always yelling at him to stick around home and mind. Sedou was the righteous one, of all his mama's sons, the one who did his schoolwork and worked extra hours at odd jobs to help feed the household. Of course that righteousness also made him pigheaded and fanatical, and got him killed for speaking his mind. N'Doch thinks writing songs is a smarter way of saying your piece then getting involved in politics. It's true he hasn't written any songs about "issues" yet, but he keeps thinking he might. He hasn't written any about Sedou either, though he's got a lot in his mind. Probably the songs about Sedou will end up being about politics, so he figures he'd better just get famous first. If you're famous enough, they pretty much let you say what you want.

There's no road the way he's going. It's a direct overland

route, a mile and a half across the dry, empty fields waiting for the fall rains that have been coming later and less often every year. The soil is as dry and hot as beach sand beneath his bare feet, and the scattered grass clumps rattle like drumrolls as he brushes past. N'Doch thinks it's odd but all the same incredibly cool that he knows exactly in which direction his grandpapa's house lies. *Exactly,* as if flashing signs or a homing beacon were showing him the way, 'cept it's right there in his head and he's sure of it in ways he isn't about a lot of other things he's had to do with much more recently and in greater detail. He's even impatient with the occasional detour around brush thickets or rocks. He can sense the deviation from the straight line as acutely as he would hear a string out of tune. *Pretty weird,* he muses, but then everything is, right about now. Why should this be any different?

He decides he'll tell Papa Dja that the dragons are research clones escaped from some top secret American zoo, like in that old vid about the dinosaur island. If the old guy questions him too closely, he'll just say that's what the girl told him, he doesn't know any more. How he'll explain the girl, he's not sure, with all her bizarro clothes and speaking German. Maybe he'd better make it a German zoo. He'll just say she showed up on the beach looking for help, which isn't far from the actual truth. It just ain't *all* of it. . . .

He's there almost before he realizes. Ahead of him, just as he remembers it, the unlikely copse of thick-trunked trees, like a handful of forest tossed down among the parched scrub to spread the miracle of leaf and shade over Papa Djawara's tiny homestead. The real miracle is, there's no barbed wire or broken glass palisade along the tops of those mustard-colored walls, and N'Doch knows the gate will not be locked. When everyone else in their right mind has taken the appropriate security precautions, Djawara has steadfastly refused to do anything but adopt a pack of mangy stray dogs. N'Doch looks around, wondering where the dogs are. There must be dogs. Papa Dja always had dogs. Out hunting, most likely, good luck to them, and leaving the compound open to surprise intruders such as himself. Papa Dja always said he had nothing worth stealing, but an intact house under trees is prime real estate. Plus, the old man grows a lot of good, safe edibles inside those unassuming walls. N'Doch knows this, and he guesses everyone else around knows it, too. There must be water underground somewhere, though no well digger's ever been able to find it. If they had, Papa Dja would've lost his house long ago. But Fâtime says the locals are afraid that if they steal from Papa Djawara, he'll put a bad spell on them and that'll be that. This wouldn't hold the gangs back, but so far, they've pretty much kept to the towns and the City. So in some ways, the old coot's nutty reclusiveness works in his favor. Fâtime says he's even managed to hold on to a goat.

N'Doch approaches the gate quietly. It's that still, amber part of early evening. Entire flocks of birds are appearing out of nowhere to settle in Djawara's trees. In town, the market stalls would be going great guns again, after the midday lull for the heat. Housewives would be bartering their last pair of shoes for the evening meal. Out here, the farmers in the villages are probably setting their chairs out in the street to fan themselves a while before falling exhausted into bed. And that's just what his grandpapa is doing when N'Doch sticks his head inside, past the broken ironwork gate: sitting under a big lemon tree, fanning himself slowly.

Like the trees and the mustard-colored walls, Djawara is exactly as N'Doch remembers him. Thinner and grayer, maybe, but the same slight, erect, round-faced man in an antiquated white tunic and woven tribal skullcap. At least he doesn't have his ceremonial robes on. N'Doch recalls asking Fâtime one time why Papa Dja wore so many clothes. She just shook her head, probably at both of them. He's always been told he has her height but his grandpapa's frame. He's not sure who shares the old man's ready but ambiguous smile. Certainly not his mama, at least not anymore. And though he'd like to think his own smile could be as complex as he remembers Djawara's, he doubts he's lived long enough for that.

The old man is smiling like that right now, easing back comfortably in one of a pair of metal folding chairs, the least bent one, facing the gate as if someone has just gotten up from a conversation and Djawara expects them back presently. N'Doch hesitates, glances behind him. The flood of memories is a surprise to him. It's hard just to stroll in to this place so pungent with his boyhood. But he can't not go in. The old man has seen him and waves him in with his palm frond fan.

"There you are, there you are. Took your own sweet time, did you? Took a nap along the way?"

N'Doch looks behind him again. Has the old geezer mistaken him for someone else? Is he losing what's left of his marbles? "Papa Dja? It's me, N'Doch, Fâtime's boy."

"I know who you are, though it's been so long, that's a miracle in itself."

"I know, Papa, and I'm sorry."

"Sure, sure. We're all sorry these days."

The bright smile belies his grandfather's dire tone. N'Doch edges in a few steps farther, both eager and reluctant. He nods at the second chair. "You were expecting someone?"

"You. I was expecting you."

"Oh." That's just the sort of thing the old man's always saying, that earns him his reputation as a crazy man. "Well . . . how are you?"

"Very well, very well. And yourself?"

"Oh, fine, real fine. And the cousins? And the neighbors? And the goat? And the garden?" N'Doch throws himself into the old-style greeting pattern, hoping to lure this very traditional old man into the right frame of mind about him. "And by the way, where are the dogs?"

Djawara's smile barely wavers. "The family won't talk to me, what's left of them, and the neighbors are afraid to, as well they ought to be. The goat's stopped milking and the garden's just squeaking by. I'm getting too old to care for it properly." He pauses for a little cough and a breath, peering at N'Doch from under lowered brows. "But the dogs, mercifully, are hale and healthy. Only I put them inside, as I hear one of our visitors isn't fond of dogs . . . I hadn't counted on that."

N'Doch's eyes narrow. "Visitors?"

"You know, you know." Djawara tosses a casual wave in the precise direction that N'Doch has come.

"Ah," N'Doch replies, thinking of how tired he's getting of being caught entirely by surprise. "So . . . you know about the, ah . . ."

Djwara nods. "Visitors. The signs were all pointing to it. If I'd read them more truly, I'd be better prepared. But as it is, it is. We'll make do, won't we?"

N'Doch nods with him, still second-guessing. Like, what if they're talking about two different things? Dragons and, say, the visiting relief workers, or the Frenchmen who try unsuccessfully to sell Djawara a windmill every year? N'Doch leans against the crumbling gatepost. "Well, Papa Dja, funny you should mention, since I was hoping you could take in a visitor or two for a while, only I'm not sure . . ." His eyes flick around the visible parts of the courtyard and the small thatched-roof bungalow at its center.

". . . there's room?" The old man leans back in his chair, palm fan waving. "You'd be surprised. This place is a lot bigger than it looks."

N'Doch sucks his teeth, says nothing. He's spent the whole trip from the rock pile inventing explanations for dragons, without a thought of what to say about why he's come.

Djawara chuckles. "Come in, come in, son. I'll make us some tea. Sit down and rest a bit till the light fades. Then we'll go out and bring them back."

N'Doch slouches into the welcome sweet shade of the lemon tree. He shakes his grandfather's small, dry hand, then sets the water jug at his feet and sits. He looks up and sees actual lemons hiding among the shiny dark leaves, like little suns among storm clouds. He can hear but not see the birds settling into the branches, chattering and resettling each time another flock lands. After a long silence, he gets his courage up.

" 'Scuse me for asking, Papa Dja, but how did you . . . ?"

"Know?" The old man takes a grateful swig from the jug. "Well, your mama told me, of course. But as I said, even if she hadn't, I'd been feeling it was time."

"I see." N'Doch considers this briefly. He's forgotten about the old man's irritating habit of finishing your sentences before you can even get them out. "How did she know?"

"You didn't tell her?"

"No way."

"Well, there you are. That's Fâtime for you. I always

said she could pry secrets out of a stone. I recall one time she even . . ."

" 'Scuse me again, Papa, but *how* did she tell you? You put in a phone since I was here last?"

Djawara frowns. "Phone? This is no rich man you're kin to. Even if I had the money, I wouldn't have one in the house." His hands sketch little circles above his head. "All those waves, you know . . . they get in the way. No, she told me in a dream, son. That's how the poor folk talk together."

Speak for yourself, thinks N'Doch. It's true his mama's always put great stock in dreams, but he's still not convinced he and his grandpapa are on the same page. Just doesn't seem possible. "So, ah . . . what exactly did she tell you?"

"That you'll need help understanding where to go next."

N'Doch gives up, sits back with a sigh. "Well, that ain't lying."

When it's dark, and the tea has been made and drunk—three ritual cups of the thick, sweet brew—Djawara dons a brightly printed robe over his worn white tunic and carefully brushes out the folds. They walk in silence back to the rock pile. The old man keeps pace through the night heat without complaint. They're almost there when he grasps N'Doch's wrist suddenly and draws him beneath the canopy of a thicket.

"What?" N'Doch demands.

"Quietly!" Djawara points upward.

N'Doch listens. After a while he hears the airy whock-whock of a hovercopter approaching from the south, from town. It's flying low, like it's looking for something.

"Damn, Papa! You got great ears!"

"Shhh!"

They watch it pass by to the east, the direction they're headed, and vanish into the night toward the north.

"Already!" N'Doch has figured to have more safe time. "Who is it?"

"Baraga, I'm fairly sure of it."

The old man does not ask how or why. "Then we must hurry."

The girl and the dragons are awake when they get there,

awaiting his return. He can see that this time they were sure he'd come back, which makes him feel predictable, and that really bugs him.

Papa Dja touches his shoulder as they step under the shadow of the rocks. "One moment. What are their names?"

"Didn't Mama tell you that, along with everything else?"

"No more than she taught you manners, it appears."

N'Doch wants to explain that his manners are fine, it's the damn situation that's making him so touchy. But the old man's frown can lay him out like no one else's. How could he have forgotten that?

"Umm, the big one's called Earth and my . . . the other one's Water."

"Don't be so afraid to claim what's yours, son."

Djawara's past him before N'Doch can think of a proper comeback. But it occurs to him maybe this is why he stayed away after all those extended visits when he was young: this man, half his size and weight, can still make him feel like a child. Pretending he's moving through the frames of some surrealist stop-action video, N'Doch does the introductions. To his chagrin, Djawara greets the girl in what sounds like pretty good German. She has some difficulty with it at first, so Djawara adjusts his pronunciation. N'Doch hears it, like a change of key in a piece of music. The girl nods and smiles.

"Didn't know you spoke Kraut, Papa Dja," he marvels sullenly.

"It's *Alte Deutsch*," Djawara says, moving on to gaze up at the dragons. "Old German. Not all that different, really. Knew it would come in handy some day."

"Hunh." N'Doch notices how both critters have withdrawn into the deepest recesses of the rocks so that their true shape and size is lost in darkness. Maybe they hoped not to frighten this elderly and frail-looking human, but N'Doch thinks they look scarier that way, looming up out of the earthly void like myths or nightmares, the pale ambient moonlight touching just the relevant detail: a giant ivory claw, the gleaming curve of a horn, a shimmer of velvet, and two pairs of eyes that seem to radiate a warmer kind of light. N'Doch backs up involuntarily. But Djawara seems to have a very clear idea what a man should do when faced with a brace of dragons. He goes right to them and stands with his arms spread wide and his chin high. He looks so small in front of them, smaller than the girl even, and painfully vulnerable, but N'Doch sees that his eyes are closed and his smile transcendent. Drawing his palms together beneath his chin, the old man bows to them deeply, and the dragons incline their great heads in solemn recognition.

Erde saw that this dark little man she understood to be N'Doch's grandfather knew his way around dragons, and liked him immediately. That he spoke her language, albeit a bit oddly, naturally increased her high opinion of him. That he seemed totally unsurprised by herself and her companions made her suddenly much more relaxed about the future of the dragons' Quest. If N'Doch was not the mage they sought, perhaps this old man was. He certainly looked more like a mage. For one thing, he wasn't going around half-naked like everyone else she'd seen. He even wore a hat, and soft leather sandals on his neat, ash-colored feet. Covertly, Erde searched the intricate patterning of his ankle-length, wide-sleeved robe for familiar alchemical or astrological symbols but all she could make out in the dim light were fish and birds, or maybe they were flying fish, which sounded at least somewhat magical.

She let him pay his proper obeisance to the dragons, then approached him with the formality and respect due to a learned elder and probable mage.

"We seek a wise man's counsel, honored sir."

"And his hospitality as well, I'm told." His bright, crinkly eyes were on a level with her own. "Both of which you shall have, such as I can offer, which I fear these days is slight."

Earth's urgent need cut through her own impulse toward at least a smidgen of polite introductory conversation.—
ASK HIM.

Erde cleared her throat. "My companion asks: Are you the mage we seek?"

This seemed to surprise him as nothing had so far. His eyes flicked up at the dragon and back again. "Why would he think that?"

—Why, Dragon?
**—BECAUSE HE SEEMS TO HAVE BEEN EX-
PECTING US.**

Erde relayed this, and the old man smiled. "No and yes,
daughter. Never and always. Waiting for long centuries,
without expectation. From grandfather to grandson. You of
all people know how it is, how it has always been."

"Not entirely, learned sir. My grandmother died before
she could explain everything to me in detail."

"Ah, then I am sorry for your loss, but you see, she
gifted you with what detail was necessary, or you'd never
have found . . ." He nodded gravely toward Earth.
". . . him. Any deeper knowledge would create an improper
anticipation. Preparation, yes, but one cannot live one's life
waiting for a thing that might never happen."

*But I'd have been happy to be even as prepared as you
seem to be,* Erde thought. "I've no wish to cause offense,
honored   sir,   but   would   this   explain   why   your
grandson . . . ummm . . . ?"

"Yes, daughter?"

"Sir, he doesn't seem to understand much about
dragons."

"Well, now, there don't seem to be many of them around
nowadays, do there?" The old man's smile hinted at her
own imperfect understanding. "But, yes, he has been a reluctant pupil. He's grown up in a world that has no use for
the old knowledge. Yet he absorbed what he needed, or
you wouldn't be here."

Erde saw the truth in that. She glanced at N'Doch, who
had moved away into the moonlight and was staring up
into the air. Despite his ignorance and disbelief, he had
finally not deserted them. He had gotten them where they
apparently needed to be.

"Papa Dja," he called now from the edge of the light.
"That copter's coming back."

Prepared, thought Erde, *but still unpardonably rude.* But
instead of scolding the youth for interrupting, the old man
turned his way and listened.

"It is indeed."

"Think it can see us under all these rocks?"

"Heat, son. The warm exhalations of life."

N'Doch nodded disgustedly. "Damn Baraga anyway. I won't let him get her."

Djawara's smile broadened. "No. I should say not."

Erde followed this exchange as best she could, but the dragons' understanding of idiomatic speech was loose at best. "What flies in the night sky that worries you, honored sir?"

"One of Baraga's hovercopters," grumped N'Doch.

The old man eyed Erde sympathetically. "She will not be acquainted with that particular type of bird, my boy. We'll speak of these things later," he reassured her. "First we must figure out how to get ourselves to safety without being sighted."

"You think it's safer at your house?"

"For a while, yes. We can mislead this pursuit."

"Really?" N'Doch brightened and began to look slyly around. "Well, then, Papa Dja—I think I can handle this. I'll have you back home in no time at all."

CHAPTER SEVENTEEN

It's crowded in the courtyard with all five of them there, but the look of approval in his grandfather's eyes is worth any discomfort. Approval, and just the slightest trace of awe. The old man may know something about practically everything but clearly, he's never experienced instantaneous transport before. N'Doch begins to think he could get into this dragon business after all.

The dogs set up a choral howl in the house. The girl reaches to reassure the brown dragon. It makes N'Doch grin to think that any critter as well armed and armored as that big guy could be afraid of dogs. He's glad it's not *his* dragon putting up such a fuss over nothing. But Djawara goes to the door and hushes the dogs sternly. Then he says something to the girl, gesturing toward the deeper shadow beneath the trees filling the little side yard. Remembering the copter, N'Doch glances upward, then around.

"So, Papa Dja—you got some kind of jamming signal hidden around here that's gonna disable that copter's sensors?" He laughs. "Some kind of cloaking device?"

"I said 'confuse,' not 'disable,' but actually I do. The birds are my cloaking device."

"Oh, yeah, the birds." Because of course the trees are full of them. Hundreds, maybe more. "Will it work?"

"Always has before."

N'Doch wonders how often his grandfather has need of concealment from the likes of Baraga. "What if they leave?"

"I'll call them back if we need them."

"Oh." It doesn't sound foolproof, but N'Doch is distracted by the big dragon, who is looking unusually squat and reptilian as he squeezes himself under the low, spreading branches. "He'll never fit."

"He will."

And sure enough, the brown guy slowly drags his bulk inward until he's disappeared beneath the leaves. N'Doch peers under the branches and sees only shadow, a limitless darkness—and the dragon's tail vanishing into it. A chill creeps up his spine.

"Papa Dja, how . . . ?"

"Don't think about it, son. Just don't."

"But . . ." He's not sure he wants the blue dragon swallowed up likewise, but she's already on her way, leaving a trill of music in his head that sounds like reassurance. When she, too, has vanished, Djawara dusts his palms lightly and gestures N'Doch and the girl into his house. It crosses N'Doch's mind that maybe Djawara's neighbors are right to be afraid of him.

Inside, it's dark, and Djawara lights a little kerosene lamp. N'Doch is about to explain the boondocks lack of electricity in the house, and then he remembers he's the only one who'll be missing it. The dogs leap around them with interest and suspicion. N'Doch makes a quick head count: seven of them this time. Seven scrawny but otherwise healthy-looking, lop-eared, evil-eyed mutts. Most of 'em good-sized ones, too. He expects the girl to freak, since her dragon's so weird on them. Instead, she reaches out her arms to gather them and gets down on her knees among them like she's welcoming old friends. They snarl and shoulder each other for her attention, but she speaks stern German to them and calms them. Then she smiles over their hairy backs at the waiting men.

"She tells them they're beautiful," Djawara translates. "That she's never seen such clever dogs. They lap it up. Dogs are fools for flattery."

"It's good you speak her lingo, Papa Dja." N'Doch doesn't mention his doubts that the dogs speak it also. "I can't talk to her otherwise, when the dragons aren't around."

"Aren't they around?"

"No, they . . ." He realizes he knows this now, without even looking. He can tell from the silence in his head. He wonders where they've gone, and how they left from that weirdness beneath the trees. "They're off hunting, probably. They'll be back."

"No doubt." The old man is smiling one of his most complicated smiles. "Why don't you teach Mademoiselle Erde some French?"

"Well, I will . . . I guess I will, when I get around to it . . . if she's still here."

"She will be." Djawara lights a second lamp and carries it onto the cooking porch at the back of the bungalow. He sets it on a wooden slab beside a basket of vegetables. N'Doch comes to hover over the basket eagerly.

"You grow all this?"

Djawara nods. "Poor shriveled things. I can't haul as much water for them as I used to be able to. But they're all safe."

"Look okay to me." Squashes, tomatoes, peppers, a few things N'Doch doesn't recognize. He picks up a long green thing he's forgotten the name of. "What's this?"

"A cucumber. Have you never had a cucumber?"

"Not for a real long time, Papa Dja."

"Hmm. Getting bad in town, is it?"

"Bad to worse." Actually, N'Doch hasn't thought about it like that before, that it might be worse now than it was before. He's prided himself on living in and for the moment, in the cool chaos of the present, where he's like the flash of the vid image, the instant of pure data always morphing into something else and abandoning its former self in the irrelevant past. But now the past walks beside him, very relevant and immediate, in the form of a young girl and a dragon, and in a surge of childhood memories loosed by this old man and his peculiar house. He'd forgotten how peculiar. All this allows N'Doch a newly parallax view of himself, moving through time, a product not of just now, but then and now, a continuum. Which now includes a silver-blue dragon that the old man used to sing about a long time ago. Standing there thinking all this while he's staring at the cucumber, it fairly well blows N'Doch's mind.

"You all right, son?"

"Yeah, sure." He paces a little, because he has to. "Papa Dja?"

The old man is slicing a squash into a battered pot. "Mmmm?"

"You know that old song you used to sing, about the kid and the sea serpent? How'd that end? I can't remember."

Djawara ladles precious water into the pot from a bucket covered with a damp white cloth. "Don't know. You'd always fall asleep, so I'd always stop singing."

"But there must be an ending. Every song has an ending."

Djawara smiles, heading out back with the pot, toward the fire pit. "Then you'd better invent one. You're the songwriter, after all."

Outside, the chatter of roosting birds is deafening. N'Doch pursues him. It's only half a dozen steps, but it feels like he's lunging after his old grandfather. He's just realized who he can blame for all this weird shit that's fallen down around him lately.

"You got me into this, didn't you! You were . . . prepping me somehow, way back when. What's the deal? Are you some kind of alien invader or something?"

Djawara rolls his eyes. "Of course not. Where do you get such ideas?"

"I see it on the vid all the time."

"*All* the time?"

"Lotsa times."

Djawara grunts. "Consider the source."

"Whadda ya mean?" N'Doch doesn't think the idea's so far-fetched, what with all else that's been going on. "But it's you knows what I'm supposed to do, right?"

"I know what my grandfather had from his grandfather and told to me so that I could pass it on to you."

"But why me?"

Djawara kicks up the coals of his cook fire and tosses on a few handfuls of twigs. Then he straightens and faces N'Doch directly. "There is no why. Don't you see? It just *is*. You're the newest link in the unbroken chain. The why is to be ready when the time comes, which appears to be now, so you're elected. Why *not* you?"

N'Doch can think of a billion why-nots, but he knows not a one of them will satisfy Papa Djawara. "But you got me into it," he repeats in helpless frustration.

"You got into it by getting born."

"But you got to at least have an idea!" He remembers the girl's red jewel, what she called her 'dragon brooch.' "Don't you have some, uh, magic sword for me or something? Some kind of, what's it, a rune book, like in the fantasy vids?"

"This is not a fantasy vid."

"Damn right! And it's no dream either, like I kept hoping!"

A few weak flames start up and Djawara sets the pot to boil on the iron grate. "Besides, if I gave you a book or a sword, you wouldn't believe in it."

"I might."

"Inanimate objects bear only the power you yourself invest them with. You're having trouble believing in a living dragon."

"Oh, I believe in her all right. I got no choice. I'm stuck with her, and you ain't got a clue to offer me!" He's shouting now but even over his own outraged squall, he hears the familiar sound. Both men freeze and fall silent.

Whock-whock-whock-whock.

Djawara points toward the sound. N'Doch spots the five swaying pillars of light, bright pendulums slicing the night sky. He imagines a huge, long-legged spider, stalking him through the dark bush. He ducks back under the porch roof. Inside the house, the dog patter stills. The girl comes to the door, and he waves her back urgently.

In the yard, Djawara murmurs, "Don't worry." But N'Doch sees he must be a little worried or he wouldn't be whispering or listening so hard himself.

The search beams swing here, there, then approach, like sharks swimming through the darkness, pulling the copter behind them. The light flows up over the compound walls and flares across the treetops, setting off a loud chorus of bird protest. The birds lift and settle, lift and settle. One roving beam slides over the cook fire and beyond, then reverses itself and returns, blasting Papa Djawara with its icy glare. N'Doch shrinks into the shadowed corner of the cooking porch. Djawara looks up, shielding his eyes against the light, and is no longer N'Doch's mysteriously powerful relative but a pathetic old man, blinking and staring up out of the bush, caught in the innocent preparation of his evening meal. The light passes by, circles the empty courtyard, scrapes slowly across the bird-cloaked trees, and moves on.

Djawara waits until the sound has faded. Then he bends to stir his pot. "I didn't say I didn't have a clue. . . "

The old man spoons out cold rice while the vegetables are cooking, then sends the dogs outside the walls to hunt, telling them to be careful, strange things are abroad in the night. N'Doch digs into his pack and presents Djawara with some of the fish he's dried back on the tanker. The girl looks puzzled when Djawara lays out a square yellow oilcloth on the floor, places the big flat bowl of rice and dried fish and squash in the center, then settles himself down in front of it.

N'Doch is embarrassed. He doesn't mind the old style cooking so much—in fact, this rice dish called chebboujin is one of his favorites. But why can't the old coot have plates and forks and a table, like folks do in town? Some old traditions are just stupid. What's the girl gonna think?

But Djawara slides a cushion toward her feet and invites her to sit. When she does, he goes about picking out bits of fish and squash with his fingers, stacking them along the rim of the bowl nearest her. He chatters away in German all the while, explaining himself, N'Doch figures, since the girl nods and reaches with the correct hand to begin the meal. He thinks it's gross, and he's amazed that she accepts the old man's word without question, like she just doesn't know any better about old people and their uncool ways and notions. Nevertheless, he drops cross-legged beside them, knowing he'd better eat the old man's way or he likely won't eat at all.

Erde was charmed by the little mage's courtly manners, and thanked him graciously before eating the first of the choice morsels he'd set aside for her. The food was delicious, and it was an effort to sit up straight and not gobble. N'Doch seemed very shy about eating at first. Perhaps he was just making sure she and Djawara got enough before he started in on it.

It seemed like years since she'd eaten a fresh vegetable, though it was only since Deep Moor. Oddly, this tiny compound reminded her of the women's secret valley, in essence if not in physical reality. She decided Master Djawara would feel very much at home in those fertile meadows, as the women would in the heat and dust here. Immediately she felt as protective of the mage and his home as she did about Deep Moor. She studied every detail of his exotic dwelling: the rough yellow walls and baked mud floor; the flat, bright weave of the fabric hangings; the low wide benches, tossed with cushions, that hugged the walls in between shelves crammed with colorful books. Then there were the mage's alchemical lamps, whose flames rose and fell on command, like the cook fire back in N'Doch's stronghold, the castle he called a ship. And she knew true magic lurked outside, beneath those modest trees whose shade had swallowed up two full-sized dragons without a trace. When she'd looked for Earth in her mind soon after, he wasn't there. She hoped they'd gone hunting again, and would bring back a load of fresh fish to swell this good man's scanty larder. She waited until he'd eaten enough to slake his hunger, then blotted her lips gently with the hem of her linen shirt and told him of the dragon's dilemma.

He listened through to the end, only nodding now and then. He seemed unsurprised by the dragons' ignorance of their own Purpose. When she was done, he got up to make tea, a thick, sweet brew that he served in tiny, delicate flagons without handles. Only after the second serving did he return to the subject, with the suggestion that a quest after an unknown grail might be all the more passionate for being fueled by mystery. Erde could see he put great value in uncertainty. To her mind, he revered it rather too much, but she'd never say so, out of courtesy. Just as she was considering how to probe him further, she felt the dragons return, sleepy and sated.

—*Dragon! Welcome! Did you bring food for this good old man?*

—**Of course. I am no ungrateful guest.**

—*You are the very soul of gratitude, my dragon. Now, we are discussing important things. You must stay awake and listen.*

—**We spoke of important things as well. My sister has remembered something further.**

"Oh, what is it?" Erde exclaimed aloud. "Oh, Master Djawara! The dragons have news!" She translated as Water explained.

—I said that there are more of us. Now I recall the others' names: They are our brother Fire and our sister Air. Air is the one we must find. Air was firstborn. She will know what our Purpose is.

"Great," said N'Doch. "So now we're looking for two people."

"A person and a dragon," Erde corrected.

"Perhaps they are one and the same," offered Djawara.

"Why do you say that, Master Djawara?"

"Because it seems likely that the eldest should be the one responsible for gathering the others when the need arises."

"But what's the need?" demanded N'Doch.

"Indeed, that seems to be the question," Djawara agreed.

With their news delivered, the dragons had gone to sleep. Erde wasn't sure how much help their news had been. "I beg you, honored sir, surely there is some advice you could offer us, to further our Quest, to help us find the Summoner?"

The mage did not hesitate. "You must go to the City."

The words struck home, and Erde wished Earth had stayed awake to hear them. The City. The idea kept reappearing in different guises, in Gerrasch's reading of his bones and pebbles, in Rose's Seeing, even in Erde's own invented Mage City, with its white towers crowding a green horizon. She'd conjured it first to give a lost and despairing dragon a goal and an image of hope, but perhaps her vision represented a truth after all, guessed at by instinct or sensed by some power of Seeing she didn't know she possessed.

But N'Doch, hearing this once the old mage remembered to translate, raised a terrible fuss.

"To the City? Are you nuts? We barely got out of *town* alive! How'm I gonna go walking into the City with a dragon on either arm? Might as well send up a flare to Baraga right now!"

"Calm, calm, my boy," Djawara soothed.

"Then don't tell her such things! Look, I know you don't want us here too long, 'cause it's dangerous for you and we'll eat you dry, but you gotta have a better idea than that! Mama said you . . ." N'Doch stops dead, hearing an eight-year-old's whine coming out of his grown-up throat.

Djawara stares him down a while, nodding and pursing his lips.

N'Doch looks away, humiliated. More quietly, he says, "Fâtime said you'd know what to do."

Djawara lets apology hang unvoiced in the air. Quietly, he pours the third round of tea. Then he replies, "You are all welcome in my house for as long as you care to make it your home. And you would probably be safe. And we would somehow manage to feed ourselves adequately—it's easier when you have help. But there is a greater need here."

N'Doch knows this. And sees that he'd hoped to avoid the urgency of it by bringing the dragons to safety in the bush. But safety is not uppermost in the dragons' minds. Not even in the girl's, despite her moments of fear and reluctance. He sees that now. He hears the music of dragon presence in his mind, pressing him to action. His shoulders droop. "Okay. So it's gotta be the City, you say. Got any idea how?"

Djawara looks to the girl, questioning her a bit like he's checking up on stuff he already knows. She tells him something that surprises him. His eyebrows arch and he nods quickly, pleased. He turns briskly back to N'Doch.

"Well, first of all, since you grew up in the City, a place-image to travel to is not a problem."

"I don't know . . . it's been a while."

"You've been there more recently than you've been here, am I right?"

N'Doch nods. Lying to the old man is hopeless.

"If you could bring them here, you can take them there, and you certainly will know your way around when you get there."

N'Doch has to admit that's also true.

"Secondly, Baraga's not the big man in the City that he is in town."

"So? It'll just be someone else after us."

Djawara dips his head doggedly. "Thirdly, your Visitors' gifts will allow them access as free as any."

"What gifts?"

"The Visitor Earth's great Gift of Stillness, which renders him invisible."

"More like a big rock. I've seen that one."

"A rock to you, who can sense his presence. Invisible to most of the world."

N'Doch shrugs. He has no way to deny this. "And the other one?"

"The Visitor Water is a shape-shifter. Didn't you know?"

"What's a shape-shifter?" But already, he does know. He sees the blue dragon in his mind, slimming to fit the close passages of the derelict tanker, lengthening to reach the high clerestory windows. "How much can she shift?"

Djawara spreads his hands in front of him, seeming to inspect each finger carefully. "Why don't you ask her?"

CHAPTER EIGHTEEN

She's waiting for him when he slouches out into the dark front courtyard, full of cheb and sweet tea and questions he's not sure he wants to ask.

She's crouched catlike, facing the door, and the big brown guy is nowhere to be seen. N'Doch can't decide whether he feels like he's on some kind of weird first date or like he's facing the Mother Superior of his Catholic grammar school. He's never been alone with her before. The dragon, Water—he forces himself to think of her by name—is both winsome and officious, both animal and somehow more than human, and the real problem is not so much that he doesn't want to relate to her but that he doesn't know how.

He stares at her and she stares back. He wonders if he should think of her as a woman, if that would be a healthy thing to do, or for that matter, if it's what she would want. He's had friendships with women before, though not many, a few older women musicians he wanted to learn from. Mostly, sex got in the way. Either he wanted it, or they did, or both did but not for long. And then, the relationship was blown. It's okay with the girl—she's way too young and anyway, she wants to be his sister. With her, he's already put sex from his mind. But Water is a grown-up, and definitely feminine. So what kind of relationship are they supposed to have? He tries to imagine having sex with a dragon. Pretty kinky all right.

He's still staring at her when she begins to sing to him. Not out loud, and he's glad of that. Any song this hot would alert Baraga's sensors immediately. The beauty of it lays him out. Even the raucous birds have quieted. In the back of his mind, the bizarre thought is born that it's the dragon who should be the big pop star. And he could make it happen, if he could just get her into a studio. . . .

But in his heart, he knows this is music for his ears only. *His* music. Someday he might remember it and write it down, polish it up for public consumption. But for now, he'll just listen.

When she's done, she's still staring at him. He feels awkward, reading expectancy in her bottomless gaze. He wonders why she isn't talking to him, then realizes he's the one who's withholding. He hasn't allowed that inner letting-go that lets her voice into his head alongside the music that seems to invade willy-nilly with a power all its own. He decides he'll wait a while yet, and sing her some of his songs. It'll be like foreplay.

He starts with a lightweight piece, about a man trying to discover if his wife's been unfaithful. It's his usual opener when he plays in the market square. The shoppers don't want anything too serious while they're busy bargaining. It's better when he has his 'board hooked up, though he's done it plenty of times without, since he can't always afford to recharge his battery pack. But he likes the melody even without. It has a certain plaintive comic sweetness to it, especially the chorus, which he's really getting into, singing away with his eyes closed, when he happens to steal a glance at the dragon to see how she's taking it. He nearly stops breathing.

There, right in front of him in his grandpapa's courtyard, in place of a silver-blue dragon, is a pathetic crumb of a man, big-nosed, stooped, a little pudgy, a lovesick nerd casting his droopy eyes about in helpless suspicion exactly as N'Doch had imagined the guy when he wrote the song. He's speechless. He doesn't understand what's happening.

The image dissolves, or rather, re-forms before his very eyes into a silver-blue dragon. The process is not instantaneous and watching it makes him definitely queasy. When she's fully herself and staring at him again, he's still speechless, and without a defense left in the world.

—*Did I get it right?*

It's all he can do to nod.

—*Let's do another one.*

Her voice in his head is light and brisk, oddly familiar.

Not unlike his own, but with an added undertone of Well-it's-about-time-we-got-down-to-business.

"Umm," says N'Doch, mostly to see if he can still produce a human sound.

—It feels pretty good. Hardly tires me out at all.

"Umm," he says again, then clears his throat. "Feels good?"

—You don't have to speak to me out loud, you know.

"Maybe not, but you know, I'm sort of used to it, okay?"

—Certainly. For now.

"Yeah. For now. So, um, then you're not used to doing this, is that what you're telling me?"

—How could I be, without you around to sing the songs?

N'Doch is rendered inarticulate again.

—I knew it from the moment I first breathed air. I've been trying to explain it to you, but you just wouldn't listen.

"Ummm. Oh." He knows now why her voice is familiar. She sounds a lot like his mother used to, before she gave up on him. "Sorry."

—Oh, I understand how hard it is at first. It's hard for me, too, figuring all this out by myself. My brother's not much help, you know.

"Your brother?" Oh, the big guy. "Really? Why not?"

—Well, he's very gifted, of course, and he has a very great heart. But he's still so young and he's like, hopelessly old-fashioned.

Deep inside N'Doch, absurdity finally brims over. He starts to laugh. First it's a chuckle, then a snort, then an outright belly laugh. It's what he's been needing and he lets it build and peak and still go on, like he's gonna laugh his guts out and with them, all the confusion and resentment and tension he's choked back since he first felt the dragon's hold on him. When he's finally done, he's breathless and gasping.

—It's not a joke, you know.

This starts him laughing again, but he's got it under control, barely. "You really are my dragon, aren't you!"

—What else did you think?

"I mean, the way you talk and all."

—What's wrong with it?

"Nothing. Hey, girl, nothing at all. And you know, you are so right. I should have listened to you earlier. Things woulda made a lot more sense!"

Now Water is wearing particularly self-satisfied expression but N'Doch is too relieved to care, now that he sees he's not going to have to talk the old-time talk and walk the old-time walk in order to get along with this critter he's been tied to by no will of his own.

"So. This shape-shifting thing. You wanna try it again?"

—You bet. I need the practice.

He goes with a different song this time, one of his favorites, about a beautiful woman he met once, walking along the beach. She'd just fallen crazy in love with some guy or other, and that's what made her so beautiful, passion that consumed her so much, she could spend an hour with a total stranger, telling him all about it. It was like living poetry. Totally unself-conscious. N'Doch had envied her. He wanted to be in love like that, still does and—as he watches the dragon's animal form slip and change and then reshape itself into the exact image of the woman on the beach—he thinks maybe he is. It won't be like being in love with a real woman, he knows that, but at least he has a clue about what to do with all these crazy feelings he'd been having. He wonders if this is how the girl feels about her dragon.

He lets the song finish, trailing out the last note. He can't help but sing it seductively. The beach woman smiles at him and melts away.

N'Doch grunts and averts his eyes. "I think I'm not gonna watch while you're doing that."

—Why?

"It's . . . well, it's kinda gross when you're in between one thing and another, you know? Can't you do it, like, *faster*?"

—NO. That is, not yet. I'll . . . work on it.

She's a lot less brisk than usual and he sees he's hurt her feelings. "Hey, look, it's awesome that you can do it. It's mega, you know?"

—But you don't like process, only results.

"No, I . . . hmmm." N'Doch decides he'll have to ponder that one for a while. "How long can you hold a shape? Only while I'm singing?"

—*Maybe. I don't know.*

"And you don't get worn out or anything?"

—*Not so far.*

N'Doch nods to himself. Once again, the old codger is proved right. But he's not about to point that out to anyone. "So, tell me. Why do *you* think you're here?"

—*Something terrible is happening.*

"Where? How? O God, o God!" He laughs, 'cause her tone is suddenly so dire and serious. Then it begins to work on him a little. "Wait, you mean, to me? You're here, like, to protect me?"

—*No, jerk. Something much bigger than that. Something much more terrible, if you can imagine such a thing.*

He answers her sarcasm with a snort. "Girl, something terrible is *always* happening. Bombs, wars, plagues, famine, you name it. How much more terrible can it get? And so what? Ain't nothing you can do about it, 'cept move quick and avoid it when you can."

—*No. There is always something you can do. I wouldn't be here otherwise.*

To N'Doch, this is pure blind faith, kind of like religion and just as stupid. Which means there is no point him arguing it with her. But he can't let her off too easy. "So you're here to save the world, huh? If you ask me, which you didn't, you're way too late. But I guess you're not likely to be talked out of trying."

—*No.*

She looks at him, he thinks, a bit sadly, and despite his bravado, he feels a definite pang, a sense he's let her down.

"Hey, listen, you're into that, fine. I got nothing better to do." He's trying to lighten things up a little. "I don't know too much about saving the world, but I can take care of the little things. Like, I got it all figured out how we're gonna get you into the City."

CHAPTER NINETEEN

Papa Djawara insists on giving the girl the privacy of the house, so he and N'Doch bed down on the cooking porch. N'Doch doesn't really mind, though he feels he has to grump a little bit so she sees it's not *his* idea to cater to her. But there are enough mats and cushions to soften the hard slab and the faint coolness of the concrete is actually a relief. And it's a novel and nostalgic pleasure to be able to sleep outside and not really worry too much about having his throat slit in the night. He figures the dogs will kick up a ruckus if anyone comes around. He'd have a dog in town, if it wasn't so hard to keep one fed. He sleeps well into the morning and is waked only by the racket of Djawara among his pots, eagerly preparing the midday meal. He's surrounded by silvery piles of fish.

"They're perfect!" he croons, scaling and gutting and laying out the fillets to dry. "They brought them this morning! Isn't it wonderful? Fish for a month! I've never seen such fish!"

"Baraga's," says N'Doch sourly. "Just hope he hasn't got each one tagged with a tracer."

The prospect of fresh fish cheb has made Djawara mellow. "Now, *that* is paranoid."

"He'd do it. He's really touchy about holding on to what belongs to him." N'Doch scratches, looks around. "So where's the girl?"

"The Lady Erde is inside, looking at books."

"*The Lady Erde?*" N'Doch mimics mincingly.

"Your companion is a baron's daughter, did you know that?"

"Yeah, so she told me. Rich girl. But hey, that was back

in 900 whatever, and she didn't bring any of it with her."
Except of course, one big red stone set in silver. How come
his dragon didn't come with a jewel? "She's no better'n
me now."

Djawara smiles. "Of course not. But if you bear in mind
that she's grown up being treated as if she was, you might
understand her better."

"I don't need to understand her. Long as she doesn't mess
with me, we'll get along fine."

"I see." Djawara lays several thick white fillets in his rush
steamer and fits it on top of his biggest pot. He carries it
carefully out to the cook fire.

"What's she want with books, anyway?" N'Doch calls
after him from the shade of the porch.

Bending over the steamer, Djawara shakes his head. "Are
you always this truculent?"

"No, I . . . c'mon, Papa, I just woke up."

"No wonder your mama didn't mind when you left
home."

N'Doch blinks at him. "I haven't left home."

"Well, that'll be news to your mama."

That slows him down a little. "Yeah? Well, I guess it's
true I haven't been around much." But he's always thought
at least she missed him. Certainly he's liked knowing she
was there if he needed someone to take care of him.

He'd like to discuss this further, but the girl comes out
of the house with a stack of open books in her arms, and
N'Doch doesn't see that his family problems are any of her
business. She greets him politely and sets the books down
on the edge of the concrete, then takes the top one out to
Djawara at the cook fire and starts questioning him about
it. N'Doch sees all the books are open to pictures.

"So, what's she wanna know?"

"Everything."

N'Doch laughs. "Guess we'll be here a while after all."

Djawara studies the page she's held up and answers her
in detail. She nods thoughtfully and goes back for another
book. Djawara says, "She's trying to find her footing in an
unfamiliar world, my boy. Seems she's not had much help
from your direction."

"Yeah? Well, I'm doing the best I can."

"I'm sure you are."

Stung, N'Doch turns away into the house. Already, he's searching instinctively in his head for the dragon. He's pretty sure she'll be glad to see him, even if no one else is.

Waking early, Erde had found herself surrounded by the mage's extensive library. She studied the books from her pallet on one of the cushioned benches. They were not at all like the books she knew and she longed to touch them. But one did not just go fingering a mage's books, it wasn't wise, so she kept her distance until she heard Djawara puttering about outside. Then she went out to greet him respectfully and ask if one of his magical tomes might contain a searching spell to help them locate the Summoner.

The old man laughed gently. "There's no magic in these books, daughter. Only the magic of knowledge." He led her back inside, then picked out a fat one and handed it to her.

Erde received the shiny, colorful object in reverent hands. The bindings were hard and smooth but worn, she could see, with serious and important usage. It did not seem to be made of leather, but it did have a pretty design of leaves embossed in fading gold on the top cover. She glanced at Djawara and when he nodded permission, opened the book carefully. Bright illuminations greeted her, exotic fruits and flowers and trees, full of fine realistic detail without a trace of brushwork. Turning page after page, she sighed in wonder and admiration.

"That's a natural history of the region," he explained. "It describes the local plant life."

Erde nodded. His herbarium, then. Every mage must have an herbarium.

He pulled down another, larger volume. "This one's an atlas. Maps of the world." He flipped through the pages. "Ah, yes, here we go." He took the plant book from her and laid the big atlas in her lap. "This is modern Germany."

At first, the page in front of her was just a maze of colored blocks and lines. She couldn't even recognize it as a map. Then he traced out the long sinuous snaking of the Rhine and asked her to name a few familiar places. The first one they located was Köthen.

The dragon calls him to come join her, she's under the trees, but N'Doch won't go into that place after her. It's just too weird. She says it's too hot and dry in the yard for her, so each stays where they are and N'Doch sits down in the less mysterious shade of the lemon tree and sings his songs to her until Djawara calls him for the midday meal.

When they're seated once more around the communal bowl, with the dragons listening in from the trees to translate and N'Doch's mouth is watering so from the sweet smell of steamed fresh fish in tomato sauce that he can hardly concentrate, Djawara announces that he knows someone in the City who might be able to help them.

It's news to N'Doch that his old uncool grandpapa knows anyone in the City at all.

"It's been many years since we were in touch, but we were good friends then and she was a gifted woman of great promise."

"Good friends, eh, Papa Dja?" N'Doch grins at him, trying for a moment of male bonding.

Djawara smiles. "Not that kind of friends, my boy. Her interests lie elsewhere. At least, they did at the time."

N'Doch nods. He knows what that usually means, but he wonders if the girl does. He wonders if they had women who love women back in 913. He hopes so, 'cause if not, he's not sure he wants to be the one to explain it to her. Like, what if she's that way herself and doesn't know it? He wouldn't want to get caught making any kind of value judgment. Not that he minds it himself or anything. *Chacun à son goût.* He just considers it a waste of good women.

"What is her Gift, Master Djawara?" asks the girl earnestly, and once again N'Doch finds himself wishing she'd lighten up for just one damn moment. He's seen her smile, but he's never heard her laugh like she really meant it.

"She speaks with the spirits and with the wandering shades of the ancestors."

Now, *this* is the Djawara N'Doch remembers. Spooks and spirits and omens and what all.

"Is she a saint?" asks the girl. N'Doch rolls his eyes.

"No, Lady Erde. She is a human woman."

"All the saints were human, Master Djawara, when they lived. But then they were touched by God." Her thin face sobers even further, but N'Doch thinks she looks hopeful. "Is she a witch?"

Djawara chuckles. "I'm not sure what she might be calling herself these days. Then, she was my father's brother's wife's sister, and didn't call herself anything except her name, which is Lealé."

"If it's been so long, how do we find her, Papa Dja?"

The old man looks momentarily bemused. "As it happens, I know where she lives . . . I think." He gets up, crosses to one of the bookshelves and takes down a slim green book. From it, he extracts a postcard. He hands it to N'Doch.

N'Doch reads it, crinkles his brow, then reads it aloud. " 'D.—When the Time comes . . . you see she's put a capital 't' . . . 'this is the place: 913 Rue de l'Eau. Kisses—L.' " He looks up at his grandfather. "Sure this is her?"

"Oh, yes."

"*Water* Street? 913?" He looks at the postmark. "When did you get this?"

"A week ago."

"After how many years?"

"Mmm . . . nearly eleven."

N'Doch lets out a low whistle and cocks an eyebrow at the girl. "Things are getting weirder and weirder."

"Or," says Djawara, "things are exactly as they should be."

CHAPTER TWENTY

Erde worked hard to convince Earth that she needed
at least one more day in the mage's library, to absorb
information that might be critical to their Quest. Then she
spent her best efforts that day trying to get Master Djawara
to accompany them to the City.

He talked with her tirelessly, while N'Doch practiced
shape-changing with Water. He told her everything he
could about the new world she'd come to, but refused again
and again to go with them. She even tried tears—he remained sympathetic but steadfast.

"It is not my journey." Djawara tossed the cushions from
one of the benches and lifted the lid. Inside was a riot of
pattern and color: piles and piles of neatly folded fabric.
"It is your journey and dragons' only. Others can and will
help you along the way, but they cannot go along. Let's
see now . . ." He lifted out a pile and sat with it in his lap.

"But Master Djawara, it's so much easier with you
around!" Erde flopped down beside him girlishly, but
somehow the fact that, even sitting, she was taller than he
was undermined the effect.

"Oh, he'll come around. He's a good boy. You'll see."
His round face was smooth and calm as he sorted through
the fabric, pulled out a few brightly printed bundles and
set them aside. "Did you ever think that perhaps you lost
your voice for a reason?"

He knew her whole story by now, and it was hard to get
around him. Still, Erde was embarrassed that he'd guessed
so easily what she thought was so difficult. "No, I lost my
voice because . . ."

"I know, I know, child. Your heart was broken. But think about it a little further. Maybe you were going to need to know how to communicate under difficult circumstances."

Erde brightened. "You mean, it was . . . preordained?"

"A big word. Perhaps too big, but . . ." Djawara nodded and shrugged. "Who knows about such things, eh? Only the gods."

She knew that she should think of the mage as a dangerous heretic because he always spoke of the Deity in plural terms. More than one God meant pagans and idolaters, at least in the Bible. But Djawara's gods and goddesses sounded rather more approachable than the stern Jehovah of the Christian Church. For one thing, you didn't need a priest every time you wanted to talk to them, and Erde had no cause to love priests after her recent experience with Brother Guillemo. And saying something was "God's will" implied being subject to arbitrary and personal whim, like the King's will or her father's. Not that King Otto's will was ever arbitrary, but her father's certainly was. "Preordained" made things sound much more orderly and under control.

So, if it was important to the Quest that she put the skills learned through two months of being voiceless to work on getting through to N'Doch, she would accept that burden. The mage had explained that certain concepts and ideals that she grew up with, such as Honor or Duty, no longer had much currency. (On the other hand, he pointed out, being a woman no longer meant being the chattel of your closest male relative, so some of the changes over the years were positive.) The main thing was, she must learn to take nothing for granted. N'Doch would truly dedicate himself to the Quest only when he decided he wanted to.

"I understand now, Master Djawara. And though it certainly would be more pleasant if you did come, I accept that you cannot. You are very wise."

"And you, child, are a shameless flatterer. Now, look in the book and see if you can make this piece of cloth look like the picture when you wrap it around yourself."

She shook out the length he handed her and gave a soft gasp of admiration. The fabric was soft, with a graceful drape, and of a deep indigo printed with cream and bur-

gundy. She'd never been allowed to wear such rich colors
as a child. "It's beautiful! Are they snakes with wings? I
can't quite tell."

"I don't know. Perhaps they are dragons. Try it on."

She gave it a few serious tries and thought she was just
getting the knack of it when she head N'Doch laughing
from the doorway.

"Papa Dja, when I said we oughta get her some real
clothes, I didn't mean dress her up like some hick from
the villages!"

Djawara stood back from Erde at arm's length. "Why, I
think she looks wonderful! This was your grandmama's
best."

"Yeah, Papa D., it's cool and historical and all that,
y'know, but . . ."

"And I thought it would make sense if she dressed like
a villager, so the City people won't be surprised when she
doesn't behave like they do."

Erde watched N'Doch rein in his mockery. More gently,
he said, "But Papa, she's a white girl. She ain't gonna
fool nobody."

"Oh."

Even Erde had to smile. The old mage had explained to
her about the different races of humans and how it mattered to some people what color your skin was. But in her
case, he seemed not to have noticed, or at least to have
momentarily forgotten. Now he pursed his lips, fussed a
little with the folds of the material and said, "Well, I guess
you're right. She would be rather an anomaly."

N'Doch let go a sigh of relief. "Yeah. I thought maybe
let her go like a tourist—Eurotrash, y'know? Which is why
she only speaks German. There are still a few brave ones
coming around, especially in the City. They're mostly really
rich folk, but she should know how to play that role all
right, eh? We'll just say she's slumming. Granmama mus-
t've had some town clothes, yeah?"

Djawara nodded and gave the lustrous fabric a final or-
ganizing pat. "A shame, really. It looks so good on her."

N'Doch is not really happy with what they've dug up for
her to wear. He lays it all out in the sun on the back porch:
thirty-year-old jeans with no decent patches and only four

pockets, and a T-shirt so uncool it actually has sleeves and something written on it. But he figures they can barter this for something less embarrassing when they get to the City. The girl doesn't seem to realize how dumb she's gonna look, truly *flat*, but at least it's more in step than what she was wearing before. He can see she likes the idea of wearing pants—apparently women didn't do that in her day. She rejects the sensible open sandals that Djawara offers her, insisting on keeping her soft, calf-high boots. N'Doch lets her. A tourist from the colder (but not so much, these days) North might wear something silly like that without knowing any better.

"As long as you look like you pay *some* attention to your image. Otherwise, you'll really stick out." He sends her inside to try it all on.

"Surely no one can afford to worry about such trifles any more," Djawara murmurs.

"Trifles? Cool has no price, Papa."

But in fact, when the girl comes back outside with the whole getup on, N'Doch thinks she looks pretty good. The jeans fit her well. He can see she's got a shape to her after all. He may be spending more time than he's counted on just keeping the guys off of her. He glances down at his own naked torso and ragged shorts.

"Um . . . Papa Dja? You got anything I could wear?"

They settle on one of Djawara's ankle-length tunics, a light blue one he says he doesn't wear any more. On N'Doch, it comes to just below his knees, but the girl seems relieved when he puts it on.

"Oh, my, that looks very good on you, N'Doch."

Already, he's itching and feeling confined. "I'm gonna hate this."

But he has to admit, it'll help him blend better with the day-to-day crowds. For the first time in his life, anonymity sounds like a good idea.

The dragons are eager. The blue one is at the end of her patience, which, N'Doch is beginning to suspect, is never very long to start with. But he likes that about her. He's impatient, too, except when it comes to making his music. Like now, he's as ready as he's gonna be, and he's been hearing copters in the air again, Papa Dja says more often than usual, so maybe they better get gone before they get the old man into trouble he didn't start.

Except, in a way, he did. But N'Doch's not going into that again, not now at any rate.

The girl has told him about this big shed kind of place she hid out in back in her time, and he thinks it's not a bad idea to start them out in the old industrial sector.

"There's lots of empty buildings out there," he explains. "Big old factories and warehouses, all closed down."

Djawara clucks sadly. "It was a thriving district in my day."

"Yeah, well, that was before they started getting everything from China and Brazil. It's one big junkyard now. Our main problem'll be finding a big enough place that don't already belong to squatters. Papa, you got anything around by way of weaponry?"

Djawara sits up a little taller. "Only my cooking knives, my boy."

This is what N'Doch has expected, but he thought he'd try anyway. "Never mind. I'll manage. But here's the hard one. You got any money?"

"You mean, cash?"

"Yeah. Only, no paper. It's worthless, y'know?"

Djawara disappears inside for a while and comes back with a small handful of coins.

N'Doch looks them over. "Not a bad stash. I know it'll be hard for you. Just give us what you can."

"It won't be hard on me. Any kind of cash is useless out here these days. If you can't eat it, drink it, or wear it, it isn't worth anything to anybody."

"Okay." N'Doch holds out his hand, then says, "No. Give 'em to her. She'll keep 'em for emergencies. So. I guess that's it. We'll be on our way now."

He doesn't really want to leave the cool shade of the lemon tree. The night before, as he lay on the cooking porch awaiting sleep, he realized that it'd been an hour, maybe even two, since he'd last scanned for copters, or reflexively searched the shadows for the lurking knife. A whole hour of feeling safe enough not to listen—what a luxury! The thought came to him, just before he dropped off, that he could live out here and be happy enough. Certainly he'd be healthier, helping the old guy dig and carry water for the vegetables, hunting with the dogs in the evenings out in the bush. But that thought was drowned out instantly by the habitual panic. Out here, he'd be nothing, everyone would forget about him, no big recording contract. He'd never be famous. He'd sing his songs, but no one would ever hear them, 'cept one old man and a few washed out villagers.

No, it was better to be going to the City. Life was in the City.

But, he told himself, when this dragon thing was over, he'd make sure to come visit Papa Djawara more often.

CHAPTER TWENTY-ONE

They waited until midnight, then bade farewell to Master Djawara and went on to the City.

Erde thought it oddly familiar, to be dropped precipitously into the dark corridors of another strange town, so familiar that she expected (without reason) the ice and cold of the brickyard in Erfurt. Instead, the City was hotter than any place so far. There was a roaring all around them, like the rush of great winds or falling torrents, and the air smelled of . . . Erde's only thought was that it smelled like Death.

Earth coughed, a raw convulsive sound. Erde felt Water warning them to silence. She pressed a little closer to her dragon and stroked his cheek.

—*It smells like our dreams.*

—*Yes, Dragon. It surely does.*

N'Doch sniffed, peered into the blackness, and murmured, "Well, folks, the honeymoon is over."

He's chosen the big parking lot beside the derelict rubber factory. He figures they can land two dragons there without running into anything, and also, it's likely to be deserted at this time of night. There's hardly enough working cars or trucks left in the City to fill up a lot this size, and those that there are, won't be out here in the Wedge.

And he's guessed right. The wide stretch of broken tarmac is clear of anything but dried weeds and rubble, with a few burned-out wrecks along the periphery. He'll steer clear of those: even charred black, a truck cab is good cover for a single squatter, armed and dangerous. The long low ware-

houses are scattered, this far out. Lots of open space between. Plenty of copters prowling the skies, but they're all
off a ways, over where he can see streetlights, where the
buildings get closer together, in town toward the point of
the pie-slice shape that gives this neighborhood its name.
And past that, the broken profile of Downtown spreads its
colored glow on the horizon as if the whole town is on fire.
And sometimes it is, N'Doch reflects sourly.

But power to the Wedge was turned off long ago, like
with most of the outlying sectors. Not enough of it to go
around any more. N'Doch is used to moving around his
own town on the blackest nights, but even he is hesitant
about charging off into the unlit streets of the City.

"Man, it's dark out here," he mutters.

—I can help, you know.

"Yeah? What d'ya have in mind?"

Water's tone is faintly superior, but N'Doch backs off his
irritation, since he's found she can usually deliver on what
she promises, and at the moment, he needs all the help he
can get. She doesn't answer him right off. Instead, he feels
this strange sensation, like she's caught hold of him from
behind his eyeballs.

"Yow." It doesn't hurt exactly, but for a moment, he's
got double vision. He must have staggered, 'cause he's
stumbling into the girl, and she's grabbing his arm for
support.

"Yow," he says again, then he and the dragon are in sync
and he can see with a clarity that takes his breath away,
like in broad daylight except it's all black and white, and
all the surfaces of things seem to be alive with tiny wormlike
movements. N'Doch knows he hasn't chewed or smoked
anything lately, and the moon didn't just come out all of a
sudden. Besides, he's pretty sure it has nothing to do with
his eyes. It's like he's *hearing* the shapes and spaces around
him: the dragons, the girl, the nearby hulk of the rubber
factory with every broken window and cracked cinder block
picked out in awesome detail. He makes himself start
breathing again.

"Wow. Radical. It's like . . . *sonarvision!*"

"N'Doch, are you well?" asks the girl.

"Yeah, fine. Just had my eyeballs turned inside out,
that's all."

"I beg your pardon?"

"The dragon . . . Water . . . she . . . Hey, can your guy, like, you know, make you hear like your own ears never could?"

"No." She thinks for a moment. "But he teaches me the scents of things that I never even knew had smells."

"Huh. Like Papa Dja used to say about his dogs: They read the air and the ground like he reads his books. But you can't, like, see in the dark?"

"Oh, no—right now I'm as blind as you are."

"But I'm not, you see. This critter has ears like Baraga's spy-eyes."

"You mean, Water?"

"She can turn sounds into images, and transmit 'em right to my eyes. So I *can* see in the dark. Cool, huh?"

"That could be very useful."

N'Doch laughs, looks at her, then laughs again. She's serious. He can't believe this girl's total lack of irony. "Well, yeah, it could. Okay, first thing is, find us a proper hidey-hole."

"Shouldn't we go in search of the Mage's friend while it's still dark?"

"Safe digs first, girl. Wandering around the City at night is asking for it unless there're a lot more of you or you're a whole lot better armed than we are."

"But in the light, we will be seen."

"In the light, we'll blend into the crowds, or at least, that's the idea. Besides, Mme. Lealé wouldn't take well to us banging on her door in the middle of the night. In the City, no one goes out after dark, girl, unless they've got trouble in mind."

With his new sonarvision, N'Doch cases the outside of the rubber plant, looking for squatter-sign: newly boarded-up doorways or broken windows conveniently shaded with tarps. The really dumb ones, or sometimes a family that's newly homeless, make the mistake of letting some lantern-light show or leaving a telltale bit of clothing hanging out of a window to dry. N'Doch doesn't detect any of that, but he does spot a heap of recently dumped rubble just below an open shaftway a few stories up. He snorts softly and shakes his head. Whoever's got the factory is careful, but not careful enough.

"Let's move on," he whispers. They haven't been absolutely silent. They may have been spotted already, and they're carrying valuable food and water that he doesn't want to lose this early in the game. "This way."

He leads them away from the factory, through the dry weeds and shattered asphalt. He's thinking of a place he crashed at once, with a guy he knows won't be there unless he's come back from the dead. It took some getting into then, but once you did, it was big inside and pretty secure. It's not far, so he heads that way. The girl is stumbling on the asphalt chunks, rattling the scattered litter of metal shards. She slows, knowing she's making too much noise, but she doesn't have his magic new Sonarvision—he thinks of it with a capital "S" now, like some new product he's invented—so he takes her hand and guides her through the worst of it. The dragons, he notices, move along in utter silence. He doesn't even bother to ask how they manage that one. He's beginning to take dragon miracles pretty much for granted.

They pass a cluster of collapsed warehouses, no sign of habitation. He recalls just in time that there's a particularly nasty toxics dump up ahead. One drawback of his new vision: it doesn't help him read caution signs in the dark, unless the print has dimension off the surface. Besides, he's willing to bet there aren't any signs. The government-of-the-moment is too busy staying in control to worry about the public welfare. He takes a detour around the site, then continues onward.

Now and then, one of the snooping copters swings a little too close by for comfort, and N'Doch makes everyone duck and hide, just in case. But since he's got them moving so slow and careful, in the interest of silence, he also takes the opportunity to use his Sonarvision to scout for salvage. He sees everything's been pretty much picked over already, and the sigh comes up from somewhere deep without his even knowing. He can never quite let go of that old scavenger's dream—even though he knows it's unrealistic—that some day he'll light upon a huge and entirely unspoiled cache of prime bartering goods. Then his fortune'll be made, and he can buy those big amps and that new keyboard that'll make him a star.

Farther along, he catches a big whiff of the dead smell,

over to the left, and leads his gang away from it. If it was light and he was alone, he might investigate, just see if anyone's been along yet to shake down the stiff. He hates doing it, but what's dead is dead, he figures, and he's turned up some valuable stuff that way. Tonight, however, he'll move on.

The girl's caught the scent, too. Her grip on his hand, light and impersonal, tightens. "Is it . . . Plague?"

"Which plague's that? AIDS? Cholera? Typhus? Bubonic?"

"Are there so many? What have the people done to make God so angry with them?"

N'Doch snorts. "God hasn't anything to do with it."

"But the Plague is God's punishment, N'Doch."

He stops short. Even before he opens his mouth, he knows his response is over the top, and some part of him wonders why. He grips the girl's shoulders, not kindly this time, and it's all he can do to keep from shouting. "Girl, let's get this straight: Diseases come from germs, not some god idea. This ain't 913 and even if there was a god then, he sure ain't here now unless he's a world-class sadist!" He can see, with his hearing eyes, that she's gazing at him astonished, a little frightened. Is it him she's scared of, or what he's saying? He gets hold of himself, lets her go, then dusts her shoulders off in comic apology. But he doubts she'll buy it as only a joke. "You believe in God, huh?"

She nods mutely, as if she can't imagine an alternative.

"Well, sorry," he murmurs. "I just hate listening to that god stuff. I grew up with the imams and the mullahs and the ayatollahs throwing their weight around, and it didn't do nobody any good but them, far as I could see. Lining their pockets, just like everyone else, 'cept they expect to be treated special."

Soberly, she nods, like she understands him now. "God is not always well represented by his representatives on Earth." She takes his hand conciliatorily. "But we don't ever have to talk about God if you don't want to."

N'Doch sees this is as far as he's going to get with this issue for now unless he wants a raging argument on his hands, which would likely attract all sorts of unwanted attention from the shadows around them. "Fine," he says. "This way."

The place they finally come to is an old peanut processing plant that fell in on itself after being gutted by fire. N'Doch suspects it wasn't very well built to begin with, but apparently the basement was, because it's still intact, beneath a protective and concealing layer of charred steel and construction debris. He locates the entrance, a narrow fire stair covered up with the same battered sheet of corrugated metal he recalls from before, lying there as if thoughtlessly tossed aside. *Man,* he thinks, *hide in plain sight. It sure seems to work. Course there could still be somebody down there, as clever as me. . . .*

He crouches a distance from the concealed stair, pondering his next move.

—*There is nobody down there.*

He starts, remembers he's not alone in his mind anymore. "How do you know?"

—*Easy. If there were, I could hear their breathing and the beating of their heart. Oh, and my brother wishes me to add: he could smell them.*

"You're sure of this, now. . . ."

—*Of course I am! Why say so otherwise?*

Hasn't she ever heard of bravado? Maybe dragons don't need any ego boosting. Anyway, he decides he'll trust her, on the basis of what her awesome hearing has managed already. He grasps the metal sheet and slides it to one side as quietly as possible. A receding darkness yawns beneath, but the air flowing up out of the hole doesn't smell any worse than might be expected.

"Doesn't seem like anything's died down there recently," he mutters. "I'll give it a try."

—*You will lose your night sight down there.*

"Yeah? How come?"

—*What I can't see, you can't see.*

He'd swear the blue dragon is smirking at him. "Fine. I'll do it blind."

"Wait," says the girl. She fishes in her pack and unwraps a squat stub of candle. She offers it to him as if it was edible.

"Way to go, girl," N'Doch crows softly, reaching into his

own pack. He's got plenty of matches but nothing to light. "What a team."

Clutching the candle stub, he eases himself into the hole. The girl makes a sign to follow, but he waves her back. It's tricky going. The steps are crumbly with broken concrete gravel. He doesn't shift his weight onto his leading leg until he's very sure of his footing. He stops at the end of the first flight, where the stair takes a turn and the dragon will lose the line of sight. His head is below ground level, so he risks the brief flare of the match through his cupped hands and lights the candle. The stained cinder block walls close in around him. The stair feels suddenly airless, narrower in light than it did with his sonarvision. He sniffs carefully but smells only the usual metallic tang. With his free hand, he reaches for his switchblade.

It gets cooler as he descends the long stair. At the bottom, the smashed-in fire door has been yanked half off its hinges. N'Doch slips through the opening and his footsteps start to throw back echoes. His rat phobia is sending warning tingles up his spine, but he reminds himself how the blue dragon has already cured him of one major killer bug, so she can probably handle a rat bite, even a sick one. Still, he listens real hard, sure he's heard a quick scuttle and rush off in the corners of the basement. He holds the candle high and moves into the cavernous interior, testing the musty, still air as he goes. The dusty hulks of boilers and air-conditioning units crowd along the walls like parked cars. A maze of pipes and ducting, bristly with char, hangs in the darkness above his head. Despite being twenty feet underground, he feels vulnerable here. But he recalls a smaller storage room, dry and empty, across the basement somewhere to the right. If he recalls it right, it has some kind of grating that lets in air.

Again he hears a rustling sound. He whirls, candle outstretched in one hand, switchblade in the other. The flame catches in something bright, reflective, quickly moving, like a weapon or someone's eyes. Then it's gone. Too tall for a rat, too short for a man. Now he hears nothing but the rush of blood and adrenaline in his own ears. He's getting the real creeps now. He's got to find that room and call the dragons down. He steels himself and turns away, though he feels the itch at his back like he's being watched. He locates the room, pretty much where he remembered. At the open doorway, he sniffs again, real cautiously: ash, stale machine oil, a faint sour tinge, nothing rotting. He's worried that his fantasies will have enlarged and improved this hidey-hole unreasonably, but it is as he'd hoped—a big cement rectangle with one lockable door, a high ceiling, a dry coolish floor, and a faint drift of air past him at the door toward the invisible outlet above. The place has been cleaned out and appreciated by at least one man he knows. He wonders if anyone found it since Habbim died. He studies it carefully, then lets the dragon into his mind so she can transmit the image to the big guy. With her there, he feels a little bit steadier.

—I could have shifted and come with you, if you'd asked me. You were never in danger.

"Yeah?" His voice startles him, erupting into the silence. "I don't know. I'm sure there's something down here."

—Impossible.

"I dunno. . . ."

The two dragons and the girl wink into existence around him. N'Doch lets out a breath he didn't know he was holding.

"What do you think is down here?" asks the girl.

Now his fear embarrasses him. "Oh, nothing. Y'know, an animal or something."

This doesn't seem to bother her too much. She shudders and shrugs like she's used to having that sort of trouble around. But N'Doch knows there's hardly any animals left in the City except rats and men. Fact is, he's not sure what it could have been, but he's pretty sure he didn't imagine it.

—Yes. You are right. Something was here.

"You mean, it was here just now and it left? How'd it get out? There used to be only one way into here."

—Well, it's gone now, whatever it was.

The dragon seems to think that should be the end of it, but N'Doch is glad this hidey-hole has a lockable door. Meanwhile, they might as well get bedded down. He sees the girl already looking around for her spot.

"You take the far corner," he says, gearing up for an argument. But she's cool with that, and he relaxes. He stopped running with gangs once he became a teenager, so he's not much used to moving about in groups. He'll feel better if he can control the layout. But he does let the dragons scope out their own territory. "I'll hang here by the door." He closes it and locks it, though it makes him feel more trapped than safe. Then, to the right of it, where the door can't swing against him if somebody bashes it in, he tosses down his pack. "Okay, rest up. Come morning, we'll go looking for Lealé."

He settles himself on the concrete with his pack for a pillow, and blows out the candle. Darkness encloses him like a shroud. The dragon must be asleep already. He knows she's there, not ten feet from him, but he still loses faith in her existence if he can't actually see her. He'd hate to sound like some little kid whining in the night, so he figures it's time he tried the mind-calling thing the girl talks about. She says you just shape your thought like an arrow and send it. N'Doch wonders if she's seen a real arrow. Maybe she has. Maybe they still use such things back in 913. He feels himself drifting and pulls himself back.

—*Dragon? Hey, Dragon! You there?*

—**Of course I'm here. Where did you think I was?**

—*No, I knew you were here, but I, like, called you, y'know?*

—**Yes . . . ?**

—*Well, y'know, I never did that before, so I . . .*

—**You woke me up.**

N'Doch is miffed. She didn't congratulate him or anything. It was pretty easy, he has to admit, but she could have at least noticed.

—*Okay. Got that. Now, since you're awake, you sure you'd know if there was something alive down here?*

—**Absolutely.**

—*You'd, like, smell it or something?*

—**Or hear it.**

—*What if it wasn't making any noise?*

—**I'd hear it living. Go to sleep.**

He tries to, but just before he does, he hears the rustle again, muffled this time, like there's something moving about out in the main basement. He gets up and checks the door, which is latched and sturdy. But then, because he's come to trust the dragon's word on things, no matter if he questions her as if he doesn't, he finds himself thinking, well, then, maybe whatever's out there isn't technically *alive*. . . .

And that keeps him awake for way longer than he likes.

CHAPTER TWENTY-TWO

Erde lay awake for a while, tucked against Earth's fore-leg, listening to the deep bellows-rush of his breathing, always more like a movement of air than an actual sound. Usually it lulled her, but tonight it seemed less soothing. She decided he was not asleep after all, only pretending to be, and not doing a very good job. *In fact,* she thought, *none of us is asleep. That's why the room feels so . . . full.* Probably they were all thinking about the next day and what it would bring. She had heard her father's knights use the same tone the night before a battle that N'Doch used when he talked about going into the City.

—*Dragon? Are you sleep?*

—**No.**

—*I didn't think so. Me neither.*

—**Good. That means you're not talking in your sleep.**

—*Do I?*

—**You used to, when you thought you'd lost your voice.**

—*But I did lose my voice.*

—**You didn't lose it. You just couldn't find it.**

—*Oh, really? And tell me, Dragon, do you know how many angels can dance on the head of a pin?*

—**What's an angel?**

—*What's an . . . well, angels are . . . never mind. It's an expression. Alla used to say that to me when I continued an argument to too fine a point.*

—**It's not too fine a point if you think about it. You actually did have your voice all along. You just couldn't use it, except when you were asleep and didn't know any better.**

—Now, Dragon, I did not lose my voice on purpose.

—Purpose is a complex thing to define, is it not?

—You sound like Master Djawara. He said . . . Wait. Did you hear that?

Erde stiffened against him, listening.

—What?

—Do you smell anything out there?

—Out where?

—Out there, in the bigger part of the cave.

Earth's body stilled. His breathing quickened. Erde waited while he did his search.

—No. I smell nothing but unliving smells. Fire smells and the smell of the forge. And the smell of those things the boy calls machines.

N'Doch and Master Djawara had explained about "machines," but Erde thought it sounded like alchemy all the same: burning certain precious substances in order to make the inanimate move. Just as the thing they named "electricity" was clearly strong air magic: calling down invisible power from the sky.

—I'm sure I heard something. Remember, your sister said . . .

—She said something had been there and was not now. I think you are tired and should go to sleep.

—Well, I'll try.

And she did, for a while, but she failed.

—Dragon?

—Mmmm?

—Have you heard the Summoner at all since we left Deep Moor?

This time, she detected anxiety in his reply and instantly regretted the question.

—I have heard nothing. I have waited and listened. Perhaps I am listening too hard.

—Don't worry. I'm sure we're on the right path. Don't you agree?

—I am eager to find Mistress Lealé.

—So am I.

—Good night.

—Good night, Dragon.

Finally, having shared her doubts, Erde fell asleep. Almost immediately, she was dreaming.

She was home again, not home at Tor Alte but in her home time, in the chill mud and sleeting rain of a battlefield. It was early evening. From her vantage on a low hill, she could see the men and the carts moving about, hurrying to pick up the dead and the wounded before dark, butchering the dead horses to feed what was left of the armies.

In her waking life, Erde had never been to a battlefield, had certainly never seen so many dead in one place or had to listen to the moans of the dying. Their agonies filled her ears. The rutted mud was black with their blood. She wanted to turn away, but the dream would not let her.

Now a man stood in front of her on the hill. The same blood and mud stained his silken tunic and spattered his fine mail. A boy in blue-and-yellow livery raced up with linens and a steaming pitcher, and the man bent to scrub the mud and blood from his face and beard. This time, Erde was unsurprised to recognize Adolphus of Köthen, but she was sorry to see, when he turned toward her, how haggard he looked, how sad and bitter. She had assumed a warrior enjoyed fighting. Again, she thought he would speak to her, as his angry glance was so direct, but again, he looked past her and called out to someone farther along the hill. She turned and saw her father, equally battle-worn, standing beside two of his vassal barons, with a tattered parchment map stretched out between them.

In the dream, she understood she was seeing her father as Köthen saw him: florid, a bit too pudgy for a true fighting man, overly proud of his mane of prematurely silver hair, brave enough but not very bright. She understood also now that Köthen was using her father to further his own ends, but that he was no longer sure that he was getting the best of the exchange.

An early darkness was falling, thick with cold mist and cloud. Köthen signaled the boy to pour more heated water into his cupped hands. He drenched his face and beard, scrubbed hard, rinsed again, and toweled off. Out on the plain, the laden carts drew together, conferred, then split off in two directions, one group across the hill where Erde stood, the other up the longer slope on the far side of the field. Following Köthen's pensive glance, she picked out a scattering of men and horses, one flying the royal standard, another the deep red of the King's Knights.

That red—the familiar red of Hal's leather jerkin, worn despite all dangers to attest to his unswerving loyalty to the King. Seeing it, Erde sensed emotion stirring, and saw how cruelly dispassionate she was in this dream, as if she had left all feeling behind to make this journey back to where the battle had finally been joined between the King's armies and the forces of the usurpers. Men had fought and died, and Erde did not know if Hal or Rainer or King Otto himself still lived. She wished she stood on the opposite hill, instead of with her father and Köthen. At least she would know the worst. But then, she realized, she'd be wondering about Köthen.

Why was this man so often in her dreams? Not only dreaming about him, but almost as if she was him. She turned back to watch as he tossed the bloodied, dirty linen to the boy.

"See to my lord of Alte, that's a good lad."

The boy bowed and hurried off toward the gathered barons. Köthen followed more slowly. Erde's father looked up as Köthen approached. He waved away the boy with the water and lifted a corner of the map to jab a finger at it.

"What's left of them will fall back and join Otto's main force somewhere around here, I figure."

Köthen nodded tightly. "Peasants. Farmers. Tradespeople. Hardly a fair contest, wouldn't you say, my lord?"

"Ah, but if we meet up with nothing more than peasants, we should catch up with the King in three days' time, and that should be that." He let the corner drop and took Köthen's elbow, drawing him aside. Köthen eased out of his grasp but moved with him to avoid insult. "The good brother has his men spreading rumors in the villages," Erde's father continued quietly. "Once Otto is dead, Prince Carl can be accused of trafficking with witches, and gotten out of your way."

Köthen shook his head. "No. Call him off. I don't want the boy harmed. He shouldn't have to pay for his father's mistakes."

"Brother Guillemo says no bishop will crown you King while Otto's heir lives. The people, at least, require a semblance of legitimacy."

"That foul priest does love the fire." Köthen's jaw tightened. "No, von Alte, there'll be no burning the Prince.

House arrest will do fine. Carl doesn't want to be King anyway. If he did, I'd put him on the throne and rule as his regent. Call Guillemo off."

"Brother Guillemo is not mine to call off, even if I might wish it otherwise. You know that as well as I do." Von Alte took a long look at the younger man before continuing. "A little late for scruples, my lord of Köthen, is it not?"

"Never too late, my lord of Alte. There'll be no burning."

Von Alte's glance slipped aside. "You may not have the say on that, my lord. . . ."

"And why is that?"

Erde's father turned, called out to the men behind him. "Bessen! Get over here and report to Baron Köthen what you heard just now."

A skinny, scrub-bearded younger knight hurried toward them. "Concerning what, my lord?"

"Concerning Prince Carl."

The man's worry lines deepened. "Right. The Prince." He faced Köthen breathlessly and bowed.

"Come on, Bessen, out with it," growled Köthen.

"An escape attempt, my lord. This morning, while you were showing yourself so valiantly on the field . . ."

"An 'escape'? As you may recall, Bessen, the Prince is a guest in my tent, free to come and go."

"As long as he doesn't go very far," put in von Alte.

Bessen nodded eagerly. "And that's just it, my lord. The Prince took advantage of your . . . generosity and tried to flee. The White Brothers foiled his attempt and brought him back."

Köthen lunged at him, grabbing huge fistfuls of his tunic. "What have they done? Is he alive?"

Bessen cringed in his grasp. "Of course, my lord baron. The Prince is safe in Brother Guillemo's custody."

Köthen shook him like a rag doll. "SAFE? You call that safe?"

Von Alte levered an arm between the two men, to pry them apart. "Get a hold of yourself, Köthen. Poor Bessen's only the news bearer."

"And that's what I'm surrounded with! Everyone reports! No one sees anything! Yet what remarkable detail they all bring to their accounts!" Köthen shoved Bessen away in disgust, then tugged his tunic straight. "My lords will excuse me while I go rescue Prince Carl from his 'rescuers.' "

"You might want to reconsider that," said von Alte.

Köthen turned back sharply ."I beg your pardon?"

"The good brother thinks the Prince is better off in his hands. You had better go well-armed and well-accompanied if you think to change his mind."

Erde felt rather than saw rage boil up inside Baron Köthen. She also sensed how well he controlled it—unlike her father, who would have raved and thrown things. Köthen's rage spoke only through a certain stiffening of his spine, a narrowing of his glance. He stared at von Alte a moment, then nodded brusquely. "I see. So that's how it is."

"That's how it is." Though her father's reply sounded smug, Erde read the terror in his eyes. The awful priest still held him in thrall.

And then she was drifting away from them, as if someone was tugging on her arm. Other voices were calling her. She resisted, wanting to hear what Köthen said before he turned on his heel and stalked away. The voices, insistent, urgent, drowned out his reply. She wanted to stay to find out what would happen to Prince Carl. She wanted to know if Hal was all right. She . . .

"Wake up, girl!"

. . . was aware of her body again. Someone was shaking her, hard. She didn't want to come back to the heat and darkness.

"C'mon, now, wake up!"

—Breathe! You must breathe! You cannot leave now!

Erde let go of Köthen and her father, let herself relax, let her chest heave to draw in the hot, smelly air. It made her cough.

"There she goes. She's okay. She's awake now." Strong hands hauled her up into a sitting position. "Whadda ya say, girl? You awake?"

—Are you returned, Lady Erde?

—I am here, dragon.

Erde flexed her hands, rubbed her face. Her body tingled, as if the whole of it had gone dead numb and was reawakening. N'Doch leaned over her, a darker shadow in darkness softened by the faintest scatter of light filtering down from above. She gripped his arm to steady herself. "I was somewhere else."

His laugh was relieved. "I'll say you were."

"I went home."

—You went there without me. Do not do it again.

That's what was so strange, Erde realized. She and the dragon had always shared their dreams since they'd been together, but not these recent ones of home and her father and Baron Köthen.

—It just . . . happened. How will I prevent it, unless I stay awake?

—I will keep watch. It is the priest who draws you.

"No!" she cried out, aloud.

N'Doch jerked his arm away. "You talking to him or me?"

—Yes. I believe this is so. My sister agrees.

—But how, why *would he do that?*

—How, I do not know. Why, because he seeks to separate and thereby weaken us. He is learning new powers. As ours grow, so do his. But I am alerted now, and will keep watch.

Now the waking, fetid darkness would be a sanctuary from the perils of her dreams. Erde slumped in dismay and felt N'Doch watching her.

"You with us, girl? You all right? It's time we got moving."

"I am fine, N'Doch. Thank you." But when she got to her feet, it was a struggle. The dream had left her weakened and trembling. "Will we break our fast before we go?"

N'Doch laughed.

"Yeah, we'll eat up, for sure. Don't want to be carrying food around in the City, not where anyone can see it, at least."

N'Doch breaks out the water and some of the fish and vegetables that Djawara packed up for them. He's hoping to actually buy bread and cheese with the cash the old man's laid on him. And wouldn't some coffee be radical. . . ?

It might be the dimness of the light falling through the grating above, but it strikes him that the girl is looking really flat out right now. He hands her an extra section of cucumber. "You wanna stay here, like, rest? Let me scout out Lealé?"

"No!" she comes back fast, like she doesn't want to miss this trip for anything. But he's worried now that she might slow him down.

"Won't he, y'know, be lonely?"

It's a nice try, but it doesn't work. She lays a caressing palm on the big guy's flank. "He will be with me, even while he's here."

He understands that she likes that part, the constant lurking presence that makes him feel crowded. "Hunh. Okay. Ready, then?"

She nods, a little too brightly to be convincing. He turns to the blue dragon. "What about you? All set to boogie?"

—Remind me.

N'Doch chuckles. "Sure thing, girlfriend. Here we go, then." He does a few soft bars of the song they've agreed on.

—More.

"You forgetful or what?"

—I like listening to you.

The pleasure this brings surprises him. But hey, why not? An audience is an audience. He sings a bit more, starts to get into it, and finishes the verse. He's moving on to the chorus when he spots the girl gazing at him in wonder and admiration. He finishes the chorus directly to her, then grins and sketches out a little bow.

She claps her hands, delighted. "Why, you sing very well, N'Doch! Like a true bard!"

"A *bard,* huh? You mean, like one of those guys who used to go around the place singing about Robin Hood?"

She looks sort of blank, but she nods. "Sometimes the bards do travel, yes, if the weather's good and the roads are passable. Mostly, they sit by the kitchen hearth and make up songs about doomed lovers and great battles, at least that's what my grandmama's bard Cronke did. And then he'd sing them for her in the great-hall on feast days. His songs always made me sad, though."

N'Doch finds himself smiling. The picture is there in his mind, and he understands he's getting it from her through the dragons—like a window opening onto the past. He *sees* the long room, hazed with smoke from the great stone fire-place that takes up one whole wall. He feels the need to stoop away from the low-slung ceiling beams, dark and rough and as big around as his thigh. Women in long skirts are moving about in the dim light, hauling pots and kneading dough, and an old man sits in a corner, scrunched up over a stringed instrument that N'Doch doesn't recognize, 'cept he knows it's an old one. He wishes he could hear the music. He's sure it would be plaintive and sweet. But there's no sound in this memory.

"Can you sing one of his songs?"

It's as if the idea had never occurred to her. "Oh, no. I could never *sing*."

"Why not? Everyone can sing."

"They can?"

"Sure. Don't you ever, like, sing in the shower?"

N'Doch can't remember the last time he was near a working shower, but he figures there's probably still plenty of water where she's come from. But she gets that blank look again that reminds him they're speaking different languages in more ways than the obvious one. "Never mind. I'll show you one sometime."

Meanwhile, behind her, the blue dragon's been going through her transformation, and he's been distracted so he didn't have to watch till she's just about finished. Even though this is the one they've practiced most of all 'cause it's easiest for her to maintain, it still gives him a chill to see his song come to life like that: there right in front of him, his little brother Jéjé, as he imagined he would have been if he'd lived to be nine or ten. N'Doch is glad he's warned the girl ahead of time.

" 'Kay, man. All set," the apparition squeaks.

N'Doch swallows hard. "Gotta work on the voice a little."

"Sure, guy. Anything you say." Now she's taken up a higher, lighter version of his own voice, which makes more sense for a ten-year-old kid, but doesn't go too far helping N'Doch feel any less weird about the whole business.

But the girl's smiling at the thing, her hands clasped in glee. "O excellent, Mistress Water! O wonderful and marvelous! What shall we call you?"

"Not Jéjé," N'Doch puts in quickly.

The boy/dragon pouts. "No? Then how 'bout . . . L'Eau?"

The girl picks up the game. "Or *Wasser!* I'll call you *Wasser!*"

N'Doch tries it. He can get his mouth around the syllables easy enough, so it seems as good as any made-up name except that anytime he hears it dragon-wise, in translation, he's gonna hear his own name, which is just about as strange as hearing his own voice. He shakes his head hopelessly. "All right, we're off, then. Stick close and keep your eyes open every minute."

The boy child salutes him saucily. The girl giggles. N'Doch pulls up short at the door. He has a sudden heart-stopping image of his younger self razzing Sedou. Now he's glad he never got around to writing songs about his older brother. "Look, this ain't no picnic, you got me? Hang tight, don't attract attention, or you get left behind."

The girl touches his arm. "She will behave, N'Doch."

His mouth tightens. He nods. He's forgotten for a moment that he's yelling at a dragon.

CHAPTER TWENTY-THREE

Up on the surface, it's already hot, though the sun has barely cleared the broken eastern skyline. N'Doch would have preferred to emerge in darkness, so as not to give away the entrance to their hidey-hole, but that chance is past and besides, he doesn't see anybody about when he peers cautiously over the top of the stair well. He gets the others out, the hole covered, and them well away from it before he halts for a reconnaissance.

There's not much left to look at, out here in the Wedge. Collapsed, burned-out buildings, rubble, dust. N'Doch picks out the distant profile of the Diouf, a half-built soccer stadium. Ran out of money after the last coup, so they never did finish the seating. The soccer team belongs to Baraga now, and plays in his private stadium for the cameras and five hundred of his most intimate friends, but on-the-rise rock groups use the Diouf if they can afford the security. The really hot groups don't play live gigs any more. Too much risk of getting blown up or shot, or having the so-called fans riot and trash the place, then having to pay up the damages. When you get big, you gotta go remote. It's the one thing N'Doch figures he'll regret about being famous, not being able to perform live any more.

The apparition stands beside him. "Move it or lose it, bro."

N'Doch curls his lip. "Who taught you how to talk?"

"You did."

"No way." But it makes him wonder. Is that what he sounds like to the girl?

He leads them away from the wrecked processing plant,

cutting across parking lots, keeping to the wide-open spaces as much as he can. In the early daylight, the buildings and the lots and the unpaved roads are all stained the same dry, hot red of the dust. N'Doch sees a few souls stirring here and there, bent over, languidly picking through the rubble, probably the same rubble they've picked over a million times. He keeps his distance and moves on.

The main road into town is still paved, but junk-strewn, full of potholes and sifted over with a fine layer of red silt.

"Not many trucks through here lately," N'Doch remarks. Lots of footprints, though. Lots more than you'd expect, given how deserted everything looks. He hears a few copters off in the distance, and waves the boy/dragon over to him. "You hear any of those gettin' close, you let me know, okay?"

The apparition nods. Being out in the open seems to have sobered it considerably.

The girl is doing what he said, sticking close, gazing about like she's trying to memorize everything. "Was there a war?" she asks him finally.

"Nah." Then he reconsiders. "well, actually, yeah—a lot of little ones. But really it's, y'know, the climate thing."

She gets quiet a moment, in the way he's familiar with now, waiting for the dragons to puzzle out a particularly opaque translation problem. Finally she says, "You mean, the weather?"

"Ha. It's much bigger than weather. I mean, the weather's the *result,* but . . . well, the way the vid guys say it, all our bombs and factories and cars and stuff have really screwed everything up, which means the air and the water and even the dirt, y'know? The whole gig." Now that he's into trying to actually explain this global warming thing, N'Doch realizes he doesn't really know what the hell he's talking about, just the garble he's heard on TV. But it's okay, 'cause this girl's not gonna know any better. He could tell her it's all a space alien conspiracy and she'd buy it just as fast. At least he's got the basic idea. "So it's getting hotter all the time and we don't get the rain any more when we should, while some other part of the world is being flooded out, which means the farmers can't hardly grow anything in either place. And then, half the time, what they do grow is full of chemicals and all kinds of toxic shit from the ground, so you shouldn't eat it even though you're hungry enough to eat the toxics raw if they was right there in front of you."

He takes a breath. She's staring at him, wide-eyed. He thinks, just in case she is picking up on some of this, maybe he should feed it to her slower, 'cause it's a big one, maybe the biggest. If she really doesn't know what "climate" means, doing a major core dump on her all at once is gonna be a waste of time. Plus get him all riled up, since nothing makes him madder than the notion of some day soon not being able to eat, drink, or breathe. But it does occur to him that he'd better start keeping her out of the sun. Pale as she is, she'll burn up like an old scrap of paper.

"At any rate, it ain't good, and it's getting worse."

Her brows knit. "People have made this happen?"

"That's what the science guys say. Course, with them, you always gotta ask who's paying their salary."

Her frown deepens. "But . . . why would you do this?"

"Hey! It wasn't me, all right? I just live here. Besides, nobody did it on *purpose*. Lotta times, you do things, you don't think about what else's gonna happen because of it."

"And when they knew what was happening, they stopped it?"

"Well, no, not exactly." He realizes now that the science part of this isn't the toughest part to explain after all. "Like, for a long time, nobody believed it, and then the scientists were scared to say anything 'cause fixing it was gonna cost so much money. Now I guess everybody just thinks it's too late."

"At home," the girl says slowly—she's mulling it over hard, and beside her, the apparition is wearing a pensive expression that Jéjé never would have. "At home, we are having wrong weather, too, except it is the opposite: it is too cold and wet. It snowed in the middle of August."

"Sounds like paradise."

"Oh, no, N'Doch. Our farmers can't grow enough either. The grain was thin and blighted. The fruit trees hardly ripened. And the kitchen gardens were blackened by frost just when they should have been producing their best."

"Hmm. Sounds bad." N'Doch is distracted by movement up ahead, a couple of thin dogs snarling over some lumpy thing in the road. He doesn't want to tangle with them or their lump. Where there's two, there's usually more, and who knows what the lump might be carrying. "This way."

He veers off the road and cuts across a dusty field that used to be a playground for the factory workers' kids. He recalls a few big metal-frame swings and a beaten-up slide, but all that's left now are the poured concrete emplacements that held their legs. The clarity of the memory surprises and disturbs him. He speeds up, as if he could walk away from it. The girl has to pick up her pace to stay even with him.

"But, N'Doch, at home we have none of these things you talk of, these . . ." She tries to reproduce the French she'd heard, having no word of her own for "bomb" or "car" or "factory."

"But you burn stuff, right? You're wearing that fancy knife, so you must melt down metal somehow to make the steel. And if it's so cold, you're probably cutting down every tree in sight just to keep warm."

"No, N'Doch, it is not like it is here. There are many trees everywhere. There are always enough trees."

"Yeah? Well, some day there won't be." But he can see she can't imagine it.

"But still, the weather is perilous. The priests say . . ." She glances his way. "Please do not be angry, N'Doch, but the priests *and* the people say it is God's will. That the snow and the ice in August is God's punishment for their sins."

N'Doch decides to be patient about the God thing for once, since the girl obviously doesn't know any better. "So what's everyone done in 913 that's so sinful?"

That kind of slows her down, like maybe she hasn't thought about it. "All the usual things that God says are sinful, I suppose—Envy, Sloth, Gluttony . . ."

He notices she leaves out the Murder and Adultery parts. "Gluttony. Now there's a sin I could really get into right now."

"It's not a joke, N'Doch."

"C'mon, girl, be real! The whole concept of sin is a joke!" He didn't expect his patience would last, though he's not sure why her innocence riles him so much. "There's no such thing as pure good and pure evil. There's only life, and getting along in it as best you can."

She stops, with the dust of her own footsteps rising around her like smoke, as if the ground was on fire. Her

eyes are dark and serious, and N'Doch feels pinned to a wall
even though there isn't a wall anywhere in sight. "There is
true evil, N'Doch. I have met it in person. And there is true
good. How can you say otherwise when you have known
a dragon?"

Now that's interesting about the dragons. She says it
without a trace of doubt in her mind, but when N'Doch
sneaks a backward look at the image of his dead brother
trotting along behind him, he knows he's not so sure. Pure
good, in his book, should not be so fuckin' weird. But to
get her moving again, he says, "Yeah, I'm sure you're right.
We'll talk about it later."

In the far corner of the field is a big tree. The old men
used to hang out in its shade, drinking their endless little
cups of sweet tea and arguing politics. Sometimes Sedou
would be there, N'Doch remembers, arguing with them.
There's no one sitting under it now, and the tree itself is
scarred and leafless. But N'Doch decides to take advantage
of its thin shadow for old times' sake. When he was little,
venturing forth in his first kid-gang, this tree marked the
end point of the Wedge, where the factories and warehouses—often the goal of the gangs' scavenging forays—
blended into the blocks of walled residential compounds
and the narrow streets of the commercial districts. He leans
against the tree, surrendering to the memory, then shakes
himself alert. He can't get caught standing around out here
in the open. Having safely passed the dog pack, he heads
back to the boulevard, which will take them through the
DMZ into the City proper and the comparative anonymity
of the daytime crowds. The address Djawara has supplied
for Lealé is in one of the more stable, conservative neighbor-
hoods, which means he'll have to play the role and blend,
if he doesn't want to get stopped.

He surveys his little entourage for a final reality check
before they hit the inhabited zone. The girl looks pretty
convincing, now that she's sweated up a bit. Except, of
course, she's white. The apparition would convince anyone
but N'Doch. Or his mama. Amazing how something like a
song can conjure a person so totally—with details, even,
that he didn't know he remembered, like how Jéjé's skin
was the lightest in the family, so much that Fâtime's girl-
friends teased her about who the father might be. It occurs

to N'Doch that with his own dark skin, the pale girl, and the apparition in the middle, they might be taken for a family. Which is an okay cover, after all. He wonders if the girl will mind. Maybe she won't even notice.

The low-slung buildings are closer together here, lined up more or less regularly along the dusty street, with alleys and empty lots between. The DMZ is the buffer between the full-out war zone of the Wedge and the residential districts of the sometimes working poor. N'Doch leads his group past used furniture stalls, junkyards and car repair shops, all boarded up now, plus a couple of derelict gas stations. One still has its chain-link intact and some dogs inside, plopped in the shade but ready to spring on any intruder. It might be doing business now and again, if the owner has a buddy in the current government or can luck into a black market score to fill his tanks.

Past the DMZ, things begin to come to life—a few people are moving about, mostly men and conservatively dressed, but real people with homes and televisions, not squatters. They're doing their day's chores before the midday heat settles in. Watchers, N'Doch calls them. He divides the world into the Watchers and the Watched. The Watchers live only vicariously. The Watched live on television. He counts himself as being Watched-in-waiting, and hopes he doesn't have to wait a whole lot longer.

Along the ragged curbs, the single-story shops are still mostly closed, their once-bright facades sun-bleached to pale yellows, pinks, and salmons, their carefully hand-lettered signs chipped and faded. But here and there, a steel accordion gate is half-open, a corrugated metal blind is raised, even an awning is partly extended. No merchandise hangs around the doorways. Nothing is displayed out front, nor for that matter inside, N'Doch suspects. In this part of town, you just have to know who's selling what and when they might have it, as well as be pretty well known to the seller, or he won't even let you into his store, never mind do business with you.

"We'll just move on through here," N'Doch urges as the girl starts to lag, wanting to peer inside the shadowed doorways. "Folks aren't gonna like you staring like that."

"Like what?"

"Like a tourist." Which is what she is, N'Doch reminds

himself. He'll know he's into the real City when everybody
they pass doesn't step aside to avoid them or stop to glare
after them as they go by. He's encouraged to see a water
seller's stall that actually has a customer, and two old men
under a scrawny tree playing checkers with washers and lug
nuts on a curling paper board. Finally they move through
a gang of small boys kicking a much-patched soccer ball
around in the middle of the street, and N'Doch relaxes his
pace a little. People actually live here, Watchers for sure,
but still, people who won't immediately try to rip him off.
They live in boxy cinder block houses with tiny concreted
front yards, invisible behind high stucco walls with steel
mesh gates. N'Doch lived in one himself for a while, half a
mile or so away, before things got so bad, before Sedou was
killed, before . . .

He'd known that's how it would be—like it was going
back to the bush and Papa Dja's, only worse—the flood of
memories he'd rather not be swimming in, struggling to
keep himself afloat.

"Damn!" he says softly.

"S' up?" asks the apparition.

He gives it a look, and the way it hauls back from him
tells him the look was not kind. The girl sees it, too.

"Is something wrong, N'Doch?"

He's not used to it, having his feelings work him over
like this. He feels like a boxer on the ropes. To cover, he
grabs at the apparition and cuffs it playfully. "Nothin's up,
kid. Nothin' at all."

Erde sensed that something was still not right between
N'Doch and his dragon, but because she had bonded so
instantly with Earth, she had little advice to offer them.
They'd have to work it out on their own, as she was sure
they would.

Besides, she couldn't concentrate on N'Doch and
Water—or Wasser, as she had dubbed Water's shape-
shifted form. She could only look around and around, trying to soak in all the newness and make some sense of it.
Entering this strange town, this City, was like stepping into
the intricately painted pages of her grandmama's illuminated Bible, where every leaf or flower, even the stones in
the walls of the ancient sacred cities of the Holy Land,

looked exotic and unfamiliar, nothing like the lands around her father's castle. Not the ruddy dusty street, not the pale, petal-colored crumbling walls or the sparse, dry vegetation or the dark skin and bright clothing of the inhabitants. And, of course, there was the heat, the constant heat. Perhaps it was the unrelenting sun that made everyone's skin so dark. Perhaps if she stayed here long enough, she would be burned as black as N'Doch.

As they moved deeper into the City, there were more people in the streets, and the buildings got taller. Soon they were tall enough to cast a shadow along one side of the road, and of course everyone chose to walk on that side, so it began to feel like a crowd, almost like the crowds in the towns at home on festival days, except this crowd was neither joyous nor rowdy. Erde thought this particularly strange. Except for the children, or their parents disciplining them, all these people were rushing here and there in total silence, keeping strictly to their business. No one stopped to greet an acquaintance or exchange a bit of gossip, perhaps because there were so few women about. As the crowd thickened, the men even shouldered and shoved one another, and no one stopped to apologize. If one of them pushed her hard enough, Erde worried, she might stumble and be trampled by the throng. Or get separated from N'Doch, who was slipping between the moving bodies with the speed and ease of an eel through swamp grass. She'd be left behind and he'd never know he'd lost her until it was too late. Of course, Earth could come instantly to rescue her, but Erde could just imagine what sort of terrible panic that would cause, if even a half-grown dragon materialized in the midst of this crowd. She snatched at N'Doch's arm, but he shook her off surreptitiously.

"Not here!" he hissed. "Hold on to the kid if you want. Nobody'll mind that."

To his surprise, she gets it right off.

"Is it improper?" she asks.

He nods. "In public. In private, men and women do whatever they want together." He glances back, grinning, but she's looking both shocked and curious, and since he's not hot to be the one filling her in on the facts of life, especially right here and now, he lets it drop.

"We're getting close now," he says, but she's already distracted. She's stopped dead in front of a barred-up shop full of televisions. The window actually has most of its glass left. Only one row of the vids are on, a big enough expense but the least a shop owner can get away with and still expect to sell anything. One of the early morning series is playing. A couple of teeners have stopped to watch. The girl is being shoved this way and that, but she's staring at the bright line of repeated images like she's never seen a TV before. Remembering where she's come from, N'Doch realizes she probably hasn't. Hard to imagine such a thing. A few guys pull up to stare with her, in case she's spotted something they don't want to miss. N'Doch doubles back through the crowd to stand beside her before she and the apparition get 'napped right out from under his nose.

She doesn't have to look up to know he's there. That dragon thing again. It keeps unnerving him. She reaches for his arm, then stops herself halfway, so her hands gets left floating in the air.

"What magic is this?" she whispers.

The older guys glance at him, check themselves in the cracked window glass and move on. The kids are glued to the tube, and ignore them. N'Doch can see the girl is scared. "Only electronic magic. Remember I told you about electricity?"

She nods dubiously. "How are the people in the windows made so alike? Are they golems?"

"Those aren't windows. And those guys aren't really there. It's only a picture."

"Someone has painted them?"

"Not exactly . . ." He can see this is gonna be a hard one.

"But they move. They're so . . . like they're alive."

"Well, they are, only not there in the box. Somewhere else." He tries to see the vid images the way she must be seeing them, as something alien and inexplicable. He fails.

"What's it for?" she asks finally.

"To watch. Whadya think?"

"Why should we watch what other people are doing? Isn't *that* improper?"

"They're actors. They get paid to be watched."

"Why?"

For a moment, he's at a loss for words. "Look, um, the

vid . . .those boxes . . . they show all the daily series, and you can hear all the big groups play, and see the sports, y'know?" His voice trails off. She doesn't have a clue, though he can see she's trying hard to get one. He has a sudden vision of his mama, alone in her little cinder block house with the box going all day long, the steady reassuring background noise of her life. "It tells you stories," he says finally, "and keeps you company."

"Oh," she says wonderingly. "Stories."

She lifts her hand toward the window, as if to reach through the bars to touch the dancing images. N'Doch grabs her wrist.

"Unh-unh. Might bite."

She recoils, stares at him, then back at the screens as if she expects the vid characters to leap out at her, teeth gnashing.

"I mean, you might set off the alarm, that's all." He sees he's freaked her a little, but since she doesn't know what's what, it won't hurt to have her thinking twice before she goes around laying her hands on things. "Let's move, okay? You'll see plenty more vids around. Everyone's got 'em."

She follows, but her brain's obviously on overdrive. "Master Djawara did not keep one of these companions."

N'Doch laughs. "Papa D. thinks the box is evil."

"He does?" She stops to stare back at the shop again. "Why? Is it *black* magic?"

He motions the apparition to pull her along faster. He's impatient now, tired of having to explain things all the time. He wants to get on with finding Lealé. "Depends on who you ask."

"If it was black magic, the Church wouldn't let it be shown out like that, in public daylight."

He likes that phrase, "public daylight." As if there was any other kind. "The church ain't got nothing to say about it. This here's the Land of the Prophet."

"You mean, like Isaiah or Ezekiel?"

"Mohammed. You never heard of Mohammed?" He grins, 'cause he's never been devout, only so much as he's needed to get by the imams. "You a pagan, girl."

Instead of the laugh he expected, he gets a frown. She turns pensive. "Brother Guillemo says so, too. He called me a witch."

"You keep time-traveling and running around with dragons, what d'you expect the brother to think?"

"I know," she agrees seriously.

"Hey." He shoves her gently. "It's a joke. You really oughta lighten up, girl. I mean, this is some old guy way back when, right? You're here, in 2013. Whadda you care what he thinks?"

She shakes her head. "He's there now, even as we speak. He haunts my dreams. He'll be there, still after me, when I go back."

N'Doch can see that this Guillemo guy is a real bad thing in her life. "How do you know you gotta go back?"

She blinks at him, opens her mouth, then shuts it again.

"Bingo. Never thought of that, didja?"

She licks her lips, then purses them. "No, of course I will go back. I must go back, when the Quest is fulfilled. I am sure of that. But . . ." She tosses him a sidelong little glance, impish almost, the closest thing to humor he's seen in her so far. "Perhaps in a country where there is so much magic all around, it is not so terrible to be called a witch."

CHAPTER TWENTY-FOUR

When he finally locates Water Street, and the address that Papa Dja has given him, it's a narrow side lane, rutted and unpaved, with the usual walled yards and cinder block boxes at the back. No names on the gates, only faded numbers, but the street is pretty clean, not much litter around. N'Doch rings the bell at Number 913.

The gate is solid sheet metal, scarred as if someone had been beating on it with a sledge. A little sliding panel is set at eye level. N'Doch rings for several minutes without result.

"Gotta be patient," he assures the girl. "Just gotta wait 'em out."

The apparition is scuffing his feet in the dust, his hands shoved deep into the stretched-out pockets of his shorts. N'Doch remembers these shorts now, except they were *his* shorts, not Jéjés, and were particularly prized for being the match to a pair worn by his favorite pop star at the time. And that's what weirds him out. The time was ten years ago and he hasn't seen those shorts since. Or the pop star.

"She ain't in there," says the apparition.

"I said, you gotta be patient. People don't just come racing out to see who's knocking. They might be watching their show. They might feel safer not being home."

The apparition shrugs. "There's someone in there, yeah. But it ain't her."

N'Doch's fists ball up on his hips. "How the hell do you know?"

The girl looks right and left. The street is empty. She lays a warning hand on his arm. "Surely you've seen by now . . . if she says she knows, she knows."

Damn! He's forgotten again. Of all the shapes the dragon

could have pulled out of his mind, it had to be this one? N'Doch guesses he should be grateful she's not walking around looking like his mother. Or Sedou. This last notion leaves a hollow ache in his gut that he'd rather not have to deal with. He resolves to stop thinking of the apparition as his brother Jéjé. He reaches to ring again. "Gotta at least find out if she lives here."

The little panel jerks open on squealing tracks, just a crack. "Who is it?" demands a voice.

It's a woman's voice, despite its gruffness. N'Doch assumes his best public persona, the one that always charms the ladies. "We're looking for my grandpapa's dear old friend, Mme. Lealé Kaimah. Is she at home?"

"Yeah? Who's this grandfather?"

"He is M. Djawara N'Djai."

"And who are you?"

"I am his grandson, N'Doch N'Djai."

A pair of crow-footed dark eyes scrutinize him through the narrow crack. "Lealé doesn't live here anymore."

"Excuse me, but my grandpapa received a postcard from her just last month giving this as her address."

A short pause on the other side of the gate. "What do you want with her?"

N'Doch lets a whiff of the bush spice up his performance. "We're just into town, my family and I. First time, y'know? Papa Dja asked us to look Mme. Lealé up, see how she's been all these years."

"Huh," scoffed the voice. "Looking to sponge off her, more likely, now she's found something steady for herself."

N'Doch lets his shoulders droop. This woman wants abject humility. "No, no, Madame. In fact, my grandpapa was not even sure that his old friend was still living until he received her card."

The voice chuckles. "Oh, she's living, all right."

"Then I may report to him that she's well?"

"You can go see for yourself. I guess you sure are new in town, 'cause it's no mystery to anyone local where Lealé's living these days. You know where's the Marché Ziguinchor?"

"No, but I'll find it, I'm sure."

"Yeah, well, you go down there. Ask for the house of the Mahatma Glory Magdalena."

"The what?"

But the panel slams shut as N'Doch leans toward it. He almost rings again, but he's pretty sure he's gotten all he's gonna get out of this woman.

"I think she means 'who,'" notes the girl. "The Magdalene was . . ."

"I know, I know." He doesn't, but he's tired of being informed all the time. He stands chewing his lip for a moment. "The Ziguinchor. What's Papa Dja doing knowing someone who lives there?"

"Then you do know it?"

"Oh, yeah. But I wasn't about to tell her that."

"Why? What is it?"

"A part of town where rich people play, but not the kind like Baraga. He's bought himself some respectability, at least. The Zig is where the rich and famous go when the old money won't have 'em around." He doesn't know how to say it to the girl, but he's wondering if Papa Dja's old pal has made her success working in a pleasure house.

"Is it far?"

He shakes his head, but he's thinking that the Zig is the sort of place he'd rather go by himself, not dragging some white girl and a kid after him. He'll have to turn down offers for them right and left, and somebody might get argumentative. But he's got nowhere he can stash them meanwhile, so he'll have to risk it. Better in the morning than later on. At least a tourist will be less of a novelty there. He's never seen the Zig by daylight. It's the one part of town that doesn't even get started until after dark.

He leads them back to the main drag, and all the rush and bustle on the boulevard. They're just crossing to the shade on the north side when he hears sirens coming. His first thought is, *Run!* But he can't, with all this new responsibility. He hurries the girl and the kid onto the sidewalk, against the charred wall of a boarded-up house. The crowd stops and lines up along the curb to stare at the oncoming vehicles.

The girl moves in close, looking up at him wide-eyed. "What is it?"

N'Doch bites back an impatient reply. Probably she saw him tense up, and it worried her. It's not her fault she doesn't know anything, but he's just not cut out to be a tour guide. "Somebody famous."

"A powerful lord?"

N'Doch laughs. "You're thinking, like your daddy, hunh?"

"No, N'Doch. My father wasn't very powerful. I used to think he was, but that's because I was a little girl. Now I see that he wasn't as powerful as he wanted to be, and that's why he allied himself with Brother Guillemo. To get more powerful."

He blinks at her. This story of hers is beginning to sound interesting. Maybe there's a song or two in it. "Well, that's the way of it, isn't it? Power and money." He stands up tall to see over the heads of the men in front of him. The lead pair of motorcycles have just run the signal at the intersection, their headlights flashing. Behind them are four more, rolling along two by two, a stone's throw ahead of the limo. Behind the limo, more flashing lights and the sirens of the rear guard. N'Doch lets out a low whistle. What blows his mind is not the numbers or the noise, but the style and splash.

The six lead cycles are bright cherry red. All their chrome parts are polished gold. The riders are uniformed in opaque black helmets and glossy black boots, and skintight gold bodysuits set with bits of mirror, so that each is shaped by darkness top and bottom and by edgy, dancing sparkle in between. The limo itself is mirrored gold all over, even the windows, and entirely anonymous. No logo, no flag, no banners, none of the usual personal advertising. Not even an initial.

"Who is it? Who?" the crowd murmurs.

The hot air is full of guesses and pronouncements. Even N'Doch finds his cool ebbing away. The sirens fill his ears and set his blood pounding. The bright heavy sun, rising toward the midday heat, pales to insignificance before such brilliance, such blinding spectacle. He imagines the frosty interior of the limo. He smells the soft leather of its seats, the sensual perfume of the woman next to him as he rides across town to the studio to shoot his latest music vid. Maybe it's two women, and they're chatting softly while he, aloof, gazes through the gold-tinted window at the people who've lined the streets to stare at him with fascination and envy. And then a new thought enters his fantasy: Will he remember where he's come from, when that day arrives? Will he remember that it was him once, lining the streets? He'd like to think it would, but . . . hey, why should he? Nobody else does, once they've made it.

The limo slides silently past. Behind it are another six cycles, roaring and flashing. When they've all gone by, the street seems vastly empty. The crowd mutters and complains.

The girl is entranced. She cranes her neck after the tail-lights, clapping her hands in glee. "Oh, a golden carriage, oh wonderful! Is it a king?"

"You think everyone rich is a king? We don't have kings here, you get it?" Like the crowd, N'Doch is left aroused and dissatisfied. "Don't know who it was, anyway. A publicity stunt of some sort, maybe. Who'd go to all that trouble and expense, otherwise; without telling you who they are?"

He's aware now of a low keening sound in that place between his ears where the dragon music has staked its claim. He looks around, realizing he's lost track of the apparition. He spots the kid balled up in the corner of a gated doorway, shoulders hunched, his hands pressed hard to his ears. "Oops," says N'Doch.

He slips through the dispersing throng to catch hold of the kid and help him to his feet. The girl is there instantly, wrapping her arms around the boy-thing, crooning to him soothingly. This time, N'Doch thinks, it's she who's forgotten the kid's really a dragon.

"Musta been the sirens," he offers. "Hurt his . . . her ears." He assumes it's pain. What's a dragon got to be afraid of?

"No," the girl replies. "Well, yes—mine, too . . . but not only. Mostly, it was the badness, she says."

He finds himself staring at them, this alien white girl with her arms around *his* dragon. "So why can't she say that to me?"

The girl looks up at him. "But she does. She will. She wants to. But you have to listen."

"Hunh," N'Doch says. They've been this route before. But he thinks maybe he'll just give it a try, for the hell of it. See what it's like. "So, remind me—how do I do that?"

She cocks a dark eyebrow at him reprovingly. "You know how, N'Doch. Just like you do it to understand me. Like you do it when you want to. Only you also have to do it when you don't want to."

"Hunh," he says again, but then he's more interested in something else. "What'd she mean, the 'badness'?"

"It was a feeling she got." She releases the apparition and urges it gently toward him. Sounding just like Papa Dja, she says, "You ask her."

N'Doch lets out a breath, feeling already like he's conceded something. "So. What did you mean?"

The apparition shimmers, seems to swell and shrink with its own breathing. N'Doch throws up both hands, palms out.

"Not here! You can't! Don't change!"

The apparition shakes its head, shivers and settles back into a steadier reality. "Sorry. Just kinda threw me there, y'know?"

"Umm . . . no. I don't."

"In the car, I mean. Not bad, exactly. Something . . . wrong."

"Yeah . . . like what?"

The boy-thing shrugs, as if its panic had never happened. "Don't know, bro."

N'Doch lowers his hands. "Great. All that fuss for an I-don't-know."

"It's a warning," says the girl.

"Right. 'It's a sign! It's an omen!' You sound like Papa Dja."

"You could do worse," notes the apparition. "At least he gets it right some of the time."

Unfathomably irritated, N'Doch rounds on him. "Whadda you know? You never even met him!"

Now the apparition looks truly offended.

"Of course she did," puts in the girl hastily.

N'Doch presses both palms to his temples and squeezes hard. Yes! What was he thinking? "Sorry! Sorry. Okay? You two are making me crazy. Look, it's time to move.

We gotta check out this Mahatma Glory Whosits while it's still daylight."

"Magdalena," say the kid and the girl together.

N'Doch sighs. "Whatever."

CHAPTER TWENTY-FIVE

They're still on the outskirts of the Ziguinchor when N'Doch begins to see the signs. Posters in shop windows and pasted on the walls. A billboard, erected hastily on the roof of someone's house, alongside an old satellite dish. Even little stickers, brand new, in all the colors of the fluorescent rainbow, blooming on the faded doors and gateposts. He's used to having political broadsides and government proclamations plastered up all over the place, but this is different. These are almost . . . decorative.

He points them out to the apparition and the girl. Carefully, the girl sounds out the words.

"Glow . . . rye? Sorry, the letters are funny. Glowree? Glory!"

Impressed, he nods. "It's her. That's the place we'll find Lealé."

The image is the same everywhere: the dark face of a woman superimposed on a bright four-pointed star. It's shaped like a compass rose, like he's seen on old maps in the history vids. The woman is smiling beatifically. "That's all it says, 'Glory,' but it's gotta be where that woman was talking about." He's kind of relieved, 'cause this face don't look like it's selling sex or kinky games. Still, you never know. "Maybe Lealé's joined some kind of religious cult."

The girl shudders. "Oh, I hope not."

"Why? You know your Bible stuff, sounds like. I'll let you go ask her where Lealé is."

She eyes him sideways. "But, N'Doch, I do not speak her language."

He snaps his fingers, an oversized gesture. "Damn! Right again!"

Her brow creases, then smoothes. Her eyes lighten and she grins, sketching a little bow. "Ah ha," she says, then nods for him to lead the way down the street.

N'Doch thinks, *Now we're getting someplace.*

The stickers and signs soon become elaborate arrows pointing the way. N'Doch just follows them.

"That Water Street woman sure was right about this place being no trouble to find," he remarks. But the closer he gets, the uneasier it makes him. This Glory person doesn't look to be leading a very private life. There's sure to be lots of people around, and awkward questions about the kid and the girl. He wonders if he can manage to hunt up Lealé without getting tangled in this Mahatma's dubious business.

They come around a corner finally and there in the wide square is the ramshackle four-story pile of crumbling yellow stucco that houses the Marché Ziguinchor. N'Doch thinks of the coins Papa Djawara has given him. He thinks of cheese and bread and oranges. Oranges! Maybe even a tidbit of chocolate, that fabulous luxury of luxuries. But the market is closed, and the ring of outside stalls as well. It's nearing noon. Both vendors and customers have fled the heat. Those with no place to go have staked out niches in the shade. The bundle of rags tucked in each corner is a person napping. N'Doch's timing is off again, but it's no disaster. He's hoping, despite his disclaimers to the woman at 913 Water Street, that Lealé will be good for at least one full meal in the Glory woman's kitchen, and a cooling siesta in his grandfather's name.

Besides, now that he thinks about it, he's glad the stalls are closed. He wouldn't want the girl to have to see some of the stuff they sell in there besides food. But he oughta find shade for her pretty quick, he sees. She's damp and flagging, and paler even than usual. She may not know to drink enough, though N'Doch notices the apparition is sure putting a big dent into the water bottle he made it carry.

Still, he lingers by the south entrance to the market, staring pensively at the big, barred wooden doors. Litter has blown up in piles against them, like they haven't been open in a while. There used to be showers of neon here, people night and day, and music blaring into the streets. A resourceful kid could always find what he lacked at the Zig.

All sorts of deals going down, lots of biz, the very center of biz, even in the hottest noons. Maybe at night, it still is. N'Doch hopes so, 'cause right now, it's looking real drab and down on its luck, falling apart like everything else.

The apparition taps him on the arm. N'Doch turns, and there's the place.

"Yee-ow," he murmurs.

It's a big stone building, a mansion really, filling one entire end of the market square. It has white columns and an upper gallery with wrought iron railings, like from colonial times, even to the magenta riot of bougainvillea cascading from the balcony. N'Doch recalls there was some kind of hotel here before, but he doesn't recall these elegant columns or that lacy iron gingerbread, or the ornate but massive gates in tall white walls topped with razor wire. The place even has its own driveway. He especially doesn't remember the mammoth light-box sign over the front portico, the beaming woman in the golden four-pointed star. Above, her name in glowing block caps: "GLORY." Underneath, a legend: *In this sad world, a bridge to the next.*

N'Doch eyes the impressive guard house between the motor gate and a smaller pedestrian gate beside it. He supposes an entire system of locks, screens, sensors, alarms, and monitors—and armed bouncers.

"I guess Lealé's come up in the world, all right," he mutters. "If she's in there. Question is, how're we gonna get *us* in? Probably need a password and our own personal bar code."

"Go knock on the door," says the apparition.

"Sure thing, smart mouth. You got 'rich boy' stamped on your forehead?"

"It says 'Welcome.' "

"Where?"

The boy-dragon points. Sure enough, over the pedestrian gate, in gold letters. *Bienvenue.*

N'Doch fights through a twinge of resentment. The real Jéjé never lived long enough to learn how to read. "Well, it don't mean us, you can bet on that."

"You won't do it, I will."

And before N'Doch can stop him, the kid is sprinting across the square. The girl starts after him, swaying a bit in the sun, then looks back. *"Kommen sie nicht?"*

"Huh?" The damn kid's fallen down on the translating job. N'Doch holds his ground a moment, then groans softly and follows. Got to get the girl inside before she drops. Besides, he's just noticed the shiny new street signs on the mansion's corners: *Rue de la Terre.*

The kid waits for them at the walk-in gate, then just as N'Doch is catching up, he raps on it sharply. It swings open to his touch. N'Doch can see that the gate itself is a metal detector, but the smiling guard in the bullet-proof booth waves them in like the host at some swank garden party.

And inside the walls, that's exactly what it looks like—the aftermath, at least, of a really *big* do.

A shallow, tiled yard runs the width of the building, dotted with fancy fruit trees in big ceramic tubs. People are lying about everywhere, curled up beneath the trees, asleep on the stone benches in between. At least, he assumes they're asleep. Smiling too peacefully to be stiffs, even on their hard beds of tile and stone. Maybe the place is a pleasure house after all. But the sleepers look to be sleeping normally, not napping off a high of some sort.

The girl nudges him. At the far end of the yard, several slim young guys in white robes are wandering about watering the bright, lush flowers overflowing the bases of the potted trees. One is picking up scattered bits of clothing from the tiny oval of green inside the circular driveway. N'Doch stoops and rakes his fingers across its manicured velvet. "Unnh. Real grass . . ." He wants to get down and roll in it.

But he sees the girl eyeing the white-robed guys with serious suspicion. He doesn't think any of them looks like much to contend with, but he waits anyway, to be spotted and told to get the hell out, like all the other times he's been told the likes of him don't belong in someplace he'd really like to be.

Instead, the guy scavenging the clothes bundles up his armload and comes over, smiling. "My, my, aren't we up early? Hello, I'm Jean-Pierre. How can I help you?"

N'Doch is tongue-tied for the split second it takes for the apparition to pipe up.

"We'd like to see the Mahatma Glory Magdalena."

"Danke," adds the girl hastily.

The guy's brows lift. "Oh, I'm afraid it's much too early

for that. She won't be up for hours yet. But you're welcome to wait. The line starts around the corner to the right. Of course, there are . . ." He waves a languid hand at the litter of sleepers. ". . . a few petitioners in front of you already, but it shouldn't take much more than a few days. Will it be cash or credit?"

N'Doch eases himself forward. "For what?"

The guy takes N'Doch's measure and pumps a little more warmth into his smile. "For your Reading, of course. You are here for a Reading?"

N'Doch judges that the same charm he puts to work on the ladies might work with this Jean-Pierre. He smiles back, heavy-lidded. "Well, no. Actually, we're searching up an old friend of my grandpapa's. At the last known address, they told us to look here."

The guy's warmth dims perceptibly. "Ah. An elderly gentleman, then? We have no elderly gentlemen working here. Perhaps your informant meant he is on line, awaiting a Reading. You are welcome to look around, but I do hope you won't disturb any of our guests unnecessarily. They all need their sleep."

N'Doch smiles ingratiatingly, though it pains him to do so. "I'm sure they do. But it's not a gentleman we're looking for. It's a lady, and not so elderly. I'd guess she'd be in her fifties."

"She's here," says the apparition suddenly.

N'Doch turns. "Hush, now."

The girl catches on. She slides restraining hands onto the apparition's shoulders. N'Doch gives her a little nod, already turning back to the young man. "Her name is Lealé."

The guy's face goes briefly blank, and then his smile returns. N'Doch imagines a robot checking a data file, but he knows that look: the momentary shutdown of the bureaucrat who's just received a piece of information he doesn't know what to do with.

"What was that name again?"

Bingo, thinks N'Doch. He conjures up a pleasant innocence. "Lealé Kaimah."

The guy backs up a step. "Well, now. Let me see. Why don't I just go on inside and check the records for you? Anyone waiting in line will have signed the reservations book. Perhaps your friend has already been and gone, happily enlightened."

"My grandfather's friend, she is. From long ago."

"How lovely. And what did you say your grandpapa's name is?"

"I didn't. It's Djawara."

"Yes. Well, then, I'll just go check." The guy escapes up onto the colonnaded porch and into the house.

"Sure lit a fire under him, didn't we?" crows N'Doch. He's not used to people being polite to him, for whatever reason.

"A toady," scoffs the apparition. The girl nods, like she knows all about it.

Erde sank gratefully into the shade of a column but kept herself alert. Despite the exotic and unfamiliar setting, she recognized in this white-clad man the tone and body language of a courtier. This was not like any court she had knowledge of, but instinct told her that she must not take anyone or anything at face value. Politics, flatteries, and subterfuge had ruled at Tor Alte, even during her grandmother's more open reign. Erde wondered what the Mahatma Glory Magdalena had done to acquire the kind of power that the presence of courtiers implied. She knew it meant the woman could be dangerous. If not dealt with properly, she could stand between them and finding Master Djawara's friend Lealé.

When the young man in white had vanished through the broad double doors of the manor house, N'Doch said quietly, "Stay put. I'm gonna have a look around. Drink some water, huh? You look awful." He started away, then halted. "Listen, if the guy comes back, let the kid do the talking. Speaking Kraut to 'em will only make 'em think we got money."

Erde nodded, uncorking her water jug. She'd finally figured out that N'Doch spoke a kind of Frankish, some future version of the language she'd heard from visitors riding into Tor Alte from west of the Germanies, in the same way that the German that Master Djawara spoke was a future version of her own. She didn't speak much Frankish, beyond the few polite phrases of greeting and farewell that

would be expected on formal occasions from the daughter
of a noble house. But she was sure she could learn it.

She watched little Wasser scuff around the white-paved
driveway, and opened her conscious mind to her boon companion waiting a morning's walk away in the war zone.

—*Dragon, how are you?*

—**I am sleeping.**

—*You are not. You are awake and translating.*

—**The part of me that is not awake is sleeping.**

—*Brilliant Dragon! Part of you can sleep while another
part is awake?*

—**Yes. Only now, all of me is awake.**

—*Poor Dragon. I'm so sorry.*

Erde's smile, repressed mentally, came out physically.
She caught Wasser grinning at her mischievously.

—*Well, Dragon, answer my question, and then you may
go back to sleep, however much of you wishes to.*

—**Yes!**

—*Will your sister teach me this Frankish tongue that is
spoken here?*

—**Ask her. She is awake.**

—*Dear dragon, I cannot, unless I ask her in German,
which her current boy-form does not speak. Therefore, you
must stay awake to translate even if I do ask her myself.*

A giant dragon sigh rumbled through Erde's mind like
the echo of a distant avalanche. Still grinning, Wasser
nodded.

—*She says, yes, she will teach you, if you will
teach her.*

So, while N'Doch had his look around, the lessons began.

Expecting to be stopped and strip-searched at every step,
N'Doch wanders the grounds in a way he hopes looks suffi-
ciently casual. But his notion of stumbling across some secret sector proves bogus. There are people sleeping
everywhere he turns.

The right side of the mansion has a row of tall curtained
French windows opening onto a wide flowered terrace. The
stone is white, the flowers are pink. It's all like some kind
of vid set, except for the sleepers. Here, where there's shade
from a few ginkgo trees, they're lined up back to back, head

to toe, like in some sort of fiendish dormitory, or like one of those makeshift morgues they throw together after some war or natural disaster. It gives N'Doch the creeps, looking at them just lying there like that.

At the end of the row of windows is a big door with a canopy as long as the terrace is wide, all draped in gold and white fabric, something glittery with sequins. N'Doch goes up close. The sequins are shaped like four-pointed stars. He doesn't know much about fancy fabrics, but he's beginning to get the drift here. He tries the massive and elaborate brass handle on the shining white door. Locked. No surprise there. It's even less of a surprise when he continues around the back, where there are more tall, curtained windows facing a graveled car park and a six-car garage. Out on the gravel, two of the white-robed young guys are hosing down the mirrored gold limousine.

Even though it's not a surprise, N'Doch has to work to stay casual-like. He's gonna actually get close to the thing, maybe get a look inside. The gravel is dark with many price-less gallons of perfectly good water. He can see it's clear coming out of the hose. Course, that doesn't mean it's safe. N'Doch guesses the flashy motorcycles have had their wash and are already stashed in the garages.

He slouches over diffidently. "Want some help?" He knows a little lightening of the work load can often be bartered for information.

But the guys in white stare at him like he should only dream of being allowed such a privilege. One of them smiles, though, the same even smile N'Doch has seen enough of already in this compound. It's beginning to make his teeth itch.

"Oh, no, sir, but thank you. The Mahatma would never wish a Guest to soil themselves for her sake."

N'Doch thinks: *With all that water, you'd end up being cleaner than you arrived.* "Oh," he says. "I see. Okay for you to, though, huh?"

His offer of worker solidarity falls on deaf ears. "We don't mind, sir. As her devoted disciples, such onerous tasks are our honor and our duty."

"Natch," says N'Doch. If the Mahatma Glory won't be up for hours like the guy at the door said, who was it out parading around in her limo? He'd like to hang and check out the fabulous car, but probably it wouldn't do to look too curious here. "Well, see ya."

"Our best wishes for your Reading."

"You bet."

He follows the driveway out of the car park, across the back of the house and around the left side. He finds a little grove of trees, some thick-leafed tree he doesn't recognize, rising out of a carefully mowed square of lawn. N'Doch slows, studying it. Here, there is not a sleeper in sight. Weird. That soft grass under those heavy trees looks like the coolest, most comfortable place for a lie-down in the whole compound. He sees no fence or keep-out signs, no guard post or dogs. Somehow anyone coming here just knows to stay away from this spot. He'd expect at least a scrawny pigeon in the grass, the one or two that haven't already been netted and eaten. This should be a perfect refuge for 'em. He gets a little chill, staring into this silent green emptiness. It reminds him of the weirdness beneath the trees at Papa Dja's. At least there, there were birds.

He stores his search data in a corner of his brain and goes off to find the girl and the kid. They're hunkered down in the shade on the front steps, tight as you please, playing some sort of word game in two different languages. It takes him a while to realize it's a two-way vocabulary lesson.

The girl looks up. *"Bonjour, monsieur N'Doch,"* she chirps proudly.

N'Doch grins. *"Mais, bonjour, mademoiselle."* Pretty neat. No dragons between 'em or nothing. *"Ça va?"*

She throws a quick one back at the apparition. The kid nods encouragingly, like a grown-up.

"Oui, monsieur," says the girl. *"Ça va tres bien, merci."*

N'Doch applauds, and she blushes. "She's a fast learner," he tells the kid.

"I'm a good teacher. *Sprechen Sie Deutsch*?"

"Oh, no, you don't. Leave me outa this."

"But why, N'Doch?" asks the girl. The dragon translation program has kicked in again. "It's fun!"

"Schooling's never fun. I know what I need to know, y'know?"

The minute he's said it, he hates how narrow it sounds,

but he can't take it back. It's a show of weakness to second-guess yourself.

The girl's brow furrows. "No, I guess I don't. Don't you always want to be learning new things?"

"If it's useful stuff, sure I do." He's digging his hole deeper, he knows it. He can't seem to stop himself. Seconds ago, he was delighted to hear her speaking his language, but something about her dead earnestness just needles him badly. "Wouldn't want to waste my time otherwise."

"It's a waste of time to be able to talk to me?"

"Hey, we're talking now, ain't we?"

Her frown is deepening. "I mean, to each other, without the dragons."

N'Doch looks away, yawns. "I say, if it ain't broke, don't fix it."

The girl tips a handful of white pebbles from palm to palm, says nothing. The apparition leaps up and sticks its little Jéjé nose right in N'Doch's face, scowling.

"You're mean, big brother, that's what you are!"

"I ain't your brother."

"So much the worse for you!"

N'Doch sees the apparition's outline waver, and panics. "No! Don't do it! I'm sorry! I didn't mean it!"

The girl catches at the kid's hand. "Wasser, please. Let's not fight. We've more important things to worry about."

Erde heard an echo of herself in N'Doch's petulance, the younger self who rebelled against her father's arbitrary dictates. But it was Earth, now waked fully by the sharp turn of the conversation, who offered an explanation.

—*He is rebelling, too.*

—*Against what? No one here's telling him what to do.*

—*In a way, you do. By setting a superior example.*

—*He doesn't think it's superior. He thinks I'm stupid.*

—*He thinks you think it's superior. He doesn't quite believe it's who you are.*

—*Well, this is very mixed-up, Dragon.*

—*Yes. Especially since he also suspects he's given up something in order to become as clever as he is about survival, something he suspects you still have.*

—*What?*

Earth maundered about a bit, rumbling gently in her

mind, as if he wasn't so sure of this grand theory of his after all. But their philosophical reverie was broken by Wasser's sharp little elbow digging into Erde's ribs.

"Hsst!"

"Listen!" N'Doch agreed.

There was a commotion inside the house. A woman's voice raised in querulous demand, and a hubbub of lower voices explaining, placating, apologizing. In the tiled front yard, the young men in white set down their watering cans and eyed each other anxiously.

"Sounds like Her Gloryship is awake after all," N'Doch murmured.

The front doors burst open, both of them, in a great sweep of gleaming paint and polished brass that scattered several of the young men who had gathered to eavesdrop on the argument inside. A tall, ebony-skinned woman strode out in a flurry of color and motion, yards and yards of glimmering white silk and bright, multicolored scarves and beads, hundreds of strands looped about her long neck and her bare, dark arms and woven into the intricate architecture of her hair. She halted on the top step, the back of one hand pressed to her brow, her eyes closed, her back gracefully arched. The young men in white rushed to gather about behind her like angels in the heavenly choir.

Erde wondered if she was meant to curtsy. Out of pure habit, she almost did.

N'Doch stared up at the woman openmouthed. "What an entrance!" he breathed.

"They're here!" declaimed the woman, who had to be the Mahatma Glory herself. There was no mistaking her from the images plastered on every fence and doorpost, like the Virgin Mother's on her holy Feast Day. "They've come, as I predicted. The doubters laughed, but I said they would and they have come to me!"

She opened her eyes and turned her fiery glance on her visitors in order of height: N'Doch first, then Erde, and lastly, little Wasser. Her gaze lingered there and narrowed. The boy-dragon shivered and shrank against Erde's side.

"They tried to keep you from me, said you weren't important. The foolish ones! What do they know about the world and eternity, ah?"

Erde thought of raving priests and white-robed henchmen in another time and place. She shifted an arm and hugged Wasser protectively.

Then Glory spread her own arms with a tinkling of beads and little bells hidden within the shimmering folds of her robes. She offered them the blinding, beatific smile of her painted image. "Come to me, children. Your journey is ended."

"I hope not," the apparition muttered, his voice muffled by Erde's T-shirt.

N'Doch said, "This could be interesting."

PART THREE

The Call to
the Quest

CHAPTER TWENTY-SIX

Erde had been schooled in courtly manners and presentation from the earliest age. Her elders had drilled her constantly, for she would naturally be the focus of much attention, being a baron's daughter and probable heir. She'd felt about it the way she felt about learning to dance: a series of moves designed to produce a given outcome, a collection of predetermined masks she was required to put on. She'd resisted her training, and had often been punished for it.

The Mahatma Glory Magdalena's presentation caught her entirely by surprise. She had never laid eyes on such a woman: so grand, so spectacular, so histrionic, all arms and hands and braided, beaded hair flying in every direction. Dignity and decorum were the basis of court behavior, seen at its best in the dignity of Erde's beloved grandmother, the late baroness, a woman of no small presence herself. But to stand in the Mahatma's presence was like standing in a gale. Every word she uttered, every move she made called attention to itself. A welcome from this woman was writ in capital letters, given with tears and sighs and lightning flashes of her brilliant smile. Entirely undignified. And yet, Erde admitted, her charisma was such that you gladly let it buffet you in the face, even if it threatened your balance. You just HAD to watch her, to see what outrageous thing she would do next.

And what she did next, after she'd finished declaiming about the foolishness of her overzealous protectors and the perfidy of anyone with the temerity to doubt her predictions, was to swoop down on her three visitors with the same grandiose flashing of tears and smiles. She enveloped each of them in a smothering hug, finishing with Wasser, who was trying so hard to be invisible behind Erde's right hip that she was sure the boy/dragon had actually shrunk in size. Wrapped in the silken folds of Glory's robe, Wasser looked five years younger than the putative ten-year-old who'd walked through the gates. Erde hoped the dragon knew what she was doing. It wouldn't do to draw attention to herself by exhibiting unusual abilities.

"Precious children!" Glory exclaimed, though Erde did not see how the woman could think of N'Doch as a child. "Brave children! Come all this way to see Glory! Glory hallelujah!" She glanced around at her slack-jawed acolytes and threw up her arms. "I said, glory hallelujah, brothers!"

"Glory hallelujah, sister!" they chorused, though none of them looked very happy about it. "Amen, amen, amen!"

Glory's hot-ember eyes narrowed. "For I have seen the light. . . !"

"Oh, yes, sister! Amen!"

"And with God on my right. . . !"

"Amen!"

Roused by the noise, a few of the sleepers groaned to their feet and shuffled over to join in on the chorus. Glory's smile brightened, like a fire fed by the addition of kindling.

"There is truth in my sight!"

"Amen, sister, amen!"

Beads and bells tinkled as Glory lowered her arms and pressed her palms together. "Amen," she repeated with obvious satisfaction, then turned back to her visitors. "Now, dear and blessed, dear and foreseen travelers, rest from your trials, from your terrible journey."

It wasn't all that terrible, Erde would have reassured her, if she'd been further along with her lessons in Frankish. But Glory seemed to be enjoying her own version of their story. The light in her eyes, Erde saw now, was not unlike the hot glint that filled the bard's eyes at home, old Cronke, when he was deep into the recitation of a favorite tale.

"So, enter this humble house, good children! Bring to Glory's hearth the heavy burden of your terrible tidings, and lay it down! Glory hears all! Glory sees all! Glory will ease your load!"

And Erde wondered: *Which particular terrible tidings does she have in mind?*

* * *

N'Doch has felt the sudden gust of chill air expelled through the doors as the Glory woman flung them open. It makes him eager to get inside even though he has his doubts about the wisdom of venturing into what is clearly a crackpot's lair. But he's never been into an air-conditioned space that he didn't immediately get thrown out of. He'd like to know what it's like, this rich man's luxury. Maybe it's no big deal, really, but he thinks it probably is.

So against his better judgment, against all the accumulated cunning gleaned from a life in the streets, N'Doch lets the Glory woman take his arm on one side and the girl's on the other—he sees the girl's got the apparition well in tow—and sweep them up the shallow white steps like a small herd of sheep. Or whatever. N'Doch has never seen a sheep, but he knows their reputation for going willingly to the slaughter.

The white-robed toadies fall over each other in their haste to haul open the massive double doors, so that Glory and her guests pass through into the house without a break in stride. N'Doch sees only darkness inside, and pulls back a bit. Glory urges him inward. The doors, as tall and wide as any he's seen, breathe closed behind him with barely a whisper.

He's in a dim, cool hall, so dim he can't be sure how high or wide. He wants to stop, wait a bit for his eyes to adjust, but Glory is drawing them down along thick carpet he can only feel. His strongest impressions are sensual: the plush carpet; the caress of perfumed air cooling his skin, wicking away his sweat; the soft murmur of voices in other rooms, like the steady wash of the sea on a calm night. It's a spooky thing. He'd like to be *seeing* a lot more than he is.

"Hey, girl . . ." he ventures casually, into the darkness.

"I'm here," she replies. "And Wasser, too."

He feels a little better, though Glory's grip on his arm is disturbingly strong. He wonders briefly if his usually unerring instinct for gender has played him wrong. But he's seen the womanly curves of her body shaping her robes and now can't help but notice her rounded hips and full breasts as she holds him tight to her side. Experimentally, he leans into her a little so her breast rubs against his chest. Her nipple is hard. Apparently she's enjoying this scene she's

creating in more ways than one. N'Doch is more curious
than ever, but the oddness of it makes him doubly wary.
Like, maybe it's fear. He's seen that. But he can't say that
this woman looks like she'd be afraid of anything.

Finally his eyes adjust, but by then, they're at the end of
the hall in front of another set of double doors. N'Doch
barely has time to register the polished hardwood paneling,
outlined with a glint of gilt, when the doors are drawn aside
by white-sleeved arms and are swallowed up into the thickness of the door frame. N'Doch is freed as Glory raises the
arm that held him, moving into the room and signaling behind her without looking.

"Water! Warm water, soap, and towels for Glory's
guests! Then food and drink! Quickly! Hurry now!"

She flies about the room, beads jingling, hands and arms
in motion, and a small battalion of toadies swirls after in
her wake, drawing drapes and shades, flicking on lamps,
plumping pillows, pulling giant upholstered chairs and otto-
mans away from the walls into the room. N'Doch takes up
a position at the epicenter with the kid and the girl, like in
the eye of the storm, watching and wondering just what the
hell this is all about.

Shimmering white tablecloths are spread. Water is
brought in big white porcelain bowls. A soft white towel is
put into N'Doch's hands. Because he can't think of any
reason not to, he dips a finger into the nearest bowl. The
water is warm and clean. It doesn't smell or sting. N'Doch
rinses his hands, then his face and neck. Now he's really
aware of the cool air, chilled at such inconceivable cost.
It's actually raising goosebumps on his forearms. N'Doch is
amazed. He thought that only happened when you were
scared shitless. He asks himself, has he ever been this cold
before? He thinks he would remember if he was, and can't.

He watches the girl, sees how easily she falls into being
waited on, how her cool brief smiles and calm nods look
almost professional, like he's seen actors do it on the tube.
He sees the apparition observing her carefully, doing exactly
what she does. The toadies and acolytes seem surprised, like
they're not used to being treated graciously. He figures he'll
just give it a try. He's gotta be at least as good an actor as
the girl is.

The Glory woman washes, too, though N'Doch can't

imagine that she needs to, seeing as she supposedly just got up, plus took the time to get dressed to the nines like she is. She's got three attendants dancing after her like their lives depended on it, one holding a bowl, one the soap, and the third a whole pile of towels. She seems to notice them about as much as she would the furniture. She's in motion all the time and they have to stay alert to keep up with her without slopping suds and water all over the ankle-deep carpets. N'Doch wonders why she won't sit still, if maybe she's nervous or something, or like, did she take in too much of the precious white powder when she woke up this morning?

He thinks of the sleepers on the ground outside, and imagines the whole compound seething with people charging about at the speed of the Mahatma Glory Magdalena. It makes him laugh. But when he hears voices down the hall, a deep man's voice pitched to carry above others, and he sees Glory go on the alert, N'Doch realizes she's been listening, real hard all along, and part of her nonstop movement is simple wariness.

She goes to the door, trailing attendants, and calls down the hall, promising an immediate arrival. N'Doch notes the trill of coquettishness that brightens her voice and offers just a hint of submission. Then she whirls back into the room, tossing her towel aside without looking to see where it might land.

"Children, dear children," she declaims, circling, her eyes still drawn to the door. "Forgive your naughty Glory for abandoning you so soon after your arrival. But she won't be long. She just *must* bid a very special Guest good-bye, and then she'll be back to you in an instant!" Gathering her skirts, she wheels out the door and away. The attendants gather in the hall like storm refuse and stare after her.

So now, of course, N'Doch is dying to know who's this "special guest," this guy with *cojones* enough to make this astonishing woman hop to so fast.

"Wasser is not happy here," murmurs the girl at his elbow.

"Can't he speak up for himself?" N'Doch is enjoying the spectacle. He doesn't want his curious adventure brought to a premature end by some little kid's failure of nerve.

The girl gives him an odd, impatient look. "She's only warning you. There is something unusual here."

N'Doch snorts. "You don't think I can see that? You think I spend my life in air-cooled mansions with fresh water and servants at my beck and call?" No, but I'd like to, he finishes silently.

"Not that kind of unusual," she whispers. "Dragons don't notice human comforts. Or discomforts, for that matter. It's like what she said about the golden horseless coach. There's something . . . wrong."

Dragons. Right. Distracted by luxury and longing, he'd once again forgotten. He tells himself he really cannot afford to keep doing this. "Okay. Warning taken. Let's play it out, though. Sees where it goes."

She nods, dipping a corner of her towel into her basin. She pats delicately at her pale, sweated forehead. The towel comes away red with dust.

N'Doch grins. "Better just stick your whole face right in there, if you want to get that off." But he knows she won't. It wouldn't be . . . ladylike.

At last the washing ritual is completed. The basins and dust-ruddied towels are whisked away, and a regal spread of bread and fruit and cheese is laid out on the shining tablecloth. N'Doch thinks it looks like an advertisement. He checks it out pretty carefully, to assure himself it's real and safe and no one's pulling a fast one. He sees the girl holding back and tells her to go ahead, who knows when she'll ever see another meal like this one. When a steaming pot of coffee is wheeled in on a silver cart, he's sure he's died and gone to heaven.

"Eat, children. Help yourselves." Glory swoops back into the room like a gust of hot wind. Her brilliant smile and mobile hands urge them toward the table. "You must be dry and famished from your long and arduous travels."

To N'Doch's disappointment, she offers nothing further about her "special guest." Instead, she hovers briefly, pointing out delicacies, watching them as if to make sure they eat. She even grazes the food herself a little, commenting on the quality of this or that, and he wonders sourly if he's seen the extent of her, if she's like so many other star performers: all bombast and stupid small talk. He promises himself he will not be like that when *he's* a star.

Then suddenly, she's off again, shooing the remaining acolytes from the room. "Leave us, leave us! Glory knows
you're eager to hear the message they bring us, but first, you
must let the dear children eat and you must let them rest!"

It seems to N'Doch that the young men all give him a
look and go reluctantly, like maybe they don't trust him
with her or something. And he's not too busy piling food
on a plate not to notice when Glory locks the doors behind
the last of them. She does it quietly, so quietly and carefully
that N'Doch would be worried if it weren't for the fact that
somehow he just knows it's the people on the *other* side of
the door she wants to keep from noticing. When she's slid
the bolt home, she rests her forehead against the rich wood
for a long, still moment. He sees that she's breathing hard.

When she finally turns, she's no longer the flamboyant
Mahatma Glory Magdalena. Her smile is gone. Her eyes
look weary, haunted. Gathering herself, she glides swiftly to
the table and past it, murmuring, "Say nothing. Not a
word." She gestures them to gather up their food and follow. She's dropped the mask so suddenly that N'Doch is
left a little dizzy. The girl, however, seems relieved, as if
this new Glory is a more expected one.

"Lealé?" she whispers.

Still in motion but without all the arm-waving, the
woman agrees less with a nod than with a roll of those
haunted eyes, a look that also tells them to hurry, that no
real conversation can be had until they get to where she's
leading them. At the same time, she's muttering to herself,
"I didn't know, I didn't know."

N'Doch thinks she looks confused, but he's more concerned right then with his own humiliation. How'd the girl
figure it out so quick? It was the dragon told her, he's sure
of it. *His* dragon. He elbows the apparition urgently. "You
could have clued me in first, kid."

The boy/dragon blinks up at him, echoing Lealé. "I
didn't know."

"Yeah, sure."

"Really."

"Yeah?"

So maybe the girl's more on the ball than she looks. This
is a hard one for N'Doch, but he figures he'll learn to live
with it. Meanwhile, he reflects, the confusion of identities

in this caper is really getting out of hand. He decides to
think of the woman as Lealé, since she's the one Papa D.
sent him looking for.

And now she's saying in her regular "Glory" voice,
"Bring your food and drink, children. We'll go in here
where we can be comfortable." A deep archway in the far
wall divides the big room from a smaller alcove where there
are soft couches, big enough for sleeping or making love,
and low tables and some kind of music N'Doch can't quite
make out. He guesses this little area doesn't have the hidden
mikes and cameras she seems to be worried about. It looks
comfy and all, but when they're all there and setting down
their plates and glasses, and N'Doch is getting ready to
really tuck into his food, Lealé eases past, touching each
one of them on the shoulder. When she has their attention,
she mouths silently, "This way."

She moves back to the archway, leaning one hand against
the wall beside it, then makes an abrupt turn to the left
and vanishes.

The girl and the kid follow right her after like it was
nothing. N'Doch swallows, but knowing what he does
about surveillance sensors, he understands he better not
react visibly to what he's seeing. And he hates the idea of
leaving all this good food behind. So he palms an orange
off his plate and assumes an easy slouching pace across the
alcove until he's under the arch and able to see the slim
opening where the paneled thickness of the arch has swung
noiselessly aside. A dark narrow passage yawns. A hand,
Lealé's, reaches out and snatches him inside.

CHAPTER TWENTY-SEVEN

Waiting in the dark for N'Doch to join them, Erde squeezed Wasser's hand. It was chill, she noted, and the palm slightly damp, but what else would one expect from a dragon named Water? She was delighted by this new turn of events: the sudden shifting of identities, the magical appearance of a secret passage. Wonderful omens, each of them. Signs that the Quest was finally on its way again.

"Is this what was 'wrong'?" she whispered eagerly to Wasser. "Things not being what they seem to be?"

"No." The boy/dragon shivered. "Nothing ever is."

"True enough. But some things are even less what they seem . . . or more. Oh, I don't know. Anyhow, have you any better idea what it is, what you're afraid of?"

"I'm not afraid. Who said I was afraid? I'm . . . horrified."

Erde silently considered this mysterious difference.

"Same body language, I guess, different emotion."

"Oh. Horrified by what?"

Wasser gave an impatient snort. "By the wrongness, of course." Erde could hear him scuffing his feet in the darkness. "Maybe the right word is 'outraged,' " he concluded.

"Hurry now, children. It won't be long before they notice. Up ahead is a place we can talk."

With N'Doch in tow, Lealé propelled them forward. The passage was pitch-black and wide enough for only one body at a time. Erde was forced to lead the way with a hand braced against each enclosing wall. But now she noticed something ominous. Reaching behind her, she drew Wasser close to murmur in his ear. "It's gone awfully quiet in my head all of a sudden."

"Yes. I felt it as we stepped through the door. Wherever this place is, it isn't here."

As little sense as that made, she knew exactly what he meant. "He'll be worried," she whispered.

"He'll be frantic."

"You're doing very well translating on your own now."

"Yes." Erde could hear the boy/dragon grin. "I am, amn't I."

"Aren't."

"I knew that."

"Did you really know we were coming?" asked N'Doch behind them.

"Wait," Lealé replied. "Until we get there."

"We're between the walls, huh?" he marveled.

"Yes," Lealé murmured, but Erde thought her tone a bit doubtful.

"Your surveillance rig isn't high-tech enough to reach inside the walls?"

"Not this wall."

"Cool. Lead shielding, eh?"

"Not exactly."

Erde took in their conversation with half an ear, partly because she was worried about Earth, now totally isolated in his underground burrow, and partly because Wasser's German had only recently been lifted from her own head. It did not include words for much of what they were discussing. More important, she was distracted by a peculiar but somehow familiar sensation. Feeling her way along this lightless passage was not exactly the same, but certainly reminded her of how it felt when Earth transported her someplace. The same feeling of "otherness." A kind of deafness within an echo, a tingling kind of numbness. Only, instead of being instantaneous and then over, before you were really aware of it, the sensation went on and on like a dull ache, not rising or falling in intensity.

"Hsst!" Wasser jogged her arm.

A square of green light shone ahead—how could she not have seen it before?—an enlarging square rather like an open window. She seemed to be moving toward it, but at an oddly unpredictable rate. For a while, it would grow steadily, then it would stay the same for what seemed like minutes, though Erde knew she had not slowed her pace. Occasionally she would glance behind her, unthinking, to check on the others even though it was too dark to see anything. When she looked ahead again, the square would have suddenly enlarged, and she would be sure she was almost on top of it, ready to burst through into whatever mystery lay beyond.

"You could at least tell us where you're taking us," N'Doch muttered.

"To the only safe place. Everywhere else, I am watched. It's the price of fame. But this place no one knows about except . . ." Her voice faded, then as quickly recovered. "I call it my 'Dream Haven.' "

"Say it again?"

"It's where the Dreams come to me."

"Hunh. Seems like everyone's having dreams lately."

Erde knew Lealé had stopped short when she heard N'Doch's soft explosion of breath as he ran into her.

"You're not the Dreamer, surely," Lealé said.

"Sure, I have dreams, I guess. Doesn't everybody?"

"I mean the dreams you remarked upon."

N'Doch was silent a moment. Erde tried to will him to keep his silence, tried to nudge Wasser to still him before he said too much. "No," he admitted finally, "that would be her, I guess. Mine are pretty ordinary. But she's been having some real humdingers."

"Yes," Lealé replied slowly. Erde could almost feel the woman's eyes boring into her through the darkness. "Yes, I know. And I am meant to warn her against them. I see that now."

"So you did know we were coming."

"I must tell her not to listen to them. Except . . ." She broke off, as if changing her mind or suddenly losing her train of thought.

"Don't think that's gonna be necessary," N'Doch went on, oblivious. "She's already . . ."

"Wasser," Erde murmured, "Ask her if she saw us in her dreams."

But N'Doch's ears were keen. "Hey, girl, how 'bout me? I can do that now, remember, just as good as him."

Erde doubted it, but she could see how much it meant

to him, so much that he'd forgotten (or conveniently ignored) the fact that it was thanks to Wasser that the translations entered his head in the first place. He didn't even seem to have noticed that there was currently one less link in their communications chain.

"Then you must do it," she said to him. "But don't tell her about my dreams, ask her about hers. Did they tell her about us? What did they say? Why does she need to warn me? Ask her if . . ."

"Whoa, slow down, girl. I'll get to it."

His insistence on always appearing casual was, Erde thought, his most irritating characteristic. After all, some things were more important than others. Some things were worth getting excited about. But N'Doch had to behave as if nothing in the world mattered at all.

"So that's how you knew we were coming, Sister Lealé, from your dreams?"

But Lealé did not answer, and just then the passage widened and they were in a tiny empty room, lit only by the watery light from a wide doorway directly in front of them. This was the elusive green square that had led Erde through the darkness. It looked out on a bright grove of slender, smooth-trunked trees. Three broad steps of translucent stone led down to a flawless lawn that looked but did not smell like it had been fresh-cut minutes ago with a very sharp scythe. And there was something odd about the trees. A prickle up her spine made Erde halt just inside the opening. The others gathered beside her.

N'Doch spoke first. "So, are we there?"

"Yes," Lealé murmured. "This is my Dream Haven."

"Pretty weird lookin' trees out there."

"They're all the same," Wasser supplied.

"Yes," said Erde. "How remarkable. Every one of them, exactly alike."

"Cloned, must be," N'Doch remarked. "This is kinda like your little park out back, 'cept those trees are, y'know, normal."

"I see you've been exploring already." In a brief flash of humor, Lealé deftly parodied his answering shrug, then turned serious again. "I think it is sort of my little park out back, but whenever I go in there, I never end up here. It's very confusing."

"What happens when you go out there from here?"

"I never do."

"There's someone out there," Wasser said quietly.

"Oh, no, dear," Lealé assured him.

"There is."

N'Doch eased forward. "Let's go find out."

Lealé grabbed his arm. "No! You can't!" When he looked back at her in surprise, she let go but her eyes begged him. "Really. I never go out there. He wouldn't like it."

"He?" N'Doch gave her a sly look. "Aahh. The guy down the hall."

Lealé laughed. "Oh, no. Not him." Then she sobered and fell silent. Her moods were so mercurial that Erde was unable to make sense of them. The pale green light from the grove flowed over her anxious face as if it had substance, like smoke or water. *This is how it would feel,* Erde mused, *if you could live at the bottom of a clear lake.* She noticed how oddly steady the light was, as if every branch and leaf in the entire grove was utterly motionless. As still as the grave, she found herself thinking, then made herself stop, because of the chill it gave her. She remembered certain spring mornings at Tor Alte when the castle on its barren crag was wrapped in fog, and the sunlight seemed to come not from above, but from all around, as if trees and rocks, everything, even the fog itself, were aglow. *This place,* she decided, *is not of this world.*

"Then who is it you're so worried about?" N'Doch prodded.

"When I do my readings," Lealé offered finally. "I call him my spirit guide. My clients prefer to be able to envision their contact with the Infinite. Actually, I don't know what he is. I just know when he's here."

"Here? You meet him here?"

"He speaks to me here."

"Only here?"

"Yes. He calls me and I come."

Erde's ears pricked up at her use of the word "call" but N'Doch only nodded.

"Seems obvious to me—it's him out there, whoever he is."

Lealé shook her head. "He doesn't speak to me from out there. He's . . . somewhere else."

Watching the grove, Erde saw a flicker of movement. "Wait!"

Lealé started. "What? What is it, dear?"

Erde pointed, then let her hand fall. "No, it's gone."

N'Doch shifted his weight onto the first of the white stone steps. "You saw something?"

"It's nothing. That's how it always is," Lealé said. "Especially lately. I'm sure I'm seeing something, but he always tells me to pay no attention, and there's never anything out there really."

But Erde knew she'd seen something. "Did you see it, Wasser?"

The boy/dragon shuddered. "I felt it. We're very near now. . . ."

"Near to what?"

"Knowledge."

"I tell you, it's nothing," Lealé insisted.

"How do you know," countered N'Doch, "if you never go out there and look?"

"Please. Don't."

The fear that had been building in Lealé's voice finally drew Erde's attention away from the grove. Looking back into the darkness, she noticed that it was no longer so dark, and that the room was a little larger than she'd thought. She could see the walls now, paneled wood below and an intricately repeating pattern of some kind above, like a tapestry, only smoother and more abstract. It didn't seem to have any particular color. It just reflected the watery green glow pouring in from the grove.

"He doesn't want me to go there," Lealé continued. "He's been very clear on that score. And he's . . . not very pleasant when he's crossed."

N'Doch made a broad show of looking around. "I don't see any gate here, no bars or signs or nothing."

"I know. It's . . . like a test. He asks very little of me, but if I disobey him, he won't send the Dreams to me."

He folded his arms. Erde could see stubbornness rising in him like sap. "Okay, but he's not sending me any gigabillion-dollar dream scam, right? So you just stay put like you're supposed to, and I'll go have a look around."

Lealé grabbed him again, and a flare of the Mahatma's fire burned in her gaze. "Listen, it's you who've shown up like beggars on my doorstep! I don't even know who you are! Now, I've been generous because you invoked the name of my friend, but I'll not have you calling my Dreams a scam! My Dreams are true ones!"

"I thought it was you who sent for us," N'Doch retorted.

Lealé held on to him even more intensely. "Who are you? I don't even know why I sent that card! I need to understand why . . ." She broke off again abruptly and drew her hand away. "Forgive my rudeness."

"Hey, no problem. And my name's N'Doch, just so you know. Try to remember it. Someday you might see it plastered all over town just like yours."

"N'Doch, then. Is that why you think I'm a fraud? Please understand, then: It's not the fame I crave. I do have to promote myself in ways I'd prefer not to, but that's to get the people in. To get their attention, so they know there is hope for them. To support this house, this place of peace and safety, so they can come here and be helped. People need truth in their lives!"

N'Doch avoided her earnest stare. "Don't get me wrong. I'm all for turning whatever gimmick you got into making your name and fortune. I hope to do that myself real soon. But this spirit guy, he's your thing, not mine. My thing's something else at the moment, a lot of questions that need answering, and one of them just became: What's out there?"

"No! You mustn't! You can't!" Lealé's hands began to lift and fly about her in random fitful movements. Erde saw finally that simple envy was making N'Doch misbehave. In his desire to win, he was ignoring what was sensible. She stepped between them.

"Remember that Master Djawara sent us here to listen to Mistress Lealé, not to frighten and insult her."

"Aw, girl, this is stupid! We're here, why not just check the place out? It's just a bunch of trees."

"You know better than that by now, surely?"

"What is she saying?" asked Lealé.

Wasser turned away from the grove for the first time.

"Anyway, we certainly shouldn't go out there without telling my brother. I don't want to leave him stranded, in case we . . ."

"So tell him!"

"I can't."

"Why the hell not?"

For a moment, even to Erde, Wasser seemed tall and threatening in the eerie green glow. "Listen."

N'Doch blinked, and listened. "Yeah? So?"

"Listen *inside*."

N'Doch lowered his eyes, then quickly raised them again. "Hey. Where'd he go?"

His smaller self again, Wasser replied, "I don't think he went anywhere. Question is, where did *we* go?"

"Hunh." N'Doch's shoulders slumped. "Okay. You win. But, Sister Lealé, it seems silly to bring us here if it's so risky for you."

Lealé had been watching their exchange with narrowed eyes. Erde wondered what she'd made of it. "It's less risky than everywhere else."

"Right, so you said. The listeners. So who's listening?"

Lealé took on an entirely new face, world-weary and amused. She waved a dismissive, bright-nailed hand. "Oh, that's a whole other story. It's not really fit for children, and it certainly doesn't concern you."

"It does if you can't feel good about us talking where they're listening."

She gave him a quick, seductive smile. "It's just a jealous man, you know?"

N'Doch's sly grin bloomed in reply. "Ah! Now we get to the guy down the hall."

"Yes." Her smile turned faintly bitter. "Keeping track of his investment. Really, it's not your problem. I just don't want him knowing about all this." She gestured around the dark recess and outward, toward the grove. "Where my dreams come from or this . . . other business."

"The business of the card you sent Papa Djawara."

Lealé's nervousness returned. "Yes."

N'Doch glances around the cramped dark space. He sees low cushioned benches set along the wall that he hadn't noticed were there. In fact, if you'd asked him, he'd have sworn there was no place to sit before.

He sits. "Okay. You wanna talk. Let's talk."

The girl and the apparition join him. The kid grabs the seat nearest the door, probably so he can keep an eye out for any goings-on in the weird park thing. Lealé does not sit. She paces, not the smoothest thing to do in a space that small. N'Doch can see she's as nervous as a cat.

"I need to start at the beginning, if the story's to make any sense at all. You see, Djawara and I grew up together. We were distantly related." She turns to face N'Doch. "He is truly your grandfather, Djawara is?"

Her doubting makes him huffy again, but the girl is watching him, so he nods in a way he hopes looks noncommittal.

"I should have guessed it would be someone close to him. But I recall him mentioning, when we were still in contact, that he'd lost a grandson or two."

"Three. I'm the fourth, the one he wasn't close to, for a while at least."

Still pacing, she stops in front of the apparition, her face softening like women always do around little kids. "Is he your grandpapa, too?"

The apparition shakes its head.

"What's your name, then?"

"Wasser. It means 'Water.'"

N'Doch is still not happy with this name, has not once yet used it.

Lealé turns to him. "An interesting coincidence. Your name in Wolof is also . . ."

He nods. "Water."

Lealé looks to the girl now. "And yours, my dear?"

"Erde," the girl says, just a bit late.

"A lovely name."

The girl nods. *"Danke."*

"It means 'Earth,'" says the apparition, his child's eyes narrowing on Lealé. N'Doch wonders if the kid means it to sound so much like a challenge.

But Lealé brightens. "Ah. Like my little boulevard outside. Then it must be right." She starts up her pacing again. "I'll go on with my story."

"So, as we were growing up together, Djawara and I, we discovered we shared interests that set us apart from our other friends and relatives. Interests in the past, in history, in the old myths and customs. Djawara, particularly, was a gifted storyteller. He could expand his tales indefinitely, until they became entire sagas based on the adventures of some mythic hero. Later, when I did a little study myself, I discovered that he'd invented most of what he'd held us so enthralled with. When I put it to him, he admitted it readily enough, even seemed pleased with me for finding him out. Then he swore me to secrecy and confessed that he did it to distract himself—and us—from his growing obsession with the one tale that he hadn't invented, at least not consciously, the one tale he just somehow *knew*."

"The boy and the sea monster," N'Doch murmurs in spite of himself.

"Yes. The very one. He told you?"

"He used to sing it to me, when I was little." *Before I decided he was just too uncool to be with,* N'Doch reminds himself ruefully.

"It frightened him, I think," Lealé goes on. "This tale that would not leave him alone, whose central figure—the keeper of the ancient ways—he finally realized was himself." She stops in mid-pace and lets her gaze drift to the floor. "I had my own . . . dilemmas . . . at the time. I was having strange, well . . . visitations. Dreams and visions I couldn't explain. So when Djawara came to me—hoping, I'm sure, for a dose of healthy skepticism—I met him instead with encouragement and belief. I thought, well, if my much respected friend was being overtaken by some inexplicable fate, then my own bizarre experiences might be valid too. So, you see, each of us became the other's proof of sanity, and thus we were bonded for life."

She sighs and leans her head back, smiling, and she's beautiful again. N'Doch can tell she's picturing the young Djawara in her mind, and wishes he could be there to see him, too. "Later on," she continues, "When the events of our lives led us apart, we promised to be available for each other whenever our spiritual lives reached a crisis. For many years, they never did. Then I began having a kind of dream I'd never had before."

For the girl's sake, N'Doch asks, "When was that?"

"Two months ago," the girl puts in abruptly.

He frowns at her. "Let her tell us, huh?"

Lealé asks, "What did she say?"

"She said, two months ago, but that's just . . ."

"That's right. She's exactly right." Slowly, Lealé turns and looks at the girl, like she's seeing her for the first time. The girl smiles, like she's trying to look helpful, but Lealé shudders, moans a little, then drops right down in the middle of the floor cross-legged and buries her head in her hands. "Oh dear oh dear oh dear!" she wails, rocking back and forth. "I knew it I knew it I just knew all this was much more complicated than it seemed at first, much more than he said it would be! Oh dear oh dear oh dear!"

N'Doch sees tears and all, but he's not quite convinced—the change came on her so sudden. But the girl jumps up right away and kneels at Lealé's side, and puts both arms around her like she's known her forever. *Women can do that,* N'Doch reflects. And here comes the apparition now, only he goes around the front and sits facing Lealé, taking her hand more like a woman would do than a little kid. N'Doch thinks maybe the two of them are getting a little carried away, and he stays put, waiting for his part in it to come clear to him. Lotta times, since all this began, he's felt more like a glorified tour guide than this so-called "dragon guide" he's supposed to be. Like, where's his converted armored personnel carrier with the bullet-proof viewing windows, so he can say stuff like, "and on your right, ladies and gentlemen . . ." He's heard the patter. For some weird reason, the tour APCs broadcast it over their exterior speakers as they troll along the city streets and byways. Maybe they're trying to prove those rich foreigners riding in there in air-conditioned comfort are actually learning something useful.

Meanwhile, the girl is saying, "There, there," and other meaningless stuff made even more meaningless by the fact that she's saying it in German, like she's forgotten that Lealé's not a subscriber to the dragon comnet. But the apparition is translating softly in its little-kid voice, and to N'Doch's surprise, all this fuss seems to be having some results. At least Lealé has stopped her wailing.

"There, there," parrots the apparition, its small hands soothing Lealé's knee. "It's all right."

Lealé takes a breath, a long shuddering one, then lets it out in an even longer sigh. "No, you don't know . . . it's not all right! I should never have told him about Djawara and our pact. I never expected it to come to anything, you see, but now . . ."

"Tell us, Mother Lealé," urges the apparition while the girl murmurs and pats. "Tell us about your dreams."

"I can't!" She hunches up, whispering suddenly. "Not here! He might hear me!"

"Seems like you got overhearing problems wherever you go," N'Doch comments sourly.

"Mother Lealé," whispers the apparition, "surely if he can call you into this room, he can hear you wherever you are."

"Yeah," N'Doch agrees. "So it doesn't really matter, does it, and that's supposing he's listening at all."

Lealé eases herself back onto her heels. She looks a bit cornered but maybe a little comforted and, N'Doch could already tell, always willing to accept an excuse to talk about herself.

"Well, okay, but I refuse to say anything bad about him." She palms tears from her cheeks. N'Doch can see her preparing for a long recital. "Before, you see, my dreams were entirely random. I'd have one every now and then and there'd be someone in it I knew, so I'd go tell them about it and interpret it for them. And I was often helpful to them about some problem they were having, which made me feel good, like I wasn't going through all this weirdness for nothing. Then word got around, though, and people I didn't know came by looking for readings, and sometimes these people would offer me money, and we were poor, so I'd take it."

She shifts a little, her eyes wandering to the walls. N'Doch notices she's placed herself with her back to the door and the still green grove outside. "But then I felt they shouldn't go home empty-handed, so I looked them over as hard as I knew how, and made stuff up best as I could, to satisfy them. Yes!" She slaps her knees lightly with both palms and stares her challenge all around. "I've said it! I used to take money for fakery. But, children, if you understand the world at all at your tender age, you know that all people really want is an exciting performance and close personal attention to their mundane little problems. One way or another, I *always* gave them their money's worth! But then . . ."

Lealé takes another deep breath, steadier this time, and flicks a glance at the girl. "But then one night, about two months ago just like you said, I had this new kind of dream. It was a very specific dream, full of very precise information about some guy I'd never seen before in my life, like watching a vid-doc on the tube or something. I thought it was odd at the time but I didn't worry myself too much about it until later that day, the guy himself—the *exact same guy*, no doubt of it, I could tell you what he looked like even now—he knocks on my gate over on Water Street asking for a Reading.

"Well, needless to say, I gave that guy the Reading of his natural life, and he went out of my house and made a whole lot of money in some business deal, the crucial detail of which had been revealed in my dream! When I heard that, it gave me a chill. Then I had second dream like that, and again the stranger I dreamed about showed up right after, and it kept on happening. Then word really got around fast, and . . ." She stops, breathless, then looks around at each of them as if for sympathy, and shrugs.

"And *presto!*" N'Doch supplies. "You're the Mahatma Glory Magdalena."

Lealé nods as if she can't quite believe it either. "Except that it's not me doing it. Oh—I dreamed this house myself and made it so. Or rather, I learned how to make it so. He taught me."

"This spirit guy . . . ?"

She laughs full-out this time. "Oh, no. Sorry. The *other* one. My investor. I dreamed him once and he showed up."

"And saw you had a gift could make you both a handsome living."

"Yes."

"Which now you don't want to let go of."

"Do you blame me?"

N'Doch stretches his legs. "No way. I'm in awe of your achievement, sister." But it seems to him there's one big detail missing. "So the spirit guy . . . when did he put in a personal appearance?"

Now Lealé hesitates, licking her lips and searching the corners of the room, as if even to speak of him invited his unwelcome presence.

"Please, Mother Lealé," begs the apparition on cue, even though now it's looking just as scared as she is. "Tell us."

"One night I dreamed about me, finding my way to this hidden place. When I woke up, I went and found it, just as the dream had told me. While I was there, I grew drowsy and must have dozed. He came to me then. It was . . ." She's talking so quietly that N'Doch has to lean in to hear her. ". . . after my second dream about Djawara."

"What'd you dream about Papa D.?"

"At first it was just . . . about him. Later, it was about the visitors he would have . . . you. Only not you, exactly. I never expected he'd be sending children. . . ."

N'Doch thinks she's called him a child just about once too often. "What *did* you expect?"

She shrugs uneasily. "Just that there'd be more than one, and that one would be a Dreamer . . . like me."

The girl's been real quiet for a long time, listening, but now she starts murmuring into the apparition's ear.

He says, "Erde asks if you are sure your dreams of Djawara came from your spirit guide? If it was he who sent the dreams, then he must have known all about Djawara already. If he didn't know, he couldn't have sent those particular dreams."

"You mean, they were just . . . dreams?"

"Perhaps," says the kid.

"But they were true dreams, or you wouldn't be here."

"Why should that surprise you? You are, after all, a Dreamer."

N'Doch jumps in. "Anyhow, you haven't betrayed Papa D. after all, so you don't have to worry."

Lealé glances at him, then away. "It isn't Djawara I'm worried about. Djawara is a man of power. He can take care of himself. It's . . ." But she can't quite bring herself to say it, so a silence falls in the dim little room.

"It's us," says the apparition finally. It gets up and walks to look out the green, open doorway. "Isn't it."

Lealé nods. "He wants you . . . done away with. And I was supposed to do it. When you got here."

The apparition smiles at her gently. "I thought you said he didn't ask very much of you. . . ."

But N'Doch's had enough. "Who is this guy anyway? What's he got against me? I don't even know him!" He knows it's nuts, taking death threats from spirits seriously when he doesn't even believe in spirits, least he didn't used to. But that was back when he didn't believe in dragons either. "Sounds like a major raw deal coming my way, and for nothing!"

"Be cool, my brother," the apparition advises from the doorway.

"*You* be cool," N'Doch snaps back.

The kid turns, standing taller and older, silhouetted against the livid green. "You're surprised only because you've forgotten who and what you are, what I am, what we are, and what we must do."

Lealé watches with a mixture of awe and agitation, so that when the kid comes toward her again, she recoils, leaning back on one hand, twisting herself defensively to one side.

"Mother Lealé," the kid says in a soft voice that fills the room. "It is absolutely vital that you tell us everything about this 'spirit guide' of yours. What he says, how he looks when he comes to you, *everything*."

N'Doch is watching, too, and not real happily, 'cause the older the apparition makes itself appear, the more it looks like Sedou.

Lealé shivers, staring up at her pint-sized inquisitor. "Who are you? *What* are you?"

N'Doch thinks, *Well, I guess the gloves are all off now, aren't they?*

CHAPTER TWENTY-EIGHT

Erde had observed Wasser's handling of Lealé with admiration, but she did wonder how much his/her true nature the boy/dragon thought was safe to reveal. Something that Lealé had said provoked this display of strength. Apparently Wasser had decided that the woman had information he needed to know sooner rather than later.

"What kind of spirit might this be that visits Mistress Lealé?" she asked, thinking to gentle the moment away from confrontation.

"There are no spirits," Wasser replied gravely, with his eyes still fixed on Lealé. He looked as though he might pin her to the ground if she but moved an inch.

"No spirits?" Lealé managed. "But I . . ."

"There are only Powers, and humans with a gift. I am one such, and I wish to know what other seeks my end."

It was a tone she had never heard out of Wasser or even Water, before. Quiet, but full of intimations of ancient strength and grandeur. Erde backed away a step and sat down along the wall. She saw N'Doch do the same, both of them leaving the floor to what both of them knew was a dragon with a serious purpose in mind.

"First, describe this 'spirit' to me. Don't leave out the smallest detail."

Lealé's brow creased. "I don't see what . . ."

"Not the smallest detail. I do not ask without reason."

"What if he hears and comes after me?"

"I will protect you."

Lealé grinned weakly. "I think you'll have to grow some before you take him on."

"If it will make you feel more confident." And right

there in front of her, he did, each moment looking less and less like a little boy and more like a man. Erde saw N'Doch ease himself backward along the wall.

Lealé stared, caught between terror and curiosity. But she was not undone, having already lived much of her life with the miraculous and inexplicable. "What is your gift?" she asked shakily.

O clever dragon, Erde thought. *Offer a choice of truths and let the hearer make the wrong one.*

"I have many. Tell us about your dream-giver."

Lealé blew air softly between pursed lips. "Well, he is very vain . . . he'll probably love hearing me describe him. He's very handsome, you see. . . ."

"He's human, a man? He comes to you as a man?"

"Oh, yes, he surely does. He's tall and broad-shouldered, with perfect ebony skin and the flashing golden eyes of a warrior."

"He's got gold eyes?" N'Doch asked dubiously.

Lealé was caught up in her description now. "As gold as the rising sun. And his voice is very deep and resonant."

"Of course it is," muttered N'Doch. "And he's able to leap tall buildings in a single bound."

"How is it that I look as I do?" Wasser reminded him quietly. "There are humans with the gift to take on the aspect most desired."

N'Doch glared at him. "You are certainly not what I most desired."

"Consider it further, my brother."

Erde was grateful when N'Doch folded into a thoughtful silence for a while. It was clear to her, as it would have been to any woman, that Lealé's relationship with this "spirit guide" was rather complicated. She seemed now to be consulting her inner portrait of him, or it, and her expression had grown definitely dreamy.

"He has very big hands with unusually long nails, which he keeps up very carefully. In fact, he paints them."

"Yes," replied Wasser softly. "Long nails. Anything else?"

Lealé giggled briefly. "Oh, he won't like me telling you this, but it's his choice, so he must think it makes him look good." She lowered her voice to a breathy gossip's whisper. "He always wears a lot of gold jewelry. All sorts of it, anywhere you can imagine! Places even I wouldn't have imagined!" She sat back with a pretense of offended modesty. "Isn't that peculiar?"

N'Doch started to chuckle but Wasser only grew grimmer.

"Ah. Golden eyes, golden metal," the boy/dragon said tightly, turning to gaze out on the grove again. "What color does he paint his long nails?"

"Gold! What else?" Lealé leaned forward intimately. "And detailed with exquisite miniatures of beautiful naked women, a different one on each nail—I mentioned he was vain, didn't I?" She grinned as if it were a great joke, but Wasser's tense back told Erde that it was not.

"What else?" The boy/dragon now seemed the reluctant one, and Lealé the eager raconteur, spurred on by N'Doch's appreciative laughter.

"He has a right to be vain, beautiful as he is, but he's also very proud. He's always boasting of how powerful he is. And he has a terrible temper!"

"What does he do?" asked N'Doch.

"Oh, he can't actually do anything physical, but he can take my Dreams away and make my life completely miserable!"

Wasser turned. "He cannot manifest?"

Lealé shook her head.

"A Power, then, surely," Wasser concluded. "It's as I feared."

But N'Doch looked enormously relieved. "Then he's not gonna be, like, jumping out of bushes to slit my throat or anything."

"Not him, no."

"So what does it matter?"

Lealé's mouth tightened. "You can't imagine how much it matters. His tongue is as lethal as any blade."

". . . as corrosive as acid," murmured Wasser from the doorway.

"Yes," she said to his back. "Exactly."

"O, I fear, I fear," he whispered, as if to himself.

N'Doch shook his head. "Not me, man. I'm real glad to know some spook who's said he wants me dead can't actually make it happen."

Wasser sighed, as if exhausted. "Anything more you can tell us?"

Lealé shrugged. "Well, let's see . . . he smokes."

N'Doch laughed out loud. "You got a spirit that smokes?"

"No." Wasser turned toward Lealé, his face darkened by shadows and foreboding. "He comes in smoke. He comes wreathed in its tendrils, as if accompanied, and perhaps here and there a touch of flame."

"Yes," breathed Lealé. "How did you know?"

"You know who this is," Erde murmured.

"I have an inkling now, oh, yes, I do, a terrible inkling. But perhaps this is his idea of a prank, a way to make his presence known and demonstrate his superiority at the same time."

"A prank?" repeated Lealé, sobering. "No, I don't think so. Not when I tell you how many ways he'd figured out that I could murder you. If he's who you think he is, would he want you out of the way so badly?"

"If he's who I think he is, he is capable of anything."

"Hold it . . ." broke in N'Doch. "I thought you said he couldn't . . ."

"If he can't manifest a physical presence in this plane," said Wasser impatiently, "he has only to coerce a human agent into doing his bidding. By giving them gifts, and promising great wonders."

Staring down at her hands, Lealé nodded.

N'Doch snorted, scanning the dark walls, the invisible ceiling. "Wow. So maybe bringing us here is one of the ways, huh?"

"No," said Lealé mildly.

"And why not?" Wasser inquired, just as mildly.

Her bittersweet smile seemed to be admitting to a fatal weakness. "He didn't tell me it'd be killing children. I guess I just don't have it in me."

"I am glad of that, Mother Lealé."

"But you know, he'll only find someone to do what he wants. And, of course, I will be ruined. I should have known things don't come this easy." She thought for a moment, then frowned gently. "He got one thing wrong, though. He told me to expect four of you, not three."

This seemingly minor bit of information seemed to drain the last gleam of hopeful doubt from Wasser's eyes. He hunched, let out a soft moan. His whole outline seemed to waver.

N'Doch leaped to his feet. "No! Don't do it! Not here!"

Erde moved to comfort him, but the boy/dragon caught him/herself and steadied. "It's time we got out of here. I must warn my brother." He started down the receding dark passage, then threw over his shoulder angrily, "My other brother!"

CHAPTER TWENTY-NINE

When they get back to the alcove, N'Doch sees the food's still sitting on the plates like nobody's touched it. In fact, his coffee's still hot, which makes him wonder about how much time they'd actually spent in that weird dark place. Maybe not as long as it seemed.

And now there's a lot of knocking on the door out in the main room. N'Doch checks behind him to see if they'll have some explaining to do, how they went in with a little kid and came out with a full grown man. But the apparition has returned to kid form. N'Doch breathes a sigh of relief.

Lealé motions them toward the sofas in the alcove and mimes eating. "Rest, children, and we'll talk later," she says in her Glory voice. "I must return to my duties." She draws heavy, embroidered drapes across the archway and lets herself out between them. N'Doch can hear her unlocking the big double doors and exclaiming in full-blown Glory persona, "My goodness, what *is* all the fuss about?"

The reply is murmured and unintelligible.

"What did you think?" Glory comes back. "Of course I'm ready! Are the afternoon candidates assembled? I hope you remembered to . . ."

The thick wooden doors shut behind her. The big room is silent. N'Doch gets up to sneak a peek through the drapes, and feels the now familiar itch inside his head. He turns to reply out loud, but the apparition quickly raises a finger to its lips.

— *We'll take no chances.*

N'Doch nods. It'll be an effort, him not being real experienced at it, but he's beginning to see real advantages in this silent communication. As soon as he goes to the right place in his head, he feels the big guy's presence there again and hears his rumbled greeting. He's surprised how glad it makes him.

And now he guesses it's safe to ask:

—*What'd you mean, your* other *brother?*

—**Our brother Fire.**

—*And he's, y'know, like you? A dragon?*

—**Of course.**

Her voice in his head is irritated, and in front of him, the apparition frowns. But its gaze is oddly distant and N'Doch's almost sure it's frowning at the possibility of Fire and not at him at all.

—**And if Fire were to take a human form, it would likely be as Lealé has described.**

The girl's voice chimes in, softer than her spoken voice.

—*Surely not, Mistress Water! A dragon works only for good!*

—**Whatever gave you that idea? Brother, perhaps it's time to relieve this child of some of her illusions.**

The girl looks dumbstruck, and Earth's reply, when it comes, is humble.

—**I did not recall what our brother Fire was like until just now.**

—*We gotta go talk to this asshole, then!*

N'Doch turns to the hidden archway, where the paneling had swung inward so readily at Lealé's touch. He presses on the wall and nothing happens. He feels around a bit, searching for a seam or crack to tell him where the hinges are. Nothing.

"Damn!" he murmurs. He tries to picture exactly where Lealé placed her hand just before she vanished, and feels around some more. Still no luck. The apparition joins him but stands back after a while.

—**We will look very suspicious to anyone monitoring the surveillance system.**

N'Doch shakes his head. He's beginning to understand why they need him around after all. He's like their technical expert.

—*From what she said, I got the idea there was only sound sensors in this part of the room.*

—*That doesn't seem very thorough.*

He wonders how much detail he's gonna have to go into.

—*But look at all these big plush sofas and things . . . maybe the big bankroll himself wants a little privacy in here from time to time . . . you know what I mean?*

The girl looks back at him blankly, but N'Doch feels Water's knowing assent in a whole new corner of his mind, a place apart from where all four of them spoke together. He hopes the images that ran through his mind along with the thought of the bankroll on the sofas have stayed in that special corner as well. He figures they must have, or the girl would be blushing something fierce. What's odd about all of this is he's just recalled what Papa Djawara implied about Lealé preferring women. Maybe when he said her interests lay elsewhere, he meant she was hot for some other *guy*. Certainly now that he's watched her operate, N'Doch's inclined toward that explanation. He realizes now that Lealé's a hard one to read. She's like a whole lot of people rolled up into one.

—*So we can't get back in there till Lealé tells us how. What'd you wanna do, then? You think she expects us to just hang around here?*

N'Doch looks longingly at his plate still mostly full of food. He sees the girl has edged herself closer to her own plate in order to pick at it surreptitiously.

"You hungry, girl?" he asks aloud.

She nods, and N'Doch grins. It's beginning to feel like she really is his baby sister. "Then, first things first, I say. Let's eat."

It's just about the best meal N'Doch can ever remember. He tries not to stuff himself so much it'll slow him down, but it's hard. His reflex is to eat when the food's at hand, 'cause it'll likely be a while before you see it again, especially food like this—safe, fresh and delicious, with such a variety of tastes and textures all at once. He's not used to being able to choose to eat *this* instead of *that* simply because *this* might taste better.

After a while, he looks up. The apparition is waiting none too patiently in front of a full plate.

"Eat up," N'Doch advises. "You don't get it much better than this."

The kid makes a little Jéjé face, entirely out of sync with the voice in N'Doch's head.

—*I can't eat in this form. The parts aren't all in the right place.*

N'Doch doesn't know why, but it makes him laugh.

—*You mean, if I sliced you open right now, it'd be a real biological surprise?*

—**Wouldn't be a pretty sight.**

—*Kinda like it isn't when you're changing, huh?*

—**Probably so.**

Sitting cross-legged on the edge of the sofa, struggling not to get lost in cushions too deep for his small body, the apparition's really looking like his dead little brother. It makes N'Doch remember stuff he'd forgotten, moments of stupid kid-jokes, moments of shared conspiracy, the few moments they'd had to feel like brothers before Jéjé was gone. Moments sort of like this. He grins across the girl's dark head, bowed over her plate.

—*Whadda ya say, think we oughta go exploring a little?*

The apparition nods, and the girl looks up. She's been listening in.

—*As soon as is possible, we must find some place for Earth to join us.*

She's right, of course. N'Doch gives it some thought.

—*There's a big garage out back.*

—*What about the park you and Mistress Lealé spoke of? Is there cover?*

—*Not much. Besides, I got a weird feeling about that place.*

The apparition hops to its feet.

—**Let's go take a look.**

The girl's been eating slowly. N'Doch waves at her to keep at it.

—*You stick close and hold the fort, case Lealé comes back.*

Her eyes widen in protest.

—*She won't expect you to talk to her or anything. Just keep an eye on her, y'know? Follow her around like you're glad for another woman's company.*

He thinks it's a pretty clever ruse, but the girl nods so pensively that N'Doch suspects he's touched a true nerve. It makes him wonder about her a little. Like, maybe she's got a mother somewhere worrying about where she is, like his mother worried about all her sons, and lost them anyway, all except him. What would it do to poor Fâtime, so worn and numbed by loss, to see the spitting image of her youngest standing right in front of her the way the apparition's there in front of him now, ready for an adventure? He thinks it might just finish her off.

He jerks his head at the kid gruffly, the way older brothers get to do, and lifts his hand to the girl.

—*You can always just pretend you're asleep. And if you need us, just give a yell. We'll come running.*

She nods. She doesn't look all that worried, actually. She knows, as he does, that she can monitor them every step of the way through the big guy.

N'Doch turns and parts the concealing draperies with a finger. He surveys the outer room, counting a camera port in every corner.

—*No way we're gonna get outa here without them seeing. Better just look like we know where we're going. I'll go first, see if I set off any alarms.*

He pushes through the heavy curtains and wanders across the room to the food table. It's all still there, laid out like a gang leader's funeral supper. Though he'd been sure he couldn't possibly cram in another bite, N'Doch finds a few things he hasn't tried and starts nibbling. It's a good enough cover, and so far, he's heard no bells or sirens, no Jean-Pierre flapping down the hallway, screeching like some big white bird. Course, all the most expensive systems give silent alarms: some bright red readout below a bank of sleek monitors in an office somewhere full of fast guys with guns.

The apparition joins him and pretends to pick at the food for a while. Neither of them have any trouble producing the right body language of two bored young men tired of being cooped up inside.

—*You ready, bro?*

The apparition grins at him. As one, they turn and head for the door.

CHAPTER THIRTY

It was odd, Erde thought, the lassitude that came over her when she was left alone in the alcove, enclosed by its thick draperies and its strange furniture, as softly cushioned as a feather bed. The cool air smelled faintly of perfume, and the light was dim and golden, like a dying fire but as miraculously steady as the sun's own light. This, she supposed, was Master Djawara's "electricity", which she had not yet seen close up. The lanterns that made it were tall and thin, like brass bells turned upside down on the top of pike poles, and did not flicker. For the first time since arriving in this world of 2013, she was not hot and sweaty, she was not uncomfortable or dirty, and she was not hungry. She thought perhaps she should be a bit more nervous than she was about being left on her own in a strange house, but the rich food and the sudden comfort were making her irresistibly drowsy.

—*Dragon, I need to sleep a little. Will you watch over me and wake me up within the hour?*

—**I will, as best I can from such a distance.**

—*Not so far, really, and they will find a place here for you soon.*

—**I am eager for that.**

—*As am I, dear Dragon.*

Erde settled herself into the deepest cushions, in the farthest corner. Perhaps if someone looked in here, they wouldn't even notice her. Her last thought, swimming up through the layers of drowse just as she fell asleep, was: I hope I don't dream.

But of course she did.

*   *   *

She thought she woke in darkness, but then the darkness showed a dim light through a crack across from her bed. A lantern in the outer room, she decided sleepily.

—For shame, Dragon! You've let me sleep far too long.

She yawned and stretched, awaiting his reply, his expected excuses about how badly she needed her sleep. But the dragon's answer did not come. Then she realized that, stretching, she could not feel her body. She tried to sit up and had no awareness of limbs. No sensation at all except a creeping dread. She was not awake. She was dreaming, and the air in the room was damp and chill, and full of the snap and groan of wind among tent ropes.

She watched the lighted crack, her only anchor in the blackness, and understood she was looking through a slit between lowered tent flaps. Outside, the light dipped and flared in the breeze. Torches, then. One at least. And no other sound but the wind.

Suddenly, as if she'd arrived in this dream just at its moment of crisis, she heard the soft thud of running feet, feet trying not to make noise, encumbered by the weight and rattle of weapons and armor.

She heard a frightened voice cry, "Halt!" and heard it just as quickly hushed, followed by a hurried conference, low and urgent.

The tent flap was snatched aside.

"My lord!" A half-dressed squire, painfully young, stood in the opening. "My lord baron! Are you awake?"

"What? Yes!" growled a voice so close to Erde's side that the shock alone nearly woke her up, a voice shaking off sleep like a dog shakes off water. "Yes, fool, I'm awake. What is it?"

The boy hissed to the man behind him, then took a torch from him and stepped aside. A tall and burly soldier stooped into the tent and went down on one knee. The torch at the opening lit his mud-spattered face and heaving chest, and the grim rage in his eyes.

"Wender. What . . . ?" The man on the cot came up warily on one arm. The edge of the torchlight touched the rough gold of his beard, and Erde could confirm what she already anticipated: Adolphus of Köthen.

"My lord, they've taken the Prince."

"What? We had men guarding his tent."

"Dead."

Köthen sat up, swinging his legs to the ground. "All?"

"Throats cut, all three of 'em, with the Prince's own dagger, my lord, conveniently left behind."

"What of the priest's men?"

"A showy mess of surface wounds, but all likely to recover, probably by morning if circumstance doesn't intervene. I'm tempted to let it. Each claims to have seen the Prince fighting 'like ten thousand demons.'"

"Ah, Carl, poor lad." Köthen ran angry hands through his sleep-matted hair. "Is there a trail?"

"Two, my lord. The one we're supposed to find, and then the other. I sent six of our best to follow the second, and came to fetch you."

"All this without arousing notice?"

Wender smiled, and Erde pitied the man who got on his wrong side. "Aye, my lord."

"Pray they find him. Pray six will be enough. Have you horses ready?"

"In the copse."

"Tell that silly boy to douse the torch before he announces us to the entire camp. His little fire should be enough to keep the dark away." Köthen heaved himself out of bed. "Help me dress."

Before the torch could be extinguished, Köthen walked into its flickering light. He was naked. Erde tried to look away, but the dream-state did not allow her the luxury of modesty, and in the slowness of dreams where a few seconds can seem an eternity, she found herself made breathless at the sight of him. She'd never seen a grown man naked. She thought men were probably ugly without their fashionably form-altering clothes. Even Rainer, that fine figure of a young man she'd convinced herself she was in love with, even in her most romantic fantasies she'd always pictured him fully dressed.

But this man was beautiful, naked or clothed. She could not help but notice his efficient grace, or how the muscles moved under his skin as he bent to snatch up his clothing, or how the failing torchlight glimmered gold on the hair of his arms and chest and thighs. The intimacy of the moment shamed her. Surely Baron Köthen would be appalled if he knew. But she could not look away. She thought she could look at him forever.

Then he moved out of the light and threw on his shirt and undertunic. Erde was released from her disturbing fascination and had a moment to consider the dire news about the Prince. She wondered where her father's hand was in this latest plot.

Wender shook out Köthen's mail and held it high for the baron to shrug into, easy enough as he was at least a head taller than Köthen and several stone heavier. "It seems this priest will make you King, my lord, whether you like it or not."

Köthen laughed sourly. He slipped on his blue-and-yellow tabard, then bent to pull on his boots. "And when Otto and his mysterious champion are dead on the field, and I've rallied the people around me with the promise of victory and peace, how long do you think I will survive?"

Wender grunted. He turned away and came back with Köthen's sword and dagger. Köthen took them wordlessly and buckled them on.

Outside the tent, the torch had been upended in the squire's little campfire. The two men hesitated, straining through the high sighing of the wind to pick out other, man-made noises. The moon was bright. Köthen squinted at it suspiciously.

"Back to bed with you," he murmured to his waiting squire. "Or at least pretend to be, as if I were still inside asleep as usual. Have you your weapon handy?"

The boy shivered and patted the long knife on his hip.

"Good lad. Protect yourself if the need arises." Köthen nodded to Wender then, and followed him off into the night.

The horses were waiting with another dozen men in a copse of aspens out of hearing of the encampment. With the moon to light their way, they quickly picked up the trail of those who had gone ahead along the muddied road.

"He hopes they'll mingle with the track of ordinary travelers," noted Wender. "But only brigands and soldiers travel in a time of war."

Köthen grinned. "Well, we know which of us are the soldiers. . . ."

Erde found herself galloping through the moonlit darkness as if she were a hawk on Köthen's shoulder. She could almost forget she was dreaming, but for the rock and rise of Köthen's body on his racing horse, in such sharp contrast to her own smooth surreal flight.

But cushioned as she was by the unreality of the dream, she could not shrug off the lurking dread. Köthen's presence somehow held the dread at bay. She recalled how he had protected her from the priest in the barn at Erfurt, even though she was a stranger and the ally of his enemy. Being with him flushed her whole body with warmth and a sense of well-being. But she knew that this strange euphoria was but a thin tissue between her and the terrible things she sensed were about to happen, and could do nothing to prevent. The dread was real and could not be avoided forever.

They rode hard for a good while until Wender judged they might be closing on the men he'd sent ahead. The ground was half mud, half ice, and pocked with puddles frozen just enough to make a noise when horses' hooves crashed through them. Where the trees folded over the road, straining out the moonlight, Wender slowed them to pick their way along more quietly, listening ahead. Soon Wender pulled up, his hand raised for a halt. Köthen rode up beside him.

"A light, my lord, though the trees off to the left."

Köthen cocked his head. "No sounds of battle."

"No. We'll go in on foot, in case our men are yet waiting to engage."

The baron nodded. He seemed to have no difficulty taking direction from an older and more experienced adviser. "Quickly, though, in case they've been taken unawares."

The company dismounted silently and left two men behind with the horses. Köthen drew his sword. Several of the soldiers armed their crossbows. They left the roadside and crept into the trees, seeking the quietest path through the sodden leaves and matted underbrush, avoiding the brighter patches of snow and ice where a man's footfall would sound as loudly as a shout.

Those ahead did not seem to be making any great effort at silence. They'd lit two torches already and soon a third flared to life. Erde could hear horses milling and snorting, and voices that were restrained but not muffled. Wender waved his company forward, signaling one man to Köthen's right and taking up the left-hand guard himself.

They were well within range when a voice ahead sounded an alert and the torches were doused in an instant. But that single word of command told Wender what he needed to know. He signaled his men down, then whistled sharply, three ascending notes and one falling.

"That's Hoch," he whispered. "I'm sure of it."

A whistled reply came back immediately, the same four notes in reverse order. Wender rose and moved on ahead.

They came down into a snow-swept clearing, broad enough for a circle of moonlight to make its way through the overhanging trees. Hoch's men relit the torches while Hoch came forward to meet them. Erde saw in the man's eyes the dread she'd been shoving aside. Köthen saw it, too.

"What is it, Hoch? What have you found?"

Hoch had a thin, intelligent, worried face. Erde thought he looked more like a guildsman than a soldier. He swallowed nervously but looked his baron in the eye. "The worst, my lord."

"The Prince?"

Hoch dropped his glance, nodding.

"Dead? Already?"

"Dead, my lord. Within the hour."

Köthen swore and looked away. Then he glared around at the waiting men as if searching out someone to blame for this outrage he'd been so sure he could prevent. His men stood their ground silently, their heads bowed, absorbing the heat of his rage and giving him back their trust. It moved Erde deeply that Köthen, even as he was at that moment, a dangerous and angry man swinging a naked blade so that it flashed in the torchlight, would never turn his rage on his men. Her father's men would have retreated well out of range, as far as was possible with honor, in such a situation.

Prince Carl dead. Murdered, she supposed, and she had no doubt by whom. The mad priest's plot was proceeding.

Was it possible that he—and evil—would somehow win the day?

Finally Köthen took a breath, lowered his sword, and sheathed it abruptly. "Show me," he growled.

Hoch offered a slight bow. He motioned to one of the torchbearers, and led the way.

The young Prince lay crumpled at the foot of a big tree. He was small for his age, having not inherited his father Otto's height. His feet were bare and battered. Not at all the figure of a King or warrior, Erde mused. He'd been a studious boy, she recalled Hal mentioning. Her heart went out to him: a scholar, doomed by birth to be a pawn in the vicious games of men more powerful and ambitious than himself. He was dressed in the soft robes he would have worn for retiring to bed. Clearly, he had not been armed. One torn end of a long sleeve had been folded back to cover his face.

Erde searched for blood or wounds. There were none anywhere on his slim body, except on his torn and muddy feet. Then she noticed the rope disappearing beneath the covering sleeve. Hoch took the torch in his own hand and raised it in order to illuminate a stout overhanging branch of the tree: Another length of rope dangled there, its loose end hastily slashed.

Hoch cleared his throat. "We cut him down not five minutes before you came, my lord."

The men in Wender's party shifted and muttered.

Köthen stared up at the offending rope. "He will call it a suicide and discredit the whole of Otto's line. Why? This Prince was not his enemy. Are there no depths to which this man will not sink?"

No, Erde wanted to shout at him. *Not a one! I could have told you that! Hal tried to tell you in Erfurt, but you wouldn't listen!*

Köthen raised his voice to be heard around the clearing. "Let not a man of you believe that the Prince died by his own hand!"

Wender laid a feather-light hand of warning on his baron's sleeve.

Köthen shrugged him off brusquely. "Yes, yes, Wender, I'll be quiet. For now, at least. But later . . ." He knelt beside the body and briefly lifted the concealing sleeve.

"Forgive me, my Prince. I tried to keep you safe as best I knew how."

Wender waited, sucking his teeth, then said quietly, "We could undo the shame at least, my lord."

Köthen gave his lieutenant a shocked look that slowly turned to bleak acceptance. He rose, flicking the sleeve back into place. "Do it," he said, "then swear the men to secrecy."

"Aye, my lord."

Wender sent the men scurrying—to untie the rope from the tree, from the Prince's neck, to burn the evidence and scatter the ashes, and finally to do the necessary violence to the corpse. Köthen moved away, out of the gathered circle of torches, away from the busy clot of men. He moved like a man in physical pain, sorry for the death of an innocent, Erde thought, but also deeply disturbed by the sacrilege of this pragmatic desecration. Köthen would go to confession and do his penitence, and still carry this guilt on his soul forever, even though he had allowed it for all the right reasons, to honor a monarch he himself was trying to usurp. Watching him brood, she ached for him. Her desire to reach out to him grew so intense that she could almost believe it was possible, by sheer force of longing, to walk out of her dream-state and into Köthen's reality.

This was a new idea, and even as swept up as she was in dream-induced fantasizing, the fact that she was considering it seriously quite took her aback. Her intention shifted a bit more toward the rational with her sudden realization that she had information that might ease Köthen's guilt: If what Hal and Rose had surmised about Rainer's parentage was true, a rightful heir to the throne might still exist, that is, if Köthen and her father hadn't already killed him off unknowingly. But she had heard Köthen's brief reference to Otto's "mysterious champion," and was sure it could be none other. If Rainer lived, and if he was the true Prince, Köthen could forget all this needing to be regent in order to keep the country together. He could join Hal and establish Rainer as Otto's heir, and this alliance would crush the offending priest like a bug. And then they could all run the country together. Erde thought it a grand and glorious vision, a future one could look for-

ward to. It was nearly—minus Rainer—what Köthen himself had offered Hal at Erfurt. It was a perfect plan and
would solve everything. The hell-priest would at last be
defeated.

She was very aware of being without substance in her
dream-state, but her other senses were fully intact. She
could see and hear and smell. Perhaps she could simply
speak to Köthen without leaving the dream at all . . . why
had she not thought of this before? And what harm could
it possibly do to try? She focused on him very hard and
thought of speaking, as she did when she spoke with the
dragons.

—*My lord of Köthen.* . . .

Her dream-voice was like the whisper of night wings. She
could hear it . . . but could he?

A thrill shot through her when she saw his head lift
slightly and his eyes sweep the darkness in front of him
as if listening. She had never expected to make contact
so easily and now she was almost tongue-tied. What
should she say to him? How should she introduce herself,
a person he hardly knew, his enemy? How explain to him
what was happening? She recalled how long it had taken
N'Doch to accept the joining of minds. Köthen, she suspected, considered himself a rationalist, a pious man but
not much given to superstition. How could she put words
into his head without him thinking he was losing his
mind?

—*My lord of Köthen* . . .

It sounded so formal. Then she remembered what Hal
had called him.

—*Dolph* . . .

His head jerked this time. His eyes widened. She watched
a faint flush of fear race through him. She decided she
would not introduce herself at all. It was not her identity
that mattered, it was her message, and now she realized
she must convey it quickly. Even in her disembodied state,
she suddenly felt faint. Each effort to bridge the gap between Köthen and herself sucked energy out of her like
water down a drain. It was a greater gap than she'd imagined. She had to tell him her message before she lost the
strength to do it.

*—Baron Köthen . . . Dolph . . . a Prince may live still . . .
find Hal and ask him. . . .*

Köthen shook his head hard, then pressed his temples
with both hands and let out a strangled cough. "Hal?" he
murmured.

A sentry's whistle off to the left distracted him. Quickly,
Wender joined him at the edge of the darkness, and Köthen
was once again all business.

"Visitors, my lord."

"Indeed. How convenient. Have you done what you
must?"

"We have."

"Prepare His Highness for transport, then, with the
honor due his rank. And, Wender . . . don't be too quick
about it, eh?"

"Will he come himself, do you think?"

"He expects to find his Christmas goose still trussed
and hanging."

Wender grinned his flat, dark grin. His eyes flicked off
through the trees toward the road, where the approach of
men and horses was no longer a suspicion. "Sounds like
he's brought a whole regiment. And enough torches to light
a town."

"Or burn it. Better send some of the men into the woods
to cover us, in case in his madness, he decides to murder
us all and lay the blame for Carl's death on me."

"What head will he have left then to crown, my lord,
having so long ago lost his own?"

Köthen's laugh was a short bark. "Why, I suppose von
Alte's next in line, poor fool."

Wender snorted and went off to prepare the body. Köthen drew his sword, set its point to the frozen ground, and
leaned on it gently, awaiting the priest's arrival.

Now Erde's terror stirred in earnest. From the time her
dreams of home began, she knew Fra Guill would enter
them sooner or later. Even in his absence, his black aura
pervaded them. Her dream-state connection with Adophus
of Köthen, her supposed enemy, was a mystery and a surprise, if now increasingly a pleasure. But from the day the
hell-priest first presumed upon the hospitality of her father's court, from when his thief's eyes picked her out and

followed her everywhere, when in the barn at Erfurt he had sniffed her out of hiding despite her disguise, she knew that her fate was entwined with Guillemo's in some grim and awful way. In fact, if there was any way she could manage to wake up, now was the time to do it. But she was unable to wake herself from these dreams as she had learned to with ordinary nightmares. So she withdrew inward as best she could, and imagined concealing herself in Köthen's shadow.

Even so, when the first of the white-robes appeared, pale ghosts moving between the black columnar ranks of trees, each with its own huge torch, she thought of the lost souls wandering in torment, the souls these white ghosts had put to the torch at Tubin and the other "witch-ridden" towns. And she wondered if it was possible to die of terror while dreaming. Only the thought of the dragon waiting for her a thousand years away gave her the strength and the reason to master her fear, the way the man beside her was mastering his loathing and outrage in order to gain control of himself, and the situation.

The priest's forces fanned out as they entered the clearing, a long arc of hooded men in white, mounted on tall white horses. Köthen did not move from his casual pose, but his eyes took them in, counting. Erde counted twenty, and was relieved not to find her father among them. Apparently he was not included in this particular conspiracy. Did that imply that Josef von Alte was losing his usefulness to Brother Guillemo? Erde feared for her father's life if he was.

A space left in the center of the ranks was filled at last by Fra Guill himself, unhooded but wearing a full soldier's breastplate over his white monk's robe. His tonsured hair was no longer the madman's rat's nest it had been when she'd seen him last, but his face had grown gaunt and sallow. His eyes receded so deeply into their hollows that they appeared as two shards of ice glimmering in wells of shadow.

He spurred his horse forward. "Abroad so late, Köthen? Or is it early?"

If Köthen noticed the lack of honorific in the priest's greeting, he did not show it. Erde took this as a frightening sign of how far the tables of power had already turned. It occurred to her to worry for Köthen's safety as well as her father's.

"Late, Guillemo, much too late, in fact. But so are you, it seems."

"The battle against Satan knows no clock. Late is early, is it not? And so, what finds you here?"

Köthen tossed a nod behind him. "A little business. What finds *you* here?"

"Our hardy pursuit of that Satan's minion, Otto's treacherous spawn, who's made a bloody and murderous escape this night."

Köthen leaned on his sword hilt a little more heavily and replied dryly, "He'd hardly have been trying to escape, Guillemo. He's barefoot and in his bedclothes."

The priest's eyes narrowed until their light was virtually extinguished. "You have news of the villain?"

"I have news of the Prince, if that's who you mean."

Erde wondered if Köthen was hoping to make Guillemo beg. He was goading the priest, for some hidden reason or because he could not restrain his hostility completely. Either way, she wished he would stop. Was she the only soul in Christendom besides Hal Engle who understood how venomous Fra Guill really was? When she'd faced him last, in Erfurt, he'd seemed wily but entirely mad. Now he appeared to have regained possession of himself. Erde was unsure if this was better or worse.

"You've caught up with him?" Guillemo sat up ever so slightly to peer past Köthen toward the huddle of men on the far side of the clearing.

"In a manner of speaking."

"What's the news, then?"

"Your heart's desire, Guillemo. The Prince is dead."

"Ah." Instantly, the priest crossed himself and bowed his head. A moment later, twenty white-robes did likewise, sending a rustle of wool and rosaries through the damp, still air. "Did he confess his dread villainy and call on his Savior before being given his end?"

Köthen seemed to be working a bad taste out of his mouth. "I doubt he was given the chance. He was dead when we got here."

The banked glimmer in Guillemo's eyes flared up again. "Ah! Distraught, then, with the weight of his bloody deeds,

as a ray of goodness pierced his heart and made him see
his . . ."

The priest had an infinite supply of self-serving rhetoric,
as Erde clearly recalled. But Köthen had had enough. "Carl
was murdered, Guillemo. By brigands, one supposes, unless
you have any better ideas."

"Murdered? You've seen it . . . him . . . yourself?"

"You know me, Brother. I never take anyone's word
for anything."

"I'll go to him, then. To offer whatever poor words might
be allowed to intercede for his tarnished soul."

Köthen cocked his head, still leaning on his sword. "Be
my guest."

The white-robes remained in their long array as their
leader rode across the clearing. The torches made way for
him, and a man-at-arms leaped forward to hold his horse
as he dismounted. As he moved into the crowd of soldiers,
Köthen jerked his sword out of the ground and strode
after him.

Wender met him just outside the circle of light, stooping
to pick up Köthen's hurried murmur.

"I don't like it. He's taken it too quietly."

"Grace in the face of being outmaneuvered, my lord?"

"Not even a possibility. Stay by me."

They found Guillemo on his knees beside the Prince's
corpse, peeling back the wrapping of cloaks and oilskins
with his own too-eager hands. Hoch and Wender had artfully arranged the layers to allow exposure of the Prince's
wounds with a minimum of effort. Guillemo wished to see
a little more. He yanked and burrowed until he was satisfied, and all Köthen could do was stand and watch. Erde
wished he would move off a bit. She had little stomach for
being forced to observe the poor mutilated body at such
close range. But she did note how all evidence of Carl's
true cause of death had indeed been erased by Wender's
careful butchery.

Guillemo studied the wreckage carefully. He touched his
finger to a ragged gash, then smoothed the blood between
finger and thumb, sniffing at it cautiously.

Wender muttered at Köthen's side, "More like a chiru-
geon than a priest."

Köthen watched and waited, and soon had his answer.

Guillemo sniffed his bloodied fingertips again, rubbed them together and sniffed again. Abruptly, he cried out and sprang to his feet.

"Water! Ho, water! Quickly, on peril of my soul!"

A man-at-arms grabbed a waterskin off the nearest horse and ran over, shoving it at the priest with both hands in frantic bewilderment.

"Pour it for me, fool! Quickly, on my hand! Or else we'll both be damned!"

The nervous soldier drenched Guillemo's hand, water spilling everywhere, even on the Prince's body. The priest then raised that hand, dripping, and held it out from himself like it carried some treasure or disease. "A torch, now! Bring me a torch!"

A torch appeared, and Guillemo directed the man to angle it toward the ground so that the flame swelled and leaped upward, overfed with fuel. With slow ceremony, Guillemo passed his wet hand through the dancing flame, several times, back and forth, until the soldiers murmured and gasped and took a step or two backward, away from him.

A mere carnival trick, fumed Erde, yet see how it amazes and subdues even these hardened fighting men.

At last, Guillemo withdrew his hand from the flame and held it up to show how it remained unsinged and unscarred. "A virtuous man has no need to fear the purifying flame," he remarked. Then he turned slowly toward Köthen. "But you, my lord baron . . . what unlawful devil's ritual have you been enacting here?"

Köthen went entirely still. Erde could see he was suddenly and exquisitely aware of the trap that yawned before him, reeking of brimstone and the black smoke of the stake. If he told the truth, his earnest sacrilege would be for naught. Poor Carl would have only an excommunicant's grave in unconsecrated ground. To deny the deed would mean lying to a priest, God's representative on Earth, and there were a dozen men present who might not be so willing as he was. A moment later, Köthen relaxed. Either he'd found an opening, or he was simply brave enough to fake it.

"Since when is it unlawful to bring a King's son home for burial?"

"You wish me to believe that you found him like this? With the devil's own sign cut into his mortal flesh?"

"What? Where?"

Guillemo pointed. "There!"

No sane man, nor an honest one, would have traced out a pentacle among the crisscrossed wounds on the Prince's chest.

"I don't see . . ." began Köthen. He turned to Wender. "Do you see . . . ?"

"Of course he doesn't, for foul magic has hidden it, from all but a wary and knowing eye!" Guillemo met Köthen's furious stare for the length of a breath, the gleam in his own eyes already victorious. Then he rounded on the nearest man, the frightened one who'd brought him the waterskin. "You, my son, for the salvation of your immortal soul! You tell me what's gone on here! What terrible unholiness has this godless man led you to commit?" Without looking, the priest raised his arm and pointed at Köthen.

"This is nonsense, Guillemo," scoffed the baron, but Erde could see he knew it wasn't. "We have more important tasks in front of us."

The priest turned, his head high, shoulders flung back. His eyes seemed to have found their former life, and filled the hollows below his dark brows with flash and danger. "My lord of Köthen! What could be more important than a man's immortal soul?"

Just lie to the man, Erde pleaded desperately. Had she been there in reality, she would have flung herself at Köthen whatever the peril, and begged him not to pursue this futile debate. Like his mentor Hal before him, he refused to believe that the craft inspired by lunacy could win out over the craft inspired by reason. But Erde was sure that he'd soon learn, as Hal had, how easily men are swayed by superstition and terror.

Wender had apparently reached the same conclusion. From the moment the debate was joined, he'd begun to ease himself backward through the cluster of men. Now he moved casually along the outside as if trying for a clearer view of the action, grasping certain elbows, prodding certain backs as he worked his way around the circle. He got concealed nods in return, and those men, four, six, seven of them, keeping the rest of the onlookers between them and the long line of white-robes across the clearing, backed off slightly and quietly readied their weapons. Their eyes strayed to Hoch, who would give the order. When Erde looked for Wender again, he was gone. Slipped off into the woods, she guessed, to alert the hidden reinforcements.

Meanwhile, Köthen was saying, "Nothing is more important, good Brother, unless it be the bringing of peace and order to the land, so that its people have time and security enough to tend properly to their spiritual well-being!"

Guillemo rolled his eyes and groaned as if hearing the worst sort of blasphemy. "Oh, dear Savior! Forgive the day your loyal servant agreed to an alliance with this unbeliever!"

"You go too far, priest! How dare you question my faith?"

"Who better to question it than a man of God?"

Köthen spread his hands and turned to the men around him, seeking a show of their support, a sign that they knew where Fra Guill's posturing was leading and would have none of it. Erde felt a moment's pity for him. Hal had said that men's willingness to follow him was Köthen's greatest strength. He'd risen to power on their loyalty and support. When he searched their faces now and saw loyalty ebbing away, as she did, he would know he had lost them, and losing them, had perhaps lost everything.

But would the realization be enough? Or would he keep flailing away at the priest's apparently invincible juggernaut of unreason? She must tell him to forget reason, forget honor! Tell him he must back out of the trap while he still had a chance, for once closed, it would open again only as the flames rose up around him at the witches' stake!

She *could* tell him. She was there, at his ear. . . .

—. . . *Run, my lord baron! . . . you must save yourself!* . . .

Köthen shook his head, a negating shudder.

—. . . *Listen to me! You must flee!* . . .

He brushed the air dismissively with his hand.

Guillemo gasped and pointed. "Ah! See! See how the Dark One speaks to him even now! But you cannot put off Satan so easily, can you, my lord baron, as if you were swatting a fly!" He lifted both arms and bellowed, "O, down on your knees, Adolphus of Köthen! Confess to the Lord your vile sins of trafficking! Throw yourself on His mercy, for it is infinite!"

Köthen was breathing in the tight, measured way of a man readying himself for desperate action. His gaze remained fixed on the priest, though Erde was sure he'd rather be scanning the dark woods for help and rescue.

—. . . *Dolph, behind you! Your man is behind you!* . . .

She had little strength left for this urgent speaking across centuries. She gathered herself for one last try.

—. . . *Now, Dolph! Run! Or I swear, HE WILL BURN YOU!* . . .

Guillemo froze, both arms still raised toward the cold night sky. "What?" he whispered.

And Erde learned that she had not lost all bodily sensation in her dream-state: She distinctly felt her blood run cold.

He took a step toward Köthen. "What do I hear?"

"You hear nothing!" Köthen snapped.

"Do not deny it!" Guillemo hissed. "She is here!"

This time Köthen did not have to feign bewilderment. "What 'she'? There is no 'she' here."

The priest edged another step closer, sniffing like a dog on a scent. His blazing eyes searching the air around Köthen's head. He seemed to have forgotten the rapt audience he'd been playing to so fervently a moment before, but the sudden change in him only frightened his listeners more. Erde noticed to her horror that, deep in their hollows, his eyes were the same green-gold as the eyes of a snake.

"Is it possible," he murmured to Köthen, "that you do not know?"

"Know what, priest?"

"The witch-girl. She speaks to you. It's her voice you hear in the night sounds. . . ."

Köthen's nostrils flared. "No. . . ."

"It is." Guillemo moved closer, within a pace. "What does she say to you?" He slithered sideways, circling, his voice pitched low and far too earthy for a cleric. "You hear, witch? He minds you not. Come, speak to one who's worthy of you!"

Erde shrank from him in panic, as his aura invaded her dream space.

—*Wake! I must wake! Dragon, help me!*

—*He cannot, witch.*

The hell-priest's mouth had not moved. His voice was in her head.

—*And you never shall wake. . . .*

—*I will! I will!*

But there was smoke twined in his hair and tiny flames danced around his body, and his green-gold eyes pinned her like prey. He was the hell-priest and he was not. He was something more, something Other. He would swallow her, eat her alive, he would snuff her, smother her, he would . . .

—*HELP ME!*

She grabbed for Köthen and felt the hot shock of contact. He felt it, too, and moved at last, jerking himself aside as if to confront the one who'd touched his shoulder. But his hand by instinct stayed to his sword hilt, and Guillemo sprang back, bellowing.

"To me! Ho, to me, knights of God! We are under attack!"

The Other in Erde's head lost hold. Her dream-self shot off like a stone from a catapult, careening away, away, toward blackest emptiness, toward the void. But just before the void, something caught and held her, something soft and strong and infinite. And a voice spoke to her, as light and as large as the stirring of air.

—*He cannot help you, but I can. . . .*

And then she was ever so gently repulsed from the edge of the darkness and sent back toward the light, drifting slowly. She could not propel herself back to the clearing. She hadn't the strength. She could only float helplessly and watch from a distance as . . .

Hoch's order rang out. Köthen's head turned to the sound of horses behind him just before the charge of the white-robes drowned it out. He drew his sword and with infinite trust in his lieutenant, backed off in the direction of Wender's approach. Hoch's men were already halfway to their horses, preparing to meet the charge. A few of the remaining soldiers got hold of themselves and backed away with Köthen, leveling their own weapons at those who remained undecided.

Köthen yelled to the stragglers, "Come on, think, you fools! Since when does a madman speak for God? Come now, while you can! He'll show you no more mercy than he's shown me!"

The priest raced in among them, screeching hellfire. Most of them broke and ran, terrified. Hoch drew his horsemen up in a line between his baron and the priest, and the white-robes were almost upon them when Wender swooped down out of the woods with a big gray horse in tow and lifted Köthen bodily into its saddle.

"Two to one's my count," he shouted over the clash of steel and hooves and leather. "Do you wish to fight another day?"

"I do, indeed," Köthen rasped, reining in his horse so that it danced and circled. "I've been fool enough for one night! Get the men out of here!"

Wender signaled Hoch to pull the men off and retreat.

"Wait!" Köthen yelled. "We must see to the Prince!"

Wender snatched at the gray horse's bridle before Köthen could turn back. "Already seen to." He pointed as two men raced past, one with Carl's swaddled body slung over his horse's shoulders. "Quick, my lord! He'll have them after us!"

"Only for show. I'm more useful to him now as a living threat of witchcraft than a dead one!" Köthen urged his horse forward anyway. "Wender!"

"My lord baron?"

"Name your reward!"

They were moving away from her now, a dozen men low over their horses' necks, ducking branches, fleeing through the dark woods faster than Erde, in her weakness, could follow.

"A speedy escape, my lord!" called Wender, "And after that, the hell-priest's head."

"That you'll have to stand in line for. But I'll use my influence, if I have any left!"

Their voices were fading. She wanted to go with them, to share in the euphoric bravado of the escape, to know that they were safe. But she only drifted. . . .

"But first we shall deliver this sad Prince to his father."

Even this did not catch Wender by surprise. "Aye, my lord, we shall."

And then she heard only the thudding of hooves as they faded beyond her hearing entirely, and beyond her consciousness.

CHAPTER THIRTY-ONE

Waking up was a surprise, almost as if she hadn't expected to. But she had to be awake, or she wouldn't have been so painfully aware of her body. She was as weak as a newborn and ached in every joint, as if she'd been put on the rack. She was lying facedown with her limbs sprawled as if she'd fallen or been tossed down from a height. She flexed her hands. Her fingers clutched something prickly-soft. She managed to turn her head and lift it slightly. She was lying on grass.

Grass! For one joyous moment, she thought she had ended up at Deep Moor. But this grass was much too short. Tiny even blades, each one the exact copy of the next, and entirely without scent. Unnatural. She pressed weakly against the ground and it gave a little like ground should. But it released no rich, dark smell of loam, no bright sweet-green pungency of a sunny valley mead.

Erde struggled to pull herself up. When she called for the dragon and got no response, she knew exactly where she was. No, not exactly. She knew where she was . . . she just wasn't sure where *that* was.

Just sitting up left her breathless. She remembered the dream, every moment, and recalled how this weakness had come upon her, how every word she had murmured in Baron Köthen's ear was like breathing her life's blood into the wind. She fell back on one elbow and looked around: perfect green lawn stretching as far as she could see, endless receding ranks of the smooth-trunked trees that N'Doch had called "cloned."

How ever did I get here? she wondered.

She pondered her catapult journey to the edge of the

void, and decided that not all of her travel had been a dream-state illusion. Just like she had actually *touched* Baron Köthen's shoulder. That had been real, certainly. She could recall the sensation as if it was imprinted on her fingertips: the silky feel of the tabard sliding over the hard mail beneath, the smoothly jointed links close-textured like her grandmother's beaded purse, and warm from the heat of Köthen's body.

Erde blushed, thinking of him. She missed him already. It was absurd. It was ridiculous. How had she allowed this to happen? She knew that young girls were meant to be romantic, but this was worse than falling in love with Rainer even though she'd thought he was dead. At least Rainer was only nineteen. Köthen was at least thirty, he barely knew she existed and he lived a thousand years away. She'd never even had a conversation with him. The one time she'd met him in person, she'd still lacked her voice. Perhaps she was merely homesick. The raw dangers of 913 were at least more comprehensible than the mysteries and complications of 2013. She hoped that when she grew up, she'd finally become sensible enough to fall in love with someone she could actually spend some time with.

Meanwhile, here she was in Lealé's "Dream Haven." That she had come from a dream to here warranted thinking about. She wished the dragon were there to discuss it with her. She wondered how much time had passed while she'd been dream-shifted to her home time, and was anybody likely to be looking for her yet?

What she needed to do was get up right away, if she could manage, and find the doorway to Lealé's little room. Then she could follow the passageway back to the house. Standing up was difficult, but not impossible, though once she got there, her balance was unreliable. She was, she realized, enormously thirsty. Hungry, too, although eating would require far too much energy. She staggered a little, turning step by step to scan the odd forest in all directions for a sign of where the door might be.

When she'd completed her circle—though it was hard to tell exactly, with identical views at every angle, if she really was back where she'd started—she steadied her balance and thought she had better try it again. At her next sideways turn, she let out a small shriek of surprise. A small table stood in front of her, right there on the grass where she was sure there had been no table before. It was a delicate sort of table, with a single carved central pedestal and a short, lace-trimmed square of snowy linen covering its top. Not at all the sort of object she would have missed the first time around, especially as it contained a clear glass pitcher full of water, a plate of lemon slices, and a dainty glass tumbler, all set out on an oval tray of finest silver.

Erde stared. Having just come from 913, the world of the hell-priest, she wondered if this was some sort of a trap. N'Doch, she recalled, never drank water unless he knew where it had come from. But she had a feeling about this water . . . a good feeling. A feeling that emanated from the forest around her, as if someone was whispering in her ear—as she had whispered in Köthen's—that she mustn't worry, everything was perfectly all right . . . at least for now.

But if it wasn't a trap, it could still be an illusion. She was questioning reality now the way N'Doch questioned the safety of anything he put in his mouth: by habit. In the world of her growing up, reality had not been in question. Everything was real, even witches, magic, and dragons, all things that N'Doch's world had decided not to believe in. Lately, even she had questions about witches, having been labeled one herself, and most of what she called magic, Master Djawara called "science." The only thing she was really sure of was dragons.

So to prove that the water was real, she drank it. She felt a lot better for it afterward. Almost up to putting her mind to the problem of not having seen even a hint of a door, or anything but trees, the same tree, over and over and over again.

When they get past all the sleepers, most of them up and about by now, N'Doch and the apparition head straight for the odd little park. It's the only place he's seen so far that might be big enough to hold a dragon. He can feel the big guy in his head, but not so clear as he can when the girl's around. He's a little worried that she's fallen asleep and they're letting her, even with this thing about, like, *going in* to her dreams. But they're the dragons, he figures. They gotta know what they're talking about.

They walk along slow, so's not to alert one of the "flappers." This is how he thinks of Glory's henchmen in their flowing white gowns. He's teaching the apparition how to saunter, how to do it with authority, so you don't get bothered on the streets by just anyone thinking you might look like a mark. The kid's not real good at it yet. Sauntering doesn't really suit its dragon nature. But N'Doch thinks it's worth a try anyway.

At the edge of the park, the apparition stops along the gravel path and stares into the trees like it was reading a book.

"What?" asks N'Doch. He figures it's okay to talk aloud out here, with no one around to listen. He doubts if the big bankroll's likely to be bugging the woods.

The apparition points toward a corner of the park, where the trees are the thickest. N'Doch looks, then shrugs.

— *Look carefully.*

N'Doch sighs and looks again. And then he notices that, everywhere else, he can see the far surrounding wall through the straight smooth trunks. In that one corner, he can't. *The trees must be thicker there,* he thinks, though he sees no change in their spacing.

— *I'm going in there.*

"Sure, okay. Let's go."

The apparition shakes its head, puts a finger to its lips.

— *You stay here at the edge and watch me. Keep in constant contact and tell me when you lose sight of me. If you lose contact . . .*

— *I'll be right in there after you, don't worry.*

— *No! Tell my brother Earth, if you can hold that connection, or go wake up Erde immediately and tell them both what has occurred. If you come in alone, we may both be lost.*

"Easy, man. Glory ain't gonna let the punks and muggers hang around where they could be hurting her business, y'know."

— *Do as I say!*

N'Doch sulks, but when the dragon gets this tone on, he knows he's gotta pay attention. He scuffs the gravel, looks around for something to lean against.

— *I'm gonna look like some terrific kinda guy, letting my small bro wander off into the bushes by himself.*

The apparition turns just inside the first row of trees and flashes him a grin.

 —*Just tell 'em I went in there to pee.*

N'Doch watches, trying not to look like he's watching, in case *he's* the one being watched. The apparition pads off purposely through the trees, exactly like it's looking for a likely spot. N'Doch smiles. *This kid's all right,* he thinks. Maybe Fâtime won't have a coronary when she sees him, if N'Doch prepares her right.

The trees don't seem to be closing in around the apparition as he goes, though by now he's already farther in than he should be able to go, judging from where the wall is everywhere else. N'Doch checks it out to either side and checks back. The kid's still walking. N'Doch thinks maybe the wall takes a big jog out there where he can't see it. No reason, after all, why the lot has to be square.

And then, between one step and the next, the kid is gone. Like, in a heartbeat.

"Yo!" N'Doch sputters. He takes a few long steps forward, and then remembers.

 —*Hey! You there? You all right?*

 —*Yes, of course. Why?*

 —*You disappeared!*

 —*Really?*

 —*You didn't, like, step behind a tree or something?*

 —*No. Wait a minute. Keep watching.*

An instant later, he's there again, waving through the trees like some kind of tourist. He vanishes again, reappears, vanishes, reappears.

"Awesome," N'Doch murmurs.

 —*What does it look like from there?*

 —*Like you're switching yourself on and off like a light. What's it look like from there?*

 —*Come ahead and find out.*

N'Doch scans the view in both directions. One flapper by the garage putting the final polish on the Glory Car's headlights. Whole bunches of "guests" moving about in the front yard, paying him no mind whatsoever. N'Doch saunters into the trees. Before he gets to him, the apparition vanishes again.

 —*Hey!*

 —*Just walk straight. You'll get here.*

He stops, glances back at the house. Hardly seems like he's covered any ground at all. He shrugs and keeps going. Ahead of him is nothing but trees, and he's thinking he's gone wrong somehow when all of a sudden, he's there.

The trees open out into a big grassy clearing, shaded by overarching branches. In the middle of it sit two dragons. N'Doch looks behind him again. The house and grounds are right there, not a hundred yards away.

"Total bizarro," he remarks, and turns back to the dragons. It's kind of a leap for him, seeing her in dragon form again. He was just getting used to the apparition. But he can't help but notice all over again how beautiful she is.

"Lookin' good, girl," he muttered.

They're both sorta grinning at him.

"Guess you guys figure you're safe here. . . ."

—As safe as any place around here, and a lot more comfortable.

"You're pretty glad to be out from underground, huh?" he says to the big guy, who flexes his muscular neck, looks around and seems to shrug in a pleasantly ironic fashion.

—My name is Earth. I was born underground.

"Oh. Right. Sorry." N'Doch has to admit it's about time he started calling the big guy by his actual name. It's just, well, it sounds weird going around referring to someone as "Earth." Of course, it's no weirder than everyone calling *him* "Water."

—You weren't born underground.

—I was. Under the mountain.

—No, that was later. *We were all born together, at one instant, out of elemental matter. You don't find that under any old mountain.*

Earth looks both interested and mournful.

—You are wise, my sister. You recall so much of our beginnings.

—Not enough, or I'd have some idea what our brother Fire thinks he's up to.

"What's his problem, this brother of yours?"

—He was always the most volatile.

"He's like his name, huh?"

—As are all of us.

N'Doch considers, and has to agree. "Can't wait to see what *his* dragon guide looks like."

—*If he's awake, he must have heard the Summons. Why would he be plotting against us?*

—*Did I mention he was also the most devious?*

—*Sister! A dragon would never be devious!*

Water pulls her sleek little head back as far as her long neck will allow, and stares at the big guy as if he's from Mars.

—*No wonder that girl of yours has such anti-quated notions!*

N'Doch just has to laugh. "She awake yet?" he asks Earth, sort of to let the pressure off him. This Water gal is beautiful, but she's not too long on tact.

—*I have not wanted to wake her. Perhaps I should . .*

—*We were going to make a quick food run, is what he means. You already got to eat, remember.*

"Hey, go for it. I'll take a walk back and check in on her. Listen, you think Glory . . . I mean, Lealé knows about this place, y'know, what it does in here?"

—*It would explain why she thinks it's the same as the wood outside her "Dream Haven."*

"Is it, do you think?"

—*There are intriguing similarities, but until we've gone there . . .*

"Yeah. Who can tell? Okay, you guys go eat. I'm heading back."

He intends to check on the girl all right, but what he really has in mind is a closer look inside the house. Now he's got himself free of all his recent encumbrances, he figures he can do it pretty quick and pretty thorough. Never know what he might find in there.

He looks for a back way in, but there's only the front door and the big ceremonial side entrance for the "guests," and they're lined up two deep out there, winding all the way around the neat stone terrace a few times and ending up down on the lawn.

Got her hands full this afternoon, he thinks. He wonders if her spirit guide gives her a Dream each for every one of these poor suckers, how he could possibly have the time, especially if he's busy plotting against his siblings. If he is this Fire guy, that is.

Another dragon. N'Doch wipes his brow on his forearm. That's all he needs.

He finds the front door unlocked but not unguarded. Two flappers are sitting up beside the columns in lawn chairs, fanning themselves. N'Doch opts for sheer chutzpah, and strolls right by them with a smile and a little wave. They nod at him, none too graciously. Apparently the word's gone out that he's here at the Mahatma's invitation.

He's glad to be back in the air conditioning again, though the central hallway is so dark, it really does give him the creeps. Maybe the Mahatma's trying to save money on electricity. He puts his hand to the first big brass knob he sees. He turns it quietly, expecting resistance, but it opens easily into bright, even light and the sounds of keypads, cooling fans, and drive hum. Under that, work chatter. An office. Well, if he'd had light enough out in the hall, he could've read the sign on the door. He backs out silently. No point disturbing the daily maintenance of the Mahatma Glory's financial empire. Now he wishes he'd had the nerve to ask Lealé how much it costs for one of these Readings of hers.

The next door down is already open. N'Doch peeks into a long dim room full of sofas and draperies and china lamp bases, sort of like the alcove off the dining room, only richer and more formal. Huge vases of flowers decorate carved ebony tables so polished you could see yourself in them. There are dark paintings with heavy gold frames and their own hidden spotlights. It smells like leather and cigar smoke and, well, money. It's exactly how N'Doch imagines the rich people live, except this room doesn't look much like anyone lives here. More like it's for people to come to now and again, and pretend that they do.

He thinks he'll just try it on for size himself, seeing there's no one here trying to stop him. He goes in, strolls around a bit. He sees a newspaper, actual printout, sees that it's about everywhere else in the world but here and passes it by. He picks an oblong silver box, looks it over longingly, then opens it a crack. Out flows the heady thick aroma of expensive tobacco. He's tempted. He's not much for smoking cigars, but the barter value on the street is astronomical. He sets down the box, exactly as he found it. It won't do to go getting acquisitive this early in his stay. Plenty of time when he's leaving to lift the odd little treasure or two.

He strolls around a bit more. He spots a minute silver coke spoon on a tiny silver tray. This really tempts him— it's so portable. But he moves on, feeling virtuous, until a glimmer of crystal and amber draws him toward a shadowed corner and a whole tray of decanters and glasses, the big round kind with the stubby stems. N'Doch whistles low through his teeth and selects a decanter at random. He lifts the diamond-shaped stopper, and an even headier scent curls out and around him like a finger beckoning. This summons he cannot refuse. Besides, who's gonna know? Isn't that what it's here for? He pours a few inches of the golden liquid into a glass, then replaces the decanter as carefully as he did the cigar box. He carries his prize around a bit, just liking the bulbous smooth feel of the glass in his hand. Then he spots two big leathers chairs with high backs flanking a brick fireplace. There's a coldflame log burning cheerily in the grate.

He eases himself down into one of the chairs. The leather groans under him as sweetly as a woman. He kicks off the horrible plastic sandals that Papa Djawara made him wear into the City, and digs his toes into the deep pile of the carpet. He is memorizing every sensation. He tries to convinces himself otherwise, but deep in his heart, N'Doch does not really believe he'll be rich someday, some fantastic overnight sensation. He knows that's a line he's bought from the media, 'cause he had no other line available to him at the moment, no other way out he could believe in. He raises the glass to his lips and touches his tongue to the liquid, then leans back, savoring the deep bite, the honey that burns to the back of his throat and sends its sweet heat up into his nostrils.

Tears come to his eyes, and he tells himself it's the liquor. He doesn't brush them away. He stares at the dancing fire that produces no heat, and slowly consumes the entire glass, the finest Armagnac. When it's gone, he carefully sets the glass down on the table beside him, and falls asleep.

CHAPTER THIRTY-TWO

By accident of repetition, Erde discovered that the little table with the water on it was only there after she had consciously thought about it. She'd look for it and find it gone, then turn back a moment later, and there it was, the lovely slim pitcher filled once more to the brim with sparklingly clear water. And the glass was newly clean and dry each time.

There is something in this wood, she decided. Logically, it was the same something that both she and Wasser had caught just a glimpse of from the doorway to Lealé's dream room. *And it knows that I'm here,* she concluded. *It hears me thinking somehow.* Since it offered her water when she was so thirsty, it must be a benign presence.

"Hello? Are you there?" Her voice echoed softly among the trees, less like a ricochet than as if her call was actually being repeated over and over. A faint rustle among the leaves made her turn, but there was nothing there. Would it put in an appearance, this presence? If she thought of food, would it feed her as well?—for as her strength began to return, she really was feeling hungry. Ravenous, in fact.

And lo, as she kept turning, there it was: another, larger table, full of food. But this table had a more familiar aspect, as if its mysterious conjuror had plumbed Erde's own memories to produce a feast such as might have been laid in sunnier days at Tor Alte. For there was the lustrous pewter table service, and the dragon-embossed gold goblets that her grandmother the baroness had used on ceremonial occasions. And there, the tall gold carafe that matched the goblets, a gift of His Majesty King Otto, to whom the baroness always raised a toast whenever the wine was poured.

Erde reached a tentative finger to its rim. Perhaps it would all just disappear. But the carafe remained, smooth and weighty to her touch. She stroked the crisp, brown curve of a rye loaf, still warm as if snatched mere moments ago from the bread ovens and rushed up the long stone stairs to the banquet hall. . . .

No! I am not at Tor Alte. You cannot make me think I am.

She stared around at the endless progression of copycat trees and identical blades of grass.

"Who are you? What do you want with me?"

The leaves stirred like a sigh. Erde's short-cropped hair ruffled, as from a gentle caress, and was still. She felt an overpowering urge to eat, and could not come up with a good enough reason to resist.

What a comfort were the familiar smells and tastes and textures of home! Though it was odd that she could eat so much and not feel as stuffed as she did at home every feast day. She wondered, if the dragon was here, would the weird wood produce a brace of sheep for him, or a nice fat goat? He must be very tired of eating fish.

The thought of the dragon brought her out of her reverie. She was much better, much stronger now, really she was, even though the meal felt so strangely light in her stomach. What had made her think of Earth, when she'd been so lost in nostalgia? It was almost as if someone had called his name to remind her.

"Was it you?" she asked rhetorically.

Again came that odd, faint stirring of the leaves. Erde felt it then, the Presence. Calm, huge, unthreatening, but beyond her understanding.

"Please tell me. Who are you?"

There were no words, yet she knew she'd been answered. And what she heard was a call for help.

He wakes with a start and thinks he must still be dreaming: a fireplace, big leather chairs, rich carpet underfoot? *This ain't my life.* And then he shakes off the rest of his sleep, and remembers. The empty glass is still there on the table beside him.

But it was the noise that woke him. The old, clipped

"wock-wock-wock" of a copter, coming in close. Out in the hall, doors are opening. Habitually hushed voices are heating up to an anxious pitch. A whispered conference convenes right outside the door of the long parlor. N'Doch strains to catch a word over the racket of the copter, but nothing he hears makes any sense. Flappers come and go down the hallway—he hears the nervous snap of their long skirts rather than the soft pad of their footsteps along the carpeted floor.

His first, not-entirely-rational thought is that the copter is coming for him. It's what he's always thought, when the pursuit was on and he happened to be nearby, that he was the quarry. And sometimes he was. But he's been taking a pretty raw look at himself, and he can't muster that old fantasy anymore. It used to make him feel important, alive. Now he's had a glimpse of how egotistical paranoia really is.

On the other hand, the copter is damn well coming closer. He can hear it right over the house, hovering, its rotors agitating even the air inside the room, inside his lungs, the very blood in his veins. The paranoia is an old habit. He'll be caught in a place he does not belong. N'Doch shrinks into his chair and thinks hard about what to do. Break and run is the obvious thing, but it's probably too late for that. And then, there's the girl to think about. And the dragons.

The dragons. It's like someone stuck out a hand with an offer of help. N'Doch lets a little of the panic go. He's not alone in this venture. He's got a couple of powerful friends, after all.

So he feels around in his brain for that still unfamiliar spot. It's like when he was learning to play, how his hands had to search out the right notes, only it's harder 'cause he can't be looking at the inside of his brain like he could cheat and look down at the keyboard. But he knows when he's found it now, at least. It's shaped just right, like his inside-self is a key fitting into a lock. Only this time when he tries it, the dragon isn't there.

Damn, he thinks. *Still out stuffing her gut.*

But the fact that she could be back any minute keeps him from falling back into the panic, lets him listen to the roar of the copter's descent like he just *knows* it's coming for someone else. Like, maybe Lealé hasn't been keeping up on her protection payments, so the militia's staging a little raid to teach her a lesson.

Outside, the copter settles, somewhere out back on the grass. The high turbine whine chokes back to a steady growl, then the engine cuts off and it's only the rhythmic swish-swish as the rotors slow down. N'Doch thinks you could write a whole symphony with the range of sounds that a copter makes. Whoever it is out there is planning to stay for a while.

The bustle out in the hall has quieted down, too, but N'Doch expects that's because they've all run outside to deal with this latest unexpected arrival. Judging from the way they treat him, he guesses the flappers don't much appreciate random events dropping in on them. Now might be as good a chance as any for him to move around, find a better place to lay low, maybe check on the girl. And he's just about to do it: he's bid good-bye to the best chair he's ever sat in and he's up with his sandals in his hand, gliding across the dim room like the shadow he's often been called by both his friends and his enemies, when the front doors burst open, and light and people and noise stream into the hall. N'Doch hightails it back to his tall-sided chair by the fireplace, where he makes his lanky body as small in it as he knows how to do.

"You need help, is that what you're saying?"

It was like that night above Tor Alte, when her small, quiet life was changing forever and Erde found herself faced with a creature out of ancient myth, demanding to be fed. She felt powerless and ignorant and in no way up to the task.

But the Presence had given her food and drink, and those had revived her, so the least she could do was find out what sort of help it thought it needed. At least she had some experience at this sort of thing now. She thought of Rose and Deep Moor, and Rose's "Seeings." She settled herself down on the grass and cleared her mind.

"Speak to me, then, however you can."

But nothing at all came to fill up the mental space she had cleared. Instead, the leaves rattled, and the wood became suddenly animate. Things began to happen around her. A tiny brown mouse scuttled across her feet and pounced on a grasshopper. A swallow swooped right past her nose and snatched up a gnat. A spider spun its web in the grass.

Erde took all this in very thoughtfully. Then she ventured, "Something is after you?"

The leaves stirred a bit more loudly. Erde would swear she heard negation in their dry rustle. Then a large ginger cat with yellow eyes bounded out of the woods with the brown mouse held delicately in its jaws. It crouched in front of Erde and set the mouse down between its paws. The poor mouse darted this way and that, desperate for escape, but the cat's paws were everywhere it looked.

"Ohh, I see," murmured Erde. "Something already has you."

Prey and predator vanished. The wood stilled. Calm again. Gratitude. Assent.

Erde couldn't imagine how anything could hold this Presence a prisoner. It was so huge and open and . . . well, but it was true, she had to admit. It didn't feel powerful, at least not as she'd learned to define the word. It didn't feel strong or aggressive or overbearing. Still, it must *have* power. It had conjured up food out of thin air . . . or had it? To Erde's surprise, she heard her stomach grumbling again. Could it be? Had her wonderful feast been only an illusion?

Around her, the trees lifted their branches and sighed with regret, and then they renewed their wordless plea for rescue.

The front doors hiss shut. The hubbub flows down the hall.

"Jesus H., JP, I can't see a goddamn thing in this place! Why don't you people get some light in here?"

It's the bankroll, N'Doch is sure of it. He remembers the voice from earlier, the sort of voice that's always louder than anyone else around it, a voice used to giving orders and speaking for attribution. The bankroll himself, heading N'Doch's way.

"Least you know how to keep a decent temperature! Christ, it's hot out there!"

N'Doch hears Jean-Pierre, the head flapper, doing an

apologetic tap dance at the same time he's trying to use all
these low, calm tones calculated to make the bankroll shut
up and listen. N'Doch can't believe the idiot thinks it'll
work.

"Of course she's busy!" the bankroll retorts, "She better
be busy! She's gotta pay for all this! She's got expenses!
One of them is your goddamn salary, and you don't want
to be losing that at a time like this. So get your ass in there
and tell her I need to see her . . ." He pauses, and N'Doch
can almost hear a sharky grin spreading across his face.
". . . as soon as she can make her charming self available."

They're right there at the parlor doorway. N'Doch curls
deeper into his chair.

"You know, monsieur, I'll do everything I can but when
the call is on her, she . . ."

"I know, I know. She's 'apart from this world.' Isn't that
what you always tell them? Kind of like being asleep, isn't
it?"

"Not unlike that, monsieur."

"Fine. If she was asleep when I came, what would you
do?"

"I'd wake her up, monsieur, of course."

"Well . . . ?"

"Monsieur, I'm only doing . . ."

"Your job, I know. Look, JP, here's the story. I'm a good
boy. I make appointments. I come here on time, when I'm
scheduled. I could just as easily make her come to me—I'm
a busy man and the world's in crisis. But I don't do that,
do I?"

"No, monsieur . . ."

"So when something exceptional comes up, I expect a
little respect, you know what I mean?"

"Yes, of course, monsieur. I've sent . . ."

The bankroll sighs. "Don't send, JP. Go. You go. Now.
You get me?"

N'Doch can't hear Jean-Pierre's reply. He figures the guy's
mouth's gone too dry to manage even a syllable. N'Doch
has about zero sympathy for the flapper flunky. *You get,* he
quips silently, *what you get paid for.* He hears the bankroll
come into the parlor, trailed by placating voices.

"Please have a seat, monsieur."

"Would you like a drink, monsieur?"

"Perhaps you are hungry, monsieur?"

"The PrintNews is right here, monsieur."

The bankroll snorts. "Get it away from me. I got enough problems already without having to read about 'em. Give me a big brandy and a little privacy. I don't plan to be staying long. Come to think of it, I'll take the privacy first. Get out of here, all of you. I'll see to myself."

A flat, deep voice says, "Sashsa and me'll be right outside, sir."

The bodyguard, N'Doch surmises.

"Thank you, Nikko. Sasha, if Marco calls, I'll take it in here."

The bowing and scraping and whining dies down until all N'Doch can hear is the bankroll pacing about at the other end of the parlor.

"Jesus Christ!" he exclaims again, and lets out an explosive sigh.

N'Doch smiles, picturing the bankroll's tension dissipating into the room in radiating lines of cuss words and insults to the staff. This dude he can almost feel sorry for. Then the pacing turns purposeful and heads N'Doch's way. He tenses. But it stops partway, replaced by sounds of glass clinking and liquid being poured. N'Doch's just dying for a peek at this guy. He figures he could sneak a look now, while the dude's busy at the bar. He eases his body forward just enough to peer around the high winged back of the chair, but the leather creaks and he's gotta make like a statue before he's moved far enough for the full view. All he sees is half a dark, slick-haired head on the well-tailored, medium height shoulder of a man in a business suit. European or mixed. Ordinary enough, as far as it goes.

Finally, there's Lealé's voice, trilling down the hall. The bankroll moves back toward the door with his brandy to meet her.

"Oh, hello, Nikko. Is he in there?" She rounds the corner. "Ah, darling! Back so soon? You should have warned me— I'd have sent the car." It sounds to N'Doch like Lealé's thrown herself bodily into the bankroll's arms.

"Stow the car. Haven't you heard what's going on? Food riots at the Ziguinchor, right outside your door!"

Lealé takes on a pouting tone. "Oh, dear. Again?"

"Your man out front was smart enough to lock the gates."

"I hate that! You know I hate that!"

"This is no joke, Glory. Word got out somehow about the next price hike, and the shit hit the fan. Why'd you have to pick this neighborhood, right in the middle of everything? There're plenty of safer places."

"Oh, darling, it couldn't be any other place! You know what the dream told me. It'll be over soon out there, like it always is. I come from there, remember? People must just stand up and shout about things every once in a while, but they'll settle down again, once they remember that shouting doesn't do any good."

"This time, I'm not so sure . . ."

"Ooo, you're so grumpy! You didn't come all this way to be grumpy. Come here. Oh!" Lealé giggles. There's the small clink of a glass being set down, then the rustle of her robes and a moment of heavy breathing. "See? You just couldn't wait to hold your Glory again. Here, let me close the door."

"Now, none of that. I don't have time. Besides, you'll make Nikko nervous. He's feeling jumpy today."

"Awww, what is it? Another bomb threat?"

"There are always bomb threats. There's not enough explosive made to supply all the bomb threats we get in a month."

"Poor darling . . ."

N'Doch is sort of relieved there's gonna be none of "that," just a mini-lecture on the perils of doing business. Sitting over here in the dark is like watching the daytime vid when only the sound is working. But the news of the food riots crowds into his mind. *Close call*, he thinks. *We were just there. It must've all started when the marché opened up again for the afternoon.*

"Look, Glory, I just had the damnedest dream."

"Now, darling, what has Glory told you about sleeping in the middle of the day?"

"That's what's so damn peculiar. I wasn't asleep."

Lealé laughs, low and throaty. "A daydream, was it? Was Glory in it?"

"Yes. You were." But there is no intimacy in his reply.

"Excuse me, sir." A soft male voice chimes in at the door. "Mr. D is on the line."

"About time. Ask if he's seen the numbers this morning. No, give it here . . . Marco! You seen the . . . yeah! What's the deal? All of a sudden, they're killing us! . . . yeah . . . no, I'm at . . . I'm in a meeting right now. Shouldn't be long . . . well, get on it, man! I'll be back to you."

Now N'Doch gets his first real twinge of envy for the bankroll. Before the music thing grabbed him so hard, and he was running with the Needles Gang, he'd had a phone for a while. Some deck jockey had fixed it so it fed off a random selection of purloined access codes. He could call anywhere, for as long as he liked. Now, *that* was power. He can still feel the lightness of it in his hand, like it was nothing, but that phone was more lethal in its way than any hand weapon. Then one day he up and sold it to buy his first set of amps. It seemed like the right move at the time, but since then, there's been times he's wondered. *Hindsight's twenty-twenty,* he tells himself, *so meanwhile, back to the soap opera. . . .*

"Sasha, here! Get this thing outa my sight! And hold the calls now, got it?" The bankroll paces a bit more. N'Doch guesses that Glory's just sitting there watching, waiting for him to work it out. "It's a bad time, Glory, a bad time. You better be making enough to support the two of us."

"Oh, darling . . ."

"No bullshit, Glory, and to tell you the truth, it's not just me. Things are about to fall down around our ears, I can feel it. And then there's this damn dream! It was . . . like the ones you have."

"Kenzo, dearest, you're not supposed to be having that kind of Dreams . . . let Glory do that for you! She'll take the worry out of it."

Kenzo? N'Doch's not sure he's heard her right. He supposes there's more than one "Kenzo" in the business world, but . . .

"Fine," the bankroll growls, "but I had it anyway."

"Then you better just sit down and tell Glory all about it."

As the bankroll spins out the long and torturous dream-strand that's shaken him so badly, N'Doch listens hard, not to the words, but to the voice, which he is now trying like crazy to identify. But he can't quite be sure, and finally he knows he's got to risk it. He *has* to get a real look at this dude.

He moves as slowly as he knows how, tries to time his moves with the rhythm of the bankroll's speech, so the voice'll cover the creaking of the damn chair. *No good spy,* he thinks, *would ever sit in a leather chair.* He gets his head and shoulders twisted around, then leans out over the arm of the chair. He gets a clean shot, a full-face view of the guy with his hands in the air, sketching a particular detail in his narrative. Once the input from his eyes reaches the processing part of his brain, N'Doch nearly stops breathing.

Omigod. *Baraga!*

CHAPTER THIRTY-THREE

Now that she knew the truth about her less-than-substantial meal, Erde was no longer so confident about how recovered she felt, or about the apparent comfort of her current situation. If the Presence was a prisoner in this wood, could that not mean that she was also? If she couldn't leave and couldn't eat, starvation became a real possibility. And how could she even be sure the Presence was telling the truth about itself? Perhaps it was holding *her* prisoner.

Certainly, she needed to talk to it further, but an in-depth discussion was going to prove difficult if the only way the Presence could communicate was by making the wood and its creatures act out each intended meaning. There was a game at home something like that, intended for long winter afternoons by the fireplace. But Erde didn't feel much like playing games, even in the interests of communication. It seemed that the Presence could manage to convey its emotional state, particularly assent or dissent. It just wasn't very good at actual information. So perhaps if she asked only questions with yes or no answers, she might make more progress.

For instance: "Do you know a way out of this wood?"

The leaves rose and fell, rose and fell. Negation.

"Does that mean I'm a prisoner, too?"

A definite stirring. Negation.

Erde pondered the apparent contradiction. "You mean . . . I can get out, but you can't?"

A stillness, tinged with melancholy. Assent.

Perhaps it would tell her about its own situation. "Are

you a prisoner because of something . . . you did?" she asked carefully.

A sudden rotating gust snatched at Erde's clothing and tousled her hair. Fistfuls of leaves detached and threw themselves in her face.

"Please! Please! I'm sorry! I apologize!"

The gust died as if it had never been. Fallen leaves were nowhere in sight.

"If you have all this power, why can't you just leave?"

No response at all. Not a yes or no question.

Erde chewed her lip. "I can't say why, but I believe you. And of course I'd like to help you, but I don't see how I can." She found herself thinking about the dragons again, both of them this time, and recalling how Earth had at first been able to talk to her only in mind pictures. Finally, an understanding bloomed.

"Is it the dragons' help you want?"

Not a leaf or blade in motion. Total assent.

She couldn't figure out a way to shape, "How did you know about the dragons?" into a yes or no query. If the Presence had known she was thirsty and hungry without her saying so out loud, probably it had learned about the dragons the very same way.

"I'm sure they would help you if they knew, but they're never going to unless I find a way out of here."

The silent wood came alive again. The ginger cat, the brown mouse and the blue swallow all appeared from different directions and met on the grass at Erde's feet. Once there, all three of them promptly settled down and went to sleep.

Erde stared. This really was like a child's game. "Is it something about sleeping?"

Assent.

"You need to sleep now?"

Negation.

"Ummm . . . you think I need to sleep?"

Assent.

"But I don't want to sleep! I want to get out of here!"

A long silence. Assent and reassurance.

And as she watched, the three sleeping creatures woke up, not as animals usually do, instantly on the alert, but stretching and yawning like humans. Then, as one, they looked up and about them, as if in realization, then jumped up and took off joyfully, each in the direction it had come.

"Oh, dear," said Erde. "I think I understand. I'm still not awake yet, am I?"

Assent, softened with sympathy.

"So, to get out of here, I have to go to sleep in my dream, this dream that I'm still in, then I have to wake up, and hope that I've woken up for real this time."

Assent. Assent. Assent.

She had said she didn't want to sleep, but suddenly, she did. The urge was so overpowering that even she knew it wasn't her own. She wondered if the Presence understood that the chances were about even: She could end up in 2013 with the dragons, or a thousand years earlier. She thought of Köthen, and decided it didn't matter. Either would be preferable to starvation for an eternity in this weird, weird wood.

As she lay down and tried to prepare herself for any eventuality, she noticed a queer thing: A long line of soldier ants were picking out a very eccentric trail through the velvety grass. They were . . . Erde yawned. Sleep was approaching faster than she'd expected . . . spelling out letters? Words? Why not? In a dream, anything was possible.

She lifted her head the barest inch, all she could manage as sleep rushed toward her. Words, definitely words.

They read: RESIST TEMPTATION.

He flattens himself back into the deepest part of the chair. At first, he can't even think.

Baraga. *Here.*

His heart races. He stares into the fireplace, sees only darkness.

Baraga. *Baraga!*

But the roof doesn't cave in, and the man at the other end of the parlor continues his recitation as if nothing has changed, and finally, N'Doch gets hold of himself.

Kenzo Baraga, the Media King, the man he now and forever most loves to hate, is sitting not thirty feet away from him. The slick-black Asian hair of Baraga's Japanese mother might have clued him in if he'd been thinking, but . . . whoever would have thought? Kenzo Baraga, in person, right in this room. And what's he doing? Not forging dreams and deals or ending careers and hopes, like he's supposed to be, no—he's complaining about some stupid dream he's had! N'Doch can't believe it.

Not that he supposed the Big Man wouldn't have problems. But they should be world-class problems, and Baraga should be eating 'em for breakfast, not be sitting there pouring his heart out like a schoolboy to some fawning woman! But in a way, N'Doch likes it that the Big Man's got a soft side. It humanizes him.

"I'm on this road," the Media King is saying, "and it's hotter 'n hell, and dusty. The road is crap, like it was paved once, a very long time ago and never kept up. And I'm alone, and walking, can you imagine? My . . ." He stops, and in the still room, everyone listens as sirens wail past outside the gates. "So my clothes are all torn, and all I can see, everywhere around me, is burned-out buildings."

"There, you see?" Lealé soothed. "It's just the riots that have you worried."

"I had this dream *before* the riots started. And besides, this place looked like a city, or what's left of one, but I knew .. in the dream, I knew it was really my life, my business, all of it. Everything! Everything I've built, gone up in smoke!"

"I know you've been very anxious lately, darling, but . . ."

Now N'Doch's brain is working overtime. He recognizes opportunity when it finally comes knocking. It may take some pondering, but he'll be damned if he doesn't figure a way to turn this bizarre coincidence to his advantage.

Briefly, he reviews his options. First, he could just go up and introduce himself to the Big Man as Lealé's . . . as Glory's dear friend of a dear friend, then work the conversation around to asking for an audition. N'Doch's mouth twists. Yeah, right. Probably the next thing he'd see would be the business end of Nikko the bodyguard. The Media King's not known for being free with his time to unknowns like N'Doch. Besides, if he's as jealous as Lealé says, he might jump to the wrong conclusions and think his woman's taken a younger lover. That would about finish his chances right then and there. No, the only way is, he's gotta figure out some pressure he can bring to bear. Which means, entirely powerless as he is compared to Baraga, that he's gotta either have something the Media King wants, or something he wants to keep from everybody else.

N'Doch hears other copters in the air outside, and the occasional crack of a sniper's rifle. Probably chasing the rioters out of the square. If things get worse out there, Baraga will probably bolt for his safe-hole on the beach, but meanwhile, the recitation continues.

". . . suddenly there's this guy in front of me in a spotlight, all decked out in gold, with this huge wall of flame behind him—great pyro, you know? And this amazing looking woman . . ." Baraga pauses. N'Doch hears him take a sip of his brandy. "In fact, he's pretty amazing looking, so I think he must be one of my groups, but the guy's not wired or anything, and I don't see his backup anywhere. I can't even hear them—it's like the sound's gone dead—and I really want to, 'cause what if they're *good*?"

"I think it must mean that you will hear them," offers Lealé. "Perhaps very soon. And they will be good, and your worries will be over."

"That'll take a lot more than one group."

Lealé laughed. "I know, darling. We all need people to start making some money again."

"The hell with that. I need a better way to make 'em spend what they already got on me now! I need a miracle! And even that it looks like somebody's got to ahead of me . . . !"

Yup, nods N'Doch. Salesmanship or blackmail. His only choices.

But the catch is, he's got nothing to sell but his talent, and that ain't worth anything until Baraga gives him a chance and an audition, which he's not gonna bother with unless he knows it'll be worth his very valuable time. N'Doch sees opportunity slipping away already.

He takes a gingerly look at the blackmail angle. He's done it before once or twice, mostly for food, real small-time stuff, when he was really desperate. Trying to blackmail Kenzo Baraga would be raising the stakes into the stratosphere. But if his information is good and he can hold on to his nerve . . .

He knows the dream-reader angle is nothing. All the big business types check in with their tarot lady or astrologer or feng shui master before making the big decisions. But, for instance, N'Doch knows—the whole world knows—that Baraga is married to the vid mega-star Francinetta Legata. Does the spectacular Francie know that her husband hangs out with the Mahatma Glory Magdalena for reasons other than sound business advice? Does he care if she knows? What would she give for the information? N'Doch sighs. He'd probably be fool enough to just let her take him to bed. None of this is sounding like much so far, he's gotta admit.

And then, because all along he's been listening with at least half an ear to the conversation at the far end of the room, his brain's autopilot registers a word that drops out of the sky like his next shipment of manna.

". . . dragons . . ."

The desirable Francie is backburnered in an instant. N'Doch switches over to full manual and listens with all his instruments.

". . . or something that looked like dragons. I saw 'em on the tapes myself when they rolled it back for me. And two kids with 'em. Ask Nikko, he was there. And six of my crack beach patrol. Can you believe it? Some asshole's managed to gengineer dragons, and he's keeping it a secret!"

Again, Lealé's throaty, sexy laugh. "You mean, he's not telling *you* about it."

Wait a minute, N'Doch realizes. This isn't his dream anymore. This is us. He's talking about *us*!

"I had all the labs checked. Only a handful of people left who could pull off that kind of work since the university closed down, and I own most of 'em. Or did. I fired 'em all this morning. Dragons! Can you imagine the market share for real live dragons? Nikko! Get in here!"

"Yessir, Mr. B."

"I'm telling her about the dragons."

Nikko clears his throat. "Saw 'em with my own eyes."

"Well, where are they?" Lealé laughs.

"Lost 'em," says Nikko.

"But were they big? Really dragon-sized? How ever did they manage to elude the beach patrol? And those terrible dogs!"

Baraga pauses, and N'Doch knows exactly why. He's just at the part that's gonna be real hard to explain. "Well, that's the thing. They just disappeared."

"Oh, into the water?"

"No. On the spot. Right out from under the noses of six sober, tough-minded men. And the damned dogs. Two dragons, two kids. They were there and then they weren't. I got that on tape, too."

He's got us on tape. N'Doch realizes he's chewing his knuckle to shreds. *I can't put the touch on him—he'll know me for sure.* At first he feels exposed, trapped, but then in a little breathless moment, it occurs to him that he's just been handed the tools he most needs and was sure he did not possess: something to sell and the status necessary to get the Media King to listen.

The grin comes shooting up out of the depths of him, fastens itself onto his face as if of its own accord. He has no control over it. He has a hard enough time choking back the laughter that wants to rise up with it. Terrified, exultant laughter, filling him until he's sure he'll burst if he can't let it out somehow. But he can't. Not right now. 'Cause, of course, *this could be it.* Right now could be that chance in a million he'd just finished convincing himself he wasn't ever gonna get. That's the exultant part. The terror part is, if in dealing with Kenzo Baraga, he doesn't play his cards just right, he could end up even worse than he was before. He could end up dead.

First thing is, he's got to talk to the dragons. A few special appearances? Shoot a few vids? Maybe even a series. What's the big deal? He's sure they'll go for it. And if they don't, well . . . he'll just have to cross that bridge when he comes to it.

PART FOUR

The Meeting
with Destiny

CHAPTER THIRTY-FOUR

Baraga takes up his dream narrative again, and doesn't seem ready to end it any time soon. Eager now but still bound into the enforced idleness of his hiding place, N'Doch starts plotting out a dragon-based miniseries in his head. All he has to do is tell the story of his own adventures with the dragons, right? Featuring his shape-shifting blue beauty, of course—that'll really wow 'em—and then he'll write songs to go with it. A musical miniseries: a brand new concept! The Media King'll love it!

He's distracted as the intermittent sniper fire out in the market square changes abruptly to the chatter of automatic weapons. At the other end of the room, Baraga breaks off his recitation to listen, then grunts pensively and calls in his bodyguard.

"Nikko, send someone to check with ground security, make sure the place is fully sealed off. Sasha, get Amahl on the line, see what you can find out about this."

"You might want to think about wrapping it up here, Mr. B.," remarks Nikko.

"Nah. We'll wait till we know there's . . ."

The floor shudders, twice, like a cough. Two dull thuds sound in the distance.

"Huh," says Baraga. "How far, you think?"

"Coupla miles," Nikko replies smoothly. "Southwest."

"The Presidential Palace?"

"Could be."

"Well. That'll teach the old bastard. Security, Nikko. The gates."

"I'm on it, Mr. B."

N'Doch hears the tinkle and rustle of Lealé's robes. Her

cheery bells and beads sound more anxious than seductive
now. "What is it, Kenzo? What's happening?"

"A little more than somebody expected, I'd say." Baraga
moves around restlessly. "Why wasn't I told about this?"

"I have Mr. Kemal on the line, Mr. B."

Listening to the secretary's breathy uninflected voice,
N'Doch pictures him in slippers and long hair neatly tied
back in a bun.

"You talk to him. Glory, get me an update from Print-
News. They better be on top of this, or they're history
tomorrow."

"Mr. Kemal says he's getting mixed reports from the copters," the secretary murmurs. "But there does appear to be
action in the area around the Palace."

"Don't give me appearances," Baraga growls, "Give me
facts! Tell him to get someone in there to find out what's
going on! Jesus! What do I pay these people for?"

N'Doch gets a tingle of anxiety himself. The energy is
rising in the room as Baraga moves into gear. It's like someone turned up the volume and it's contagious. Normally,
during military actions, N'Doch just heads for the deepest
ground he can find. He's not sure if being around Baraga
when the bullets are flying makes him safer or more of a
target.

"We're as sealed off as we're ever gonna be in this place,"
reports Nikko from the door. "I still think you oughta consider getting out of here, Mr. B."

"Taken under advisement."

"Someone might have seen us come in, y'know . . ."

"Nikko, I hear you."

"Yessir, Mr. B."

"Mr. Baraga!" The secretary has finally been shoved off
his even keel. "Shore Patrol just intercepted mortar fire!"

"What? They're shelling my house? Get birds in the air
and clean 'em out!"

"They're already on it, sir."

"Shelling my *house*? Who the hell do they think they
are?"

Lealé hurried in rattling a sheaf of facsimile. "Here you
are, darling. Not very good news, I'm afraid."

Baraga grabbed the stack. A strained silence thickened the
air while he read. "So that's it," he muttered finally. "Glory,

clear your people out of the office. I'm gonna be needing it. Right now. Nikko, Sasha, come with me."

N'Doch waits for the silence to settle in again at the other end of the room before he peers around the back of his chair. Empty. Free at last. He hops up and goes straight for the PrintNews that Baraga's scattered behind him as he left the room. PrintNews is expensive. He doesn't get to see it very often. It's also the only real source of straight news there is—all the vid news programs have evolved toward news as-you-want-it rather than news as it is. N'Doch doesn't see any problem with this. Real news isn't high on his priority list. Actual events in the world, or even in other parts of town, don't affect his own life directly, and by the time they affect it *in*directly, it's too late to do anything about it anyway. He gets his news on the street.

But suddenly it seems kind of important to know who's bombing MediaRex Enterprises in the middle of an ordinary coup attempt, and why? He gathers up the printout and scans through it. Phew! So dry! Like reading an upgrade for software he's never laid eyes on. Names he doesn't know, factions he's never heard of, like the whole thing is written in code. Only he knows it isn't, not if you're caught up on the basic information. It makes him feel insignificant, reading about all this plotting and politics he wasn't aware of, and that makes him huffy. He tosses the papers aside. If Baraga ever needs the latest on street barter values and local gang infighting, N'Doch knows who he can turn to.

Someone's turned on the bright lights out in the hallway. Anxious flappers shuttle this way and that, plus a couple of what have to be Baraga's security guys. One or two glance at N'Doch through the open doorway, but since no one stops or comes in after him, he decides it's safe to mingle and move about, as long as he keeps out of Baraga's line of sight. Or maybe the bodyguard Nikko's.

He goes out into the hall, eyes the crowd jammed in around the door to the office, and heads the other way, toward the dining room. If the girl is awake, she won't have a clue what all the noise is about. And, holy shit, what about the dragons? When they went off to eat did they go back to Baraga's beach? He knows they're magical and all, but he doubts they're immune to a well-placed mortar shell.

He slips into the dining room, snatches a few bites as he

cruises past the food table, and pushes through the drapes into the alcove. The girl is tucked away in the farthest corner, tossing and turning and gasping for breath as if she's fighting with something in her sleep. He sits down beside her and nudges her gently.

"Wake up, girl. Easy now. You gotta wake up."

She thrashes around, whimpering and panting, but she doesn't wake. N'Doch remembers the first time she had this dream trouble. This time it looks like she's losing her battle. He grabs her up in his arms and shakes her hard. She cries out and gulps in air. Her eyes pop open, and she stares at him mindlessly for a moment, then throws herself shuddering and heaving against his chest. Her arms tighten around his waist like she's keeping from being pulled away from him.

N'Doch lets her hold on. He pats her back awkwardly. She's talking at him in Kraut, long breathless murmurs broken by sobs. He keeps patting until finally she gets her breath back and quiets down. Meanwhile, he's searching around his mind to see if the dragon's come back on-line yet. Probably not, or he'd be understanding what's all this the girl's so unhinged about.

Suddenly . . . yes! There! In a rush, like doors and windows flying open, light flooding in. Connection, comprehension, all at once. N'Doch feels like he's been plugged in direct to the socket.

—*'Bout time, girl. Where you been?*

—*Are you safe?*

—*For now, at least. Are you?*

—*My brother had to fix a small wound in my side.*

To N'Doch's surprise, something like a fist tightens around his heart.

—*You got hurt?*

—*On the beach, there was metal flying through the air. I'm fine now. But because the healing uses up his strength, we had to search for more food. But everywhere else, we found death in the water. All the fish are dying.*

Another red tide washing in, N'Doch thinks. *Must be a really bad one.* He's worried now. His dragon has been wounded. What if the big guy hadn't been around? Would she have died? Maybe Baraga's right. Maybe the world really is falling apart. He remembers now what Water had said, under the trees in Djawara's courtyard. That she was here because *something terrible is happening.* N'Doch is beginning to believe it.

—*The girl's been dreaming. I think she had another bad one.*

—**Yes. She's telling my brother about it now. She needs to be near him now. Can you bring her out to the Grove?**

—*Sure, no problem.*

Actually, it is a problem, since he sure ain't walking her out the front way, past Baraga's eagle eyes. But N'Doch is glad for a task. He's feeling helpless among all these high-power shenanigans, outside the gates and in Lealé's office. He gets the girl up and mobile, though she's refusing to let go of him for more than a few seconds at a time. So he lets her take his hand and he leads her into the outer room. Passing the food table, he thinks twice and stops.

"We ought to stock up."

The girl is ready and willing. In fact, she's putting as much food in her mouth as she is into the big linen napkin he hands her to tie up as a carry-sack.

"Whatcha been doing in that dream," he kids her, "to make yourself so hungry?"

Her eyes get round. She shudders and shakes her head, and he knows when she lets it out, it's gonna be a hell of a story.

At the big double doors, he pauses to picture the plan of the house in his mind, lining up the rooms he knows inside with the entrances he's seen outside. He guesses the ceremonial side entrance must lead into a room that's right across the hall, but when he cracks open one of the sliding doors, he sees only a blank wall opposite. It makes him skip at least one little breath when he notices, under the newly brightened lighting, that the wallpaper is patterned with dragons. *How much,* he wonders, *does Lealé know that she's not telling us about?* He sticks his head out farther.

At the very end of the hall is a small door, so small it looks like a closet. N'Doch points it out to the girl and raises an eyebrow. She shrugs and nods.

"Okay. Let's go for it."

He makes her walk slow and steady, so she looks like she

knows where she's going. When they get to the little door, it's locked. But it's an old-fashioned key lock, as old as the house is and never updated. N'Doch thinks fast, scanning the list he carries in his mind of every object currently available to him and their relevant uses. He needs a shiv and doesn't have one on him. His knife blade is too thick. He starts down the list of what he knows the girl's got, and stops at the image of the big red jewel she's got pinned inside her jeans. He'd wanted her to leave it at Papa Dja's, but she wouldn't hear of it. *Good thinking, girl.*

"Quick!" he whispers. "Gimme the dragon thing, you know, the jewel . . . your grandmama's pin!"

She blinks at him. He mimes fiddling with the door, and she gives him back a steady, searching look while she pulls her right-hand pocket inside out and unpins the red stone. He sees her overcoming heavy reluctance in order to hand it over to him. He smiles at her. "You'll have it back in a minute."

In less than that, he's used the pin's long-pointed fastener to pick the lock. They're inside a narrow inner hallway, lined with doors. The blood red stone is warm in his palm. He remembers how he'd felt sure it was alive, when it was stolen and resting in his pocket. As jewelry goes, the thing's unnatural, but he finds that comforting now, and lets his thumb trace the miniature dragon carved into its polished surface. He hands it back without a qualm. "That did the trick, huh?"

Now her eyes are full of admiration for his cleverness. N'Doch laughs. She's an easy mark if she's wowed by an easy piece of juggling like that. But it makes him feel good anyway. He starts checking behind doors down the hall. Most of them are closets, filled with the long white tunics that the flappers wear, and shelves full of linens and candles and boxes of incense. But the door at the end leads them into a small antechamber, hung with soft, sound-absorbing draperies, and from there through a curtained arch into darkness.

They both stop short at the archway. They are in a huge, domed room. It's the deep blue of the zenith just after sundown, and it sparkles with a thousand electric stars. In the center, a big golden throne waits in a lavender spotlight.

"Oooh," marvels the girl, turning to stare all around her.

"Look later." N'Doch has just noticed the ring of chairs set one next to the other all around the wall. There's a "guest" seated in every one of them, sitting, dozing, staring in meditative poses, or chatting with neighbors. He grabs the girl's hand and makes a beeline for the outer door. He's almost there when a "guest" rises to stop him, a youngish woman who lays a pleading hand on his arm.

"Will the Mahatma return to us soon? Will I have my Reading today, do you think?"

"Er . . . she's busy right now," he replies helplessly.

She grips his arm harder. "Please, ask her to hurry. I do so need her to tell me what to do about Mama."

"Do whatever you feel like," N'Doch wants to say, and finds that he actually has. He doesn't know why but he's unreasonably pissed at this woman. "Go out into the streets. See what's really happening. Go read a PrintNews."

The woman stares at him. Cautiously, she draws her hand away. N'Doch moves on.

Outside, the light and heat are blinding, even though it's getting on toward late afternoon. The sky is a lurid yellow, thick with dust. He hears sirens and gunfire from several directions now. Copters race and hover like birds of prey, and off to the south, twin plumes of oily black smoke curl up from the Palace district. Another coup, no doubt of it. Since none of the past coups have ever seemed to change anything, N'Doch can't see why this one should get Baraga in such an uproar. Can't he just lay low like everyone else until one side or the other runs out of ammunition?

N'Doch suspects now that the answer could be found in a detailed and daily reading of PrintNews. He has that sinking feeling he gets when he's understood something big enough to make him realize how little he knew before he understood it.

On the terrace outside the door, groups of "guests" are gathered around the vid screens built into neat stucco pillars here and there. He takes the girl over to look, certain for one insane moment that the vid stations have seen the light at the same moment that he has, and are broadcasting actual news of the coup. But the "guests" are watching one or the other of the late afternoon series with total absorption, as if completely unaware of the chaos outside the gates. N'Doch finds himself angry at them, too, and he drags the

girl away quickly to avoid a scene he's not sure he would
even be able to explain to himself.

He leads her around toward the back, sticking close to
the house, staying under trees and behind bushes where he
can. He makes her trot briskly across the open lawn and
gravel driveway between the house and the grove. A few
shots ring out, but they are distant, random fire. N'Doch
slows once they've reached the trees, but the girl runs on
ahead of him, following the call of her dragon, eager to see
him after so long. Of course, it hasn't been so long, just
since the morning, but even N'Doch will admit it feels like
an eternity. By the time he's made it to the clearing, she's
already got herself pressed up against the big guy between
his paws, with his great horny snout bending over her protectively. But she looks up at N'Doch with a wondering
gaze and exclaims, "He thinks I've heard the Summoner!"

Water shifts and stretches her neck.

—*I think she's heard someone else entirely.*

N'Doch senses the dragons' restless, edgy mood. *Don't
want to rush this,* he thinks. *I gotta sell it to 'em right, or
they're not gonna buy it.*

He smiles, he hopes ingratiatingly. "Well . . . when you're
done arguing about her story, I'll tell you mine."

CHAPTER THIRTY-FIVE

"**B**ut what temptation could it have meant?" the girl is asking.

N'Doch is stretched out on the soft thick grass. One part of his brain is wondering why it's so much cooler in this clearing than it is outside. The other is watching the girl for a sign that she's kidding, because he just can't believe she doesn't know the answer to her question. Of course, she can't see what her face does when she talks about this dude back when. She thinks she's telling out her dream story like it could've happened to anyone, like it's just some coincidence she's dreaming about this guy, but if he could hand her a mirror to look at, the glow in her eyes might just about blind her.

N'Doch considers her question answered, and wants to move on to the next one, which is, *what's wrong with her being tempted*? This Köthen sounds like a courageous dude and he's straight with his men and all, and him being a baron like the girl's father should make him just about right for her, at least as far as N'Doch sees it.

So he says all this, and the girl shakes her head, then blushes furiously and clams up. Both of the dragons stare off into the trees that rise around in an oh-so-perfect circle, pretending like they're not even involved in this conversation, so for a while, there's a silence so big you could drive a couple of APCs right through it. Instead, N'Doch sits up, and drives through it himself. Might be a leftover from his irritation with the Glory-guests, but he's suddenly tired of coddling the girl like she's in nursery school. Time she grew up a little.

"So what's the deal? You hot for this dude, or not?"

An instant later, he wishes he could be the girl hearing Water's relayed translation. First, she looks blown-away astonished. Next she gets stony mad. Her whole body pulls itself up and gets taller.

"What'd you say to her?" N'Doch's just sure the blue critter's got a smirk hidden somewhere.

"In my father's court," the girl gets out finally, "such insulting remarks would not go unpunished."

N'Doch spreads his hands. "Where's the insult? You like a guy's looks, what's wrong with that?"

"To imply that I would have such base thoughts, such . . ." But she can't even say it out in words.

"C'mon, girl, don't get all huffy. It's just sex. It's no big deal."

Water finally decides to lend him a hand.

—It is a big deal if it's what she's supposed to be resisting.

N'Doch is dogged. The girl is still stonyfaced and looking away from him, but he won't have one of his favorite pastimes being labeled base or insulting. "It's not the sex that's the big deal, y'know what I mean? The sex is just the bait. The question is, why is the trap being set?"

—Point taken.

"Yeah, it's pretty simple, don't you think? Something wants her back there, so it puts this cool handsome dude in her path. She said herself it might be the loony priest calling her into these dreams." N'Doch is surprised to hear himself discussing all this as if it's a series of rational events with your normal type of cause and effect. Maybe he's starting to take this "Quest" thing seriously.

The thought of the priest makes the girl set her high-toned anger aside. "Yes, it could be. He was there in my head and he said I would never wake . . . Oh. I can't ever go to sleep again."

—I will watch while you sleep.

—Watching may not be enough, brother. Whatever Power is doing this, it seems sure it has found a weakness worth exploiting.

—But surely, sister, I can protect my companion. . . .

—Can you? I wonder. I am inclined to suspect our brother Fire in this also, using the priest as he would

have used Lealé. He will know our secrets and our ways. Our companions will be vulnerable to him.

The big dragon rose up on his haunches and dipped his horned head. For some reason, N'Doch thought of a great tree tossed with wind.

—*You are too free with your accusations, sister! You offer no proof of Fire's involvement but your own suspicions.*

—*You will recall, brother, that I remember him and you do not.*

Earth draws his head into his shoulders until his neck's nearly disappeared. Making himself like a rock, N'Doch notes. Stubborn. But N'Doch likes him for wanting to believe the best about this other brother he has no memory of. So maybe he's dead wrong, but you gotta hand it to the big guy for trying. N'Doch would never stand for someone dumping all over Sedou.

"If it is Fire, who saved me from him?" asks the girl. "And who is the prisoner in the wood?"

—*It's the Summoner. It must be!*

—*Whatever saved your companion's life fought off a dragon. The only power capable of thwarting a dragon is another dragon.*

—*That's assuming it was Fire who threatened her, but . . .*

—*Who would know to seek a dragon's help but another dragon?*

—*Sister, listen! I recognize this Presence from my companion's report, this Voice that is not a voice. It's the One who's been calling me since I awoke!*

—*But, brother, you don't think it odd that our sister Air has not been heard from?*

N'Doch has learned a thing about dragons: They love to argue. Particularly in ways that seem to lead the debate away from the obvious solution, like they wouldn't want all the fun to be over too quickly. N'Doch has no patience for this. He figures they should be doing it on their own time.

"Why can't it be both?" he demands loudly. He's glad to have the fourth dragon brought into the mix, 'cause then he won't have to be waiting for any more of 'em to turn up.

Both dragon heads swivel to stare at him. The girl, bless her, actually giggles. N'Doch guesses she'd prefer answer to argument also. So then it's another one of those APC-sized silences, during which N'Doch notices for the first time that he hasn't been hearing the sirens or gunfire from outside, even though, looking through the trees toward the house, he can see torn shreds of smoke rising from the streets beyond the compound wall.

He gets up. "You guys just give it some thought, eh?" He turns away and walks into the first row of trees. The air around him feels very . . . well, *blue*. He still hears nothing, but then, as he moves farther in, faint sounds come to him, more like cap pistols and mosquitoes than gunfire and copters, even though the house is no more than two hundred yards away. He backs up a few steps into silence, moves forward back into the zone of sound. He grunts and returns to the clearing. Everyone there is in exactly the same position they were in when he walked away. "You know," he says, "there's something weird about *this* wood, too."

The suddenness with which the debate was stilled told Erde that N'Doch had hit upon a true understanding. He did have a gift for cutting to the simplest explanation. It was not a gift the dragons appreciated, as fascinated as they were with the subtle and the complex and the ambiguous. But this time, his answer was so compelling, he got no argument.

Earth's inner rumble was hopeful.

—*Could it be? Our sister Air is the Summoner?*

—*There is logic to it. She is the eldest.*

Water fastened onto the idea as if it had been her own.

—*But who could hold her prisoner?*

—*I think why is the only unanswered question, brother.*

"If you go into the wood, maybe she can tell you," Erde offered. "Maybe she just couldn't speak to me."

"We oughta go back and check it out." N'Doch wandered restlessly, obviously ready for action. "We'll have to really work on Lealé to get her to let us in again." He paused. "But first . . . are you ready to hear why that might be even harder than it should be?"

Erde thought she might have sensed reluctance in him,

but told herself he was just pausing for effect, the way Cronke the bard used to do at a particularly critical point in a story. "Of course," she said, to hurry him along.

N'Doch smiled, but not his usual easy smile. It was something much more complicated. "Most times, this'd be about the worst thing that could happen. But now I'm not so sure. I got an idea that might turn it in our favor. Guess who Lealé's rich boyfriend is . . . ?"

It would have been safer and more sensible to stay behind in the grove with Earth, as N'Doch suggested, but Erde felt that Duty refused her such luxuries. Besides, if she stayed behind, she'd have nothing to distract her from the disturbing thoughts that N'Doch had put into her mind about Baron Köthen. To think she might be in love with him was one thing—young girls did that sort of thing all the time. It was perfectly proper. But the possibility that she might be having . . . lustful thoughts? The very idea shamed her. Surely she was better brought up than that. Yet N'Doch seemed to think such thoughts were natural, as he put it, "no big deal."

So the strange noises and tension outside the grove seemed preferable to the strangeness inside her head, even though N'Doch did warn her that it might be getting dangerous out there. She understood that a battle was being waged, not with crossbows and lances but with the terrible weapons called guns. N'Doch described their magic to her: They shot many arrows without shafts and they could kill at a very great distance.

Water would come with them of course, so once again, N'Doch sang the song about his lost youngest brother that enabled the dragon's transformation. Erde thought he sang it even more poignantly than before, and she was delighted to see little Wasser again.

N'Doch took the lead on the way out, cautioning them both to stay alert and move quickly. With shame, Erde recalled how she had once questioned his worthiness as a dragon guide. She hadn't then understood how very different this new world would really be, how different would be the knowledge and skills required for survival in it.

He stopped as they emerged from the deepest part of the grove, just where the outside sounds became audible.

"Here's where they start being able to see us again." He hunkered down to survey the compound. Erde could feel that heat radiating toward her in waves. A few more steps forward and it would close around her again, making the sweat rise on her instantly and filling her lungs with dust.

N'Doch touched her arm suddenly and pointed. A thing shaped like a dragonfly sat on the grass at the far end of the grounds. As they watched, parts of it began to rumble and rotate.

"Someone's leaving," N'Doch murmured. "The Big Man himself?"

Several men sprinted from the side of the house toward the dragonfly thing. Wasser counted under his breath. Just as the men disappeared into the machine's belly, a series of loud pops came from over the compound wall, like the noise of ice breaking up on a river in spring.

"Ha! Missed!" N'Doch's wide mouth curved into a tight grimace that was almost a smile. "Hard to tell, but it looked like him to me. Damn!"

Erde glanced at him sideways. She would have thought he'd be relieved if his enemy Baraga was leaving. Now he wouldn't have to employ the elaborate ruse he'd described, by which he could protect them all by turning this terrible man's greed and self-interest to their own advantage. It had sounded like a very risky proposition to her, largely because it did involve putting themselves into Baraga's hands. Earth had not liked this scheme overmuch. He remembered the dogs at Baraga's beach. So Erde was glad that the man was leaving. Not having to deal with him at all seemed by far the most preferable situation.

But N'Doch was crestfallen. As the dragonfly lifted into the heat-shimmered air and glided away into the smoky yellow sky, he watched after it as if it had robbed him of some priceless treasure.

"Damn!" he said again.

"It will be easier to talk Mistress Lealé into helping us now," Erde reminded him.

"Yeah. For sure." But his tone was so dispirited, she couldn't even ask him why. He waited until the dragonfly was out of sight, then waved them to their feet and forward. When they cleared the last of the trees, he made them speed up for a run across the open lawn to the house.

Again, Erde heard that odd, sharp crackle in the distance, like embers popping in a fire. Gravel sprayed up a few feet to her right.

"Keep low!" N'Doch hissed. "Head for the bushes!"

Gravel and dirt spattered Erde's cheek, from the left this time. Wasser sped forward. N'Doch grabbed Erde's hand, nearly yanking her off balance.

"Move! They're shootin' at us!"

He ran, she ran, then he shoved her hard down behind a thick row of bushes hugging the side of the house. Wasser was already there.

"From the south, I think."

N'Doch nodded, catching his breath. "Didn't expect this quite so soon." Together they scanned the rear of the compound: the long low building that stabled the riding machines, the high wall behind it, and the crumbling facades of the buildings that crowded up against the wall and gazed down into the grounds, Erde imagined, with envy.

"The roof, over there?" N'Doch pointed.

"Likely."

"We'll go around the other side, then, out of their line of fire."

"Why are they shooting at us?" Erde asked. "We are not their enemies."

"They don't know that," N'Doch retorted. "They're shootin' at anything that moves. You ready? Let's go."

Erde crept after him in the shadow of the bushes until they reached the front corner of the house. N'Doch stopped to reconnoiter. Erde saw the "guests" all huddled up against the compound wall in groups, or crouching singly behind the wide stone bases of the planters.

"Good." N'Doch chewed his lip nervously. "They've left the doors open a crack in case anyone's brave enough to make a run for the house."

Wasser said quietly, "Looks like someone already tried."

Out on the little grass plot in the center of the gravel drive, a woman lay sprawled on her face, moaning. Blood leaked from her upper back. Erde moved instinctively to help her, but N'Doch caught her and yanked her back hard. "No!"

"But she's down, she's hurt. Surely they'll let us retrieve the wounded?"

His look seemed to pity and envy her simultaneously. "What kinda wars you been fighting in, girl?"

Just then, the front doors opened wide, and two of Lealé's white clad acolytes raced out across the gravel and grass to haul the woman to safety.

"Now!" N'Doch grabbed Erde's elbow, dragging her with him as he leaped up onto the columned porch and shoved through the open doorway. "In, woman, in!" he yelled at Lealé, who was standing beside the door. "You're in range!" He bundled Erde and Wasser inside after her, then held the door as the acolytes retreated inside with their bloodied burden.

N'Doch is impressed with Lealé's calm. No womanish fainting away at the sight of blood. For that matter, the girl's not either, though she does look a little shell-shocked by the sudden violent turn of events, all blown up around her like a thunderstorm. Probably she's not used to stuff happening this fast.

Lealé hovers over them briefly. "Children! Children! I looked and you were gone! Are you all right? I'm so glad you're safe!" And then she's off down the hall, directing the flapper rescue team into the dining room. "In here. Lay her on that other table! Quickly! Call Millet!"

"Stick close," N'Doch warns the kid and the girl. He trails after Lealé, moving through milling knots of anxious flappers and guests who have fled inside. The cool perfumed indoor air is heating up with the rank smells of sweat and fear. He passes the doorway to the long parlor and shoots a glance inside. More guests, crowds of them, some talking in frightened whispers, most of them huddled around vid screens that were hidden before behind the fancy wood paneling.

For the second time in one day, N'Doch entertains the wild fantasy that what they're so riveted to is the news of the coup, and once again, he's proved wrong. The late afternoon series is playing on all screens. He studies the faces of the watchers for a moment. The Watchers. Their eyes stare like they're drinking in the screen, like if they stared hard enough, they could be in there, a part of somebody else's story instead of their own. Why aren't they worried about what's going on at home, whether their house is being ransacked, whether their wives or husbands or children are being shot in the streets? *Probably they are,* N'Doch thinks, but it's like they've forgotten how to do anything about it. All they know how to do is watch.

Suddenly he knows there's something *he's* gotta do, and he drags the kid and the girl back down the crowded hall to the office. The door is closed but not locked. He ducks inside, hauling the other two with him. "Close the door," he whispers to the girl.

This seems to be the only room that hasn't been invaded by "guests" and panic. The head flapper Jean-Pierre is there with a few others, all of them busily clicking away at various keypads, muttering figures and names at each other. They barely glance up as N'Doch comes in. A last-ditch effort, he imagines, to reroute Lealé's business dealings around changes resulting from the coup. He sees there's PrintNews scattered everywhere. It's overflowed the output bin at the terminal. The service is working overtime, and here are a group of people who may actually read it. The business people. The money people. The people who know the real meaning of power. N'Doch is amazed he hasn't understood this before.

He parks the girl by the door to keep watch, for what he's not sure, but it makes him feel better as he ventures into this cool, white, alien space. The apparition shadows him as he goes straight to the PrintNews terminal and takes the latest sheet as it peels out of the slot. As he reads, the apparition reads over his shoulder.

What he sees shocks him. It makes denial rise up in him like the instinct to run, but he guesses he's got to believe what he's reading. If this ain't the truth, the truth ain't to be had. But it tears away the foundation of a notion he didn't even know he'd relied upon until he sees it crumbling. He knows things are bad. It's all around him, every day. But still, there's this notion he's buried inside himself, that things aren't really as bad everywhere else in the world as they are where he is. That somewhere, even though he can't get there, things are better, there's still hope.

If PrintNews tells true, there isn't. It's just another fantasy like every other fantasy he's been sold, 'cause there's bad shit coming down *everywhere.* He's got it right in front of him in black and white.

Half of Europe underwater, for instance, and the Amazon basin, and parts of Asia he's never even heard of. Huge storms everywhere, and crop failures, item after item, a long list of national emergencies and requests for relief, desperate cries for help muffled by the dry news service prose. He sees stuff about countries moving their capitals to higher ground, about the tides of refugees rolling inland, about governments collapsing under the strain. Revolution, violence, repression, anarchy. The weight of this steady progression of disaster bears down on N'Doch until he has to look away.

"Jeez . . ." breathes the apparition.

N'Doch's impulse is to grab the nearest responsible person and shake them until their bones rattle. He wants to scream, "Why didn't you tell us?" But there's no one in this room worth grabbing. The responsibility lies much higher up than skinny head flapper Jean-Pierre, and what's worse, it lies within himself as well. N'Doch sees he's been wrong all this time to think of himself as one of the Watched, or even Watched-in-Waiting. He's a Watcher, just like everyone else, taking what he's given as information and image, and buying right into it, same as his mama does. His particular fantasy is different from hers, is all. It's still a fantasy.

He leans his forehead against the terminal and lets out an explosion of breath. It seems to come from the bottom of his feet, an exhalation of pure rage and frustration.

"I used to razz Sedou," he tells the apparition. "Say he was living in a fantasy world if he thought he could change things by messing in politics." N'Doch saw himself as the pragmatic realist, the artist and independent loner, out for what he could get from the world. But what's coming clear is how he's been taught to want only what the world thinks is good business to sell him, assuming he ever gets rich enough to be able to afford it. The world, and by "the world" he's beginning to mean Baraga and those like him, the real power brokers—they don't want him to want freedom, they want him to want things, comfort, fame. They'd rather he didn't have a true awareness of how fucked up things really are, so they trained him not to want it.

But knowledge is power, or so it seems to N'Doch as he stands with just that sort of information held slack in his hand. What burns him the most is that this realization has probably come too late. He's never sidestepped the current of life like he thought he had, not even for a moment. He's right there in the torrent, caught up in the tide of events, tumbling head over heels along with everyone else.

"Hey, bro?" murmurs the apparition. "You okay?"

"Yeah," he replies curtly, but he isn't. His mind is a seething mess. He's blind with rage and panic and humiliation.

"I think you're not . . ."

N'Doch thrusts the paper in the kid's face. "Well, look at this!"

"I know. I did."

"Doesn't it make all your 'quest' shit look pretty silly when laid up beside the end of the world as we know it?"

The apparition blinks at him with the dragon's bottomless dark eyes. "Not if preventing the end of the world is the object of that Quest."

N'Doch thinks, *Man, haven't we been through this already?* " 'Saving the world' is just a phrase, kid. It means you're a do-gooder, which I know you are, and that's fine. But you can't take it literally."

"I can. I do."

"I mean, it doesn't mean you gotta try to do it single-handedly."

"It might."

"What?" N'Doch really has to laugh. "You?"

"Us. Not as we are but as we will be."

N'Doch feels the conversation spinning off from the crisis at hand back toward the realm of the unreal, where as far as he sees it, no solution lies. *These dragons are as bad as Baraga.* "And what will we be?"

"Eight, eventually. Four dragons, four companions. A synergy of power."

"Great. One dragon you can't find and the other one's trying to kill you."

The kid's brow furrows like he's having a complicated thought. "That must be part of the Work."

"What is?"

"Overcoming the obstacles. Solving the mysteries. All leading toward the awakening to power."

"We don't have time for all that!" N'Doch grabs up another sheet of PrintNews and shakes it like a club. "What's it got to do with today and tomorrow and how we're gonna get ourselves out of this mess?"

"Everything! Have you been listening to me at all?"

In his head, N'Doch hears/feels a blast of music, a gale that almost knocks him flat. He sags against the PrintNews terminal. He's breathless and shaking. He understands that the dragon has just lost her patience with him. "Okay, okay. Okay. We'll do whatever you want."

The apparition sighs. "I want to do what you said, before you let revelation sidetrack you."

N'Doch is exhausted. He glances at the girl, still guarding the door. She watching him, and her eyes are soft with sympathy. "And what was that? Remind me."

"Lealé."

"Oh, right. Lealé." His brain feels pummeled, but another piece of his new analysis has just clicked into place, and he sees a direction, at least, in which a solution might lie.

They collect the girl and shove their way back along the long hallway, more crowded even than it was before, and into the dining rom. A group of flappers, plus an older woman N'Doch hasn't seen before, are gathered around a long table at one end, working on the gunshot wound. He sees another "guest" lying on the floor, wrapped in a table-cloth. He can't tell if the guy's dead or alive, but he figures no one would've risked life and limb to drag him in if he was gone already.

Lealé's pacing in small circles at the other end, talking rapidly into a phone like the one Baraga'd had with him. N'Doch is glad she's smart enough to stay clear of the windows. Above the drawn draperies, the windows arch in a clear half-moon of divided glass. He sees thick sunset colors in the light, and gathering darkness in the sky above. He has a momentary inspiration for a song he could write about darkness gathering all around the world.

Lealé finishes her call when she sees them coming. Her eyes land on the apparition and stay there, so N'Doch lets him take the lead. It's his party, anyway.

The kid doesn't beat around the bush. "Mother Lealé, your help is needed. We must return immediately to your 'Dream Haven.'"

She waves her arms as if warding him off. "There's no time for dreams now. Don't you see what's happening?"

"I do. All the more reason."

"No! He'll find out! You'll ruin me!"

"Events outside seem to be conspiring to do that already."

Lealé turns away, a Glory turn, and shakes her mane of beaded hair. "Nonsense. This goes on all the time. Once the new leaders have settled in, everything will be business as usual."

"Mother Lealé." The kid's tone is low, almost conspiratorial. "Do you really believe that?"

Panic flares into Lealé's eyes. N'Doch can see her trying to dampen it, but it still makes her hands flutter around too much and her voice unsteady. "Of course I do."

The kid takes her arm. "We need to talk."

Probably because he's so small and childlike, Lealé doesn't resist as he leads her toward the alcove. N'Doch beckons to the girl, and follows. As he draws the curtains behind them, he sees another shooting victim being carried in. This time, it's a head wound, and it looks like a bad one. The snipers' aim is improving.

The kid sits Lealé down on a couch, then sits beside her, holding her hand. "Now listen. You had a dream, Mother Lealé, that caused you to write to an old friend you hadn't seen in years. That dream told you to expect travelers. Was it a good dream?"

Both his formality and his question seemed to puzzle her. Lealé considered. "Yes . . . I recall being very excited. I felt something wonderful was going to happen."

"But later, you had visits from your spirit guide directing you to . . . well, disable the travelers . . . permanently."

Nervous, she answers, "Yes."

The apparition nods, and N'Doch sees the nod of an old wise woman, slow and serene. "And you also dreamed of a particular place, a house that the dream led you to acquire. What was that dream like?"

Lealé looks around her like she's costing out the furniture. "I didn't dream of the house, actually. I dreamed of that grove of trees out back and felt I had to have them. When I inquired, I found the house came with them."

"A dream of trees." The apparition has a triumphant gleam in his eyes. "And then the idea to make a business there was . . ."

"Suggested by my . . . my investor, who I had helped so much by bringing him dreams in the past." She frowns, remembering. "He told me I should cut the trees down, build a new wing on the house to quarter my staff. It was our first argument ever."

"Why would he want you to destroy something so lovely? Surely it adds to the value of the property?"

"It is peculiar. He spends huge sums planting trees around his own house and grounds."

"So it must be something about this *particular* grove of trees. That he doesn't like."

"I don't know. Why does it matter?"

"Because I think I do know." He urges N'Doch and the girl in closer with his eyes. "You are a gifted receptor, Mother Lealé. There are not many such available. So, more than one entity wishing to communicate might be led to take advantage of your gifts. I believe that not all your dreams come from your spirit guide. The two we mentioned, for example: They came from somewhere else, and later your dream guide saw to it that you reinterpreted their instructions."

N'Doch is sure Lealé wouldn't appreciate the image he has of her now, as some sort of psychic ventriloquist's dummy.

"Dreams from someone else?" she asks, right on cue.

"Someone I have seen and Erde has seen, and you have seen as well, and been told to deny. The presence in the wood."

Lealé gazes at the apparition unhappily, then stands up and begins to pace.

"We must try to contact it," he continues, letting his voice follow her around the alcove. "It has been your true Work, which your spirit guide has tried to disrupt, to bring us here for that Purpose. And we must accomplish it quickly, before he succeeds in stopping us. Even this fighting now, I believe, is part of his plan."

N'Doch moves into the archway, so he can stop Lealé in case she decides to pace herself right out of the room. He wants to get this act over with and be on to finding a place for them all to lay low that isn't ground zero. He sees her eyes flick up to the top of the arch, just a flick and back, he almost didn't catch it. But now he knows he's missed a camera port in his initial survey of the alcove. He checks it out. Sure enough. Damn! But he doubts, with all this chaos going on, that anyone's bothering to keep an eye on the monitors.

Watching Lealé pace and wring her hands, Erde felt sorry for her. Unlike herself and N'Doch, Lealé had a perfectly good life that she was putting at risk. Or at least she did until the fighting broke out.

Erde considered that coincidence. War here, war at home. Could the fighting at home also be part of someone's dire plan, a someone that Water insisted must be the dragon Fire? Why would Fire wish to disrupt the Work, whatever it was, that all the dragons were being called to perform?

"Think of Djawara," little Wasser was saying, "who sent us to you in trust and full faith that you would do what was needed. . . ."

"But I don't know what that is!"

"Yes, you do."

"All right! But I won't go in there with you this time. I won't face him if he comes to punish me!"

"I don't think," replied Wasser, "that he will dare show his face while I'm around."

N'Doch bent his head to Erde's ear as Lealé palmed the wall and the paneling hissed open. "Don't forget to tell the big guy we're going off the radar."

Wasser led the way this time, down the unlighted passageway. Because he could move so surely in the dark, they were there before Erde had time to admit to herself how scared she was. What if it was Fire, and he did dare to show himself?

The dim little room was the same as it had been before, only warmer. The air was thick and close, and tinged with smoke. Wasser sniffed thoughtfully. "My brother leaves his calling card."

N'Doch grinned. "Trying to scare us off?"

Wasser approached the wide, empty doorway leading out to the wood. "More like he can't resist the chance to show how clever he is. Wherever he is physically, this room is the connection between his reality and ours. He wants us to know he's in control of it." He moved carefully into the doorway, then out onto the first wide, white marble step. He'd eased down onto the second when Erde darted forward and grabbed his arm.

"Don't go down there without some kind of lifeline, a rope or something! The door will vanish, I know it will, and you'll not find your way back again!"

Wasser retreated to the top step and stood staring out into the wood. The same trees, the same grass. Erde shivered and sat down on the edge of the step. She remembered it all too well.

N'Doch leaned against the doorway, waiting. "What d'you think, bro?"

Wasser turned. "I think . . . that's exactly what he wants. The object of this entire exercise: Lealé's dreams, the wood, everything. If I am trapped here, as perhaps my sister Air is, I cannot carry out my Purpose, the Work that is our collective Purpose."

Erde spotted movement then, among the trees. Her head jerked to follow it, but it was gone.

"You saw . . . ?" Wasser asked.

She nodded.

"Me, too." N'Doch came forward and pointed.

"No," said Erde. "It was over there."

"It's everywhere," Wasser concluded. "It's trying to attract our attention."

"To speak to us," added Erde.

"Or just trying to lure you out there where it can take control . . ." worried N'Doch.

"Here." Wasser extended a small hand to Erde. "We'll make a chain. Brother N'Doch, you be the anchor."

Erde took his hand and then N'Doch's, and stepped down onto the bottom stair with Wasser. N'Doch wrapped his free hand around one of the columns flanking the doorway. When they signaled that they were ready, Wasser let himself down onto the velvet grass and . . .

. . . disappeared. All but his hand, which remained tightly clasped in Erde's. The pull on her was light and irregular, like a fishing line bobbing in a slow moving stream. It was easy to maintain her grasp. She smiled over her shoulder at N'Doch, who said, "You know what? It's getting real hot inside this little room."

And, yes, she saw that he was wreathed in smoke. There

was even a faint ruddy flicker down the passageway behind him. "Oh, dear. What if the house is burning?"

N'Doch raised an eyebrow. "Don't even think about it."

Suddenly her hand was yanked roughly, knocking her off balance and nearly breaking both holds. But Wasser hung on hard, and N'Doch quickly redoubled his grip. Erde righted herself and hauled back against the pressure.

"Pull, girl, pull him in! Throw your weight into it!"

The wood came alive with movement, always just out of her line of sight. The smoke in the room seeped out from the doorway in darkening curls. Erde felt like her bones might separate at every joint, she was being held so firmly and hauled on so hard.

N'Doch began to cough. "Gonna have trouble breathing in here before long! Pull, girl, pull!"

A breeze sprang up, a sudden tiny whirlwind that shredded the smoke into wisps but did not stir a single leaf or blade of grass. Abruptly the pressure gave from the wood side. Wasser came flying back into view and slammed against Erde, sending her sprawling on the stone step.

"Quickly!" he gasped, grabbing at her, missing, and stumbling. "Out! We've got to get out!"

N'Doch snatched them both to their feet. The doorway behind him was a wall of hot black smoke.

"Take a deep breath and run for it," Wasser advised. "Now!"

"We'll fry!" N'Doch objected.

"Better that than an eternity in between!"

"What?"

Wasser scrambled up the steps. "I'll explain later. Come on!"

As he reached the doorway, the whole room burst into flame. He threw out his arms to hold the others back. He retreated a step, and the flames came after him.

"Trying to drive us into the wood," N'Doch yelled.

Then Wasser planted his feet. "Wait!" he cried. "Wait!" His small form wavered darkly against the sear of flame. "I am . . . I am . . .

—WATER

A roaring filled Erde's ears and eyes and consciousness, and swept her up and into darkness, a long tumbling passage where she wasn't sure if she was breathing or not,

whether it was air or water filling her lungs. She felt the
weight of heat and light behind her, driving her forward,
down and down through darkness, rivers and oceans of
darkness, until she gasped and was spat out by the flood
onto the thick wool of Lealé's carpets.

"Hit the deck!" N'Doch bellowed, and Erde cowered,
awaiting the conflagration that would finish them when all
that heat and fire behind them came exploding out of the
passageway. Instead, she heard Lealé wailing and pounding
on the wall where the opening had been until it delivered
them from instant incineration as if from the mouth of
Hell itself.

"What have you done?" Lealé screamed and wept and
pounded. "What have you done?"

"Where's the kid?" N'Doch croaked.

Erde raised her head. She was back in the alcove, dripping wet like everything and everyone else around her, but
otherwise unharmed. There was no fire. Not even a lingering wisp of smoke. Only a blank, wood-paneled wall that
no longer yielded its secrets to Lealé's pleading touch.

"Where is he?" rasped N'Doch again.

"Here." A whisper, barely audible, from the corner,
nearly drowned out by the renewed crackle of gunfire outside. Wasser was smashed up against one of the couches
like a discarded doll. Erde crawled toward him. N'Doch got
to him first and turned him over, ever so gently unfolding,
surveying his limp and twisted limbs.

"Nothing broken, little bro. You okay?"

"No . . ." His voice was weak and scratchy.

"I thought you said this asshole brother of yours couldn't
hurt anyone."

Wasser stirred. "Are you hurt? Is she . . . ?"

"No, no, lay still. We're both drenched but we're in
one piece."

"I . . . made water? Real water?"

"You sure as hell did. It was awesome, and it saved our
lives. That dude's fire was real enough also, except . . ."
N'Doch glanced up to frown at the wall where Lealé huddled, getting hold of herself.

"Except his fire couldn't leave his reality. Good thing,
huh?" Wasser coughed and groaned and tried to lift his
head. "I can't move . . ."

Glass shattered in the outer room, once, twice. A woman screamed. N'Doch ignored it. "What is it? What happened to you?"

"Weak . . . so weak . . ."

"Then you'll just have to rest up, little bro." He gathered the small slack body into his lap, trying to arrange it comfortably. He looked to Erde, his eyes troubled. "What's wrong with him?"

She leaned close and kept her voice low. "The magic she . . . he made cost all his strength. I think he found more power than he knew he had. If he's like Earth, he'll need food and rest, the really deep sleep that renews the life forces." In her head, she heard Earth confirming her guess.

N'Doch's mouth tightened. "He can't eat in this form."

"We must carry him back to the grove."

He shook his head. "Listen to it out there. We'd get cut to ribbons the minute we stepped out the door. Think of something else."

She gazed back at him helplessly.

"There's gotta be something!" he insisted.

"Sing to me . . ." Wasser murmured.

"What? Now?"

"Sing to me. Sing me your strength. Sing me . . . Sedou."

N'Doch feels the ache rise up in his gut. He tries to press it down, back down there where it's been all along, where he needs it to stay.

"I don't have a song about Sedou."

"Yes . . . you do . . . I've heard it in you."

You've no right to ask this, he thinks, *no right*! But the small body on his lap moves him beyond measure. A moment ago it was a magical being of awesome power. Now it needs him. It *needs* him.

Still, maybe he can fool it.

"You mean the one that goes like this?" He hums a few soft bars of a raunchy little ditty he and Sey used to sing together. It catches in his throat, but he gets it out at least.

"No . . . not that one."

The ache's still there, pressing on his ribs, pushing upward against his lungs and heart. It won't go back down like it always has before. N'Doch understands that the kid is right, the song is there. The ache *is* the song, and it'll come if he lets it. It'll be right there on his tongue, words, melody, everything, formed way back down over the years he's denied it. He's reminded of a woman's pain in childbirth, and wonders if it could ever be as bad as the agony of this bearing forth. He gives in to it and lets the song open his mouth.

It's a hard song and a sweet song. It jangles and growls, and then cuts away swiftly to soar on high pure notes of light, only to swoop down again, hawklike and ruthless, and plunge into darkness. He's real shaky on the first verse. The song is still drying its wings. But as the wings unfold their dark, crystalline brilliance, the singer unfolds with them, revealing the black knot of loss that he's carried inside him like a stone he swallowed and could never pass. In the light of day, the stone crumbles and lifts, each dark shard a rising note.

He's aware of his small audience—the girl, Lealé, a few others who have nosed through the draperies to listen. He can see that he has them enraptured. He's aware that the shuddering of the ground and the rattle of machine guns outside is the perfect thematic baseline for the story he's weaving. Most of all he's aware that, as his voice clears and strengthens, as he moves into sync with the song and with his feelings, the small body in his lap is enlivening, enlarging, transforming, until it's no longer the slim weight of a child that presses against his knees, but the solid burden of a man.

N'Doch clamps his eyes shut. He doesn't dare look down.

But the song has an ending, a dark inevitability he doesn't want to reach, and have to live through twice in one lifetime. The weight on his lap stirs and lifts away from him. A large hand grips his knee.

"That's a great song, bro," says Sedou's voice. "Let's end it right there."

He does, within a breath, before the inevitability. He opens his eyes and stares into his brother's smiling face.

"Sey . . ." is all he can manage.

"No," the apparition reminds him gently. "But almost."

N'Doch surprises himself with a nod. No hot flush of rage that this well-loved face before him isn't really Sedou.

He's content just to see it again, alive and whole, and know that seeing it means the dragon's back in working order.

"Hey, big bro . . . good to see you," he says, and smiles.

Somebody at the archway starts applauding. Others join in. N'Doch wonders what they think and how much they've seen, and how much of that they could possibly understand. But the applause dies quickly as explosions shake the walls, leaving only one pair of hands offering up a precise and heavy syncopation with the chatter of the machine guns. Out of the corner of his eye, N'Doch sees Lealé rise from where she'd settled in raptly to listen. The apparition's chin lifts, his smile dies.

"Making music while the city burns?" crows Baraga cheerfully. "A man after my own heart!"

N'Doch just manages not to leap to his feet in panic. The Big Man herds the other spectators away and draws the drapes tight, dusting his hands together with satisfaction. "Well, Glory! You been hiding the local talent from me?"

Now N'Doch stands up. The apparition's rise beside him is even slower and more collected. N'Doch senses a new power in the dragon, filling his brother's already powerful body with an even greater strength and presence. This dragon-form he resolves to call by name. Sedou would be honored. Baraga's eyes are on the singer, but they stray again and again to Sedou.

It's easier to face Baraga with Sedou standing behind him, easier to look into those predatory eyes, and not wince and stutter.

"Glad you liked the song," N'Doch says, amazed at how calm he sounds.

"The song and the singer." The Big Man is actually shorter than N'Doch, but wider. Big shoulders, thickly built. His glossy black hair is artfully streaked with silver. His skin is clear and Mediterranean. He's stripped off his expensive suit jacket somewhere and rolled up his silk sleeves. He holds out his right hand and gives N'Doch a broad smile. "Kenzo Baraga. You've got talent, son. What's your name?"

N'Doch shakes the Media King's hand, something he's always dreamed of doing. "N'Doch N'Djai."

"Good name. You can always change it."

Not on your life, N'Doch thinks. Naming has always

been important to him. "Sure could," he replies brightly.
"Oh, ah, this is my friend Erde von Alte." He's proud that
the first time he has to say her whole name, he gets it all
out right. "And my brother Sedou."

Baraga responds to the girl's old-fashioned little curtsy by
catching up her hand and touching it lightly to his lips. To
N'Doch's surprise, she seems to accept this as an appropriate greeting among strangers. But he notices that the
Media King is a little slower to shake the hand that Sedou
offers. Intuition grips him.

—*He knows.*
—**He suspects. But he's not sure.**
—*He recognizes me, from the tape.*
—**Perhaps. And he has a touch of Fire in him.**
—*What do we do?*
—**We have no choice. We'll hear what his offer is.**

Shots ring out and more glass shatters in the dining room.
Baraga tilts his head to listen, then shrugs and smiles. "Hell
of a time to do business, eh?"

N'Doch says carefully, "Is that what we're doing?"

"Think I'm going to let a talent like you slip by me because of some minor coup? No way. I need a kid like you
right now. Real star potential, with the right promotion and
development."

Star potential. N'Doch has waited all his life to hear those
words. And now that he does, all he can do is smile and
nod like some rube from the bush. He hates himself for it.
"That's real kind of you, Mr. Baraga."

"Kind, schmind. You know my rep, right? You know
'kind' isn't a word anyone applies to Kenzo Baraga. Business is business. We work out a deal, you and me, then I
own you, 'cause it'll cost me big to make you big. But you
turn it around and make me money, I'll treat you right. So.
You ready to talk?"

Lealé glides forward and slips her arm around Baraga's
elbow. "Dear Kenzo, give the boy a chance to think."

"It is a little . . . sudden, Mr. Baraga." Too sudden. Even
an overnight discovery is supposed to have to work a little
harder for it than just one song. He knows he should be
suspicious, but he's so, so willing to let the Media King
convince him.

"It sure is. I don't like it either. But we're smack in the

middle of a goddamn revolution—got no time for the nice-
ties of courtship. I'd like to get myself to high ground. You
want to talk turkey or not?"

It's out of his mouth before he can stop it. "I . . . yes, of
course I do."

"Good! Good! So, first thing we do is find ourselves some
place safe to talk. I sent my guys out a while ago to bring
back some secured ground transportation." Baraga glances
around the alcove, seeming to court noses. "How 'bout an
unplanned beachside vacation while we wait for all this to
blow over?"

N'Doch can't believe it. Safety *and* his chance for the Big
Break. His own scheme exactly, as if he'd laid it out himself
for Baraga's approval. But beside him, he feels Sedou shift
with what feels like disapproval.

Lealé laughs her Glory laugh. "But, darling, I thought
they were shelling your beach house!"

"Oh, we wiped them out hours ago. A hornet's nest,
nothing more. We . . ."

A huge explosion shakes the crystals in the chandelier,
and the lights flicker. Two more softer thuds follow, then a
burst of gunfire. The girl gasps and lets Sedou wrap his arm
around her. Lealé's hand flies to her mouth to hold back a
scream. The soft background hush of the AC dies into
silence.

Baraga cocks an eyebrow. "Huh."

Abruptly the bodyguard Nikko shoves through the draperies, a phone clutched in one hand and a semiautomatic
in the other. "That was the gate, Mr. B. We're down to
emergency power, and our ground transport's been held up
trying to get in through the front."

"How long can we hold the house?"

"Minutes."

"Risk it and call in a copter?"

Nikko shakes his head, brandishing the phone. "Base says
everything's getting shot out of the air. These bastards are
very well organized."

"Your suggestion?"

"Only chance is to work our way to the rear and let
ground transport come through the back and pick us up
there."

"Okay, let 'em know." Baraga thrusts his chin at N'Doch

and Sedou. "You men stick with me. Nikko, keep an eye on the ladies."

"Yessir, Mr. B. Got your vest on?"

"Always." Baraga yanks open the drapes. The dining room is a haze of smoke and dust rising in the ruddy light of sunset that pours through the shattered windows. "Let's move."

N'Doch feels Sedou's hand on his shoulder as they start after Baraga. The familiar touch about cracks his heart open. He turns, meets his brother's eyes, and sees the dragon in them, trying to act like a man she knows only from his memories.

"What's on your mind, bro?" Sedou murmurs.

"Gettin' outa here."

"Listen. Only listen."

—We've only to get to the back door. My brother Earth can pick us up there and we'll be away from here.

—But Baraga will protect us, especially if he thinks he's got a live dragon he can put on his network. Where else can we go? Anywhere in the city's a war zone. We go out to the bush, we put Papa Dja in danger. Baraga'll keep us safe. He's got the money and the power to do it.

—And the money and power to make you a star, is that what you're thinking?

If it wasn't the dragon's usual voice in his head, N'Doch would swear it was Sedou talking. It's not just the good things he's remembering now. "It's on my mind," he says aloud. He shakes off his brother's hand and moves ahead, but Sedou's voice stays with him in his head.

—We cannot be dancing to Baraga's music! We have our Work to do. We must find Fire and learn why he's turned against us.

N'Doch takes a breath.

—Okay. Then you go. I'll go with Baraga and distract him, while the big guy takes you and the girl wherever you want to go. Then you'll all be safe, and I'll still have my chance. It's a good plan. Think about it.

It's a while before the dragon replies. There are bodies sprawled on the floor of the dining room. N'Doch nearly trips on one. No one is attempting to rescue them now. Broken glass is scattered everywhere, mixing with blood and a dusting of ceiling plaster. Sedou catches up with him at the door.

—*It's not a good plan. I can't go without you.*

—Sure you can. You'll do fine.

He's glad he's not trying to say this aloud. He's not sure he could do it. He's just got Sedou back and he's giving him up so soon?

—*No, I mean, we can't. Three is not four. You are needed.*

He tries to make a joke of it.

—*C'mon, it can't matter that much. What if I died?*

—*We fail. Without you, without any one of us, the Quest will fail. If the Quest fails, my existence is purposeless.*

—*Existence is never purposeless! Life is its own purpose!*

—*Not for a dragon.*

—*So then what?*

—*I will cease, as will the others. You are needed, Dragon Guide.*

N'Doch remembers when the realization first came on him, standing in the gym in the supertanker, of the burden this "destiny" was trying to dump on him. The same hollow panic grips him. Before, he'd thought it was rage and rebellion, but now he sees that it's actually fear, fear of losing his freedom, of losing his self.

—*No! I don't want it! I didn't ask for it! What about what I need? I got the chance of a lifetime here! This is my quest! You only get one chance like this one!*

Sedou looks back at him steadily. N'Doch understands now why this brother's shape suits the dragon so much better than Jéjé's. It's not just an issue of size. Sedou and the dragon have a lot in common: The same hard righteousness lights both their gazes.

—*Remember the message offered in the wood?*

—*The girl's, you mean? Yeah, so?*

—*Take it to heart, my brother. It was meant for you.*

CHAPTER THIRTY-SIX

Erde supposed she was meant to feel safer with the giant Nikko right at her back, but she didn't. She didn't like how his eyes slid past her face, lingered on her body, then dismissed her altogether. Or how he used his burly body as a prod, herding herself and Lealé through the smoke and destruction in the outer room. Broken glass crunched underfoot. The long table loaded with food had been tipped over sideways in front of the ragged openings that are all that's left of the windows. Several people huddled behind it, a few of them looking more dead than alive.

They'd almost reached the door when the light in the room flickered again, as if even this magic of electricity was subject to wind and warfare. The bodyguard barked a warning to Baraga ahead of him, and then the room went dark. Lealé moaned softly and reached for Erde's hand. Her grip was moist and hot, like the thick damp air invading the house through its broken walls. Light fell in through the holes like light into a tunnel, enough to see by but barely, a red smoky light that raised the hair on Erde's neck. She sent images to the dragon anxiously waiting in the grove, of the ruddy shadowed room littered with glass and bodies.

—*Like our old dreams, Dragon! What does it mean?*
—***That we are meant to be here.***

Earth would think this was offering her comfort, since being where Destiny intended him to be was all he required of life. Erde hoped for a little more, and from now until they were safe again, she'd be unable to think of quests and purpose or anything else but survival.

—Sometimes I think we're in Hell. Are we, Dragon? Is it a punishment for my wicked deeds and unclean thoughts?

—You mustn't fear, child. Fear is a temptation to give in to Weakness.

—Fearing and giving in are not the same. I can do one without doing the other.

—I am glad to hear it.

Baraga listened at the door, then slid it open just enough to slip through. N'Doch and the new dragon-shape called Sedou followed him. Nikko herded Erde after them, his hands on her and on Lealé in places she was sure they didn't need to be. The hall was dark, and thick with jostling, sweating bodies. Nikko palmed a small cylinder that suddenly gave forth an intense beam of white light. Erde recoiled from it, and then wished she had one. But Nikko used it as a club, flashing its brilliance into frightened eyes, forcing a path of fear down the crowded hallway.

By the little door at the end of the hall, the head acolyte Jean-Pierre was fumbling with the lock while he balanced a pile of metal boxes in his arms. He squinted into the spear of light.

"Got it all, Mr. B."

"Good man." Baraga grabbed the key while Nikko aimed his light. They piled through the door into the lightless narrow passage on the other side. Nikko came last, ejecting a handful of acolytes who tried to follow. He slammed the door and slid the heavy deadbolt home.

"Go dark, Nikko," warned Baraga from the curtained antechamber. "We got a crowd in here." Nikko doused his beam, plunging the hot little room into blackness as suffocating as the grave. But Erde felt a tickle behind her eyeballs, and grainy shapes and shadows swam up out of the black as Water extended her night vision to her human companions. N'Doch edged up on one side of her, Sedou on the other.

—Say nothing. Your safety may depend on appearing helpless.

Erde blinked, and gave her eyes over completely to the dragon's control. By the arched entrance to Lealé's Reading-hall, she could see Baraga and his henchman listening at the draperies. Baraga reached and drew Lealé to him.

"How many, you think, Glory?"

"Could be as many as a hundred."

"Laying low, hoping nobody'll notice 'em." Nikko lifted the metal thing she knew was a gun and seemed to be weighing it. "I'll notice 'em, if they get in our way."

"They are my 'guests,'" reproved Lealé's Glory-voice. "They'll let us pass if I tell them to."

"Will they let us hop into a tank and leave 'em all behind?" Baraga retorted.

"Yes. I think they would."

From what she'd seen around the compound, Erde agreed. Besides, what N'Doch would call "the Glory thing" seemed to be their only chance to get through. She didn't really believe that Nikko's gun could fend off a hundred people, and as far as she knew, it was their only weapon.

"Should she go first, Mr. B.?"

"Yeah, then you, with the light. Ceremonial-like, you know? Like the power's just blown and we're dealing with it. I'll follow with the others."

—Setting up the order of sacrifice.

Erde felt dragon energy thrumming through the body of the tall stranger beside her.

"Nah . . ." muttered N'Doch.

—Putting himself in the middle, where he's covered.

—He'll cover us, too, like he's covering Jean-Pierre. We could make him millions.

—He'll dump anyone he thinks is extra weight.

—There's no extra weight here. Three isn't four, remember.

—Baraga doesn't know that.

—Or perhaps he does. . . .

Earth's weighing in to the conversation signaled to Erde his acceptance of Fire's treachery.

—What d'you mean?

—As my sister said, he has a touch of Fire in him.

"Oh, god," N'Doch whispered, and then told them of Baraga's dream.

—Given up on Lealé to move on to more fertile grounds . . .

—He's only got to get rid of one of us to satisfy his

dream-lord's demands. The rest he can keep for himself.

—No one could hold onto one of you guys by force, not even Baraga!

—You think so? Fire seems to have done it. For all we know, he's been giving the Man lessons.

—Yeah, but look: All Baraga knows is, he's got three people. One of them he's suspicious about, but he's still not sure who he needs and who he can do without. So we're safe until he knows.

—So you're saying: Lay low, my brother.

Erde saw the flash of N'Doch's smile.

—Yeah. I sure am. None of your dragon pyrotechnics.

—Not me. That's the other one.

Erde recognized the tone: the banter of men before battle. The dragon did so well in this new shape. Even for Erde, the lines were blurring between the big man beside her and the voice in her head. She could only imagine how N'Doch must feel about it, who knew them both so well.

"Ready, Glory?" Baraga chucked Lealé under the chin as if she was a child. "Show 'em your stuff."

Erde was sure Lealé was more frightened than she was letting on as she squared her shoulders and tossed her head, gestures made only to herself in a lightless room. Nikko drew back a thickly embroidered drape, then flicked on his magical light and let Lealé walk majestically into its beam.

An amazed murmur rolled around the dark, cavernous hall, like a gust of wind through grass.

"Glory! Glory! Gloreee!"

Lealé smiled and lifted her arms in salute and benediction. The hard white light caught on the beads in her hair and on her robe, making her sparkle like a jewel, shooting tiny flashes into the darkness to reflect in the adoring eyes of her invisible worshipers.

"Glory! Help us! Glory! Save us!"

"Children!" The Glory-voice rang out like a bell, chasing its own echoes around the unseen dome. "My dear children! You must stay calm and quiet until this crisis has passed. The power is off for a while, but I'm sure they'll have it back again soon."

The ground rumbled and shook, calling her a liar. But the petitioners only sighed and called her name.

She answered them, and as she talked, she moved into the huge space, out across the polished marble as Nikko's beam illuminated a path for her. Some petitioners were standing, most were seated in groups on the still-cool stone, pressed together for comfort. Lealé picked her way gracefully among them, bestowing a smile here and a touch there. Baraga trailed her, in the light bearer's shadow, with Jean-Pierre behind him, clutching his precious load of boxes. Erde had no choice but to follow. She noted that Sedou took up the rear, scanning the unlit vastness with the interest of one for whom the dark is no obstacle. She hoped Baraga was too focused on his own escape to notice.

As they progressed grandly across the hall, more of the petitioners stood up. They pressed in closer and their pleadings became more desperate. Lealé's pace slowed. She could no longer pass through them easily. Nikko began to ask, then demand that they move aside, but Erde could see he was unpracticed at the Glory-thing, and his harsh orders set off bouts of weeping and hysteria among the weakest, and angry mutters among those with more presence of mind. So Nikko shoved harder, and Lealé kept up her steady stream of Glory patter, soothing, seducing a path to open up behind the rough-handed bodyguard. Behind them, the petitioners rose up and followed, murmuring and pushing against Erde and Sedou and N'Doch, until Erde wanted to scream and lash out with arms and fists and anything to keep them away from her. But she didn't, remembering what Earth had told her about fear.

An eternity of seconds later, Lealé was nearly at the door. Beside the towering columns that framed the ceremonial entrance, she turned back toward the crowd, a faceless, dreamlike figure outlined in brilliant white.

"Now, my brave children, my dearest brothers and sisters, you shall rest here in safety, while Glory goes out to put an end to this nonsense! For how can the Word of Light be heard with all that going on?"

Erde heard N'Doch's brief exhalation of disgust. She laid her palm against his back to quiet him.

"Hey, girl," he whispered.

"Hey, bro," she answered, in his own Frankish syllables.

He laughed softly, put his arm around her and hugged her close. "This is where it's gonna get rough. You ready?"

Erde shook her head.

N'Doch wishes he could give the girl comforting words, but he has none. At the door, big Nikko slips the lock and eases the door open just the slightest crack to give himself a view of the situation outside. N'Doch ducks around behind him to peer around his back. Before the door swings shut, he gets a glimpse of the twisted-iron wreckage of the front gate. The pseudo-colonial guardhouse is a pile of rubble. Jack-booted soldiers in camo uniforms are pouring single-file through the gap and fanning out across the front, rifles at ready. N'Doch recalls what Nikko said about the attackers being organized. *Who are these guys?* he wonders. Why spend so much effort on just another cult house? The city's lousy with them. But none of this is a mystery to Nikko.

"Storm troopers, Mr. B. They know we're here."

The phone on Nikko's hip beeps discreetly, like just another business call coming in to enlarge the Big Man's empire. Nikko confers with it briefly.

"Fifteen seconds to the wall," he reports. "Another twelve to the door."

Baraga pats the air, palms down, a silencing gesture. His eyes flick toward Lealé, still soothing the petitioner crowd. Some of them are claiming her personal attention now, and by habit, she is trying to supply them with a calming answer. N'Doch watches the bodyguard balance his maglight on the rim of a tall vase of flowers. He does it without moving the beam, so that the light continues to embrace and magnify the Mahatma Glory even as he moves away from it with Baraga and Jean-Pierre, toward the door. Baraga looks back at N'Doch and jerks his head in a wordless summons. N'Doch feels the chill seep into his gut.

He's gonna leave her behind.

N'Doch tells himself this bothers him because he's soft-hearted where women are concerned. But it's also scary confirmation of the dragon's dead-weight theory of Baraga's escape tactics.

Nikko cracks the door open again, letting in only the slightest wisp of light as he counts down silent seconds to himself. At fifteen, N'Doch hears a grinding, tearing crunch, muffled by the heavy door. Nikko gives Baraga a slow nod.

Look behind you! N'Doch begs Lealé. He's only ten feet away from her. He's got twelve seconds, less now. He could warn her with a whisper, but he can't bring himself to do it. If he does, he could blow his Big Chance. He sees fame and fortune miraculously within his grasp, after a lifetime of dreaming, and the desire for them rages in him as hotly as sex. *Lealé can take care of herself,* he reasons, as the tanks roar up outside the house.

With his pistol held at arm's length, Nikko yanks open the door. Jean-Pierre hugs his boxes and runs for it. Baraga wraps an iron arm around N'Doch's waist and propels him forward.

"Keep your head low, kid."

N'Doch bucks back. He has to at least try. "No! You're leaving her! You can't . . ."

"You want to live and be famous? Two four-man tanks. There's no room."

N'Doch doesn't count heads, he struggles, not even sure why he's doing it, if he feels the way he says he does. The Media King is stronger than he would ever have imagined. The iron arm around his waist is replaced by one around his throat. Baraga drags him through the doorway. N'Doch can't see Sedou, but he guesses the heavy drag on Baraga's other side is his brother hauling on him.

The tanks are firing rounds into the front yard, keeping the assault force down in cover. But bullets are pinging against the tanks' armor and zinging past N'Doch's ear. He's still arguing with himself, telling himself to just relax, let the Media King toss both him and Sedou inside the goddamn tank where they're safe. Nikko can get the girl.

"Nikko!" Baraga shouts. "Get him off me!"

The *girl*!

Off to the side, past Baraga's stranglehold on his neck, N'Doch sees the girl dart out of the door. She's got Lealé in tow, and she's moving fast, using the tanks for cover like she should, except she's not heading toward them, she's . . . *running for the grove*!

He tries to choke out a yell, but Baraga's got him so tight, he can only gag for breath. Now he sees Sedou, grappling with the bodyguard, unable to shake him loose.

"Which one of you is it?" Baraga hisses. "Which one of you's the dragon handler?"

N'Doch takes a wild guess. Maybe Baraga doesn't know. Maybe he thinks *both* the dragons are stashed somewhere else.

"All of us!" he gasps.

"That's not what he told me."

"Then he didn't tell you much!"

The girl's out in the open now, and the rain of gunfire intensifies.

Nikko has Sedou pinned against one of the tanks. Sedou's struggling to fight him off, struggling to hold on to his human-form, failing . . .

—Sedou! The girl! Stop her!

The Sedou shape waves, resettles, wavers again. Nikko lets go and backs off from it in horror. He levels his pistol at its head.

"Nikko! No! Don't hurt it! Take the other one!"

If he'd been thinking clearly, N'Doch realizes, he'd have seen the way it was going down. But then Baraga finally makes a mistake. He looses his hold on N'Doch's throat to watch the man they'd called Sedou melt and dissolve before his very eyes and reform into a living creature out of myth. A dragon. N'Doch jerks himself free, off balance, and falls hard on his side. He rolls to his feet just as Nikko levels his pistol at the fleeing women.

"Nikko! Both of them! NOW!"

The bodyguard gets one shot off. Lealé stumbles and drops. A sudden wind has come up. Blinded by dust and outrage, N'Doch throws himself into the line of fire.

The lead ripping into him at close range blows him off his feet. Or maybe it's the wind. He expects the agony of having his chest torn open, but there's only a tingling and a vast roaring. He expects to land hard, in too many pieces.

But he never lands at all.

CHAPTER THIRTY-SEVEN

He comes to consciousness slowly, surreally aware that he is running, has been for a long time. His lungs ache and his ribs are cramped but his long legs keep pumping away, doing what is needed without his having to think about whether he can keep going or not. He just does.

Being on autopilot lets him check out his surroundings. The air is thick and hot, and the sun's all wrong, too red and not quite round, like it might be at sunset near the horizon, except it's straight overhead. The dusty hills around him are too red, too, and pocked with shell craters. He sees he must have imagined all that blood and tearing and having his chest blown open. By some wonderful mistake the bodyguard missed, even at such close range, and N'Doch's old survival instincts took over: He finally got some sense and ran for it.

But the landscape isn't the familiar flat, dry fields surrounding the City. And N'Doch doubts that even the most organized coup could have leveled all the outlying villages and housing projects as completely as the rubble around him indicates. Plus, it all looks like it's been there a while. Layers of grit have softened the contours of the shattered walls and filled in the crevasses. He searches the hills and horizon for the smoke plumes of fire-bombing, and listens for the clatter of artillery or the wock-wock of the copters in the air.

Nothing. Just hot, dry landscape and a man running. A man who hasn't a clue where he is, or even why he's running. He just knows that he has to, something is after him, but it isn't behind him, it's all around him. . . .

N'Doch wakes abruptly, with a heaving gasp and a need

for air so desperate that it's a long shuddering moment before he can think about anything but breathing. When he gets it under control, he opens his eyes. He still doesn't know where he is.

He's lying in a bed, not just on it but in it, between sheets and under blankets, as far as he can tell. He lets his eyes rove, sees a tall wooden footboard with turned posts at both ends. The blankets are a single thick, airy coverlet. Its soft, coarsely woven fabric makes him think of his mother Fâtime at her loom.

The bed sits in a shaft of light from a small window. The bright cold light leaves the rest of the room in shadow, so while N'Doch gets his breath and waits for his heart to stop trying to break through his ribs, he studies the window in detail, hoping it will help him understand what's happening to him.

The window is square and set well into the wall, so a deep seat is formed by the sill. N'Doch sees a thin, brown cushion and a pile of what might be clothes. He wonders if they are his. The glass in the window is divided into many smaller panes, held together with thin strips of some dull-colored metal. At first N'Doch thinks there's something wrong with his eyes, but then he sees it's the glass. It's all ripply and dotted with minute air bubbles, so that his view of the outside is subtly diffused and diffracted: bare branches, furry-pointed green ones and blue, blue sky. N'Doch has never seen a sky that blue, and he stares at it until he realizes he's been drifting, probably for a long while, because when he becomes aware of himself again, the angle of the light has shifted and the sky is chased with big white and gray clouds. And now there's a woman sitting in the window seat, a white woman, paler than the girl even, dressed in white and with white-blonde hair as fine as spider silk. She's bent over some sort of handwork which she's holding up to the window in order to see. With the bright, white light, her long white dress and her own shell-like pallor, the woman is almost translucent.

N'Doch thinks he's kept still but he must be wrong, 'cause the woman looks up at him with a soft frown of interest and concern, then sets her work aside and comes toward him. Her hands on his cheeks and forehead are cool and professional. He figures he'll lay low and see what she's up to. And then it comes to him like a shock that she's a nurse, maybe a doctor. So he did get blown to bits, and somehow they've managed to stick him back together again. Only he's not sure now of how much of himself he's got left. He's forgotten to check.

The pale woman reaches her arms around him and with the impossible strength of mothers and doctors, bundles him up into a sitting position, supported by pillows and bolsters. N'Doch takes inventory and finds himself complete. Not quite like himself, and as weak as a newborn, but entirely as whole as one, too. It just doesn't make sense. The woman pats his shoulder, then reaches to a low wooden table beside the bed and fills a small clay cup with water from a stoneware jug. The crisp trickle of water inflames a vast thirst he wasn't aware of a moment before, and he drinks without worrying if the water's safe. It's cold and clear and more delicious than he ever imagined water could be. She's holding a third cupful to his lips when his next big revelation hits him, so hard he almost chokes. They did it once, they could do it again. *He's been doctored by dragons.*

Which means it really did happen. The shock of the impact and the ripping and tearing of his vital organs, it's not all a sweat-drenched nightmare. The bullets took him, then the dragons came and took him back, and carried him off somewhere . . . here. . . .

Revelation clicks in once more, and N'Doch understands where he is.

The woman sets the cup down and moves away through the shaft of light toward a shadowy door. She leans out and calls softly down the hall, and N'Doch knows he's figured right. She's speaking the girl's antique Kraut. For cryin' out loud, he's in 913!

He lets that explanation settle for a while to see how its logic suits him. He knows he's not thinking real fast or straight quite yet, but mostly he's just grateful to be thinking at all.

I died, he tells himself. *Or almost. And they fixed me.*

The miracle implied makes him shiver, and the woman comes back to the bed and pulls the covers up around his chest and shoulders. His entirely unmarked, unventilated chest.

"Kalt?" she murmurs. Her eyes look away from him, as if she lets her hands do her talking.

And he is cold, he realizes, not just from shock and revelation. It's cold in the room, and it's probably real cold outside. Now that he's upright, he has a wider view through the window, and he sees why the light streaming in is so hard and white. There's snow on the ground out there.

Snow. Real snow. He's never seen it before, except on the vid. He shivers again, and the woman goes to the corner where a small fire is burning in a narrow stone fireplace. She prods it with a metal poke and throws more wood on. She looks up at the sound of footsteps coming down the hall, light and steady, accompanied by the creak of floorboards. A second white woman comes into the room, shorter and older than the first, and rich with autumnal color in her short, graying hair and layered clothing. She has a brisk, direct presence that makes N'Doch feel obscurely chastised even though as far as he knows he hasn't done anything wrong except die and be resurrected.

"Hello," she says. Her voice is warmly resonant. Immediately N'Doch is thinking how much he'd like to hear her sing. Her French is odd and deeply accented but it's French nonetheless, and he can understand her. "My name is Rose. Welcome to Deep Moor."

Deep Moor. He recalls the name. The girl's back when haven with all the women. But she'd always described it as a paradise of perpetual summer. It doesn't much feel like summer in this room.

He wonders if his own voice will work. "I am N'Doch N'Djai."

Rose smiles. "Yes, I know. I know all about you, so you needn't tire yourself with explanations."

N'Doch is fairly sure now, but he could use some confirmation. "Am I alive?"

"Certainly. But there was doubt there for a while. The dragons worked long and hard. How do you feel?"

"Uh . . . okay." But what he really feels is *different*. If he had to describe this difference, he'd say he feels bigger, not taller or fatter, but bigger *inside*. He's been too distracted so far to search his mind for the dragon presence. Now that he does, he cannot raise them.

"The dragons," he asks Rose. "Where are they?"

"They went back, as soon as they recovered from the great effort of the Healing. They went back to rescue the mage Erde called . . ." She stumbles over the name. ". . . Jarara?"

"Djawara?"

"That's it. Did she say he was your grandfather?"

N'Doch nods, exhales, and lays his head back. He wonders if the old man will come. He's been worried about Djawara ever since going off and leaving him alone out there in the bush, never mind what Lealé says about him being a man of power. . . .

Lealé.

"Excuse me, madame . . ."

"Rose. Just Rose."

"Rose. There was a woman who helped us. Did they say . . . ?"

Rose shook her head gently. "The Dreamer was already gone when they got to her. The spark of life had fled." For some reason, her gaze flicked outward, toward the window. "Even dragons cannot make miracles."

N'Doch is not sure she's right. Mostly to keep her talking so he can hear that wonderful voice whose undertones tickle the insides of his lungs, he asks, "There's a war here, too, right? How's that going?"

Again, her gaze drifts to the window. He sees the strain in her then, the worry and exhaustion in her eyes. "The King's forces are in retreat, the barons are fighting among themselves and the mad priest is burning every witch in sight, and a few that aren't. The only good news is that Baron Köthen has gone over to Otto's side. About time, I say. But the war is the least of our problems."

Rose seems to lose herself to the view for a moment. Then she shakes herself out of her reverie. "Still, we're safe for a while yet, and we've food enough in the cellars, so you are to rest and eat and await the dragons' return. You're in good hands." She reaches and draws the younger woman within the circle of her arm. "This is Linden. She is Deep Moor's healer. Unfortunately, she speaks no Frankish, but then, she normally prefers not to speak at all." Rose smiles at Linden as if this was some long-standing joke between them.

"How come you speak French?" Instantly N'Doch regrets his bluntness. He's trying to recall how the girl acts with strangers, so he can do like she would at home, but he sees he just didn't pay close enough attention.

But Rose laughs, a throaty, complex reply to the unspoken parts of his question. "I've . . . traveled. Now—would you like to get up and move about? Here are garments on the sill. I'd say let's go for a walk outside, but it's frigid with this . . . unseasonable cold. We aren't meant to have weather like this in Deep Moor, and I doubt you're recovered enough for it. But come downstairs and join us for supper when you're ready."

The women leave him to dress, but at first, even getting up is a problem. N'Doch has a moment of terror where he convinces himself he's paralyzed. But it's more like his body's forgotten how to work, like he needs to apply conscious effort and teach it all over again how to sit up, stand up, and walk.

Different, he keeps thinking. *I feel different. Newly made. Dragon made.*

They know. These witchy women know, and they left me alone to deal with it privately. N'Doch appreciates their consideration. He gets the clothes on, pulling them over the longish linen shirt they'd put him to bed in. They're odd clothes, hanging loose and heavy on his slim body, yet meant for a shorter person. When he stands up next to these women, he's gonna tower over them. He has a hard time not thinking of the clothes as a costume, like when he first saw the girl on the beach, when he still thought this whole deal was a vid shoot. It makes him laugh now, but it's a hard laugh, full of unaccustomed irony aimed mostly at himself. He wishes he had a mirror.

But the clothes are clean and warm and comfortable, and he knows now that to ask for his own clothes back would be indulging in the macabre. Maybe their remaining bloodied shreds would make this death and resurrection thing somehow realer to him. But he didn't die, it seems, not quite. Because Lealé did.

He takes an experimental walk around the room. It's a small square white room with a dark, beamed ceiling just inches above his head, and a wide-boarded floor that complains musically of his every step. There's a wind outside now. He hears it howling in the rough stone chimney. The light at the window has gone gray and flat, and there's actually some of that snow flying in the air. N'Doch watches it for a while but it only makes him feel desolate. His limbs have remembered how to walk in time with each other, and he's chilled and hungry and thinks he'd prefer the company of strange women to the burden of trying to understand what's already happened to him, and what's supposed to happen next. He heads downstairs.

He's halfway down the narrow, steep steps, gripping the railing with both hands, when he feels the dragons' return. *Her* return.

His whole being lifts toward her, and the dragon-shaped emptiness inside him fills with her welcome. But the bright joy that sweeps through him like a searchlight is still freighted with denial, and N'Doch knows he will never fully accept this role that Fate has cast him in without his approval.

But somehow, he tells himself, he'll keep this from her. He owes them now. He owes them Big Time. So for the time being, he'll see this dragon thing out. He'll go off with her, with them, and find this bad dude Fire and see what they can do to settle his hash. N'Doch has a bone or two to pick with the guy himself. Then he'll be free to think about what comes next.

The dream swims up, as vivid as a vid running right there in his mind. He knows where to go now. He doesn't know where it is, or even *when*, but he knows how to get there.

N'Doch pulls his clumsy, new-made body together and goes on downstairs to play along with Destiny.

Melanie Rawn

"Rawn's talent for lush descriptions and complex characterizations provides a broad range of drama, intrigue, romance and adventure."
—*Library Journal*

EXILES

THE RUINS OF AMBRAI	0-88677-668-6
THE MAGEBORN TRAITOR	0-88677-731-3

DRAGON PRINCE

DRAGON PRINCE	0-88677-450-0
THE STAR SCROLL	0-88677-349-0
SUNRUNNER'S FIRE	0-88677-403-9

DRAGON STAR

STRONGHOLD	0-88677-482-9
THE DRAGON TOKEN	0-88677-542-6
SKYBOWL	0-88677-595-7

To Order Call: 1-800-788-6262

Tad Williams

THE WAR OF THE FLOWERS

"A masterpiece of fairytale worldbuilding."
—*Locus*

"Williams's imagination is boundless."
—*Publishers Weekly*
(Starred Review)

"A great introduction to an accomplished
and ambitious fantasist."
—*San Francisco Chronicle*

"An addictive world ... masterfully plays
with the tropes and traditions of
generations of fantasy writers."
—*Salon*

"A very elaborate and fully realized setting
for adventure, intrigue, and more
than an occasional chill."
—*Science Fiction Chronicle*

0-7564-0181-X

To Order Call: 1-800-788-6262

Mickey Zucker Reichert

To Order Call: 1-800-788-6262